# SHADOW TRACKER

Published in 2007 by 30° South Publishers (Pty) Ltd.
28, 9th Street, Newlands,
Johannesburg, South Africa 2092
www.30degreessouth.co.za

Design and origination by 30° South Publishers (Pty) Ltd.

Cover image by Craig Bone.

Printed and bound by Pinetown Printers (Pty) Ltd.

ISBN 978-1-920143-15-2

*Keith A. Nelson*

# SHADOW
# TRACKER

30° South Publishers

**Keith A. Nelson** was born in DeKalb, Illinois in 1951. He served in both the US Army Special Forces (Green Berets) and the Rhodesian Light Infantry. Earning a degree in medicine at the University of Rhodesia (now Zimbabwe) in 1982 he worked in medical research and was a Human Health Risk Assessment Manager on nuclear cleanups in the US. Keith lives in southern Ohio with Mary, his Rhodesian-born wife of 29 years, and has two grown children, Chris and Laura.

⌘

This book is dedicated to all of the men and women who served in the military and were taken before their time. Their courage and sacrifice will never be forgotten.

⌘

I would like to thank Chris and Kerrin Cocks of 30° South Publishers and my wonderful editor, Jayne Southern. Without their professionalism, patience and dedication this book would never have happened.

# PROLOGUE

## Rockland, Maine
## December 1, 1957

The morning was cold, but the sun rising over the North Atlantic sliced through the ice-cold, ground-hugging fog, melting the fine crystals with its touch. The air was bright when the men clustered onto the frozen field for the annual holiday trap-shoot. Besides large frozen turkeys, prizes also consisted of money, hams, slabs of bacon and other meat.

A tiny concrete block trap house lay half buried in the ground thirty yards in front of the group of men. The structure was only a few square feet and had a concrete slab roof, nearly hidden by snow and dead weeds. A slight boy of fourteen years sat on top of the structure dangling his legs off the side, trying to keep warm whilst waiting for something to happen. His job was to load the clay birds onto the throwing arm inside the bunker during the shoot. Until then, it was much warmer to sit in the feeble sun than it was to squat in the icy underground bunker.

A rusted steel oil drum burned discarded cardboard boxes and pieces of poplar and spruce limbs cut from the surrounding woods. Most of the heat went straight up into the clear sky, but enough warmth radiated from the sides of the drum to take the chill off the clustered men, who switched places when their thick clothing warmed. The shoot was supposed to begin at nine in the morning but it was nine fifteen and the men were still shuffling around and talking, with no one seeming concerned about the delay.

Most of the men were dressed in a similar manner. They wore heavy outdoor clothing made of canvas and coarse wool, suitable for the climate of coastal Maine. Some were lobster men from nearby St George, Port Clyde and Mohegan Island. A few were lumbermen from the interior, the rest were farmers from the surrounding area. Farming was difficult in the stony soil of the coastal plain but some laboured at it anyway, usually finding more success with livestock than with crops. The men were rugged and of individualistic temperament, friendly among their own, but an outsider would have found this group difficult to talk to. All brought along shotguns of various types. Double-barrels and pumps predominated, but an occasional semi-automatic was propped up against wooden racks just behind the firing points.

One of the organizers finally pulled a folding table and a chair out of his pickup and set them up. He placed a few pieces of paper and pens on the table and shouted, "Sign up!"

The milling ceased and as the men formed lines, the seated man began writing their names on the paper. With the holidays looming, all of them were hoping for a ham or slab of bacon to take home. For a dollar and a half a try, the game was appealing, added to which each man knew the meat would make his wife less critical when he returned with a little Canadian Club or beer on his breath.

No one paid much attention to the boy standing in line to sign up. His face was serious and solid at an age when most youths were still engaging in horseplay. His dark blond hair looked as though it had been cut with a pair of garden clippers and his canvas jacket was an obvious cast off, too threadbare to be of any use on the open sea. The people in this area were mostly poor working class but very proud. The boy didn't look proud however; he looked like a ragged refugee from the War in Europe fifteen years before. In the crook of his left arm rested a gun case made from a patchwork of odd cloth pieces roughly sewn together with sail cord.

Several of the men gestured at the case and laughed. The boy took no notice and signed up for three shoots: bacon, ham and a turkey. He fished in his pockets and pulled out loose change and counted out four dollars and fifty cents. The waiting men were impatient but also sympathetic. It looked like every penny the boy had and he was going to lose it all, shooting against men who were older and more skilled.

Walking over to the gun rack the boy slipped off the cover from his shotgun and, one by one, the men turned to look. The figured walnut stock gleamed in the sunlight. Not a bright reflective shine but a soft diffused glow only hand finishing and hand rubbing imparts. Few of these men had ever seen a similar gunstock. The shotgun itself was a Winchester Model 12 pump action which was common enough but, when the boy worked the action, it sounded slick and smooth. He placed the gun in the rack, then silently waited for his turn to shoot.

The rule of the game was to break ten machine-thrown clay birds from 16 yards behind the trap house. The shooter with the greatest number of broken birds won the prize. The organizers tried to squad people so they would be competing against others of roughly the same level of skill. There were always 'sandbaggers' who tried to get in with the novices and win prizes, but this practice was frowned upon and, once a man had won two prizes, he was automatically put into a higher class. The 'hunter' class included those men who were not trap shooters, who mainly used their shotguns for shooting small game. The boy was placed in this class though, because no one expected him to break many birds. Shooting trap was difficult even for experienced shooters, let alone some poor kid from the backwoods.

Pull ... *bang*. One at a time the men called for their targets and shot at them. Most waited a bit for the clay bird to fly out a distance so they could aim carefully before shooting. Unfortunately the birds flew very fast and if the shooter waited too long, the shot spread out so far the target wouldn't break. Some of the birds were hit, breaking into chips or large fragments. Others were missed and flew out to crash into the frozen ground.

When the boy's turn came he easily shouldered the full size gun and immediately called for his target. Pull ... *bang*. He shot quickly, too quickly according to those watching, but the bird turned to dust not far in front of the trap house. He repeated this on his second bird, then on all the rest. He was the only one to break all ten targets in his squad. The ham was his. The other men eyed him, suspiciously, and began to mumble among themselves.

The boy had to wait a while for his next turn. The organizer listened to complaints from the disgruntled shooters, then put the boy into an intermediate squad to pacify them. The shooters in this class were better than the previous group but none were able to beat the boy, who again broke all ten targets. The next highest score was nine, so he took away a large slab of bacon.

This time there was no questioning the boy's skill, so he was moved to the expert squad for the last event, shooting for a twenty-pound turkey. Shooters hated being assigned to the expert squad, because there were always one or two competitors who were very good and took away most of the prizes.

The best trap shooter in the area was a young state policeman by the name of Dave Armstrong and he was in the boy's squad. Dave recognized the youth as a helper in one of the lobster boats in Port Clyde and nodded to him. The boy curtly nodded back, but immediately turned away to focus downrange.

Everyone in the expert squad shot their targets, and when they were finished Dave, another man, and the boy had broken all ten. The rules stated they then had to move back to a distance of twenty-five yards behind the trap house for a man-on-man shoot-off until one winner remained.

From the increased distance the gunman had to fire at the target very quickly before it flew too far away, where the chance of the clay bird escaping the shot pattern was greater. The other man missed his second bird, leaving Dave and the boy. Both of them broke the next five birds with no misses. By this time everyone at the event had stopped what they were doing, to watch the cop and the boy shoot it out. Dave felt he was in a dilemma. He wanted the boy to win, but to lose to a kid would be devastating. The state champion trap shooter beaten by a ragged youth who cleaned out lobster boats? There would never be an end to that story, not in this community.

Finally they were both ten for ten at the twenty-five yard line, and the organizer decided that this stalemate had to end. Man and boy moved back beyond the field demarcations to approximately thirty-six yards behind the trap house. At this distance if the shooter didn't fire extremely fast, he would stand little chance of breaking the target. Dave shot first ... Pull ... he fired and took a chip off the target, but the rules stated that a chip was as good as any break.

The boy intently watched the trap house, shouldered his gun, and called for a bird. Pull ... he fired before the bird was visible. Dave knew the boy had erred and fired too soon. For a second he sensed relief that this embarrassing show would end but as the bird appeared, the boy's column of shot arrived just above the concrete roof. The clay target shattered so close to the trap house that the kid inside yelled in surprise.

He turned to look at Dave and smiled for the first time since arriving that morning. The policeman was disconcerted. What he had just witnessed had to be a mistake, a very lucky shot that could never be duplicated. Dave called for his bird and it came out a hard left, the most difficult shot from that distance, and nearly impossible to break. He fired and felt a cold wave pass down his back, "A miss ... damn!"

The youth closed the action on his Model 12 and called for his bird as he shouldered the shotgun. Again he fired early, but this time the shot pattern hit the lip of the concrete roof and bounced off and up with a puff of dust, shattering the emerging target. Muffled cursing was heard from the trap house as the trap kid was hit by a few small fragments.

The crowd began hooting and yelling at the feat they just witnessed. Dave just stood in stunned disbelief. He had a sick feeling in the pit of his stomach that this kid was playing with him, as a cat would with a mouse. Nobody, not even an experienced trick shooter, could do that with any confidence. But the boy had just done it and Dave knew he could do it again. There was some relief when no one taunted him for being trounced by a kid. The others knew they would have been beaten just as easily. There were cheers and backslaps but the boy didn't seem to notice the attention. He simply collected his meat prizes, put them in a cloth bag, grabbed his shotgun and walked off into the woods.

"Who the hell is that kid?" one of the older shooters asked Dave as people were leaving.

"Don't know," Dave replied. "I've seen him around the docks but I don't know his name."

"Well the little SOB sure can shoot a shotgun!"

"You don't have to tell me, he just whipped my ass ... and it still hurts."

⌘

Driving home along the back route to St George, Dave saw a lone figure walking between the shoulder and the ditch, carrying a heavy bundle and a gun case. He stopped and opened the truck door.

"You like a ride, son? I'm going your way and it looks like you're pretty loaded down."

The boy stopped and looked him in the eye for a second.

"You sure you don't mind, sir? I wouldn't want to put you to any bother."

"No bother at all, you must have fifty pounds of meat in that sack there," Dave said.

"Yes, sir, my grandpa will be happy. Things are kind of tight this time of year, it's nice to have something other than fish and game. I didn't tell him I was going to the shoot. He would have been mad and said it was a waste of money. Winning this much meat will take the wind out of his sails."

"What is your name, son?" Dave asked, as the boy climbed into the passenger seat of the truck while putting his bag of meat and his gun in the back.

"My name is Kurt Christianson, sir."

Dave thought for a moment as he drove off down the road.

"Kurt, was your father in the Marine Corps in Korea?"

"Yes sir, he was, but he was wounded pretty badly and is still in the VA hospital in Portland. I live with my grandfather near Port Clyde."

"Yes, I knew your father. He was a good Marine. I'm sorry about what happened to him."

"Well, it's just one of those things that happens I guess. I really don't remember much about him before the war. I was just a little kid, one or two years old."

There was a pause and neither spoke for the next few minutes as they headed east toward Port Clyde.

"Well, you can certainly shoot that shotgun of yours."

"I'm sorry about beating you sir, but it was a fair contest," Kurt said.

Dave laughed.

"Yes it was, and you beat me fair and square. I'll bet you don't know you just defeated the Maine state champion trap shooter for three years standing, do you?"

"No, sir ... really?"

"I'm sorry to say, but it's true. Where did you learn to handle a gun like that anyway?"

"I learned mostly from my grandpa, sir. He taught me to shoot just after I started to walk. He says I'm a natural shot, whatever that means. We hunt a lot, in the interior, bear and deer and things."

"You've shot a bear?" Dave asked.

"Yes, sir, five of them now, got a three-hundred-and-fifty pound male this fall near Baxter." Kurt reached into his shirt and brought out a piece of cord from around his neck. Hanging on it was a black bear claw over three inches long.

"That must have been your grandfather's lobster boat I've seen you on at Port Clyde?

"Yes, sir, and you're a state policeman, aren't you?"

Dave laughed again. "No moss grows on you, does it, Kurt Christianson?"

# CHAPTER 1
## THE CAULDRON

**Muong Nong, Laos**
**June 3, 1969**

Kurt had been closely tailing the North Vietnamese Army security detachment since they left their base camp several hours before. They were headed out on a mission but there was no way to tell where they were going. By the way they interacted with one another he had determined that there were two officers and fourteen enlisted men in the group. Following their trail wasn't a problem in daylight. With more than four or five men moving through heavily wooded terrain there was no need to track, merely to follow in their wake.

So far none of them had doubled back or set up temporary ambushes on their back trail. Their lax security was probably because no American or South Vietnamese forces were supposed to be in Laos. By international agreement no NVA were supposed to be here either but they were here all right ... by the thousands.

It was mid afternoon before the NVA patrol stopped and began to set up positions around a small clearing, as if they were settling down to wait, expectantly. He'd been alone in Laos for several weeks but, apart from his heightened state of alertness, there was some comfort in knowing that nobody knew he was here or even suspected his presence. But nevertheless Kurt had a bad feeling about the situation.

One man, practicing the art of concealment and covert movement, could operate in a triple canopy jungle for extended periods without ever being detected. As the enemy troops settled in, he moved very slowly behind their perimeter to determine their positions and which individual and weapon was where. After this assessment was finished, he retreated to the rear and waited, for what he didn't yet know.

Half an hour before sunset there was the distinctive beat of incoming helicopters. This sound caused Kurt immediate concern, because it indicated that American birds were heading into a very hostile area. To his knowledge no conventional US troops were here, nor Republic of Vietnam or RVN forces. The only other possibility was that the Special Forces CCN or CCS projects were inserting a reconnaissance team, the same way he arrived weeks ago. If this was the case, the unit of NVA he was following might be an unwanted reception committee.

Standard procedure was for the choppers to fake several inserts on possible landing zones, then to drop the team at one of them. This tactic prevented enemy that happened to be in the area from zeroing in on the actual insertion site.

The Huey sounds grew louder and changed pitch as the choppers varied their orientation. This meant they were not flying in a straight line, and were probably carrying out the dummy drops. If this clearing was chosen as the primary LZ there would be hell to pay. The reinforced squad of NVA he'd been following were now set up and dug in for a fight. Anyone exposed in the middle of the clearing would be shot to pieces quickly. The NVA would most likely let the team land, then attack only once the chopper and gunship escort left.

If the NVA opened fire prematurely, they risked the Huey door gunner and the Cobra pilot saturating the LZ and their positions with machine gun, rocket and cannon fire. Kurt didn't want that either. Area weapons of that sort were indiscriminate and his chances of being hit by friendly fire were just as good as the enemy's. With a radio there would be the possibility of establishing communications and warning off the team, but he didn't have a radio, or even a smoke grenade.

As the choppers approached a tentative plan formed in Kurt's mind. He already knew the enemy locations. When shooting broke out the NVA would never suspect opposition from their rear. Moving quickly enough he could attack their individual positions and put the ambushers out of action fairly quickly. His biggest problem would be avoiding friendly fire from the inserted team. They would be shooting at everything in an attempt to break contact once they were fired upon, but there was little choice, and little time. He had to try. Otherwise the reconnaissance team would be lost.

The familiar pressure waves of the UH-1H rotors buffeted the air as the chopper came in just over the triple canopy forest and dropped, almost vertically, into the small clearing. Like all pilots assigned to special projects, this chopper pilot was highly skilled. The whirling rotor blades only had a few feet of clearance on each side. With the chopper in a low hover, men leaped into the chest-high grass and ran to take up defensive positions. Kurt's intuition had been correct: what unloaded was a recon team, made up of two Americans and five Montonguards, more often called Yards, the friendly tribe from the Central Highlands of South Vietnam.

The seven men were disgorged in seconds and the Huey lifted up and pitched forward. The Cobra gunship escort circled at an altitude of two-or-three-hundred metres. The two helicopters flew off together to make several more fake inserts before flying back to South Vietnam. Suddenly all was very quiet on the ground.

Cautiously, Kurt crept directly behind one of the NVA machine gunners placing the sights of a captured AK-47 he carried on the enemy's neck. The reconnaissance team's communications man, a Yard, keyed his radio transmitter button twice. This indicated a clean insert, with no opposition on the ground. The team assembled, gave hand signals, and started to move off.

Seconds later a burst of AK fire shattered the silence and green tracers streaked across the LZ. Kurt squeezed his trigger, dropping the NVA RPD gunner. M-16s blazed back from the clearing, as members of the ambushed recon team raked the surrounding tree line. More than twenty automatic weapons were firing in an area no bigger than a suburban lot. Bullets buzzed and cracked from all directions and fragments of wood, bark and severed leaves rained down. Kurt knew his chances of being hit in all this initial mad crossfire were high, so he hugged the ground.

He crawled and rolled from one position to another, dispatching most of the NVA with one shot to the head or neck, both to save ammo and to prevent his location from being detected and subjected to direct fire.

There was a jarring thump as one of the NVA fired a rocket-propelled grenade towards the surrounded team. A burst of orange flame, smoke and dirt obscured the LZ when the warhead exploded. Somewhat stunned by the back blast, Kurt located the grenadier and shot him. Though probably causing casualties on the recon team, the smoke and dust from the rocket provided him some cover to move against the remaining NVA. Adopting a crouching stance, he went from one position to the next eliminating the remaining enemy soldiers with grim economy. The iron dictum of 'always secure your rear' had been disregarded by this NVA team. They died ignoring it.

Kurt quickly checked the bodies to make sure they were dead. The NVA detachment commander and his radio man were lying close together. Near the commander's body was a khaki-coloured canvas satchel and inside was a manila folder containing some papers. Kurt adroitly removed the file and stuck it in the front of his waistband.

⌘

The jungle went quiet again, broken only by the deep moans of a wounded team member. The NVA were all dead. He was afraid to approach the team's scattered positions directly. They were spooked and meeting another American wouldn't feature amongst their expectations. He carefully circled the LZ to assess the damage. Three of the five Yards were lying dead in the clearing and one, the radio operator, was lying down holding his right side, seriously wounded. The Americans proved harder to locate.

Finally Kurt manoeuvred around enough to see a large man hidden in a thicket. He wasn't identifiable at first, due to the dense cover and the man's blackened and bloody skin. Kurt eventually recognized him as Joe Cordoza, a One Zero team leader from the CCN Project, based in Da Nang. It looked as though the blast from the RPG explosion may have damaged his eyes. Joe was just standing still, in cover, waiting to be discovered by the NVA, anticipating the jolt of an AK round that would finish him ... if he was lucky.

"Hey, Joe, are you taking a nap in there?" Kurt yelled. "What the hell are you doing? I need your call sign if you want to get out of here."

Joe recognized the voice. It was the new kid who went missing a couple of months ago, an MIA. He figured he was dreaming or hallucinating and his mind, already in shock, was racing with questions for which there were no answers.

"Goddamn," Kurt said. "Give me your call sign so I can radio for an extract to get you out of here."

Through swollen and parched lips Joe finally spat out, "Krait, the call sign is Krait."

"You CCN guys like the snakes, don't you?" Kurt asked. "Maybe, if you used bird names as call signs you could fly the fuck out next time."

Kurt moved out into the clearing and recovered the wounded Yard's radio, surprised it was still usable. He carried it back to the thicket and began to transmit to Covey, the Cessna bird-dog that was always in the air covering Command and Control operations.

"Covey, Covey this is Krait, I repeat, Krait. We are hit and have casualties. Request immediate extraction, three KIA and at least two wounded, perhaps more, over."

The radio hissed for a few seconds then came alive.

"Krait, this is Covey. I copy last transmission. What is your location, over?"

"Covey, I don't have exact coordinates," Kurt continued. "We are just off the primary LZ, use those coordinates, over."

"I copy you, Krait. Are you currently hot? I repeat, is the LZ hot? Over."

"Negative, Covey," Kurt said into the mike. "I repeat, negative, not currently hot but situation is very fluid ... over."

The radio was silent for a few seconds.

"Krait, message relayed, chase is en route. Report any changes ... over."

"Roger, Covey, many thanks." Kurt continued into the mike, "Covey, I have coordinates of an NVA troop concentration to relay to fast movers as follows ..."

Kurt relayed the eight digit coordinates of the NVA base a few clicks away, which he'd been watching for the past week, from where the now annihilated security detachment had departed earlier. The bird-dog pilot acknowledged the transmission and signed off.

Kurt went to the wounded Yard and pulled him to cover. Fortunately the recon team members always carried medical supplies with their gear. Cutting away his clothing to expose the full extent of his injuries, he applied two pressure bandages to the wound. The man was very weak and his survival was questionable. He also found some ophthalmic ointment in a medical pouch to put in Joe's eyes to help his corneal burns.

⌘

A flight of F-4 Phantoms were first to arrive on the scene. The jets were several times faster than helicopters and were en route to targets in North Vietnam, when they were re-routed. The flight leader had been monitoring the open transmission and wiggled his wings as he passed overhead, heading toward the nearby NVA base.

From a concealed position, 57mm anti-aircraft fire burst forth. The lead F-4 released two shiny aluminium napalm canisters just short of the coordinates Kurt had given. A momentum of four hundred and fifty knots carried the containers of gelled gasoline in a long trajectory, arcing them directly into the target, where a huge fireball was seen a moment later.

Close on the heels of the lead aircraft, three more F-4s released their loads of snake eyes. The one thousand five hundred pound high explosive bombs looked almost graceful as their drogue fins deployed to slow their fall in order to avoid damaging the low-altitude fighters. The bombs flashed consecutively throwing huge amounts of soil, plant material and wood into the air above the target. Kurt felt the ground shock a few seconds later and, after a delay, the rolling air waves slapped like angry surf.

This flight of fast movers was on a mission to take out bridges, power plants and other large stationary targets in North Vietnam with these specialized munitions. The heavy bombs were not designed for anti-personnel use. Cluster bombs or smaller high explosive bombs would have been a better choice in this situation. However, the Air Force pilots knew that anti-aircraft fire was very intense in the North. Consequently they took the opportunity to divert to a more lightly defended target whenever the option arose.

After the explosions the 57mm gun emplacement stopped firing and only a handful of green tracers from sporadic AK-47 bullets were fired futilely into the sky at the retreating jets. The aircraft departed leaving sooty contrails; only the popping of ammunition and other ordinance, cooking off at the NVA base in the intense heat, echoed through the trees.

⌘

At first barely audible, the regular beat of chopper blades could be heard as the extraction birds came in from the east to pick up the remnants of Recon Team Krait. Kurt grabbed a smoke grenade from Joe's webbing, pulled the pin and tossed it into the clearing. A few seconds later the chopper pilot's voice crackled over the radio.

"I have purple smoke, Krait. Chase is inbound."

"Chase, I confirm purple," Kurt replied in his mike. "Hover and drop stabo hooks."

While the chase choppers were still on approach to the LZ, a pair of Bell Cobra gunships shot directly overhead and peeled off to either side. The Cobras wore First Cavalry markings which was good news to Kurt. These boys, like their namesakes a century before, liked to hunt things down and shoot them.

"Krait, we have your position," One of the Cobra pilots transmitted. "How can we be of service?"

"Roger, gunships," Kurt replied. "Vector three-zero-zero degrees at two-five-zero-

zero metres is a large NVA position, likely battalion size. A flight of fox fours put the hurt on them but AA batteries may still be operational. Use caution."

As Kurt spoke, tracers from a 57mm anti-aircraft gun streaked across the pale blue sky, attempting to tag one of the Cobras. The boom, boom, boom of the gun firing followed a few seconds later. The range was long but the NVA gunner's marksmanship wasn't bad. The pilot of the targeted aircraft cursed into his radio and cranked his ship sharply to port to maximize his speed at right angles to the anti-aircraft gun.

The pilot of the other Cobra, orbiting on the other side of the team's position said, "Got 'em."

The second chopper was hovering behind a rise that was just out of sight to the AA gunner. When his nose became lined up with the target, the pilot pulled up his collective and popped up so he was pointing directly at the position.

The manoeuvre took balls. The Cobra was at a dead stop: if the AA gunner had him in the sights, he was as good as dead. But before the NVA operator could crank the barrel of the big 57mm cannon around, the Cobra pilot unleashed a fiery stream of 37mm ZULU rockets from a pod beneath his stubby left wing. Because he knew the range, the stationary helicopter was like a fixed platform and the rockets were dead on target. The bursting of the rocket warheads was followed immediately by larger secondary explosions as the 57mm gun's ammunition stockpile detonated.

"Scratch one AA site," Kurt said to himself.

Only occasional small arms fire emanated from the vicinity of the destroyed NVA base camp and the ridgeline above it. At this range it wasn't a major threat to the extraction mission but it would be foolish to underestimate small arms fire. One lucky AK round could still kill a pilot or blow off a tail rotor.

The Cobras were on the offensive now. The pilot of the first gunship, angered by the close call, swept the ridgeline with his General Electric Minigun, which despite its name was a powerful rotary cannon that fired one hundred rounds of thirty calibre ammo per second. His wingman fired what remained of his ZULU rockets at suspected positions. Like two terriers hounding a fox, the deadly snakes were doing what they did best.

Kurt keyed the mike.

"Good work, Cobras. Make them stay put until I get these guys hooked up."

The first of two chase Hueys appeared near the dying smoke grenade. It wasn't possible to move all of the dead and wounded soldiers to the centre of the clearing for a helicopter landing, that would take too long. Instead, one-hundred-foot lines with stabo hooks on the ends were thrown out from both sides of the chopper by the crew.

In spite of the Cobra's suppressive fire, the intensity of small-arms impacts near the clearing was picking up. The surviving NVA had figured out what was happening and were trying to find their range. Out of his side vision Kurt saw an RPG-7 ignite from halfway up the ridge and streak toward them, but the shot was futile. The range was too long and the arcing rocket exploded in mid air. After four hundred or five hundred yards and four seconds of flight time RPGs self-destruct. The NVA either didn't know the limitation of the weapon, or didn't care.

Leaping off the skid of the hovering helicopter, a soldier slid rapidly down a line thrown out of the door. The man wore a flack jacket, a chopped off M-79 grenade launcher clipped to his harness, and half a dozen double-0 buckshot canister rounds in a bandolier over his shoulder. Hurriedly unhooking from the line he scanned the area for dead and wounded but stopped, shocked, when he saw Kurt. Seth Wilson was one of Kurt's Special Forces classmates, now a C&C chase medic, one of the more exciting jobs in SF.

"Christianson!" Wilson yelled over the rotor noise. "What the fuck, you're supposed to be dead or captured. Aren't you?"

Wilson was both confused and frightened; his eyes looked like those of a scared cat as he reached for his M-79. Kurt knew that a venomous thought was developing in Wilson's mind ... turncoat. There were rumours circulating that some of the captured or missing special operations people had gone over to the other side. This possibility was very real to Wilson, who at the moment was hanging his butt way over the line.

Kurt knew there was no time to explain the circumstances. The only answer was immediate positive action.

"I've stabilized the wounded," Kurt yelled at him. "Two are serious but neither is imminent. Let's get them hooked up and out first."

Ducking low, Kurt darted into a nearby thicket and, with one arm, lifted Joe Cordoza by his patrol harness. Even thought he was a large man, Joe looked like a floppy rag doll as he was hustled to the ropes and clipped to a stabo line.

Withdrawing the uncomfortable manila envelope from his waist, Kurt quickly folded it in half and buttoned it in the side pocket of Joe's jungle pants.

"Joe," Kurt yelled in Joe's ear over the rotor wash, "give this to S-2. Don't forget, it's probably some good stuff."

"This one is superficial," Kurt continued to Wilson. "He may have internal blast injuries, I can't tell. The third has three rounds through the left thigh, left pelvis and right bicep. Seth, you go with them and I'll hook up the bodies on the next chopper."

Grabbing Wilson by the harness, Kurt clipped the stabo hooks on to his shoulder links. Looking up at the belly of the chopper, the crew chief craned out of the door looking for a sign. Kurt gave the palms up signal and immediately the chopper lifted off with the four men suspended by long lines. The Huey was an old B-model and the weight of four men added to the crew made for a maximum load in a hover at this temperature and altitude.

In order to achieve more lift the pilot nosed the aircraft ahead to gain forward air speed. This meant that the men on the lines were dragged through the tops of the trees for a distance. Wilson, Joe and the radio man knew the drill and balled themselves in foetal positions to avoid being caught in a tree. The critically wounded Yard didn't have the reserves for the manoeuvre. They were almost clear, when the Yard's foot became stuck sideways in an upper fork of a tall tropical hardwood. The tree limb began to bend like a giant spring but wouldn't let go of the trapped foot.

Kurt couldn't see what was happening due to the thick foliage, but the radio sprang to life as the pilot assessed the situation. The chopper slowed its forward speed and the whine of its turbine engine increased in pitch. The stabo line with the wedged Yard on the end was acting like a deadly anchor and the results could be disastrous.

Kurt then heard the sharp but muffled thump of the M-79 firing then the chopper and lines swung free. The Yard was now missing his lower left leg. His bloody jungle pants hung down below his knee in tatters, folding up under the severed limb as the wind struck it. Wilson had blasted off the Yard's leg with an M-79 buckshot round. The last glimpse Kurt had of the retreating chopper was Wilson grabbing at the Yard's leg. He would try to put a tourniquet on the wounded man while airborne. The chopper and the four hanging men disappeared over the treetops and were gone.

Kurt spoke into the radio again, "Chase Two this is Krait, I have bodies to hook up, send your ropes down. Over."

"Roger, Krait," the pilot replied, "are you coming with them ... over?"

"Negative," Kurt said. "Krait out."

He dashed to the bodies of the remaining Yards. All of them were small and light, maybe eighty or ninety pounds apiece. Kurt drew his Randall and cut off their gear, which they wouldn't need anymore. Weapons, grenades and food he couldn't carry would be cached.

He went over and lifted the larger American Two-Zero out of a stand of bamboo where he died, and cut off his combat gear. The Yards were clipped on the extraction ropes easily, but the American was heavy and it took what remained of Kurt's energy to carry the body over and hook it up. He gave palms up to the crew chief and skyward they went. As the chopper flew off, the lifeless bodies dangled and bobbed in the rotor wash, the last dance for all of them.

Kurt felt his energy spiralling down with the waning adrenaline surge. This was the really dangerous part, the team and aircraft were gone but he was still here, surrounded by pissed off NVA. Equipment had to be cached and distance put between him and the enemy, quickly. He hoped the NVA reaction force didn't have dogs this time; he was almost out of CS powder.

## CHAPTER 2
### HOME FROM THE HILL

**July 5, 1975**

The heat began to dissipate as the I-95 approached the sea near Portsmouth, New Hampshire. From there, the old Highway 1 split off and crossed into Maine winding along its serpentine coastline. From this coastal highway many other roads branched off and fed into the finger-like projections of land jutting into the North Atlantic. The open-top Jeep drove noisily over the hard surface. The tyres were off-road models, and the hum of the rubber knobs on concrete emitted a continual buzz.

Summer's tourist rush was beginning and station wagons, convertibles and campers were stacked up at the toll booths. Ninety degrees in Boston a short time ago was being replaced by coastal air that was twenty degrees cooler. Beyond Portland the traffic thinned out making cruising at seventy-five miles per hour possible, without being assailed by state troopers. The mid-coast was still some distance from the interchanges of Portland but, aside from a few slow motor homes, it was mostly good running.

Coastal Maine was one of the few places in the country where a person could still find himself seriously lost with little trouble. Kurt assumed residents preferred it that way. The farmers, lobstermen and fishermen were all very independent people and many of the gravel and side roads were deliberately left unmarked, as a 'need to know' philosophy prevailed.

In the old town of Thomason, grey stone and barred portals heralded the Maine State Prison on the right. Just beyond that, Highway 135 branched off, in front of the Knox Mansion and headed for Port Clyde, where his journey would end.

Kurt swung the Jeep to the right following one of the unmarked feeder roads heading into the pines just past the turnoff to St George. Three quarters of a mile further on, another path, virtually overgrown and easily overlooked, branched off. Slowly negotiating the rutted dirt track, a small spruce windfall obscured the access and had to be cleared.

The Jeep came to a halt just short of a piece of rusty anchor chain that was bolted across the entrance to the old house. Nailed to the trunk of one of the big pines, just above eye level, was a grey weathered piece of wood. In the late afternoon light, the name 'Christianson' was still visibly etched into its surface. Parking his jeep outside the barrier, he leapt across the chain and walked the short distance up the remnants of the driveway.

The small house was run down. Some of the neglect could be attributed to deterioration that had occurred since the death of his grandfather, but the old man hadn't been one for property maintenance anyway. Nature always took over very quickly when man let go. The exterior of the house was an unpainted and weathered grey, with one corner of the small front porch threatening to collapse. The windows had been covered by boards on the inside but surprisingly, the glass was intact, as was the roof. Even though most people in this area were poor, they respected the property of others and to Kurt's eye there was no sign of any break-in, vandalism or intrusion.

Just over the front door of the house was nailed another sign made of the same old weathered wood, inset just enough to protect it from direct sun. Kurt remembered when his grandfather had brought this plank of wood from the beach after a storm. He said it was a piece of oak planking which had come off a ship that sank to the bottom of the bay centuries ago, and waves from a brutal storm had churned pieces up on to the beach. In the old Scandinavian tradition, the name Christianson was deeply burned in the wood, along with Norse Runes that spelled out both this name and the name of the house.

Walking around to the back, he prised up a brick that formed part of a cistern, and found the house keys, still there. The brass had oxidized with time to a greenish colour but not enough to ruin the metal beneath. Using the key and some encouragement, the door finally opened. Inside, a thick layer of dust covered the floor, indicating that nobody had set foot in the place for years.

Only cracks of light filtered in through the shuttered windows, though the partially open door illuminated the sparse furniture, utensils, the wood burning stove, a rough hewn pine table and two wooden chairs. On one wall, almost obscured by a film of dust, was a picture of a Maine lighthouse; on another was a faded print of a Viking longboat with its red and white striped sail unfurled. Kurt remembered how this picture fascinated him as a child. Staring at the image on cold desolate afternoons, he had imagined sailing on such a boat to all parts of the earth. His grandfather sometimes told stories about those ancient days, stories that still left vivid images. There was little more in the house to see, so he closed the front door and walked around to the attached shed.

The little wooden skiff was on its old trailer in the shed, as he remembered. One of the tyres on the trailer was flat. A few strokes with the hand pump, still hanging on the shed wall, inflated it for the time being. A small two-stroke outboard motor also hung on the wall. It had been drained of fuel some time ago. Kurt had remembered to bring a five gallon can of fresh oil/gas mix up with him. He pulled out the spark plug on the outboard, cleaned off the gummy residue, and hooked up the motor to the skiff. Kurt backed up the Jeep to the trailer and attached the ball of the trailer to the rear tow hitch.

As a boy Kurt had taken the skiff out to Burnt Island just off the point of St George and camped there on rare mild summer nights. The island wasn't large enough to be occupied and the steep rocks made it an unlikely spot for a casual stop by sea-going tourists. From a vantage point on the island, all activity on the Cape and Inlet could be seen. With a burst of almost juvenile excitement flowing through his veins, he opted to go there that evening.

⌘

The grocery store in Port Clyde, run by the Kelly family, hadn't changed in at least fifty years. Tourists liked its quaintness; locals shopped there because it was the only store in the area. He parked the Jeep and went in for supplies for the night. In the past the proprietors had always catered more to the tourist dollars than to the locals. As a child Kurt remembered going down to buy a few groceries, having only just enough money, or sometimes not enough. He was either made to wait until all the other customers had been served, or often totally ignored ... a ragged boy not worthy of attention.

At the counter, an older incarnation of the same woman who had been so aloof years before, now rushed to help, which Kurt found amusing. Unlike the dishevelled youth, few could ignore his presence now. The scruffy child of the past was over six feet in height and two hundred pounds, with piercing blue eyes and the arms and shoulders of an athlete. His dark blond hair was finally growing out since his release from the Army, the ends bleached almost white, contrasting sharply with his tanned skin. Lately, his mere presence attracted attention, something he found a little disconcerting. Used to being ignored as a child, he preferred the comfort of anonymity.

The woman checked out his purchases while smiling coyly at him, and he couldn't help himself.

"You don't remember me do you, Mrs. Kelly?" Kurt asked in a soft voice, so only she could hear.

The woman looked puzzled for a few seconds and her eyes remained blank.

"No," she said. "I don't recall you."

Kurt smiled slightly and shook his head.

"Don't worry ma'am," he replied. "It's not important."

That part of his life was past and could be forgotten. He was a new man. A feeling of elation passed over like a summer cloud as he left the store and walked to the skiff. That sense of pure joy was puzzling but felt good. It was such a beautiful evening on the coast.

⌘

The skiff, loaded with a few camping supplies, was tied up to the pier next to the larger, sleeker runabouts. The bigger boats belonged to the people who had summer homes on the islands, and cruised about on large yachts during the warm months. They used their runabouts to make grocery runs and commute to the handful of small restaurants and bars dotting the nearby coast. Most of these people had money far beyond Kurt's comprehension.

The small, beaten-up, dirty skiff floated at its moorings, like a sparrow among peacocks, but it served its purpose. Fortunately the little two-stroke outboard motor had been stored properly by his grandfather, and only took a little coaxing to get it started. The old Swede had looked after his machinery, if not his house.

The outboard motor sputtered and smoked as it came to life. The engine wasn't very powerful but, because of its diminutive size, the skiff took off at a good clip towards the outlet where the St George River flowed into the ocean. Kurt slowly circled the shoals where fresh water flowed out and mixed with the denser salt water beneath. Idling the motor and riding with the current, the skiff drifted further to sea before he shut it down.

Finding schools of fish was a skill he had learned at such a young age it had become instinctive. He took out a stout fibreglass pole mounted with a sea casting reel. He then baited a number six hook with a blood worm which was set just above a two-ounce lead sinker and vigorously cast towards an eddy current that looked promising.

Are the stripers running? Kurt asked himself. The question was answered a minute later when the pole began to jerk violently. The hook set firmly and a nice two-foot striper reeled in. With fresh bait, he tossed the line back and quickly snared another striper and an eighteen-inch mackerel before the drift ended. Mackerel is an oily fish which he had never liked, so he threw it back.

Restarting the motor, he ran the skiff back to the river's mouth and began to drift out again. After the third striper was in the boat, Kurt started the motor and headed out to sea. Except for the tide eddies, only light ripples broke the ocean's blue surface and the little boat ran smoothly.

A handful of small islands rose from the blue waters just beyond the river's mouth. The islands were hilltops from another era, carved and partially submerged by glaciers in the last ice age. Further out was the picturesque and idyllic Mohegan Island, linked by ferry to Port Clyde. Hopper Island, which was uninhabited, passed by to the port side. Another fifteen minutes of easy running led to the shore of his old campsite.

Burnt Island was only a couple of hundred feet across, just large enough to offer a dry perch and a good view of the nearby coast. Running the skiff on to the shallow gravel beach, he dragged the boat further on to shore before unloading the camping equipment. He pulled a wetsuit top, mask, fins and snorkel from a duffel bag, and quickly donned them. The sun was dropping fast and there would be little light in the depths if he didn't hurry. The water was still cold at this time of year hovering at about sixty degrees; cool enough to put an unprotected swimmer into hypothermia in minutes.

Jumping into the clear cold sea sent a shocking rush through his body. An underwater ledge surrounding the island dropped off quickly into a jumble of rock sheets and boulders. Swimming away from the island on the surface for a hundred feet or so, Kurt jackknifed his legs straight up into the air and his body slid vertically beneath the water. A weight belt with fifteen pounds of lead slabs neutralized the buoyancy of both his body and the foam rubber wetsuit top. A few strong strokes drove him to the rocky bottom at twenty to twenty-five feet down. While descending, he pinched the rubber nose pouch on the mask and blew air from his lungs, up into his ears. Without this manoeuvre his ear drums would burst from the pressure.

The light was very dim in the late afternoon at that depth, but experience dictated where to look on the jumbled, rocky sea floor. Scanning the bottom, an armoured feeler protruded from a crevice, waving back and forth in the surge. From his right leg he unfastened a chrome-plated dive tool that looked like a pry bar with a rubber handle and quickly enlarged the crevice. Maine lobsters were tricky to snare and snorkelling made catching them very challenging. Reaching into the crevice, he grabbed the lobster by the rear of its carapace to avoid the claws. The lobster was a nice two-pounder. Shooting to the surface, Kurt turned over on his back and finned to the island, holding the thrashing creature with a firm grip.

Catching a lobster barehanded was technically illegal. Lobstermen were very powerful in the State of Maine and, according to law, no one except licensed lobstermen were allowed to collect the clawed delicacies. His grandfather had been a lobsterman, and Kurt agreed that those who earned their living from the sea should be protected from poachers, and he would never consider tampering with another man's traps. However, he felt strongly that collecting fruits of the sea for personal use was a right, like breathing air. He flipped the lobster into the aluminium skiff, where it could not crawl up the slick, steep sides and it helplessly scraped in attempt to escape.

Going back in the water and diving on the shallow rocks closer to shore, Kurt collected some small green sea urchins, a bunch of clams and mussels, and some small crabs that attempted to hide and scuttle under the rocks. All of this undersea harvest he stowed in a net bag clipped to his weight belt, then swam back to shore.

Removing the divesuit and other gear, he stood naked on the beach towelling down thoroughly in the transient onshore breeze. Higher up on the island, a flat sandstone shelf formed a natural depression and acted as a shelter from the constant winds. It took several trips to carry up all the supplies, including a carrier of dried oak splits for a fire. Years back there had been firewood that could be harvested on the island, but now little remained.

With the entrenching tool head set at ninety degrees, he quickly excavated what remained of the old fire pit. It looked as though the pit hadn't been used for quite a long time; however the constant wind and rain on the island made it impossible to date anything that was exposed.

He re-dug the shallow fire pit, stacked rocks around the perimeter and piled a handful of dry oak splits in the centre. With that finished, he took a trioxane bar from the backpack and nestled it underneath the stack of wood before lighting it with a match. In the past, fires were started with matches, some dry kindling and persistence. The ever-present winds on the island did their best to extinguish all small flames. The trioxane bars, or heat tabs as they were called in the Army, were made of a chemical that was only one step away from RDX explosive, which burned with an intense heat that wind could not blow out. In moments the fire was burning brightly, casting swirling shadows on the rock ledges of the small enclosure.

Kurt removed kitchen utensils from his duffel bag, including a small but deep cast-iron frying pan, a small bottle of cooking oil, plastic bags of powdered milk, flour and seasonings. On a nearby rock he placed the three striped bass, made a few deft cuts on each with the razor-sharp Randall knife and carefully peeled away fillets of white meat. He tossed the fish remains down on to the rocks below. Between the gulls and the waves they wouldn't last long. He placed the lobster near, but not in the fire to firm up the meat, before it was removed from the tail and claws and placed in the hot oil with the fish fillets. Small portions of the urchins, mussels and crabs added variety. This seafood stew was prepared in the same way his grandfather had made it years ago, using only simple, storable ingredients and fresh fish from the clean, cold waters of Maine.

⌘

A beautiful evening descended over the mid-coast while Kurt slowly savoured the stew. Several angular sails caught the waning sun, contrasting sharply with the now deep blue, almost black, ocean. In the distance, a sprinkling of lobster boats plied the deeper waters, the fishermen on board picking up and checking their traps in the productive summer season.

Kurt felt good being back here, the only place he had ever called home. His ancestors had fished in the waters of the cold North Atlantic for centuries. Maybe there was some magnetic attraction to this heritage, or perhaps it was just comfort in familiarity. The rocks, the wind, the waves were all primal elements of nature that could fill voids in a man's being. For the first time in recent memory he was enjoying a few hours of unmitigated peace. Instinct told him he needed to recover from recent events and focus on the future.

He cleaned the dirty dishes at the water's edge with sand and sea water. The darkness was very close and deep shades of indigo over the harbour were all that remained of the day. A boat emblazoned with coloured lights and full of young adults buzzed by, heading from Port Clyde to the outer islands. As the boat flashed by, too close to the rocks, Kurt glimpsed beer bottles and ice-cream cones. The occupants didn't see the man who was watching them from the shore.

The fire died to red embers and small blue flames appeared and disappeared with the dying breeze. Lying on a foam pad beneath a camouflage nylon poncho liner, the smell of salt-laced North Atlantic air and the sound of waves crashing on rocks were natural narcotics. His eyes grew heavy and a dreamless sleep gently enveloped him.

The moon woke him in the small hours of the morning. The orb seemed iridescently silver in its intensity. Kurt rolled towards it and saw its reflection in the ripples of the ocean, like an infinite luminous pathway to the heavens. He drifted asleep again before any unwanted thoughts could disturb this long sought after peace.

⌘

Morning split the unified darkness of earth, with a soft red horizon and pale violet sky. Fond memories of time spent on the island as a child resurfaced as he brushed his teeth with seawater and baking soda. The pistol and knife blade were well oiled, because salt-spray eats steel voraciously. He removed all signs of his presence by rearranging the fire pit rocks into a random pattern, and mixing the ash with sand. Violent storms would do that anyway, but removing tracks had become a habit, if not an obsession. The skiff loaded with all the gear, he prepared to depart the island.

With the sea nearly deserted, the motor on the little skiff turned over slowly as it made its way back to Port Clyde. The lights from several fishing boats working deep waters were still silhouetted against the horizon. Tying up to the floating dock he found the stairs leading up were steep because the tide was a good twelve feet lower than it was the previous evening. The stripers would be running soon.

The small restaurant near the dock was just opening for business. Kurt remembered eating there only a couple of times, years ago, when eating out was considered extravagant. A young couple seemed to be running the place now, maybe a husband and wife. He ordered a large cup of coffee to go and two fresh doughnuts that must have been picked up in Belfast that morning, at the only bakery in the area. Taking the breakfast outside, the sunrise began to light the eastern sky like a distant explosion.

⌘

The deep indigo of the pre-dawn hours had been chased away, replaced by the promise of a bright summer's day on the Maine coast. The rocky shoreline, brightened to shades of grey, brown and light green. Kurt walked down the length of the Port Clyde pier and sat on the end of the docks, taking in the smells and sounds of his youth, which now seemed like a vacation in some exotic place. The salt air carried a chill north-east breeze, that he found comforting and couldn't be more different from the stifling jungles still vivid in his mind.

The Lady Anne majestically circled in from the St George River. She was resplendent in her environment, and she bobbed and swung on the early morning swells like an athlete warming up for the day's challenges.

The Lady Anne was a highbred mix of fishing boat and tourist yacht. Dave Armstrong had commissioned her to be built at the Bath Ship Works, in the same place heavy commercial and naval vessels had their keels laid. Her sturdy forward boom allowed huge blue tuna, sometimes weighing a thousand pounds to be easily reeled in, yet other accoutrements were those rather befitting luxury yachts. This configuration gave Dave the versatility of conducting tourist cruises in the summer season and commercial fishing during the cold months.

Disrupting the idyllic scene was the chatter of people parking cars and carrying coolers and supplies down to the boat ramp. Kurt was always annoyed by the presence of tourists. Raised by his grandfather and growing up as a lobsterman gave him a sense of identity with this raw and picturesque coastline. He always sensed that the tourists. looked at the locals as a curious and crude people who were nice fodder for vacation photographs, but not worthy of further association. Dave suddenly emerged from the bowels of the ship as his paying customers began to arrive, and Kurt waved to him. Dave froze in his tracks, looking like he'd seen a ghost. With a few strides of his powerful legs Dave bounded off the boat, over the ramp and on to the dock, and was standing next to Kurt a few seconds later.

"Well, hello, Kurt!" Dave said with genuine pleasure. "I didn't expect to see you, I heard you were in school."

"Had a couple of weeks between semesters," Kurt said. "Thought I'd come up. I finally had the nerve to face the old place."

"Well, it is a pleasant surprise," Dave said, patting him on the back with a calloused hand that felt like seasoned wood. "I hope you can stay awhile. Lady Anne is running well. Didn't get a chance to talk to you, but all of us do miss the old man."

Kurt nodded and looked toward the ground. He knew he would have to discuss his grandfather sometime but he wasn't ready now. It was only after he arrived back from overseas that he heard the news about the incident. The old man had always taken chances and often went out alone when he shouldn't have, but he was a master seaman and his drowning didn't make sense, especially since it happened in fair weather.

"Hey, why don't you come with us on the Lady Anne today?" Dave asked him. "We can talk. I'm just taking these folks from Boston out around Mohegan Island. We should be back this afternoon."

"I appreciate the invitation, Dave," Kurt responded, "but I have some things to do, plus it wouldn't be fair to your passengers. Those people would rightly be annoyed if you weren't entertaining them as part of the tour package."

Dave nodded his head.

"You're probably right. It's a cross we all have to bear to live here. Often I'd rather use them as bait than entertain them. Will you be around tonight? Why don't you come over to the house? You've never seen it."

"Sure, Dave, I'd like that."

"Good," Dave replied. "Come over about six. I'll put some fish on the grill."

"See you then, Dave," Kurt said as he walked off. "Don't let those city folks get on your nerves."

⌘

Kurt spent the rest of the morning prowling around favourite haunts on the mid-coast, visiting the images remembered from childhood. The Maine coast was unique in the world. Glaciers had scoured huge channels along the courses of ancient rivers leaving a series of bays and peninsulas that projected into the North Atlantic like fingers of a great hand. Huge quantities of fresh water flowing into the ocean from the rivers were continually mixed by the highest tides variations on earth, over fifteen feet between low and high tide. The constant supply of nutrients and continual churning created a cauldron of sea life. Schools of fish, crabs, clams and lobsters thrived in the environment and continued to have large populations despite two hundred years of intensive fishing.

The primal power of it all had impressed him as a child and still took his breath away. The faces of the rock cliffs glistened with salt spray as rollers came in, breaking on the shore with a crash, time and again. The sea was a perpetual motion machine. It would never cease, would never stop until time itself ended. Man was insignificant here and, despite the will to dominate, man would never dominate this, which made this place so special. The sea was continuous and touched all places in the world. Desert sands and icecaps, steaming jungle and barren shores, the sea saw it all. But the Maine Coast was the only place the sea called home.

Kurt ate lunch in a small outdoor café in Bristol, while reading newspapers in the warm sun until early afternoon. The Seaside Cemetery was a few miles further to the north at Point Pleasant. The cemetery was located on the side of a hill overlooking an inlet. Huge hardwoods and conifers kept most of the gravestones in deep shadow, and the freshening sea breeze always felt cool in their shade.

Kurt normally thought of cemeteries as depressing and pointless places but they did link the past and present and, in the vacant lots waiting to be filled, the future. All the hopes, ambitions and achievements of the people who had lived and died in this community lay beneath this patient piece of earth.

Kurt didn't know the location of his grandfather's grave. While alive the old man never spoke of such things and would not have been concerned about a burial plot. Kurt knew that Dave had made the arrangements discreetly. Dave was like that, one of those immensely practical and generous men, who without complaint looked after the dreamers and the wanderers like the Christiansons.

Walking through the older grave stones there was no sign of fresh digging in the original area: there was no room left. Newer burials were located at the perimeter of the cemetery. Further down, the land sloped towards the inlet in which the water's flow perpetually changed direction, dictated by the rhythmic tidal flux. Here would be the perfect resting place for a fisherman who would go to sea no more. This thought turned prophetic when a lone grey headstone appeared further down the slope.

On drawing closer, this headstone was noticeably different from the others. There was no inscription on the side facing the other markers, because it was positioned at an angle parallel to the shoreline. Kurt circled around the grave slowly, as if the ground would crack underfoot. He felt ridiculous, since there was no one alive here but nevertheless he approached with trepidation. His dead grandfather lay beneath the carpet of new green grass and wildflowers. Burial was something Kurt never understood. Why trap a body beneath the ground, to wait for insects to claim it? It made more sense to burn the dead, releasing their remains quickly.

The inscription of the headstone came into view on the far side. When he saw it he stopped and read the inscription.

Rulf Christianson
Born 1903 in Ellsborg Sweden
Died 1969

*Home is the Sailor Home from the Sea*
*And the Hunter Home From the Hill.*

The last line of a poem by Robert Louis Stephenson was very appropriate for the old man, almost as if it had been written for him before he was born. Not just a sailor and a hunter, but the very best of both, and here was his final resting place. Around the perimeter of the headstone was a decorative motif, but on closer examination a series of Norse runes appeared, linked in the form of an undulating serpent.

The interpretation of runic inscriptions had been taught to him as a child. Reading runes was not like reading words. Kurt quickly scanned the engraving but his skills were long out of practice, and no clear message formed. The headstone was made of fine granite and immaculately carved. He would have to thank Dave for the dignity so generously bestowed upon his grandfather.

⌘

Dave's house and marina were set in a hidden and picturesque cove on the banks of the St George River, about eight miles inland from Port Clyde. Massive but unpretentious, the house was constructed from rough hewn logs and cemented beach stone. Pine and cedar trees melded with fractured boulders resulted in a structure too massive to be washed or blown away, even by nature's might. Dave's boat, the Lady Anne, was berthed up against his personal dock on the river, like a purring cat resting after an active day.

Fragrant smoke curled around from the rear of the house on wispy tendrils, drawing Kurt to the food. A spacious patio connected the back of the house via a walkway to the river dock. The patio, walkway and dock were all constructed of hand-split native cedar, which had a large amount of natural oil and resisted deterioration. Dave stood in the centre of the patio at his custom-built barbecue, poking at the fire with a long metal fork. The grill was made from bisected fifty-five gallon drums and spouted yellow flames from its belly.

Kurt walked up to Dave, who was startled by his presence.

"God, I didn't even hear you, Kurt. My hearing must be going."

"That's a really nice grill, Dave. Where did you buy it?"

"I'll have you know," Dave replied, pretending to be piqued, "that beauty wasn't bought, it was custom built. Things are a little slow in dry dock from time to time and the welders like to keep busy. I did trade a rather nice bluefin tuna for it though."

"Cooking with wood not charcoal?"

"Yes, sir," Dave responded with pride. "If you use fruitwood like apple, pear or cherry, it imparts a very subtle but wonderful flavour. I need to burn it down a little more though ... beer?

"Definitely."

They sat in chairs that were handmade from solid wood planking and finished till smooth with marine spar varnish. The deck overlooked a natural harbour formed by a meander in the St. George's River. It was nearly eight o'clock and the sun was on the wane, but this far north the evenings persisted for a long time in late June.

Kurt took a swig from a bottle of locally brewed Shipyard Ale.

"Not bad, at least it has some hops. You have certainly carved out a beautiful place here, Dave. In fact if I was the settling down type I'd work for something like this."

Dave got up and stood by the railing overlooking the water and his boat.

"Anne and I worked for this dream home all of our lives," Dave said quietly towards the river. "I spoke about my plans to your grandfather on several occasions; he always rolled his eyes but when I started building the place he came over and helped me clear and dig. Great old guy your grandfather, I miss him."

"I miss him, too," Kurt talked around his beer. "I always thought he was a nasty old cuss and I guess he was, but he became a part of everything he touched."

"My wife and I saved every penny and built this little piece of paradise we always dreamed of. Just before it was completed she was diagnosed with breast cancer and went downhill very fast."

"I'm really sorry to hear that, Dave," Kurt said.

"It's ironic," Dave mused, "that just when you think you have everything under control and you are finally achieving your life's ambition, the hand of fate comes down and smacks you senseless."

"I guess all we can do is roll with the punches," Kurt said. "We can't alter fate."

All was silent for a few minutes. Water in the tidal river was reversing directions. The influx from the sea was waning and the flow down river was beginning to dominate, causing eddies and swirls to form.

"So now I have this place to myself," Dave said aloud. "The kids visit once in a while, but you know how kids are? They have lives of their own. You know what I do like about it though?"

"What's that, Dave?"

"I can shoot off my back deck into the river and not bother anyone."

"I smell a contest in the air," Kurt said grinning. "You'll never live down that day at the trap range until you beat me, will you?"

Dave laughed and walked in the back door, emerging with a black nylon satchel, which looked like an emergency police call-out bag. He set it down on the table in the middle of the deck and from it removed two pairs of ear muffs, protective glasses and a blue Smith & Wesson 38 special revolver. Kurt recognized it as a Model 14 Targetmaster, a gun that had little power but fine accuracy.

"See the stump?" Dave pointed across the bend of the river to a remnant of a gnarled pine trunk, emerging from the muddy river bank. The tide had now begun to run seaward rapidly.

Kurt nodded.

"Most hits out of six wins," Dave said. "Of course, I do have the home court advantage. The stump is about seventy-five metres away and the sights are set for a six o'clock hold. I'll go first."

Dave positioned himself in a classic bull's eye shooter's stance, grasping the revolver with his right hand and extending it directly in front of him, his left hand in his back pocket.

The muzzle of the pistol barked and rose slightly from the recoil. Water splashed just below the tree stump, forming a temporary cavity in the muck. Dave cocked the hammer, fired again, and a cavity formed just to the left of the stump. Dave nodded in satisfaction. Now he had the elevation and windage. The gun fired a third time followed by a dull *thunk* as the soft lead wad cutter struck the stump. The revolver fired three more times in succession and three more times the bullets burrowed into wood.

"Four out of six isn't bad," Dave said with some satisfaction as he swung out the cylinder and began to reload the pistol with loose ammo from a cardboard box.

"Don't worry, I'll use mine," Kurt said.

Kurt unzipped his windbreaker and pulled a silver revolver from a shoulder holster. The gun had a shorter barrel than Dave's but was of heavier construction. The finish wasn't shiny and polished but had a dull brushed appearance. The grips were carved and polished from a piece of highly figured wood.

"I didn't even know that you were carrying," Dave said with surprise. "What is that?"

Kurt pointed the gun at the deck and unlatched the cylinder.

"It's a four-inch Model 29 44 magnum," Kurt said. "I had this piece sandblasted and hard chromed to prevent corrosion and cut glare."

Kurt tapped the ejector rod. Six cartridges rose up and he checked them.

"Ears," Kurt said as he swung the revolver into a two-handed triangular stance.

As the gun came up, Kurt pressed evenly on the trigger, causing the hammer to come back smoothly. The moment the pistol reached the apex of travel, the gun fired. In the gathering dusk the muzzle flash lit up the deck like a lightning strike.

Dave saw another small flash in the centre of the stump and pieces of wood were blown clear, landing in the water and surrounding mud. Before the debris settled Kurt fired a second shot and then four more so fast it was hard to distinguish individual reports. The air near the target was suddenly filled with smoke and debris. Consecutive flashes lit the stump and nearby water in pulses. Then all was silent except for the sizzling sound as the last of the debris settled to earth.

The tree stump was ruined. Large chunks of wood were missing and fragments were lying on the muddy embankment. The remnants of the stump smoked, as if it had just been bombed.

"Just what the living hell was that?" Dave questioned loudly, gawking at the scene.

Kurt took off his ear-muffs and opened the cylinder of the revolver.

"It's special ammo, Dave. There is priming compound in the hollow nose and it's sealed up. It goes off on impact. The fragmented bullets dump their energy quickly. Works well, don't you think?"

"You can buy that ammunition?" Dave asked.

"No, I make them up myself," Kurt replied. "The old man taught me how to reload ammunition to save money and I figured the rest out by myself. The trouble is a 44 magnum will pass through the target wasting a lot of energy on the other side. This technique prevents that from happening. A hit with one of these and the party is over."

Kurt wiped down his gun with Dave's silicone rag, replaced the spent cartridge cases with fresh rounds, and placed the revolver back in his shoulder holster.

"Six out of six as I counted them," Kurt said. "You're buying the beer."

"Bought and chilled already, I'm a step ahead of you," Dave laughed.

⌘

They drank local beer and ate fresh tuna steak and grilled corn on the wood burning creation of which Dave was so proud. The flavour was bold and subtle at the same time, better than anything Kurt could remember except, of course, for the fish stew he'd made the previous evening, but this tuna had to be a close second.

Dave talked about the frustrations of his charter boat business he ran in the summer and how difficult it was becoming to catch the big bluefin tuna anymore, even in deep water.

Dave was a man with fingers in many pies. To be successful in an economically depressed area like coastal Maine, a businessman needed to diversify. He also discussed conducting some sea trials on boats that were being constructed in the nearby Bath shipyards. The boats were custom built for supporting offshore oil drilling operations in places like the Gulf of Mexico, the North Sea and other locations. Maine had some of the best shipyards, as well as the most skilled boat builders in the world but the completed products had to be tested before they were delivered to the user.

The boats would be taken for seaworthiness trials locally, Dave explained, then ferried to a New York shipyard for the installation of final fittings prior to delivery. A unit was due for completion in a few weeks in preparation for delivery to the west coast of Africa. Kurt knew there had to be a purpose to this dialogue. Dave wasn't prone to discussing things in such detail unless there was a reason.

"I'm putting together a crew to drive the boat over, Kurt. We could use you. You're strong, know boats pretty well and should have some of those sea legs left. The trip is rough and physically demanding, but you're young and the pay is good. I imagine you could use some extra money for school?"

Kurt swirled his beer in the bottle, the liquid subtly reflecting the deep yellow glow given off by the half dozen citronella candles burning on the perimeter of the deck.

"Sounds interesting, Dave, thanks. And you're right, I've signed up for school this fall and the money would definitely help. It's pretty hard to live on the GI Bill. The truth is I'm finding it hard to focus on school right now. Maybe it's too soon, you know, after ..."

"I know what you mean, Kurt. It takes time to readjust. It took me several years after Korea to make any sense of my life. Eventually, though, you'll put it into perspective and move on."

"Dave, can I ask you something?"

"Sure, Kurt, go ahead."

"How well did you know my father?"

Dave looked a little startled in the flickering candle light. His hesitation in answering revealed more than words could.

"I knew him fairly well; it's a small community. We were in Korea at the same time but not in the same unit. You probably don't remember him, do you?"

"No, I guess not ... only vaguely. I remember being taken to the VA hospital as a little kid and being frightened, that's about it."

"He came back on a prisoner exchange." Dave looked at the deck as he talked, not at Kurt. "From what I've heard, he volunteered for a special Marine unit that worked with the Navy Underwater Demolition Teams, an extremely hazardous job. He was concussed in an explosion while reconnoitring a potential amphibious landing site on the North Korean coast. He was never the same after that. The doctors said he had permanent brain damage from the blast.

Kurt nodded.

"My grandfather never spoke a word to me about him. Every time I asked, he stayed silent. I've always wondered … if he …"

"Be assured he was a brave man, Kurt, always going beyond what was expected. But he was mortal like all of us. People are killed and injured in war; you know that better than anyone."

"Yes, it's just hard not knowing. Not knowing him or what he was like, it's always bothered me."

"He was a lot like you."

"How was he like me?" Kurt met Dave's eyes in the flickering light, with the beseeching stare of a child, pleading for answers.

"Well, he was leaner in build than you but he had the same physical strength, determination and fearlessness. Yes, you are a lot alike. The fruit doesn't fall far from the tree, as they say."

"Thanks," Kurt said. "It's good to talk about it. There's always been a big gap and even a little information helps me a lot. He died when I was four and that's when my mother left, just disappeared. It's lucky my grandfather was around to take care of me or I'd have ended up in an orphanage. It was hard on him too, raising a child at that age."

"Well, I can say he did a great job, Kurt. I really don't know a whole lot more or I would share it with you."

Kurt nodded and excused himself. He knew Dave was sailing early tomorrow and needed his sleep.

"I'm heading back down to Massachusetts tomorrow. I suppose you need an answer soon about the job?"

"I'll need a yes or a no by the end of next week," Dave replied. "If you don't accept, I need to find someone else."

"Sure, I appreciate the offer, I'll let you know."

⌘

The night was a dark one and with the low cloud cover coming in from the sea, no moon shone. Kurt didn't want to stay in the old house; there were too many ghosts there. He slept in the storage shed with the door left ajar. When the rain came just after midnight, the drops on the metal roof drowned out his thoughts and a fitful sleep finally came.

One strange dream was of small dark men with jagged teeth and constant smiles. They lived in a desert of hot fine sand and intense sun where it never rained. Like most disconnected dreams it made no sense, but left a feeling of unease that persisted. Perhaps this desert was the antithesis of the Maine seacoast, why else would he be dreaming of it?

Before dawn he arose and packed up. The rain had ceased long before but a heavy fog had rolled in and engulfed the entire mid-coast region. Fog was beautiful in its own way, though most of the lobstermen and fishermen would disagree. This morning the grey denseness was almost palpable, as it moved and swirled like an odourless smoke between the trees and the house. Looking towards the yard light, individual particles of moisture seemed to pass in front of the bulb.

After turning off the yard light and locking the shed, Kurt checked the house before turning the key in the lock and replacing it beneath the brick. He turned once more to look at the house and wondered if he would ever see it again. The best thing would be for Dave to just sell the property, then it wouldn't be a worry anymore.

The restaurant in Port Clyde was open at this early hour. A yellow glow through the big windows was visible when he drove within sight, like a safe harbour for a lost ship in the pre-dawn. The young owners were bustling about making ready for the day, though Kurt was the only patron. The couple whispered to themselves and glanced at him as he drank coffee and ate a large fresh sweet roll. Kurt was irritated by the rude behaviour until the woman approached him. She had a pleasant face and a round body.

"Mister, you're that soldier that was written about in the paper, aren't you?" she asked cautiously. "The paper said that you went missing or were captured in Vietnam and then were found again months later."

Kurt swallowed before answering.

"Perhaps, ma'am, I haven't seen the papers here."

"Okay, I'm sure it was you though. You wore a green beret in the picture."

Kurt nodded to her.

"You see, my older brother was killed two years ago over there. He was in the 173rd Airborne Brigade. Did you know it? That unit I mean?"

"Oh yes, I sure did. They were one of the best," Kurt replied.

The woman nodded eagerly before continuing.

"They sent us a Purple Heart medal and a Bronze Star, after they shipped Tommy home.

"I'm very sorry for the loss of your brother, ma'am," Kurt said. "A lot of good men died in the war, many friends of mine."

The woman shook her head again and looked down at the table.

"Well, it's nice talking to somebody who was over there," the woman continued. "It gives a little comfort. Tommy's gone and all we have now is a box and some medals. I think he is still over there somewhere wandering around, his spirit is anyway. He liked the woods, you know; he was a good hunter and fisherman. It doesn't seem right that he was killed and others weren't. You wonder why. I don't think there has been a single night I haven't woken up and seen his face, lost, over there in the jungle, trying to get back home."

Kurt could sense the poor woman's grief. This was multiplied by the nearly sixty thousand boys lost in this soon to be forgotten war. Every young man was a vital part of a family, with friends, relatives, girlfriends, fiancées and classmates. Each loss left an irreparable hole. Secretly he knew that his own reported disappearance may have played a role in his grandfather's death, but he didn't want to dwell on that now, it was just too painful.

"We all ask that question ourselves, ma'am; but there's no answer. The best we could figure is that it was just where you were when the bullet or shell came. It's just fate, or as my grandfather used to say; 'Where you're standing when the serpent strikes'. Remember your brother for the good man he was and that's the way he'll always be in your hearts and minds."

"Well, I don't mean to keep you," the woman said as she got up from the table. "I can see you are getting ready to hit the road."

"Yes, I'm heading back to college, I don't know for how long but I'm doing my best."

"Good for you," the woman said. "Don't end up like me working in a restaurant; it's for the birds. Would you like to take a couple more doughnuts with you on your trip? They're on the house."

"Thank you, ma'am, that would be nice."

The woman smiled at Kurt and selected the two biggest doughnuts from the glass display case and put them in a white bag to take with him.

"By the way, my name is Joyce. If you come back this way, please stop in again. It's been nice talking to you."

"I certainly will do that, and thanks again ... Joyce."

Kurt held up the bag and smiled as he walked out the door. The eastern sky was brightening and the fog was beginning to push inland. The trip back shouldn't be too bad. He hated driving in thick fog; it tempted fate.

There was that word again. Fate took poor Tommy and, for the rest of her life, that sweet woman would be haunted by the death of her brother. Why do the most innocent people have to always shoulder the greatest burdens in this life? Now there was a question that defied an easy answer. He tried not to think about it for the rest of the trip.

# CHAPTER 3
## WANDERER

When the I-95 swung away from the coast, the heat returned with a vengeance. It would climb well into the nineties today, away from the cooling influence of the sea breeze. The landscape became flat and featureless; pines, rocks and sandy soil made it apparent why Maine was a poor state.

Kurt crossed the bridge at Portsmouth, New Hampshire, and drove through the sprawl of the huge Naval Shipyards, where a destroyer and a light cruiser were undergoing refitting. Massive cranes intersected the skyline in crazy angles as they hoisted rebuilt subsections into the huge vessels.

Kurt suddenly felt very tired. It may have been dehydration or the lack of air conditioning in the jeep, or perhaps it was the thought of heading back to school. The reality was only now starting to register. With one semester under his belt already since his discharge from the Army, the prospect of sitting in classes this summer and listening to droning professors seemed unbearable. His grades were good thus far, because he applied himself with maximum effort. He thought it pointless not to give of your best.

Earlier he'd fantasized about going to MIT but, even if he could meet the admission standards, there was no way to pay for a semester there, let alone two or three years. The GI Bill, as good as it was, did not enable returning soldiers to enroll in prestigious Ivy League schools. Also, Kurt wasn't sure he could last another three or four consecutive years in a high pressure academic environment. The war had changed him. School just didn't compare to the excitement of combat and that insatiable 'itch' for action that grew every day.

His fields of study had been narrowed down to the geosciences or mining engineering. With the former there was the possibility of working in the open air for a petroleum company. With the latter he could go into production mining, work that required physical labour and being outside. He realized that his nervous energy and requirement for activity could not be fulfilled in an office; that would be equivalent to a prison sentence. Staying in the Army would have been fine, if that had been an option. Working in forestry had been another possibility, but discarded when he saw the pay scale. Being born poor was a curse which he intended to exorcise, not prolong.

He pulled up in front of the small rented house. A room-mate who attended the same school, had gone home for the summer. Slowly he walked around the house to see if there were any signs of disturbance or entry marks.

Some strange occurrences had recently made him edgy. The phone would ring but the line would be dead, or only the faint sound of breathing was heard. Also, on a couple of occasions he suspected he was being tailed by a white van while driving.

Maybe it was all just post-combat paranoia; he hoped so. Whether or not these events were related to his recent experiences in the army he didn't know, but gut instinct told him to err on the side of caution.

Finding nothing unusual, he opened the front door and went in.

The house was hot and stuffy from being closed up for several days, so he opened all the windows, in the hope of a breeze. After drinking a quart of cold water from the fridge, he switched on the TV and sat in the only comfortable chair in the house. The TV was just a distraction, white background noise. Some political talk show was on but nothing of interest and sitting upright, he fell into a light, almost trance-like sleep. The television continued to spew raw sound, driving words and phrases into his semi-conscious mind.

"Guerrilla camps attacked ... casualties ... atrocities ... international condemnation ... civilians ... bush war ..."

From far away, deep in his drowsing mind, questions surfaced, dragging him back to consciousness. "What war? It's 1975 and Vietnam is over; what are they talking about?"

As he awoke slightly he heard a word come out of the newsreader's mouth.

"Rhodesia."

"Rhodesia," Kurt's mind tried to wrestle with the word to find a familiar chord, "Rhodesia. That's in Africa somewhere."

As he stirred and became fully awake, the news report shifted gears to the weather. Tornadoes in the mid-west, rain in the north-west, drought in the south. The previous report didn't register any longer.

Now the sun was down, Kurt decided to go for a walk to shake off the lethargy, and stretch his legs that were cramping from the heat and inactivity. Was the restlessness only in his mind, or was his body provoking the restless thoughts? It was sometimes hard to know which force drove which.

⌘

As twilight became darkness, he strolled along the banks of the river. The area was very picturesque and historic, but too built up for Kurt to feel comfortable. The brightly illuminated skyline merged with the last wisps of sunset to form colourful chaotic forms reflected in the running waters.

Like the reflection, Kurt thought, life changed constantly, substance and form were always in flux, forever shifting. The best anyone could do was to grab a piece of the speeding landscape and hang on. This complex country seemed to be too large and mature to notice the contributions of an individual. Deep within he felt he had something unique to contribute, but he was struggling to identify what it was. To survive here they wanted you to change your identity and become some insignificant and unrecognizable cog, hopelessly lost in the bowels of this great machine that glowed in the jumbled waters.

Watching water sweeping out to sea always conveyed the feeling that nature was futilely trying to cleanse the blight that had taken over the land. In spite of her best efforts more clutter appeared, more roads, more buildings and more houses, covering everything once sacred. How could you feel part of this? When would men come to their senses and see what they were doing to the world in the name of progress?

Just before ten o'clock Kurt headed back to the house. The temperature was still warm but the intense heat had broken and sleep should be possible if not comfortable. The raw purity of the Maine Coast had left its stamp again. Maybe he should just go back and live in the family property and fix it up ... and then do what? There would be no next generation of lobstermen or fishermen. As for working on a tourist boat like Dave did ... that was out of the question.

Open windows, with the help of a slight night breeze, had cooled down the house. When the phone rang, to Kurt's surprise the call was from Joe Cordoza, the man he had saved years ago on that aborted SOG mission. He thought about Joe often but had never got around to contacting him. Rumour said that Joe had recently divorced and retired about a year ago to a little town in New Mexico, where he was blacksmithing. After trading pleasantries, Joe surprised Kurt by inviting him to New Mexico. There was a Special Operations Veterans Association meeting being held in Las Vegas the following weekend and Joe wondered if Kurt was interested in it attending it with him. There was a mining school Kurt was considering at New Mexico Tech in Socorro, so the trip seemed logical. He could be back in time for summer school the following week. The agreement made, Joe told him to call from the airport on arrival.

A worn Eastern Mountain backpack accommodated everything needed for the brief trip and a call to the airline confirmed the time of the next flight. He opted for standby status, which made sense since the flights going south that time of year were seldom fully booked. Leaving Logan in the early hours, the flight arrived at Albuquerque International at nine o'clock the next day.

⌘

Tired, but re-invigorated by the desert scenery on approach, Kurt waited for the backpack to come around on the luggage carousel. He'd had to check in the backpack because it contained items not allowed in the passenger compartment. As it looked like a student's beaten-up travelling companion, Kurt had little concern about anyone stealing it.

People walking around the airport were a mellow assemblage of ranchers, Hispanics, students and other ordinary people free from the urgency and bustle that typified most big city airports. This atmosphere felt relaxed and non-threatening, which was a plus for New Mexico already.

After collecting the backpack, he approached a pay phone to call Joe. He passed a large picture window that looked out onto the vista of a bright morning in the desert. The air was breathtakingly clear and the rolling sand and scrub covered hills merged with the mountains in the distance. Without further deliberation he decided to walk.

He dropped some coins into a vending machine by the exit and received two lemon-lime drinks which were pushed into the backpack before heading through the door. The airport was located to the south-west side of Albuquerque on an elevated mesa. In close proximity to the airport were Kirtland Air Force Base and Sandia Laboratories. Kirtland was the place where the Air Force Para Rescue crews were trained. Kurt recalled that on one occasion in Laos, men trained here came in with miniguns blazing from the door of a Big Sikorski HH-53 helicopter to rescue a downed pilot.

As he walked away from the airport, a variety of military aircraft were parked along the far reaches of a nearby runway; National Guard A-7 Corsairs, C-130s, C-123s, C-7A Caribous crowded the tarmac, making his pulse quicken at the sight.

Sandia Laboratories was on the other side of Kirtland. Although the buildings were well known and visible, there were rumours they harboured some of the most sensitive and classified operations of any facility in the country. The brains working in Los Alamos, in the northern part of the state, designed nuclear weapons and other exotics which the engineers and technicians at Sandia made into working devices. It was also said that Sandia, named after the Spanish word for watermelon, which it resembled at sunset, was hollow and enclosed a large nuclear weapons repository. For a place that seemed so relaxed on the surface, Albuquerque was a tiger laying in wait.

A couple of kilometres west of the airport terminal and obscured by a brush covered hill, Kurt unpacked and reconfigured his equipment. He moved the 44 revolver from the main compartment and put it in the side pocket of his pack, where it was readily accessible. A Randall combat knife, carried through the war, he tied upside-down on the left shoulder strap of the backpack. He then wrapped the knife with a small green towel which was secured with two rubber bands, making it available but not visible. A military lensatic compass and a signal flare pen, contained in a clip pouch, he secured to the right shoulder strap.

Kurt knew that other casual hikers would find it strange he carried all this gear. However, being both a woodsman and a soldier, he knew it was much better to have equipment and not need it, than to need it and not have it.

Unfolding a generic Rand McNally map, Kurt took a bearing for a destination between the small villages of Tome and Bosque Farms, on the eastern bank of the Rio Grade River. That way the river wouldn't have to be crossed. Not being able to shake the military tactics made him feel foolish sometimes, but that was how he saw the world and thus far, it worked.

The morning coolness still hugged the shadows but the rising sun was clearing the eastern mountains and immediately felt intense in the desert air.

Kurt stopped and removed his backpack and stripped off his travelling shirt, replacing it with a thin camouflage T-shirt. On the map, lying between his current location and his destination was the Isletta Indian Reservation which he'd have to cross. From this elevation it appeared mostly undeveloped barren desert, interspersed with patches of rough vegetation and undulating hills. The surface soil didn't appear to be sand, but fine gravel that could survive scouring desert winds.

At the crest of the mesa, the Rio Grande Valley snaked below. From this vantage point the vista was magnificent. To the far west, near the uranium mining town of Grants, loomed the forested slopes of Mount Taylor. To the north the Jemez Mountains surrounding Los Alamos were barely visible, immersed in a purple veil. Looking southward, South Baldy near Socorro was the recognizable landmark. Doing a quick calculation in his head, he estimated an area sixty miles wide by one hundred and thirty miles long, or some five million acres, could be seen at once. You couldn't do that in Maine.

The land on which he walked was currently used for animal grazing. Meandering paths beaten down by hoof prints intertwined on the slopes. Otherwise there were few fences, roads or other man-made developments. At the bottom of the slope the black-topped sinuous highway I-47 broke the continuity. It ran parallel to the Rio Grande River, which was obscured by the heavy growth of cottonwoods, poplar and other trees that managed to tap into the running water supply in this otherwise arid country. The trees faithfully followed the river as a ribbon of bright green, cleaved through an ocean of brown desert.

⌘

He heard the old man before he saw him. The still air on the calm morning seemed to magnify sounds. A faint scraping and rustling came from the other side of a rise just before the I-47 road embankment, and Kurt slowly circled around to approach the source of the sounds. On the opposite side an old man was stooped over, placing discarded cans in a plastic garbage bag. Kurt stopped and stood quietly, twenty feet behind him, for a few seconds.

"Getting to be a hot one ... ain't it?" the old man said without turning.

He had been sure the old man hadn't seen him yet.

"It sure is," Kurt replied, trying not to sound surprised.

The old man straightened up and slowly turned around. Despite the heat he wore a tattered suit jacket and an old blue work shirt. His pants were threadbare khaki, with frayed bottoms. Bright yellow cord, probably clothesline, held the pants on his bony hips. Crudely made sandals, fashioned from discarded truck tyres and hemp rope were on his feet. A faded and bent black cowboy hat rested on his head, with a band of rattlesnake skin just above the brim securing a large golden-eagle feather.

The old man's hair was long and braided into two grey ropes which hung below his shoulders; his face was brown and fissured. Chocolate eyes, rimmed by yellow sclera dotted with tiny red spots, had wispy films of opacity clouding both. Though he looked beyond redemption, Kurt perceived a sharp mind hidden beneath the worn-out exterior.

"Don't see many white people walking through these hills," the old man said. "You running away from something?"

Kurt grinned at the old man's incisiveness and boldness.

"No, nobody is chasing me. I'm just heading down the valley to visit a friend."

"Most people drive." The old man shrugged towards the road, visible just over the escarpment.

"You can't see the country very well from the road," Kurt told him.

Kurt swung off the backpack and put it on the ground and sat down on the dry earth, leaning against it.

"Like a drink?" Kurt asked the old man as he unzipped the top pocket of his pack.

"Sure," the old man said, nodding his head.

Kurt handed him one of the 7-Ups. The cans were still cold, but in the dry air there was no condensation.

"Why are you collecting cans?" Kurt asked.

"They give me money for 'em at the recycling place down in the South Valley. I don't need much money, just a little bit sometimes … but it's hard to get that little bit."

"Don't you get a pension or government money, or whatever?" Kurt asked, thinking the government took care of the remaining Indians to some degree.

"I live with my daughter and son-in-law," the old man said, "but they get to the government cheques first, and spend most of it at the liquor store the same day so it doesn't leave much. They get some food stamps, which keeps their two youngsters eating, anyway."

"The world isn't a pretty place is it?" Kurt asked.

"Oh, the world is a beautiful place." The old man swung an arm behind him indicating the surrounding countryside. "It's just that man isn't too beautiful; we make it very hard for ourselves. Instead of caring for each other, we're greedy and foolish. We hurt ourselves with bad decisions each and every day."

As the old man spoke Kurt picked up a dot on the western horizon, the crystal clear air creating little interference. The shape of the aircraft was unlike anything he'd ever seen. Sleek, yet large and flying low and fast, it passed just to the north of them a few moments later, its engine noise drowning out all other sounds. The exhaust ports from four massive turbofans were nestled in the plane's rear section, but were only applying a fraction of their potential power on final approach.

By the unique shape Kurt knew the aircraft was a B1B, probably a prototype because they were not in service yet. Kirtland AFB did shielding experiments and other tests such as blasting the planes with electronic signals to simulate nuclear explosions. An article he'd read said that the electronics bay of the B1B was lined with pure gold to suck up the nuclear electromagnetic pulse, so delicate instruments wouldn't be damaged.

The old man had stopped talking as the aircraft passed by. His head turned, moving in sync with Kurt's as they both watched man's latest defence creation sink into its lair. The old man spoke again when the desert silence was restored.

"Like I said." He nodded in the direction of the plane's disappearance.

"I wonder how much one of those costs?" Kurt voiced.

"In dollars or cans?" the old man asked.

They both sat in the silence sipping their drinks. They were sitting in shadow where the heat hadn't yet penetrated. Kurt noticed that the towel wrapped around the knife he'd tied to the shoulder strap of the backpack had slipped down a little, revealing the handle. He moved to cover it but he old man had already seen it.

"That's a very nice knife you have there," the old man said. "It's a Randall isn't it?"

"You have a good eye," Kurt replied. "Yes, it's a Randall. It belonged to a friend of mine who didn't make it through the war. He only had a mother back here in the States and, when I wrote to her, she told me to keep it. She didn't even want his body back. She said that if he liked war so much just to bury him over there. The Army didn't want to do that and I heard they arranged for a plot in Arlington."

The old man looked puzzled.

"So the knife is yours now, huh?" he asked.

"Well, not really," Kurt explained. "It may sound strange but I've always thought that knives and other personal items have a soul or a spirit attached to them. Maybe it's pretty small when compared with a human spirit, but it's still there. Part of the owner becomes attached to the object perhaps, I don't know. He was a good friend of mine and I wanted to keep it, until ..."

"Can I see it?" the old man asked almost apologetically. "I've heard about those Randalls."

"Sure," Kurt said, as he reached up and unsnapped the strap that held the knife in place and handed it over, handle first, with a smooth movement that startled the old man.

He took the knife slowly and balanced it to test the centre of gravity, which fell just behind the guard at the index finger, as it should. He turned it in his hand inspecting every detail. There were a few dings and scratches from use, but the knife was still in good condition. The old man gently scraped the blade over his left gnarled thumb nail and peeled off a fine curl.

Kurt knew by the way he handled it that he was a master with a blade. Only very experienced users knew those subtle tricks.

"The handle is stag horn," Kurt explained. "Indian ... or Asian stag, I mean. It's not slippery when wet like most materials."

"Well, it certainly is beautiful." The old man felt it one last time, then handed it back handle first.

Kurt subtly shook his head.

"No... the knife is yours now," Kurt said.

"I... I can't take this. I don't have any money, only that bag of cans. It wouldn't be right."

"You don't understand," Kurt said. "The knife doesn't belong to me; I was just carrying it until the next real owner could be found. I don't believe in chance. Not much anyway. There was a reason I walked from the airport and we met today. You found it, or it found you, nothing more needs to be said."

While he was talking Kurt undid the bands that fastened the leather knife sheath to the pack strap, and handed it over.

"I don't know what to say. Nobody has ever given me anything like this." The old man carefully slipped the broad polished blade into the protective leather cover.

"You don't need to say anything." Kurt hesitated. "This may not mean anything to you but the original owner of that knife was a Navajo from Window Rock." Kurt pointed to the northwest.

"Oh, it means something, all right," the old man mumbled.

Kurt didn't understand what he meant and the look on his face indicated he didn't want to explain the comment.

"Tell me one thing, was the original owner a brave soldier?" the old man asked.

Kurt looked at the old man for a moment. His dark eyes, though clouded with cataract, seemed to bore through him. There was a hunger for the answer to his question.

"Yes, he was one of the best," Kurt told him softly. "No one ever doubted his courage or loyalty, not for a second."

From around his weathered neck the old man took a worn brown string. On it was threaded a silver and turquoise amulet about an inch across. Kurt recognized the figure on the amulet as a Thunderbird or Native American eagle he'd seen before, but he couldn't remember when ... or where.

"You take this," the old man said. "It will protect you as long as you wear it. That's what they say, anyway. Look at me. I'm still here."

Kurt hesitated, "Are you sure? That looks very personal. I'd feel awkward about taking something like that."

"No, you must take it and wear it. I don't need protecting anymore. Nobody would want to bother with this old bag of bones."

Kurt took the string and put it around his neck. Later he would put the charm on the cord with the bear claw he'd worn since a child. He felt embarrassed about taking it, but was unable to turn down such a spontaneous and heartfelt gesture.

Swinging the backpack off the ground and over his shoulders, Kurt gave a half-wave to the old man, who was still squatting in the dust studying the unexpected gift. Without looking up he said in a low, even tone, "Good hunting, young warrior. Don't go looking for trouble, enough will find you anyway."

Kurt thought about questioning the comment but decided to let it pass. Some things were best taken at face value and left alone.

"Take care, sir," Kurt uttered and headed off down the road embankment.

The old man sat in the same spot for quite awhile even after the sun became hot. Reaching back he removed a dark, tattered wallet. The leather was almost worn through and it contained no money, only an old photo with dog-eared corners. Despite its faded condition the picture was clear enough to see the image of a young Native American soldier wearing a green beret and holding an M-16 rifle. It was a posed picture, but the image clearly showed the handle of a knife which was fastened on the man's web belt.

Stag horn is very distinctive, with its light and dark stripes, and seldom are two pieces exactly the same. The old man rotated the handle until it faced forward as it did in the picture. The markings matched perfectly.

Standing up, he placed the last two cans in his bag. The bag was full now and it was time for him to go.

⌘

Kurt moved down the escarpment, crossed the highway, and joined a gravel road leading into the centre of the Isletta Reservation. Half a mile further down was an old mission building, a general store and several gift shops surrounding a main square. Noon was approaching and his stomach was grumbling. Adjacent to the general store, was a covered area protecting several shaded old picnic tables. Despite it being near the lunch hour, the tables were empty.

A stray mongrel was sniffing at a discarded ice-cream wrapper which someone had thrown near, but not in, a trash barrel. Judging from the animal's rib cage, dog food must have been in short supply.

Kurt bought some Indian fry bread from a vendor in a wagon set up on one side of the store. The fry bread was unleavened, made from fresh ground local grain, and cooked in an iron skillet. It looked appetizing when freshly made and still warm, but he imagined it would be solid and indigestible in a very short time. Inside the store, he bought a small block of cheese, a small jar of mayonnaise and a carton of orange juice from the pretty young cashier. She smiled at Kurt keenly, like an attractive bird of prey. Her look made him self conscious; his body image was still that of an awkward teenager, not the six foot one, two hundred pound man he now was.

Three dogs now prowled around the picnic area. They all had their noses circling the ground near the empty tables. As Kurt prepared his meal all of the animals stopped their sniffing and stared up at him, panting expectantly.

Placing the backpack on a table, he reached for the Randall, stopped short, then remembered the old man. Behind his right hip was a little birch handled, short bladed puukko, which was more suited to the task anyway. There was far too much bread for his sandwich, so he used the razor-sharp blade to slice the large flat loaf into quarters. He tossed a quarter to each of the three dogs that were still watching his every move. Two of them grabbed their pieces from the dust and proceeded to voraciously wolf them down. The third dog, the thinnest of the three, wandered over to her piece and just sniffed at it. When the other two dogs had finished theirs they tried to take hers away, but she bared her teeth and let out a vicious growl, backing them away.

"More worried about protecting it than starving," Kurt thought. "Dogs are almost as weird as people."

"You really shouldn't feed them, they won't leave you alone now."

Kurt was surprised by the voice but tried not to show it. The pretty cashier from the store was standing very close, within touching distance. Not hidden by the counter anymore, she looked lithe, graceful and confident. A simple, floral dress hung perfectly on her frame. Her black hair shone like a raven's wing in the sunlight, falling to the middle of her back. She was erect with her head held high.

"Sorry," Kurt replied. "They looked hungry."

"You can't feed everything that's hungry," the girl said. "You'll only make the problem worse. You're not from here, are you?"

"No, I'm not," Kurt replied, "but I suppose you are."

"Yes, I was born and raised right here in the Pueblo, but I won't be here much longer."

The girl had her arms crossed in an assertive manner. The shyness or vulnerability usually present in a person of her age was absent. A very determined bearing was evident, and her eyes were steady, on his.

"What are you doing here? You don't look like the normal visitors we get, taking vacations and seeing how we 'Indians' live." The girl's statement had a tinge of sarcasm, though no bitterness was apparent in her voice.

"I'm just heading down the valley to visit a friend I haven't seen in years," Kurt told her, pointing south, "and I hope to go visit New Mexico Tech in Socorro."

"Are you going to school there?" she asked, her voice rising in pitch slightly.

"Maybe, it's one of the schools I'm considering."

"What are you studying?" she asked, now dropping her arms to the sides and moving a step closer to Kurt.

"I'm studying geology and mining but I'm just in my first year, I haven't decided which subject to major in yet. I know I couldn't work in an office. That would drive me crazy."

The girl smiled at the comment.

"There's not many of you guys around anymore," she said.

"What do you mean by ... 'you guys'?"

"I mean warriors," the girl said. "You are a warrior, aren't you?"

"Well, I did spend some time in the army," he laughed. "Maybe that qualifies me as one."

The girl now had a trace of smugness in her face.

"I knew it."

Kurt took a long drink from the carton of orange juice and half-heartedly offered it to the girl. She refused, shaking her head subtly.

"You seem to be a sharp judge of character, but you haven't even told me your name," Kurt said.

"It's Rose. My mother named all four of us girls after flowers, she likes to garden."

"Well, Rose, I'm Kurt, it's nice to meet you."

Kurt put out his hand to shake. She lightly grabbed his hand with both of hers and didn't shake it as expected but began to feel his palm with her fingertips. The act surprised Kurt but he didn't resist because the sensation was pleasant.

"What are you doing Rose, reading my palm?"

"Not your palm, your whole hand," Rose explained. "I think you can tell a lot about a person by studying their hands. They are the window to the soul you know."

"That's funny," Kurt countered, "I always thought that was the eyes; 'The eyes are the window to the soul' or so I've heard anyway."

"A common misconception," Rose said. "If you think about it, everything that we do in the world, we do with our hands. Our eyes just see things. Our hands are what make us human."

"And my hand?" Kurt asked.

"I think it's very complex and needs further study," Rose said as she let go of Kurt's hand.

"Do you always do this to strange men, Rose? It could be dangerous."

"No," she said, "only to guys with nice hands."

"You know, girl, I can't put my finger on it but I think you got me in a corner here."

"What do you mean?" Rose responded.

"I think it means I have to see you again so you can finish studying my hand."

Rose smiled. "Well, if you came by some evening, I *might* be available."

"Are you sure it would be OK, there isn't a big boyfriend or anything I should know about?"

"No," she said, "and even if there was, I think you could handle it."

"Well, I'll have to borrow my friend's car, but I was going to need it anyway to go to Socorro."

"Why don't I go with you?" she asked. "I know the area. There's not much around here but I can show you what there is."

"Alright, give me your number and I'll give you a call tomorrow to make arrangements."

Rose smiled and took a pen from a pocket on her dress and took Kurt's arm. Slowly and deliberately in large numbers she wrote a telephone number.

"I won't wash the arm, Rose. Ever," Kurt laughed.

Kurt threw his trash into the bin and without looking back walked through the scrub and fields of the Rio Grande Valley escarpment. The three mongrel dogs trailed him for a time, but dropped out one by one as they realized they weren't following an easy meal.

# CHAPTER 4
## STRANGERS

Kurt heard the strange sound over half a mile away in the still, hot air of mid-afternoon. At that distance it sounded like a ping, ping, ping; then it would stop then start again. As he drew closer it changed to a clang, clang, clang. The sound was definitely metallic in nature, but unfamiliar. Circling the source at a distance, there was no way to see what it was through the thick stand of cottonwoods that grew at the very edge of the Rio Grande Valley.

Downwind there was the sudden smell of hot metal and charcoal fumes, not unpleasant but pungent and distinct. Nearer to the sound, he made a slow rotation around the double-width mobile home, which was mounted on a permanent concrete foundation on a gravel patch set in the middle of the Bosque, or river valley. In front of the house was parked an old burnt-orange Chevy El-Camino, with a stripe painted down its side that had probably looked sporty when new. Twenty yards from the back of the house sat a pre-fabricated building designed to be a small garage or storage shed. In front of the shed was a large awning, supported by aluminum poles.

Beneath the awning was the source of the sound. Joe was hard at work on a large black anvil pounding an object held in tongs, with a hammer. Kurt assumed the man was Joe Cordoza because that's what the mail box in front of the house said. He wore a baseball hat, heavy leather gauntlet gloves that came nearly to his elbows, and a dark apron that covered his front. He also had on glasses with black or dark purple lenses. The work looked terribly hot for this time of day, but Joe was totally focused on what he was doing and didn't hear Kurt approach from the rear.

Joe stopped pounding, put the hammer down, and flung off his right gauntlet. Sliding the dark glasses up on his head, he looked at the object still held in blackened iron tongs. Not satisfied with the light under the awning, he walked over until the piece was hit by afternoon sunlight. Kurt saw the object was a crude knife blade. Evidently Joe's eyes didn't focus too well up close, as he held the tongs at arm's length and rotated the blade to examine its contours and surface. Only then did Joe sense someone in his presence, and he turned suddenly.

Joe's movements seemed cumbersome owing to the protective gear, and it took him a few seconds to recognize Kurt. They hadn't seen one another in nearly six years.

"Hey, I thought you were going to call," Joe said. "I put a bell outside so I could hear the phone. I thought maybe you had missed your flight, or decided not to come." Joe walked to his shaded workbench and put down his equipment and remaining glove, before extending his hand towards Kurt.

Kurt grabbed Joe's hand. It was like grabbing a wet towel. The man's entire body was soaked from exertion and heat.

"I decided to walk from the airport and see something of the country; it looked interesting when the plane came in," Kurt replied. "Riding in a car isn't the same."

"Kurt, it doesn't surprise me that you'd do something like that. It's a long way though, nearly twenty miles. You must be pretty tired."

Kurt shrugged off the comment and looked at the piece of metal Joe had just placed on the anvil to cool.

"Just what in God's name are you making there, Joe? It's awfully warm to be pounding red-hot metal."

Joe laughed, and only now noticed he was soaked with perspiration.

"I started forging custom knives a few years ago to keep myself occupied; it is kind of lonely now the wife and kids are gone, so I started doing this as a hobby and began to sell some pieces. It doesn't make a lot, but it helps supplement the retirement money a little. I see you made it across Isletta without being scalped."

"The natives were friendly to me, very friendly. I think they do all their scalping now at the general store."

Joe laughed.

Kurt stepped towards the blade lying on the anvil, putting his face near it. The metal had lost its red glow but the blade and business end of the tongs still radiated heat to the point where he had to lean away.

"What kind of steel is this? It looks ... layered," Kurt asked. "I've never seen anything like that before."

"Only in a museum maybe," Joe responded. "It's new steel based on a very old technology, called Damascus. It's made of very thin layers of hard and soft metal fused to each other. A blade made this way is incredibly tough and flexible."

"If it's old, how come you say it's new?" Kurt asked. "If that question doesn't sound too stupid."

Joe laughed and shook his head.

"No, that's a good question. For centuries it was a mystery how the ancient sword smiths manufactured this steel. Even with all of our technology we couldn't figure it out. Then a few years back a blacksmith and knife maker by the name of Bill Moran re-discovered it. So everyone is making Damascus now; it's the new fad."

"How do you make it?" Kurt asked.

"It's pretty simple really," Joe explained. "You just weld a piece of hard steel and a piece of soft steel together and heat the piece up and fold it, just like making toffee. It's not that easy of course, the temperature is critical, but after a dozen folds there are hundreds of thin layers in your blank, then you make your blade out of it."

Kurt continued to stare at the rough blade, intrigued by the mosaic patterns.

"You could get lost in the swirls."

"I had a lot of failures at first; I think I was using the wrong materials. Then at a mineral show last year I picked up a chunk of metal that I figure must have been a meteorite. It was dead soft iron and when I welded it to high strength nickel steel it worked like a charm. This blade here is the last of it."

"That's amazing," Kurt said. "Ancient and the modern combined to make a strong composite. What is this blade design, it's interesting?"

"This pattern is a fighting knife I designed," Joe continued. "The blade shape is like an Arabian scimitar with a lot of sweep but also with enough point for penetration. It should be quite effective for close combat."

"I'd like to see it when it's done," Kurt said.

Joe removed the heavy leather and denim apron and laid it on the workbench. His clothing underneath was wet where the apron had touched but within seconds a ring of white appeared, as the moisture evaporated in the desert air.

"Let's go inside where it's cool," said Joe. "I think we could both use a beer."

⌘

Inside was a refrigerator full of Coors cans, a welcoming sight to Kurt. Both men downed two, straight from the can, then they each poured another beer in a glass mug, to enjoy at a more relaxed pace.

The interior of the house was spartan. Joe spoke of how his marriage of twenty years began to disintegrate when he left the army, blaming the split on a series of little things, not on one blow up or disagreement.

Kurt suspected that Joe's marriage ended for the same reason a lot of military break-ups occurred. People spent too much time apart and when they did get back together on a full time basis, they found themselves strangers.

"The two years in SOG really changed me," Joe mused. "I didn't think so at first. It's pretty hard to analyze yourself, but I think my wife saw differences right away. We didn't communicate much. I pulled back and stayed in my own little world. She wanted me to sell insurance but the thought of wearing a suit and being nice to people in order to take their money made me sick, and I mean real puking sick. When I started to make knives she didn't understand. To me it was something I could do and not have to face people every day, which was what I needed at the time. That stress does something to you; I'm not the same man that I was."

"I know exactly what you mean, Joe," Kurt said. "I think of it this way, most people have no idea of what we've been through and they really don't care, because it's beyond their comprehension. People watch movies and television for their little dose of adrenaline and then go about their safe, routine lives. None of them have been hanging from a helicopter at the end of a rope with green tracers coming up at them, or trying to patch up a buddy who is leaking blood faster than they can stop it. They haven't been alone in the jungle with bloodhounds and a company of NVA Regulars on their trail. That changes you, Joe. It has to change you."

"I know what you're saying," Joe interjected, "but what the hell do we do about it?

We have to come back and live in a society we risked our lives to protect. When we came home we were treated like strangers and outcasts. We're no longer a part of this country we enriched with our blood."

Kurt shook his head. "It's one hell of a dilemma, Joe, and I wish I had an answer. I'm a lot younger than you are but I feel exactly the same way. At least you can semi-retire and take it easy a little, but I can't. I have another twenty or thirty years before I can do that. I'm trying to join the system and be one of them, but it's not working. I say to myself 'give it time and I'll come around', but I don't think it'll happen any time soon. I constantly crave something I can't even define. Whatever I do seems only a stop-gap. I'm always looking ahead to something else but I don't know what it is, or if I'll ever find it. I feel lost, without a compass or a map of the area of operations."

Both men were silent for awhile. Kurt felt depressed at the truths both of them had just expressed, but talking about it had to be therapeutic. Theirs was a private world only fellow veterans could understand. Even psychiatrists and psychologists were pretty clueless about post-traumatic stress syndrome, and the personal devastation suffered by returning combat soldiers.

"Yeah, I think we're going to have a good time in Vegas," Joe said as he swirled his beer, changing the subject. "I'm looking forward to seeing some of the guys again. Besides you, I've only had contact with a couple of the old crew. Several of the old team members I talked to were anxious to see you. We all want to hear what happened to you; no one seems to know."

It was predictable that the conversation would drift toward what happened in Laos six years before. His third beer half finished, the exercise, alcohol, heat and empty stomach were all working in concert now. A silent expectation fell over the room like dense smoke.

Kurt hated explaining himself. Applying logic and after-the-fact analysis to what happened in war was only of interest to historians, voyeurs and non-participants. Things of this nature could not be explained or rationalized by those who were not there. Worry, concern and guilt about past actions were pointless and needlessly poisoned the mind.

He could reflect on past events providing he wasn't expected to explain what his thinking or motives were at the time. Joe looked at him expectantly. The beer hadn't dulled the eyes of his friend. Joe needed to understand and had every right to ask.

Kurt began, "Remember when the Command and Control teams started to go missing in Laos, Joe? No survivors, not a trace. They just vanished."

Joe simply nodded at this rhetorical question. He knew the events well enough. Some of his friends had been lost, sucked into a mysterious black hole from which none of them had ever emerged.

"Something was seriously wrong with our cross-border operations," Kurt continued, "but no one had the balls to admit it. I came to the conclusion that one man operating independently could find out why our teams were vanishing. When I was deployed with Recon Team Viper and we were hit just off the LZ, I helped to extract the team but I didn't go back with them, I stayed in Laos."

Joe interrupted, "That's when we thought you'd been captured and you were reported as MIA. Two spike teams were launched to locate you, but they didn't find anything."

"Yeah, I felt bad about that," Kurt said looking at the floor. "I never meant to endanger any recovery teams but in my opinion, there was no other way to get information except on the ground where it was happening. I couldn't tell anyone what I was up to either. For one, any plan like that would have been refused by our superior officers. Also, if there was a leak inside as we suspected, the NVA would know I was there and would have hunted me down. This way I was off the books, so to speak."

"I guess that makes sense," Joe said. "What happened once you were there?"

"Initially, I hung out near a large NVA unit supporting transportation down the Ho Chi Minh Trail, and just observed them. I discovered the unit was split into two sections. The primary group was a transportation section that hauled munitions and supplies down the trail. The NVA soldiers were mostly young recruits building roads and carrying supplies on their backs and on bicycles. Attached to them was a smaller security element. I focused on them because they were more interesting. There were the message couriers and they also controlled incoming and outgoing electronic communications."

Kurt looked up at the slowly turning fan turning overhead, took a gulp of beer and continued, "I began to follow this security section when they patrolled. Mostly they carried out standard perimeter and point security for their transportation section, as you'd expect. But twice they went out on night patrols and received aerial deliveries by light aircraft. I heard the aircraft clearly but couldn't see them. I was too far away and the plane was blacked out. I didn't think the gooks had this kind of support. I always assumed we owned the skies except for MIGs in the north."

"The patrols didn't cotton on to your presence at all when you were tailing them?" Joe asked.

"No, they didn't," Kurt replied. "You could tell they were very confident that they were the only ball team on that field, and I always used maximum concealment. I could have done them some damage but that would have been a one-off thing, and that wasn't why I was there."

Kurt paused, trying to arrange the facts in his head before he spoke.

"So everything was pretty mundane until one afternoon when the security squad suddenly became very agitated after receiving a radio message. They quickly mobilized a heavily armed patrol, which looked more like an ambush team to me. I figured they expected something coming into their operational area and they wanted to get there in a hurry.

I trailed the patrol for a few clicks and set up some trip wire booby traps I 'borrowed' from them to cover my back trail. The patrol was obviously marking their route, so reserve troops they left behind could assist them quickly if needed. I wanted to slow down any possible reaction force, even if it meant blowing my cover."

"That was my team coming in then?" Joe asked expectantly.

"Correct," Kurt replied. "Their co-ordinates were right on the money. Unknown to you, Krait was dropping in almost on top of the NVA transportation battalion. By the sound of the choppers approaching, your pilots pulled at least half a dozen fake insertions, but the gooks only went to the primary LZ. Somehow your asses had been compromised in a major way. They knew exactly where you were going to land."

"Not a coincidence maybe?" Joe asked.

Kurt just shook his head dismissively.

"The NVA patrol set up a C-shaped ambush surrounding your primary LZ and after you landed they shot your team up pretty badly. I had the feeling they were under orders to capture Americans and kill the Montonguards. I came in behind their command post and then swept their line as quickly as I could before I reached you."

"Jesus, Kurt, you took out the whole element," Joe exclaimed. "How many were there?"

Kurt looked at the lumbering ceiling fan again and shrugged.

"About fourteen or fifteen I think. Fortunately they stayed in place. Once their commander was dead, they didn't move, but that's how the NVA worked; it was their Achilles heel and I took advantage of it."

"I can't remember too much myself," Joe said softly. "I thought we had a clean insertion and then, when we were moving off the LZ, all hell broke loose. I tried to organize my team to return fire then everything went blank. The next thing I recall was your voice. I could barely hear and could only see a little light. I remember thinking, if this is what being dead is like, it's not so bad."

"That's because one of the NVA fired an RPG at the centre of the LZ," Kurt said, "and you were hit with the ground blast. I nearly caught the back blast on the other end. I didn't see that grenadier until after he fired the rocket. After I hooked you up I put the package of material I recovered from the dead NVA commander in the pocket of your jungle pants and told you to take it to Intel, remember?"

Joe began to rub his face and eyes with the palms of both hands, as if the pressure would conjure up long suppressed images and memories. The mind has a tendency to block out traumatic events for the sake of self preservation. Resurrecting them on demand wasn't an easy task.

"Yes, I remember, and I did turn it over ... I think," Joe said slowly as if he had to extract the words from his mind one at a time. "I told the medic who bandaged me up at the launch site to take the file to S-2, and as I recall he said he would. Then he injected me with morphine and I don't remember anything after that. When I got out of the medical ward at Na Trang I remembered, and went up to S-2 to make sure they received it."

"And had they?" Kurt asked.

"That was the strange part," Joe continued. "They gave me the cold shoulder at 5th Group S-2, as though I was a drunk with no money who had just walked into a high-class whorehouse. Colonel Belgrave himself came out and spoke to me, which I thought odd at the time. S-2 denied ever getting a file or documents I brought back. Then he told me to drop the issue, so I never talked about it after that."

"Did Belgrave or any of the others inquire about what was in the file?" Kurt asked.

"Belgrave didn't, but a staff sergeant warden from the S-2 shop did ask me that question. I told him I didn't know because my eyes were too burned to read anything and I'd been in pretty bad shape. That seemed to satisfy him and he didn't ask me anything else. I thought the whole thing pretty strange, but I didn't pursue it any further."

"What was in the package, Kurt?" Joe asked, leaning forward.

"Like I told you, Joe," Kurt replied. "I took it off the dead NVA officer and put it in your pocket. The shit was starting to come down and I was directing air strikes so there was no time to read anything. I thought it might be good and timely intelligence and of value, that's why I sent it back with you. Too bad they lost it."

"They may have received it," Joe added, "and just didn't want to say anything. You know how spooky that business is."

Kurt nodded in agreement.

"S-2 is a strange bunch all right. Well, at least we did our bit, even if they screwed it up."

⌘

Kurt stared out the front window of Joe's house which faced towards the east. Above, the desert the Monzano Mountains loomed clearly against a pale blue sky. Monzano, Kurt thought, means 'apple' in Spanish. It didn't look like a place to site an orchard, but the higher altitude on the slopes might attract more rain ...

"Joe, did anyone else know about this?" Kurt asked. "I mean our people, operations folk?"

"Just the chase medic, Wilson, who took the file to S-2 for me," Joe said. "But he was killed a few weeks later. I heard his rappelling rope was severed by ground fire. He fell a hundred and fifty feet, didn't have a chance."

"Sorry to hear that; Wilson was a good man."

Kurt finished the dregs of his third beer. Three was enough.

"When you came in from Laos what happened?" Joe asked. "How were you received? There was a total blackout on any information about you. You ceased to exist."

Kurt thought for awhile before replying. Since this had happened he had never told anyone the details. Maybe it was time to tell someone; it was hard to keep these things bottled up for so long.

"I was across the border for a little over three months, but I knew I had to come back. After the incident with your team and the air strike on the NVA battalion, they knew someone was there, and they were constantly searching. It was just a matter of time before they found me.

Instead of trying to cross back into south Vietnam to be bombed or shot at by friendly fire, I travelled in the other direction and finally made it to Long Thieng, our not-so-secret base in central Laos. The spook station chief there was a man by the name of George Barlow, ex-Special Forces and a real gentleman. He treated me like a lost brother until word got out that I was there and they flew an Air America chopper from Khe Sahn to get me. The situation deteriorated after that."

"No hero's welcome, huh?" Joe asked.

"Hardly. When I arrived in Khe Sahn a call was made to Da Nang and they flew down and picked me up a few hours later. I was kept incommunicado for two weeks while I was debriefed, if you could call it that. I was interrogated just like the enemy; in fact from the way I was treated, I thought I was the enemy."

"After your disappearance there was a rumour floating around that you had gone over to the other side," Joe said. "But after you rescued what was left of Krait, everyone involved told the debriefing people what you did, and that you saved the lives of team members and killed a bunch of NVA. They should have put you in for a Silver Star for that one Kurt, maybe even a DSC."

"I don't deserve any medals, Joe, and I understand why they were pissed off. My actions were out of order but the very last thing I would ever be is a traitor. That really bothers me, that anybody would think that."

Kurt cleared his throat and sat silently for a minute.

"They told me that the only reason that I wasn't court-martialled was that they didn't want the negative publicity because classified projects were involved. I was reprimanded and sent back to the States and given a bullshit job at Fort Bragg. I knew they were watching me closely the whole time I was there."

"That's no way to treat a good soldier, a real shame," Joe said.

"Well, like we used to say; fuck 'em all but six, and save them for pall-bearers."

Both men laughed at the familiar irreverent Special Forces humour. The joke broke the spell and they moved on to discuss people they had both known and what they knew about them now. They even had another beer each.

"Well I'm getting hungry hombre," Joe said, "and I'm going to take you out to dinner. I hope you like *real* Mexican food."

⌘

They went to the Old Town section of Albuquerque, which was originally built in the 1700s. The traditional adobe structures were mixed with new developments, although the plaza still had an air of antiquity about it. They went to a restaurant that had been serving the same food since Joe was a child. The Chile Pepper offered what could be called 'authentic' New Mexican cuisine. Joe warned Kurt about the heat of the genuine, locally grown red and green chillies used to flavour the food. Kurt took the warning in good humour, until he had taken a couple of bites of chilli rellano and the full blast of capsicum hit home. Several bottles of Dos Equis took the edge off of the burn, although he knew that the peppers would have to run their course.

Joe explained that the peppers caused a release of chemicals in the body called endorphins that gave you a high, of sorts. Whether it was Joe's suggestion or the endorphins Kurt didn't know, but the surroundings became brighter and more intense. Except for the now fading burn in his mouth, he found the sensations pleasant and strangely relaxing. He thought it was unfortunate that this food was so regional, and that he'd never had it before.

⌘

The next day Kurt borrowed Joe's old El Camino to visit the New Mexico Tech campus in Socorro, where he was thinking of enrolling in mining school. Joe had some knives to finish and ship off before he could go to Las Vegas anyway. What Kurt didn't tell him was that he was driving up to the Sandia Reservation first to pick up Rose.

Rose was waiting outside the grocery store where they had met the previous day. She wore a pink floral dress and her long hair shone, glossy and black in the sun. Kurt thought her slim form looked elegant in the way a model looks on the cover of one of those women's magazines. She smiled as she climbed into the beaten up funny-coloured car-truck as if she was stepping to a limo in front of a luxury hotel.

The drive to Socorro was a short one and Kurt had the opportunity to speak to several members of the faculty who were in the process of grading final exams. The summer semester hadn't started yet and the campus was quiet. The school, located in the high desert with a spectacular mountain backdrop, was small, picturesque, and felt right, but he was still undecided about his major.

Geology and mining engineering were good fields, but he felt no passion for the work. Nothing offered even a fraction of the excitement he craved. Perhaps it was inevitable he would have to bite the bullet and become a cog in the big machine, one of the anonymous masses. He wondered if he could tolerate such a life for weeks and months, let alone for years and decades.

Collecting the required paperwork from the school's admission office was straightforward, leaving them free to explore. Rose suggested they stop at a famous eating place she had heard about, but had never visited. Kurt agreed, and they headed over to San Antonio, New Mexico, which unlike its namesake in Texas, was a tiny hamlet just up the road from Socorro, on the opposite side of the Rio Grande.

⌘

The Owl Cafe was an old local roadside diner that had expanded by necessity, not by design. The façade of the building was constructed to look like a giant owl, now weathered and pitted from the blowing desert sand. The wooden owl didn't look bright-eyed and alert anymore, but was a survivor in this bleak desert. The restaurant earned its reputation by making the best chilli cheeseburgers in the known world and keeping the prices reasonable. The Owl also had an extensive bar which the local ranchers and labourers frequented because it was the only decent watering hole in the area.

Kurt and Rose walked through the door, intent on one another and gave little thought to the occupants, some of whom had been camping out on the well-worn bar stools for much of their uneventful lives. Like much of the South-west, the local economy was depressed, with at least as many ranch hands and oilfield workers hanging out looking for work as were actually employed. This was bad news for most sectors of the local economy, except for the bars.

They found a seat near a wall in the dimly lit dining room and Kurt ordered a pitcher of beer and two glasses from the waitress. He was expecting some comment from the waitress regarding Rose's age, but she didn't blink and returned with the beer. Kurt smiled and shook his head and Rose chuckled as he filled the glasses.

"They really don't care out here, as long as you behave yourself," Rose said as she sipped Budweiser from the iced glass.

"You been drinking for long, girl?" Kurt laughed. "Is there something I should know about?"

"Well, we don't hold our liquor very well," she replied. "You have to watch us, you know."

"I don't mind watching you at all, Rose. It would take me a while to grow bored with that."

Rose eyed Kurt coyly. The combination of the beer on an empty stomach and the presence of the attractive and interesting girl made Kurt feel he was spiralling to a plane where he hadn't been for a while. Maybe, he thought, life was starting to settle down a little. The war was loosening its grip at last and perhaps it was time to relax and enjoy some of the good things in life, like the company of the girl sitting across the table.

They ordered two of the famous cheeseburgers, which were as huge as advertised and layered with locally roasted green chilli peppers. Kurt recalled the meal the previous night and the pain it inflicted, but felt that maybe a repeat performance wouldn't be as bad. He hoped not anyway.

A few minutes into their meal they heard a strange warbling sound coming from the bar. It came again before Kurt realized what it was. One of the drunk locals sitting at the front bar had turned around and was making a poor imitation of an Indian war whoop, followed by others laughing.

Kurt's good mood evaporated in a flash. Unable to tolerate ridicule, a legacy from his upbringing, blood rushed to his head and chest and his muscles hardened. Rose saw his reaction and tried to calm him.

"It's okay, Kurt, he's just a drunk. Don't bother with him, it's happened before."

Kurt tried to ignore it but knew it wasn't working.

"You know, Rose, the reason I fought for this country is so everyone could live their lives in peace here and be free. I know that may sound stupid and idealistic but it's true. Then we come to a place like this, minding our own business and some worthless drunk insults us and everyone thinks it's funny. I wonder sometimes who the real enemy is; we don't need to go to a foreign country to find one. The son of a bitch is sitting right here on a barstool."

"Well, there is nothing we can do about it other than leave," Rose said in a hushed voice. "I'm underage and if there's trouble, you know who's going to come off worse."

"Hey there, squaw boy!" The voice came from the same drunk, and set the rest of the people at the bar laughing again.

"That's enough," Kurt said evenly as he stood up.

Rose attempted to grab his arm.

"Don't get in a fight, Kurt," she said with an edge of desperation. "We don't want any trouble."

Kurt could tell that Rose was intimidated by the cultural difference, by the situation and by the perceived strength and ruthlessness of these people. She had seen enough drunkenness, racism and cruelty to last a lifetime and she wanted no more of it. Her face pleaded with him.

To leave the restaurant they had to walk past the drunk and his friends, which was unfortunate. If there had been rear entrance they would have taken it to avoid any confrontation, as Rose requested, but that wasn't an option. Kurt put money on the table.

"Rose, you go first," Kurt said. "Don't look at anyone, just keep your eyes straight ahead and don't give them any reason to say anything. I'll follow."

Her eyes pleaded with him. "Don't ..."

"Don't worry; I'm not going to cause a problem if I can help it."

Rose nodded and walked out of the café. Kurt followed a couple of paces behind. As she passed the loudmouth drunk, Kurt took stock of his opponent. The forty-year-old at one time might have been wiry and physically fit, but the years of drinking had taken their toll. His arm and shoulder muscles had withered away and he had a beer paunch. His grizzled face, although brown from exposure, looked waxen and unhealthy. Kurt thought it was remarkable that such a poor specimen could be as stupidly obnoxious as he was, but there was 'no telling fools' as his grandfather used to say.

The drunk and a couple of others sitting near him made lewd faces at Rose as she walked by, but said nothing because she didn't make eye contact. Kurt had passed the drunk and was nearly to the door when the words struck him from behind.

"Bet she's a nice piece of ass, ain't she, squaw boy?"

He felt icy coils race up his spine and spin him around. Kurt slowly walked back and stood directly in front of the drunk, who was now more then a little disconcerted. Like all loud-mouths and cowards, he furtively glanced around for assistance. All the other patrons kept their places.

Eyes red with rage, Kurt leaned close to the man, whose breath smelled of alcohol.

"You are a loudmouthed, drunken asshole," he said, enunciating each word clearly and distinctly.

The drunk began to visibly pale and quiver, as if from a sudden attack of Parkinson's disease, but failed to articulate a single word in his defence. Kurt felt sickened that he was even confronting such a pathetic individual and turned away in disgust. He suddenly sensed movement and quickly turned to see the drunk hauling back his right arm with a beer mug clutched in it. Before he had a chance to swing, Kurt grabbed his forearm with his left hand and wrenched it, forcing the mug to drop to the floor and pushed him hard against the bar railing.

With a single precise punch with his right fist, Kurt hit the drunk in his right side, feeling and hearing ribs crack as they were compressed against the wooden rail. The man slumped to the floor holding his side and whimpering.

"You didn't need to do that!" One of the other patrons said. "You hurt him bad ... look!" The speaker who was wearing a dirty grey Stetson pointed to his friend, now lying on the floor.

"He'll live," Kurt said dismissively as he headed to out the door, "and next time he might consider being more polite. But I doubt it. He's one dumb bastard."

Kurt walked out of the café and saw Rose anxiously standing by the El Camino.

"What happened?" she asked.

"Nothing much, just giving a lesson in courtesy and civility. Let's get out of here."

⌘

They drove back on to the I-25 and headed north up the Rio Grande Valley.

"Kurt, are you in any hurry to get back?" Rose said as the sun began to set in the west, casting the long shadows of mountains on desert sands, now brushed by pink and red hues.

"Not really, what did you have in mind?"

"Turn up here at Highway 60 and head west," Rose told him.

"Where are we going?"

"Just drive. I want to show you something. It would spoil it if I told you."

They turned and headed west on the highway, which became more remote the further they drove. The desert of the valley became more mountainous and scrubby juniper and stunted hardwoods covered the undulating landscape. Driving with the windows open, the air became scented and balmy and the sky turned progressively darker blue until features were no longer distinct, but blended form with shadow. The moon was rising, illuminating the landscape with touches of silver frosted light. The air was so clear here it didn't soften its razor sharp edge.

"Over there," Rose finally said. "Pull over here."

Kurt did as he was told, pulled into a lay-by on the left of the highway and switched off the engine and lights of the El Camino. Only then did he look to the south to behold the spectacle. Between the highway and the distant mountains was a great flat basin that was once an inland sea, now called the Plains of San Agustin. In spite of approaching darkness, huge, pure-white discs scattered on the floor of the basin glowed ethereally. The scene was breathtaking, unlike anything Kurt had ever witnessed.

"My God, what is this?" he said in a hushed, almost reverent voice.

"I told you it was worth the drive," Rose said, not answering the question, but smiling at the response.

"But what ...?"

"It's called the National Radio Astronomy Observatory, Very Large Array, or VLA for short," Rose said. "From what I understand they listen to things way out in space, radio signals and stuff. Do you want to get a closer look?"

"Sure," Kurt said and nodded, unable to take his eyes off the stark white shapes.

Rose reached into the back seat of the El Camino and clasped a blanket that Joe kept on the seat. They climbed out of the car and walked down a barely discernable trail that wound from the pullover, down a slope, and up to the crest of a nearby hill. The view would be less obstructed there. Finally they reached the sandy dome, spread the blanket, and sat down. The rising moon now bathed the radio antennae in surreal light, making the discs stand out like beacons in the dark landscape.

"God, Rose, this has to be the most beautiful sight on earth," Kurt whispered.

"It is spectacular, but I do find it a bit ironic."

Kurt turned towards her at the comment. "Why ironic? I don't understand."

"Well, for many centuries my people tried to connect with the spirits and the stars," Rose replied. "They held rituals, took potions and fasted nearly until death in order to communicate with the spiritual world. The most important thing in our existence was to try to understand our existence."

"Go on," Kurt urged.

"Well, the whites came and conquered our society and left the old ways in tatters. Their Christian religion thought of our traditions as inferior, and overwhelmed us with their rituals and beliefs. The really sad part is that we believed them and fell into the subservient role."

"It's a terrible legacy," Kurt said. "One we will never be able to reconcile. But why does it make this ironic?" Kurt waved at the scene before them.

"Don't you see?" she replied. "After totally destroying our religion and traditions, what does the white man do but build huge ears out here in order to listen to the stars and the spirits? The same thing we were doing for thousands of years."

"Despite our science and technology we still don't know, do we?" Kurt asked.

"No," Rose replied. "People of all races or cultures are in the same predicament. No one really knows what it's all about, so they keep searching."

Kurt stared intently at the giant white discs that were silently listening for the faintest whispers from somewhere out there. What would they tell us? And if there was a message, did we really want to know?

Kurt looked over at Rose again and was surprised. She was lying back propped up by her arms. Her body was perfect and her bare skin shone like satin in the moonlight.

# CHAPTER 5
## ENEMIES

"Well ... it looks like you had a good time," Joe said.

Kurt arrived back at Joe's place a little after one in the morning looking tired and not a little sheepish. Joe was still up, reading.

"It's been an interesting day to say the least," Kurt replied.

"No harm done, I hope?"

"No, everything's fine."

Kurt's response didn't sound all that convincing to Joe, but he didn't want to press for details.

"What do you say we get some sleep and leave for Las Vegas in the morning?" Joe asked.

"That sounds like a good plan to me ... goodnight," Kurt replied, as he walked back to the spare bedroom.

Kurt switched on the room light. The knife was lying in the middle of the bed, strapped into a leather belt sheath. Removing the blade, the layered Damascus steel Joe had been forging was now finished and stunning, even in the dim light. The surface was satin smooth and the cutting edge so sharp it caught when it barely touched a thumb nail. The handle was shaped out of ancient, fossilized mastodon ivory tusk. The material was not white in colour but a dark yellow, with veins of blue and green running through its structure because it had been buried beneath the arctic tundra for thousands of years. The balance seemed perfect as he lifted the piece and it felt surprisingly light in his hand. This beautiful and deadly work of art was Joe's way of saying thank you for saving his life.

Whilst admiring his gift, Kurt opened the window and breathed in the cooling desert air as it flowed into the room. The moon was high, silhouetting the dark Monzano Mountains to the east. The image of the great white discs and Rose were hard to dispel; he could still smell her musky sweetness. Drifting off, he dreamt of being lost in a vast land, where everything was still wild. He was the sole human and had to survive on strength and wits alone. Awakened by the sun rising over the mountains, he felt as tense as a bow string.

⌘

They drove to Las Vegas through the vast and remote desert south-west. Crossing the Hoover Dam at midday revealed a sparkling blue Lake Mead backed up behind it—a massive man-made reservoir quenching the parched land.

Arriving in the gambling Mecca mid-afternoon, intense daylight dulled the glittering night-time oasis into a dusty, tacky blight on the desert landscape. After checking into the hotel and showering and changing, they went downstairs to the hotel bar to see if anyone else had arrived.

The Special Operations Reunion was being held at the same hotel, which was convenient. The annual meeting had been first held a few years before, as veterans returning from Indo-China and elsewhere realized that getting together was a popular idea. The men who were invited to these conventions were not wishful thinkers or armchair warriors, but the real thing.

⌘

Most young people who served in the military did so out of some sense of duty to their country, to their family, their God and all the other icons of civic responsibility inculcated from infancy. Young soldiers, sailors and airmen served with the perception that their 'real life' lay back in the farm, hometown or city, with an accompanying wife, mortgage, kids and car payments. Young people weren't supposed to enjoy time spent in the military; it was a patriotic duty to be performed at personal sacrifice.

Covert operations have always been practiced by a breed of men different from those filling the ranks of the regular military. The qualities that made for a good special operative such as absolute independence, boldness bordering on recklessness, the tendency to be secretive and the possession of little emotion would mean troubled careers in any other branch of the military, or in civilian life.

There is an unwritten law that says whenever rules are made or generalizations cast, there are those who live to break the mould. Special Operations people volunteered for dangerous missions not primarily out of duty or responsibility. They did this dangerous and thankless work because they loved what they did and for that reason alone they were damned good at it. When a person does something because they think it is a duty, one tier of performance is met. When something is done out of personal passion, an entirely new level is achieved.

Special operatives had two strikes against them in the eyes of the public. Firstly, they did things the government and people needed to be done but didn't want to admit to and secondly, they enjoyed the work. They not only enjoyed the work, they lived it, revelled in it, and would usually keep doing it until they were dead, incapacitated or just too old to continue. Aside from the public denial and vilification, the government and military planners knew the truth. Since the inception of the OSS in the desperate days of World War II, special operations were proven to be a cost effective and viable alternative to warfare on a larger scale, especially once atomic weapons were introduced. Special Operations was the silver surgical bullet the Cold War required, but their missions were kept in deep shadow, away from the public spotlight. For whatever duration a state-sponsored conflict might last, it was guaranteed that covert operatives were there before, during and after.

These people spent time in places that were never admitted to in public, and their exploits were unknown to anyone except those working in darkened offices, deep in the bowels of the defence establishment. Successful missions were generally met with denials and cover-ups, as were failures.

The pilot, Francis Gary Powers, was a good example of a covert operative who was treated shamefully by the country he defended with valour. A brave, dedicated and decorated combat pilot, Gary Powers was shot down over Russia while piloting a CIA U-2 spy plane in May of 1960. He barely managed to claw himself out of a destroyed aircraft at extreme altitude, and was captured upon landing.

Powers was finally released from Soviet prison to the great embarrassment of those who actually ordered the mission. Upon his return he was treated like a pariah, not for performing his heroic duty but for being caught. Such is the fate of the special operative, despised by enemies and vilified by the very society he risks life and limb to protect.

⌘

Vietnam started as a covert war but quickly became a massive conventional effort which became a victim of its own excesses. Special operatives were there, but their best efforts were to no avail as the lumbering oversized military beast panicked and ran off the cliff, chased by screaming politicians and journalists.
Just two months before Kurt and Joe arrived in Las Vegas, the NVA rolled into South Vietnam virtually without resistance. It was not difficult for their side to win, because in our angst we had pulled the opposing team off the field.

It was understandable that Special Operations' veterans were disappointed by the turn of events in Vietnam, but it was no surprise to them. These men seldom engaged in 'what if' mind games, or wore an aura of defeatism when things didn't turn out as planned. They knew they had done everything possible, given the suffocating restrictions.

Regret and remorse about what could have, or should have, been was the domain of politicians, not special operators. This legacy ensured that society labelled Special Operations' soldiers a branch of military misfits who were not to be spoken to or about in polite company. Society often fails to understand the need for 'down and dirty warfare'. The former members only solace when not working was to seek the company of one another, because only they understood.

Now, like bees to nectar, the thought of socializing, drinking and partying with their peers drew them to Sin City annually, as members of one of the most exclusive fraternities on earth. Kurt and Joe were both veterans of this small shadow world, lost somewhere between admittance and denial, between trust and deceit, between bravery and insanity and, indeed, between war and peace.

⌘

Because Joe had been in the Special Operations community for over twenty-five years, he knew many of the people present. Kurt had been involved only briefly and knew only a few, so Joe took him around and introduced him as 'the guy who saved my life on my last mission in Laos'. Joe then moved off with a couple of old buddies and Kurt walked around by himself.

The word about his presence must have spread quickly because people began to look at him when he walked by; not real looks but curious glances with aversion, once eye contact was made. This treatment was uncomfortable, and he wondered why he'd been talked into coming here. He realized that being such a small community, news of his disappearance while on a mission was still on the tongues of many. The real story was known to only a very few.

"God Damn, I can't believe who is in front of my eyes! It's Casper the friendly fuckin' cross-border ghost. How ya doing, you slick bastard?"

Kurt immediately knew Dahl's irritating voice even though he hadn't seen him in the six years since they had been on a brief mission together. Dennis Dahl was well on the way to becoming falling-down, commode-hugging drunk, so Kurt just smiled and let the comments bounce off. He didn't like loud, obnoxious drunks but some concessions were necessary to spend a weekend at this reunion.

A man could certainly drink without being obnoxious. Kurt recalled Jerry (aka Mad Dog) Shriver who taught him to listen to ground sounds and was the best reconnaissance man ever born. When he returned from a mission, he would go to the NCO club and buy a case of beer. He would then sit in a corner and drink it all himself without saying a word to anyone. Everyone knew better than to talk to Jerry unless he spoke first. He was a man of integrity who didn't use the excuse of alcohol to brag about himself. He didn't need to.

Dahl, on the other hand, handled his booze in the manner typical of too many GIs. He put his arm around Kurt and continued to talk too loudly about too little. Kurt found physical contact with this drunk repulsive. He freed himself from Dahl's grip, said he was running late to meet someone and would catch up with him later.

Kurt walked around the main function room. The walls were gaudily decorated with posters and emblems of the Special Forces' arrowhead and the Studies and Observation Group or SOG patch. The SOG emblem was a white skull wearing a green beret with a snake entwined and slithering out of an eye socket. The other unit insignia, including the Command and Control North (CCN), Central (CCC), and South (CCS) logos, surrounded the SOG emblem. The Studies and Observation Group had an interesting past but its very existence was known to few outside the Special Operations community. There was a veil of tight secrecy and deception that had been placed on the unit, the missions and the men who performed them.

Kurt suddenly felt a sensation like heat, followed by a chill on the back of his neck, and turned in time to catch a short bald man moving his head too quickly in the opposite direction. Kurt's mind fogged for a second then he knew who he was: former Lieutenant Colonel Belgrave.

Belgrave had been the commanding officer of Special Forces 5th Group Intelligence or S-2, and also the senior officer participating in Kurt's interrogation upon his return from Laos. Most of the time Belgrave had sat impassively in the interrogation room while others did the questioning.

Kurt wanted a 'read' of the man, even just eye contact to see how he would react. However, Belgrave wasn't staying and was already moving away, quickly. No doubt he was surprised to see Kurt at the reunion, but there would be time over the next couple of days to corner him.

The party was spread out across the main function lobby into the hallway and into several of the side rooms. There were small groups of men huddled together telling war stories. Periodically there would be raucous laughter before they settled down again. One group was playing cards and smoking cigars; others were roaming and drinking, while they could still walk, knowing if they stopped they would fall over.

The last, and probably the most dedicated group, Kurt always referred to as the pussy hounds—out to bag a woman, any woman, and this reunion was quickly becoming what the intelligence wienies used to describe as a 'target rich environment'. Females of all sizes, ages, shapes and colours were drifting in. Some were obviously Las Vegas hookers looking for some quick and easy money, while others were just having a good time mingling with these wild men, whose reputation preceded them.

While he was eyeing the backside of one of the targets, Kurt felt a tap on the shoulder.

"Kurt Christianson, I'll be damned!

He turned and saw Jeff Warden, a former staff intelligence specialist assigned to 5th Special Forces Group Headquarters in Na Trang, and a former Special Forces classmate. He remembered that Jeff had been one of Belgrave's assistants at S-2 and the man Joe referred to when they discussed the NVA file Kurt had recovered. What was he up to greeting him like a long lost friend, when they had never been close? To his credit Jeff seemed to be one of the few sober individuals in the room and came across as slick … very slick indeed.

"Are you going anywhere in particular?" Jeff asked.

"Not really, Jeff, just checking out some of this," Kurt nodded to the well-rounded rear of one of the girls prowling through the room.

Jeff laughed out loud, "There's plenty of that around here, but that one will cost you big time."

"I'm too broke to worry about it, Jeff. How have you been anyway?"

"I'm doing well these days, thanks," Jeff said quietly. "I have an interest in several businesses here in Vegas, as well as the family business in LA, so there's little time off. Why don't you come over here with us, Kurt? We have a table in one of the quieter rooms and there are a couple of the guys I'd like you to meet."

Jeff was the consummate diplomat. Kurt was amazed how some people naturally had that gift; what ever the situation, they were on top. They weren't necessarily the brightest or the best but they were slick, good looking, well-spoken, urbane and just had a way with people. Jeff was so good in fact that Kurt found himself following with no reservations at all.

Jeff led Kurt to a table in the back corner of one of the side rooms where seven or eight people were seated. The men looked serious and subdued in comparison with what was going on elsewhere, but the table wasn't full so Kurt didn't feel like he was intruding. He recognized two of the people. All of the men smiled at him but Kurt could sense something odd. He assumed it was his imagination and the pressure of these surroundings.

"Some of you know Kurt Christianson," Jeff introduced him. "He worked at CCN in sixty-nine and seventy and set a record for the longest cross-border operation on record by an American. Kurt, I'd like you to meet Bob Newman, Charlie Ruff and Cliff Daniels.

With a peristaltic wave the men sitting at the table nodded their heads in recognition, not of the man but of the deed. Bob Newman, who had five tours in the Projects, stood to shake hands with Kurt. Newman had one of the best records and reputations in Special Operations in Indo-China. At nearly six and a half feet tall and blond, he would never pass for an Asian, under any circumstances. He led the team on the first operationally HALO free fall jump of the war. On his last operation in Cambodia he stepped on a small 'toe popper' mine and lost his right lower leg, so he was currently in retirement selling insurance in California.

"Glad to finally get a chance to talk to you Kurt," Newman said in an open gregarious manner. "I wish we could have worked together. Didn't you run with Mad Dog for a while?"

"Only a short time, unfortunately," Kurt replied. "Jerry disappeared on that Bomb Damage Assessment in Cambodia while I was … gone."

Simultaneously, everyone at the table collectively bowed their heads at the mention of Jerry Shriver. They also knew that anyone who referred to Mad Dog by his first name knew the man intimately, and that in itself was a badge of honour. Although dead for years Mad Dog was still revered by this group. Kurt smiled. Newman didn't emanate any bad vibes and he began to feel slightly more comfortable.

Kurt began to talk about Mad Dog and everyone listened, then individually recounted their personal experiences with the legend.

"Remember when Jerry went back to the States on leave just to get one of the big 444 Marlin lever guns to use in the tunnels?" Ruff said. "Jerry was skinny enough to wiggle down those VC tunnels but he needed a gun that would stop the gooks with one shot; in that kind of tight space a wounded gook was big trouble. That lever gun blew a hole in them as big as your fist, so they went down pronto and couldn't shoot back. As far as anyone knows that was the only lever action rifle used in the Vietnam War."

Slowly the stories moved on from the exploits of Mad Dog Shriver and began to shift to direct questions to Kurt, who had become famous or more accurately, notorious, in his own right, with one difference. Most of the stories about him were based on rumour. No one knew exactly what he'd done or why he did it, except for Joe.

Kurt was warming to the attention but felt apprehensive about being open about his past. That wasn't his nature. A bottle of Knob Creek Bourbon, to which Kurt was partial, appeared on the table. He was surprised to see his favourite bourbon, but thought it was just good fortune. Two fingers of the rich amber Kentucky spirit was poured into a clear tumbler, and it was every bit as smooth as he remembered.

A short time later he was telling the men at the table how he had operated solo in Laos for months, and all of them seemed to have a very keen interest. Except for an occasional question of clarification they listened intently. None of them tried to interrupt his monologue or steal the spotlight.

About an hour later the bourbon bottle was finished and Warden, looking around as if planning a major conspiracy, pulled out a flat, dark-coloured pint flask from under the table. From the flask he poured a small quantity of liquid into a tumbler and held it aloft for those at the table to see.

"Does anyone care to join me?" he asked in a hushed voice.

Even in the dim light the liquid was emerald green and almost phosphorescent. Kurt had never seen anything like it before, and asked, "What the hell is that, Jeff?"

Warden smiled coyly, "Absinthe."

Newman said, "That stuff is poisonous, isn't it? Where'd you get it?"

"It's toxic only if it's made wrong. A friend of mine in San Francisco makes this brand," Jeff explained.

"Does he know what the hell he is doing?" Ruff asked.

"Of course," Warden said. "He's the best, and no bad affects at all, just the good extract. As always, only the best for my friends, I wouldn't give you guys any garbage."

"I don't know about that, Warden," Ruff said. "But I know you can afford the best, and you wouldn't drink it yourself if it wasn't."

"I've heard of that stuff before," Kurt interjected. "It's made from wormwood isn't it?"

"That's right, "Jeff replied. "That and some other ingredients that he won't disclose. Gives you a rush like no other drink."

"Fucking worms!" Ruff backed away from the table in simulated horror. "I'm a hard bastard but I ain't drinking worm juice. I won't even eat that little worm in tequila."

Warden shook his head in dismay.

"Charlie its wormwood, wood ... It's a plant not worms. It has nothing to do with insects at all."

After Jeff poured half an inch in everyone's glass, they held their glasses in front of them looking at how the iridescent green liquid sparkled, even in the dim room lights.

"Come on guys, let's not make it too obvious ... cheers." Jeff put his glass to his lips and downed the liquid in one swallow. The rest were more cautious and hesitant but all of them, including Kurt, drank the potion. Kurt expected it to be bitter like most herbs and he wasn't disappointed. He finished the glass and could feel the emerald liquid slide down his throat and pool in his stomach like molten metal. He washed it down with more bourbon, which seemed to neutralize the bitter taste.

"Wasn't this the stuff Van Gogh drank before he cut off his ear?" Newman said.

"Yeah, but don't worry about that," Warden explained. "That guy was a whacky artist, an unstable SOB anyway. He didn't cut his ear off because of absinthe."

"Jesus," Newman continued. "Hide the fuckin' silverware, Ruff's gonna start hacking ears off."

"Fuck you, Newman," Ruff growled. "I wouldn't want your stinking lily-white ears, anyway."

"It's that Indian blood in you, Ruff," Newman countered. "A little green firewater and you'll be collecting body parts; well, stay away from mine."

"Fuck all of you," Ruff said. "See if I ever drink poison with you guys again. What's so bad about this stuff anyway? I feel fine."

"Hey!" Daniels spoke for the first time. "Maybe this is like that worm juice they drank in Dune. Remember that science fiction book? It was blue and gave whoever drank it magical powers. It was squeezed out of the baby worms, not those big grown up motherfuckers."

"Well, Daniels," Ruff said, "you ain't gonna get no magic powers, you dumb fuck. Jeff already told us that this didn't come from no real worms anyhow, not even baby giant worms. Anyway it's green. Magic worm juice doesn't come in green."

"Who're you calling a dumb fuck, Ruff?" Daniels stood up. "How would you like me to pull off your head and shit down your neck?"

While the bizarre banter continued, Kurt felt a strange sensation starting in his middle and working its way to his limbs. The feeling was a combination of relaxation and euphoria with a weird, underlying agitation. It was the latter feeling that concerned him. By nature Kurt always felt on edge, and he didn't need anything tipping the scales.

He shouldn't have drunk the absinthe.

Kurt excused himself and stood up to leave but Jeff Warden jumped up and walked with him.

"Where are you going, Kurt?" Jeff asked. "I didn't get a chance to ask you any questions."

"I have to walk around," Kurt replied. "That stuff made me feel strange."

"It does that sometimes; it's only temporary and if you keep moving it will burn off. You looked pretty tense and in need of some relaxation, if you know what I mean." Jeff laughed at his own comment.

Kurt stopped and looked at him.

"What do you mean, Jeff? Are you doing the pimp thing too? You shouldn't need to do that kind of work with your successful businesses and all."

Warden laughed but it was a dry, forced laugh. Kurt's sarcasm hit a nerve; something ugly hovered just below Jeff's smooth exterior.

"Hardly," Jeff said, not betraying emotion, "but if you are feeling that way inclined, just make your way down to The Aces; it's a little off the strip about six blocks west of here. Ask for Monique. You couldn't mistake her if you were blind. I'll tell you what, I'll call and tell her you are coming down. Just tell her you know me. You won't believe this chick. She used to work in the porn industry. She really gets into it; a genuine freak, no play acting with her, and she craves good-looking muscle men."

Jeff hit Kurt firmly in the upper arm. Kurt saw it coming and tensed. Jeff's hit landed solidly but didn't move him at all.

"Sounds interesting, Jeff, but first I'm going to walk around a bit and see how I feel."

"You'd be a fool if you don't, partner," Jeff said. "She leaves town for a week starting tomorrow morning so you'll miss out. It's a chance of a lifetime, I guarantee it."

Kurt waved and took the elevator down to the hotel lobby where the gambling was in full swing.

When the elevator doors closed Jeff Warden looked at his right hand and said to himself, "Christ, like a fucking brick wall."

The fake corporate smile melted from his face, and what replaced it was a mask of black anger, mixed with fear.

⌘

The lobby was in chaos. Kurt drifted through the masses busily throwing their money into the gambling machines. Some of the people playing the one-armed bandits looked as if they were enjoying themselves. Others had a haunted look of desperation as though trapped in a place from which there was no escape, eternally pulling handles in search of an elusive happiness. Kurt subconsciously held his breath as he walked through the lobby. He didn't want to inhale the air and become infected with this compulsion.

The concrete on the street and sidewalks was still hot, radiating the heat baked into it during the day by the fierce sun. Neon lights were in full force now that darkness had settled in, blinking to entice, blinking to attract, but with each pulse his nerves screamed a little louder and he wanted to be away from it. He felt like a walking zombie. The absinth was like nothing he had ever consumed. Maybe it was a legendary poison. He became angry with himself for being gullible enough to drink it.

Only Jeff's last words were clearly remembered—there was an exotic woman only six blocks away waiting for him, and how foolish he would be to blow this opportunity ... foolish. He looked down and saw his feet floating over the hot concrete beneath, the hot pavement permeating through his shoes, heading away from the neon, away from the crowds. He found himself heading towards the place described by Warden. Three blocks down the strip he turned left. Once off of the main strip, Las Vegas looked much like any other town in the South-west.

Two blocks further down he saw The Aces and it looked dark and remote, the antithesis of everything on the strip. The club was a seedy, old and run-down shell that had probably looked ramshackle even when new.

The Aces sat back, off the road, behind a newly constructed strip mall. There was a gravel parking lot along with a sign in the middle, a neon ace-of-hearts playing card. Muffled music could be heard leaking out from the front and side doors of the club as people walked in and out.

Standing in the shadows of a tree observing the place for a few minutes, Kurt noticed that the people leaving were mostly couples, whereas those going in were alone or in groups. Prostitution was legal in most of Nevada, but not in Clark County where Las Vegas was located. He assumed this was to keep the strip clear of obvious excesses in order to attract family tourism and gambling but here, well off the strip, it seemed to be business as usual.

He watched several of the couples leaving the building. One pair got into a car and drove off. Others walked a short distance to a nearby apartment building. The routine was clear; there was no attempt to even hide it.

A few minutes later an Oldsmobile sedan pulled into The Aces parking lot with two men in the front seat. This was unusual because the occupants didn't immediately get out and go into the club, but sat in the car and watched the entrances for several minutes before driving off slowly. Kurt remained shielded from their view by a large tree. The pair could have been law enforcement but they didn't have the right look, even for undercover police. When they drove off Kurt dismissed them as irrelevant.

Common sense should have told him to give this place a miss, but common sense wasn't currently dictating his actions. He was in a mixed state of agitation, euphoria and aggression and he knew what he was doing and that there was no way to halt the process. His attraction to danger and challenge in any form was drawing him further in and he felt powerless to resist.

What he didn't realize was that a suggestion had been planted whilst he was in an altered state. This suggestion had burrowed deeply into his mind and taken root. Like a launched torpedo he was running on a predetermined course. We like to think that our actions originate from 'free will' but more often than not another force is at the helm and we are just riding along, not really in charge.

After a few more minutes of observation Kurt went into the club. Inside, the establishment was actually fairly spacious, nor as crowded as the number of cars would indicate. The centrepiece of the room was a dark, polished, semicircular wooden platform used as a serving bar, and doubling as a stage for the dancers. A number of men stood against the bar, or had stools pulled up at the edge of the platform. The strippers would start at one end of the semicircle and slowly gyrate around the curve to loud music. After the dance, the strippers would climb down and mingle with the observers, soliciting tips from them, which were eagerly stuffed into their thongs like dead green butterflies.

The crowd seemed pretty tame, and the two hefty bouncers standing near the entrance with their arms folded looked intent upon keeping it that way. The rest of the room was occupied by ordinary tables and chairs seen in any cheap eat-in restaurant, except they were in near darkness. Dancers who weren't performing or getting ready to perform, were sitting at the tables talking one-on-one with customers. Kurt sat down at an empty table against the far wall and ordered a beer from a non-dancing waitress. He didn't want any more to drink, but having something on the table would make him look less conspicuous.

After a few minutes with no invitation or eye contact, one of the off-duty dancers came over and sat down at his table. She was short and thin with badly bleached close-cropped hair. Her eyes looked directly at him but even in the dim light they were flat and expressionless.

"Hey, big guy," she said in a raspy voice, "you looking for some company tonight?"

Kurt didn't respond to the rhetorical question. If he said no, she would ask him what the hell he was doing in this place. If he said yes, she would say "well here I am", so he changed the subject.

"Worked here long?"

She looked confused by the question. Kurt reasoned that is wasn't the type of question she was used to fielding.

"Couple of years," she finally said. "Why, does it make a difference? Are you gonna buy me a drink?"

Kurt nodded and the girl signalled the waitress who brought over a Coors. At least she wasn't drinking champagne, he thought.

Kurt looked the girl directly in the eyes seeking a response, some flicker of life through the hardened exterior. Under his steady gaze, she blinked rapidly and then her eyes began to shift around like those of a frightened child.

"Where are you from, girl, and what are you doing here?" Kurt asked, trying to make his voice soothing and non-threatening.

Her toughness evaporated; it had never been more than a thin veneer.

"My name is Bonnie, Bonnie Scott, from Montana originally, Billings Montana. My daddy worked in the copper mine but he was a mean drunk, so Mom and I left. She worked as a dealer in the pits but met a guy and I haven't seen her for a while."

For the next few minutes as Kurt listened to the girl's story, he doubted if anyone had ever bothered to ask her about her life before. She was just a frightened child of eighteen or nineteen who needed friendship so desperately that she would accept it from anyone.

When she stopped talking, Kurt moved closer to her so no one else would hear.

"Bonnie, do you know a Monique who works here?" he whispered.

Bonnie reacted as if Kurt had thrown icy water in her face.

"I didn't think you were that type," she said in a huff, and stood up to leave.

"Hold on," Kurt held her arm and felt hard little pieces of scar tissue buried in the skin on her waif-like, butter-soft forearm. She slowly settled back in her chair without any further coaxing.

"Look, I just was hoping you could help me out with some information."

"Are you a cop?" she asked.

"No, look, I'll square with you," Kurt's mind was racing as he explained. "I was hired to investigate some ... shall we say financial irregularities and her name was mentioned. That's all I can say. Please don't discuss this to anyone."

Kurt thought he had lied convincingly, since his story seemed to be working. It was obvious that there was no love lost between Monique and Bonnie, and it is easy to convince someone that a person they don't like is either a thief or in trouble. It's the ultimate vindication, just human nature.

Bonnie looked around the room then settled back in her chair and crossed her arms.

"Yeah, that figures," she said with a measure of haughtiness. "The stuck-up bitch. I hope you bust her good, put her in jail where freaks like her belong."

"Wait a minute, Bonnie," Kurt interrupted. "I'm not busting anyone remember? I'm just collecting information, or trying to."

Kurt felt his head becoming a little clearer. Hopefully the effects of the absinthe were wearing off. The ongoing mental challenge was helping to burn through the fog.

"What can you tell me about Monique?" Kurt asked, feeling like a junior detective asking questions. "Why don't we move back there so no one else will hear?"

Kurt ordered two more beers and they moved to the table furthest away from the action. The only people sitting within possible earshot were too engrossed in one another to eavesdrop.

"I first saw Monique about eighteen months ago," Bonnie said. "About six months after I started. You could tell right away that she didn't belong in a dump like this. She is a high living, big money, party girl. Everyone wondered what she was doing here and the rumours started flying around. One of the other girls swore that she saw Monique, I don't think that is her real name by the way, in a porn film a john made her watch; you know, the leather, chains, whips and stuff. I'm not into that shit at all, I want you to know, I think it's sick and perverted. Then someone else said that there was a snuff film in circulation."

"You mean where someone really gets killed?" Kurt asked.

"Yeah, talk about sick!" Bonnie shivered with a revulsion that was genuine. "The girl was supposed to be chopped up on camera, very slowly from what I hear, with a man and a woman doing the chopping. I never saw it myself, thank God, and I would never ever want to. But a guy I talked to said he paid two hundred bucks to see it, and he swears that one of the killers in that movie was Monique. I guess she had a mask on, but her figure and boobs gave her away; there ain't no one else built like that."

"So what's she doing here then?" Kurt asked.

Bonnie took a long drink of her Coors like she was trying to quench her anger.

"In my opinion," Bonnie whispered conspiratorially, "she has been put on ice here till things cool down. You know Vegas, money talks and bullshit walks. You pay off the local cops and they'll look the other way as long as you don't cause any trouble."

"So she came here by herself?" Kurt questioned.

"No, the owner of the place, or a partner, comes in to talk to her from time to time. Chats with her and then leaves. He sticks out here too; he's too much of a pretty boy. Looks like big money and drives a BMW."

"What does this guy look like?" Kurt asked, already knowing the answer.

"Blond hair, brushed back, tall, not very heavy, and usually wears grey suits."

Kurt nodded unintentionally.

"So do you know him?" Bonnie asked, seeing his gesture.

Kurt hesitated; he didn't want to give away any more information to the girl than necessary.

"Maybe, he does fit another description I have but … Look, Bonnie, I really appreciate the information. I don't want to take up any more of your time. I'd like to give you …" Kurt reached for a clip of bills he kept in his shirt pocket.

Bonnie subtly raised the palm of her hand and shook her head to stop him.

"No, I'm glad to help you out. If you can help to bust that bitch I will be a happy girl."

"We'll see," Kurt said softly.

Bonnie's face suddenly brightened.

"Hey, if you are around tomorrow," she said, "why don't you come by when I get off and we can go some place and have a good time, no charge or nothing, you're a nice guy. You won't believe what tricks a girl learns after a couple of years in this business." She reached her hand under the table and grabbed Kurt high on his left thigh and slid her fingers towards his crotch, when she froze momentarily.

"My God, what the hell are you hiding in there?" she whispered.

Kurt smiled at her.

"Does that mean you are withdrawing your offer?"

"Hell, no, I love a challenge," she said as she discreetly put her hand back on the table.

"I think I'll be in town tomorrow. What time should I come by?"

"Oh ... About twelve-thirty or one, what ..."

Bonnie straightened up in her seat and looked toward the entrance.

"Well, speak of the fucking devil, look what just walked in."

Kurt moved his eyes toward the door and knew it must be Monique. At about five nine or five ten she had a startling face, crisp and clean like a fashion model. Her hair was short and jet black except for a sprinkling of frosted highlights. She was dressed, like the other girls who worked in the club, in a black mini-skirt and a tied halter-neck top. No doubt to blend in, Kurt mused. Monique's legs were long and tapered and there was hardly any flare at her leather-wrapped hips and ass that ended in a tiny waist. Her chest was a real show stopper though. Her breasts were straining the halter, defying confinement.

"Wow," Kurt exhaled reflexively, not trying to look at her directly but having little luck averting his eyes.

"Yeah, she's something else, isn't she?" Bonnie mouthed quietly so only Kurt could hear. "It's too bad she's such a total bitch."

Monique scanned the room stopping briefly on Kurt and Bonnie sitting against the far wall, then her eyes continued on.

I stayed too long, Kurt thought, she's looking for me.

Monique went backstage, and came out a few minutes later wearing a costume and high heels. She gingerly climbed up the stairs leading to the crescent bar. As she began to move to the music it was obvious that compared with the other dancers, she was a professional. Those long firm legs weren't developed sitting on bar stools. Once her body was exposed it looked more like a caricature or an artist's fantasy than real flesh and blood. Her body was firm and sleek except for her perfectly shaped but massive breasts that seemed to defy both gravity and the laws of nature.

Her act finished, she made her way around the bar and let the enthusiastic men place bills between her breasts, which she cupped and supported with both hands. Most of the other dancers were given singles; Monique was collecting nothing but fives, tens and twenties, and a lot of them. Quite a decent haul for twenty minutes work, Kurt thought, even for a high-dollar chick forced to slum it for a while.

Kurt got up and nodded to Bonnie.

"I'll see you tomorrow." He made his way over to an empty stool that had opened up at the bar. Monique was just moving to this section when Kurt sat down. He quickly pulled out a ten dollar bill and held it out. She opened up her cleavage and, when Kurt put the bill in, she closed her breasts and his entire hand was buried in soft flesh up to his wrist. They felt real and warm, not like bags of silicone like he expected. Her nipples were the size of small cookies, and about the same colour.

She leaned close to him and softly said, "Jeff told me to say hi."

Her breath smelled of mint and musk and for a few moments Kurt was speechless, momentarily paralyzed by this human Venus fly-trap. Monique's face wore a smooth and well practiced business smile, no doubt used with all the customers.

"Why don't you go have a seat at one of the tables and I'll be over when I finish here?" Her eyes bored into him like hot skewers. She released his hand and proceeded down the line to collect bills offered by the other enthusiastic customers.

⌘

After, she sat down at his table and ordered a drink, a club soda, Kurt noted.

"How long have you known Jeff?" she casually asked.

Kurt didn't answer immediately—he was studying Monique, trying to figure out her angle. She seemed far too classy to be a local bang one buddy would throw to another.

"I knew him years ago in the army, just ran into him at a convention today."

"I see him occasionally, less these days though." Monique stirred her drink with a little red swizzle stick which was a pointless action for soda water.

Kurt could sense that she was acting. Something wasn't right about this situation, but Jeff was right about one thing, this woman was the most attractive and beautiful creature he'd ever seen up close. Turning her down would be an unthinkable act for any sane male. The allure and underlying danger of the woman caused an adrenaline rush that, mixed with the absinthe, made Monique's image more intense.

"Well, any friend of Jeff's is a friend of mine, as they say." Monique put her hand on Kurt's arm and began to play her fingertips on his muscles. Her sharp nails were painted blood-red and looked like miniature daggers.

"What are you into big guy, a little rough stuff maybe?" As she said it, Monique purposefully pressed her fingers into the skin of Kurt's upper arm, causing pain as the nails dug deeply, though he didn't flinch.

"Not really, I'm a conventional type of guy when it comes to those things."

The nails released their pressure.

"You're not boring, are you? I really don't like boring men very much," she said. "There are other girls here," Monique nodded in the direction of the stage where another dancer was performing. "They do the boring work with the boring people. I do, well, the more sophisticated and challenging work. If Jeff referred you ..."

Monique stopped talking. Kurt looked into her eyes and even in the gloom and shadow could see something he didn't expect or even understand. He didn't know if he was looking at desperation, hunger, fear, aggression or something else entirely. Monique radiated danger. Kurt wasn't about to leave, not now.

"I live just a couple of blocks from here," Monique said with authority. "Let's go."

"Don't you have to dance again?" Kurt asked.

"Maybe later; I'll let the crowd change over. They get cheap on you if you go around too often. It's a waste of my time."

Monique got up and led him out the fire exit on the side of the building. The door opened out and was only supposed to be used in emergencies. One of the brawny bouncers moved in their direction to close the door. Kurt quickly sized up the bouncer as one of those big, inflated, biker-types who had become too fat. He knew that he could take down that pile of blubber in seconds, but his ominous-looking figure evidently served its purpose.

They left the club and walked up the road toward Monique's apartment. She was strangely quiet, unlike Bonnie who couldn't stop talking. Monique must work out or run, Kurt thought. It would be hard to maintain a figure like that and that level of muscle tone without heavy exercise. She didn't seem to smoke or drink either, which was very odd considering her 'occupation'.

From the walkway, they turned into a courtyard leading to an apartment complex. The exteriors of the older buildings were Spanish style stucco. Brick archways framed the entrances of each apartment building leading into the common courtyard. She directed him to a darkened building set in the far corner of the complex.

He found the lack of lighting a bit strange but perhaps all of the units were rented out to girls who worked at the club. That would explain it. They walked by assorted vehicles parked along the street and in covered carports attached to the buildings. Garages were hardly needed in this climate. As they passed near an Oldsmobile Delta 88 something prickled the back of his neck but he was so entranced by the woman and under the veil of absinthe nothing else registered at the moment, not even the obvious.

Monique stopped at the bottom of a flight of concrete steps leading up to the second floor and fished in her purse for keys. Kurt stood watching her thinking, "Jesus, women and their purses."

They finally went up the stairs and Monique reached a door and inserted her key. The veranda covering the doorways was also dark, too dark.

Kurt began to wonder why there was no security lighting on the front of the buildings. Luckily Kurt's night vision had always been extraordinary, and darkness had never been much of an issue. While others had a difficult time patrolling in the triple-canopy jungle at night, he had always coped well.

Instead of turning the key and entering the apartment Monique slowly turned around with her back to the door and without saying a word held her arms out to Kurt. He approached and she circled him around the waist and pulled him close. She leaned forward and placed her mouth on his and latched on to his lower lip with her teeth, not biting hard enough to draw blood but using enough pressure to send electric shocks down his spine. Her breasts were so large it was not easy to be face-to-face. Monique began to undulate in his arms like a snake, pushing her pelvis into his thigh and moaning. If she's faking this, Kurt thought, it's damn good acting.

She moved her hands to his chest, pushing him away far enough to unbutton his shirt. Placing her hands on his chest first she rubbed hard with her palms and then raked her sharp ruby nails across his skin. Monique knew exactly how much pressure to apply, scratching the epidermis and sending the nerve endings wild, but not drawing blood.

Kurt went rigid, his entire body going into spasm from the sensation. Monique then reached up and untied the loose knot from behind her neck, and her massive breasts seemed to spill out. She took Kurt's hand in hers and placed them on her breasts and clasped his thumbs and forefingers together encouraging him to squeeze her swollen nipples.

Monique began to moan even louder. Kurt thought someone was bound to hear but the place seemed pretty deserted and he didn't want to stop. This woman was …

Kurt was watching Monique's face and eyes. Her right eye reflected a faint star from a streetlight a block away and then without either of them moving, it disappeared. The slight change would have been missed by most, but to Kurt it was like a bucket of ice-water being thrown on a horny dog.

He released the girl and spun around quickly on the ball of his left foot, thrusting his bent left arm over his head as he did. He saw an object held aloft, behind and above him, a tyre iron or crow bar attached to an arm. With his elevated left hand Kurt grabbed the arm just below the object and held it fast. It had just begun its downward swing and had little momentum so he managed to hold it where it could do no harm. Then the attacker came into focus, long dark greasy hair and about one hundred and forty pounds against his two hundred; it was no contest. The man looked shocked, unable to decide what to do next.

With his right hand Kurt reached behind his belt where the little razor-sharp puukko knife lay hidden. Experience enabled Kurt to use the knife by feel and he inserted it, blade up, at a point just above the attacker's belt then sliced upwards. There was a sound like a zipper being opened as the man's thin T-shirt and abdomen were bisected. Only the tip of the knife was used—just enough to penetrate the skin and underlying muscle. Kurt had made this same manoeuvre on many occasions when cleaning game.

He kept the blade moving vertically with some force until it hit the attacker's sternum with the grating sound of metal striking bone. Kurt then tipped the blade back and kept the edge cutting until it jumped off his opponent's chest and struck his chin with a "tic" and the momentum carried the blade through one nostril and above the man's head.

Kurt rotated his assailant's arm aloft and twisted it inwards. Turning the little blade, he brought it down across the attacker's biceps muscle just above the elbow, using enough edge to sever the muscle body, but not going deep enough to cut the brachial artery that lay close to the bone. Then Kurt released his opponent. The tyre iron, destined to shatter the back of Kurt's skull, fell to the veranda floor with a loud clang, where it took a chip out of the painted concrete surface.

His right arm now extended and useless, the attacker went down on his knees and with his left arm and hand tried to hold in his now bulging and exposed viscera, but this position only increased the pressure in his abdomen and made matters worse.

The moment the man dropped down Kurt spotted another and potentially more deadly problem. The other Oldsmobile man was standing at the top of the stairs. In the dim reflections from the streetlights he could vaguely make out a heavy Webley .455 revolver in his hand. The would-be hit man was young with straggly light hair that went past his shoulders. He was obviously inexperienced with weapons from the way he was holding the revolver with one hand and shaking.

Kurt had Monique behind him and the gunman's partner kneeling in front. Attacker number two was more than likely convinced that the tyre iron would have done its job and the gun wouldn't be needed. Now he held a shaking gun, and faced an indistinct target in the dark.

Kurt knew that the revolver was double action only and the trigger pull was long and horrendously hard. The old Webleys didn't go off by accident, but the man had likely begun the trigger pull. Kurt dropped the puukko from his right hand and grabbed the kneeling man by the throat but it was slick with blood, so he grabbed hold of the man's hair and lunged forward with one movement, throwing the injured attacker towards his partner. If the gun went off the body would block the bullet, and a heavy slow .455 slug wouldn't travel all the way through a man.

The gutted attacker slammed into his partner causing the gunman to lurch backwards and tumble down the stairs, the unfired revolver still clutched in his right hand. Young and flexible, the gunman managed to roll with the fall onto the landing and was beginning to get to his feet when Kurt bounded down the flight of stairs in three leaps.

Kurt back-fisted the gunman directly in the face with his right hand and with a sweep of the left arm knocked the revolver, spinning, onto the landing where it clattered down into the brick courtyard.

Kurt grasped the gunman's right upper arm with his left hand and, with an explosive movement, rotated his right elbow into the side of the man's face. There was a pronounced *thud* as the powerful blow struck home. The man's head flopped to the side as Kurt followed it up with a rapid second strike. With the second blow a muffled cracking sound confirmed neck vertebrae separating. Kurt let go of the man's arm and he fell on the landing like a bag of grain. Kurt watched the gunman's chest heave as foam appeared on his lips.

The first attacker was now lying near the top of the stairs trying to hold himself together with his good arm and screaming hideously. Kurt surged back up the stairs past the screaming man.

"Shut up!" he spat harshly between his teeth as he stooped for the blood-covered puukko. The attacker continued to wail, loudly.

"I said shut the fuck up!" Kurt snarled louder. Again the man paid no heed.

Kurt looked at Monique still standing in front of the locked door; she hadn't moved or attempted to flee during the altercation. Her eyes shifted from Kurt to the screaming attacker. It was excitement Kurt saw on her face, not the terror one would expect from an innocent witness.

Kurt reached over and grabbed her blouse and with a downward snap pulled it completely off. The thin material gave way and she stood there wide-eyed with both breasts free and bouncing, exposed.

Wrapping the torn blouse around his right hand, Kurt picked up the tyre iron and swept it towards the screaming man, striking him solidly in the jaw with the bent end. There was a cracking sound and the screaming was replaced by a gurgle. Kurt flung the steel bar across the railing into the courtyard below where it clanged loudly. With a piece of tattered blouse Kurt tried to wipe blood off the blade and handle of the puukko.

He slowly walked over to Monique and watched her breasts move as she breathed heavily. She didn't try to cover her nakedness but stood tall as if she had just finished running a race and won. She stared at Kurt expectantly, not saying anything but her excited eyes told the story.

"You love this shit, don't you, bitch?" Kurt asked when he was about a foot away from her face. "You don't care who gets hurt do you? Them, me … you?" He took the puukko and flicked Monique's left nipple with the point.

Monique continued to stand there but now started to shiver and a soft sound was heard as her bladder emptied down her leg and pooled on the floor. A familiar hot, musky smell permeated the air. A fine ribbon of blood began to flow from her left nipple and detour towards her navel.

Kurt slid the little knife back into its sheath.

"No matter what I did to you, you wouldn't tell me a thing, would you?" Kurt knew there would be no reply. She would never say another word to him. He had beaten her at her own game. "No doubt Jeff will be disappointed. I'd hate to be in your shoes, Monique."

He grabbed her forcefully and smelled the pungent mix of blood, urine, sweat and fear that mingled with the hot desert night. It was an exhilarating cocktail that heightened his senses to a new, raw intensity.

He grabbed the back of her head with his left hand and pulled it to his. His mouth went over her full perfect lips and seizing the lower one with his teeth, he bit down. Her soft tissues crushed with the force, and he tasted the metallic flush of fresh blood. Monique's entire body went rigid and then began to buck in powerful orgasm, but he held her fast until it played out, then he released her.

"I liked it, too," he whispered in her ear.

Kurt walked a few steps to the stairs and turned.

"Tell that coward Warden not to insult me by sending dickhead boy-scouts to kill me. You'd better call the ambulance for those idiots." Kurt swept his arm in the direction of the two attackers. "If they get here soon they may be able to salvage something."

He turned around as if to leave, and then spun around again.

"And Monique, you *are* beautiful. It would have been fun."

# CHAPTER 6
## RUNAWAY

Kurt was a mess. Blood covered his hands, arms and clothes. If he was seen in this state he would be reported immediately and any more trouble was the last thing he needed now. There was no telling how much influence Warden and his gang had on the local authorities. He suspected a one way trip to the desert would be the result if he was detained, or turned himself in. Escaping from Las Vegas undetected was essential. From the apartment complex where Monique had orchestrated the ambush, he cut across backyards, heading obliquely for the Strip. He needed to contact Joe, if Joe was still an ally. Recent events cast doubt on everything and trusting anyone, from this point on, wasn't an option.

In one backyard a garden hose was lying extended on the grass. The owner must have been watering his small flower garden and left the hose out, instead of reeling it up. The house was dark and quiet and the hose was attached to a standpipe in the yard. Easing open the valve, he hosed himself off. The blood was fresh and it came away easily from his skin and clothes. His clothes were still stained, but it looked like dirt or grease to a casual observer. Body heat and the low humidity began to dry both skin and clothes rapidly. By the time he approached the Strip he was merely damp.

Police sirens wailed in the background; there was little doubt where they were headed. Working by instinct, Kurt approached the hotel from the rear and staying in the shadows, made a slow reconnaissance of the parking lot. Ten minutes later he saw it. Like all good special operatives, before arriving in Vegas Joe and Kurt had made arrangements for an emergency. Kurt hoped Joe remembered and was still a friend. The El Camino was easy to spot in the parking lot. On closer inspection, Joe was sitting in the driver's seat, drumming his fingers on the top of the steering wheel.

Moving to within hearing distance of the El Camino and not seeing anyone else in the vicinity, Kurt let out a soft whistle. Joe recognized the sound immediately and cocked his head. Kurt repeated the call and Joe climbed out of the car, locked it and casually strolled toward a nearby street. Once there, he turned and walked away from the busy Strip.

Kurt remained in the shadows looking for anyone observing or following Joe. Seeing nothing suspicious he strode briskly on an intersecting course, keeping to the clutter of cars and buildings, and checking to his rear occasionally.

Continuing his casual pace, Joe detoured into an alley separating two stores at the back of a small shopping mall. Kurt made his way around the store and met him coming the other way in the darkened alley. From here they could easily see anyone approaching, and they had two escape routes. Joe looked nervous and continued to scan both entrances to the alley when Kurt approached.

"Jesus, I'm glad we managed to link up," Joe said sounding relieved. "I picked up some information from one of my old teammates who knew something was up and that you may be in trouble. I looked around and couldn't find you anywhere. I recalled we agreed to rally in the parking lot if we got separated and … "

In the dim alley Joe surveyed Kurt's dishevelled state and stained clothes.

"What the hell happened?" Joe asked.

"Your warning is a little late," Kurt replied. "A couple of street goons tried to collect on a contract, but didn't fare very well. I heard an ambulance go to pick them up a few minutes ago."

"You didn't kill anyone, did you?" Joe asked.

"I don't think so, but I'm not sure."

"I hope not," Joe said. "Bodies cause a lot of problems in civilian life, not like the old days."

Kurt's adrenaline high, built up by the events in the club and fight, was crashing around his ankles and he was in no mood for small talk. The situation was both confusing and deadly and he needed more information to out-manoeuvre whatever forces were conspiring to kill him.

"Joe, what the fuck is going on? Why are these people out to kill me? And why am I here? My patience with all this crap has completely run out."

"Look Kurt, I'm on your side, you saved my life and I will never forget that," Joe said with a desperate edge to his voice. "I had a call a couple of weeks ago from Colonel Belgrave asking me to contact you and bring you to the convention. I thought it a little odd, they knew your address and number, but they wanted me to invite you. They offered me a thousand bucks if I got you to come and, frankly, I need the money. I thought they just wanted you there because of your exploits; because Mad Dog is dead and you're one of the few living legends of SOG."

Kurt studied Joe's eyes and body language in the dim light and saw both fear and remorse in the man. Joe wasn't lying to him.

"That's alright. I'm not pissed at you. It sounds like you were just being used. But from what you just learned, why …?"

"From a former teammate who is now in the Pentagon," Joe said, "I hear there is some real crap hitting the fan in DC. There's a Congressional inquiry about covert operations in the war involving CIA, NSA, Special Forces, you know the whole thing. SOG has come under scrutiny because we were tied in to most of them. They are lifting the rock and the bugs are scurrying for cover."

"What the hell is the purpose of a public investigation?" Kurt asked. "We were just doing what the government told us to—kill and destroy communist aggressors."

"I know, it doesn't make a lot of sense, but Watergate and Nixon's resignation last year turned the Washington political machine on its head. What's going on now is partisan politics at its worst, using the legacy of covert operations to embarrass some politicians and bolster others. We're stuck in the middle. A cornered dog bites back.

It seems the Pentagon has accused the CIA and other government agencies, most likely the Department of State, with making secret deals with the North Vietnamese at the Paris Peace Accords."

"That's not news," Kurt said. "We already know that they sold us down the river. And they smiled for the cameras when they did it."

"Yes, but specifically the Pentagon is openly accusing Department of State of serving up SOG teams to the North on a silver platter as part of the accords."

"Shit," Kurt exhaled, "sacrificing us so they could make their deals. We knew there were leaks but ..."

"You know the North Vietnamese hated SOG with a passion," Joe continued. "It appears that one of the compromises reached in the negotiations was to eliminate the SOG cross-border teams. They were exposing NVA forces which were operating illegally in Laos and Cambodia. Your little one man crusade held that up for awhile, and was an embarrassment to the negotiators."

"Hell, Joe, I've always been an embarrassment, but that's water under the bridge now, the Reds rolled into Saigon. It's all over. So ..."

"Just stay with me a minute, Kurt," Joe said. "So our side agreed to step-up the supply of information to North Vietnam, to show their good intentions so the talks could continue. The conventional means of leaking information by spies and double agents wasn't effective or fast enough. The Phoenix Program was neutralizing communist agents quicker than the North could field them."

"So how were they getting the information to the other side?" Kurt asked impatiently.

"They were giving the NVA information by using the simplest and most direct way," Joe replied. "Hand delivery."

Kurt stared at Joe, not understanding what he'd just heard. The light clicked on.

"Covey flights," Kurt blurted suddenly. "Those planes I heard were ours, weren't they?"

"Right," Joe said. "Using some foreign contract pilots from Air America they were sending out maps, LZ locations, call signs, one time code pads and even IDs of team members, directly to NVA intelligence in the field. When the enemy had that information, our teams had no chance once they hit the ground. It was like a handful of ants being dropped on an aardvark nest."

"Fucking murderous traitors," Kurt hissed.

"Yes, in a major way," Joe said. "But someone by the name of Kurt Christianson threw a monkey wrench into their well-oiled wheels."

"How did I do that?"

"Remember the documents you took off the NVA detachment commander and buttoned in my pocket before I was airlifted out?"

"Yes, I thought the Intelligence wienies would find it useful."

"Useful!" Joe almost shouted. "If that goddamn bag had contained a nuclear bomb or flying saucer plans it couldn't have stirred up more trouble. I lied to them. When I was flown from the FOB to the hospital in Na Trang my eyes had cleared sufficiently and I looked in the bag and saw all of this shit, but all I could do was turn it in. Wilson knew I had it and there was no way to get rid of it, so I just played dumb."

Kurt was silent, trying to think the situation through. Joe continued, "You sent material dropped off by a Covey flight a few days previously, straight to MACV Intelligence, who of course knew nothing about the treason. You ruined the whole day for the high level State Department sell-outs and a few others. I didn't want to tell you any of this because I thought it had all cooled down and been forgotten, but considering recent events you'd better know what you're up against."

"Christ, I should have looked in the envelope but we were under fire and there was no way to do that at the time," Kurt said.

"You would have never figured it out then, anyway," Joe said. "It was just a fluke. You weren't playing the game predictably. You caught them with their dicks out. Now you're just a wildcard they can't afford to leave on the table. When it happened it took some fancy footwork by those involved to cover up everything; payoffs, promotions, contracts … you know. Now all this recent political throat-cutting and recriminations are bringing the bad smell back to the surface."

Joe looked at the rough concrete and litter in the alley and shook his head before he continued.

"This thing's really screwed up. They're convinced that I didn't know about the material because my eyes were injured. They are convinced that you do, because you sent it, but I'm the one who knew all along. I also knew you didn't know and thought it best left that way. Now they think if you testified in front of a Congressional Committee or the press, a bunch of high-level officials would hang and they aren't going to let that happen."

"I haven't talked to anyone about what happened since the war, why would I start now?" Kurt questioned.

"That's because you are a man of integrity, Kurt, and those slimy politicians don't even know the meaning of that word."

"Who covered up on our side?" Kurt asked. "Someone had to know about it."

"You probably know the answer to that. The S-2 commander and a staff intelligence specialist in C Team Headquarters in Na Trang were the two traitors from our side. It was a very neat operation with very minimal involvement. State found and turned the two snakes in the woodpile."

"Belgrave and Warden," Kurt voiced, confirming what he suspected.

"Right again, so now you know why they want Kurt Christianson gone. If your ass was subpoenaed by the inquisition their cover-up would fall apart, and some high level rats still feeding from the government trough would have a tough time explaining things. As far as they know, you're the last link in the chain. The only reason I'm still alive is that they believed my story about not knowing the contents of that bag. I trust you with this information. No one else knows and if they find out I'm a dead man."

"I'd never say anything, Joe, but what the hell do I do now? I can't fight these people. Belgrave and Warden are just the tip of the iceberg. If high-level government types are out to get me, it's just a matter of time."

Joe bowed his head slightly and nodded in agreement.

"Kurt, in my opinion you have two choices, but neither of them is very attractive. One is to go to Washington, call a press conference, and testify about all you know. But if you do that, the powers that be are going to use every trick in their book to discredit you, and you may end up sharing space with a 45 slug for your trouble. The other option is to disappear."

"Disappear? I'm not a damn magician, Joe."

"No, I mean get out of the country, somewhere remote with no extradition treaty with the US, so even if you're subpoenaed they can't get to you. Also, it's very difficult for these people to extend their fingers that far; there are diplomatic considerations. Stay away for three to five years and all this shit will most likely blow over. You're young and that time won't mean much in the long term; it beats the deep six anyway. It's your best chance Kurt. Do you have any ideas where you could go?"

Kurt was silent for a few seconds before replying, "I think so."

"Good, I'll help you all I can but I don't want to know where you go."

"I think I can arrange that myself," Kurt said. "If you get me to Reno I can take it from there. I don't like the idea of leaving Las Vegas by public transport right now, and I certainly don't want to go back to your place."

Joe walked back to pick up his car. He'd managed to remove a few of Kurt's things from the hotel room and put them in the trunk. He didn't see Warden or Belgrave on his way out the side door. Hopefully they were too busy focusing on Kurt to watch him. He drove around for a few minutes to check he wasn't being tailed. Kurt met him at a pre-arranged location, on a dark back street, and they headed out of town by an indirect route that linked up with Highway 95, which headed north to Reno.

⌘

The Nevada Desert at that time of night was as dark, bleak and barren as a land before time. Very little traffic moved at that hour and the speed limit was unrestricted, so they cruised at eighty to ninety miles per hour. In the small hours near Tonopah, they checked into an old motel for a couple of hours' rest. Kurt needed to shower and change his clothes in order not to attract attention. The bloody clothes were cut up and thrown away in a dumpster down the street from the motel.

The following morning they ate breakfast on the road and Joe dropped Kurt off a block from the bus station in Reno. It was more difficult to monitor travel on buses than it was on aircraft. At this point state or local police wouldn't be involved, only a few spooks with limited manpower.

After thanking Joe, Kurt carried his backpack to the bus station and paid cash for a one-way fare to Kansas City. The journey to the East Coast was accomplished in stages, by buying tickets for the next leg of the trip randomly to avoid a traceable pattern.

Two and a half days later, a Trailways Bus pulled into Portland Maine and Kurt felt totally exhausted. He checked into an inexpensive hotel in town and slept for ten hours, awaking in the early evening.

⌘

Kurt called Dave from a public pay phone on a street corner and asked if the job on the boat crew was still open. Dave seemed happy to hear from him and said the boat was currently undergoing local sea trials. The following week both boat and crew would depart from the Bath Shipworks to New York, where the boat would undergo final fitting before travelling to the West African oil fields. Dave explained that the politics in that part of the world were shaky, and the multinational petroleum companies were desperate to maintain production in these fields. The cost of required equipment to keep the wells operational was of little consideration.

Dave mentioned he had to go to Freeport, just up the Coast from Portland, to pick up supplies from the LL Bean warehouse. It was only a short bus ride there, so Kurt said he'd meet Dave at the store at noon the following day. After the phone call, Kurt walked to the Portland docks and ordered a huge plate of Damariscotta clams, harvested near Boothbay. It would be a while before he would see Maine seafood again, so he vowed to take full advantage now.

After eating, he went to the local YMCA and paid a one-off fee and lifted weights, swam in the pool and ran laps in the gym until exhaustion set in. Travelling disrupted workouts and his muscle tone was suffering. It would be difficult to stay in shape on the boat. Perhaps the continual effort required of a crew member would help a little.

⌘

LL Bean had been selling sporting goods and outdoor clothing from their Freeport,Maine location since the turn of the century. Originally selling only fishing and hunting boots, their product line was continuously being expanded to offer all types of sportsmen's clothes, camping equipment, fishing tackle and multitudes of accessories. The company did most of their business by mail order, but locally they had a large warehouse where customers could wander around and select items from tables and shelves. Bean's was the best place to buy rugged seafaring clothes and other gear at a reasonable price.

Dave and Kurt went shopping and Kurt picked up a lined nylon windbreaker, canvas pants, deck shoes, socks, a waterproof flashlight, a sealed document pouch and a few other small items he thought necessary for the trip. Dave paid for everything, since it could be billed to the client. After leaving Bean's they also stopped at a supermarket and a drug store to buy canned food and medical supplies, before driving back to Dave's place in St George.

On the trip to St George Kurt spoke, "Dave, I know it's a little bold of me to ask but could I borrow your pickup and go down to Massachusetts tomorrow and collect some of my things? I also need to put my jeep in storage before I leave. I'll put gas in the pickup."

"Sure, you just come back from somewhere?" Dave asked.

"I was out in New Mexico visiting an old army friend last week."

"I was out there once," Dave said. "I don't know if I could stand living in that part of the country. Too dry and too far from the sea."

"It is different," Kurt said, "but it has a beauty all its own. Everyone has their own definition of paradise. I guess I haven't found mine yet, I'm still looking. Have you been to Africa before, Dave? What's it like there?"

"I've been to the West Coast three times delivering boats and I went to Kenya, hunting, once. To answer your question, asking what Africa is like is like asking what North America is like. Here we have everything from Alaskan glaciers to Guatemalan jungles. Africa is even bigger and more diverse. I find it a strange, primal place. I think mystery still inhabits that continent. It's always seemed ironic to me that all of us came from there originally and wandered off somewhere, yet it is still the most poorly understood place on earth. You may find paradise in Africa but then again, you may find something else entirely."

Dave was quiet for a few minutes, sensing Kurt's questions were not just of an inquisitive nature, but had a deeper purpose.

"Are you coming back with us or are you staying on a bit longer?" Dave asked, scratching the beard he was growing in preparation for the voyage.

"I was going to talk to you about that, Dave," Kurt said. "I'd like to travel around a little after we arrive, and I wondered if there was any provision for that?"

"Well, I don't see why not. I can pay you when we get there and I'll just leave you with an open return ticket, or give you the cash equivalent. Either way is fine with me, but then you'll be on your own."

Kurt nodded, "Thanks, Dave, I appreciate it."

"Kurt, you're not in trouble are you?"

Kurt looked at him then away towards the pine-flanked road ahead. Dave was very perceptive—being an ex career cop probably had something to do with it.

"There are all colours, sizes and flavours of trouble, Dave. There is some serious crap going on but this time the colour is green, not blue and it's pretty big and somewhat bitter. You really don't want to know any more."

Dave drove on for a few minutes before he spoke again.

"Yeah, Africa is a big place. It wouldn't be difficult to become distracted over there for a while."

⌘

The next morning Kurt drove the borrowed Ford pickup to the small college town where he'd been living. He really wanted to go to the rented house, but given the circumstances it was too risky. If his enemies were serious, the house would be under surveillance and he would blunder straight into a trap.

Fortunately, foresight, training or old-fashioned paranoia had taught him to cache a few items in other locations. A bank safe deposit box contained some cash, travel documents and a small hideout, or 'just in case' pistol. These he collected with no problem. Some heavier gear and clothes were kept in a small rental unit, partly because he didn't have room at the small shared house, and partly in anticipation of such an event. He would mail a letter to his roommate on departure with instructions about his jeep, things remaining in the house and mail.

Returning to St George the same day, Kurt was introduced to the other two crew members who would be making the trip with them. They were selected based on their technical abilities and the fact that they were young, single guys who volunteered to make the voyage. Al was a tall, lanky farm-boy who appeared a little 'slow' until near marine engines, where he was transformed into a wizard. Dan was a short redhead and a prototypical electronics nerd. If either of those systems were to break down on the trip, they would be vital.

Kurt, Al and Dan went with Dave on the last of the sea trials before they took the boat down to New York to be outfitted. Kurt suspected that it would take time to restore his sea-legs. It had been many years since he'd gone out with the lobster boats and feeling sick on a long transatlantic voyage wasn't a pleasant prospect.

The vessel they would be taking over to Africa for delivery, temporarily named the Lil' Katie after Dave's daughter, wasn't pretty or graceful but it was a very solid and rugged piece of equipment. The shipwrights at the Bath Shipworks had done a superb job. As oil rig tender, the vessel was designed to take the constant abuse of cargo and personnel, being loaded and unloaded, under the worst conditions. Her one thousand two hundred HP diesel engine provided more than adequate power to cruise and manoeuvre.

During the trials they ran the vessel at high speeds over rough seas, to ensure the performance of the engine and to check the seaworthiness of the hull and controls. With a few adjustments everything seemed to run smoothly and Dave gave his stamp of approval to the vessel. With some relief Kurt felt his sea-legs kick in.

The night before they left for New York, Kurt told Dave he was leaving behind a trunk and, if things worked out on the other side, he would send a forwarding address. They closed up Dave's place on St George since it would be unoccupied for several weeks. All gear and supplies were loaded aboard the Lil' Katie and the engine kicked over just before dawn. They split the calm blue waters of Coastal Maine and headed out to sea. Kurt wondered privately if he would ever see this cherished coast again.

He watched the diminishing coastline, as if a beautiful lady was walking away, and felt a twinge of sadness. Maine was a hard place to leave. All the events of the last week had taken their toll. There should be some excitement about this new adventure but, for the first time in his life, Kurt didn't feel in control of his destiny. His mood was one of sad numbness as the last of Maine faded from view, so he went to work helping the others stow gear for the voyage.

⌘

After a smooth run down the coast on light seas, Lil' Katie and crew arrived at the Port of New York mid-afternoon. The Bath Shipworks in Maine had built the hull, installed the engine, electrical components and power train for about half of what the same work would cost elsewhere. However, a specialist contractor located at a New York facility was contracted to finish the boat over the next week or so before they made the transatlantic crossing.

The four crew members unloaded their personal gear and provisions and stored them in a secure area at the maintenance support building, while the technicians got busy with the modifications. They checked into two small motel rooms located very close to the maintenance facilities and for the next week rotated twelve hours on and twelve off observing and sometimes assisting with the around-the-clock fitting out of the Lil' Katie.

From a stripped hull and power train, the boat quickly began to take shape as the workhorse she would become once on the other side of the Atlantic. Heavy duty winches, radios, radar and tropical hardwood decking with non skid surfaces were laid down. Storage lockers and sleeping bunks were installed below. The fitting crews worked hard and efficiently. Dave would receive a bonus from the oil company for every day he could beat the scheduled delivery date, justifying the overtime paid to the workers.

The following Friday afternoon only minor adjustments and checks had to be made on the boat before departure. Dave surprised them when he said they would be staying in New York City for the weekend, at the company's expense, and departing on Monday morning for Africa.

⌘

From the shipyard the four of them caught a cab to a hotel in Manhattan—Kurt felt he was entering another world. This was his first trip to New York, besides changing airplanes and driving through on the I-95. The traffic, the press of strangers and the vertical real estate all seemed big, inhospitable and a little threatening, but mostly it was the lack of control in these surroundings that made him uneasy. The people swarmed around and didn't look at one another.

After checking into the hotel, showering and changing clothes, they all split up to do their own thing. Dave, a man of culture at heart, wanted to see a Broadway show he'd heard about. Al and Dan, the pair hired from the Bath Shipworks, wanted to go directly to Times Square and investigate 'the action' as they described it. Times Square was awash in peep shows and porno shops, which did lucrative business by entertaining the likes of Al and Dan. When the pair told Dave where they were going, he frowned but thought it best for them to get it out of their systems before the crossing.

Dave gave them a two hundred dollar advance on their pay, told them all to have a good time, but to meet back there at six for dinner. Kurt was feeling jumpy and anxious and knew it was due to the lack of exercise. He'd seen a YMCA nearby, so he put his exercise clothes and swimming trunks in a cloth laundry bag and caught a cab. The facility was well equipped but had seen better days, and the old gymnasium smell permeated the air.

After warming up carefully to prevent sprains or tears, Kurt used the lat machine and did curls and dumbbell butterflies before hitting the bench. His 'max' bench press had dropped to three hundred and sixty pounds from its peak of over four hundred, not surprising after a break in training. The amount of weight he was pressing drew a few stares, mainly because he didn't have a bodybuilder's physique even though he could lift in the competitive range. He worked his muscle groups to the point of failure while pushing to his limit. It was strange how strengthening was accomplished, he thought; you have to destroy the old to become stronger. Nature worked in mysterious ways.

It took two and a half hours of intense workout to reach a state of physical exhaustion. When finished, Kurt felt that warm glow which only intense exercise brought about, and was much more relaxed than when he came in.

Aside from a few serious bodybuilders, most of the people using the facility wore expensive, brightly coloured workout clothes and seemed to only toy with the weights and machines. It looked as though most used the gym as just another place to socialize and chit-chat with friends, not seriously train. One man in particular kept eyeing Kurt, and seemed to be shadowing him. He was middle aged, with an average appearance but looked too soft and urbane to be athletic. Kurt ignored this intrusion, but when he moved too close in the locker room, his constant presence became an irritant.

"Do you want something?" Kurt finally said to the man in calm voice, trying to sound non-threatening.

Sitting on the bench the man looked at him with a strangely disconcerting smile. It wasn't a smile that one man gives another and his eyes were different, like soft round pools.

"My name is Roger and I've been watching you work out and I must say…"

Having just returned from the shower, Kurt took off his towel and turned towards him. Roger's eyes dilated and he stopped speaking in mid-sentence, his mouth agape.

"And what is it you want?" Kurt asked as he put one leg on the bench and dried himself, mocking the man who was behaving like a helpless child.

"I want …" his voice stopped again, unable to continue.

"Yes, speak up," Kurt persisted. "You want what?"

"I'd like to go out with you," Roger mumbled unable to take his eyes off of Kurt's crotch. "How much?"

Kurt looked at the ceiling as if he was thinking then looked down at the quivering man again, and grinned.

"Well, Roger, I'll tell you what, you can probably buy just about anything in this city with money, but not me. Do you understand?"

Roger looked disappointed. He said nothing more, jumped to his feet, grabbed his clothes and moved out of sight, to another locker across the room.

Two weightlifters were coming in just as it happened, and began to laugh as Roger ran off.

"Did that guy try to hit on you too?" one of them asked Kurt.

Kurt just shrugged and didn't reply. At one level he'd been offended by being propositioned, but the man was no physical threat. He just didn't understand some things or people, and probably never would. He figured when people became too far removed from the natural world normal behaviour broke down.

"Big cities, they're not for me," he said to himself as he walked out the door of the gym on to the street.

⌘

After dropping his things off at the hotel and having nothing better to do, Kurt decided to visit Times Square and try to find Dan and Al to make sure they were staying out of trouble. They were country hicks like Kurt. The main difference was that that both of them had 'victim' written all over their faces. If any harm came to either of them the departure might be delayed and, given the situation, Kurt wanted to leave quickly.

Walking the crowded streets, he looked at the store windows and people, taking in all the sights and sounds. The smell of the air itself was also different. Vehicle fumes mixed with cooking smells from restaurants, dust from the roadway and the subtle, but acrid, smell of the multitudes of people all perspiring in the heat, which formed a unique odour. The day was clear but even that wasn't obvious. The sun couldn't strike the streets because of the massive buildings, which gave the impression of walking at the bottom of a great walled canyon.

Kurt headed in the general direction of Times Square, a place familiar only on the annual New Year's Eve broadcasts hosted by Dick Clark. Al and Dan were probably prowling around the bowels of the place and spotting them would only be by luck or chance. Kurt spent half an hour walking the strip, looking inside the peep shows, X-rated arcades and adult novelty shops. The people on the street were young and old, rich and poor, black and white, long haired and short haired but were mostly men with desperate eyes. A picture of an animal carcass came to mind, dead for a week and now infected with a multitude of insects all feeding off the spoils.

Was this the fate of all of civilizations? Kurt mused. Do the once great and noble ideals and labours inevitably degenerate into this sort of ruin? Did all of the 'more and more' eventually yield 'less and less', fewer great animals and more insects? If this was so, was a society so bravely defended by so many, worthy of defending at all? Or was this all a cosmic joke, a losing battle of colossal irony?

Like most self-directed questions Kurt didn't have the answers and, along with all of the others, they were filed in his dark recesses.

⌘

Dan's red hair was visible from a block away. The bright red mop shone brilliantly in the dusky human sea, like a fishing bobber would in the green Atlantic. Kurt laughed to himself, thinking that if the boat sank it would be wise to stay close to Dan in the water. The search and rescue aircraft would see that hair for miles. Walking quickly, he caught up with the pair just as they were about to enter yet another arcade.

"Hey, guys," Kurt shouted to be heard above the street noise, "you having a good time?"

Al and Dan turned around simultaneously.

"Kurt," Dan blurted excitedly, "you have to come with us man, these places are really incredible. We've never seen anything like it!"

"What's the use of looking when you can't touch the merchandise?" Kurt asked.

Al and Dan looked at one another. Neither had thought of this.

"What are you talking about man, these movies are great!" Dan replied. He sounded as ecstatic as a hog rolling in shit.

Kurt shook his head. Al was just grinning from ear to ear, perfectly portraying the 'country bumpkin gone to town'. His mouth was stuffed full of small jelly bear gums, a pound of which he clutched tightly in a white bag. Unfortunately he wasn't swallowing as fast as he was stuffing. A multi-coloured ring of saliva and jelly formed around his mouth as he chewed. Al joyfully offered his bag of candy.

"Those things will spoil my dinner," Kurt said. "And clean off your face, you look goofy."

Al looked confused at the response and reached in the bag for another handful.

"Speaking of which," Kurt said as he looked at his watch, "it's almost time to go back to the hotel and meet Dave."

"I think we're going to stay here," Dan said, waving both his hands to indicate the street. "This place is great, tell Dave we'll meet him later on."

"Look, guys," Kurt said sternly. "I don't want to spoil your party, but when the boss says meet back at the hotel at six o'clock, that is just what we are going to do. He may have some information he wants to give to us, or changes or something."

The unlikely pair looked at each other again and then both lowered their head in resignation.

"Look," Kurt said, "if it's cool with Dave you can come back later tonight. The atmosphere will be better then anyway. I don't see how you two can get excited about this in broad daylight. I'll even come with you to make sure you stay out of trouble."

They reluctantly agreed to the plan and because they were late hailed a cab back to the hotel, arriving just before six. Dave took them to an early dinner at a nearby Italian restaurant. At dinner he told them he'd checked the boat that afternoon and it would be ready for release as scheduled on Monday morning. This was good news; all of them were anxious to get started with the trip.

After dinner Dave went back to his room early, but Kurt decided he'd better keep his promise and accompany Al and Dan so nothing would happen to them prior to departure.

⌘

Night transformed Times Square from a dull, garish, sun-washed, seedy business district into an X-rated neon wonderland. The streets were lit up at least as brightly as Las Vegas, maybe more so, if such excess can be quantified. The encroachment of night, accompanied by colourful man-made luminescence, imparted a carnival atmosphere to the surroundings, a fact not missed by Al and Dan as they wandered the packed streets, turning their heads in every direction but straight ahead.

The people in the Square had changed in character with the light. Gone were the businessmen and casual shoppers who, during the day, infused a modicum of normality to the crowds. During the electric non-night a totally different breed of inhabitants dominated their presence, causing Kurt to wonder what planet he was really on. Gaudy, spiky, leather clad and freaky were some adjectives that passed through his mind as Al and Dan were herded along the walkways. The atmosphere didn't seem threatening, just bizarre and degenerate in a way that was hard to describe, let alone comprehend. Kurt figured he was in no position to pass judgment on things that had no significance in his world, so the scenes rolled by, but true to form, he made sure his immediate surroundings were secure.

After awhile, Kurt began to relax and even enjoy the crazy people and sights, after rationalizing that this place was all about entertainment, not real life. He was just an observer not a participant.

Young men and women sported brightly dyed hair in a multitude of bizarre shapes. They also had pins, rings and other assorted metal objects skewered through parts of their bodies. How ironic, he thought that he'd spent a great deal of time trying to avoid being pierced by metal, yet here people actually paid to have it done. He couldn't imagine these folks working on lobster boats, or in coal mines, or cutting timber. Perhaps when people had too little to keep themselves busy they, like bored parrots, started to pluck their own feathers and become self-destructive.

Kurt looked at Al and Dan oggling the people and sights and shook his head in mirth. He waited on the street while they both went into several arcades and came out again, only to spot yet another they had to go into.

"You'd think that both of you just came out of a prison or a POW camp the way you carry on," Kurt told them.

"What do you mean by that, man?" Dan seemed genuinely hurt by the comment.

"I mean you are acting like school kids on their first outing; it's a little excessive isn't it?"

"We're just having fun," Dan said. "You don't have to come along with us and chaperone; we can take care of ourselves, man."

Al nodded in agreement with Dan, but wasn't speaking, which wasn't surprising. What did surprise Kurt was that the tall, skinny, gangly farm boy with a genius for marine engines had his mouth packed with something again, even after eating what looked like half a tray of lasagne for dinner.

"Well, that may be so," Kurt said, "but if you guys don't get back in good shape we won't be able to sail, and that will piss Dave off. I for one don't want to spend two weeks on a small boat with a pissed off captain."

"I told you, we'll be okay," Dan reiterated.

"You're damn right you'll be okay," Kurt barked, "because I'm not going to let either of you out of my sight until we get back to the hotel, got it? Have a little more fun but let's go back in another hour or so."

Passing by a trendy uptown bar, even the odd couple agreed that having a few beers and watching the 'classy' women in such a place was preferable to sticking quarters into grainy, soundless-sex loops. The decision was a no-brainer for Al anyway because the bar served snacks. Each of them had several beers, and emerged on to the street at eleven thirty.

Kurt decided to walk back to the hotel instead of hailing a taxi. This was partly economics and partly to burn up the nervous energy of his charges so they wouldn't be tempted to hit the streets again later.

The activity on the streets was winding down a little and once away from Times Square, the character of downtown changed yet again. During the day these streets were bustling with taxi cabs, cars, trucks and busy people dressed in expensive business attire. At night, long shadows from the abandoned monoliths stood in dark vigil. The three men could hear the soft plodding sound of their own footsteps on the pavement. A few vehicles passed by, but they had their windows rolled up even on this warm night.

"Are you sure we are going the right way, Kurt?" Al asked with trepidation in his voice.

"Yeah, don't worry," Kurt replied. "We're headed in the right direction, I walked it this morning."

"I think we should get a cab," Dan said, beginning to whine as his legs struggled to keep pace with the other two. "I really think we should."

"No, we all need the walk," Kurt said. "We're going to be cooped up on that boat for a long time and need the exercise."

As the three were mid-block, a pair of figures turned the corner ahead of them and began to walk down the sidewalk in their direction. Kurt picked up on their stride, which wasn't strolling or leisurely as might be expected this time of night. The two men were walking purposefully, at a pace that would be used when emotional levels are high, and with great intent.

Kurt's finely tuned alarm system jumped from yellow straight to red. The pair approached rapidly. Their body language said they were young males, one tall and lanky, the other shorter and more stoutly built.

Kurt spoke quickly to Al and Dan who were still oblivious to the developing situation.

"Stay behind me and don't let anyone get behind you!"

Al and Dan instantly became attentive and slowed their pace as Kurt moved in front of them. The two strangers were directly in front when the tall man stopped squarely in Kurt's path. The heavier man moved to the side flanking them. They were throwing a good manoeuvre, Kurt thought, there was nowhere to go and if he did blow through, Al and Dan would be trapped.

Reluctantly, Kurt slowed and stopped, checking over his shoulder quickly to see if anyone was behind them. Both men had their right hands in their pockets and their left hands free, the universal sign language for, 'I've got something in here, and I'm ready to use it'.

The tall man spoke, "You want some shit, man? I got what you need … grass, speed, coke…"

Kurt was now little more than an arm's length away from the self-proclaimed pharmaceutical salesman. If a gun appeared, he would have to get it quickly; his heavier partner was further away, but hopefully would move a little slower.

"No thanks, we're just going back to our hotel," Kurt said with a neutral voice.

"You dudes ain't from around here, are you?" the tall one asked. "Where you all from, man?" His words seemed conversational, but the tone was threatening and Kurt didn't like it.

"We're from up north," was all he offered.

The tall man began to chuckle

"Up north? You all must be from the North Pole. Now what do you dudes want? I ain't got all muthafuckin' night."

"I told you, we don't want anything," Kurt snarled. "Now get out of our way, you stupid street-ape."

Kurt made the inflammatory statement to provoke the ambushers before they could organize themselves further. While the tall man was talking, the big guy was moving around and would soon be behind him. Kurt would then have enemy on both front and back, making Dan and Al vulnerable.

Reacting to the fighting words the tall man's face metamorphosed into a shocked scowl, as he began to withdraw his right hand from his pocket.

Kurt launched his body directly towards the tall man to his front. While moving forward, he brought his right arm across his chest with his fist placed high at his own left clavicle. At the correct distance from his opponent, he powered the back of his fist forward with as much force as he could muster. Putting all the power of both his moving body and extending arm into the blow, the tall man took the hit directly in his face.

When he struck, the blow sounded like a watermelon had dropped out of a high rise building onto the sidewalk. Kurt felt nose cartilage and facial bones collapse and crush into heavier structures beneath. The man flew backwards from the force of the punch and spun into the concrete wall, stumbled, then crashed to the pavement.

Using the force of the first blow on the tall man's face as a push off, Kurt sprang across to the flanker and with his left arm tied up the big man's right arm just as he was trying to withdraw something from his pocket. Facing the second opponent, Kurt hooked his right heel behind the man's right leg, dropped into a crouch and surged upwards with the palm of his right hand open.

The big man took the full force of the upwards blow below his jaw and, although tipping the scales at more than two hundred and fifty pounds, he was driven straight up into the air. He fell backwards, hitting the street with the sound of head and bones smacking the pavement.

The tall man had partially recovered and was trying to crawl away on his hands and knees. Blood ran down his ruined face and dripped heavily onto the sidewalk. The blow had fractured his lower eye sockets making meaningful vision impossible. He looked like a cockroach someone had half crushed with their foot, trying to drag itself to safety. Glistening on the sidewalk at the beginning of the blood trail was a cheap silver automatic pistol.

The big man lay on his back over the curb without a sound or movement; his open eyes calmly staring at the black starless sky between the buildings.

"Jesus Christ!" Dan shrieked at the top of his voice. "Bruce Lee, he's a fucking Bruce Lee. Did you see that? Holy shit, I've never seen anything like it. .. goddamn! Did you kill this one Kurt, he looks dead?"

Kurt reached out and grabbed Dan's open collar and shook him. His red hair flew around like a mangy rat in a terrier's mouth. Al stood in silence with his mouth wide open. The box of coloured jelly beans he'd been eating lay on the sidewalk, sprawled like bits of precious jewellery beneath the shadowy streetlight.

Kurt quit shaking Dan and put their faces very close. Dan was dazed and stunned, but now he could focus and became even more terrified. Kurt's eyes were savage, his pupils fully dilated leaving no colour, only a deep blackness.

"Shut the fuck up, you little jerk. Not one more word. Now let's move!" Kurt's voice was deep, rough and evoked immediate compliance and cold fear.

They walked away rapidly from the scene, turning another street, heading back to their hotel indirectly. No one said a word. When they finally arrived, Kurt spoke to the pair in his regular voice, devoid of menace.

"Don't mention this to anyone, even to Dave, or talk between yourselves. This *never* happened, you understand? It is very important."

Kurt looked at them, and they both nodded their head in agreement.

"Thanks," Dan said. "You saved our asses, I'm sorry I freaked out but I never ..."

"That's okay," Kurt cut Dan short and waved his hand in dismissal. "Now let's go get some sleep."

# CHAPTER 7
## OUTWARD BOUND

The ship-fitting crew had worked around the clock preparing the Lil' Katie to specifications provided by the oil company. Installation of accessories included winches, storage lockers, loading ramps, long range fuel tanks, state of the art radio and navigation gear and marine radar. The engine was thoroughly checked and the fuel-pump and filter system were upgraded from the temporary units installed for their short trip down the coast.

A transatlantic crossing in a vessel this small was a risky undertaking but the urgent need for the equipment in the newly developed Cabinda oil fields, near Angola, outweighed the risk. When completed the boat was as durable as a miniature battle ship, essential for her future of loading and unloading cargo and workers to and from off-shore oil rigs.

Another day of sea trials would normally have been carried out before sailing but, during the refitting, Dave personally checked out the work and found it all to be above specifications. Dave was not a risk taker by nature. His plan was to give all systems a run through after departure while still in range of Coast Guard coverage. The day's acceleration in the delivery schedule would also net them a nice bonus.

Part of the large inventory of supplies they were taking with them on the crossing included spares for nearly everything that could break, with all the appropriate tools to do the repair job if needed. Dave and Al could both disassemble and reassemble a marine engine blindfolded. The electronics and radar were another matter but technicians tested everything and gave all systems the thumbs up. Dan brushed up on the electronics operation manuals and was satisfied.

At six in the morning on the day of departure the diesel engine was fired up and using the twin differential screws, that gave the boat superb manoeuvrability, the Lil' Katie threaded her way out of the harbour and into the open ocean. The throttle was kept at twenty percent until they were clear of traffic, but even that setting gave them a speed of fifteen knots. The bright yellow hull not only sported the flag of her new owners but was also very visible against the green waters of the Atlantic.

Weather reports for the crossing looked favourable. The hurricane season was still a couple of months off but violent tropical storms could appear off the west coast of Africa with little or no warning. The craft was strong enough to survive nearly any storm conditions, but navigating a small boat through violent seas was to be avoided if at all possible. Dave was at the helm and Dan and Al were busy performing final checks on all the mechanical systems and electronic gear.

Supplies were stowed where the manifest specified, with everything that should be tied down or placed in the lockers secured. The last thing they needed was for a large object to become airborne when they hit a rough spot. Extra fuel was stowed in fifty five-gallon double-walled drums, secured vertically to support members on either side of the inner hull. A pair of electric transfer pumps with manual back-up could distribute the fuel from the drums to the fuel tanks, as needed.

Dave reckoned that they were in for at least eight days of hard running to the west African coast if everything went as planned. There they would refuel and then it would be another four days' travel down the coast to their final destination of Cabinda, and the oil platforms off of northern Angola.

Kurt completed the few chores he had been assigned and came forward and stood next to Dave as he steered the craft through the final marine buoys and into the open sea.

"Kurt," Dave said barely audible above the engine noise, "I noticed a little tension between you and the other two this morning ... anything serious?"

"No," Kurt answered. "We were in the wild part of town the other night and got into a bit of a ruckus. I was just trying to get them away without being hurt and I might have leaned on them a little too hard."

Dave nodded and said, "I appreciate you looking after those two but we don't need any tension on this trip, we all need to pull together. Whatever it takes to settle this thing down between you guys, go ahead and do it. Even if you have to eat a little crow, it's not that bad after the first mouthful."

"Sure, Dave." Kurt replied. "I was meaning to talk to them anyway after we got going. They both definitely know their stuff and seem like hard workers. I don't want any problems either."

"Thanks, Kurt," Dave responded and changed the subject as was his nature when something was resolved to his satisfaction. It was a habit after all those years in the police.

"We have to work out a schedule," Dave continued. "I figure eight or six hour shifts. What do you think?"

"Either is fine with me, but I think that sixes will be better for the first couple of days."

"So be it," Dave agreed. "You take the wheel at twelve, Dan at six and Al at midnight. We will run sixty percent throttle which will give us twenty-five knots or so."

Kurt listened. The engine was running smoothly and the ride seemed to be free from the vibration and harmonics that plagued many small boats.

Later that afternoon Kurt said a few words to both Dan and Al. They both acted a little reserved, still in shock from the incident, but both seemed to be coping. He wouldn't push it; things would be okay. Time has a way of easing stressful events.

Kurt grabbed a snack and a couple of cans of soda and headed for the bridge just before noon to relieve Dave at the wheel. Dave stayed awhile and seeing that Kurt was comfortable with the controls, and that the radar indicated there was no other traffic in the immediate vicinity, he left the bridge and went down to get something to eat.

Kurt adjusted the throttle to seventy percent then back down again to get a feel for the response. Both of the differential props were locked at one hundred and eighty degrees, the RPM read two thousand five hundred and all instrumentation was in the green.

Half an hour later Kurt noted that they had drifted slightly north of his bearing so he corrected it. Ten minutes later he noticed the drift was back and became a little concerned. The wind was running seven to ten knots from the west, which in itself would not cause this amount of course variation. Kurt had a gut feeling that something was wrong, but he didn't have enough experience with this type of boat to determine the nature of the problem. He thought that perhaps one of the props was out of alignment, even though they were thoroughly checked before they left, nor was there any obvious vibration or bad harmonics that a fault like that would cause.

A few minutes later Dave appeared back on deck with a sandwich in one hand and a can of Pepsi in the other.

"Running okay?" Dave asked rhetorically.

Kurt was silent for a moment, eyeing the gauges and the compass.

"I don't know. It feels like something is causing the boat to veer to port. I don't think it's the wind; it may be the way the Gulf Stream is running, but we should be clear of that by now."

Dave put down his food and drink and Kurt explained to him what he was seeing and feeling. After a few minutes on the controls Dave reluctantly nodded in agreement.

"By golly, I think you're right. Something's funny here, not much but enough to notice. It may be the port screw is turning a little slowly, but that would indicate a transmission problem. God, I hope not. Maybe it's damaged or has a bad bearing?"

"Or we got something wrapped around the prop shaft in the harbour." Al said from directly behind them. "I checked the engine and transmission and everything seems fine. If there is something wrong it has to be external. I say we shut her down and have a look."

"Better here than further out," Dave agreed. "From here we can limp back or get a tow from the coast guard if we have damage we can't repair.

Kurt volunteered to look and went to get the mask, fins, snorkel and dive suit from the side locker where they were stored.

Dave brought the engines back to an idle and the screws were disengaged. The engine was then shut down. Dave didn't want to risk having a diver in the vicinity of the props with a running engine with a potentially faulty drive train. The swells were only a couple of feet high but, when power was cut, the boat started to bob like a cork and rock from side to side. Kurt rolled backwards over the transom entering the water as taught in the army dive school in Key West.

Swimming to the rear of the boat, Kurt jack-knifed under the water and with strong, even fin strokes, circled the props and looked for any obvious damage or tangles from fish nets or debris. The two props looked intact and identical. He ran his hands over the cast bronze blades and detected no dents, dings or roughness. Out of breath, he surfaced, and saw the faces of the other three crew members hanging over the stern, watching intently.

"The props look fine; I'm going to check the shafts," Kurt said in a muffled voice, his nose trapped in the dive mask.

Jack-knifing down again he went deeper this time, avoiding the sharp prop blades and coming up beneath the shafts, he tried to hover, but the rocking boat made that impossible. The Lil' Katie was unique. The craft had long, exposed twin drive shafts that allowed each prop to be controlled independently at low speed. This allowed almost unlimited manoeuvrability in and out of oil platforms. This was important when loading and unloading cargo on floating docks, when currents and wind could be uncooperative.

Kurt reached up and stroked the starboard drive shaft, which felt smooth. Moving over to the port shaft the problem became apparent. Nylon netting was wound around the shaft, almost enveloping it in a ragged sheath. This could explain the propulsion problem; acting like a brake the entanglement could cause enough resistance to slow the rotation of the starboard drive shaft, causing the boat to veer in that direction. Due to the cooling effect of the water and the smoothness of the shaft, the material stayed tightly wound and didn't burn off. It would take a few minutes of serious cutting to remove it and then the shaft could be inspected for damage. The task would be too laborious for surface diving and breath holding, so Kurt swam to the rear of the vessel and surfaced.

The three men were still awaiting his word.

"The port shaft is wrapped with nylon," Kurt shouted to them. "Probably an old fishing net when we were leaving the harbour. It's going to take a while to cut it off. Would one of you attach a regulator to a scuba tank and pass it to me?"

Al went to the locker for the equipment and Dave asked, "Do you see any obvious damage?"

"I can't tell until the stuff is cut off, but doesn't look like it," Kurt replied. "I'll give it a good eyeball after that netting is removed."

Al climbed over the stern and stood on the rear platform and handed Kurt an eighty cubic foot U.S. Divers aluminium scuba tank with a Poseidon regulator hooked up and with the air turned on. First Kurt put the mouthpiece in and checked that he could breathe easily, wrestled into the straps while the tank was still being held by Al, and buckled the clasps. Al also handed him a rubberized pressure proof flashlight which Kurt turned on, noting it was bright even in daylight. Without further delay he rolled under and made his way back to the entangled shaft.

He took out the combination dive tool, pry bar, and knife from its leg mounted rubber sheath, and it quickly became apparent it wasn't the ideal tool for the job. A soft rubber handle was fused to a flat rectangular pry bar which was bent up at the tip. One side of the bar was sharpened and the other side had saw-teeth. The nylon material encircling the shaft was so tightly wound it was rock hard and difficult to cut away. Kurt first tried the saw-teeth but that didn't work because they just caught on the material. Then he tried the sharpened edge and began slicing the tangled netting lengthwise, trying to strip it away from the drive shaft. This worked better but was still slow going. The nylon line came away in layers but the whole mess was connected, and soon it was hanging everywhere, obscuring his work.

Eventually most of the nylon came free, but it didn't drop away and looked like it was attached further forward on the hull. This seemed odd, the hull was smooth and there shouldn't be anything there to hang onto. Kurt made his way forward to where the shredded netting was tethered, and froze.

The object couldn't be seen clearly because of to the veil of netting, but even then it had a distinctive shape that was instantly recognizable. When he shone the flashlight on it there was no question. It looked like an ugly green bread pan with spider-like legs. Several fragments of netting were hung up on it. Kurt understood immediately how the entanglement of the drive shaft occurred. A piece of floating or submerged net had caught on the object and the rest swung to the rear and wrapped around the shaft; a stroke of luck maybe. Kurt swam closer and studied it carefully.

His initial assessment was correct; it was a standard issue US Navy limpet mine. Used by the underwater demolition teams since WWII to blow up ships, the several pounds of torpex high explosive it contained would blow a hole five feet in diameter in the hull of a warship. Attached just beneath the port gas tank of this small vessel, it didn't take much imagination to picture what it would do if detonated. Since the pivoting magnets on either side of the mine held it directly against the outer hull, the physical incompressibility of water worked in its favour. When detonated, the sea would serve as natural tamping, so most of the explosive force would drive up through the hull into the ship.

Kurt tried to clear his mind before he did anything. This mine must be for him; it couldn't be for Dave or the boat. Business competitors just didn't go to these lengths. But who knew about his trip? He hadn't told anyone. That mystery would have to wait, for now he had to deal with the problem in front of him.

Kurt carefully cleared away the strands of netting from the mine and the frayed cords fell down, but not away from the boat. The netting was still tethered by a few strands to the drive shaft. Kurt knew a little about limpet mines from his army dive training. As part of the military diving course they had to attach and then find and recover similar dummy mines from the hulls of ships moored at the dock in Key West. He knew they were attached and released by a cam mechanism. Once attached to a metal hull, the permanent rare earth magnets were too strong for the mine to be pulled off directly.

These vicious explosive devices could be set with a variety of timers and detonators. Whoever attached it would most likely want it to detonate in mid-ocean, away from any potential third party witnesses, where it would be easy to blame something else for the loss of ship and crew. Blowing a boat up in a New York harbour would draw far too much attention. That meant the mine was perhaps set to go off in a few days but that was no help; it could just as easily go off in ten minutes.

From its outer appearance the mine looked like government surplus. That would work in the favour of whoever placed it, because if found, it probably couldn't be traced with any degree of certainty. Anti-lift detonators could have been installed on it, though Kurt doubted that. If the mine had been discovered by workmen before the boat left, there would have been a lot of heat to bear if it had exploded.

He wondered if he should tell Dave and the others. Should they leave the boat just in case? Working on gut feel, he decided not to tell them unless he couldn't clear it. As expected, the cam lever had been removed from the device but his dive tool, made out of non-magnetic Stellite, could perhaps be placed in the cam slot and used as a surrogate lever. It was now or never, indecision and hesitation had to be thrown aside.

Placing the dive tool in the cam slot, Kurt applied pressure and it slipped out without moving the attachment. A little shaken, he tried the manoeuvre again with the same result. He then forced the tool further in to the slot by rocking it so as to feel it catching on the engagement lever. Bracing himself against the hull of the boat and applying heavy downward pressure on the dive tool, the cams rotated, followed by a loud 'clunk' as the magnets disengaged from the ship's hull. The green metal brick fell away into Kurt's arms and he clung to it tightly. He vaguely remembered from his training that if released into the open sea, a crush depth would be reached and the timing mechanism would collapse, detonating the mine. He didn't want it to detonate anywhere near the ship; it still might inflict some serious damage.

Still clinging to the mine, Kurt swam to the rear of the boat, where the troublesome but life-saving netting was still attached to the port drive shaft by a few threads. The bulk of the fishnet was floating gracefully in the current beneath the boat, looking like an angel's veil. He tied one of the loose threads to a magnetic leg of the mine and cut the net free from the boat. The net would act as an expedient underwater parachute and slow the mine's descent, but they still needed to get away, quickly.

Dave, Al and Dan were shocked to see Kurt nearly fly out of the water and pull himself up and onto the rear platform as he shouted.

"Start the engine and move out now! Don't question, just do it!"

Dave ran to the bridge, kicked over the engine and immediately put the boat into gear. The craft surged ahead while Kurt was still sitting on the entry step hanging on to the railing above him. Falling off now could suck him into the screws. Kurt tossed his gear up to Al and was straddling the rear gunwale to climb into the boat when he felt the solid thump of the mine detonating. No splash was seen on the surface because of the depth. Immediately Dave backed down on the throttle and yelled back to them, "What the hell was that?"

"Nothing, we're okay."

Al and Dan looked puzzled but knew better than to say anything. They both knew something strange had just happened, but having been close witnesses to Kurt's temper inhibited them from asking questions.

⌘

The Lil' Katie was running fine now, straight and true with none of the drift that was noticed before the incident. They spent the remainder of the day running at seventy percent power in an attempt to make up for lost time. As evening fell, the sea became very calm, smooth and vast, as if the ocean was the entire world and land had never existed. The course Dave selected would take them south into equatorial waters on their transit to the African coast. Winds and tides in this zone were minimal, a fact that had given sailing ships grief for centuries, but worked to the advantage of a powered craft attempting a swift passage.

The coming of the first night on the open ocean served to soothe everyone's nerves and showcase the beauty that remained in these lonely stretches of the earth. To the stern, the setting sun stroked clouds in high reaches, throwing orange and red illumination with the brush of a mad painter. Ahead of them sea and sky blended into a single azure body which only parted when the stars, free from the dust, smoke and haze of land masses, burned through the twilight, establishing a line between heaven and earth. When darkness settled in, the wake of the boat, already churning pure white, became luminescent. The glow was not an illusion, but billions of the sea's smallest creatures fluorescing, their only means of protesting a disturbance in their micro world.

Solitude and natural beauty always left Kurt in a philosophical mood, but he was beginning to understand that philosophy didn't answer any of life's problems. It merely conjured up more. Delving into questions usually gave him a good feeling when he started but, ultimately, he encountered nothing but dead ends and disappointments. Maybe his brain just wasn't wired to resolve the details of life, or even to understand much of it, only to participate to the maximum in its adventures.

But what was the purpose? What unseen forces were trying to kill him, make him disappear into the sea without a trace? No answers were forthcoming as the smooth sea split cleanly for the steel bow that was headed towards Africa, adventure, escape and the unknown.

Rest came easily when he finally turned off his thoughts and felt the cool salt mist on his skin. He climbed into a summer-weight sleeping bag and propped himself at an angle on the rear deck, to better watch the ship's wake disappear. Just before sleep overtook him he recalled the desert and the white discs pointing to the unknown reaches of space, searching.

⌘

The next two days passed quickly and nearly incident free. They were running ahead of schedule, which seemed to please Dave. Early in the morning on the third day, a pod of Atlantic bottlenose dolphins surrounded the boat and for a while, kept pace. At twenty five knots the dolphins were swimming at full tilt and their perpetually smiling faces seemed to enjoy the company. After about twenty minutes they departed. An hour later, Kurt thought he saw a whale blow in the distance, but he wasn't sure because he'd read that there were few whales left in the open ocean. He wished he could shut down the engine so he could put his ear to the metal hull. A whale's call could be heard from much further than they could be seen.

On the fourth day the weather began to deteriorate. Dark clouds appeared to the north-east and although their course was heading south, it didn't look as though the weather could be completely avoided. Swells developed on the ocean surface, and the boat began to bounce as it ran into them. Dave explained that in this part of the world tropical storms formed spontaneously. A small disturbance off the West African Coast could meander west, pushed by the trade winds and, if conditions were right, would be a full blown hurricane by the time it reached the Caribbean. However, most of the storms just wandered a short distance and fizzled out.

Their radar was now picking up squalls to the north and east, so their course was adjusted to skirt around the leading edge of the weather. On the adjusted course they reduced speed which decreased the chop, but the roughness persisted for the rest of the day.

⌘

During this time Kurt spoke with Dan. His withdrawal and avoidance of Kurt indicated that the night in New York still bothered him and, if possible, Kurt wanted to clear up any bad feelings. Kurt approached Dan who was sitting on top of a locker near the stern sipping a coke, staring out at the heaving green Atlantic.

"Hey, Dan," Kurt said, trying to sound upbeat. "I wanted to tell you I'm sorry for what happened the other night. I should have taken your advice and taken the taxi; it would have avoided that ... unpleasantness."

"Don't get me wrong, Kurt," Dan said, "and I think I speak for Al as well. We appreciate what you did for us; you may have saved our lives. It's just that ... I've never seen anything as violent as that in real life. At first it was exciting, like watching a TV show or a movie but, later on, it really started to bother me. You really hurt those guys and we didn't call for help or anything, just left them lying there. They might've died because we didn't call for help. Doesn't that bother you?"

Kurt walked over, grabbed a can of Coke out of the cooler and sat down on a locker near Dan before he answered.

"In a word, Dan, no ... it doesn't. Do you think those street hoodlums would have helped us if they'd hurt or killed us, as seemed to be their intent? They would have left us to bleed to death on that street after they shot us or stuck us with knives. That's what they would have done."

Dan contemplated for a few seconds before he continued.

"You're probably right, but as I see it, that isn't the point. We are supposed to be better than that. We have responsibilities to fellow human beings, don't we?"

"Dan," Kurt responded, "just because a person walks, talks and breathes doesn't make him or her valuable to mankind. Those thugs were out to rob people and they didn't care who they hurt or killed in the process. Your compassion is wasted on them, save it for those who deserve it."

"But don't you feel anything?" Dan asked, his voice rising with emotion. "Don't you feel some guilt for doing that to another person?"

Kurt looked down at the burnished red teakwood decking on the boat. It was tough wood; it would probably outlast the boat.

"I really don't know anything about guilt. I know the definition of the word but have never felt it personally. Guilt is an alien concept to me."

"But that's not ..." Dan interrupted. "That's not human; we all feel guilt."

"The way I see it," Kurt said, "and it's only my opinion, is that people are split into two distinct groups, the grazers and the predators. You're either one or the other. Do you think a lion has any guilt if it has to kill another animal, or even one of its own, in a survival match? I seriously doubt they lose any sleep worrying about it. They only have one rule, and that is survival."

"People aren't animals, Kurt, don't forget," Dan interjected.

"On that point I disagree with you, Dan," Kurt said. "If being a hunter from an early age has shown me anything, it's that we *are* animals. People are a bit smarter than many other species, but we're animals all the same."

"Well, I think you are dead wrong there, Kurt," Dan said sharply. "God has chosen man as a special creature on this earth, separate and distinct from animals; we are able to feel and we have responsibilities to our fellow man."

"You think that way, Dan, because you are a grazer," Kurt stated getting up from his seat. "You will never and can never see things as I do, and vice versa. I just have one bit of advice. When you are standing around chewing your cud feeling warm about the world and the wolf is eyeballing you, don't curse the guard dog."

⌘

Traversing the centre of the Atlantic, there was very little traffic. A container vessel and then a warship of unknown origin passed at some distance, but great expanses were unoccupied, probably because Dave had chosen their route away from the busy commercial corridors most of the way from the US to Africa.

As they approached the west African coast, traffic increased suddenly and considerably. The primary sea lane from the Middle East to Europe skirted the Cape of Good Hope in South Africa and carried much of Europe's oil supply up the west coast. Supertankers were too large to squeeze through the Suez Canal and had to take the long route. The ships were massive and lined up from north to south, like a waterborne railroad following invisible tracks. The West was still recovering from the oil shortages earlier in the decade, and these great vessels were hauling crude oil to run the engines and to lubricate the wheels of the modern world.

⌘

Kurt knew they were near Africa before they saw it. Fishing trawlers were now a fairly common site. They generally worked in offshore currents inhabited by schools of commercial fish. Prevailing breezes were gradually shifting from west to east and subtle and mysterious smells were borne on invisible tendrils. Scouring winds picked up fine sand from the arid Sahara and smoke particles from the fires that swept through grasslands and forests, as well as odours of lush vegetation-rich soil surrounding rivers and lakes. The resulting mix was tumbled aloft by clashing air currents, only to gently settle offshore beyond the turbulence.

Kurt inhaled deeply and the scent and taste made his pulse quicken and mind stir out of the numbness caused by days of vibration and pounding of the ocean voyage. The smell told him that what lay ahead was Africa, the birthplace of man and land of a billion dreams. Kurt had never been there but, strangely, felt like he was returning home after a very long absence. On the eastern horizon a hazy ragged brown line began to emerge out of the endless expanse of water and the crew watched as it loomed, ever larger.

Directly to the front a white wake suddenly appeared and, at the tip of the wake, was a swift vessel that looked intent on interception. Dave took the wheel from Al, throttled back to thirty percent power and steered ten degrees starboard to avoid a collision, if for some reason the other craft hadn't seen them. The white plume grew in size then changed direction to remain on an interception course.

"We've got company boys, stay cool," Dave told the other three, who were all clustered around him on the bridge.

"Who the hell are they?" Al asked, his voice high pitched from stress.

"Don't know yet," Dave responded, "but I hope to hell they aren't pirates. They usually wouldn't bother a petroleum company ship, but you never know. Kurt ..."

"Yeah?"

"Is the shotgun loaded with double-O buckshot and accessible?" Dave asked.

"It's in the port locker," Kurt answered.

"Good," Dave said. "Go get it and stay low and out of sight, understand?"

"I got it," Kurt replied as he disappeared down the steps.

"Dan and Al," Dave continued, "go to the back of the boat and look busy, look normal. Play with some tie downs or something; stay low."

The fast craft was bearing down on them. Kurt looked over the transom and saw a green and black flag flapping from a standard on the bow of the approaching vessel. The flag was probably good news: Kurt doubted if pirates would bother to fly a flag but then again, it could be a decoy. Dave kept the boat throttled back to fifteen knots and remained on course, so there was no appearance of trying to evade or outrun the approaching ship. About two-hundred metres away the approaching vessel throttled down and altered course in order to come along the port side of the Lil' Katie.

As the foreign boat came up alongside them it became clear the vessel was a naval gunboat or fast attack craft of some sort, not some beaten up pirate boat.

Kurt's initial impression was that is was a French vessel, though he had limited knowledge or experience with these things. A crew of three men, wearing olive drab life jackets, were visible on the bridge. One of the men was driving the boat; another was sitting, in close proximity to a pedestal-mounted 1917 machine gun, on the starboard side of the craft just behind the driver. The operator's left forearm was draped across the firing handles but the gun was pointed skyward and to the rear.

The third crew member was strapped into a swivel chair behind a 50-calibre Browning Heavy Machine Gun, positioned on a rotating mount amidships, the massive barrel and ventilated shroud pointed towards them. The operator was constantly adjusting the gun's position so he could rake their deck with fire from the deadly weapon with a push of his thumb. Kurt knew the futility of any resistance to this threat. The 50-calibre could cut them to pieces in seconds and, if they were firing incendiary rounds which was normal in a naval application, the Lil' Katie would be not just be reduced to debris, but burning debris.

Dave waved to the approaching crew in attempt to display friendly intent, but the men in the gunboat didn't wave back, only eyeballed him. The driver of the gunboat was now talking into a radio mike with one hand as he guided his craft in a 360 degree orbit around them. The 50-calibre gun operator, using the flexible pivot, kept them in his sights the whole time, though Kurt noticed that the gunner had removed his thumbs from the firing buttons. Their actions at the moment indicated there was no anticipation of imminent hostility, they were just going through the motions. Kurt, Al, and Dan all made their way up to the bridge.

Kurt spoke to Dave first, "What do you think?"

"I believe it's a Senegalese naval vessel just checking us out." Dave replied, "I never thought about it but we are probably putting out an hellacious radar signature. The steel from the winches and assorted fittings would make us look like a much a larger boat. They probably thought we were a small warship on the radar screen. We are also heading towards land and are currently inside commercial sea lanes. They are just keeping track of what is going on in their territorial waters, which is understandable."

"Sure looks like these guys mean business," Al interjected. "I'd hate to piss them off."

"You're right," Dave said. "It's best to keep your nose clean over here. When dealing with armed men it is wise to be very diplomatic, even if it means greasing their palms or even kissing ass a little. That is a lot better than being floating target practice, or winding up in some mouldy jail cell waiting for someone to bail you out. We have to play by the local rules over here. Uncle Sam is a long way off and can't do much for us."

After two more orbits of the Lil' Katie, the Senegalese gunboat apparently lost interest in this mundane commercial vessel. Without any communication it departed as quickly as it appeared. Kurt recalled the words Dave had just spoken "can't do much for us". That was good news in some respects. Whoever was after him would find the pressure harder to apply over here. The thought crossed his mind that shedding one form of danger may mean acquiring others that were even worse.

⌘

Their plan called for refuelling and re-supply at Dakar, Senegal, an old French colonial commercial port located on the apex of the West African bulge. After refuelling they would make their way south by commercial sea lanes to Cabinda Province, just north of the outlet of the Congo River. Dave explained that Cabinda was currently disputed territory. Positioned north of Angola's northernmost border, the province was actually closer to Zaire. The Portuguese historically laid claim to the area but, with oil discovered there only recently, Zaire was beginning to flex its muscles. Lucrative deals made by hungry petroleum companies with both powers no doubt played a large part in keeping the province relatively conflict free, thus far.

Portugal's sudden pull-out from her African colonies, Angola and Mozambique, the previous year, brought the spectre of political instability to the entire region but, in the short term, oil companies were desperate to keep the productive fields and their revenues flowing, so a tenuous 'business as usual' mentality prevailed.

An hour and a half after their encounter with the gunboat, the Lil' Katie prepared to dock in Dakar. After slowly weaving through considerable traffic of fishing vessels, container ships and small oil transporters, they found a berth at a side dock and tied up. Jumping onto solid land again was a very strange sensation after a week of continuous bobbing in the Atlantic. Working on lobster boats all his youth, he'd never been out for more then a day. It was uncanny how the body adapted to unusual environments, then protested about going back to normal.

After tying up Dave told them, "I know you are all anxious to walk around but be patient, we have to be cleared by customs first, which may take awhile."

Over the next two hours, several pairs of uniformed armed men walked by, glanced in their direction, then continued with their patrols. Approximately two and a half hours after they had tied up to the dock, the afternoon shadows making the sun slightly more bearable, a pair of what must have been customs and immigration officials strolled at a leisurely pace down the boardwalk of the dock and stopped at the Lil' Katie. One of the men was in his thirties and the other must have been Kurt's age. They wore identical dark aviation-style sunglasses and lightweight tan uniforms.

"Who is the owner of this vessel?" the senior of the two asked.

"I am, sir," Dave said as he raised his hand.

"Can we come aboard?" the same official asked in French accented English.

"Certainly," Dave replied, as he indicated the boarding steps on the port transom.

"Merci," the official said and he carefully stepped aboard, followed by the younger officer.

"You are American?" the senior customs official asked.

Kurt noted that though the official's English was accented with French, there was a definite tribal dialect in the mix.

"Yes, all of us are American," Dave responded.

"You are fortunate that I speak English so fluently," the official said. "It makes this process much easier."

The customs official had a refined, almost elegant, bearing but it was obvious he was already hitting on them. He wasn't wasting any time.

"May I see your passports and the registration papers of your vessel, please?" he said with a very businesslike demeanour. It was a well-practiced act, intimidating without being overtly threatening.

Dave acted calmly and politely. He bowed his head slightly and turned to get the paperwork.

"Yes, sir, I will just be a minute," Dave said, as he headed down the stairs behind the bridge, to the small safe in the forward hold where the documents were kept.

With Dave gone the two officials surveyed Kurt, Dan and Al. All of them were standing in close proximity on the hot bridge. When the senior official turned and looked towards Dan with his shaded eyes, Dan smiled and blinked like a puppy dog being stared down by his master. Both of the officials smiled in response. Kurt noted it wasn't really a smile at all but a look of contempt, a private joke between them. When the pair turned their attention to Al, he immediately lowered his eyes to the decking pretending to look for something, the universal body language of fear. The joke continued.

While this was happening, Kurt assessed the officials for any immediate threat they might pose. If it came to blows, which he hoped it wouldn't, both of them could be downed before they could draw their concealed pistols. Unfortunately, the gendarme patrolling the docks would be formidable and unforgiving if anything violent occurred.

When the officials focused their attention on Kurt, they saw something they weren't expecting. Kurt was watching them like a lion watches an antelope take a drink. Both of the men could sense that he wasn't playing the game like the others; the difference was enough to stop them cold.

The senior man reached up and grabbed his dark gold-framed sunglasses by the right arm, slowly peeling them from his face. The purpose was to bare his eyes to his opponent. Eyeball to eyeball intimidation was a potent weapon, whilst also a weapon of last resort. The eyes were said to be the window of the soul, but Kurt thought that definition inadequate. A window by nature is passive. The eyes were more like telegraphs, revealing exactly what you needed to know about a person's capabilities and intentions.

The corners gleamed with wetness and the pupils were dilated even in the harsh afternoon light. There was distrust, given away by the wrinkled brow line; there was also an air of arrogance of someone who always got their way. More dramatically, there was a veiled undercurrent of pure hatred or fear bubbling to the surface. Kurt found it difficult to separate the two emotions of hatred and fear. They were so close as to be inseparable, and ran together hand in hand, like evil twins. Kurt bored into that pair of dark eyes, until they finally turned away.

"Here you are, gentlemen," Dave's voice was pure relief from the mounting tension. "I'm sorry about the delay; I had difficulty opening the safe. Unless you use the combination regularly, you forget."

Dave was being more talkative than normal. He sensed the charged atmosphere on his return. Each customs official was handed two passports. Sandwiched between Kurt's and Dave's was an American hundred-dollar note. The senior man spotted the cash immediately and put his sunglasses back on his face. The pair of passports was gently lifted from Dave's hand with two fingers and with a practiced, almost indiscernible move. The official then slid the bill out and slipped it into his right jacket pocket. He proceeded to open one of the passports and study it.

Dan and Al's passports were given to the younger official and between them a fifty dollar US note was folded. Kurt rolled his eyes. Dave knew the rules; even blatant corruption had a protocol that must be followed. The reference to being conversant in English had indeed meant the official wanted something additional in return for his language abilities, and Dave had deciphered the message correctly.

Each of the passports had a valid Senegalese visa obtained in New York several days before they departed. When the senior man opened Kurt's passport he stared at the picture intently, then looked as if to confirm his identity. He initialled the visa stamps, then abruptly closed the passports and handed them back to Dave. His partner followed suit. The older man then took the boat registration from Dave, giving it a cursory glance before handing it back.

"Everything looks in order, gentlemen," the older official said. "Do I have your permission to check the cargo?"

It was a rhetorical question; refusal of such 'permission' would likely result in seizure of the boat and cargo as well as probable detention of the crew. Dave quickly agreed with the request, and motioned with his right arm for the officials to proceed.

While the others stayed on the bridge, Kurt wandered back to the stern and took a cold can of Mountain Dew out of the cooler. The Senegalese officials roamed around the ship randomly checking stowed gear. An actual smuggler could have easily concealed a great deal of contraband without fear of compromise. These guys were just going through the motions, not really searching.

Locked in a port below-deck compartment on the Lil' Katie there was a Remington 870 pump 12-gauge shotgun as well as an old 30-06 P-14 Enfield rifle. Most vessels carried some type of armament, and normally nothing was said if it was kept aboard, though technically a customs official could get awkward and make an issue out of it if they felt so inclined. Fortunately neither official asked for the compartment to be unlocked.

Seemingly finished with their cursory inspection, both men strolled forward to the bridge and spoke to Dave.

"What are your immediate plans, Captain?" the senior man asked.

Dave looked visibly relieved that this inspection was nearly concluded.

"We have to fuel up and purchase some supplies and then we will be on our way down the coast. We are on a tight delivery schedule."

The senior official grinned. Kurt knew that Dave had just given them an opening. Never expose your weakness or soft underbelly to your opponent. Dave should know this, but everyone could be careless when their guard was down.

The senior man turned slowly to his partner as if communicating an open secret, but the younger official remained passive and expressionless as he had throughout the visit.

"I will show you where you can purchase diesel fuel," the older official said. "Also for your other provisions I can recommend this shop. The man extracted a card from the top pocket of his uniform and handed it to Dave. "I can vouch for their, eh ... reliability."

With that the pair climbed the transom and stepped out on to the dock, stepped up the ladder to the pier, and walked briskly away.

"Well, that wasn't so bad. Those guys seemed helpful," Dan said.

"As long as they can keep sticking their hands into our pockets and getting fistful of money, they'll be helpful all right," Kurt said. "I don't know about you guys but I vote to fuel up and get the hell out of here. Spending a night tied up to this dock doesn't strike me as a smart thing to do. I bet you a week's pay those two are getting a cut of what we pay for fuel and supplies. I also wouldn't be surprised if they told some buddies where to find us tonight."

"Don't be so confrontational Kurt," Dave interrupted. "That's just the way things are done over here. You have to apply a little grease to the wheels to accomplish anything. And next time, try to avoid giving people the evil eye. It's best to just nod your head in agreement, with whatever they say, and not look at them directly."

"They are as corrupt as shit, Dave, nothing but criminals," Kurt spouted.

"They are predatory, no doubt," Dave agreed, "but they know how far they can push. They don't want to piss off an oil company which does business with their government or they might lose their cushy jobs and have to go back to picking cocoa beans on the plantation. Their official pay probably sucks but, as you saw, the tips and benefits are good. We just have to play along and everyone is happy."

"Yeah, but it still stinks," Kurt retorted. "I hate corruption. It just isn't … right."

Dave shook his head impatiently.

"Well, if you are going to spend any time over here, you'd better get used to it. Sometimes I think Americans do themselves a disservice by being so moralistic. We expect everyone to be the same way, and we're disappointed when they aren't. I'm afraid we come across as an arrogant bunch of numbskulls."

⌘

They drove over to the fuelling point and while Kurt stayed with the vessel and supervised filling the tanks, Dave, Dan and Al went to the recommended store for food and other needed supplies. When it was almost evening and they hadn't returned, Kurt was thinking of leaving the boat to find them when they appeared, each carrying a large cardboard box.

"Goddamn charged us an arm and a leg for this stuff," Dave complained. "I could have got it much cheaper in Manhattan."

"Get any beer?" Kurt asked Dan.

"What I call beer and what they call beer are two different things," Dan said. "It's cloudy and has chunks of white crap in it. It was cheap enough but I gave it a pass, don't think my stomach could take it."

Dave laughed at him, "That's what they call traditional or native beer. It's an acquired taste and, speaking for myself, I never acquired it, either."

"It's getting dark," Al said. "I think we should spend the night here."

Kurt shook his head at the suggestion.

"No fucking way. I say we split. I don't want to sound paranoid but we are safer out there." He pointed to the ocean.

Dave and Dan were ambivalent about what they should do, but eventually sided with Kurt. Dave paid their fuel bill, which was at least fifty percent more than it should have been and, with the big diesel engine fired up again, the Lil' Katie headed towards the red sky and dark water.

⌘

Following a heading of one hundred and ninety degrees, they set off with the goal of merging into the sea lane that served as an unmarked marine highway paralleling the African Coast. Now approaching the equator, the surface conditions of the sea were glassy smooth.

Occasional lightning bolts from storms deep in the African interior pulsed blood red and orange in the eastern sky. The intermittent light silhouetted the ghostly form of a nearby super tanker hauling crude to a thirsty Europe, a silent dreadnought conveying energy on a massive scale from one part of the planet to another. Despite its huge size, it too, was just another piece of flotsam on this vast expanse of tropical water. Late that night, Kurt was lulled to sleep by the vibration of the engine, the soft languid air and distant flashes. He felt he was travelling back into the womb.

The sun broke the horizon the next morning precisely at six a.m. GMT. Days and nights near the earth's middle were of almost equal length all year around. When they crossed the equator it would no longer be summer, but officially winter as they proceeded further south. As the sun cleared the hazy line on the horizon that was Africa, the heat, uncomfortable even at night, began to mount. Wind generated by their twenty-knot forward speed did little to cool their skin. It felt more like hot air from a furnace blower.

As the day progressed everyone in the crew grew lethargic. Heat and the lack of any real exercise on the small boat over the past week, took its toll on their patience and energy. Staying sufficiently alert to pilot the boat safely was a challenge, but they managed by changing drivers more often. All found the food they brought along to be unappetizing, except for the canned fruit, candy bars and soft drinks.

Al asked if they could stop the boat and go for a swim, but Dave and Kurt didn't think it was a good idea because these waters were the ideal habitat for large sharks. By the end of the next day the Lil' Katie was approaching the upper reaches of the cooler Benguela Current which flowed northward from Antarctica and skirted the west coast of Africa. Fishing trawlers appeared on their horizon and the cooler water stole some of the fierceness from the heat.

That afternoon they encountered a brief but violent squall, which tossed the boat about and soaked everyone, but after the stifling heat it felt wonderful. The storm subsided as quickly as it erupted.

⌘

Early on the morning of the fourth day out of Dakar, the oil platforms of Cabinda loomed into view above the low foggy patches that hugged the water. Dave smiled broadly at the success of the trip, and the good cheer was shared by the crew. Several test and production platforms comprised the complex of the international oil company to which they were delivering the Lil' Katie. In the centre of the nest of massive steel structures on stilts, was the main production platform and offshore headquarters of the corporation.

After almost two weeks at sea and a successful crossing behind them, Dave opened up the throttle beyond ninety percent and circled the huge rig, throwing a white rooster tail in their wake. They remained far enough from the base of the platform to see the working decks far above. With Dave at the wheel, Kurt, Al and Dan stood on top of the boat and waved frantically. On their second orbit a cluster of oil workers could be seen lined up at the railings, waving back.

Cutting the throttle to just above idle, they docked the boat on a pier built beneath the giant rig. When the men leapt off the boat onto the solid dock they all immediately experienced vertigo, with a mild wave of dizziness from the radical switch from a moving to a stationary world. The heat and saturated atmosphere beneath the platform added to the discomfort, but this subsided in a minute or two.

Workmen in thin blue coveralls, metal hardhats and sunglasses jumped into the Lil' Katie to help remove the crew's personal gear. After the vessel was inspected and signed over from Dave's care to the company, she would start her real but unglamorous life here, hauling workers and gear between the rigs and the mainland. All four of them thought it sad to leave her. She'd done a fine job of bringing them safely across the huge ocean.

A service elevator from the upper levels of the platform descended and a tall thin man dressed in spotless work clothes stepped out, accompanied by several others. His hair was grey and cropped close to his head like a military officer. He extended his hand to the newcomers.

"Carl Simmons," he said in a loud Southern drawl. "I'm the boss of this old rig, welcome aboard." He shook their hands and they all introduced themselves to the tall Texan.

Carl strode over to the Lil' Katie and looked her over, and the others in his entourage followed.

"Well, I see ya got her here in one piece alright," Carl said. "She looks in great shape. Give ya any trouble?"

"No, sir," Dave offered. "The engines ran smoothly, all mechanical systems seem sound, and thanks to my crew," Dave waved his arm to indicate the other three, "we made excellent time."

"Ya sure did," Carl said, with a voice like a foghorn. "Wasn't expecting you for a few more days, but then, we thought you might disappear like the last boat and crew."

"Disappear?" Dave asked in a hoarse whisper.

The crusty Texan dipped his head for a second and solemnly nodded before looking up and continued the discussion, unfazed.

"Now I think of it, y'll might not have heard about the incident. We wanted to keep it quiet while the investigation was still going on. A couple of months ago another crew was bringing a tender over after a refit. She came out of the gulf, not the east coast like you all, but just vanished. Some say she made port in Dakar but nobody has been able to confirm it. We are still looking but we've got no leads so far. It's a real shame, but I'm sure glad you came through okay."

Kurt swallowed and felt his nausea return briefly. He remembered the limpet mine, and the strange hostility of the customs agents in Dakar.

"My God, that's terrible," Dave said. "It's a good thing you talked us into leaving Dakar, Kurt."

The Texan removed a large dark cigar from the upper pocket of his tropical weight shirt, clipped it, and lit up, savouring the first draw.

"You fellas look like you could use a shower and some hot chow, how about it?"

There was no dissent among them at the offer and the mystery of the missing boat was soon forgotten. They all climbed into the service elevator and, when the door closed, they shot up several hundred feet above the Atlantic.

# CHAPTER 8
## INTO AFRICA

**Petroleum International Production Platform**
**off the coast of West Central Africa**
**August 7, 1975**

Kurt stared at the green Atlantic far below his perch high on the oil platform. The cold water had a perpetual haze, like a thin veil that protected the ocean's surface. Most of it would be burned off by the midday sun, although the low fog would never disappear entirely. The air-conditioned living quarters of the massive oil rig provided welcome comfort after nearly two weeks on the boat. Now clean and filled with copious amounts of hot food, he began to focus on what should be done now that he'd arrived in Africa. The plan had been to do some serious thinking on the way over, but the stress and challenges of the voyage prevented that.

The idea of working in the developing oil field off the African coast seemed plausible and would also be fairly profitable. Initial inquiries indicated he could work as a crew member of the Lil' Katie, since he knew how to operate the vessel, or work as a labourer on one of the many rigs recently built in these waters. On reflection, neither prospect sounded that attractive. The oil platforms really weren't Africa but a piece of displaced America, sitting on stilts, in the south Atlantic. Enemies could find a person working on the rigs without any trouble, and accidents in this dangerous work environment happened all the time. If anything, it would make their job too easy.

Kurt made his way to the cafeteria. Dave was sitting alone at a small table drinking coffee and reading a three-day old *New York Times*. Kurt sat down at other side of the table until Dave noticed him and looked over the top of his half-frame reading glasses.

"Sleep okay?" Dave inquired.

"Not bad," Kurt replied. "This place is like being half way to heaven, isn't it?"

"Seems that way," Dave said. "The inferno is only a short distance away though."

"How's that?" Kurt asked.

Dave pointed to the paper lying on the table in front of him.

"An article says there's big trouble taking place pretty close to here."

"What sort of trouble?" Kurt looked closer at the paper but it was upside down.

"Here," Dave slid the newspaper across the table. "In Angola there are several factions fighting for dominance now that the Portuguese have pulled out. The Russians are backing the Cubans, who are involved, and the South Africans are backing another bunch. The Americans ... Anyway you get the picture. Sounds like a place to stay clear of."

Kurt then remembered that they were actually in Angola, specifically just off the

Cabinda Province. He figured that the former Portuguese colony must have claimed the territory at some point. Who knows what the situation was now?

From the view offered through windows of the cafeteria, they were high enough to see the Angolan coastline to the east. It wasn't what Kurt had imagined Africa would look like. The land was dry at this time of year and there was constant suspension of dust which blurred the boundary of where the sea ceased and land began. The coast looked like a fuzzy brown smear.

Kurt looked up from the paper.

"If we're technically in Angola and the country is chaotic, how do we get out of here now that the boat has gone?"

Dave rocked back in his chair, nearly tipping it over.

"Don't worry," Dave replied. "The company has worked it out. I talked to the guy on the platform who arranges travel. They're now bypassing Luanda and using air connections out of Brazzaville, located just up the Congo River. It's closer anyway. We'll rest here for a couple of days then they'll chopper us to the Brazzaville Airport where we'll make our connection. From there we'll take a commercial flight to London or Paris, and then to New York."

Kurt thought for a few seconds.

"I've made a decision, Dave. I'll go with you to Brazzaville and then I'll see where other flights are headed. The situation in the States I mentioned before we left is pretty serious. I need to stay out of the country for a while, at least until things cool off a bit. I figure as long as I'm here, the *where* part is solved."

Dave took off his reading glasses and rubbed his temples.

"Fair enough, I'll pay you in US currency when the company settles up with me later on today, or tomorrow morning. If you're not going back with us I can also convert the amount of your return air tickets to cash. They even issue travellers' cheques here; these company guys are really organized."

"Thanks, Dave; that's the way we'll play it then. I hear they even have a gym on this thing. I really need it."

⌘

On the morning of their second day on the hotel in the sky, the former crew members of the L'il Katie loaded themselves and their luggage into an old UH1B Model Huey helicopter that sat like a fat, dirty duck on a helipad located on the top deck of the oil platform. The helicopter was painted mustard yellow beneath the carbon soot stains. 'Petroleum Helicopters' was stencilled on its side, though the words were barely legible. Petroleum Helicopters, Kurt discovered, was an aviation company that supported offshore oil and gas platforms all over the world. They bought surplus Vietnam-era helicopters for next to nothing and manned them with ex-Vietnam War pilots. Flying into and out of places no other company would fly guaranteed large revenues for the company. Few knew or cared that Petroleum Helicopters wasn't exactly what it seemed.

The Huey pilot was leaning against the aircraft wearing green shorts and T-shirt, and holding a flight helmet under his left arm. Vietnam veterans nearly always knew one another on sight. This pilot's looks and dress made his status a certainty, so Kurt gave him a high-five slap. The passengers loaded up and buckled in to the nylon seats just as the turbine began to spin with its distinctive high-pitched whine, a sound that pierced the skull.

Kurt noticed that the co-pilot's seat was empty and tapped the pilot on the shoulder, motioning for permission to sit up front. The pilot nodded and Kurt unbuckled from his position in the back, moved through the open side door and climbed into the left front seat. Buckling into the body harness he grabbed the headphones and mike set hanging on a hook and put them on. Now Kurt could converse easily with the pilot over the internal intercom.

The pilot performed his checks and, with the rotor spooled up, raised the collective control. The skids of the aircraft lifted off the deck a few inches. The helicopter crept ahead until its nose just cleared the edge of the helipad. The surface of the hazy Atlantic Ocean was visible hundreds of feet down.

The pilot suddenly pushed the control forward and the aircraft fell off into space, diving straight for the water. A veteran of many helicopter flights, Kurt knew this manoeuvre was used to pick up airspeed and put less strain on the engine, but the sudden dive was unexpected and felt like a plummeting roller coaster. Looking back, Kurt saw Dave and the others clinging tightly to the aluminium and canvas seat fixtures, thinking no doubt that they were going to crash. Kurt chuckled to himself and turned to the front just as the aircraft pulled up, banked to the right and wheeled around the base of the rig fifty feet over the water.

"I like the way you fly," Kurt said to the pilot over the intercom mike.

"Thanks, man. I like to have fun but it pisses some of the execs off, so I cool it a bit when I transport them. The drillers and roughnecks love it though; it gives them something to talk about when they're laying pipe."

"My name is Kurt Christianson, yours?"

"It's Andy, Andy McDonald. Glad to have you aboard, Kurt."

"How long have you been flying this gig?" Kurt asked.

"About eight months over here. I was in the Gulf off Louisiana for two years and before that I did a year on the North Slope of Alaska. Left Nam at the end of '72. Where did you serve?" Andy asked.

"I was in SF, worked in the recon projects, mainly CCC and CCN," Kurt replied.

"No shit, you're Special Forces, huh?"

"I *was* Special Forces, you mean," Kurt said.

"No man, that's like being a chopper pilot. Once you're in you're never out. If I wasn't flying choppers I'd be thinking about it all the time. Don't tell me you came over here with the fucking Peace Corps to help out some poor villagers?"

"I don't know what I'm doing," Kurt said. "Just going to sightsee a little for now."

"Right," Andy replied, "I can hook you up with a tour guide if you're interested. This tour guide is in need of some warm bodies that won't run for the bush when things get a little intense, if you know what I mean. Pay is pretty good too, from what I hear."

"I'm always open to suggestions," Kurt said into the mike.

"You got something to write on?"

Kurt reached for his upper left shirt pocket where he always kept a small spiral notebook and mechanical pencil. Ink would run with sweat or damp, pencil lead didn't.

"Shoot," Kurt said.

The pilot gave him the address and contact name which he copied into the notebook.

"The FNLA, huh?" Kurt asked, "Are they a pro-American, pro-West group?"

"Hell, I think so," Andy responded. "They aren't commies, I know that much. But shit, you never know over here. They may be friends one day and flying the hammer and sickle the next. All the groups do whatever seems in their best interest at the moment. You have to watch your butt when dealing with any of them. Remember, if you get into trouble over here, Uncle Sam doesn't know your ass from a crocodile's ass."

"So I heard," Kurt said.

⌘

Immediately to their front lay the vast Congo River delta where rainfall, collected from thousands of square miles, converged and emptied into the south Atlantic. An abundance of fishing boats and small ships were spread haphazardly across the chocolate-coloured waters of the delta. The helicopter was flying very low, only about one-hundred feet above the water, weaving through the boats, avoiding any with tall masts.

"I'm going to get a little more air under us and hug the north bank of the river," Andy said. "I don't want to be popping up on Congolese radar by surprise. They have a couple of air defence artillery sites this side of Brazzaville and they might try to use us for target practice. The south bank of the river is Angola. There's all kinds of strange shit going on over there. Six months ago there were no problems; now any dingbat with an AK may want to try their luck shooting at a helicopter, and they don't care who's in it."

The helicopter pitched up and by the time they crossed the north shore of the Congo, they were at five hundred feet altitude and climbing.

"I'm going to level out at two zero (two thousand feet) and vector in to Brazzaville approach," Andy said into the internal intercom.

Palm trees and crude wooden docks and piers fought for space along the river's edge. An occasional dirt road broke through the jungle canopy near the water. People working on the docks and balancing in the small boats turned their heads skyward; occasionally one waved at them. Dock workers were visible because some wore stark white clothing to ward off the intense sun. This contrasted with the darkly-aged wood and even darker, chocolate-coloured water.

Structures near the river consisted of clustered groups of small wood, tin and tar-paper buildings mixed with the more traditional African grass rondavels. They numbered from a few to hundreds, and composed irregular towns and villages that sprawled along the north bank. Just inland the true tropical forests began, patchy as a result of continuous clearing and overgrowth. A wispy blue haze was pervasive. Cooking fires and burning vegetation generated continuous smoke that rose, swirled and mixed in the stifling air beneath them.

"This is one hell of a river," Andy said to Kurt over the intercom. "Goes right up into the heart of Africa. Some of its branches haven't even been explored by westerners yet."

"Sure is a big mother," Kurt replied. "You could take a boat up there and disappear for a long time."

"Yeah, maybe forever; rumours are that some of the tribes up there are still cannibals," Andy mused.

"They'd have to be pretty damn hungry to chew on my tough ass," Kurt said.

They both laughed but Andy's laugh seemed nervous. He often flew alone over remote stretches of this tropical forest. On those flights it wasn't difficult to imagine bright eyes, painted faces and teeth, filed sharp as daggers, watching him from the endless jungle.

⌘

Less than two hours later the chopper made a slow straight approach into Brazzaville. They landed on a piece of tarmac adjacent to one of the old, run-down, colonial-era maintenance buildings that were situated some distance from the airport's main terminal.

Andy wisely wanted to stay well clear of the primary and secondary approaches to the main runway. Though Brazzaville attempted to operate in an orderly manner like most airports, wild and renegade pilots were not uncommon in this part of the world. Since road systems into the interior were bad to non-existent, missionaries, miners, hunters, farmers and the military relied primarily on air transportation. All types of functional and non-functional aircraft cluttered the airfield in testament. Poor maintenance, over-familiarity, lack of qualified supervision and tropical lethargy resulted in a high rate of aircraft accidents.

On the taxi way in front of the main terminal sat a Boeing 737 and two turboprop commuters awaiting passengers.

As the Huey's rotor wound down and they unloaded their bags, a lone incredibly thin soldier wearing a plain baggy camouflage uniform made his way towards them from the maintenance building. He ducked low to avoid the slowly spinning blade, although the aircraft sat on level pavement and he was in no danger of being struck.

"Good afternoon, gentlemen," the soldier said stiffly with a heavy accent.

All of them nodded and said hello or good afternoon. The soldier's face was rigidly impassive.

"Welcome to the Republic of the Congo. Bring your luggage and follow me, please."

Andy finished shutting down, quickly inspected the aircraft, and spoke to Kurt.

"I'll hang around and make sure you get through customs before I fuel up and fly back to the rig."

The thin soldier marched in front of Dave, Al, Dan and Kurt and led them to a desk to one side of the entrance foyer in the main terminal. The bags were heavy and awkward to carry, and all four of them were soaked with perspiration before they reached the building. The customs' area was manned by a short and very heavy man perched behind a counter on a three-legged stool. He tried to cross his arms in attempt to appear casual and disinterested as they approached, but his bulk made the manoeuvre difficult.

The official was wearing the same type of uniform as the skinny soldier but the material was stretched to near bursting, and adorned with coloured and metallic decorations and braids. Kurt saw a set of ornate gold parachute wings displayed prominently on his left chest. He wondered if the man had been much thinner when he received them, or if they had to rig him up for a cargo drop.

That thought made Kurt grin, a gesture that was immediately picked up by the fat official who stared intently at him, soft beads of perspiration glistening from his exposed skin. Kurt stifled the grin and looked at the floor, which seemed to satisfy the official for the moment.

"Passports!" the official shouted at them even though they were standing close by. His eyes moved to on a clock mounted on the wall behind them. It must be near lunch time, Kurt thought.

Dave had possession of three passports, but not Kurt's. He placed three folded twenty-dollar bills between them and handed the stack to the official. When the documents were separated, the bills fell to the desk and the official inadvertently grunted when he saw the money.

"What are your destinations?" he said, examining the visas and pictures in the passports.

"We're flying to Kinshasa and then to Paris and New York. We're Americans returning home," Dave volunteered.

The big man slowly closed the passports and held them up in his left hand like a deck of fanned playing cards. The American eagle was clearly visible on all three.

"I would certainly hope so," the official said as he handed the passports back to a red-faced Dave. "Carry on."

Turning his attention to Kurt the customs official scowled noticeably and asked, "And you?"

Kurt handed over his passport.

"I will be staying in Kinshasa a few days then catching a flight out. I'm sightseeing."

The customs official slowly moved his eyes up from the passport in his hand to Kurt's face positioned immediately in front of him. His eyes were sullen, like those of an old hound dog that has just been scolded.

"Sightseeing ... in Brazzaville? That is funny; we don't get very many sightseers here Mr ... uhhh," he looked at the first page of Kurt's passport, "Christianson. In fact you are the first one in recent memory. We have many missionaries, hunters, UN officials and salesmen but we have very few sightseers."

The big man held Kurt's passport in his left hand and with his right hand resting on the desktop, he not too subtly rolled his thumb and forefinger together. Kurt reached into his shirt and extracted a money clip from which he took a fifty-dollar note. He carefully took his passport, inserted the folded bill and handed it back. The official opened the passport, slid the bill into his palm and a look best described as smug satisfaction crossed his face.

The passport was quickly handed to Kurt.

"Enjoy the sights, Mr Christianson. I assume you have nothing to declare."

Kurt responded with negative head movement.

"Remember, sir, the Democratic Republic of the Congo is a peaceful land," the official unexpectedly declared. "We enjoy harmony among our citizens and neighbouring countries and we like to ensure it remains that way. Good day to you."

He dismissed all of them with a wave and the group proceeded into the small run-down terminal.

Kurt spoke to Dave, "Peaceful? That's not what I heard. There are so many warring factions around here they have to take a number to get noticed."

"It sounds like a standard line," Dave replied. "If you get into trouble they can say they told you so, and this definitely looks like a place where you don't want to get into trouble. I'm glad we're flying out in a couple of hours. Be careful Kurt, it's a different world over here."

"I'll probably only be here a day or two at most, then I'll probably go to Johannesburg and look around South Africa a bit. I hear it's a little less threatening down there. Anyway Dave, if anyone asks … you don't know where the hell I went."

"Right, that won't be a problem," Dave replied.

Kurt sat with Dave, Dan and Al in the lounge talking about their voyage until it was time for the three of them to board the twin-engine commuter turboprop for their hop to Kinshasa in Zaire. Just prior to boarding, they all shook hands in farewell and Kurt said to Dave, "I'll be contacting you about where to send the trunk I left at your house."

"Be glad to help you out any time, Kurt. Just let me know and it's as good as done."

Kurt watched the aircraft depart and felt a pang of loneliness immediately followed by a real concern about where he was and what was going to happen next.

⌘

Outside the airport he hailed one of the numerous Peugeot taxies that plied the dusty potholed streets, and asked the taxi driver to recommend a reasonable hotel. The first place the driver stopped at was too run down and dirty to even consider. The next stop was at an establishment that seemed more reasonable, from the outside anyway, but by international standards it wouldn't have rated half a star. Named the Vieux Jardins it was probably a decent place in colonial days but, like so much else in this part of the world, neglect had allowed it deteriorate beyond recovery.

After checking into his room, Kurt went for something to eat at the combined hotel dining room and bar. Afterwards he walked the hot, dusty and chaotic streets of Brazzaville to get a first-hand view of the city and its inhabitants. Bicycles, taxis, transport and military vehicles fought for the limited space in the main streets. Middle-class men and women in suits and vibrant dresses mingled seamlessly with workmen, soldiers, transients and beggars on the packed walkways.

Little shops lining the streets advertised food, clothing, radios and other goods but looking inside it was clear that most had little or no merchandise to sell. The limited items produced locally could be purchased cheaply, but imported items seemed terrifically expensive when they were available. Goods most westerners took for granted were not to be had, making an urban life difficult at best. Many of the people looked like they lived in the countryside where they could subsist on much less, and commuted or walked into town.

At the end of the afternoon Kurt was unimpressed with the place and felt uneasy. With events unfolding nearby there seemed to be a palpable underlying tension amidst the typical third world activity. Perhaps it was like this in Warsaw or Brussels just before the Germans invaded, or on the streets of Saigon just before the NVA tanks rolled in. Something bad was in the air, although no one could articulate what it was. A state of denial dominated, so people just continued about their business.

That night, he lay atop his bed in a room in a once ritzy colonial hotel now gone to seed. The windows were wide open to allow the little breeze to flow through and remove the stagnant air; at least that was the theory. However, it only exchanged stagnant air with more stagnant air, which carried with it mixed smells of rotting fruit, dust and the heavy pall of backed-up sewage. Across the street and half a block down was a bar, or beer hall as they were called here. Raucous laughter filled the air until midnight, after which the noise tapered off, as the place closed and drunken customers drifted off singly or in loud groups.

He remembered that he must go to a pharmacy tomorrow and buy some chloraquine. A single pill taken weekly would prevent malaria spread by the insidious mosquito that was still a big killer over here.

Kurt stared at the ceiling through the haze of cheesecloth mosquito netting draped in a canopy around his bed. The cracked plaster on the ceiling struck by reflected streetlights made intricate but subtle patterns. With a little imagination and an exhausted mind these patterns looked like a relief map of trees, rivers and roadways.

He pictured the rocky coast of Maine, a wild sea churning white foam on dark rock and the ceiling matched his thoughts. He thought of the thick jungle and limestone karsts of Laos and, almost keeping pace with his mind, the ceiling subtly shifted to mimic the new scenes. Just before drifting off into a light, troubled sleep the ceiling changed again into the harsh and rocky high desert. Mountains surrounded a vast barren bowl. Brightly illuminated by moonlight, pure white discs sat in the hollow pointing at the stars listening, silently listening, bearing witness.

⌘

Kurt arose while the sky was still violet. His sleep had been restless—it always was the first night in a strange location—but all seemed quiet so he dozed for another fifteen minutes before the city came to life.

Not yet daylight, he looked out of the window and was surprised at the level of activity on the street. Vendors were pushing handcarts loaded with produce to their stalls; pedestrians were walking, enjoying an early start on the day while it was still relatively cool. The Congolese were early rising people. Many of them lacked electricity and, like the West before Edison, most went to bed just after sunset and by sunrise they were on the move.

Just outside the hotel a boy was selling an English language newspaper, so Kurt bought a copy and carried it rolled up under his arm. Walking down the crowded street he spotted a small café offering a few wrought-iron chairs and tables scattered on the walkway, competing with the foot traffic. A waiter quickly appeared and he ordered black coffee and a croissant, hesitant to trust anything more substantial until he'd been in the country a few days and his stomach had a chance to adapt to the food and water.

The headline in the paper was about the instability in Angola, which in regional terms was only a stone's throw away from the Republic of the Congo.

According to the news article this little country seemed like a bug caught between two rolling boulders. A wrong move or political alignment could mean disaster for a small state. To the north was the formerly pro-Soviet, now pro-West Zaire run by President Mobutu. To the south was the formerly Portuguese colony of Angola where armed pro-Soviet, pro-West and unaligned nationalist factions battled for power. Far to the south and west, but never out of range of influence, stood the colossus of South Africa and her desert colony of South West Africa, referred to as Namibia by many. This little backwater Democratic Republic of the Congo was in an unenviable situation.

If the DROC supported the socialist or communist factions, Zaire and the West would be on its case. Support the western factions and, if the communists won next door, the Republic would be put on the communist's 'domino list'. So what is a small poor country to do when surrounded by mass confusion and political fluidity? The logical answer was to take no sides but trade with all of them, profiting from the uncertainty. That's just what the DROC seemed to be doing, attempting to be a Switzerland of the African continent.

Kurt shook his head at it all. What could one person do in this cauldron of confusion that would make any lasting difference? Probably nothing, but it was exciting to be here anyway.

⌘

The address and contact name the helicopter pilot gave to Kurt was located on the southern outskirts of Brazzaville. The distance could be walked from his hotel but Kurt decided it would be more prudent to take a cab through unknown territory. He sat reading the rest of the paper and sipping the bitter chicory-based coffee until eight in the morning. By that time, daily commerce was in full swing and the noise, movement and exhaust fumes made him anxious to get moving.

Before hailing a taxi he went into a pharmacy and bought some chloraquine and Lomotil. The Lomotil was in case his gut suddenly reacted to the strange water and food. In Indo-China this medicine had been referred to as the 'little white cork'. He took two chloraquine tablets immediately, with a familiar six-ounce bottle of Coke purchased from a street vendor. No matter where you went in the world, he thought, Coke was always there.

When given the address, the driver of the little Renault R4 taxi drove him to a light industrial area near the wharfs past the southern boundary of the city. The large, mainly dilapidated structures looked like warehouses used to store goods for transport up and down river by boats and barges. This dusty and nondescript area was inhabited by old flatbed transports, pushcarts and small groups of African workers.

The cab stopped in front of a building that looked like any other except it had a hand-painted black and yellow sign that said 'FNLA' tacked beside the door. He paid the driver who anxiously took off down the dusty, litter-strewn access way. Kurt had the notion that the cab driver was nervous here, which didn't make him feel comfortable either.

He knocked on the door next to the sign and waited; there was no response so he knocked again, more forcefully this time. A military Land Rover parked in an alleyway beside the building looked as though it had been driven recently. It was a British vehicle with right-hand drive. Further back in the alley was a fairly new camouflaged Mercedes Benz Unimog two-and-a-half-ton 6x6 transport, which Kurt knew was a very durable and expensive piece of equipment. Just as he was preparing to knock for a third time the door opened a crack. The interior of the building was as dark as a cave due to the brightness of the morning sun and intense reflection off the surrounding walls.

A shiny black face and pair of yellow eyes, overgrown with small blood vessels, peered out. The eyes shifted back and forth studying him for a moment before saying, "Que voce quer?" Portuguese, the language most of the oil rig workers used.

"I was sent here to see a Mr B," Kurt said to the person in the darkness. The weathered eyes just stared back at him for a few more seconds.

"Who sent you?" the voice finally asked in heavily accented English.

"A friend of mine sent me, a helicopter pilot. I have come a long way."

"Wait a moment," the voice said, then the door closed and he was again standing alone in the dusty street, which grew hotter by the minute.

⌘

Kurt stood looking at the door for five minutes wishing something would happen, but also beginning to wish he hadn't come here. The situation didn't feel too encouraging so far.

Finally he heard footsteps, heavy distinct footsteps, then the door opened. Before him stood a very large African soldier who was at least six feet tall because Kurt looked him directly in the eyes. The soldier must have weighed at least two-hundred-and-fifty pounds of solid muscle. He wore Portuguese camouflage fatigues tucked into polished brown boots. On his head sat a nicely moulded and weathered black beret with a black and yellow crest which matched the sign by the door. A set of ornate gold jump wings was pinned through the material on the left of his shirt. Kurt recognized them as the same wings as those worn by the customs official, Portuguese most likely.

This soldier must have been a product of Portugal's colonial army and it would be assumed that he was still a member, except Portugal bailed their military forces out of the region two years before. He wore gold pips on his shoulder epaulettes, indicating the rank of field grade officer. He looked Kurt up and down like he was examining an item he was considering purchasing, all the while wearing an expression that remained passive and seemingly disinterested.

"How can I be of assistance, saaah?" he said in a deep, resonating voice that had no doubt been developed while commanding troops on the parade field.

"Good morning, Major," Kurt knew that his recognition of the soldier's rank would do two things. First it would demonstrate his military awareness and secondly, it would show respect for the man standing before him. The tactic seemed to be working. The man broke into a slight smile. "I was sent here to talk to a Mr B."

Damn! He thought, at least the pilot could have given him the proper name. This sounded so ridiculous coming out of his mouth.

The soldier's expression went back to neutral.

"I am Major Fernandez, adjutant to General Holan Roberto. I know of no Mr B ... as you say. If you wish to come in, I will make some inquiries for you."

Kurt was hesitant about going inside but decided he had little choice but to follow through. The major led him into the darkened building and into a room furnished with only a small wooden table and two chairs. It looked like a police interrogation room. Before he closed the door the major said, "Please do not leave this room unless you are escorted. I am posting a guard outside and he will help you if you need assistance."

The language was very diplomatic but Kurt realized that he had just been made a prisoner. The room was small and the air stagnant and very hot. The only ventilation was from two perforated cement blocks on the upper corners of the rear wall. Inside, the room had been painted light green long ago but the paint was mottled with dark stains. The floor was covered with cracked and chipped red tiles. Vibration came from a vehicle starting next to the rear wall of the building; maybe it was the Land Rover.

When the vehicle pulled away an eerie silence engulfed the room. One hanging bare light bulb served as the room's only illumination and it cast a shadow on the broken floor of Kurt sitting in one of the chairs.

⌘

Time crawled by. Out of habit, he checked his watch every couple of minutes. On several occasions soft mumbled voices could be heard in the background. After an hour and a half of waiting Kurt's bladder was suffering the effects from the pot of coffee he drank at the cafe.

He got up and softly knocked on the door, which opened up a crack to reveal the same set of yellow eyes, but this time the owner could be distinguished. It was a soldier in a camouflage uniform wearing the same beret as Major Fernandez.

"I need to use the bathroom," Kurt said, trying to hide the edge of desperation in his voice. The yellow eyes blinked.

"Toilette," he said hoping the soldier would know French.

The word seemed to be understood. The soldier closed the door and shouted something in Portuguese. Running footsteps were heard; then the door opened wide and the same soldier stood in the entrance, now flanked by two other camouflaged men. The soldier who answered the door was only wearing a Browning 9mm pistol on his belt but the two flanking soldiers carried AR-10s, big automatic rifles that fired a 30-calibre NATO round. Kurt remembered vaguely that the Armalite Corporation in the US made some of these guns for Portugal in the 1950s.

The trio led him to an attached restroom that had a lavatory and urinal but no door. They watched with boredom as he relieved himself. As he was led back to the room he glanced around the building but there was little to see. Boxes, equipment, duffel bags and filing cabinets were haphazardly piled in the hallway and side rooms. One of the guards opened a cardboard box and offered Kurt a warm bottle of Coke which he gratefully accepted, before being locked into his room again.

Another hour passed when he heard the vehicle engine again as it pulled in adjacent to the wall of the building. He held his breath as footsteps approached and the door opened a crack. He saw someone studying him carefully.

⌘

"Well, I'll be goddamned if it isn't Kurt Christianson, the terror of the Ho Chi Min Trail."

The door flew wide open and George Barlow burst through. His dark, curly, short-cropped hair was almost white with dust and he wore faded standard US military issue green jungle fatigues and scuffed jungle boots with nylon sides. He was next to Kurt in a second and grabbed his hand.

"What are you doing in this hellhole, boy? I'd figured you'd had enough the last time I saw you."

Kurt was startled by the presence of the man whom he'd last seen in Long Theing, Laos when he came in from the war.

"Jesus, George, what a pleasant surprise," Kurt exhaled. "I thought for awhile I'd really screwed up and was a goner."

"What's the matter, the boys haven't been hospitable?" George asked. "I probably need to give them some coaching in etiquette and social graces." Then he laughed in the same hearty spontaneous way Kurt remembered.

"No, they were fine. I just didn't know what I'd got myself into."

"Well, hold that thought, it's not Disney World; What are you doing here? Just come to have a look see, or coming to help the cause?" George asked.

"Well," Kurt replied, "since I don't even know what the cause is yet, it may be premature to answer that. Actually, I came over with a boat crew and a chopper pilot on the oil rig gave me the address of this place."

"Oh, Andy flew you, did he? He's one fine pilot. A little wild sometimes but under pressure he's one of the best; he flies for us sometimes. That outfit Petroleum Helicopters he works for is really owned by the Company, if you know what I mean. Andy flew almost continuously when An Loc was under siege, mostly medivacs and supply runs. Had two choppers shot out from under him and a half dozen others that were heavily damaged. Yeah, Andy McDonald and the Mad Medic, now that was a pair," George shook his head almost wistfully.

"The Mad Medic?" Kurt questioned.

"Flying medivacs with Andy was another guy, whose name eludes me now, but everyone called him the Mad Medic. He had a fancy degree from Harvard or some other Ivy League school ... a Ph.D. in psychology I think. For some weird reason he joined the army and became a medic in the Rangers. Flew medivacs during the last part of the war '71 and '72, even flew chase for SF recon teams too, I think. During the siege of An Loc, which lasted over two months, he volunteered to stay there the whole time and take care of the wounded. Of course the conditions there were hell—constant bombardment and scarce medical supplies. He did his best, a totally fearless man, but he watched hundreds of people die and he couldn't help them, then he was badly wounded himself."

"Really, where's this Mad Medic now? Did he make it back?" Kurt asked.

"Yes, but I heard he went over the deep end after that. According to those who knew him he was never too tightly wrapped to begin with and after An Loc he became very strange indeed. He was nominated for the Distinguished Service Cross but when he found out about it he refused even to be considered for a medal because he thought he failed his mission by not saving everyone. In reality he saved a whole lot of lives, maybe hundreds, but he may be one of those who could only focus on failure, not success. From what I understand he came over to Africa with Andy and then they parted company. No one has heard from him in a while.

"Anyway ... enough of that. I'm sure you're sick of this room," George said, switching gears. "Let's go find something to eat; then I'll give you a tour of the base camp."

⌘

They walked out of the darkened building into the startling sunlight. Major Fernandez was supervising the loading of wooden crates into the Mercedes Unimog.

"Major Fernandez, I believe you met Mr. Christianson," George said. "He's the American Green Beret you have heard stories about; you know the one who gave the communists so much trouble in Laos some years ago." The big major turned and looked at Kurt, his expression slowly changing from impassive to surprise.

"Yes," Fernandez said in a deep baritone, "I have heard some stories."

Kurt shook his head in embarrassment.

"Are you going to fight with us?" Fernandez asked Kurt directly. "We can use all the assistance we can get, especially from experienced soldiers like you."

"I appreciate the offer, Major," Kurt replied, "but I'm just here visiting Mr Barlow. We go back a long way."

"Finish loading this equipment," George said to Fernandez while looking at his watch, "and I'll meet you at the assembly area at fourteen hundred hours. We'll hold an operations briefing at fifteen hundred for tonight's activities. Be sure everyone cleans their weapons and has all their gear together. We'll hold a detailed inspection before departure."

"Yes, sir," Fernandez replied, coming to attention and clicking his polished heels together.

George and Kurt climbed into the Land Rover and sped off down the dusty cluttered alleyways towards the centre of Brazzaville.

Kurt spoke first, "I didn't want to ask you back there, George, but what is the story here, if I may be so bold?"

"Well, my boy, welcome to the most fly-by-night, chicken-shit operation in the entire history of warfare," George laughed as he said it but Kurt could tell there was a sharp edge to the comment.

"I had the misfortune to stick my head into an office in Langley at the wrong time, and I was shanghaied for this gig. We're supporting Mr Holan Roberto of the FNLA, unofficially of course. He is a long time African nationalist who fought against Portuguese colonialism in the '50s and '60s. His bank of insurgents made their reputation by massacring farmers and settlers in remote areas of Angola. Once they tied the occupants of a small town—men, women and children—onto logs and ran them through a sawmill one at a time, so family and friends could see what was going to happen to them. A couple of them were lucky enough to escape and tell the tale. He's a real fucking gentleman, but now in the scheme of things he's a good guy and a US ally."

"It's always the same bullshit," Kurt mumbled.

"We, or should I say the FNLA," George continued, "have influence on this side of the Congo River, the northern sectors of Angola and some pockets further south, but not as far down as Luanda. Our major opponents are the MPLA run by a guy named dos Santos. The MPLA have turned pro-communist. They occupy the centre of the country and along the Atlantic coast, including Luanda. As you may have guessed, these divisions are primarily tribal. The MPLA are currently Soviet backed, so Cuban proxies are arriving as advisors, bringing lots of toys with them. The MPLA have been pretty disorganized in the past but, with Cubans and Eastern Bloc weapons pouring in, they're becoming more dangerous by the day."

George almost ran into the back of a truck which suddenly came to a stop for no apparent reason. After cursing the driver, he found a way around the truck and continued, "In the more remote eastern and southern regions of Angola there is another group called UNITA, led by a very charismatic and dynamic man named Jonas Savimbi. He is a nationalist but officially aligned with neither the West nor the Soviets. The South Africans are supplying him with intelligence and equipment. His tribal group is very loyal and his force can't be underestimated."

"Where is Holan Roberto now?' Kurt asked.

"That's another interesting twist," George replied. "Roberto is President Mobutu's brother-in-law. So he spends a lot of time in Zaire trying to squeeze his relative for money and supplies."

"Then how does the United States fit in the picture?" Kurt questioned.

George paused before answering, "That's a good question. Four months ago when I arrived, we were receiving some material through the black operations pipeline but it slowed to a trickle and now it has stopped. I really don't know what is going on but I've received no order to disengage. It seems the senate inquiries in Washington have put the brakes on covert operations worldwide. Those politicians don't understand there are both lives on the line and promises to keep. This is the kind of crap that gets people in the field killed and, unfortunately, we happen to be those people."

⌘

They pulled up to a small hotel with an attached open air patio. George turned to Kurt.

"I come here quite a bit. The place has a half decent atmosphere, and a taste of the old colonial ways that aren't quite dead."

They chose a table at the far edge of the eating area for privacy and ordered from a waiter formally dressed in a stark white shirt and black pants. The midday heat was becoming oppressive, even with the shade provided by the large umbrella over their table. After ordering their food they spoke in a subdued manner in an attempt to keep their conversation private.

"So what's the story, George?" Kurt asked. "How are you going to whack these commies flying in if our uncle has put the screws on supplies? This situation sounds pretty bad to me."

"We've had to shift gears a little from our original plan," George answered. "Our first goal was to mount an offensive in the northern provinces and set up a separate tribal-based state. But with the Cuban influx and the de-escalation of support from our side, the best we can hope for is holding actions until the situation becomes more defined. Holen is sure we can remain in control in some key villages and territories in the north because of those tribal loyalties; we have sanctuary on this side of the river for the same reason. The MPLA and Cubans are concentrating their efforts on securing Luanda and keeping Savimbi out of their hair. We've already gone up against some of their flankers sent to the north for security. For now, the FNLA is viewed by the MPLA as just a nuisance to be dealt with after they have achieved their primary objectives."

"So resistance is fairly light then?" Kurt questioned.

"We have fairly good intelligence from the villagers so we have avoided any heavy concentrations of MPLA troops or their Cuban advisors. They predictably conduct vehicle convoys on the main roads then withdraw back to more secure bases. We've shot it out with a couple of small elements, probably reconnaissance patrols. We've killed a few of them and they've killed a few of ours. It's a tit for tat kind of thing, nothing of any real consequence. We did manage to surround and capture two Cuban advisors last week and we brought them across the river for interrogation."

"Get anything from them?" Kurt asked.

George shook his head.

"No, not much. And believe me they would have told us if they knew anything. These local interrogators are as nasty as they come. Both were just draftees who didn't want to be here and only knew their individual assignments."

"What did you do with them?" Kurt asked.

"They are being held prisoner in a couple of pits out near the base. They keep them tied up in the holes with steel grates on the top, next to the latrines. You'll see for yourself this afternoon."

"What are your short-term plans then, George?"

"We've been making forays across the river a couple of times a week. Mainly setting up caches of weapons and ammo, the little that remains in our inventory, anyway. Hopefully Holen will come through with some more hardware and cash. Otherwise we'll be lucky to maintain the small force we have, let alone expand to any effective size. If we stop our operations all together, the little momentum we currently have will be lost and the troops will get frustrated and leave. If that happens our backers will lose confidence and the whole movement will die."

"It sounds to me like it may be best to shut it down temporarily, at least until Washington decides if they want to back a dog in this fight," Kurt said.

"You have a point and that is probably the only logical thing to do, but it's my personal commitment and I'm reluctant to close it down. Even our minimal force could make a big difference to the outcome of this war, given the circumstances. If we can show even some military victories, that will increase our visibility internationally. Everyone wants to back a winner."

"You're a romantic, George," Kurt shook his head, almost laughing. "You see all of this as a personal crusade, don't you?"

"Of course I do. Why the hell else would I do it? Because it's fun?"

"That's really not such a bad reason George, if you think about it."

They paid their bill and drove for forty-five hot dusty minutes to the FNLA forward base camp cut out of the thick brush along the banks of the Congo River.

# CHAPTER 9
## HEART OF DARKNESS

The FNLA base looked like a transient labour camp rather than a military garrison. Several squat concrete block and tin roofed structures were the only permanent buildings, and these had seen better days as storage garages for agricultural and maintenance equipment. These crude quarters served as headquarters, communications, supply and sleeping billets for officers and senior NCOs. A couple of dozen faded and ragged canvas tents were also scattered about the perimeter of the camp in a loose defensive ring.

The cinder block buildings were protected on the river side by overgrown earth ramparts. Behind the mounds were trenches dug four feet deep and three feet wide. The trenches were prevented from collapsing by sandbags and rough timber reinforcements. These trenches ran beyond the protection of the earthen ramparts so, if under attack, defenders could jump into the trenches and manoeuvre laterally and return fire at the attackers. Beyond the perimeter tents were areas relatively clear of trees and undergrowth. Aiming stakes, made of wooden laths with bits of flag tied on their tips, were positioned in the ground at various distances to define fields of fire for the defending gunners.

"Is that your handiwork, George?" Kurt asked as he stood in the centre of the camp and surveyed the positions.

"I just beefed up what they had. Holen and his senior brass thought it was a waste of time building defensive positions in a secure area, but I tried to convince them otherwise. It's an attitude of discipline that has to be instilled in the troops. If they're sloppy in base camp they will be sloppy when we're working on the other side. We learned that the hard way with the Mong in Laos. I've seen a lot of improvement already. These guys will never be a ranger battalion, but we have to work with what we've got. Let's go have some coffee over at the HQ and you can meet some of the men."

George put a hand on Kurt's shoulder and squeezed then withdrew his hand suddenly.

"Damn you're solid; don't feel like regular flesh and bone."

Kurt laughed. "I worked with my grandfather rowing small boats and hauling lobster traps for twelve hours a day when I was a kid. The exercise must have done some good, although I sure hated it at the time."

"Well, I'm jealous as hell. I'm turning to flab in my middle age," George said.

"Middle age? You can't be more then what ... thirty five?"

"Thirty-six, but thanks for the compliment. This is a young man's game and I don't feel young anymore. When I leave here I'm going to go back to the property I bought in Wyoming and breed horses, cows and anything else that feels like breeding. Hell, I might even have a kid myself, you never know."

"Don't fool yourself George, you love this shit. They'll be pushing you on patrol in a wheelchair when you are eighty."

Both of them laughed, but the laughter died quickly.

⌘

At three-thirty the group planning to cross the river that evening met in their informal briefing area. There were a total of fifty-seven individuals, no more than a platoon in a regular army. They were an unlikely mix of Angolans, Congolese, two Portuguese nationals, a Greek and a Briton. George and Kurt were the only Americans present. George had constructed a sand table on a cleared patch of earth behind the HQ building. Already etched in the soil with a pointed stick were the Congo River, the entry and exit points and the roads leaving from the southern bank of the river to their destination along the northern border of Angola.

George stood holding his carved stick while the rest of the group sat or kneeled around the display. Kurt thought that this must be one of the oldest practices in military science, sitting around in the dirt drawing and discussing strategy. The Romans, the Greeks, even the Egyptians probably did the same thing, and it was still one of the most effective training tools.

George began to outline their mission for the evening while pointing at the impromptu map to illustrate.

"At twenty-one hundred hours we will send a recon patrol across the river into Angola, here, to establish a beachhead on the other side ... here. When the landing area has been secured they will flash a light in code to this side. The abort signal will be SOS or any combination other than the designated one. If clear, we will move the main body across at twenty-two hundred hours. As before, the recon team will stay with the boats to ensure their security."

As George talked, he paused at every other sentence as a Portuguese translator repeated his words. Most of the men could understand and speak English to some extent but full comprehension was only possible in their native language. George understood Portuguese well enough to ensure that it was being translated correctly.

"Our Angolan assets will have two vehicles. They will pick us up at twenty-three hundred hours and we will proceed to checkpoint Bravo which will be our point of departure. We will then de-bus and maintain two foot patrols and when we come to the fork in the road here, we will follow the left fork for approximately five kilometres to checkpoint Alpha, here. This position is just on this side of a shallow ravine. Vehicles coming down the road will have to slow down for the ravine so that is why we established it as our ambush point. Intel sources report that there will be a small Cuban and MPLA convoy coming along this route to re-supply their northern outpost at Zombo. The target is expected to reach our position mid-morning tomorrow, according to our latest information. We have to do a good job of cover and concealment tonight so we aren't spotted by the enemy in the morning. If they detect us before we trigger the ambush, they could dismount from the vehicles to manoeuvre against us."

George paused and waited for the Portuguese translation to complete before continuing.

"We will place two command-detonated vehicle mines fifty metres this side of the ravine surrounded by a cluster of anti-personnel mines in the road, and on the shoulders. These will be placed to slow enemy troops in case they aren't killed in the ambush and try to assault our position. Remember where you place the mines; if possible, we want to pick them up again when we're finished."

George stopped talking for a minute and lit his pipe, which allowed time for the translator to catch up and answer any immediate questions. When the translator stopped talking George continued.

"They probably won't allow much distance between their vehicles. We want to stop the main supply truck or trucks and kill the occupants. We don't want to destroy the supplies and munitions, we need them. If they're lax and send the whole convoy together, we'll blow the mine on the lead truck, and then fire up the others. Are there any questions so far?"

There was murmuring from the men but no questions, so George continued his briefing.

"When the mines are detonated, the machine gunners and the RPG gunners open fire immediately. We don't want them to have enough time to get the vehicle mounted machine guns in operation. The claymore mines will be fired next. Their purpose is to eliminate the driver and soldiers. RPG gunners, remember to aim at the engine or the hard body of the trucks. If you hit canvas, the rocket may pass through without detonating. We are counting on the blast of those rockets to kill or stun the occupants until we can work them over with our machine guns."

George took another draw on his pipe and scanned the troops to see if there were any looks of confusion. He failed to detect any so he continued the briefing.

"Machine gunners: be sure to take out any visible mounted guns on the trucks first. They are our biggest threat, so don't let anyone get to them, or if a soldier is manning one, blow him off of it right away. Then rake the cabs, the bodies and anyone jumping out. Our goal is to kill all the occupants and take their equipment. We've not going for prisoners this time."

George took a long swig from a green plastic canteen before resuming; the afternoon heat and lack of breeze near the river made the briefing area uncomfortable.

"Flank security, keep it tight and join in the ambush but your main job is to keep any surviving troops from flanking us or getting to our rear where they can push us into our own mines. Our trucks will be hidden in a ravine about two clicks from our ambush position. After the threat is neutralized, we will attempt to salvage any usable supplies from the convoy. When our trucks receive our radio signal, we can load up any salvage and personnel then move back to the river without delay. If something isn't right, the stick commanders or I will give the abort signal and we will sit tight and let the convoy pass. We have no support on this operation, no air cover, no reaction force, no choppers and no artillery. Everything we do must be to maintain the advantage and always err on the side of caution. Are there any final questions?"

Several hands now went up now from soldiers who wanted more detail about their specific roles. George answered all of them succinctly and with a calm demeanour. After all questions were dealt with, he glanced at this watch and said, "Okay, get your gear ready, we will have a complete inspection at nineteen-hundred hours. Your weapons should be sighted in but, if you aren't sure, we are making a run out to the firing range in half an hour. Let your squad leader know if you need to go. Dismissed."

George walked over to Kurt.

"So, are you staying here, or are you going to come along and see how we play guerrilla war on a shoestring?"

"Hell, I'll be happy to go if you'll have me," Kurt responded. "It sounds as though you could use an extra gun."

George nodded his head in agreement while emptying the ashes from the bowl of his pipe. "You got that right. We are pretty thin on the ground. Besides, these people are very leadership dependent. If they see someone doing it right with confidence, they will copy but they're just as liable to follow a bad example and, God knows, that's not hard to find."

"I need some gear and a weapon," Kurt said.

"Come to the office and we'll put some together for you."

"Where are the Cuban prisoners you talked about?" Kurt asked.

"Oh them … they're over there," George pointed to the edge of the perimeter. "Let's go have a look."

⌘

A small concrete open-top latrine sat on the edge of the camp's cleared northern perimeter. Kurt smelled it before he saw it.

Ten paces to one side of the latrine a young soldier attired in camouflage squatted, holding a black G3 rifle across his knees. He stared passively at two heavy steel grates secured to the ground with heavy wooden stakes. The grates covered open square pits, were a metre and a half wide by two and a half metres deep. They looked like unused latrine holes. Kurt approached cautiously and peered in. At the bottom of each pit was a naked man, his hands and feet bound together with coarse hemp rope. The stench wafting from the pits was overpowering, making him almost retch.

First one, then the other, of the wretched men looked up at Kurt. Even in the dim depths of the pits their eyes shone. Their faces looked swollen and bruised but this was obscured by matted dark hair and scraggly beards. The faces of both men registered fear, with a faint glimmer of hope as they saw the new face, a fresh Western face with dark blond hair. Perhaps they thought he was the Red Cross, a UN official, or help of some other kind.

"What the hell are they doing in there?" Kurt asked. "These holes aren't fit for an animal."

The African soldier stood up from his squatting position and responded to the question before George could.

"But suh, they are not animals ... they are not that good ... they are Cubans! They burn villages, they kill families, steal food and rape our women. An animal would never do such a thing. They will stay in these holes until they die!"

"That's enough, Corporal, back to your post," George told him sternly.

"Yes, suh!" The soldier saluted George then spun around, walked over to one of the pits and spat a large wad of saliva between the bars. He then moved back to his original position and resumed his squatting position.

"I know it looks bad but some things are beyond the control of advisors. I tried to get them housed above ground and get them better treatment but the men became very hostile when I suggested it. We don't need bad feelings right now, so I conceded. Not very strong of me, is it?" George asked.

"You're doing what you have to do, George. I feel sorry for the poor bastards, they're probably just draftee peasants, but if either of us was caught we'd probably be in for the same."

"Yes, or even worse," George volunteered.

"You said there was some gear for me, George?"

"Right, let's go take a look."

Kurt was handed a well worn G3 rifle. It was a 30-calibre selective fire, originally designed in Germany after WWII, now manufactured under license from Heckler and Koch in Portugal and other countries. The rifle was heavy and bulky, with a reputation for extreme reliability. He was also handed a like-new Tokarev pistol taken from one of the captured Cubans. It was rather crudely built, but fired a high intensity bottle-necked 7.62mm round that was originally designed for the old broom handle Mauser pistol at the turn of the century.

George also managed to find Kurt a clean and fairly new FNLA camouflage uniform. The pants fitted but the shirt was too tight in the arms, so Kurt cut it off at the shoulder and used it as a vest. A set of canvas chest-webbing with pouches and a couple of canteens were also included. George then remembered he had an extra pair of US jungle boots that were too big for him, which fitted Kurt well.

They all cleaned weapons then secured equipment and loaded magazines. Several of them jumped into the Unimog and drove the four kilometres to the east and away from the river. A makeshift rifle range was bulldozed into the ground in a naturally occurring depression that was probably an old river washout. Old piecemeal wooden frames were hung with man-shaped silhouette targets, yellowed with weather. The targets were positioned fifty yards from an uncovered firing platform. Kurt didn't want to mess with the targets, so he fired at some rocks that were mixed in with the soil that had been pushed up into the sandy backstop.

The G3 was firing low and to the right so he adjusted the sights using his pocket knife blade until the point of impact was about three inches directly above his point of aim at fifty metres. They were using 1950s vintage surplus ball ammo so accuracy wasn't superb but, for this type of shooting, precision wasn't needed. He also ran a magazine of ammo through the Tokarev, but due to its fixed sights no adjustment was possible. In any case the pistol would only be used at close range if things really went to hell.

⌘

Back at base camp the soldiers taking part in the raid stood for inspection. Kurt assisted George and Major Fernandez and found that there were several soldiers with dirty weapons and webbing and backpacks that weren't rigged to be as noise and rattle-free as possible. Instead of cursing the troops and threatening them like Major Fernandez was doing, George and Kurt quietly helped the men disassemble their weapons, clean them, and tie down loose gear with some green duct tape.

At twenty hundred hours they were ready to move to the boats. This was done in two loads with the Unimog. Kurt, George and Fernandez followed the last truck load of troops in the Land Rover.

The reconnaissance team was placed across the river an hour before the scheduled crossing to secure the landing area, and then the boats returned. The pilot of the craft began watching the opposite shore with a pair of high-magnification field glasses.

"Do you see anything yet?" George breathlessly whispered to the boat pilot after a steep and slippery climb down the river embankment.

"Nothing, suh. I expect another fifteen to twenty minutes before they will signal. Everything looks quiet," he said calmly.

Kurt stood next to George and looked out over the dark waters of the mighty Congo. The dark surface looked oily and placid. To the west the sky still had traces of orange streaks rapidly subsiding into deep tropical blackness. Insects chirped and hissed softly in the reeds that cluttered the shoreline. Frogs of different types croaked intermittently.

Suddenly a staccato of deep sound and vibration struck them. The sound reflected off the surface of the river and could be both felt and heard. Kurt immediately squatted and brought his rifle forward. George laughed softly at his response. Kurt quickly scanned the water but saw nothing.

"Hippos," George said. "A big male looking for a date on this fine evening."

"Goddamn scare the hell out of you," Kurt stood up feeling a little embarrassed.

"Remember this is Africa. Plenty of things over here will gnaw a piece of your butt if you let your guard down. There are lions, hyenas and leopards in the bush and big crocs and hippos in this river."

"Are hippos dangerous?" Kurt asked.

"Yeah, they have an evil temper. Sometimes bull hippos get territorial and attack a small boat. They have incisor teeth that look like scimitars. More people are killed by hippos in Africa than by any other animal."

"Suh, the signal," the boat driver walked up to George and handed him the glasses. George took them and looked. On the far bank he saw a green light blinking the Morse code letters C - L - R, then paused and repeated.

"Let's load up; it's a go." George spoke along the embankment in a whisper loud enough to be heard by ears that were listening intently.

"Si," Fernandez responded immediately and he turned to organize the troops into their planned crossing elements.

"These look like decent boats, George," Kurt said quietly.

"We took delivery of these US Navy inflatables a few months ago when the pipeline was still open. They were flown in from Norfolk with a team of SEALS and other personnel to train the drivers and mechanics. Those Navy guys run a first class operation, I must say."

There were three boats tied up to wooden pilings driven into the embankment. The reeds and shrub growing along the river's edge effectively concealed the boats and the activity.

All talking was kept to whispers as the soldiers divided into three teams, descended the embankment, and climbed into the 15-man inflatable boats with their weapons and equipment. George got in the lead boat and signalled the drivers to start the engines and move out. The engines started with a gentle purr and settled to a hum. Water sloshing into the pilings and riverbank made more noise than the engines themselves. The lead boat pulled out followed in sequence by the other two. Kurt rode in the last inflatable. If there was trouble with the landing he could better cover the first two boats.

The distance across the river was further than it looked initially. Kurt estimated around two miles. If it wasn't for the floating pieces of vegetation and other debris from upriver, the water looked like a lake on a windless night. George kept the pace slow to minimize a visible wake and put enough space between the craft to prevent a single mortar round or gun emplacement from doing damage to all of them. But all was quiet and aside from the hippo grunts and an occasional fish jumping, nothing else moved.

Kurt looked up the course of the massive river making its way from the African interior where it disappeared into the deep blackness of night. He remembered the novel by Joseph Conrad, *The Heart of Darkness*. It struck him that he was talking about this same river, the Congo. In the book, the further you moved towards the river's source the more savage conditions became. Conrad equated travelling up the river to plumbing the depths of man's soul. Instead of journeying up the river tonight they were crossing it to get to the beast. It was the more efficient and modern route to insanity. He shivered at the thought of the symbolism all around him.

They were crossing the river not venturing up its course, though in their case the latter would be the safer journey. Cannibals and madmen would be easy going compared with engaging the MPLA and Cubans equipped with modern arms. Journeying up the river into the unknown was out of vogue now; the world was too impatient, too knowledgeable.

⌘

The boats landed softly, discharging troops who rushed to secure a beachhead before unloading their equipment. Upon landing Kurt volunteered to conduct a clearance patrol to ensure that no hidden surprises awaited them. George agreed and sent two experienced soldiers with him. They paralleled the bank of the river for about a half a kilometre and then swung in an arc of that radius around their landing site. All seemed peaceful and on their return George sent a coded radio message for the trucks to meet them at the pickup point, which was on a frontage road one-hundred metres south of the landing site. Two green two-and-a-half ton cargo trucks with painted-over Portuguese military markings arrived twenty minutes later in a totally blacked out state.

After loading up, the two vehicles travelled in convoy for thirty kilometres or so on a fairly well developed but washed-out dirt road, then turned east for another twenty kilometres following old tyre ruts before they stopped and disembarked. George led the soldiers to a pre-selected overgrown clearing that had been roughly hacked out of the bush, and spoke to them in a loud whisper as they gathered closely around.

"This is rally point Bravo as marked on your maps. If things go to hell we will regroup here; it can be defended fairly well. The first ones back immediately set up a perimeter and challenge anyone coming in. The password tonight is Mango, I repeat Mango. Don't forget it. We will leave three men here with a 12.7 heavy machine gun, a 60mm mortar, some spare rockets and extra ammo. If we're chased, let our people pass through the perimeter, then lay waste to any pursuers. The trucks will be concealed in a ravine about a click west of here. Okay, squad leaders, perform a head count and field checks. Major Fernandez will lead us to the ambush position. He scouted the location a couple of days ago. We head out in ten minutes. Are there any questions?"

There were none.

The ambush site was about five clicks east of rally point Bravo. The terrain was deceptively difficult to move through at night due to thick low bush, vines and creepers that pulled back with each step. They made their way in single file. Some of the troops had patches of white cloth the size of a postage stamp sewn on their backs just below their collar. It looked like a laundry tag but at night it provided just enough contrast for the man behind to focus on, so the column wasn't separated.

Low hanging acacia trees had iron-hard thorns on their branches that could penetrate any clothing or pierce eyes, so the men were careful not to 'spring' branches into the faces of those following. Fortunately, Major Fernandez knew the route fairly well. As the men walked, jackals could be heard yipping, a hyena barked and the indistinct low growl of a big cat echoed in the distance.

The selected ambush site fronted a dirt road and seventy metres to the rear they set up rally point Alpha, which was to be their immediate staging and fall back position. At three in the morning the group had formed a tight defensive perimeter at Alpha.

George then took a team of soldiers trained in laying mines to the ambush site. Kurt volunteered to provide security for the mine laying team and George agreed. While vehicle, anti-personnel and claymore mines were being placed in the road, Major Fernandez began to position soldiers in pre-selected locations by leading them from rally point Alpha to the ambush locations two at a time. By using this technique, a bunch of people weren't milling around the ambush site making noise and unnecessary tracks. In the light of day when they planned to spring the attack, any disturbance could be picked up by sharp eyes and the tables turned on them by the enemy, with deadly consequences.

At the centre point of the ambush, Fernandez placed two light machine gunners and their assistants about 20 metres apart. Linked 200-round belts of ammunition were loaded in each gun and each assistant gunner had two more belts at the ready. The two light machine guns formed the hub of the blue and red fire teams and each team was supported by a half a dozen riflemen, each armed with either a G3 or Belgian FAL auto loading rifle and several loaded 20-round magazines.

Each fire team also had a grenadier, armed with a captured RPG launch tube, with one rocket loaded and two spares on the ground beside him. The West had no equivalent of this light, cheap and lethal rocket-propelled grenade launcher, which was a mystery to Kurt. The RPG was effective against a variety of targets including light armour and bunkers as well as personnel. Fortunately, the communists made them in great quantities and shipped them to their allies by the boatload. They weren't too difficult to obtain, you just had to take them away from the enemy.

Flanking security elements were positioned on extreme ends of the fire teams. Their main function was to prevent opponents from performing a counter ambush manoeuvre by flanking and attacking the weak ends of the ambush position. By using such a tactic correctly, the enemy could quickly roll up and destroy an unprotected ambush team. The secondary mission of flank security was to lend support to the ambush as riflemen when the firing commenced.

Located immediately behind the main body of the ambush was the command team. This included Major Fernandez, George and the communications man. Kurt knew the FNLA trained together and that it was not wise to interrupt the cohesiveness of a team by putting an unknown in their midst, so he stayed close to George to be used if and when needed. George controlled the 'hot wires' that would command-detonate the anti-vehicular mines and the pair of claymore anti-personnel mines placed in front of the embankment, covered with dirt for concealment.

The plan was to disable the vehicle or vehicles in the centre of the kill zone between the two fire teams, using the command-detonated anti-vehicle mines buried in the road. Next, the claymores would be set off which would saturate the target with hundreds of white-hot steel ball-bearings. Finally, the target would then be subjected to machine gun and rifle fire. The plan seemed to border on overkill, but the hallmark of an ideal ambush is that everyone in the kill zone dies quickly, with no return fire.

⌘

The African bush was hinting at light in the eastern sky. Grunts, squeals, muffled howls and roars of the animal world settled to silence in the period just before dawn. The men were told to keep quiet but signs of nervousness included throat clearing and fidgeting with equipment. These subtle sounds were common with troops awaiting violent action. In other circumstances there would be concern about giving their position away, but Kurt sensed that at the moment there were no other people in the area.

With the speed of sunset the previous night, the daylight overtook them swiftly and the still-moist night air was burned away by a sun whose presence became increasingly fierce with each increment above the broken tree line. Most of the men were protected by the shadow of rocks, bush or the elevated road embankment that acted as natural cover. The rattle of canteen caps became a regular sound as the men quenched their thirst. Kurt disliked working with groups of soldiers like this. It was hard to keep them covert and there was always noise and movement. He knew he could keep very still for days, but it often proved impossible to instil that same discipline in others. The company of other armed men made everyone too confident, even in perilous situations like this, an attitude too dangerous in this work.

With George's permission, Kurt moved around quietly in the rear of the ambush party from position to position checking on the men. He made almost no sound and usually surprised the soldiers when he appeared directly behind them. Two riflemen were nodding off due to the exhaustion of moving the previous night and the warmth of the morning, but a sharp pinch on the back of the thigh instantly cleared their cobwebs. Kurt also closely examined the roadway and embankments now that daylight would show up any tracks or marks that could give away their presence, but the site looked clean. George and the mine laying team had covered their tracks well.

Sixty or seventy metres to the rear of the ambush position grew a very old and large sentinel African teak tree. Kurt approached George.

"Can I borrow your field glasses? I think I can get a good view of the road from the upper fork of that big tree, in the rear. I'll climb up the back so I can't be seen from the road. In these dry conditions it should be easy to spot the convoy coming from quite a way off. When I spot something I'll try to estimate the size and dispersion, and then come down and report. That way we'll be able to get a heads up anyway."

George nodded and handed Kurt his compact Zeiss binoculars. Leaving his rifle and chest webbing at the base of the tree, he carefully scaled the rear side by gripping old knots and rough bark until he reached the first projecting limb. The upper fork was over forty feet off the ground and once he was in position, it offered a fairly clear view of the dirt road that wound its way towards them from the west. The ambush position was well selected, located on a slightly elevated crown in otherwise flat terrain. It was just before ten o' clock.

Kurt carefully scanned the road and surrounding landscape. In the distance he could see several kraals and rondavel huts so characteristic of the rural African countryside. Each group of huts was surrounded by an irregular patch of land claimed from the bush and planted with corn or vegetables. A scattering of goats and cattle grazed under wild acacias which provided much needed shade. An adolescent herd boy was driving a small group of multi-coloured goats across the road a couple of kilometres west of their position. Kurt thought it amazing that grazing animals could find subsistence in this harsh landscape. This scene seemed pulled out of the pages of *National Geographic*. Half an hour later he spotted dust plumes.

⌘

The appearance of two distinct plumes was significant. It meant that the vehicles or groups of vehicles were separated by enough distance to allow dust to settle before the next group passed. The vehicles were still a few kilometres off and although Kurt wanted to warn the team, he also wanted a better visual of the potential targets. The vehicles were travelling at a fairly slow speed, maybe thirty kilometres per hour he estimated. This could mean the enemy was being overly cautious, which wasn't a good sign. The ambush teams needed to remain undetected.

The vehicles drew closer. In the lead was a standard two-and-a-half ton 6 x 6 cargo truck with a canvas top and a manned 12.7mm heavy machine gun mounted on back of the cab. Following at some distance was a Mercedes Unimog with an uncovered bed, with what looked like 12 to 15 armed soldiers seated on side benches in the back. Like the lead truck, the second vehicle also had a heavy manned 12.7mm machine gun mounted just behind the cab. An armed cargo truck with a heavily armed escort and was running quite a way behind ...shit...

Kurt bounded down the tree trunk as fast as he could, scooped up his rifle and other gear and, bent over at the waist, sprinted to George and Major Fernandez, who were watching him. Kurt crashed into their position and began a rapid-fire situation report.

"Seven or eight minutes out, two vehicles," he held up two fingers. "Transport in lead with troop carrier following two to three hundred metres behind. Twelve to fifteen troops on the rear truck, maybe more on transport; it's covered and I can't see. Mounted 12.7s are on both vehicles."

"That doesn't sound very good," George interrupted. "We're too bunched up. If we take the lead truck the escort will get us and vice versa."

"Right," Kurt said, as he nodded in agreement before continuing.

"I figure we will either have to let them pass by, or I'll take one team of men down the road three hundred metres towards the oncoming trucks. I'll let the first truck by. As the first truck approaches you, trigger the ambush and neutralize that twelve-seven. My team will take out the rear truck after you have initiated. It means splitting our forces in half but that's the only thing that'll work. If either twelve-seven stays in operation we'll be chewed up."

Major Fernandez had a puzzled and frightened look and glanced nervously from Kurt to George. George had a look of concentration as he was trying to focus on what was being said. He only waited a few seconds before responding.

"I recommend we go with the plan, Major. Kurt has made the correct assessment. We didn't come all the way here just to hide in the bush."

Fernandez stared intently at Kurt, as if looking for something in his face before saying anything.

"You take the Blue Team," Fernandez said in his booming voice, not concerned about noise discipline any more. "Blue, go with this man," he shouted to his squad leader. "Do exactly as he says, and hurry, the enemy is almost here!"

He then repeated the essence of his command in Portuguese.

Kurt ushered the light machine gunner, six riflemen and single grenadier through the bush to the position he'd selected from his vantage point in the tree. When Blue Team arrived the cover wasn't as good as he hoped, but there was no time to make changes at this point.

He positioned the fire team on the edge of the eroded road embankment that had marginal but, hopefully, sufficient cover. For the plan to work the first truck must pass by them without being alerted. They quickly settled into their positions and Kurt covered the men with loose vegetation as best he could. Everything grew very quiet again except for the irregular breathing of the men, winded from their sprint, and the buzzing of a few midday tsetse flies in search of a blood meal.

The snarl of diesel truck engines broke the silence. Kurt caught an odour coming from the soldiers lying near him; it was a familiar smell, like stale cat urine but was actually raw fear exuding from their skin. Their bodies were preparing to kill or die. He gave his final directions.

"Under no circumstances are we to fire at the first truck, unless they fire at us first. I will shoot first. I'm going for the twelve-seven gunner on the roof of the second vehicle. Do not fire until I do. Then focus on the machine gun on the cab and then the back of the truck. Everyone else, shoot into the back of the vehicle and fire on the soldiers when they jump off. RPG ... " Kurt looked at the grenadier, gripping his bamboo firing tube with the cone shaped rocket, sitting on the front end, "aim for the cab or mid-body. Reload and keep firing. And for God's sake don't point the back of that tube towards any of us."

An English-speaking soldier quickly translated what Kurt said to the rest of the troops. Kurt prayed that he didn't screw up the translation.

The grenadier was positioned by Kurt at the near end of the fire team, both to keep better control over this key weapon and to have quick access if the man was hit. Unfortunately there was no time to set up claymores or set a command-detonated mine in the road. They had to rely on individual firepower to take out the heavy machine gun and the occupants of the troop carrier.

A minute later the lead truck seemed to burst from the bush two-hundred metres up the road. It was doing twenty kilometres per hour and throwing up a plume of dust behind it. Fortunately, the dust was settling over on the opposite side of the road due to some subtle, unfelt air movement and wouldn't obscure the second truck when it arrived.

The lead truck was a canvas-covered beaten-up 6x6 cargo truck of Soviet manufacture, similar to both the vehicles used on the Ho Chi Min trail in Laos and the ubiquitous American duce and a half. Both the driver and the machine gunner looked lethargic and bored, which was a good thing. A very alert man may have detected their hastily assembled and poorly camouflaged Fire Team Blue, just behind the embankment.

As soon as the lead vehicle cleared their position, the trailing truck came into view. As suspected, the second truck was a Mercedes Unimog and it looked nearly new. A 12.7 MG and gunner were clearly visible on top of the cab, with the large deadly barrel pointed forward.

Kurt hadn't been certain of the distance between the two trucks. If he underestimated and Fire Team Red ambushed the lead vehicle while the trailing truck was still short of their position, the Unimog would stop before reaching Blue's kill zone. If this happened both teams were vulnerable to fire from the wicked 12.7 mounted gun, as well as the enemy troops once they dismounted. If the trailing truck stopped within their kill zone, or even between the two ambush teams, neutralizing them would be easier, but still not a sure bet.

Kurt rose into a kneeling position with his G3 to his shoulder. The Unimog was about seventy-five metres from them and closing quickly. He saw a man standing at the ready at the rear of the 12.7mm, hanging between the firing handles for support as the truck heaved down the rutted road. In two seconds that gunner could bring a hail of devastating fire down upon both fire teams due to his elevated position. Kurt stayed very still and waited.

When the front wheels of the cargo truck were parallel with the buried vehicle mine, George triggered the explosion. The ground vibration was felt just before the roaring air blast was heard three hundred metres away by Fire Team Blue. This was followed quickly by a loud but less intense bang as George blew the claymores into his target.

Kurt stood up with his G3 in firing position. On hearing and seeing the blast up the road, the Unimog came to a halt about twenty metres short of Fire Team Blue's position, brakes screeching and dust flying as it slid. The twelve-seven gunner was quick. The moment the truck stopped, orange flames were visible from the end of the barrel and concussive waves from the firing struck the soldiers of Team Blue as the gunner sprayed heavy bullets toward the embankment near the halted lead truck.

A brown, bearded face crouched behind the firing handles of the twelve-seven, peering through the circular anti-aircraft sights to aim his shots. Touching his front sight post to the gunner's chin, Kurt carefully pressed the trigger of his G3 and felt the rifle recoil. The 30-calibre NATO round struck the Cuban gunner just above the bridge of his nose, blowing the rear of his skull to pieces. Kurt saw the man's field hat fly off and a pink cloud of vaporized brain and blood form, momentarily, in the air. The body flopped back into the truck bed and the big gun was silent.

A split second after he fired, a fusillade of rounds burst from the MAG light machine gun and rifles of Fire Team Blue, striking the Unimog like a hail storm. Enemy soldiers were beginning to leap over the sides of the stationary vehicle. Several of the Cubans and MPLA troops had rapid firing, drum-fed RPD light machine guns which were deadly when brought to bear.

Kurt sprinted behind the fire team to get abreast of the vehicle. Bullets began kicking up the dirt around their positions as enemy soldiers began to fire in their direction. A *whump* was heard, indicating his grenadier had fired an RPG, which streaked toward the truck but struck too low and right of centre. The shaped charge warhead flashed, striking the undercarriage of the Unimog near the middle wheel, blowing the wheel off and bending the axle, spraying metal shrapnel on the legs of several soldiers who were using the truck for cover.

Arriving at a position parallel to the truck, Kurt closed in slightly, taking single well-placed shots at the scrambling Cubans and MPLA as they sought cover behind the crippled vehicle. He struck four enemy soldiers with centre hits before they could return fire. An RPD gunner tried to spring across the dirt road toward cover on the other side, but he fell in the road with a bullet to the upper torso.

Remaining in their original positions, the MAG gunner and riflemen of Fire Team Blue continued to rake the vehicle from stem to stern. The remaining enemy, taking cover behind the Unimog, spun and fell from the bullets passing through the sheet metal body. A second thump was heard and a second RPG rocket streaked briefly to the truck, striking it this time in the right side of the windscreen, blowing the upper part of the cab to shreds.

"Cease fire," Kurt yelled, waving his hand above his head. The MAG cut immediately but the rifle fire continued sporadically for a few seconds until everyone got the word.

Kurt slammed a fresh magazine in his G3 and indicated to the fire team, by hand signals, that he was going forward and for them to stay put and cover him. He sprinted into the road and swung behind the ruined vehicle. Several Cubans were wounded and still moving. One had dragged himself to the opposite side of the road. Methodically, a round was fired into the head or chest of every moving soldier, as well as the ones who appeared dead, in case they were faking. As he approached the vehicle to inspect it more closely, a man crawled out from beneath the bed and put his hands above his head.

"*No me tire, por favor,*" he said in a quivering raspy voice.

The soldier's face and uniform were bloody, having been peppered by RPG fragments, but remarkably he had missed being shot. Kurt indicated with his rifle barrel for him to move out from under the truck. The frightened and dirty soldier tried to obey, inching on his stomach, trying to move forward with both hands still raised. Kurt reached down, and with his left arm lifted the prisoner half into the air by the shoulder and dropped him face down in the dirt road telling him to *estancia*, or stay put, using the little Spanish he knew. The soldier froze, trembling from shock and fear.

Kurt jerked open the cab door of the truck, rifle at the ready, and had to jump clear as the body of a Cuban soldier inside nearly fell on top of him. Judging from the insignia on his shoulders, his new tailored uniform and aviator style sunglasses, he must have been the commander of the destroyed contingent. The left lens of the glasses was shattered into flakes and mixed with blood and the jellied remains of an eye. He had also taken several other hits in the body and his left side was chewed up by shrapnel.

Standing on the truck running board, Kurt looked at what remained of the driver. The second RPG fired by the grenadier had hit its mark and struck the truck window in front of the driver, blowing his upper body into pieces too mangled to identify.

Shooting from Fire Team Red had ceased also. Kurt stepped in front of the shattered, smouldering truck. He pointed to the two troops nearest him in the ambush team and signalled for them to join him, but for the others to remain in place. The pair of young African soldiers sprinted forward, their eyes wild and excited. This was probably their first taste of blood, Kurt thought. Fortunately one of the two spoke English and was able to translate for the other. He told the non-English speaker to guard the prisoner and the other soldier to follow him in a check for spoor, on the opposite side of the road, from enemy that may have escaped.

They went up the road twenty-five metres and then cut back into the bush and parallelled back ten metres from the road. In this way they would cut across any tracks left by escapees running from the scene. Parallel with the destroyed truck, Kurt picked up tracks and blood spoor. It was not just blood but had traces of pink froth in it, indicating a hit in the lung. A man with this wound wouldn't go far. But a wounded enemy was even more dangerous than a healthy one. His dying act may be to fire an RPD or throw a grenade at them.

Before following the spoor, Kurt and the young FNLA soldier walked another twenty-five metres parallel with the road to check if any others had crossed over. This search proved negative so they looped back and picked up the trail of the wounded man a little further in. Kurt indicated to the young soldier to stay to his left and cover that flank, and he would cover ahead and the right flank as they followed the trail.

After covering about one-hundred metres, Kurt sensed that there was something in a thick tangle of thorn bush to their immediate front. He dropped to one knee and signalled to the soldier to do the same. The young soldier did not obey immediately but stopped and tried to peer over the vegetation to see what was to their front, just as a burst of automatic fire shredded the vegetation around them. Kurt could see muzzle flashes in the tangle and caught the glint of green tracers as bullets streaked nearby. One of the rounds struck the standing soldier with an audible slap, throwing him down and backwards. Kurt aimed his G3 rifle, just above and slightly to the right of the flashes, and rapidly fired half a dozen rounds into that area.

One of his bullets sounded as if it had struck flesh, but he wasn't sure. The hostile firing stopped. Kurt crawled over to the downed soldier who was lying on his back looking up wide-eyed and expectantly. Blood was flowing from a red furrow beneath the soldier's right armpit. Kurt removed a compression bandage from his trouser leg pocket, ripped it open and pressed the absorbent side on the centre of the wound. He placed the soldier's good hand on the bandage and pressed. The soldier understood, and attempted to press as best he could in his weakened state. Using a motion of his right hand but no words, Kurt instructed the wounded soldier to stay where he was and not move.

Crouching as low as possible and angling laterally, Kurt moved to a position that flanked the quarry, stopping every few seconds to look for movement. All was deathly silent. Approaching the expected position in a low crawl, he saw a Cuban lying face up, an RDP drum-fed light machine gun by his side still supported by an extended bipod. This made a very stable firing platform even for a wounded man. One of the G3 rounds had passed through the gunner's mouth and blown off the side of his head.

Kurt picked up the RPD and two drums that the dead Cuban had stowed in pouches on his webbing. He then walked back to the injured FNLA soldier, who was still lying on his back pressing a now blood-saturated bandage into his wound. Replacing the bandage with a fresh one, Kurt took two green cravats stowed in his gear and tied them around the soldier's armpit and chest to hold the bandage on tightly. The soldier's face winced in pain but he made no sound.

"You're going be okay. I know it hurts like hell but let's get you back and get the medics working on it," he tried to reassure the soldier.

Bending down, he lifted the wounded soldier and placed him over his left shoulder like a sack of grain. With his right arm Kurt scooped up both of their G3s and the RPD. With this load he couldn't manoeuvre in the bush so he just bulldozed his way back to the road suffering the scratches, cuts and jabs of the briar and acacia thorns.

When they arrived back at the road, George and half of Fire Team Red had moved over to Team Blue's ambush position and a dozen weapons were trained on him as he emerged on to the road.

"Get the medic for this man; he has a serious wound," Kurt said, his voice harsh and barely audible from the hot dry air and lack of water.

The two nearest soldiers shouldered their weapons, relieved him of the wounded man and carried him to the far side of the road to shade. A small soldier of Portuguese descent rushed to the wounded soldier with his medical pack and began administering aid.

George looked at Kurt who was encrusted with dirt, debris and dried blood. George thought he looked like a bulldog that had just killed its opponent in a pit fight. No matter how torn up or injured the dog was, the only thing that mattered to it was winning. If Kurt had a tail, George knew it would be wagging now.

"Excellent job, but what the hell happened in there? You're not hit, are you?" George asked, pointing to the bush where he had just emerged.

"No. Wounded Cuban, followed blood trail in, was well hidden, shouldn't have taken the young guy in with me. Cuban had an RPD, shot him."

George noticed that Kurt's sitreps, or situation reports, were always delivered in a rapid-fire skeleton narrative devoid of adjectives and elaboration. He then told Kurt, "For our part we blew the mine under the front end of the supply truck. The claymores put the driver and two guards out of action and all we had to do was finish them off. The truck was carrying some ammo, mortar bombs and tinned provisions. We can use most of it. We are lucky the mortar shells weren't ignited. Our trucks are on their way to the pick-up point and will be here in ten or fifteen minutes. When they arrive, let's load up and get the hell out before a reaction force arrives. In the meantime, pull everyone back to rally point Bravo and put them in a defensive perimeter. We can't afford to be standing here with our peckers in our hands, gloating about what just happened."

The combat unit arrived back at the staging area on the south bank of the Congo River by late afternoon. Though considered 'safe' territory, they put out a loose defensive perimeter anyway, then ate and drank at leisure. A civilian fishing boat, covertly on contract to FNLA, was radioed and came over to pick up the wounded man and the prisoner. Everyone else waited until nightfall to move across the river in the tactical boats, to prevent undue attention.

⌘

In common with all victorious soldiers through the ages, a victory celebration was spontaneously planned. A large bonfire was built in the fire pit near the HQ building, and an impala and two young goats were put on spits and roasted over the flames. Local African beer, Portuguese wine and some hard liquor in the form of clear sugar cane distillate were distributed to the men. Fernandez confiscated all weapons and explosives from the participants and locked them in the HQ building prior to the celebration, except for George's and Kurt's handguns, which they kept on their belts.

The exhilaration from having survived such a dangerous mission was infectious, and the upbeat mood among all the participants was palpable. Both Kurt and George also knew it would go a long way to instil confidence in the new soldiers. Several soldiers who didn't participate in the mission were assigned to security posts on the perimeter of the camp. In addition to the roasted meats, traditional coarse bread baked in clay beehive-like ovens, thick cornmeal porridge and boiled vegetables were passed around in pots. Kurt thought it tasted better than anything he had ever eaten, with the exception of fresh Maine seafood, and even then it was a close call.

George seemed to be enjoying himself, within his puritan limitations, Kurt observed. He would indulge on occasion and have a drink or two, but never to excess. George was a strange and incongruous mix of conservative civil servant and ruthless warrior. Whatever shaped the personalities and destinies of men, be it inherited traits, environmental influences, or a combination of the two, the theory was severely tested in George. Most people could be pigeon-holed pretty quickly, some took longer and a few remained dauntingly enigmatic and challenged anyone to ever understand them. George was definitely in the last category, bestowing a subtle uniqueness that lay beyond his chiselled features glowing in the firelight.

George sat close to the fire, carving off singed pieces of antelope with the blade of a captured communist bayonet, with a refinement that might be displayed at a black tie function. The ivory grips of his 45 automatic glowing softly in the firelight

He turned and casually said to Kurt, "The boys are talking about you." George nodded his head toward another larger fire where the activities were becoming raucous. The words and shouting were unintelligible to Kurt because most were in Portuguese and African tribal dialects but he imagined the tales regarding the day's fighting were growing taller and more improbable with each swig from the bottle. A couple of the soldiers accompanied their renditions with pantomime, simulating crude re-enactments of what had transpired that day. These actions were always followed by either hearty endorsement of the play-acting by the others, or rapid condemnation and dismissal.

George, far from the casual observer, spent several years with the National Security Agency (NSA) as a linguist interpreting radio intercepts for up to 12 hours a day through static and frequency drift. Though appearing to be disinterested in the noisy chaos occurring nearby, he was assimilating all that was said and could probably have written it down, word for word, an hour later.

"You're the big hero, now," George said quietly. "I haven't heard that you can walk on water or spit grenades like melon seeds yet, but I expect that is coming."

"Oh, that's bullshit," Kurt blustered, embarrassed. "It was just an ambush and I fucked it up by taking that soldier with me and getting him wounded. I should have gone in alone."

"But you didn't, and I'll tell you why you didn't," George said.

"Oh, now I suppose you're a psychologist too, huh?" Kurt snapped.

"Yes I am, but that's beside the point," George replied.

"Look, Kurt, it's hard to see it from your perspective but others can see it right away. Most men have to train very hard and acquire much experience to become even adequate soldiers. Some never do and many are killed in the process. You on the other hand were born with this talent. Who can explain it? Soldiers want to emulate you, work with you, and hold you in some sort of awe. Don't you see that's an important part of this work?"

"That's all bullshit, George. How do you know all of this? Besides this time, I've only worked with you once before."

"That's true. I shouldn't tell you this but I'm going to anyway. You caused a big uproar when you walked into my camp in Long Theing. The other brass didn't know what the hell you were about. At the debriefings they put you through in Da Nang, some of those guys who looked like Intel weinies were doctors and psychiatrists who were flown in from Fitzsimmons Hospital in Colorado. At first they thought that you may be a collaborator or double agent of some kind but a review of the facts, and the testimony of men who were with you in the field, didn't support this. Absolutely no one believed that a lone man could pull off what you did, let alone survive to tell about it. Two years after it happened I managed to get a copy of the report through a contact. Their conclusion was that it was all true as far as they could determine, and you were just different, unlike anyone they had ever evaluated before."

"Well, it certainly is nice of them to share that with me," Kurt said sarcastically. "For years I've had to live with the stigma of traitor or wacko, when all I was trying to do was fight their war the best way I could."

"You know how the system works as well as I do," George replied. "It makes no provisions for the rights or feelings of an individual, only what's good for the system, whatever that may be at the time. Anyway, predictably the conclusion of the report was that you were a disruptive influence but were not criminally liable in any way. There was some talk of making you an instructor at the Special Warfare School in Fort Bragg but the nays won out because they didn't understand you. That's the sad reality, Kurt, but I'm glad you're here now. You are one hell of a gifted soldier and it is their loss."

"I appreciate the support and honesty, George, but I still burn when I think of the arrogance of those bastards."

"Get over it, there will always be bastards," George laughed.

"You're right as usual, George, but I think I prefer Cubans firing to my front, rather than my countrymen sticking in a knife from behind."

"Amen to that, brother."

George uncharacteristically took a long swig from a green bottle of cheap Portuguese wine.

⌘

There were several women, either from the local villages or from northern Angola, who had joined the soldiers at the other campfire. There was an occasional scream or loud shrill laugh as the drunken soldiers took turns grabbing or groping them. Aside from the expected rough behaviour, everyone seemed in good spirits.

One of the women, clothed only in a plain dark sack dress, slowly strode over to the smaller fire where Kurt, George and several of the officers and NCOs were seated. She was an African Portuguese mix. Her skin shone like burnished copper in the firelight and her thin dress material highlighted large breasts on her otherwise thin body. She was young, maybe eighteen or nineteen, with a pretty face and a shy smile.

She walked boldly in front of George and said something to him in Portuguese. Her speech was rapid, soft and melodic. George shook his head slowly and looked embarrassed. The girl turned at a slight angle, pointed to Kurt, and repeated the words. George also indicated 'no' to her a second time. The girl then laughed and said something loud enough so that it could be heard over at the other fire. The men surrounding the yellow flickering flames were all looking their way and, immediately after she made her statement, they burst into raucous laughter. The girl then left the small fire and walked back to the group of boisterous men, looking satisfied.

"What the hell was that all about?" Kurt asked. 'I really don't like being the butt of a joke told in a foreign language."

"They put her up to it. Probably gave her a handful of escudos," George said. "She asked if either of us wanted to screw her and I told her no. She said just as well, she'd heard that Americans had small ones that couldn't make a woman happy anyway."

Kurt stopped chewing and looked over at the men who were pointing, laughing and slapping each other in alcohol-induced glee.

"Ignore them. They are just having some fun at our expense, trying to bring us down a notch or two so they will feel more comfortable."

"That's a bunch of psycho babble, George. See it for what it is ... a challenge."

Kurt stood up and the laughter from the other fire died immediately.

"Sit down, Kurt, you'll either make a fool out of yourself or start a fight. You don't need either," George scolded, like a school teacher.

Kurt ignored George and all eyes were on him as he walked over to the larger fire. His features were only illuminated by random yellow pulses of the flickering flames.

"I seem to have missed the joke, would someone tell me what is so funny?" he asked the group.

Several of the soldiers furthest away still grinned furtively, as if the few extra feet of distance and intervening bodies conferred protection. Those nearest him were either stone-faced or looked at the ground. To be within an arm's reach of such an angry man was not comfortable. One of the NCOs that spoke English addressed him.

"We mean nothing by it, sir. We are just having some fun."

"I understand that, Sergeant, but it is never wise to make fun of what you don't know. Bring that girl over here," Kurt pointed at the girl.

She was led over by one of the men, reluctantly. She held her head back as if anticipating a blow from the American. Kurt tried to look directly into her eyes but they were turned away from him like a frightened puppy. He put out his hand and with strong fingers turned her face toward him and coyly smiled.

"Sergeant, tell her that the reason I turned her down was that I didn't want to hurt such a delicate flower with my huge American thing but, if she wants to have it, she knows where I will be."

The Sergeant translated and the whole group laughed uproariously. Even the girl's face broke into a coy smile when she knew it was only words she would be receiving. Kurt then put his arms around her shoulders and gently squeezed. Her body seemed like warm putty, and didn't resist at all. Kurt walked back and sat next to George again.

"Honour restored, my commandant," Kurt said quietly.

"Pretty smooth, I must say, for an enlisted sort. But what happens if she takes you up on your offer?" George asked.

"If, George?" Kurt sounded surprised. "I'm counting on it."

# CHAPTER 10
## ON WINGS

In the six weeks Kurt worked with the FNLA contingent, a total of eight more operational actions were carried out. These included two vehicular ambushes of Cuban and MPLA troops and supplies, a raid that was conducted on a small outpost that was overrun and destroyed, plus five sabotage missions, including mine laying and placement of demolition charges in a power substation supplying a northern province of Angola. From a strategic standpoint the combined effect of their efforts was minimal, but covert wars of this nature relied as much on propaganda value than on the actual impact to the enemy. The local and international press, waiting impatiently for anything to happen, jumped at the opportunity to report every incident. Holan Roberto in turn was happy to feed that fire, even if it meant exaggerating the truth to make the FNLA more newsworthy.

Favourable publicity was much sought after by all sides during a war but this also had a downside. As articles about the conflict appeared in the newspapers, magazines and electronic media around the world, volunteers were drawn to the cause. Additional manpower was always needed to flesh out an undermanned and struggling fighting force. The low level of military skill possessed by the local population required that much of that expertise come from the outside.

Because the world press began to publicize the previously unknown war in Angola, young men from all over the world who read the news accounts began to drift in. Their motivations included curiosity, wanting to prove their manhood, running away from the law, or seeking glory, adventure, or money. Unfortunately these were all the wrong reasons to fight in a dirty, thankless war. In the end, however, their intentions did not matter since possession of a warm body, the ability to fire a rifle, not to mention gullibility, were usually the only qualifications needed to sign up with one of the warring factions.

Men found their way from Europe and the US to Brazzaville and Kinshasa in ones and twos. One day a stocky swarthy man in his late 20s was brought to the camp and introduced as Colonel Cullen. His shifty eyes and seedy appearance set off Kurt's alarm bells. After Cullen left, Kurt spoke to George about the situation.

"If he is a colonel then I'm a major general. That guy is a nutcase with a violent streak; you can see it in his eyes. He'll be nothing but trouble, George."

"I don't disagree with you, Kurt, but Mr Roberto has given direction to hire any reasonable volunteer as long as they can march and carry a gun. He doesn't want to turn a capable soldier away. It's a lot like the French Foreign Legion. Why kill off local people and be subjected to all the political fallout, when you can hire foreigners whom nobody cares about? There is some method behind this madness."

"So we are going to hire and trust our lives to anyone who can piss and chew gum, but not necessarily at the same time," Kurt scoffed.

"Goddamn it Kurt, I have my orders and we need people. Like they say, beggars can't be choosers. If they aren't up to scratch when they get here, we'll have to train them."

"Yeah, and I've seen a troop of baboons howling around the camp you could train better and faster than some of the volunteers. It's dangerous George, we'll wind up with a gang bang on our hands," Kurt said.

"You know a Dan Gerhardt, ex-Special Forces?" George asked.

"I think so. He was in HALO school with me, I believe."

"He'll be coming tomorrow. Holen hired him in Kinshasa," George said.

"From what I remember, Dan was a decent sort of guy, kind of quiet, kept to himself. Well shit, looks like we are putting together a circus and we'll have to dress the clowns accordingly, and assign them rings."

Kurt scratched at his reddish-blond, unshaven facial growth. He was beginning to feel like he looked. Everything, including clothes, skin and equipment was becoming impregnated with the red ochre tinted African soil. Like all the other troops he'd begun to smell like a blend of fermented sweat, rations, smoke and gun oil. There was a growing comfort in the role he couldn't quite understand.

⌘

"So what are we going to do with this motley crew, George?" Kurt asked. "We can't keep nipping at the enemy's heels. That isn't going to amount to shit. I expect the boss wants some major victories to strengthen his political position."

George was unconsciously giving his thousand yard stare in the direction of the Congo River and Angola. The smoke from George's pipe rose vertically in the stillness. His silence was telling but when words came, they were direct.

"Holen wants us to take out a sizable fixed Cuban or MPLA base. I'll need your help on this one, Kurt. If we are to have any chance of success, we will need to make use of your reconnaissance skills." George didn't look at Kurt directly as he spoke.

"Hell, George, don't be so glum, that's what I do best. I thought you were going to ask me to train some more of those damn recruits. All I ask is for the freedom to do it my own way. Do you have any targets in mind?"

George puffed on his pipe and nodded.

"Holen is considering that question as we speak. I suspect we'll know something very soon. As politics are shifting so rapidly, time is of the essence. If the FNLA doesn't get some sizable victory under its belt, everyone will forget about us. It's a lot like an actress in Hollywood. If she isn't looking at her next picture she's looking at being a waitress."

"Well, that's a bit troubling. Using political directive for our actions instead of strategy spells big problems to me. When do you think this action will be conducted?" Kurt asked.

"Very soon," George replied. "The FNLA command and their backers are anxious, naturally."

"Well, we can get organization and planning underway for an assault, and when the word comes down we'll at least be prepared."

"That's what I had in mind," George said. "I'm going to put you in charge of target reconnaissance, I just wanted to let you know beforehand. I'll let you pick the troops to go along."

"Thanks, George. Don't worry, we'll make a big splash for the boss and try not to get our asses blown away in the process."

"Well, just do your best, Kurt. I really appreciate your participation. I'll see you in the morning."

George walked off, but smoke tendrils from his pipe lingered in the gathering dusk after he left, swirling in the little eddies and currents of warm and cool evening air before they finally disappeared.

⌘

Kurt lay in his bunk beneath the green gossamer of mosquito netting. The darkness was nearly total. The open windows of the concrete block building were covered by a coarse wire mesh to stop grenades from being thrown in. He was nearly asleep when the door creaked slightly and a figure entered. His hand grasped the nearby Tokarev but the movement was furtive, not aggressive. The light was too dim to discern objects, but other cues such as air movement and shadows told him the intruder was moving closer ... maybe a thief.

Instinctively, he placed his left arm across his head to protect it and pointed the pistol at the approaching figure. The intruder stopped near the bed and very gently lifted the mosquito netting on one side. Kurt knew who it was by her smell. A sweet odour coupled with a mysterious muskiness struck his nose and he relaxed his guard. Someone intent on violence or mayhem exudes a distinctive smell which assaults the nostrils.

He reached up and stroked her arm with his hand; it felt soft and delicate. Gently he drew her in and re-set the netting. She lay down beside him; her body rigid and her heart quivering like a frightened animal. To calm her, he took his fingertips and gently and slowly ran them over her silky-soft skin. After a minute or two her breathing slowed and her body relaxed, becoming soft and compliant.

Her fingers began to make small circles on his bare chest and abdomen, feeling the shape of his defined pectoral and abdominal muscles. Kurt lay absolutely still, focusing on this light, gentle touch which was so different from his recent harsh and brutal experiences.

The gentle touch brought forth images of other times and places. Floating underwater in a warm Florida spring in complete darkness, the water almost skin temperature, with no sensation except the small eddies of current caressing bare skin. Standing on the very peak of Mt Katadin in northern Maine watching the sunrise break on a glorious summer morning, chilled from the pre-dawn climb, the earth still and silent. Memories of sitting silently in a triple canopy forest after a late monsoon rain, listening to the drops of water cascade from leaf to leaf, then softly falling to the crumbling ground cover.

Now curious fingers worked, picking up tempo and shifting a little lower with each orbit, navel, then lower ... pausing. She inhaled sharply then let out a moan. The running partners of fear and pleasure took hold as she carefully explored her prize.

Kurt let her do what she wished, remaining passive, concentrating on the sensations whilst still alert to background sounds, his fingers still only a few inches from the pistol. He could feel the heat radiating from the girl as her skin flushed with mounting excitement. In the humid stillness this brought on a fine sheen of perspiration, which caught the very faint filtered light of the newly rising moon, making her skin glow like a satin ghost.

Her hands, fine boned and delicate, stroked and rubbed his scrotum, thighs and cock with a soft, light touch. The hardness of his body and the underlying power fascinated her, but it also made her fearful and indecisive, and she hesitated about what to do next.

Sensing this, Kurt rolled to the side and grasped her upper thighs and firm buttocks with his hands and slowly eased her on top of him. Her youthful body felt light and supple in his hands, which now pressed and stroked her more firmly as his desire rose. She readily complied with his direction and let out a long low moan as he entered her and began to slowly slide in. She remained still for a few moments and then began to move, at first almost imperceptibly, then with increasing speed as she accommodated him.

Her large breasts were swaying and vibrating with every movement. Kurt reached up and with thumb and forefinger felt her firm rubbery nipples, the tissue hardening and swelling at his touch. The girl's moans grew louder, her motions more extreme and erratic. With a forceful downward thrust she managed to envelop his entire length. Kurt felt warmth welling up, the tightness and movement making delay impossible.

He grasped her warm damp pelvis and held it still while he came. Unable to move her hips she thrashed back and forth like a dying creature, her breasts brushing against his chest. It had been a long time and in the past few weeks there had been little privacy or thought about such matters. The intensity was overwhelming, and the spasms seemed to go on and on, much longer than usual.

As he relaxed he could feel the girl's body, in full contact with his own, tremble and flutter. Her breath was rapid and raspy. She smelled erotically musky and pungent.

Slowly she slid off and curled next to him as her breathing slowed. In slow motion she reached a hand over and grabbed his soft wet cock, and gently milked it. Her hand moved down to massage his balls but stopped as sleep fast overcame her. Kurt fell asleep more slowly, becoming aware of the changes made by the moonlight and shadows that fell in the room. He dreamed of climbing a steep mountain, something he had never particularly liked. With each step up the slope he always slid back down the loose surface. The more effort he put in, the more he slid back, always ending up in the same place or losing ground. He awoke in a tense chill just before dawn.

Only half awake, the girl reached over for him but her hand only grasped air and the rough muslin sheet. She opened her eyes to an empty room. Only the smell lingered, a deep musky scent, similar to the den of a wild forest animal which was both frightening and exciting. Her nipples began to contract and harden with the thought, and she felt a cold trickle on her thigh and abdomen. Feeling both a sense of glowing serenity and awe at the sheer power of this man, she longingly wished he was still beside her.

⌘

The FNLA operational element stared intently at the sand model in front of them. It wasn't actually sand but fine powdery soil, once mud but since pulverized by vehicle tyres, people's feet and animal hooves. Eminently recyclable, the material would revert to mud again come the rains. A model of the selected target had been constructed from some old drawings and pictures, as well as the memories of two ex-Portuguese colonial army soldiers who had been there and were now members of the FNLA. Cubans and MPLA now occupied the Vista del Sol colonial military facility. The word had come down from Mr Holen Roberto that the FNLA military branch was to conduct a raid on the compound and the forces that occupied it as soon as possible.

There were uneasy feelings about such a rushed operation. Both George and Kurt were aware that political decisions translated into action always seemed to lead to a screw up, and they had no reason to believe this was an exception. Kurt made eye contact with George and nodded for him to follow. The pair walked into the bush surrounding the camp as the early morning sun cast long, surreal shadows on the dark green vegetation.

"Let me check it out first before we hit it," Kurt insisted. "Moving fast it will take me two days at most. You could be leading the troops into a big fucking ambush if anything has leaked. This thing has a bad smell to it already."

"I don't know if we can do that," George replied. "Holen's orders were explicit, he wants us to hit the base in forty-eight hours and twenty-four would be preferable."

"What's the basis for his decision, George? Why so quick?"

George shook his head as he tried to light up his pipe.

"Nobody ever tells us. It's probably a way of maintaining authority, a culture thing perhaps. It's just the way these things happen here. There also may be some intelligence source that he doesn't want exposed. All I know is that we are heading across the river and we are going to shoot this place up, like it or not."

"We have to drive most of the way to the target by vehicle," Kurt said. "It's too far to patrol, especially with the ordnance we need to pack."

"I know," George replied. "We'll have to use vehicles we can muster from across the river. Right now we can secure two Unimogs and a jeep with an MAG mounted on a floor pedestal. That will have to do unless more assets become available, which isn't likely. We need to move fast, get as close to the target as possible, hit them hard and get the hell out."

"That's all wishful thinking without tactical reconnaissance, George," Kurt offered. with concern in his voice. "More than likely the Cubans have already set up, or will set up, an ambush between Vista del Sol and the Congo River. On the whole they aren't very good troops but they're not total idiots. They aren't going to leave the road from Brazzaville open. They know we are here and if we blunder into them, they will eat our little raiding party for lunch."

"What are your thoughts then?" George asked.

"Ideally, we would have time to reconnoitre the target thoroughly before we put together the final plan but ... " Kurt was cut off in mid sentence.

"Big but ... we can't do it," George insisted. "We don't have anywhere near the time that would take."

"The only alternative then is to insert a recon element on the target, which will then link up the raiding force before the strike," Kurt said.

"What precisely do you mean?" George asked.

"A person or persons will have to be inserted near Vista del Sol and conduct a quick reconnaissance of the facility. After that is completed, they'll have to travel up the road to make sure that access to the target is clear, before linking up with the assault force some distance to the north. The assault force would then be briefed by reconnaissance prior to the final staging. This operation would take place on the fly and is very time critical, but it's better than heading blindly into a possible ambush."

Kurt stopped talking and kicked at a rock in the dust. The sun was now well above the horizon and its heat was palpable, like an oven door being opened.

"And who is going to conduct this reconnaissance, as if I have to ask?" George smirked.

Kurt just grinned back.

"You know it's my thing, George, I wouldn't want anyone else to do it. I don't like working with others on this type of mission anyway; they're too awkward and noisy."

"How do you intend to insert ... by boat?" George asked.

"That's a good point," Kurt said.

"When I was a guest in the FNLA headquarters in Brazzaville I saw some military free-fall parachutes in storage, looked like squares. Am I right?"

"Nothing gets by you, does it?" George replied. "The SEAL team brought them over when they airlifted the boats. Their team was going to do a training jump in the river, but they were recalled before they could organize it. I think the parachutes are camouflaged Cloud XLs and Triconical reserves. It's all first-class gear of course, nothing but the best for our navy friends."

"Then I won't feel bad using one," Kurt exclaimed. "You know in Vietnam I tried like hell to get a Stoner 23 rifle but couldn't, but the damn SEALS could get them with no problems. I figured the only way I was going to get a Stoner was to shoot a SEAL and take his, but that never happened because they never worked externally. I'm just kidding, George. Anyway, if I'm going to use the chute I have to get a ride. That will be the tough part."

Kurt stopped and stared at the morning sky. Beyond the ground haze the air was a glorious powder blue, cleansed by the vast Atlantic. That was the same water that lapped the rocky shores of Maine. How different these places were.

George stared at him curiously, "Watching birds, Kurt? I think I can get you a ride. With any luck you can jump out of a cargo jet."

⌘

George drove the Land Rover to a small building at the far end of the Brazzaville airport complex. The cinder block and tin single-storey structure was painted colonial tropical pink, surrounded by overgrown bougainvillea and some aggressive jungle creepers. On the wide tarmac in front of the structure sat a well-used DC-8 cargo aircraft. All of its doors and the rear bay were open and it looked like the big jet was under water due to the mirage hovering on the black runway. The small emblem of a flag Kurt didn't recognize was painted on the aircraft's tail and he nodded his head toward it.

George noticed and said, "Omani."

Kurt looked at him quizzically, "Arabs ... what the fuck?"

"You've heard of Liberian oil tankers haven't you?" George asked. "Any flag will do."

The jeep pulled up to the front door of the building. Stencilled above the door in an arch were the words 'Air Trans Africa'. An African soldier appeared from around the building and strolled toward them carrying an old .303 Enfield rifle slung muzzle down over his shoulder. His disinterest was palpable. He spoke first in French but when George answered in English the soldier switched languages.

"What is your business here, sirs?" The soldier asked.

"We have a meeting with Mr Malloy, Corporal," George replied, as he handed him a rolled-up ten-dollar American note.

"Ahhh ... very well, you can go." With that the soldier meandered off behind the building again. It was clear from the dried grass still on his back that he had a spot in the shade where he was lying down.

"I know it seems pathetic," George said, "but it's better off like this. They could be strip searching us everywhere we go."

George knocked on the sun-peeled door and a gruff voice from inside said, "Come in … it isn't locked."

The roar of an old window air-conditioning unit almost masked the voice. When they entered the building the air was so cool it almost took their breath away. A big red-faced man was lounging behind an old chipped wooden desk, cluttered with stacks of papers that looked like manifests, inventory lists, or some other paperwork. The man rose and extended a beefy paw to George.

"Nice to see you again, Yank," he said, when George grasped his hand.

"Jack, this is Kurt Christianson."

Jack looked Kurt up and down.

"I say … are you one of those otters or seals or whatever they call themselves?"

George laughed and turned to Kurt, "Mr Malloy has helped our navy boys move some gear around on a couple of occasions."

Kurt noted that the man spoke English with a strong accent he took to be South African.

"Mr Malloy is based at Salisbury, Rhodesia, but carries cargo to and from a variety of places. What do you call yourself, Jack … a sanctions buster?" George asked

"That's right," Jack said. "A modern day privateer if you will. I've just traded a Caravel for a DC-8 and there you have it. Say, do you blokes want a bottle of snake piss? I'm buying."

Jack held up a green bottle with a red and yellow label imprinted with a coiled green cobra, with its hood flared, ready to strike.

"It's the best beer brewed in Brazzaville and I'm taking several hundred cases down to Windhoek. Strangely, some of the folks down there have taken a liking to it."

"Don't mind if we do, Jack," George said, with Kurt nodding in agreement. "That's very hospitable of you."

Jack removed two bottles from a plain cardboard case sitting on a chair directly in front of the noisy air-conditioner, and opened them with a metal bottle opener lying on the desk. The beer was cool but not cold. Kurt thought it had a heavy body, more like malt liquor than beer but, in the circumstances, it was just fine.

Jack sat heavily on the desk and looked from one man to the other.

"So what can I do for you blokes? Got some cargo I can expedite?"

George folded his arms and scratched his chin as he often did when he was thinking of the best way to phrase a difficult question.

"My request is a little different this time, Jack. We need a man delivered to the Angolan coast and the best option seems to be by air."

Jack took a swig of his Cobra and waited for more, but George was silent.

"Go on," Jack finally said.

"I trust you with this, Jack, because I know you Rhodesians are fighting the same battle we are."

"One man dropped by parachute?" Jack said. 'That's not much of an attack force."

"It's more of a reconnaissance mission," George explained. "Intelligence gathering, you know. The other option is by sea but because of time constraints that's not practical."

"When do you want to do this?" Jack asked.

"We'd like to leave as soon as possible," George replied.

"Well, like I said, I'm flying the DC-8 to Windhoek tomorrow afternoon on a regular cargo run after we pull some maintenance and load up. Let's look at a map."

Jack pulled a detailed flight map out of the top drawer of his desk.

"I've avoided flying over Angolan airspace since the political unrest began. They have a few old rust bucket Mig-17s and one or two 19s they like to put up occasionally to scare foreign aircraft. They haven't shot a commercial flight down yet, but it's just a matter of time before the silly bastards do. If they thought a transport was supporting aggressors, I don't think they would hesitate to blow it out of the sky."

Jack pointed to a pencilled line drawn on his air navigation map.

"Currently, I take off from Brazzaville and follow the north bank of the Congo out over the Atlantic and then vector south, notify Luanda control, then stay at least twelve miles out and parallel to the coast. I usually prefer twenty miles. That way there are no surprises and they can watch me on their radar the whole way down. If I got closer they might get nervous and launch a Mig or two to take a look. I don't think this route would do a parachutist much good unless you wanted to swim like a fish in that bloody cold water."

Kurt stepped forward and traced a path on the map with his finger before speaking.

"I don't know, maybe. What altitude are you at when you're ... here?"

Kurt pointed to a spot on the flight path that was just south of the coastal town of Vista del Sol where the Cuban and MPLA military base was located.

"Oh, about twenty to twenty-two thousand, but altitude's not critical unless there is other traffic in the vicinity, which there usually isn't."

"So you might be able to go a little higher, say twenty-four to twenty-six thousand at this location and hug the twelve mile line?" Kurt asked.

"I don't see a problem there," Jack told him.

"Remember we would have to keep the cargo bay depressurized until you jumped, so you will need oxygen. I have oxygen masks on-board but if you removed it at that altitude, you won't stay conscious very long."

Kurt nodded thoughtfully.

"If I can take a few hits on the way up I'll be okay. I've jumped from twenty-four thousand before without oxygen and after I jump, I'll drop to breathable atmosphere pretty quickly."

"That sounds reasonable," Jack agreed. "You show me your release point and I can switch the light beside the loading door from red to green when we arrive. My crew chief, Jeffrey Cooke, would be with you until the drop; afterwards I can re-pressurize the cargo bay. The crew chief will also be wearing an oxygen mask. If you black out or anything, he will be able to handle the situation."

Jack stopped talking and looked at both men. His face reflected a calm, business-like demeanour.

George scratched at his hair; he seemed uncomfortable.

"As far as payment... "

Jack halted him mid-sentence by holding out his right arm, palm facing George.

"There are only two things that motivate me. Unfortunately money isn't one of them. As you may know I was a Spitfire pilot in World War Two. I flew in the same squadron as the Rhodesian Prime Minister himself ... I'm pleased to say. We shot down some Me109s, Dorniers, Henkiels and also lost a lot of good friends, but I wouldn't have missed it for the world. I still think about it every day and have for over thirty-five years now. Flying these lorries with wings is a living but it's far from exciting. Looking at young Kurt here, willing to risk his neck parachuting into a hostile war zone, makes me feel young again and a part of me wants to go with him. I'm too old and fat for that, but I'm glad to do whatever I can to help."

Jack took a long swallow from his green serpentine bottle, finishing it off. He sat the empty down on the top of the old cluttered desk. Kurt looked at the bottle. The cobra on the label stared directly at him with unblinking, ruby red eyes.

"The other thing is," Jack spoke again, "we all must do whatever we can to stop those communist devils. If they are successful in Angola, they will use that country as a platform to launch attacks all across Southern Africa. I don't know, maybe it's inevitable, but I just can't believe the whole world is going to sit idly by and let it happen. The Huns seemed pretty dammed indestructible in 1939 too. Well, I've said my piece; the ride is on me, no charge."

"Speaking of wars and all, how are things going in Rhodesia, Jack?" George asked.

Jack looked at him with a serious expression and spoke in a lowered voice, "I can't say exactly but, from what I hear, the guerrillas are infiltrating deeper into the country. Nothing big scale as yet, although the farmers are definitely feeling the pressure, and the odds are it's definitely going to get worse before it gets better. It's the nature of these things. Look at Malaya. The boys chased the insurgents down and dealt with them, but it was like catching fish in the sea. You get some of them and that looks good and makes you feel good, but you can never get them all."

Jack made a move to get another beer but abandoned his action in mid-stride. He self-consciously patted his belly. He turned to George and Kurt again and switched subjects.

"So, if we are leaving tomorrow afternoon for a drop at six in the evening, you need to be aboard the aircraft by three thirty. A cargo truck will be coming from the warehouse to load the aircraft at that time. Dress in work overalls and pack your gear in a couple of wooden canned fish boxes that we will provide. Customs people are watching our operations and they do a quick inspection before we leave. They won't be suspicious if everything looks normal. When you get aboard just come forward and sit in the engineer's seat in the cockpit until we are underway. Do either of you have any questions?"

George and Kurt looked at each other and shook their heads.

"One more thing," Jack added. "You will probably be packing weapons and grenades or whatever. Please have the guns unloaded and everything else very well secured. A stray round through my fuel tank would cause me a bit of concern. I do miss the war but I've definitely outgrown the need to pilot a burning aircraft."

"Don't worry, sir. I'll need every round I can carry when I get on the ground, no need to squander it elsewhere," Kurt said with a half grin.

Jack laughed and got up from the table.

"Well, there we have it then. If you two will excuse me, I have to make out some manifests or we will never get off the ground tomorrow. Show up midday at the warehouse in town; you know where it is George, you've been there before, so we can well ... box up your luggage."

"Thanks a lot, Jack, see you tomorrow," George waved behind him as they headed for the door.

⌘

They drove into town where the local populace was stirring again after taking an afternoon break from the intense heat of early afternoon. After parking and strolling around to check if anyone was tailing them, they stopped at another outdoor café. George ordered a local beer and a plate of cold pickled fish. Kurt thought that a bit risky and ordered bottled sparkling water and a well-cooked steak. Any gastric upset tomorrow would not be welcome. He wanted no more complications for the mission.

"You know, George, it's only the night before a mission that the world comes into focus."

"How do you mean?"

George was attempting to separate the fine fish bones from the flesh, and having some trouble. He carefully bit into a piece and quizzically chewed it before reaching in and pulling out the offending sliver of bone. Then he repeated it twice before he was confident he could swallow the mouthful.

"If you get one of those bones stuck in your throat, you'll regret it," Kurt chided.

"What I mean is, I can feel everything so intensely. The lights, the smells, I get what I call a giddy sensation in my throat, it tightens up and tickles at the same time ... you know."

George looked at him with uplifted eyes.

"No, I don't know what you mean."

"You will if you get one of those bones stuck," Kurt parried.

"You're an adrenaline junkie, Kurt." George pushed his partially eaten fish to one side.

"You mean like a drug addict or something? No, I live healthily, or try to under the circumstances."

"Well, partially," George wiped his mouth on a napkin. "When most people are scared they go to shit. Good soldiers learn to cope with it. Intense training and simulating combat puts a lid on their anxiety for awhile, but it's still there. But you, you suck it up like a sponge, you love it, revel in it. The only time you feel really alive is when you are in mortal danger and your adrenals are pumping hormones into your blood. Everything else is just grey to you, isn't it?"

"So is this Mr Psychologist talking, or should I say, Dr Barlow?" Kurt asked.

George shook his head as if dismissing the sarcasm.

"It's not all that uncommon; football players, racing car drivers, skydivers, a lot of them live for the rush. That's why they choose to do those things. You fit that profile exactly; it's just that you've chosen a game that plays for keeps every time you do it."

"You're probably right again, George, but you know what?"

"What?"

"God help me, but I love it!" Kurt said, too loudly.

George remembered the phrase they all used to shout in Special Forces training. They yelled it when everything seemed hopeless, or when they were impossibly tired and hungry, or they had to walk another twenty clicks with packs at night in the mountains. It might as well have been the rallying cry of Saint Jude, the patron of lost causes.

"That's my boy," George said, grinning. "Let's kick some ass over there."

⌘

When they arrived back at the FNLA base camp that afternoon, George said, "I've got a surprise for you Kurt, let's go over to HQ."

Once inside the office, George shut the door and pulled what looked like a metal footlocker from the corner of the room.

Opening the lid revealed equipment fitted neatly in nested spaces.

"What do you have there, George?" Kurt asked, peering at the polished metal.

"Some toys I think you'll like," George responded. "When the SEALS came down they brought with them some equipment I requested. Originally, I ordered two dozen of these but we only received two. The government in their infinite wisdom ... I won't go on. Anyway, this box contains a new model FNC .223 folding stock carbine with twenty magazines and special hollow point ammo."

"Goddamn, I heard rumours that they were going to make a smaller version of the FN rifle. So this is it, huh? Cool."

"And that's not all," George continued, "also in here is a modified Browning 9mm with a removable Military Armaments Corporation suppressor. The silencer is screw on and comes with six thirteen round magazines of 147 grain sub sonic ammo. It's whisper quiet. Both weapons are sterile; they have no serial numbers or markings. There is also a set of compact FM voice scrambling radios in the box, much lighter than the PRC-25s we're using now. Their range is limited to five or six miles but they'll be useful for the link up we're planning."

"You've been holding out on me, George. You had this stuff all along."

"Yeah," George admitted reluctantly, "but because there were only two, the other troops would whine about favouritism if anyone else got one. Anyway Kurt, *you* could use a muzzleloader and still be deadly with it, but I thought given the mission, you might need them now."

"Thanks, George, and there's still enough light to test fire them."

⌘

The team leaders were briefed in the operations area by lantern light until the small hours of the morning. Based on the best geodetic and geographic maps they could obtain, Kurt picked out RVs, or rendezvous areas, near the target that looked like they might have reasonable cover, and were in close proximity to the planned route of approach.

After parachuting in south of the target, Kurt would make a reconnaissance of Vista del Sol, then move north and link up with the assault force at one of the selected RVs. Because it was difficult to anticipate the timing of either party, or the fact that one or more of the RVs may be unsuitable, flexibility had to be built into the plan.

If no link-up occurred at RV#1, which was closest to the target, Kurt would make his way to RV#2 and so forth, until link up occurred, or they were close enough to use the scrambled radio sets. The plan seemed acceptable to George, who added some details before giving it his stamp of approval.

"When we link up or establish voice communications, I will give my recommendation for go or no-go and how we should implement the plan, based on what I've seen. Is everyone okay with this?" Kurt asked.

All parties indicated their agreement.

"I recommend that the assault party carry as many weapons and as much ammunition as possible," Kurt continued. "There will be no re-supply if things go to hell, and we can't rely on captured weapons or ordinance. Even if compromised, the assault party has a good chance of blasting its way out if it stays tight, and has enough firepower."

George scowled at the map, and cocked his head sideways, as if something was misaligned. He directed his next question to Kurt.

"So your contingency is, if we don't link up with you or establish voice communications, we abort?"

"That's up to you, boss. If neither occurs you can assume I'm out of the picture, for whatever reason. You can decide then, either go forward with the assault, or go to plan B and head for home."

George lit his pipe again; it kept going out in the damp environment.

"You know a hell of a lot is riding on your performance, and you will have no one to blame but yourself if things go south. It's primarily your plan." When George spoke, he looked through upturned eyes. The soft tissues around the orbits were dark, like they were bruised.

"Enough of the pessimism, George," Kurt said. "With a little luck we can pull this off, but surprise and firepower are our only assets in this case. If the enemy is tipped off and is waiting for us, we are screwed ... period. If there is even a hint of a security breach, abort the damn thing. I can find my way back okay, so don't risk anyone's safety for me." The members of the group went over the plan in detail once more. Kurt would have two days to recce the target then meet up with the assault force. Then they would finalize the plan of attack, incorporating Kurt's latest information, and move on Vista del Sol, hitting it in the early hours, when unsuspecting troops are traditionally at their lowest state of alert.

George finally addressed the cadre when the briefing ended.

"We have our manpower, equipment needs and tactical planning addressed. Consider this the mission warning order. I will draft a standard five-paragraph field order in the morning and we will read it to all participants just prior to isolation tomorrow. Are there any final questions?"

All was quiet.

"Okay everyone, thank you and try to get a good night's sleep. It will be your last chance for a while."

⌘

Kurt slowly walked to his sleeping quarters. The outline of a figure floated in the shadows near the building. If not for the movement, the shape would have blended in perfectly with the soft shadow and vegetation hugging the darkened walls. When he stopped walking the figure approached, head bowed shyly. She wore the same type of one-piece dress as before but of a lighter floral print. Still barefoot, her hair was now pulled back and tied with a piece of twine: and the fragrance of flower-scented cologne followed her. Slowly she raised her head and looked him directly in the eyes. Hers were dark placid pools.

"What are you doing here so late, you should be sleeping," he whispered.

"I ... I was waiting to see you," She replied with a melodious softness that harmonized perfectly with the night air and subtle stirrings of the surrounding jungle. Her English was a seductive blend of Portuguese and tribal intonations.

"You must have been waiting here for hours?" His voice had an edge or concern, or perhaps irritation, he didn't know which, but her absolute patience somehow bothered him.

"It is all right, I wanted to see you." Her reply was so deceptively simple it was confusing at first. He was coming to realize that African thinking was very different from his own. A Western woman would have long since given up or been seething if made to wait so long, but in Africa nothing is achieved easily. Patience and persistence are seldom rewarded, and sacrifices are borne without complaint. It is a culture where few results are expected, even after monumental effort is expended.

Kurt glanced around cautiously then motioned with his head for her to follow him inside. Once in the room she shrugged off her dress and let it fall around her feet. Her flesh felt like warm butter in his hands, and that too seemed to blend with the dark softness of the tropical night.

⌘

George drove Kurt to the Air Trans Africa shipping warehouse in the heat of midday. The Navy Cloud XL parachute had been carefully repacked that morning in the hallway of the FNLA headquarters building. The packing tags on the reserve were current so they left it alone, trusting a Navy rigger in Virginia Beach to have done his job properly. The parachute backpack assembly was placed in a wooden fruit box and nailed shut; the combat gear was stowed in a similar box. Kurt donned a set of old workman's coveralls provided by ATA. They were worn through on the right knee and the armpits had a pungent odour, courtesy of the previous wearer.

The delivery truck finished loading at the warehouse at about one o'clock. Saying farewell to George, Kurt climbed into the cab with the driver and the truck wound its way to the airfield amidst the bicycles, pedestrians and pushcarts. Once they arrived at the airfield and began to unload, the ATA loadmaster checked off items from his manifest which included tinned fish, beer, fruit, canned meat and tanned hides. The cargo was then carried up the ramp of the aircraft by labourers and secured with straps in the hold. Without prompting, Kurt carried his two boxes forward, secured them to the floor near the forward bulkhead, then went through to the cockpit and sat in the flight engineer's seat as instructed.

External auxiliary power was already connected, so the aircraft ventilation and cooling systems were running. This kept the temperature in the cockpit bearable, but it was still very hot due to the greenhouse effect of the sun through the windscreen. In the sweaty stillness the borrowed overalls began to reek even more, so he wriggled out of them, crumpled the tattered cloth suit into a ball and jammed it under the seat. The smell would probably make the real flight engineer wonder about his own hygiene, until he discovered the source. Kurt was clothed in nothing more than a pair of military green shorts, a worn grey t-shirt, and a pair of FNLA issued Bata smooth soled anti-tracking tennis shoes, but it was more than enough cover in the heat.

An hour later, loading noises from the back of the DC-8 ceased, and the truck drove away. Shortly thereafter the sharp footsteps of what he assumed were customs officials checking the cargo were heard. From the noises made they were poking, prodding and sometimes kicking but not opening any of the boxes or crates. In other words they were going through the motions, each with crisp one hundred dollar US currency notes in their shirt pockets. Kurt didn't stick his head out to look down the cargo bay but it probably wouldn't have made any difference. In a few minutes the footsteps departed down the loading ramp and the aircraft was quiet, except for the external generator and hum of the air handling system.

Kurt then heard a single set of light footsteps and the crew chief, Jeffrey Cooke, appeared with a sweating litre bottle of Coke and a paper bag clutched in his hands.

"Reckoned you'd be a mite thirsty waiting up here, mate," Jeffrey was about thirty years of age, trim, sharp and spoke with a soft Cockney accent. Kurt took him for an ex-member of the British military.

"I don't care what Jack says about you, I think you're a saint," Kurt joked as he relieved him of the bottle.

"Well, compared to old Jack, I am a saint," Jeffrey laughed. "That man is the biggest outlaw on the African continent, but I worship the ground 'e walks on, he's just that sort of bloke. Don't worry, 'e filled me in on what's going on wiv you. When I was wiv the RAF I worked wiv SAS more than a few times, so I've got yer covered. I've never dropped anyone solo, though. You must either be brain damaged or have balls as big as a Cape buffalo's to go it alone, but ... that's not my concern." He put up his hand in the universal sign of indifference.

"I brought yer some sandwiches, didn't think you'd eaten in a while," Jeffrey threw a brown bag towards Kurt, which landed on the cockpit floor.

Kurt looked down at the bag lying at his feet but made no attempt to retrieve it.

"They aren't cucumber, are they? I've heard rumours about what the British have done to sandwiches ... and it's a mortal crime."

"Well, ain't we the fussy one?" Jeffrey shot back. "Layin' up 'ere in yer skivvies, starving to death, and ya' complain about my sandwiches. The trouble wiv you Yanks is you 'ave no breeding, or sense of appreciation."

Kurt picked up the bag and carefully peeked inside as if something was going to fly out at him.

"Breeding, hell, you're wrong there, we breed a lot, that's why there are so many of us."

"See wot I mean? Yer just confirmin' what I said, and there's no cucumber sandwiches in there, mate ... they're Marmite."

Kurt sniffed the bag contents and looked up.

"I don't know what that is, but it sure smells funny."

⌘

Long shadows were growing on the tarmac when Jack and his co-pilot entered the aircraft and took their positions in the cockpit.

"Sorry about the long wait, lad, but I wanted to get you in before customs inspected the cargo. Sometimes they sit across the airfield and make sure nothing else is loaded. Mostly they are decent chaps but they don't like to be made fools of."

Jack's face then became serious.

"All right, listen to me," Jack continued. "I have to pressurize the cockpit but we are going to leave the cargo hold un-pressurized until you are dropped. It's going to be cold in there but you won't be at altitude for long before we arrive at the release point. I'll keep her low; about twelve thousand feet until we are ten minutes out, then I'll rapidly climb to twenty-four thousand. You and Jeffrey both have oxygen masks. The climb to final altitude will be your warning. Jeffrey will open the starboard-bay side door six minutes out. Over the intercom I will give the signal to go and the light over the door will also switch from red to green. Exit vigorously and don't get hung up on my aircraft. We have no winch to pull you back in; if you get towed we will have to cut you loose, conscious or unconscious. Do you have an automatic opener on that chute?

"They are built into the chutes, sir," Kurt told him, "but I have disabled the system. I've never trusted automatic openers and I have no idea when these were last checked and calibrated."

"Glad to hear that," Jack said. "If one of those blows prematurely the chute can snake out of the door and could take down an aircraft. I don't know if that's ever happened to a DC-8, but I sure don't want to be the first. Jeffrey checked the oxygen system this morning and each of you has a full bottle. At altitude, that should last you half an hour or more, which should be sufficient for our purposes. We don't plan to be at altitude in a depressurized state for more than fifteen or twenty minutes before we return to normal."

Jack pulled a worn air navigation map from the side pocket of his flight overalls, unfolded the map, and put his finger on a point along the intended flight path.

"We are going to release you here?"

Kurt nodded to confirm the location.

No mark was made on the map. If, for some reason, the aircraft had to make an unscheduled landing and Jack was detained for questioning, it might be difficult to explain. Kurt went to the back, grabbed a crow bar from the tool box and peeled the lid off one of his secured boxes. He fished out his tactical map and folded it so only the coast was exposed.

"Confirm that the coastal wind will push me towards shore this time of day?" Kurt asked.

"Right," Jack looked up at him. "Offshore winds are pretty dominant in this area around sunset. The sun heats up the air over the land during the day but, because the air is usually very dry and clear, it cools off rapidly at dusk. The air mass over land contracts and the breeze from the ocean rushes in to fill the void. You will probably only notice it below five thousand feet, but then count on say … ten to fifteen knots at most."

"I'm counting on it," Kurt said. "I'll need it to push me inland; otherwise I may have to swim, and that won't be any fun with the gear I'm carrying."

"I would take you closer in to shore but Luanda might get spooked and launch an interception. I'll do my best," Jack told him.

Kurt extended his hand toward the veteran pilot.

"Thanks, Jack, in advance. I appreciate the risk you are taking."

"And thank you lad, for fighting the war against this pestilence. Remember, if things don't work out here or you feel like a change, Rhodesia would welcome you. I personally know most of the senior military officers, including Kenneth Wallis, Bernard Hicks, and Reed Donovan. I'd be glad to put in a good word for you any time. Take care of yourself, son."

With that Kurt turned and moved into the cargo hold of the aircraft. Jeffrey shut the connecting door, and with a soft hissing the cockpit was sealed off and pressurization initiated on the other side.

Kurt and Jeffrey finished unloading the two boxes of gear. The first box contained combat equipment Kurt would carry on the jump. Most of it had been scrounged from the supplies the SEALS left behind during their training mission. Included were black battle dress shirt and trousers, and a new ALICE rig which was the US military's latest rucksack made of light weight aluminium and nylon. Civilian hikers and backpackers had been using comparable equipment for years, but the government's glacier-slow evaluation and procurement system was just getting around to issuing them to the military. Kurt thought fleetingly that this ALICE rig was the first of its type ever to be used in combat, and no one would know.

The FNC .223 carbine George had given him had its stock folded and was placed in a green canvas drop bag. The drop bag was an old piece of gear probably dating from WWII or Korea and used for jumping with M1 carbines, but it fitted the FNC just fine. The Browning 9mm pistol was also in a green canvas flap holster that buckled shut. He would wear the pistol, without its screw-on suppressor, so he could access it if need be while still under canopy. The rifle would have to remain in its case until after landing.

The ALICE rig was hooked up with an 'H' harness which wrapped around the backpack leaving two clips on the top. A fifteen foot long 'lowering line' was then attached to the clips and Z folded on the frame of the ALICE rig with rubber bands. The other end of the line would be tied to Kurt's parachute harness. When in the air, the rucksack would be held snugly against his thighs with thin break-cord. Just before hitting the ground quick releases would be pulled and the rucksack would drop fifteen feet. This would do two things. At night it would give a warning of about one second when the rucksack struck the ground before the jumper did. It would also prevent the jumper's legs from being entangled with the rucksack and being twisted or broken on landing.

The drop case containing the FNC would be tied along his left side just behind the armpit. The last thing that would go on was a compact inflatable life vest the SEAL team was kind enough to leave behind.

The idling engines of the big jet suddenly roared and the cargo bay shook. Both men sat down on boxes and braced themselves during takeoff. They should be strapped in but, in the circumstances, thought that precaution was unnecessary. Jeffrey grabbed a headset hanging on the wall and put it on. He listened intently for a few seconds then looked up at Kurt, giving him the thumbs up sign. This meant that the main tower had just given clearance for the aircraft to taxi and they would be taking off shortly. A few moments later Jack wheeled the plane around and gave it full throttle. With a surge the four-engine DC-8 sped down the tarmac.

The two men had no windows in the cargo bay and had to rely on the movement and G-forces acting on their bodies to feel what was happening. Dim lights over the external door and on the ceiling of the bay were their only sources of illumination. The aircraft picked up speed and rotated off the runway with a leap. Rough travel over the chewed-up tarmac transformed into smoothness, but the roar of the engines and associated vibration were deafening. Unlike a civilian airliner, the DC-8 cargo version was stripped of all non-essential weight, including insulation that served to dampen the engine noise.

Kurt sprang to his feet and began suiting up. They were about twenty minutes from the target and there would be no second passes. This mission depended on his ability to jump from a cargo jet over the ocean at almost five miles altitude, land undetected in hostile territory, infiltrate the enemy position, gather essential intelligence, then find and brief the raiding party. Missing the jump window would blow it all.

Fortunately, Jeffrey had previous experience with parachute jumpers and was able to help him get into the tandem rig parachute, secure the webbing and correctly arrange the equipment. Working together they were done in less than ten minutes. The cooler air at higher altitude felt wonderful on their skins. The perspiration that had saturated their clothing was now drying before their eyes, leaving a white dusting of salt. The DC-8 was now at twelve thousand feet, just leaving the mouth of the Congo River and on the way to Namibia over the South Atlantic.

A minute later the aircraft banked to the left and began to climb sharply, which caused their ears to pop. Both men pulled down and put on the oxygen masks that were hanging from the ceiling of the bay. Holding up his left hand full of fingers and the index from his right, the crew chief gave his lone paratrooper the sign for six minutes out. Jeffrey then moved to the starboard door and tied his harness to thick nylon webbing which was belayed to a connector on the exposed frame, thus shortening the line to prevent the possibility of falling out of the door. With no one to help, he would be beaten to death on the side of the aircraft or freeze in the wind, whichever came first.

Jeffrey spun his finger around, indicating for Kurt to turn for one last check of straps and equipment. Kurt complied and felt some tugging and pulling before a stinging slap on the cheek of his ass, a jumpmaster signal for, 'You are ready'.

Jeffrey slowly opened the starboard door by pulling the internal handles down and back. As the door opened the noise and wind were violent. Jack had throttled the engines back as much as possible, but the DC-8 had to keep airspeed of at least two hundred and sixty knots to maintain altitude.

Light from the open door was intense even though the sun was nearly touching the horizon of the vast blue Atlantic through a haze of mist that hugged the surface. Looking out of the open door there was only ocean to be seen. Kurt was trusting Jack to release him at the right place. If he landed even a little too far out, he would not be able to swim to shore in this cold water, even with a life vest. The ocean was flowing north from Antarctic waters and the current was strong, cold and running parallel to the coastline.

Jeffrey had his right hand pressed against the headset in order to hear Jack's voice above the din of the wind swirling through the open door. Kurt stood with his toes hanging into space and grabbed the edge of the door. The fifteen-degree aluminium felt numbingly cold, even through thin leather gloves.

Leaning out and looking down and forward, he was looking at the inboard turbo-jet engine blasting a trail of hot gas. His exit would take him through its turbulence momentarily. Mentally, he talked himself through the exit sequence and how he would have to stabilize and slow down, before deploying his square canopy parachute.

Jeffrey looked at him and gave final thumbs up, meaning the drop would be momentary.

Kurt lowered himself into a semi-squatting position and placed his right foot halfway out of the door, hands gripping both sides of the door frame. The crew chief swept his hand across his body and dramatically pointed out of the door. Kurt sprang into the rarefied blue air, using his legs to power the leap and his arms as a guide to hurl his body into space.

# CHAPTER 11
## TRAPPED

Kurt leapt from the door of the DC-8 and spun 180 degrees to the right, legs drawn up with the front-mounted rucksack clasped firmly between his hands. Now facing to the rear, his back was struck by the full force of the five hundred kilometre-per-hour wind and jet exhaust. This move was necessary to slow his forward velocity prior to opening the main parachute canopy. If the chute was deployed at too high a speed, it would be shredded or damaged. The rig had a built-in reserve chute but now, twenty kilometres out over the North Atlantic, only a functioning main square canopy could fly him safely to land.

"One thousand, two thousand," his body held tightly he counted out loud as taught in jump school, "three thousand," this way of counting slowed down the time rush, "four thousand," so the parachute wasn't opened too quickly, "five thousand." Turn!

Now slowed somewhat, he arched his body, spread his arms and legs and pushed his stomach out. The manoeuvre caused the airflow to turn him around. Now facing forward with limbs spread widely, his air speed began to diminish quickly. Looking up, he saw the retreating form of the DC-8, the setting sun lighting up water vapour contrails from the jet engines. The fast moving air roared past his ears and pushed against his body like a giant invisible hand.

His body began to stabilize and rotate to face earth. He needed to deploy the parachute as quickly as possible. Every second delayed meant another seventy metres falling straight down towards the cold ocean. He glanced down at his parachute harness for the rip cord ... it wasn't there.

Damn ... he forgot ... the SEALS blackened even the shiny chrome handle making it hard to see. Grab for it ... pull.

The canopy opening sounded like a dozen bed sheets in a windstorm. The tremendous force of deceleration jerked his harness violently as his decent was slowed from two-hundred and seventy kilometres-per-hour to twenty-five. The huge rectangular nylon wing then began to fly as it was designed, accelerating to fifty kilometres-per-hour forward speed.

Looking up, the black inflated cells of the Cloud XL nearly blotted out the sky. He reached up on the front suspension risers and grasped the steering toggles from their elastic keepers and pulled down on the left toggle until he faced directly towards the nearest shore. He would have to reach land in the eighteen minutes he'd have under canopy, but it looked so distant ... too distant.

The Angolan coastline was cast in tones of dark green, brown and tan, stretching infinitely in both directions beyond the bluish-green Atlantic below. The land and sea were separated by a thin light ribbon of surf froth and beach sand. Inland, barely discernible tendrils of smoke from cooking fires snaked upwards, but air movement merged the spaghetti-like wisps into a thin layer of haze that hugged the dark vegetation.

Kurt carefully steered the canopy directly for the closest landfall. With the parachute's forward speed of fifty kilometres-per-hour, a touchdown on land didn't look promising. Noting the altimeter and angle of approach, he estimated impact nearly a kilometre out to sea. Swimming that distance was possible, but he would have to ditch the heavy equipment, which would make his situation even more precarious once ashore. The predicted ground wind would have to materialize if there was to be any prospect of making dry land.

As anticipated, this section of Angola looked very sparsely populated. Aside from a few fires from the native kralls buried in the thick bush, there was little sign of habitation except for a dirt road that snaked between the beach sand and the tree line. Scanning up and down the length of the coastal road, no vehicles or dust plumes were visible.

The sun had not yet set judging by the slight warmth on his back. However, in the few minutes since the parachute had opened, the scene below had become rapidly enveloped in shadow as the sun began to sink. The dust-free air over the Atlantic prevented a lingering twilight, so nightfall would happen very suddenly.

Breathing became easier as the altimeter needle passed through the ten thousand feet mark. The air was also warmer and contained the smells of dust, salt spray, vegetation and fires, absent at higher altitude. The hissing of the surf piling up on the sandy beach became louder, as did the hum of the wind through the nylon suspension lines and rustle of the nylon wing as it changed shape in response to the denser air.

As time passed and his altitude diminished, Kurt became increasingly concerned about a landing location, imagining the struggle of releasing himself from a parachute harness upon hitting the water. However, another rough estimation of his speed, relative to the water's surface, now indicated he was moving faster than before. A strong evening sea breeze must be pushing him towards the shore. If this persisted, reaching land should be possible.

Selecting a landing area became imperative, as the rapid descent in altitude brought with it darkness. In the few minutes since last looking at the ocean below, individual waves were no longer visible. The ocean was now a continuous dark green but the breakers on the shore ahead looked like white foam, almost luminous in relation to the rest of the scene.

Ninety seconds later the dark square parachute and its suspended cargo glided over the beach at an altitude of two hundred and fifty metres. Thanks to the onshore wind, there would be no splash down, but a suitable landing area on shore was still not apparent. From the air, little could be seen except the surf, the light beach sand and the faintly visible dirt road running almost parallel to it. If this were a sport jump Kurt calculated he would cross the shore, make a sharp 180 degree turn, then with the wind in his face, brake the canopy and set down gently in the soft sand just behind the breakers. However, despite the quiet thus far, landing in such an exposed area might result in being seen and quickly compromised.

With no better landing area apparent, he glided for the cover of some indistinct low bush several hundred yards behind the beach. Just prior to landing, while passing over the beach road, he caught a brief flash of light on the road to the north.

⌘

Darkness obscured the ground at the landing site. Just before impact there was the familiar sensation of ground rush, the rapid blur of bush, patches of earth and other indistinct features. Experience told him this occurred at thirty to sixty metres above the ground. Reaching down he released the two nylon straps that secured his rucksack to the parachute harness. The rucksack dropped away and hit the end of its five metre tether with a sharp tug. Kurt knew he must 'flare' or put the brakes on the canopy to convert most of the forward speed to vertical velocity, to slow the rate of descent. If this manoeuvre was timed correctly, the jumper could literally step on the ground. But to get it right, the altitude had to be estimated correctly.

Coming in with a breeze at his back and with no way to see the ground beneath, flaring the parachute too soon would result in a canopy stall and a drop to earth similar to falling from seven metres. However, if he didn't flare soon enough, he would hit the ground at fifty or sixty kilometres-per-hour, equivalent to leaping from a car travelling at that speed.

Kurt applied half brakes, a compromise that would slow down his forward speed but also prevent stalling, then three-quarter brakes as the ground approached. He felt a wrenching tug on the harness and in an instant realized he was heading into the ground, face first. He released the steering lines completely, just in time to cover his head and face with his arms. There was a thud and a cracking sound on impact ... then all was very quiet.

For several seconds he thought that the sound was a bone breaking but, aside from the numbing pain of a hard impact, everything moved and he could breathe normally. The rucksack at the end of the drop line had snagged a tree or bush and acted as an anchor, pivoting the canopy and jumper over, slamming him into the ground.

Some dry branches on the ground were broken on impact which must have accounted for the sound. Besides being slightly stunned and receiving a few abrasions, he was intact. Kurt unclipped the parachute harness and unbuckled the rifle drop case, fishing out the FNC carbine and a full magazine of ammunition. After the rifle was operational, and he checked that the Browning pistol was also secure, he felt a little less vulnerable.

From the parachute harness, he traced the other end of the drop line to a fork of windswept scrub where the rucksack was lodged. The rucksack frame had suffered a minor dent on one side but otherwise the gear was serviceable. Working quickly, he balled up the harness, lines and parachute canopy, crammed it under a bush and hastily covered it with loose debris. Hopefully, at a later time some tribesman would find it and make a nice shelter for his goats or a canopy for his bed, compliments of the Navy SEALS.

With the housekeeping out of the way, Kurt focused on his situation. The flash he'd seen while crossing the road was worrying. It might be nothing but ...

Rapidly but quietly, he moved fifty metres from his landing site, sat absolutely still, and listened. The offshore wind was gradually dropping now that darkness had settled, but even the slight whistling it made in the beach vegetation would obscure subtle sounds coming from the direction of the road. If there were any pursuers in the area they were probably smart enough not to use lights, talk or slam vehicle doors.

Five minutes later there was a scent on the breeze. It was there for a fraction of a second and then gone. The air blowing in from the Atlantic was as clean and untainted as any on earth, and yet ... there it was again. The breeze was swirling air randomly around the broken groundcover. Kurt thought it might be his imagination but the smell was that of a cigarette. This was both good news and bad news. If it was trackers, then those conducting the search were either novices or just plain stupid. Anyone who allows smoking while tracking an armed opponent has a death wish.

Trying to remain hidden by the low dense vegetation, Kurt slowly and quietly began to move north, parallel to the beach road and the light he'd seen earlier. After several minutes of moving and looking, he homed in on a small point of orange pulsing then fading. It was hard to estimate the distance at night when looking at something small and stationary.

Had the mission been compromised this quickly? His first instinct was to move fast, to put distance between him and the possible pursuers. Reconsidering, he knew he had the advantage of stealth and thought it better to know who or what might be after him.

His eyes were adjusting to the darkness now, and he moved in the direction of the orange glow. Arriving at the coastal road about two hundred metres north of where he landed, he recognized the silhouette of a vehicle parked just off the road about fifty metres further north. It was an open-topped Land Rover or similar bush vehicle, with what looked like the shape of a man sitting in the front. If a party was patrolling, they may have left the driver back at the vehicle.

Should I neutralize this bunch, or evade them and proceed with the mission, Kurt wondered. Have they been tipped off? Or did they just happen to spot my parachute coming in?

The basis for the decision to infiltrate south of the target, was that there were no reports of aggressor activity in this area. Therefore static or mobile security patrols were unlikely to be encountered here. If the Cubans or MPLA had warning of his infiltration, then the entire mission was compromised and should be aborted. On the other hand, if this was just an incidental patrol, then the plan could still go ahead. Taking out this group would initially draw the enemy in the wrong direction, but it would also put them on alert.

Kurt needed to know who or what he was facing. Dealing with average military troops was one thing. Tracking a lone stealthy man at night was far from easy, and unskilled pursuers could be shaken off without much problem. It was experienced trackers he worried about. That would be a different situation altogether and would call for different tactics. An experienced tracking team would also have someone watching their back trail. Tracks, like tracer bullets, went both ways.

Moving south along the beach road away from the parked vehicle, he hugged the ground and began to cast around the softer verges of the road looking for spoor, and minutes later found footprints. He listened again carefully before cautiously manoeuvring over the tracks. At ground level, it was almost totally dark but the depressions in the soft layer of sand were visible as vague shadows. He reached down and gently felt the impressions with his fingertips.

There were three men. Two wore the same military boots with corrugated soles, Eastern European or Cuban, which had similar patterns. The other set was different, very difficult to discern, smooth anti-tracking boots like the ones he wore. This finding was ominous: there was at least one expert on this team. "One tracker with a couple of clods along for security probably," Kurt thought. At least there didn't seem to be any sign of a hound or the bare feet of a Bushman. A dog could be stopped with a little CS (teargas) powder or pepper. Only death would stop a Bushman on your trail, or so he'd heard.

Kurt withdrew his Browning 9mm from his belt holster and from the pouch on his rucksack removed the high efficiency MAC silencer for the weapon. He decided to neutralize this tracking party. Nothing else made sense. His assignment was to conduct close-in observation of the enemy. A good tracker would cast around and pick up his spoor, then sneak up when he least expected it. It was impossible to watch your rear all the time when you're supposed to be watching the enemy.

The silenced 9mm was loaded with special low-velocity ammo to prevent a sonic crack. But this also compromised its knock-down power. To be effective, the shots would have to be to the head, neck or heart, which were small targets in the dark. Kurt remembered using an SOG issued Swedish K 9mm submachine gun and raking an NVA sentry across the torso. Hit with four rounds, the dying soldier still had enough spunk left to throw two stick grenades at him before collapsing. An unnerving experience, to say the least, and the last time he had ever used a 9mm in an operation.

Closing in on the party, he noticed that a set of prints belonging to one of the soldiers turned backwards periodically. The man had probably been assigned to check the back trail and already he had compromised his duties. Instead of turning fully around, squatting, looking and listening for pursuers, he was just pivoting, glancing behind and staying tight with the others. It was very dark in the bush and this soldier was afraid of the boogeyman.

Kurt upped his pace. Ideally these three should be taken down without any shots being fired, except from the silenced 9mm. Loud gunshots would bring immediate attention and draw more troops to the area. Naturally, the skilled tracker would be in the lead and he was the most threatening opponent but, in order to reach him, his two escorts would have to be eliminated first. Everything would have to move so quickly that none of them would have time to fire back. Kurt grounded his heavy equipment including his ALICE rig and FNC rifle by a prominent bush and quickly covered the gear with grass. He couldn't move with the required stealth and speed while carrying all his equipment.

Back on the trail, movement, rustling and snapping twigs could be heard above the fading sea breeze, indicating he was closing on the three men. The tailing soldier of the group casually turned to check the back trail when a 9mm slug collapsed the bridge of his nose, and ploughed through the base of his brain. After this first shot Kurt bolted forward, dodging and snaking through the dense undergrowth to get a jump on the second enemy before he became aware that something was wrong.

It was a big risk, but when a single man faces multiple enemies he must take risks. The more audacious and unexpected the actions were the better. Kurt almost made a fatal error when he ran directly into the second soldier semi crouched, listening to the abnormal rustling in the bush, expecting his partner to appear.

The 9mm Browning he carried was designed to be a fully silenced weapon. In order to achieve this, the semi-automatic operation had been defeated by modifying the lock, and the slide had to be manually racked for each shot. As Kurt rapidly approached the soldier he remembered this like a lightening bolt striking his brain. Closing with his opponent with what felt like slow motion, he moved his left hand to cock the slide of the pistol which was thrust forward with his right.

The second soldier started to react and began to lift the muzzle of his AK-47, which was slung down to his left side. The slide of the Browning pistol clacked back and then forward again as it released. Instinctively, Kurt wanted to get close to the enemy to tie up his rifle. The Browning went off with a *pfffft* the instant the muzzle made contact with the soldier's sternum. Though fatal, the shot wasn't instantly incapacitating, and the mortally wounded soldier reflexively tightened the grip on his AK-47 and the weapon began to spew automatic fire, putting rounds into the ground very close to their feet. Hot gas pulses from the short AK barrel were like flashbulbs going off in the near darkness. Kurt felt the heat and the ejected cases strike him in the upper body. A moment later, the Cuban sprawled backwards and the AK fell from his grasp and rattled to the ground.

He racked the 9mm again and fired a bullet through the front of the downed man's head, then dived to the ground and rolled away from the body. If the tracker was close, he might come rushing back to the disturbance, weapon at the ready. Alternatively he could fire a burst towards the shots and run, hoping to buy some time. Of course, if the tracker was very good, he would do neither, but would approach Kurt without being detected.

Kurt rolled seven metres before coming up hard against an impassable bush. Charging the 9mm again, he pointed it in the direction of the second soldier's body. The FNC rifle had been cached with the other bulky equipment in anticipation of not needing it but he wished he had it, now that security had been broken. He'd have to make do. Waiting and listening intently, the dying sea wind still made it difficult to hear and isolate small sounds, and the close rifle fire had also dulled his hearing temporarily.

Several minutes passed and Kurt realized that he might have made a tactical error. The tracker may have already bolted but more likely he was playing a game of chicken. With the cumbersome security troops dead, he could now deal with his quarry on equal terms. Kurt knew he couldn't stay here long. A reaction force may have already been mobilized from the Cuban base. If a large number of troops conducted an organized sweep in this restricted area it would be difficult to break through. On the other hand if the tracker thought his quarry had run, he would want to move in quickly to pick up the spoor.

A slight rustle from a section of bush, above and to the left of where he'd been looking, alerted him. He dared not move until he was certain of the target. The single shot capability of the silenced Browning was a huge weakness at this point. A deliberate movement nearby could be differentiated from the random acts of wind blowing the vegetation. The movement was smooth but intermittent. In the few minutes since the shots were fired the tropical darkness was complete. The motion occurred again, he was sure of it now. When he was fairly confident about the location of his opponent, Kurt slowly moved his upper body around towards the target, keeping the alignment of his arms and pistol constant.

Kurt eased off the silenced shot and, with a wet slap, heard it strike flesh; a moment later the surroundings were lit by a burst of automatic fire and he felt a blow on his right side, near his waist. With a surge of adrenaline Kurt sprinted towards his left, trying to get at right angles to his opponent. He was relieved that he could run despite numbness in his right hip, which he knew could mean serious damage. If his pursuer was seriously wounded he would not be able to follow him any longer. He couldn't risk closing with him again, the man was good ... and better armed than he was.

Cautiously, he felt the affected area and he knew immediately what had happened. The tactical scrambled voice radio attached to the right side of his web gear had been smashed by one of the rounds, he could feel pieces of plastic and wire fragments hanging. The radio was so valuable he had not dared stow it with the other equipment. That was a bad decision. Now there would be no voice communications possible between him and George's assault force.

Because of the sound it made when it hit, he was confident his 9mm round had struck his pursuer solidly. Whether the burst of AK fire was another instance of a dead man's reflex he didn't know. He hoped that was the case, but even if the wound hadn't been fatal it had to be incapacitating, which meant the tracker wouldn't be following spoor any time soon. With the tracking team neutralized, Kurt knew it was time to break and run from this area. He had to collect the rest of his gear and head north towards Vista del Sol.

The presence of the skilled tracker made it almost certain that this operation had been compromised from the beginning. Information could have been leaked at a high level. For all he knew Holen Roberto himself may have made a 'financial deal' with the opposition. Money in a Swiss bank account could turn the loyalties of even the most committed. Blame for the compromise was not a factor now in any case. He just had to figure out of way of getting out of this trap and try to warn off George and the rest of the team if possible.

⌘

Backtracking to the cache, he watched his back trail and surroundings carefully for several minutes before moving in to collect the gear. It was great to feel the heft and power of the FNC again. The silenced Browning he stashed in the ALICE rig for use in a tight spot. Moving parallel to the coastal road, he was seventy-five or one-hundred metres inland from the Land Rover, separated from it by a low sand dune, when a thought occurred. If the tracker was only wounded and made it back to the Land Rover, he could get back to Vista del Sol quickly and initiate a sweep.

Downing most of his gear again, next to the trunk of a large acacia tree, he crouched then crawled to the top of a vegetated sand dune lying between him and the coastal road.

The vehicle was still there and the driver was moving around, obviously nervous, pacing back and forth in front of the vehicle, smoking another cigarette. Silhouetted against light beech sand, a holstered handgun could be made out on the driver's web belt and the barrel of an AK, propped in the front seat of the vehicle. This was no combat soldier, only a driver who hadn't a clue what was happening.

Not trusting the effectiveness of the 9mm, Kurt unsheathed his mastodon-handled combat knife and sprinted toward the driver when he began to pace away. Hearing footsteps coming from behind, the driver turned just in time to receive a Damascus steel blade thrust through the left side of his rib cage and through both chambers of his heart. He shuddered, gasped, and fell in a quivering heap as blood spewed from his open mouth. He died quickly as his heart tried in vain to pump a dwindling blood supply. Sometime he'd have to tell Joe how well the knife worked.

Quickly searching the Land Rover, he found nothing of immediate value but the AK and ammo. Kurt had hoped there would be a portable radio, but there was only a large fixed unit he couldn't carry and didn't know how to operate. Uncoupling a jerrycan of fuel from behind the vehicle; he unscrewed the cap and threw it into the front seat followed by a white phosphorus grenade as he sprinted back toward the bush. Hopefully, the burning vehicle would distract and confuse both the wounded tracker and any reaction force temporarily, until he could get clear of the area.

⌘

After the Land Rover burst into flames and began to burn, lighting up the dark sky, Kurt made his way inland a few hundred metres and then swung north. The bush thinned slightly which made walking easier. Unfortunately, come morning it would also make tracking easier so as much distance as possible had to be covered by sunrise.

Kurt's first thought was to avoid Vista del Sol entirely, giving the military compound a wide berth. However, a gut feel told him he had to have a visual on it ... after all that was his mission. Climbing the crest of another vegetated dune to gain a vantage point, he ducked low to avoid being silhouetted.

Once on top of the dune, his elevated position made the Vista del Sol military base, some four clicks up the road, clearly visible. Lights were burning in and around the compound and running engines could be heard. Headlights from a pair of vehicles could be seen heading south toward the still burning Land Rover. It also looked as though other vehicles were mobilizing and heading north. This activity seemed strange and though it meant nothing concrete, an ominous chill crawled from Kurt's neck down his back and legs.

One of two things could be happening. The mission could only be partially compromised by someone who had spotted his lone parachute at dusk. That would explain the single Land Rover and four soldiers sent south. Otherwise if the compromise had been total and information regarding the operation had been leaked to the Cubans and MPLA, that could explain the deployment of forces in both directions.

Maybe it was paranoid thinking, but Kurt knew that paranoia kept people alive at times like this, and it was wise to listen to the inner voices. With the radio gone there was no hope of signalling George and the assault force to abort the operation. The distance to the RV was too great to make it on foot in such a short time frame. If the MPLA and Cubans were already deploying north, there was no chance of reaching the rendezvous in time to warn them.

His only chance of success was to commandeer a vehicle and drive it to the rendezvous point, as quickly as possible. Desperate situations like this called for desperate measures. The enemy would expect him to run and hide from pursuers. He wished he'd taken clothes from the Cuban bodies. People usually see what they want to see. With the proper uniform there would be a good chance of walking into the compound and taking a vehicle. The remaining option was to provoke mass confusion and take advantage of the chaos.

⌘

Kurt recce'd the far perimeter of Vista del Sol and quickly found what he was looking for. A wooden and earthen ammunition and explosives bunker, surrounded by an offset barbed wire fence, was situated two hundred metres east of the compound. It had been built there for safety reasons many years ago when there was no fear of being attacked, only of the explosives blowing up and damaging the base. The makeshift bunker had a corroded tin roof and was dug into the side of a sandy hill.

Cautiously approaching the bunker from the inland side, Kurt stayed in the shadows cast by the floodlights from the base. A single unoccupied vehicle, another Land Rover, was parked near the west entrance to the bunker. From Kurt's low position he couldn't see anyone, but assumed one or two guards were in the vicinity.

Staying in the shadows cast by the bunker, Kurt quietly edged his way around the perimeter, not stopping or pausing but flowing steadily like a serpent stalking its prey. Slow continuous movement makes less disturbance and noise signature than intermittent movements.

The perimeter around which he moved was elevated in relation to the entrance which gave access to the bunker from below, like a walk-out basement. This design made maximum use of earthen walls in case of a detonation. Moving under an eroded fence and a connecting wall in the back, he followed the top edge of the bunker until he was positioned behind the façade above the bunker's entrance.

The sound of footsteps on the gravel below seemed very loud. A single soldier walked away from the bunker towards the entrance gate. Kurt clasped his pistol and squatted behind the façade. The guard stopped at the entrance gate, scanned the scene, then turned his head towards the south coast in the direction of the still flickering jeep. The guard watched for a few seconds then turned on the ball of his right boot and shuffled back to his post by the bunker door, without looking up. Kurt stayed silent. He was less than a metre above the guard's head. The guard unslung his AK-47 and placed the rifle butt in the gravel at his left side, holding the barrel by the flash suppresser in a lax, parade rest position.

Kurt very slowly reached out over the bunker door to where the guard stood. The silenced 9mm auto pistol hung muzzle down, suspended by his thumb through the trigger guard. He squeezed on the trigger and it fired once, the discharge sounding like a clack, fizz and wet pop all combined. The hollow-point bullet struck the apex of the guard's head, penetrating and expanding to twice its original diameter as it travelled vertically from brain to neck, coming to rest in the upper chest. The soldier slumped like a pile of rags to the gravel, took a couple of rough breaths and then was silent.

Kurt jammed the 9mm in his belt, drew his knife and then leapt down, landing beside the sprawled body. He jabbed at the guard's throat with the tip of the blade, but there was no response.

Quickly patting down the body, he found the key to the bunker on a short cord tied to the guard's pistol belt. Except for a pouch of AK-47 magazines and some personal papers, there was nothing else on the body. The key, removed from the guard's belt, opened the archaic lock on the bunker door. He dragged the corpse inside, slinging the guard's magazine pouch over his shoulder and picking up his AK, now lying on the ground. The dead guard's AK-47 appeared to be a newer version called an AKM, made from heavy stamped steel instead of milled parts, and looked unfired.

Using a GI flashlight with a red filter taken from the ALICE rig, Kurt scanned the inside of the bunker but it took a little time for his eyes to accommodate to the darkness and disorganized clutter. Boxes of small arms ammo occupied most of the cramped space. Wooden crates of 7.62 x 39mm ammo labelled in Russian were stacked in front, nearest the door. Behind and partially hidden, were darker metal tins of heavier 7.62 x 51mm Portuguese manufactured ammo that fed the G3s, FNs and MAG machine guns of the previous colonial army. Against a side wall were several boxes of fragmentation grenades as well as cases of RPG projectiles, in flat boxes with rope handles. Several rocket launchers hung on the wall by their leather straps. After clearing away some empty ammo crates and other litter he finally found what he was looking for.

Covered with a thick layer of accumulated dust were two crates of satchel charges: canvas bags containing eight two-and-a-half pound blocks of the high explosive tetrol, strung together with detonating cord. They were designed in WWII for slinging in and destroying Japanese bunkers in the South Pacific but could be used, when strung out, for blowing up bridges, buildings or any other target. The boxes looked old and of Portuguese manufacture but the explosives were usually stable for long periods of time. Each crate contained two of the twenty-pound charges in canvas carry bags. The boxes he prised open, and tossed three of the canvas bags towards the entrance.

Opening the fourth satchel charge he activated a two-hour-delay crush ampoule detonator, obtained from the SEAL demo bag left at the FNLA HQ, and inserted it into the detonating well in the end block of explosives. He'd thought seriously whether or not to bring the detonators. However, because they were small, and often came in very handy when he worked in Laos, he'd decided to pack them. The decision was fortuitous.

Placing the primed satchel charge back in its original box, he closed the lid and stacked some ammo cases on top of it. Kurt placed two wooden cases of 7.62 x 39mm ball ammo and a crate of twelve RPG rockets and a launcher in a stockpile at the entrance of the bunker. The dead guard's Tokarov pistol he removed and tucked in his belt. After the selected munitions were outside of the bunker, he locked the door.

The tired and beaten Land Rover only started on the third try, but ran reasonably well after that. Driving to the entrance of the bunker, Kurt jumped out and prised open the lids of the crates of ammo and rockets. He put some of the munitions in the passenger's seat in the front of the vehicle and the bulkier items, including the RPG rounds, in the back seat.

The 7.62 x 39mm rounds were packed in ten-round stripper clips which facilitated loading the dozen thirty-round AK magazines he'd collected. Some of the magazines he stowed in his pockets and others in the vehicle where they could be reached. Besides the FNC and silenced 9mm there were now two AK-47s with a pile of loaded magazines, as well as a Tokarov pistol. There was a saying popular in special operations that said 'you can never be too well armed'.

⌘

The plan, which was being improvised on the fly, was to do as much damage to the Vista del Sol military outpost as possible. Then, in the midst of confusion, take the road north with the goal of reaching George and the assault force in time to warn them and, hopefully, avoid disaster. The whole scheme was desperate, but at this point there was no option but to play the cards as dealt, and it looked like a very poor hand.

A quick, covert reconnaissance of the compound would identify vulnerabilities or weaknesses that could be exploited. Driving slowly out of the entrance of the bunker with all lights off, he pulled behind a thick clump of bush standing mid-way between the bunker and the main building of the military compound. A thin crescent moon rising in the sky cast a faint light on the coastal scrub. It was a perfect night for predators.

Kurt removed one of the satchel charges and three RPG rockets from the back seat of the vehicle. The RPG launcher tube and satchel charge had straps, so he slung them over his shoulder. Loaded AK magazines weighted down his jacket and it swung pendulously when he moved. One of the captured AKs was to be his primary weapon instead of the FNC. The FNC was lighter but he had a limited amount of ammo for it, and the little rifle's firing signature was distinctive. In a close fire fight it could be singled out. Also, AKs always seemed to work, even when grossly dirty.

Oddly enough, Vista del Sol was a converted police outpost and wasn't originally designed to be a defensive fortification. Its outer walls were constructed of non-reinforced concrete block and the roof material was corrugated metal that looked dull, almost black, in the feeble moonlight. When the army took over, the old police facility grenade screens had been installed, sloping from the roof to the ground a few feet away from the walls.

Protective earthen embankments had been pushed up around the sides of the structure except for the entrance which was built from cemented round cobblestone from the nearby beach. The embankments were slightly over two metres high and would effectively prevent ground-level fire from striking the lower walls. Defenders could lay behind these protective berms and return fire from elevated positions with relatively good cover. The main drawback of the layout was that it prevented occupants of the building from having a clear field of view of anyone approaching. This was a weakness that could definitely be exploited. On the far coastal end of the building, opposite the bunker, was a small motor pool and vehicle yard. On the other side of that was a fuelling station with a pair of thousand litre above-ground fuel tanks, located on a concrete pad.

A plan formed in Kurt's mind as he moved slowly around the compound, staying hidden in shadow. The concrete block walls wouldn't stand up to shock. The roof was weakly supported but it wasn't heavy enough to do much damage if it collapsed. The fuel tanks were some distance from the building but ...?

He made his way cautiously to the rear of the main building. It was odd that no troops were currently engaged in security around the facility, but there seemed to be confused activity in the vehicle yard. It looked like they were calling out everyone to man a hastily assembled reaction force. Some troops were already on the road and the facility seemed short handed. This activity was an unexpected bonus.

Kurt hoped that approaches to the compound weren't mined, but that seemed unlikely. Vista del Sol was no border station but deep inside Angola and, until now, a direct attack would not have been anticipated. The grenade screens and defensive earthworks probably provided the occupants with some sense of security against the odd terrorist threat. The perimeter embankments were overgrown with low dense ground cover, with some thorny vines thrown in, and would be no fun to crawl across.

After pausing to check for roving guards, he moved to the base of the embankment directly behind the main building and grounded all of the equipment, except for the AK and the satchel charge. From his upper shirt pocket he removed the flat plastic case and extracted a thirty-minute crush ampoule detonator. He couldn't read the lettering on the detonator in the dark but the raised markings on its surface revealed which one it was. He'd done this before.

Grasping the satchel charge and the AK, he walked up the back slope of the earthen hill in a crouch, thorny vines grabbing at his legs. Nearing the top he lowered his body parallel to the slope so he could peer over the top without being silhouetted. The AK he positioned so he could immediately bring it up to fire, although that was the last thing he wanted to do. Through the windows of the building, he saw soldiers hustling in a state of excitement. He hoped there wasn't a trench at the bottom of the embankment's inner slope. The defensive grenade screen was attached to the upper edge of the building and was anchored to, but not touching, the ground. This left just enough room for a defender inside to manoeuvre under the screen and up the slope into a firing position.

Kurt backed down the slope several feet to prevent being seen from the inside, opened the canvas flap of the satchel charge and felt for the detonator well in the terminal block of explosive. He tried the detonator in the well to make sure the threads turned freely. Crushing this glass vial between his fingers, he rapidly screwed it back into the well. Elbowing to the top of the berm, he lifted the primed satchel charge high with both arms and aimed at the slot under the grenade screen. As it passed through the opening, the twenty-pound bag of tetrol caught an edge, and rolled to a stop about two metres from the wall of the building. He anticipated that the earthen embankment would work to direct the explosion towards concrete block wall.

Moving quickly down the back of the slope, Kurt retrieved his gear and walked in a wide radius around the compound so the soldiers in the vehicle yard wouldn't see him. Hugging the edge of the cleared brush he settled in a position about sixty metres from the main building, just on the other side of the fuel tanks and vehicle yard. It was apparent that the Cuban and Angolan troops were loading up another convoy, possibly to reinforce the one that left earlier when he was at the bunker. The thought of George and the rest of the FNLA assault force being ambushed by the Cuban and MPLA convoy gave Kurt a sick feeling, and he hoped that this scenario wouldn't come to pass.

Minutes crept by like hours. Maybe he should have just waded in and fired up the place and then made an escape. He could be heading north by now and maybe could prevent ... no ... that kind of thinking would not do. It would have been suicide to take on this number of armed opponents alone. Even if he caught them by surprise and managed to escape, they would quickly regroup and come after him. This was his only chance.

He glanced at his watch. The crush ampoules had an accuracy of plus or minus five minutes, and it was twenty-five minutes since it had been activated. He loaded the RPG tube with a rocket and cocked the under hammer. The damn thing fired like a fat single-barrelled shotgun. The air was now still, which helped, as high or variable winds made rockets fly erratically. Heavy, still air in the middle of the night was ideal. The sliver of moon shed little light, and darkness reigned.

The RPG launcher may have been a crude tube made out of plastic and bamboo but the manufacturers had the foresight to give it visible night sights, probably radium paint. The US wouldn't use that; it would be considered too hazardous. Too hazardous! In the circumstances that sounded absurd. He might get cancer in thirty years' time from radium, but it was a swarm of AK rounds in the next five minutes that concerned him. He sighted the tube on the target, waited, and tried to relax. A good aim was crucial to the plan.

⌘

The charge blew as the watch hand swept past the twenty-nine minute mark. The blast was shattering, deafening and immediately followed by pieces of concrete block and chunks of metal roof whistling down from the sky. Gently Kurt tightened his finger on the RPG trigger, trying not to be distracted by the maelstrom. The sights were kept just below the target, anticipating a sight rise in the rocket round as it cleared the launcher and the engine ignited. He felt the thump as the booster charge went off and kicked the round out of the tube. Once it had gone seven metres out, the rocket engine lit up on cue, tracking towards its target, trailing a bright orange tongue against the black sky.

The shaped charge rocket warhead struck slightly below where Kurt intended, which was the middle of the outer fuel tank. Instead it impacted the angle iron cradle the tank rested on and exploded with a bright-blue flash. The explosion ruptured the bottom of the thousand-litre tank, and petrol sprayed out over the vehicle yard in an arc. As the fuel dispersed in the air, white-hot metal fragments flew through the mixture igniting it with a loud whoosh and roar. Searing heat and a midday brightness emblazoned the inky African night. The canvas tops of nearby trucks lit up like torches, as did the clothing of soldiers as they ran around chaotically trying to escape the inferno.

"I love this shit when it works," Kurt said to himself, and proceeded to load the RPG tube with a second rocket.

The intensity of the flames ruined his night vision, but it had also outlined the remaining fuel tank sufficiently enough to take a sighting. The range and flight characteristics of the rocket were now known. *Whoosh...* the rocket was barely audible over the roar of the conflagration but it struck squarely in the centre of the remaining tank. The shaped charge ignited, blowing a cone of burning fuel directly toward the remnants of the shattered building.

"Diesel," Kurt mumbled, "just the ticket. That'll burn for awhile."

The entire compound was alight now. Ammo and munitions stored in the building were going off like strings of firecrackers, mixing with the yells and screams of the panicked and burning soldiers who were running around in aimless patterns. Several were rolling in the dirt trying to extinguish their burning clothing. Half a dozen soldiers emerged from the wrecked building, seemingly uninjured, brandishing weapons. They began to spray automatic fire at the perimeter, thinking a massive attack was underway. He put down the RPG tube and picked up the AK-47. Flicking the side lever to single-shot mode, he shot the would-be defenders, one at a time, as they presented themselves. In a few minutes the scene had calmed somewhat and he moved out, continuing to circle in the same direction in order to avoid running headlong into any trackers who might be on his trail.

Kurt looped back towards the vehicle waiting from a safe vantage point for a few minutes before approaching it, but there was no movement or presence in the area. Knowing that there was no time to squander, he jumped in the Land Rover, started it, and headed for the north road. The camp was still ablaze, flickering and pulsing in the coastal bush.

Luanda would send reinforcement troops to Vista del Sol when they got wind of what had happened but all looked quiet to the north, as he drove as fast as the beat-up Land Rover could be pushed. Two miles north of the burning compound the road crossed a steel-beamed bridge spanning a steep ravine that ran east to west. He realized he would have to take out this crossing to hinder any reaction force the enemy might mobilize.

Just over the bridge Kurt swung the vehicle off the road and into the bush, and grabbed the second satchel charge, his FNC and several magazines. Rope would have been useful but in the absence of any he took a uniform shirt lying in the back and headed to the base of the bridge. The vertical supports were rough-hewn timber logs and the spans were painted steel girders. Moving first down the steep approach and then into the black abyss beneath the bridge he felt, more than heard, a huge explosion followed rapidly by a string of secondary blasts. "The bunker," he said aloud. "Forgot about that."

He inched along the support beams until positioned approximately mid-span. Bent nearly double and trying to keep a sure footing was tricky, and a fall would result in serious injury or his death. Removing the eight blocks of tetrol high explosive from the satchel charge, he dropped the canvas bag into the black ravine below. Placing the charges beneath the centre of the bridge would surely disable it, but he considered that the span might be quickly repaired. It needed to be destroyed completely and the only way to ensure this was to string the chain-detonated explosive blocks beneath the bridge, on the vertical supports. That way the whole centre section should fail and drop, making a hasty repair impossible.

Working his way towards the east side of the span and using his knife, he cut strips of cloth from the uniform jacket, lashing blocks of explosive to the outer centre timber supports, about three metres beneath the bridge surface. The blocks were positioned cross-wise to maximize their damage capability. Playing out the detonating cord that bound the blocks together, he worked across the supports, tying blocks to the beams. Kurt was sweating profusely now. The steel girders became slick with perspiration when he grabbed them. Almost falling twice, his muscles began to shake and halfway through the job he had to stop momentarily.

He was approaching exhaustion and knew from experience this happened precipitously. This trait confounded him all his life: an immense energy could be called upon for sixteen to twenty-four hours and then, like a flipped switch, it was turned off. The energy would fade and an overwhelming fatigue would set in. But the bridge had to be rigged. Just a few more minutes!

Vibration shook the steel beams, though he heard nothing at first. In his fatigued and weakened state it might be muscle tremors or hallucinations. But the vibrations became more definite, and then a rolling, rumbling sound.

"A convoy!" he said aloud.

Balanced precariously on supporting beams beneath a bridge, he realized vehicles were about to pass over, imminently. If anybody bothered to look down they would see a man hanging there helplessly, but he had no choice other than to ride it out. Moving around to the south side of the centre vertical support beam, he wrapped his arms and legs tightly around it. The convoy was most likely returning to the Vista del Sol compound from the northern border area. The explosions and fire would be making their return a hasty one, and they wouldn't slow down or stop while rushing to assist their beleaguered comrades. That was his hope anyway.

Their running lights extinguished, the military trucks and Land Rovers passed over him at speed, sucking up both fine powdered sand and stones from the roadway, causing them to rain down on him. There were ten to twelve vehicles in the convoy travelling almost bumper to bumper. Kurt forced his face into his shirt to filter out some of the dust.

When the last of the trucks passed over, he quickly tied the last of the explosive blocks to the bridge supports. The last block barely made the west support on the other side of the bridge. Balancing against this upright, he fished for the detonator box in his shirt and removed the last crush ampoule, a fast one rated at ten to fifteen minutes. There was a chance the convoy would head back north after finding the devastation at the camp, which in the circumstances would be disastrous. After a trial fitting, he crushed the glass bulb and screwed it into the detonator well in the terminal block of explosive.

It took several minutes to emerge from under the bridge and scramble up the ravine wall. Fatigue made his whole body tremble uncontrollably, but with a final burst of energy he reached the hidden Land Rover. Confident that the road wasn't mined due to the safe passage of the convoy, he swung the vehicle onto the road and floored the accelerator. The beaten-up bush car began to shake at sixty kilometres-per-hour and didn't seem capable of much more. Five minutes later, a flash like distant lightning appeared to his rear, reflected off the low cloud cover forming along the coast. Some seconds later a distinct boom echoed across the landscape. The rear secure for the time being, Kurt pressed on to find George and the assault force.

⌘

The road was rough, pitted and full of potholes. The vehicle's rock hard suspension served well to keep a driver awake. The pale violet of false dawn washed the eastern sky with a layer of transparent indigo. Soon there was enough light to see cone-shaped rondavels, with tendrils of smoke curling into the still morning air from the village cooking fires. From memory he knew that the initial RV was near the Jamba road junction. About a kilometre west of the road was a clearing that was the site of an abandoned Portuguese logging camp. During mission planning an old aerial photo showed a rectangular clearing a couple of hundred yards across and some old structures that were in a dire state of disrepair.

He secreted the Land Rover in a tree line several hundred yards south-east of the RV's expected location. Smoke could be seen coming from that direction but the source was hidden by bush and trees. Dust from the tyres hung in a gritty cloud as it settled softly in the still air. Kurt took his FNC rifle, a pouch of magazines, and several fragmentation grenades which were buttoned in his cargo pockets. The sun broke through the ground mist with a raw flame and the still air began to heat up. The drive was rough but the break served to regenerate his flagging energy, at least enough to function.

Quietly moving thirty metres away from the vehicle into the bush, Kurt waited. There were no sounds but the buzzing and snapping of insects. Then somewhere distant a lioness roared, her voice carried miles in the still morning air. He began to move cautiously, quietly and deliberately in the direction of the RV. Every five minutes he stopped moving to listen carefully before continuing.

About half a kilometre from the southern boundary of the RV, he heard voices. They were low pitched and inconsistent, speaking either Spanish or Portuguese, which sounded similar. Stopping, he tried to get a fix on their location by slowly panning his head from side to side, but there was too much ground clutter; he'd have to get closer.

A shift in the type of vegetation indicated that at one time this was the edge of the camp clearing. Only the lack of mature trees and scarcity of accumulated forest floor litter betrayed its usage. With a year-round growing season, it doesn't take nature long to claim her own back. His grandfather's words came to mind, "We are only tenants here; don't think you're moving in for long." They were words of wisdom now mostly forgotten. The voices were louder now, words and sentences strung together. The speakers were obviously not worried about security. That was a good sign; they weren't lying in wait.

As he edged forward, gaps appeared sporadically in the thick growth. Smoke mingled with the creepers and ground tangle, smelling of both wood and other burning things. Finally, after he stealthily crept forward, a small campfire with three soldiers around it came into view through the vegetation. One soldier was seated, one squatted and one was standing.

The squatting soldier held a pistol out for the others to see. The profile of the gun looked like a US .45 automatic, not a weapon the enemy would normally have in their possession. When the pistol was turned slightly, the morning sun cast a glint of pure white grip panel. Kurt felt a wave of nausea overtake him, making his head feel light and the world began to spin. The feeling passed as quickly as it had come, replaced by a hot flush that warmed his skin and face followed by a profound and overwhelming hatred. All traces of fatigue were gone.

George was dead. Being a true soldier he would never give up his personal sidearm to the enemy. In a moment Kurt put together what must have happened. As he suspected last night, the whole operation was compromised. Their plans had been leaked. A reception party had been waiting at his landing zone, but fortunately he'd managed to elude them. The assault force hadn't been so lucky and was ambushed, probably just up the north road or even at the turnoff to the camp. The main body of the ambush party had passed over him last night on the bridge. These three soldiers in front of him were just a security team waiting for their return. The Cuban and MPLA hit their assigned target and their intelligence had told them that no more were on the way, so they felt secure in playing 'boy scout camp out' and 'show and tell'. The sad fact was that their intelligence was right ... almost.

George's body must be recovered if it was still here. The troops scrambling back to their base most likely would not have taken the time to load bodies. He estimated there were at the most five or six enemy in this stay-behind rear guard. Those not sitting near the fire were likely to be guarding the camp entrance. They were probably neophytes, green recruits, placed there so their seniors could start a fire, cook coffee and have a good time. However, even beginners in this game were dangerous because they were so unpredictable. When the shooting started, they would either come charging with guns blazing, or run so hard and far in terror they couldn't be caught.

Much as he wanted to take down these three now it wasn't the best plan. Moving low and wide he made sure there was adequate cover between the three soldiers in the clearing and him. These three weren't alert anyway; none of them was even watching the perimeter. Using a fast smooth walk he headed in the direction of the entry road, where the voices of the two-man security team were picked up from seventy-five metres away. They lay prone in a camouflaged position about one-hundred metres up the entrance to the clearing from the main road.

As Kurt approached he could see the barrel of a tripod mounted 12.7mm heavy machine gun aimed at an angle towards the main road. The gun was well camouflaged but its size and angular construction gave it away. The 12.7 operator sat behind the tripod engaged in an animated conversation with his buddy nearby, who was sitting back against a tree. Beside the second man, propped against another tree, was a shiny new AKM rifle. The powerful machine gun and the presence of their three comrades a couple of hundred yards away gave both men a false sense of security.

⌘

Manuel Garcia Sanchez had been inducted by the Cuban Army six months previously. An on-again off-again career as an art student, coming from a working-class family, made him a target for the draft. He hated the military. It ran counter to his philosophy of life, which was surprisingly liberal for one who had grown up in such a restrictive regime. To resist the call up was futile. He knew of several students who had tried, and who ended up in jail doing hard labour. Not the rebellious sort, he decided to go with the flow, get out alive and then resume his painting. One day, he thought, he could get off the island and go to Spain or France and study. He favoured the modern Impressionist style but knew he must get away to perfect it. Maybe one day a show in Madrid, then London or maybe even New York. Those thoughts made him feel upbeat. Sometimes all you had were dreams to alleviate the boredom and horror of it all, but Manuel knew his capabilities and he believed in his dream.

The ambush last night had been terrible and he tried to push it from his mind. They had been told at Vista del Sol that a force of FNLA lackeys based in Brazzaville was coming to attack them. Manuel had been dispatched with a company of Cuban infantry to this intersection where, just before dark, a jeep and two trucks had driven into the kill zone of their ambush. The 12.7 raked the trucks causing terrible damage to troops riding in the back. Limbs and heads had been blown free from torsos and blood was everywhere. The jeep in the lead was only hit with AK and RDP fire, by order of the Commandante. Three of its occupants had been captured alive with survivable wounds, two Americans and an Englishman, or one who looked like a Latin but spoke like an Englishman. The Portuguese jeep driver was killed. Another American, at least he assumed he was American, with dark hair and a handsome face, was killed outright. The Commandante had been very angry about this. He'd wanted that man alive, but he'd been riding in the back of the lead truck and not the jeep. A 12.7 bullet passed through his chest.

Just after the ambush when a radio message reported that the Vista del Sol facility was under attack and their return was demanded, the Commandante had become confused. They had just shot the would-be attackers. How could the base be under attack? The radio then went silent and they had no option but to return quickly. The company had originally planned to deploy at the ambush site and spend the night there. In the morning the attached Cuban Intelligence (DRG) personnel would thoroughly inspect the ambushed vehicles and their contents. The Commandante had decided to return to the base with most of the soldiers but leave the DRG and a small security element at the site to proceed with their work at daybreak. Manuel and Jorge volunteered to stay behind, preferring a peaceful security detail to an almost guaranteed fire fight at Vista del Sol. The Commandante had agreed, not wanting the shirking draftees in a real battle anyway.

He closed his eyes and tried to forget all about last night's carnage. The warm morning sun was beginning to relax his tight muscles. Manuel wished he had a cup of strong hot espresso, a couple of toasted coconut biscuits and some fresh fruit; that would be wonderful. The thought of good food made his stomach wrench and he started to reach for his pack to find out what canned rations he had left, probably only beans. His long black hair fell off his shoulder and shined in the sunlight but it looked greasy, it was hard to keep clean in this filthy land. He'd managed to keep the hair through army training, which had been a trick, but to him it was a sign that his spirit hadn't been broken. He thought of himself as an artist forced to wear a uniform temporarily, not a soldier.

He glanced around at the woodland around them. His artist's eye found something wrong with the scene but he didn't know what. Shades of green and brown were disrupted by ... Then he saw the figure, a monster's form hidden in the landscape, a man's worst nightmare. It moved and then there was a soft pop. Manuel was stung by a bone fragment from Jorge's head, and he felt the warmth of brains and blood as they sprayed. Then he was jolted by a hammer strike just below his neck and he fell backwards, unable to move his body anymore. The monster appeared, standing over him ... blocking his light. He tried to scream but only a gurgle came out. A bright steel blade hovered in the air, shining with impossible brightness in the morning sun. A beautiful piece of artwork, its approach mesmerized him. It was so close he could smell the oil.

⌘

The DRG officers sifted through the few documents and other material recovered from the ambushed vehicles. They squatted and sat by the fire, now burning briskly with the hardwood deadfall that littered the edge of the clearing.

The senior officer was Major Reyes, fifteen years in the DRG or Cuban Intelligence service. Reyes was a young lieutenant during the Bay of Pigs invasion and made a reputation interrogating captured enemy. He was brutal and had not a trace of compassion in his heart. A deprived, loveless, poverty stricken childhood and regular beatings from an alcoholic father had shaped the man. The repressed anger had lasted a lifetime and he knew he would have been in prison or dead by now if this job hadn't provided an outlet for his hostility. Everyone who knew him, including his own men, loathed him, which was fine with Reyes. In fear there was power and in power there was control. Reyes loved to be in control, control so denied him as a child.

Unfortunately in a short time Reyes' rising star had been irrevocably tarnished. The early and mid 1960s saw the coming prominence of Che Guevara, a firebrand and one of the fathers of the Cuban revolution. His popularity with the masses, charisma and brilliant mind made Fidel Castro nervous. Reyes was drawn into Che's sphere like a remora to a great shark, and the pairing proved to be a good one.

Revolutionaries needed to be brutal and ruthless to survive: they required the services of interrogators, strong-arm men, and killers. However, leaders could not be seen participating in such distasteful but necessary work, such was the hypocrisy of the revolutionary. Reyes filled the bill perfectly. He had no political ambitions of his own, wanted only to satisfy his aggressions and remain loyal to a powerful man who could protect him. El Che was sent on progressively more dangerous missions at Castro's insistence. The Congo, Chile, Venezuela and finally Bolivia were his destinations and Reyes went along lurking in the shadows, performing his work with enthusiasm and efficiency when he was called upon ... and sometimes when he wasn't.

When El Che was ambushed in Bolivia in 1967 Reyes was nearly captured also, but managed to elude the Bolivian Rangers who were trained and led by those imperialist American Special Forces. Months later, he had managed to make his way to the Cuban Embassy in Lima Peru, then on to Havana, where there was no hero's welcome awaiting him. Quite the contrary, his expected fate was to perish with his leader. His survival, though hard won and tenuous, had been viewed almost as an act of cowardice by his superiors. Subsequently he was shunned and given lowly and dead-end positions. This treatment only increased his already brimming hostility. Eventually much of the stigma wore away but he was never promoted beyond major and always drew less than choice assignments, like this caca-land Angola. Still, Reyes had no other plans and was doing the only job he knew. No dreams or fanciful images filled his head. Like an animal he didn't think much beyond the moment.

The two junior DRG men with him were intimidated by his presence and carried out his orders without question; thus he grudgingly tolerated them. They were looking at documents taken from the jeep they'd ambushed last night. He reached down and patted the handle of the Colt .45 auto he'd taken from the dead American. It was a shame he died so quickly, a missed opportunity, but that was all right. When he got back to the base, three live prisoners would be waiting for him. He smiled at the prospect. A scuttling sound shocked Reyes from his thoughts. He looked in the direction of the sound and saw a round object rolling towards them from the nearby trees. He thought one of the security team was rolling them a coconut, a papaya or some other tropical fruit. The first thought was one of annoyance, then anger, at their arrogance, Damn draftees, a worthless bunch, especially the long-haired one who looks like a girl.

As the thought finished, the object came to a halt a few feet away, and he saw what it was. Tangled in a mass of glistening hair was a pair of soft eyes that had a puzzled but peaceful look. The severed head caused all three soldiers to freeze with shock.

Kurt stepped into the clearing with his FNC shouldered and, with two shots in rapid succession, both junior DRG men were hit in their upper torsos. The evil little Sierra hollow-point bullets were boosted to nearly three times the speed of sound and expanded once they penetrated flesh, shredding hearts, blood vessels and lung tissue. The two soldiers fell and flopped like caught fish on dry land.

Reyes lunged for his AKM propped by the fire but, as he reached, Kurt placed a shot in the crest of his pelvis, shattering the bony ring that supported his body weight. His grandfather had taught him that trick. When hunting dangerous game like bear you did not go for the heart or brain, but first took away its ability to charge. Once it was immobile, you could easily kill it without further threat.

Reyes collapsed in a heap, his outstretched hand still a distance from his rifle. He looked up at Kurt with surprise and anger; he was not in control now. Despite his devastating and painful wound he again tried to lunge for the rifle but fell short. Kurt slowly walked towards him, the muzzle of the FNC extended. Reyes rolled slightly and reached for the gun on his belt, George's .45. Kurt fired a bullet into Reyes' right shoulder joint. The area exploded and the man screamed in agony. A quick second shot took out the other shoulder. Reyes lay helplessly writhing in the dirt.

Kurt walked over to him and gently reached down and removed the white handled pistol from the Cuban's belt. He looked at the man on the ground and saw only pain, fear, terror and sweat. The ivory grips of the pistol had a thin smear of dried blood on them, George's blood.

"Mi amigo (*my friend*) Commandante," Kurt said in his faltering Spanish while rubbing the blood stain on the pistol grip gently. "Su sangre (*his blood*)."

Reyes looked up at him, his eyes a reflection of intense hatred, then sputtered, "Americano boina verde (*American green beret*)?"

"Si, Commandante," Kurt said solemnly.

Reyes lifted his head despite the pain and spat in Kurt's direction. His lips were dry and cracked. Most of the saliva dribbled out in a white froth. A few droplets arced upwards and landed on Kurt's dirty jungle boot. In slow motion Kurt lowered his eyes, almost forlornly, then looked back up.

"You are no soldier but a perro sucio, a dirty dog," Kurt said in an icy voice. "I know what you are, your eyes tell me. A real soldier deserves an honourable death, but not you ... not you."

Kurt slung the FNC over his shoulder and kicked Reyes hard in the ribs, forcing him to roll on his front. Grabbing the man simultaneously by the back of the shirt and pistol belt he flung the wounded Cuban like a sack of grain into the fire, face first.

In agony Reyes began to scream.

"Soy muerta! ... soy muerta! (*I am dead ... I am dead*)"

Blood flowing from his open wounds began to sizzle and boil. Reyes tried to squirm out of the fire, but Kurt grabbed the cool end of a burning log and forced him back in the intense flame. In another minute Reyes stopped moving and his body curled up in a foetal position as muscles contracted. The smell of the burning flesh was choking.

Kurt turned and began to walk to the burnt-out vehicles further up the road to recover George's body. It was the only honourable thing left to do.

# CHAPTER 12
## THE DESERT

Jack was speechless when he walked into the ATA Flight Operations office, switched on the light, and saw the man he'd dropped into Angola less than a week before sitting behind his desk. Only Kurt's eyes were moving, following him.

"Is that offer still open, Captain Malloy? The lift to Rhodesia?"

Jack was flustered and stuttered a bit in his reply.

"Sure, of course, but how did you ...?"

"Survive? That's a long story and I'm pretty tired now. As you probably heard George and the others didn't make it. All of them were killed or captured. I took George's body to the consulate this morning. I drove him as far as the river, paid a fisherman to transport us across and contacted the FNLA still at the camp. The councillor officials didn't seem at all pleased but they accepted him, anyway. At least he'll go back to his family."

"When you left the aircraft the other day, I didn't think you'd have a chance in a thousand of making it out alive. You were jumping into a hornet's nest, lad. I was monitoring radio traffic on the way down the coast after you were dropped. When I arrived in Windhoek, I went to visit a friend in the police there. They were tuned in and were very interested in what was happening. As far as can be determined, the Cubans and MPLA were somehow alerted to the operation."

"We were compromised all right," Kurt replied. "There are too many leaks in missions like this. Too many people know, and there is always someone willing to sell out. As a result, a lot of good people are dead or captured. It isn't worth it."

"I know how you must feel son, but I'm a little confused by the reports," Jack said.

"Go on," Kurt prompted.

"If your main force was shot up and captured by the Cubans how ... I mean, what happened at Vista del Sol? We heard reports of dozens killed in a raid on the base. Who did that? Was there another assault force?"

Kurt shook his head in a constrained manner.

"No, we ... I hit them with some explosives and rockets so I could get out of there and warn off George and the others, but it was too late."

"You did that damage all by yourself!" Jack gasped. "One man parachuting in alone wiped out a base camp and a reinforced company of soldiers? That seems too incredible. How ...?"

"Let me ride in the right seat of the DC-8 on the way out of here and I'll tell you. Got lucky mostly, luck plays a big part in these things. George ran out of luck I guess. Anyway, Captain, I brought you a souvenir of the mission."

Kurt tossed a gold and red badge on the cluttered desk, which spun once and stopped. Jack picked it up and rolled it around in his hand.

"Cuban DRG ... intelligence. Field grade officer, I'd say," Jack said, studying the badge closely.

"He was a bad one, that's all I know. When do we leave?"

"We'll roll tomorrow at zero seven hundred sharp. Get your things together so we can box them up. By the way, I forgot I have a surprise for you. I didn't think you'd ever pick it up," Jack said.

"Surprise? I don't know if I can stand any more surprises, I've had quite a few lately."

"I think you'll like this one." Jack walked over to a wooden box sitting near the back wall. "That chopper pilot McDonald dropped it off. It arrived at the oil rig, sent by your friend back in the States I take it."

"You're kidding! I'd forgotten I'd written to Dave," Kurt sounded almost joyous. "He sent my Smith."

"Your what?" Jack asked.

Kurt scanned around for a crow bar and found one hanging in the corner of the room. The box was soon opened and packing was strewn over the floor. After unwrapping the dull silver Smith and Wesson .44 magnum revolver from a layer of oiled cloth, he opened the cylinder and pulled the action through.

"You Yanks and your six guns, it must be in the blood," Jack shook his head in mock dismay.

"Now I feel like a whole man again, Jack, thanks. Dave sent a bunch of my ammo too."

"I'm staying at the Normandy," Jack said. "You can stay there or, if you don't want to go into town, there is a bed in the attached room with a toilet and shower."

"That will do just fine, Captain."

"Help yourself to those boxes of opened canned food. It's hardly gourmet, but then neither is the hotel food, and the cans are a bloody sight safer," Jack waved as he headed out the door. "I'll see you in the morning."

⌘

Kurt packed gear into an empty canned fish box and found Jeffrey Cooke in the hanger. The crew chief greeted him like a long lost brother. Asked if he would like to go tip a few in town, Kurt declined, feeling he was approaching total exhaustion. The loss of George and the others weighed heavily and he was in no mood for celebration.

"Maybe we'll make it Windhoek then," Jeffrey said. "There are a couple of decent clubs and some of the German girls you wouldn't believe." Jeffrey held his cupped hands a foot in front of his chest holding imaginary breasts. Kurt managed a grin.

"I might take you up on that one, Jeff, but if half of that is true, we'll risk suffocation."

Jeff guffawed and slapped Kurt on the back, "Later, mate."

"Be careful with my gear now," Kurt said over his shoulder as he walked off.

"It's in the best of 'ands, mate. ATA is the only way to fly."

⌘

The DC-8 rotated from the runway at Brazzaville just as the sun was clawing its way above the morning haze and smoke.

"Another day in paradise, hey Cap?" Kurt said aloud.

"What did you say?" Jack asked removing one earphone from his head.

"Nothing, I'm just glad to be leaving this hole, not many good memories here."

Jack nodded in agreement.

"They are memories nonetheless," Jack said. "Good and bad, they are still there. Hell, in your brief life you've done things most men will never do, and you're still alive to tell the tale. There will be some great stories to tell your grandchildren when you're a fat old man like me."

"That may be true, Captain," Kurt said, "but I doubt any of them will give a rat's ass about this. Or they'll think I'm a storytelling old fool. Unless you have been there and actually experienced the events, it all has little meaning. Truth, fiction, it's all just a blur. Whatever entertains and makes people feel good is what they'll remember, not the pain, blood, suffering and loss. They won't want to hear about that."

"I'm afraid you're right there," Jack said. "It's the same with the Second World War. Being a young Spitfire pilot was both exciting and horrifying at the same time. No twenty-one-year-old wants to go down burning, but those were our prospects every day we flew. All the stories we tell are about the good times, but there really were no good times, or if there were, they were totally clouded with the shadow of violent death. There are some things you just can't tell people, you have to know it, and once you know it you spend the rest of your life trying to forget it. But ... changing the subject, you know what makes me sad?"

"What's that?" Kurt asked.

"That all of this is changing so fast. Before and right after World War Two this continent was special. It felt so good to be part of it. Now I don't know, it's not the same place anymore. All of us living here had hopes and aspirations that Africa would one day be a great empire to rival Europe or even the Americas, and it could have been. Hell, it could have been better."

"What happened?" Kurt asked.

It's hard to say, a lot of things. I guess we Europeans were engaged in too much wishful thinking. We hoped that these countries and people could see the big picture, our big picture I should say. When it came down to it they saw personal power and bank accounts first. Then when nationalism reared its head, sanity took leave entirely. Perhaps it was foolish for us whites to think that other peoples and cultures should behave in a certain manner, when we can't even get our own affairs in order?"

"What do you mean?" Kurt inquired.

"Well, I think the beginning of the end of the colonial era was brought on by the Second World War. We recruited tens of thousands of Africans to fight the Germans, mainly in North Africa. Until then, most of them thought of the white men as different from themselves. Our social complexity and technology helped promote that image, and we did nothing to discourage it. But in war that perception was shattered forever. Black men saw white men bleed and die just as they did, call for their mothers when wounded, shake with fear, smell bad when they didn't wash. War levelled the playing field. After that it was never quite the same. The mystique we wrapped ourselves in was stripped away, and the naked truth could be seen by everyone."

Jack shook his head in genuine sorrow and confusion.

"Then, at about the same time, the surge to nationalism seemed to hit all the colonies. The West and the East started to use Africa as a cold war battleground. Neither side really cares what happens to the people here. They just don't want the other side to gain control of it."

Jack was silent with his thoughts for a moment.

"I don't know where the whole thing is going now, I really don't. It feels like we are riding in one of those little canoes down a mighty river without a paddle. We're going somewhere, but we don't know where and our only thought is to keep from drowning."

"We're just dodging the big rocks, I guess." Kurt said.

"That's the truth," Jack replied. "Maybe I'm too old to worry about it anymore, and perhaps that's a good thing."

⌘

The DC-8 departed the Congo River mouth on the same course it took less than a week before. This time Jack looped further out to sea before banking to the south and flying parallel to the Angolan coast. The morning light made everything look different. They were sandwiched between the light blue of the morning sky and the deep, almost blue-black of the ocean. The dark and light browns of the coast looked like an afterthought, a sidebar to their blue reality. It all seemed so peaceful, Kurt thought. It was hard to imagine that just a few days before …

Jack was talking on his headset to someone and had a serious look on his face. He finished and looked over in Kurt's direction.

"What's the matter?" Kurt asked.

"I've been talking to Luanda air traffic control for years, and they've always been very professional and helpful chaps."

"And now?" Kurt asked apprehensively.

"They seem to have switched air traffic controllers," Jack said with concern in his voice. "Some madman is on the radio telling me that this aircraft is violating Angolan airspace. He's talking in Spanish, not the usual Portuguese. I think he is probably a Cuban."

"That doesn't sound good," Kurt said. "I wonder what our friends have in mind? We're well out of Angolan airspace, aren't we?"

Jack nodded.

"Yes, well outside. Sounds like some trumped-up provocation. I suppose we will be finding out very soon if they are serious or just bluffing."

"Should we head further out to sea? Maybe that would please the bastards."

Kurt had already unbuckled himself from the right seat and crossed behind Jack to get a look out of the port cockpit window. He craned his head to get a view of the length of coastline located east of the aircraft. In less than a minute of intense scanning, he turned to Jack.

"I have something at eight o'clock and still quite a way out sir, but it's coming in fast! It definitely looks tactical to me, not friendly." Without thought, Kurt had instinctively reverted to calling a superior 'sir' during times of crisis.

"What is it?" Jack asked.

"Saw the wings flash for a moment when they banked," Kurt said, head now stuck back in the window. "My first guess is a pair of swept wing fighters, probably MIGs. They're approaching from about 190 or 195 degrees, too close to the sun. Now, they're falling back to vector in from the rear, I think. Wait, I've lost them."

"All right," Jack said. "I have them on radar intermittently. They're trying to hide in my blind spot."

Kurt crossed to the other side of the aircraft and pressed his face to the starboard cockpit window.

"Now I see them. They are making their approach from 160 degrees and the sun coming up in the east is lighting them up like beacons."

"They don't give a damn, they are a pair of falcons and we are a fat lumbering goose on the wing. We can't outmanoeuvre or fire back," Jack said.

"Are they going to shoot us sir, or just have some fun?"

"I wish I knew what they are thinking right now," Jack replied. "The ATC sounded like he was trying to set us up. Because of our status, if we go down there will be little outrage."

"We don't have much time, sir. They look like they are in a slight climb, heading straight at us. If they go to guns they'll slice us in half. If you put on flaps and cut throttle we'll sink, and at least ruin their pass."

"My thoughts, too. I can't see them, so you will have to tell me when."

Jack went to his radio and made an emergency transmission.

"Mayday ... Mayday. This is flight 243 bound for Windhoek. We are under attack by MIG fighters. We request assistance."

Kurt waited until the closing aircraft were just within gun range. Their trajectory would take them level with the DC-8 then just above the cargo jet in a matter of seconds. If he was an attacking pilot, he knew when he would press the switch.

"Now!" Kurt yelled.

Jack applied half flaps and pulled back throttles on all four engines simultaneously. The DC-8 immediately decelerated and lurched downwards. Kurt forgot he wasn't strapped in and nearly floated. He grabbed on to the window frame and right seat back to stabilize himself and looked out the forward windscreen, just in time to see red balls of gun fire zip over the aircraft, and the silver bat-like form of a MIG-21.

The big transport shook and shuddered as the jet wash buffeted them as it blew by. The single MIG merged with his wing man to their front. The second aircraft must have passed unseen by the port side. The pair of fighters immediately initiated a steep turn to the left with the likely intention of circling the transport and making another gun run.

"They're not going to make the same mistake twice," Kurt said.

"I know," Jack replied. "That was a one-off bluff. If they are serious they will get us on the next round."

The pair of MIGs pointed their left wing tips towards the water and banked in a high speed turn around the DC-8 to come up on their tail. Jack's manoeuvre, as effective as it was in throwing off the initial attack, now put them in a precarious position. With reduced airspeed and altitude, the DC-8 was at full throttle in a shallow climb, making them a sitting duck for the circling fighters.

"Goddamn cowardly bastards," Jack shouted. "Hell, with my old Spitfire I could knock those clowns out of the air. It really takes a brave pilot to take on an unarmed transport."

They both waited in strained silence. The MIGs were already out of their field of vision. Further manoeuvring of the DC-8 would be fruitless, and might only validate the attacker's intent.

Jack repeated his radio transmission.

"Mayday, mayday ... "

Both considered the call futile. They were over one of the more remote stretches of the planet, desert on one side, frigid Atlantic on the other, and two malevolent MIGs on their tail. Their odds of survival at that moment seemed slim.

⌘

Jack suddenly changed posture, sitting bolt upright from a resigned slouch. Kurt heard a crisply accented voice come in clearly over the cockpit speaker.

"Flight 243, acknowledge your transmission, stay your course. SADF flight 33 inbound, Mamba out."

Jack and Kurt glanced at each other with the same expression of disbelief then both looked out the windscreen, scanning the sky for some sign. Kurt was the first to see, and he pointed.

"Look, the cavalry maybe."

From a vector of one o'clock high, a speck grew larger and then separated into two aircraft. Suddenly, one and then the other aircraft looked as though they had blown up, as smoke erupted from their tails.

"They've gone to afterburners," Jack shouted gleefully. "What a bloody sight!"

Two aircraft appeared larger in their visual fields. They were pointed dart-like fighters, looking nothing like the pursuing MIGs. As they rapidly closed with the DC-8, the nose of the aircraft on the left began twinkling. It was a moment before Jack and Kurt realized they were seeing the muzzle flashes of cannon fire. The tracer rounds, moving sluggishly at first due to the distance and the angle, sped up to incredible velocity and nearly intersected their flight path, but pulled away tracking high and to their left.

An ever-present cloud of doubt told Kurt that the approaching aircraft might be firing at them. Perhaps there was a new type of MIG double teaming with their comrades? He swivelled his head to try to follow the path of the tracer rounds and picked up their intended target.

One of the MIG-21s was in a steep bank trying to avoid the incoming stream of cannon fire, but just before he could break away, one of the 30mm explosive rounds struck the tip of his starboard horizontal stabilizer. The shell detonated but due to the high speed and angle of impact, most of the explosive force blew to the rear of the MIG, resulting only in a damaged tail.

Immediately the injured MIG began to oscillate, as if losing control, but the pilot recovered. He put his nose to the east and seemed to cut airspeed, a clear sign he'd had enough and was heading home. His wing man came in to guard his rear. At that moment Kurt turned toward the front and caught a pair of super sleek Mirage III fighters shoot past on either side of the DC-8.

"Turning tail and running like jackal pups," one of the pursuing pilot's voices said over the radio. "Those two may bring back some mates, so let's get you to Windhoek, Captain."

"I'm with you on that, Mamba," Jack replied.

Like flying silver spearheads the Mirages positioned themselves behind the DC-8 to cover her rear and port flanks, the most likely avenues of attack. Jack kept the aircraft steady on course. To both men, the event already seemed like a bad dream that left you pale and sweat soaked. The visions of a horrifying fire or a cold watery grave were over, and they relaxed, slumping in the seats. Soon Windhoek Control was vectoring them in for landing. The two Mirage III broke away to set down at a South African Air Force runway a few miles away from the main terminal.

"Sometimes the ground feels damn good, doesn't it, lad," Jack stamped his polished leather boots on the black runway tarmac in an exaggerated manner.

"No argument there. But that is a strange comment coming from a guy that has spent more time in the air than I have breathing it," Kurt teased. Jack only grinned.

"It was different when I could fight back. The Spitfire at the time was equal or better than anything the Huns had to throw at us. At least it was a fair fight," Jack shook his head. "But now after thirty years of relative peace on this dark continent, fighters are shooting at cargo planes for no reason. I don't like it at all."

Kurt leaned against the open ramp of the DC-8 while local workmen unloaded crates and boxes from the cargo bay onto motorized carts. He put on his dark glasses and peeled the top of his one-piece flight suit to the waist. The warm dry air blowing in from the Namibian desert felt wonderful after the oppressive humidity of Brazzaville and Northern Angola. The air smelled fresh, mysterious, with hints of spice and exotic essences mixing with the jet exhaust. His entire body began to relax and the t-shirt that was clinging to his body with sweat dried almost instantly, leaving a white lace-like pattern of salt crystals on the fabric.

A vehicle raced toward them from the other side of the airfield. Through the shimmering mirage of midday it took the form of a Land Rover painted in patchwork desert camouflage. It was moving fast and swerving from side to side, tyres chirping with each swerve, like a bunch of drunken teenagers were aboard. Two people standing on the running boards of the vehicle leapt off as the Land Rover screeched to a halt. Kurt winced as squealing brakes and diesel fumes enveloped him, ruining the tranquil atmosphere.

Both men wore thin summer flight suits zipped open to their navels in the heat. One of the men was short, blonde and stocky while the other was tall, lean, and dark with a thin moustache. The latter moved with a feline grace. Kurt stepped away from the ramp and moved toward the men heading in his direction. The tall man stuck out his hand.

"Andre Van Lunen, South African Air Force." He spoke in English, with a deep guttural Afrikaans accent.

The shorter man also caught up and thrust his hand toward Kurt. "Reinhardt Hermann." His accent was different, and sounded more German and less Afrikaans.

"Thanks for saving our asses up there, you two," Kurt said. "I'm sure those MIGs would have flamed us if you hadn't stepped in."

Andre shook his head as if dismissing the compliment before speaking.

"That's difficult to say; those Cubans have been acting very unpredictably. In the past couple of days they harassed a couple of other commercial flights; that's why we were in the air. We knew Jack had filed a flight plan and was heading on down the coast so the SAAF gave us orders to launch just in case."

"So they weren't after us in particular?" Kurt asked.

Andre thought a moment before responding.

"Again, I don't know what their intentions were. They might have been just trying to frighten you, but this time they fired their cannons for the first time. Hopefully we taught them a lesson. Nothing like a bit of air to air combat to get the old blood going, hey?"

Andre punched Reinhardt in the arm, but the stocky blond man remained expressionless and just rolled with the punch and came back to his position unblinking. Andre approached Kurt so his face was only a foot away from his and whispered, "You're the one who caused that ruckus up north a few days ago, aren't you?"

Andre motioned with his thumb to the desert just north of the runway.

Kurt just looked at him for a second, decided that he already knew, and it would look foolish to deny it. The South Africans must have a good intelligence service. How did they know he was on the plane? Perhaps the cargo loaders in Brazzaville, or the customs officials could be agents. It was impossible to tell.

Kurt crossed his arms in an exaggerated pose.

"You know," he paused, "those folks up there have a lot to learn about hospitality."

Andre was silent for a few seconds but started to laugh as Kurt smiled at him.

"You had their whole bloody army running in circles for days. We were monitoring radio traffic from here." Andre indicated with a nod of his head a cluster of buildings that sat about a quarter mile off the runway. "They still don't know what hit them."

Andre turned from Kurt to look at Jack who was standing a few feet away enjoying the sun.

"Jack, why don't you escort Kurt over to the club, it should be open now. Reinhardt and I have to fill out logs and reports and such and should be with you shortly."

Andre leaned over to Kurt again and said quietly, "Don't worry mate, old Jack could find the club blindfolded in a sandstorm."

"That's enough of your cheek, you young pip-squeak! Your daddy and I were blasting ME-109s out of the sky before he even met that beautiful mother of yours."

⌘

The interior of the club was dark and, compared with the temperature outside, the air was so cold it made them shiver involuntarily. Even though it was only early afternoon the club was bustling. Kurt shook his head. This could be any military club on any military base anywhere. Being a soldier was a tough life. Not the worst or even the most dangerous occupation, but perhaps one of the most stressful, so soldiers sought refuge in places like this. Off-duty soldiers and airmen lined the bar and clustered at tables, smoke curling up from long-ashed cigarettes. Empty beer bottles stood like scattered tombstones everywhere.

Kurt's assumption of anonymity upon entering the club was soon dispelled. Walking through the dim lighting, eyes were following him. There was no such thing as contained information on a small military base. Military people talked to each other constantly; and information and rumours travelled at breathtaking speed. He knew by the looks and reception he was receiving and Andre's greeting, that almost everyone had heard about the recent events in nearby Angola.

Jack lead them to an empty table situated along the wall and away from the noisy bar and ordered draught beers from a large blonde waitress who recognized him.

"So, Mr Malloy, who is your good looking friend here, hey?" The waitress stared directly at Kurt and spoke with an Afrikaans accent that sounded rough, and didn't do anything to enhance her femininity. Feeling bone tired and burned out, even this cornucopia of available female flesh standing nearby wasn't sparking interest. He suspected that his attitude should be grounds for concern, but at the moment he didn't care. The waitress picked up on the snub, and bustled off in a huff.

"I wish I was your age instead of being an old fat bloke," Jack said in a self-effacing manner. "You don't even have to try, do you, lad? They just beat a path to you, and you have to fend them off."

Kurt shook his head morosely, "It's not what it seems."

"What are you talking about? It seems fine to me," Jack chuckled. "You really don't know how good you've got it."

"It may look that way to you," Kurt said." But do you ever get the feeling that everyone wants something from you, and they won't quit till you're used up?"

"Don't be daft, lad. That's the way life works. Everybody uses everyone else and hopefully in the process you get some of what you want too," Jack said.

"Maybe," Kurt replied, "but I've never felt that way."

"What motivates you then? Everyone has to have a motivation, otherwise why would you be here? Something has to make you tick, money, status, adventure maybe. You've got to have a force driving you, and in the process you use others to get there. That seems to make sense doesn't it?"

The heavy beer steins were delivered. Jack threw some bills on the table which the unsmiling waitress took before walking away.

"My grandfather was a lobsterman, a fisherman," Kurt continued. "It was a low-paying dangerous job which wore him out, and finally killed him. He died with nothing, penniless."

Kurt put his head in his arm and lowered it to the table, as if he'd suddenly remembered something terrible, but he quickly looked up again.

"Maybe that was his life, son. He did the only thing he knew, and probably did it damn well. There is nothing wrong with that," Jack said.

"I wish it was that easy," Kurt replied. "You have no way of knowing but my grandfather had graduate degrees in Anthropology and Ancient History. He was a professor at the

University of Maine and visited at some of the big Ivy League schools. He was one of the most respected men in his field in his day. The smartest person I ever knew."

"And he just quit that and became a fisherman?" Jack asked. "What happened?

"My father went to Korea about the time I was born. He was a UDT frogman. That's what they called them then. We call them SEALS now. He was on a beach reconnaissance mission along the North Korean coast when he was blown up and taken prisoner. They finally released him but he had severe brain injuries due to the blast. I remember him only vaguely. He was childlike, prone to temper tantrums, and he couldn't work. It would have been better for everyone if he had been killed. Then my grandmother died of breast cancer and my mother took off with someone else about the same time. It was just me and my grandfather after that. We left my father in a VA hospital and we packed up and moved to the Maine Coast. My grandfather was born into that environment and by sheer determination he worked his way out of it. When he lost everything he must have felt some comfort in going back. I don't know the answer."

"That's a sad story, lad," Jack said. "But you seem to have survived it though; you're a fine strong young man."

"Thanks, but I don't deserve any praise. Like I said, my father was committed to a VA mental hospital and I only saw him a couple of times, but he died just before ..."

"Before?" Jack quizzed.

"Sorry," Kurt replied. "Before I joined the US Army and became a Green Beret. That was probably the worst thing I could have done to my grandfather. I was declared missing, and he was lost at sea shortly after that. They found his body washed up on the rocks."

"But do you blame yourself for your grandfather's death?"

Kurt shrugged his shoulders.

"One thing I do know is that he never wanted anything from anyone. He just lived his life out and did it as honourably as he could. Besides being the smartest, he was also the only totally honest person I've ever known. He just didn't buy into the system, and in the end decided he didn't want it or need it anymore."

"At least you knew a man of character for that long, not many people can say that," Jack said.

"Oh, what the hell," Kurt raised his voice in a change of tone, "is this a damn funeral or what? We should celebrate the victory today. Life itself is a victory and we are still alive, aren't we? Tomorrow ... we'll have to see about tomorrow."

⌘

When Andre sat down at the table with them the mood instantly changed. Kurt forgot about his lost family. By talking about them the demons had been purged for a time.

With Andre's appearance others started to drift over and introduce themselves. Curiosity motivated them more than their friendship with the young pilot. Rumours piqued their interest and, like flies to ripening meat, they wandered over on the pretence of asking questions, but mainly to listen and to feel included in the discussion.

Kurt felt self conscious about discussing his experiences. Bragging and bravado were never part of his modus operandi, and it bothered him that it may appear that way to others. Looking into the eyes of these people though told a different story. They weren't just curious; they were hungry, hungry to share in the excitement. To live vicariously in events they would never experience themselves. Then it struck him like a cold wave of water... entertainment. They wanted entertainment to brighten up their tedious lives and he was the man of the moment, so they were looking to him to provide it. Voices came from nameless faces:

"Tell us how you fucked up those Cubans up north there. How many did you get? I heard they ran like scared chickens."

Kurt was hesitant initially but when he did speak, the room became quiet and people listened to him recount what had happened. In a short time with a couple more beers he became more relaxed and listened as some of the others told of clashes on the border, and fights with insurgents in the region. Kurt focused on their tales. They were describing a whole new conflict that was developing in this remote part of the world. Strange words were thrown about with abandon, terms he'd never heard before; gomo, vlei, veldt, koppie, hotie, terr. The ring of the language was strangely provocative and he felt something begin to stir within. A new excitement was beginning to form, welling up from a core still numbed by George's death.

The dialogue became decreasingly lucid as the day, then evening, progressed. The stories were full of encounters, or more commonly near encounters with wild animals while soldiers were on patrol. The guerrilla war had not penetrated the deep bush of this region yet. Most of this remote desert country favoured no creature including man, but security patrols were sent out anyway, thus the animal stories. It was nearly midnight when Andre broke up the party.

"Tomorrow's Friday. Let's get some sleep at the officers' quarters and drive out to the ranch, maybe get some shooting in. How does that sound?"

Kurt turned to Jack and mouthed the word "shooting" and shrugged his shoulders. Jack laughed and said out loud, "He means hunting, hunting game ... animals. You have to remember that you are near civilization now," Jack winked.

Kurt nodded and stood up to leave; there'd been enough storytelling for awhile. He turned to Andre.

"That sounds absolutely splendid, my good chap. I shall be pleased to accompany you," he said with a poorly performed mock English accent, then turned to Jack and returned his wink. Jack roared with laughter and said, "You have to watch these Yanks, Andre, they have too much bloody cheek for their own good."

⌘

The OQ rooms were sparse but very clean. After a long shower, Kurt noticed that his skin was dry within seconds of getting out; there was hardly need for a towel, the desert air was so desiccating. He lay on top of his bed as images of the day's events went through his mind like a film loop. Maybe he should have been a pilot. In college the Navy recruiter had talked him into taking a written naval flight test and he did it just for a lark. Several weeks later he received a call from Pensacola. The Navy man on the other end said that after he graduated they would like him to enrol in the F-14 programme, the latest super fighters to hit the fleet. He seriously contemplated the offer. What would it be like piloting a supersonic aircraft? Would that be the ultimate thrill? Better than ...

A light wind blew in the window at that moment, bathing his naked body with the scents of Africa, a mix of sand, cooking fires, animal wallows, blooming plants and ten thousand other things mixed together into heady, incomparable incense. The warm aromatic air smoothed his skin like a woman's gentle hand, caressing, promising, coaxing. The point dividing wakefulness and sleep is hard to define. Like so much in our world, it is not a single moment but a gradual transition, a continuum from one to the other, a matter of degree. Kurt drifted and the breeze gently purged thoughts of being a pilot or anything else that would keep him from the mysterious source. His dreams were not of aircraft but of this mysterious land, brushed by the night breeze.

⌘

Awake before the sun rose, he felt refreshed with his spirit buoyed by the clean air and crystal sky. Thankfully, the mess opened early and he sat alone for a time drinking a mug of what was promoted as coffee, but was actually a bitter impostor made from chicory bark. Andre came in and half an hour later Jack, who looked half awake at best, entered. Reinhardt came in last, hair still tousled from sleeping.

Andre was out of uniform and wore a faded khaki bush-jacket, tan shorts and veldtskoene, which were a soft suede high-topped bush shoe with crepe soles also known as desert boots. He had a thin but muscular build. He appeared relaxed, but the tanned rippling muscle tone in his exposed neck and forearms betrayed a controlled tension. Kurt figured he must weigh about one hundred and sixty pounds maximum, a perfect size for a fighter pilot, or a hunter; strong, light, quick and efficient. His own arms were twice the size of Andre's, and probably three times as strong, and he felt awkward and bulky sitting next to him.

"What do you have planned for us, Andre?" Jack asked, as he piled heaps of scrambled eggs on triangular toast wedges. Kurt watched Jack's animated actions with detached interest.

"I thought we'd do some shooting if all of you felt up to it, Jack. There is plenty of game at the waterholes this time of year. Could use some game for the freezer, and we are a little short of laborer's meat as well."

Kurt instantly lost interest in Jack's breakfast and turned to his host.

"Shooting, Andre, you are talking hunting, right?" Kurt questioned, feeling tedious by asking.

"Of course, my apologies," Andre said. "My father was born and raised in Kenya and hunting is what they call shooting in east Africa."

Jack nodded, his mouth too full of food to reply. The eggs and toast wedges were gone from the plate, and Kurt was a little disappointed because he'd missed whatever manoeuvre was used to get them all in his mouth so quickly.

"As they say … a bad day hunting is better than a good day doing anything else," Kurt volunteered.

Andre cast an impassive if slightly worried look across the table. Kurt was quickly learning that American humour didn't translate well, especially with these folks.

"Indeed," was all Andre said, and "indeed" said it all.

"Let's be off to the ranch then, if everyone is ready," Andre spouted as he got up and headed briskly for the door.

The four of them threw their bags in the back of Andre's Land Rover and headed towards the interior, away from the coast that defined Namibia. Stopping on the outskirts of town to fill the tank up with petrol, as they called gas, two jerrycans that were fastened to the back of the vehicle were also topped up.

Five minutes later they were swallowed by the dunes of the desert. Vegetation here was very sparse, consisting mainly of stunted brush and fleshy cactus-like plants. Andre explained that overnight the moist air overlying the ocean condensed in the cool desert to form a layer of tiny dewdrops. The dew looked like a wispy silver veil cast over the coast, and was used by specially adapted plants and small animals as their only source of fresh water. As the sun rose, the hot rays instantly vaporized the droplets, leaving only the stark contrast of sun and sand. The coastal strip was a thin fringe where life thrived between the contrasting realities of a cold ocean and hot desert.

Soon even the sparse vegetation dwindled and the pavement ended, leaving only a solitary, dusty gravel road winding through the sand dunes and wind ridges. Now mid-morning, the sun was elevated enough so its intensity was clearly felt through the un-insulated metal skin of the Land Rover. Only the dry, whipping wind blowing through the open windows kept the blistering heat in check.

"Be sure you drink enough water," Andre shouted to them over the noise of the blowing wind. "You will dehydrate very quickly if you're not conditioned."

Kurt saw a canvas water bag hanging in the back and using a plastic cup, passed around the cool water until no one wanted any more.

The scenery changed as they travelled inland. Most coasts have a surplus of moisture because as water evaporates from the nearby sea, some of it falls back as rain on the coast. Namibia's aptly named Skeleton Coast is not like that. The Bengela Current, originating from the cold regions of the South Atlantic, flows north along the African coastline and cools off the moist air masses flowing in from the ocean. This forces the rain to fall at sea, and it never reaches the shore. It may not rain on the Namibian coast from one year to the next. The land is parched, incredibly dry, and only a few specialized plants and animals are adapted to live there.

Further inland the vegetation was still meagre but was becoming more abundant with each mile they travelled. Sand dunes and formations were becoming less dominant, replaced with brown and red hills and ravines similar to Angola, but more arid. At midday they made a final turn down a slightly improved dirt road. Andre slowed the vehicle and opened his door, standing half in and half out of the Land Rover while he navigated the ruts and carefully watched the road surface.

"What are you doing?" Kurt shouted from the back seat.

"It's a habit I got into when driving in the bush," Andre shouted back, not taking his eyes off the road. "If you hit an anti-vehicle mine, the blast will flatten you against the roof and break your neck. This way you may be thrown clear and perhaps survive."

Kurt looked slowly up and fixed his eyes on the bare sheet metal and reinforcing bar of the Land Rover's roof, then turned slowly towards the front again.

"Not to worry though," Andre continued, "we haven't found mines in this area … yet."

The Land Rover crawled up the driveway of the ranch house swathed in a plume of dust.

Stark white walls, red tile roof and a wide veranda that seemed to completely encircle the house made it look cool and inviting after the hot drive. When the vehicle stopped, they all just remained still for a few moments and listened. The harsh suspension, engine noise and bumpy roads for the past several hours had made them numb.

The silence and sudden stillness were shocking in contrast. Sounds of the high pitched chirping of colourful flycatchers and other jewel-like birds chasing around the gnarled ancient trees ringing the house intruded like subtle music. Kurt saw that there were several small wooden platforms attached to the tree trunks that served as bird feeders, a seeming oasis for winged creatures in this dry land.

The door of the farmhouse opened abruptly and two women walked out toward the vehicle. The older woman, whom Kurt assumed was Andre's mother, wore a straw sun hat and a bright yellow floral dress. She was a tall, lean woman in her mid fifties with blonde hair turned half grey flowing out from beneath the hat. Her skin was noticeably laced with fine wrinkles and freckles from exposure to the intense sun and dry air. It was obvious that she had been very pretty in her youth and that the African bush had undoubtedly taken its toll. Jack responded to the sight of her like a pleased schoolboy, totally out of character. Kurt was both surprised and amused … there was something there.

The other woman was young and lean and moved gracefully and effortlessly. Kurt was immediately intrigued. The intense overhead sun hid her features in the shadow of a wide-brimmed hat similar to the one the other woman wore. Kurt thought, Sister? Andre or Jack didn't mention a sister, or maybe a relative, cousin, or just a friend? The young woman wore brief shorts showing off athletic legs of a deep brown that looked as firm as acacia wood. Her light blue cotton top was sleeveless, and her arms were long, lean, and of the same burnished colour.

Kurt didn't want to appear as if he was staring. Although pretending to be looking straight ahead he was watching the girl's every move from behind his dark sun glasses.

The older woman reached the Land Rover and hit the metal hood with the flat of her hand, sounding a tinny thump. She quickly pulled it away not realizing how hot it was.

"It is about time you arrived," she said to Andre through the open window. "I have lunch prepared on the veranda, and you had better eat it before it all dries out."

"That's very decent of you, mother," Andre replied. "But do you have any cold beer? I'll die if I don't have a cold beer right away."

"Don't worry, I wouldn't want that to happen. We have both pilsner and ale on ice."

"Bless you, Mother, you are a life saver."

"Well, hello Jack, it's so nice to see you again." Andre's mother said through the window, smiling.

Jack seemed to flush, even though his skin was already red from the heat.

"It's always a pleasure, Francis," Jack tipped his head toward her.

"Come on out of that hot car and come into the house, it's much cooler," Francis told them. It's then that she focused on Kurt in the back seat.

"A new face, I see. Please introduce him, Andre, don't be rude. Another pilot I suppose?"

Andre rolled his eyes slightly as he climbed out of the Land Rover.

"Not another pilot, Mother, this is Kurt Christianson, an American."

"Oh," Francis exclaimed. "A game hunter then?"

"Not really, ma'am, it's a long story," Kurt said as he climbed out.

Francis grabbed Kurt's arm and led him toward the house.

"And this is Andre's sister, Diana," Francis said nodding toward the girl walking beside them.

Diana nodded minimally in Kurt's direction and said 'hello', but didn't offer her hand. He was disappointed. You could tell a lot about a person by their hand.

⌘

As promised, inside the screened veranda sat what looked like an old tin washtub filled with ice and brown bottles and also a bottle each of locally made white and red wine. Andre was immediately into it, pulling out bottles and popping their tops with an old tarnished 'church key' snatched up from the table. Hurriedly, Andre passed out the beer bottles and clear glasses so he could get to his without appearing to be a rude host. The beer tasted like cold nectar as everyone finished their first with a few quick swallows.

Francis and Diana had prepared a buffet-style meal on a long old rough-hewn table positioned against the outside wall of the house. All the food was covered with a lightweight cheesecloth veil to keep off the insects. There were cold slices of game and irregular pieces of what looked like scrawny chicken, but when he asked he was told it was guinea fowl, which was a wild bird native to the area. There were also several dessert dishes under the netting that were mostly obscured but looked intriguing. Trying not to look greedy, Kurt filled his plate mostly with meat which he'd been craving for awhile.

"Help yourself to the meat, we have plenty," Francis said.

"Thank you, ma'am, I do love game meat."

"Have all you want. And please call me Fran."

Kurt nodded at her; with a full mouth there was no way to respond politely.

They all ate and drank until almost everything that had been laid out was gone. The combination of the hot day and the sudden intake of food and beer after weeks of so little made Kurt feel tired and light-headed. He didn't feel ill or dizzy, just pleasantly detached, like his body was rebelling and taking a needed break. Between the club the previous evening and today, he was well on the way.

"So tell us how you've come to visit us, Mr Christianson?" Fran asked.

"It's Kurt, please, ma'am," he replied.

"All right Kurt, but if you call me ma'am once more I'll klap your ear. I'm Fran, I'm not that old," she replied in a mock huff.

Kurt smiled at her, still chewing. The woman had spirit, he liked that in people.

Diana watched them all quietly.

"Well," Kurt began after swallowing his food, "Jack and I were heading from Brazzaville to Windhoek and we were attacked by some MIG fighters from Angola. We probably wouldn't be alive now if Andre and Reinhardt hadn't come to our rescue."

"My brother ... the knight in a shining Mirage?" Diana said a bit mockingly.

"Hush, Diana!" Francis interjected. "I must apologize Kurt, the twins have been at each other all their lives. They still are as you can see."

"I could fly a Mirage, too, if they would let me," Diana said. "I could always drive and fly better than Andre."

Fran said nothing but gave Diana the 'evil eye'. "Continue, Kurt," she said.

"Well, there isn't much to tell," Kurt continued. "Andre and Reinhardt came in like the Lone Ranger and Tonto, and chased the MIGs away." Kurt looked at his host hoping she didn't expect more.

"The Lone Ranger ... and who?" Francis asked.

There was an awkward pause, then Jack interjected.

"Oh, that is an American cowboy hero and his Red Indian friend, I believe. Always comes to the rescue in the nick of time, good chap."

Francis nodded as if she was suddenly enlightened.

"Oh, cowboy ... I understand."

Fran still looked puzzled but Kurt didn't want to pursue the topic any more, so he turned to Andre.

"Where are you taking us shooting, Andre?" Kurt asked, trying to change the subject.

Andre's eyes picked up. He had been staring into his beer glass watching the little strings of bubbles as they formed and headed for the surface.

"There is an old wadi about forty kilometres south-east of here. It must have been formed when there was a bit more water around than there is now. When there is surplus water, it spills out of the pools onto a level plain and grass grows pretty lush for awhile. Those pools attract animals, and they come in using the grass for cover and grazing when heading for the water. I don't like to hunt there too often, I'm afraid it might disturb the migratory patterns, but once in a while doesn't seem to bother the herds. I haven't been out there in weeks, but there's been some rain in the area recently, so I'm anxious to see what the conditions are like."

"Did you study this stuff at school, Andre?" Kurt asked. "You seem to know it pretty well."

"There are really only two professions for those of us from the south-west, Kurt," Andre explained. "You are either a rancher or a game manager. Put more simply, you either tend tame beasts or wild ones. Farming and ranching never interested me, much to Ma's dismay."

Francis gave Andre a direct look which flared briefly but cooled down just as quickly.

"Sorry, Ma," Andre continued. "I went to university to study game management, and went to work for the government in the Parks and Wildlife Bureau. Then the inclination to fly hit me and I joined the South African Air Force and, as they say, that was that."

"What about you, Kurt?" Diana asked almost abruptly. "Did you go to university?"

"In the United States, Diana, we have what's called a GI Bill that pays for college for military veterans. When I got out of the Army I felt I had to use it, so I enrolled in a school near Boston; currently I'm majoring in geology."

"So you are studying rocks, are you?" Andre asked.

"Rocks and the earth sciences," Kurt continued. "It's the only thing I can think of that pays you well to be outside most of the time. I can't stand being under a roof. That's one reason I liked the military so much."

"Well, Kurt," Andre offered, "we could always use a fit chap like you to help run down these poachers."

"Sounds great, I didn't know people were paid to do that."

"I say enough of the serious talk," Andre said, rising from his chair. "Let's pack a few things and head down to the camp so we can set up before dark. If we can get there early we may be able to see what is moving and where so we can select good positions tomorrow. Jack, you are coming, right?"

Kurt knew this was a rhetorical question. Jack and Francis had been making eye contact since they arrived; there was no mistaking infatuation. Why not? Kurt thought. It's never too late they say. He winced at the thought of being that age, looking like that, with a body that didn't work as it was designed to anymore. That didn't seem real, he couldn't picture himself old, it seemed unrealistic, and he put the thought out of his mind.

Jack cleared his throat before stating rather sheepishly he would stay at the house tonight in comfort, and come out to the camp tomorrow. He would leave camping in the bush to the youngsters. Andre grinned slightly and even Fran blushed a little, despite her tan.

# CHAPTER 13
## ANCIENT WAYS

It took the better part of an hour to load the camping gear and cooking supplies, rifles, sleeping rolls, a tent and other assorted equipment into the Land Rover and flat-bed farm lorry. The trail to the camp was slow, dusty and bumpy. Though currently dry, the track was rutted with washouts, caused by occasional flash floods in the soft sandy loam. It took nearly two hours of hard travelling before they arrived. The camp was located in a natural clearing about thirty metres across, surrounded by a fairly dense growth of high grasses and thick shrub. Their approach was through heavy grass that had come up since the camp was last used. You had to know where to look to find the place.

From where they parked the vehicles, Kurt could see what looked like a footpath that began at the far side of the clearing and disappeared quickly in the thick bush. He pointed at the path entrance and asked, "That goes to the water?"

"Yes," Andre replied, pulling boxes of supplies off the truck. "Let's set up and I'll walk you down."

By the time the tent was up and the fire was burning in the well-used blackened fire pit, an orange sun was tickling the tips of the tall grass.

"We'd better shift ourselves if we intend to make it back before dark," Andre stated. "Do you want to carry the Weatherby? I'll carry the double in case we run into any nasty creatures."

Kurt nodded and was handed the polished rifle with a mirror finished stock of figured walnut.

"An American hunter gave it to me a couple of years ago," Andre explained. "He'd had a good hunt and was feeling generous, I guess. I had the feeling that it didn't mean much to him, just more luggage."

"Pretty, but not the sort of thing I'd normally use," Kurt said as he opened the bolt and checked the chamber.

"I prefer to use the big doubles myself, but that's an acquired thing." Andre stated.

Andre broke open the breach of his rifle like a standard side-by-side double barrel shotgun and inserted two gleaming brass cartridges, the diameter of his thumb, into the chambers. To the uninformed the rifle looked plain, but Kurt knew it was a classic Holland and Holland side lock chambered for 470 Nitro Express, worth at least five figures on the open market. In contrast to the solid brute power of the H&H, the Weatherby looked like a fancy toy. Andre handed over a fistful of gleaming 300 Weatherby rounds, which he pocketed.

Kurt opened his personal duffel bag and extracted his holstered Smith & Wesson revolver which he quickly strapped on. Andre eyed the rig with a mixture of mirth and suspicion.

"Only an American," Andre scoffed, "would bring a pistol to an African hunt. That's like taking a rowboat across the Atlantic."

Kurt didn't reply to Andre's remark, just grinned at him.

"Well, we'd better head out," Andre said. "Are you coming, Reinhardt?"

"I don't think so, Andre, Diana and I will stay here and finish setting up camp," Reinhardt shouted back. "Get us some meat if you can; I'm craving some fresh meat."

"We'll see what we can do, you bloody carnivore," Andre replied. "More like you need some meat to soak up your beer."

Andre turned toward Kurt, "I will lead, stay behind me about three or four body lengths. Watch our rear. Leopards have a habit of sneaking around and attacking from behind. I'm not trying to scare you, but just in case."

At first, the trail curved up and around some small hills which were in fact overgrown sand dunes. Within a quarter mile, the path flattened out and slowly descended on its approach to the swampy pans. The visibility became much better in the flats and Kurt could see a fair distance across the top of the vegetation in some places.

He could make out the subtle movements of animals in the tall grass, approaching and departing the drinking water provided by the pans. Here, freshwater swamps and meandering streams were a focal point for all of the animals in the area. There was an unusual symbiosis between the species. Every creature was aware that without water they would all perish, that somehow their mutual survival was linked and water points were shared without aggression, as if by agreement. There was some lesson here, but Kurt let it slip from his thoughts as they left the high ground and ceased being observers, to become participants at the water's edge.

Andre motioned for Kurt to close up, and they quietly approached the glass-still water guarded by a stand of dry, pithy reeds. The waning sun cast a yellow tint over the scene, blending grass, bush, sky and swamp into a unified portrait of harmonious stillness.

Andre approached the pan from behind the cover of a thick bush growing at the water's edge. He stood perfectly still for a moment, then motioned for Kurt to drop down. Scanning the pool from a kneeling position, the water just touched their kneecaps and shoes. Fifty metres ahead, a tongue of land projected into the shallow water. Several wary impala stood on the peninsula, alternately eating the rich green grass that grew there and drinking from the pan. All of the animals were constantly alert for danger. The position left the animals exposed, but they found it hard to resist filling their stomachs on the rich sweet growth.

A young impala buck stood off to one side. His horns hadn't developed their full curve yet, but he seemed nicely filled out from the rich diet. With subtle movements of his fingers and eyes, Andre indicated for Kurt to shoot one of the antelope. Kurt nodded minimally and gently lowered the Weatherby to the ground. Andre looked slightly confused until Kurt pointed to his ear, then quietly withdrew the .44 magnum revolver from his belt. Even that subtle sound of steel on leather brought all of the impala to full attention as they tensed in preparation to bolt. With a smooth, rapid and fluid movement Kurt brought the revolver up to firing position. Andre plugged both ears with his fingers and saw that the hammer was coming back as the gun was raised. The end of the barrel flashed like a stroke of lightening and a concussion pounded the air at the same instant the movement stopped.

When he saw the movement of Kurt's arm and gun, the young buck impala leapt straight up into the air instinctively. No one knows exactly why they do this. Some say it is to get a momentary vantage point to locate their attacker so they know in which direction to run. Kurt aimed for the upper neck to break the spine. On the way up the impala ram caught the 240 grain hollow point bullet in the lower chest. A cloud of dust flew from the point of impact like a broom striking a hanging carpet. With the bottom of its heart ripped out, the ram spun almost upside down from the sledgehammer strike, hit the shallow water on its back, and lay still. The other antelope bolted and, in seconds, were gone.

Andre shook has head as if trying to get water out of his ears.

"Mother of God, what kind of pistol is that?"

"A .44 magnum loaded hot," Kurt said softly, almost inaudibly, after the blast.

⌘

The gunshot caused the darkening pan to become incredibly silent. The only object disrupting the smooth symmetry of water and vegetation was the crumpled body of an impala, lying askew in the water.

"I've never seen anything like that." Andre said, loudly now they had their kill. "I've fired pistols before, mostly nine millimetres which are pretty useless for hunting game, but that thing hits like a big rifle."

"We'd better get our meat," Kurt said as he replaced the single empty case with a live round and re-holstered the revolver, "I really don't want to be toting that back after dark around here."

Kurt waded out into the shallow water to get the impala, scanning carefully for the wake of crocs as he moved. He doubted their presence in these restricted waters, but anything was possible in Africa.

Hoisting up the carcass, he estimated it to be about forty kilos, about the same as a medium Eastern White Tail deer in the US On the bank of the pool, he slit open the abdomen with the puukko, and removed the entrails. Kurt carried the body into the shallow water where he washed out the remaining blood and cooled the meat. This also lightened the load considerably, and would make the meat more palatable. If any cats were in the area, hopefully the discarded viscera would draw them, and they wouldn't bother tracking the carcass being carried back to camp.

Andre and Kurt arrived back at camp as darkness descended over the landscape, which happened with amazing speed in the southern hemisphere. To the south of the equator there was little atmospheric dust and industrial pollutants so common in the north, which diffuse light and prolong the sunset.

Reinhardt met them carrying a kerosene lantern.

"Heard the shot but it didn't sound like the rifle; I was hoping the gun didn't burst on you or something."

"No," said Andre. "Kurt was just showing off. He took it with his pistol."

"You don't say?" Reinhardt sounded genuinely surprised as he examined the ram, "Bloody good shot though, right through the heart."

"I was aiming for the neck," Kurt explained. "I didn't know they jump like jackrabbits when they are startled."

"Put the carcass down over by those trees," Andre pointed to a spot near the edge of the clearing. "We'll take the meat we want immediately then dispose of the remains fifty metres or so out in the bush. We don't want cats or hyenas coming into our camp tonight to claim it."

By the light of the lantern, Kurt quickly flayed the hide off the impala and, still using the puukko, carved off the loins from the upper back, then took the two haunches from the hind quarters. It was more meat than they would use, the cats and other nocturnal predators could fight over the rest. As he finished, Kurt sliced off a sliver of loin meat and placed it on his tongue. Andre eyed him curiously.

"Why did you do that? Do you like raw meat?" he asked.

Kurt looked at him blankly and had to think before he responded. The action was almost subconscious, without rational intent.

"I don't know. I always do that when I hunt. My grandfather used to do it with a fresh kill and I just picked up the habit, I guess."

The meat from one of the haunches was diced up and soaked for a time in cool, salty water before the pieces were placed in a pot of broth and vegetables already simmering on campfire. The fire emitted a hot blue flame and was made from dense leadwood and wild olive branches. The aroma of cooking enveloped the still night air.

They all sat around the nearly smokeless fire, sipped cold local beer out of brown bottles and listened to the night settle in. It was a magical time when the bush made the transition from harsh, hot and real, to soft, cool and surreal. First the insects and small animals began to move, followed by the larger creatures that preyed on them, and so on. Kurt heard the soft hiss of a big cat's breath in the nearby trees. The animal was beginning its nightly hunt but had no doubt smelled them. Human scent is repulsive to cats. We smell pretty bad to an animal whose olfaction is orders of magnitude better then our own. It was probably fortunate that man couldn't smell himself they way they could.

Kurt noticed that the behaviour of people also changed drastically when day became night. During the day, man is generally bold and arrogant. Technology and ruthless cunning has made him king of the realm in the light, but night was different. Being a creature of superior vision during daylight hours, we are nearly blind at night, and our sense of smell has become almost useless over the eons. At night, we suddenly lose our precious advantages. The darkness makes man feel helpless and naked; we huddle in groups, hide inside protective structures and bathe ourselves in artificial sunlight. Other forces dominate, including creatures which are perfectly adapted to the darkness. Worst of all, it is also the time when creations of our imaginations come alive, existing only to prey on our most delicate vulnerabilities.

Kurt watched with amusement how the others in the party reacted. His grandfather taught him when he was a boy to ignore his instincts and never fear the night, to use it as an ally. He had said, "If your vision fails, use other senses that man has and animals do not."

At first, Kurt didn't know what this meant but as he matured, there came a gradual awareness of powers we unknowingly possess, but which have become fallow with disuse. He remembered tracking deer and bear in the deep Maine woods, practicing what his grandfather called 'shadowing' game. Not just finding them, but following them for hours, outside of the animal's awareness. It was very difficult at first, but with time this skill improved. The deep smooth voice of the old man would say, "We are the greatest predators on earth. We have just lost our edge from all of this soft living. The wilderness will restore your power if you let her."

Of course his grandfather was right, he was right about everything. After many failures and false starts he became fully aware on a silent cold winter day at the age of twelve. For the first time he felt the energy, like heat but different, coming from the animals he was tracking. It was like an unseen halo or aura radiating from the animal that would diminish or 'go cold' with distance. If you were 'too hot' the animal became aware of your presence, perhaps by tuning into that same energy, and would run away. The trick was to keep that balance, or as his grandfather said, "Keep warm on your prey." Monitoring wind direction, and of course sound discipline, were also necessary and vital skills to be successful.

A few years after acquiring the skill, Kurt asked his grandfather if a man could be followed in the same manner. The old man just stopped and eyed him intensely. Although he never had a verbal answer, that look said everything. Later he found that humans had powerful auras which dwarfed that of game animals. It was different in quality and not easy to tune into, most likely due to interference from the large numbers of people in most places. But if you tuned in on one or two men, or even a small group that was isolated from others, they could be followed with little trouble.

His thoughts about times past were interrupted by a figure that quietly moved toward him in the firelight. The darkness affected women as well it seemed.

Andre's sister, Diana, had almost made a point of ignoring him at first. That didn't bother Kurt; he'd long given up on trying to fathom people's motives, especially those of women. It was easier to track a lemming in the arctic during a snowstorm, and probably more rewarding. She lightly perched in the grass a few feet away and stared directly into his eyes for a few moments. He found the action disconcerting and she knew it. The flickering firelight was mystical, forming unique and unpredictable shadows and dimensions.

"Your eyes," she finally said; it sounded like a question rather than a statement.

Kurt reached up towards his face with his hand but stopped short.

"What ... what about them?" His inflection was defensive.

"They're different, like cat's eyes. Sitting over there I swear I saw the firelight reflected off the back of them. You know, like a cat ... at night? But maybe I was just imagining it."

"You're the first person to notice that," Kurt replied.

"I suppose you can see very well in the dark? I would think so, anyway."

"Maybe," Kurt shrugged. "I've always taken it for granted. It's hard to know what is normal when you've never seen the world from any other eyes. But now you mention it, when I was training in the army I always thought it was funny watching everyone else stumble around in the dark, banging into trees. My grandfather taught me how to see at night when I was little by using the sides of your vision, not the centre. Maybe it is a learned and not a physical thing."

"That's interesting," Diana said. "I imagine there are a lot of things like that we don't know about ourselves."

They talked for awhile longer. Diana told him about their lives in the Namibian bush, which Kurt thought wasn't all that different from his own upbringing on the Maine Coast. The rawness of the land and the feeling of being on the edge of wilderness was the same, even though the climates and geographies were vastly different.

Diana's direct manner and melodic voice were both soothing and appealing for reasons he could not explain. Sometimes there is no explanation when things are right. There is a harmony in the universe we don't create but occasionally fall into, if fate allows it. Diana looked like the perfect young woman to Kurt. She was attractive, strong, intelligent and, most importantly, born in one of the last pieces of wilderness left on earth, unspoiled by what man had become.

Everyone else seemed to be asleep. Diana moved closer to him as the desert chill began to grab with icy claws. They sat close for awhile and watched the fire die from blue flame to yellow-orange translucent coals. Finally she broke the silence with,

"Goodnight, Kurt" and turned towards him. Her lips were soft against his and her body felt warm and supple. With his palm he reached up and gently brushed her breasts which were free beneath a khaki shirt. Her nipples were as hard as buttons from the cold air and she shivered, involuntarily, with the touch. She didn't pull away, but didn't encourage him either. Smiling, she stood up gracefully and walked to her tent.

⌘

Kurt lay looking at the stars. The Southern Cross was clearly visible and dominated the night sky. Far from feeling tired, his mind and body seemed vital and electrified. The African bush was starting to take hold. Was this the feeling of a wayward son, returning to his roots after five thousand generations? Could it be? Or was it just a fantasy made up as he went along? South-East Asia had its mysteries, horrors and beauty but for some reason always felt alien, strange, but never comfortable. This was different. Already it felt right. He tried not to think about the lovely young woman lying only a few yards away, or the possible impact she might have on his life. Women were known to alter the lives of men, changing their ambitions and destiny on a whim. It would take discipline not to be deflected by Diana. The fact that he didn't have any conscious ambition or destiny at the moment made him more vulnerable. Her kiss and momentary brush against him had the effect of a mortar bomb landing in the middle of his gut. It all hadn't sunk in yet, he needed time for the shock to wear off so he could think clearly.

Restlessness dominated the remainder of the night, waking him every few minutes to listen intently to the sounds of nocturnal animals. He drifted in and out of sleep, staying just below the surface of consciousness. Both Andre and Reinhardt woke him when they got up to relieve themselves in the bushes.

The sounds of the bush had lulled and light was breaking when he felt a nearby presence: not threatening, but it was different, unusual, and then a sharp smell like musk struck his nose. His right hand tightened on the smooth grips of his revolver, beneath the rolled-up clothing he was using for a pillow. Sitting up slowly, Kurt saw the unexpected. A small elfish, brownish-yellow man squatted in the bush about ten feet away. The camouflage was almost perfect.

"Well, I'll be ... a Bushman," Kurt said to himself.

"I think you got that wrong, boet," Andre said, walking towards them tucking his shirt in his pants. "I think it's 'he be the Bushman, you be the great white hunter'."

Andre squatted down and motioned for the Bushman to approach. Breaking his perfectly motionless stance, the small, brown, nearly naked man smiled and vocalized a part clicking, part high-pitched voice monologue as he cautiously came towards them.

"What is he saying?" Kurt asked Andre as he slid out of the sleeping bag and stood up, dwarfing the approaching Bushman.

"Squat down, Kurt, your size intimidates him," Andre said.

Kurt did as he was told and squatted next to Andre.

"Xi says that he wants to hunt with you today," Andre translated. "He saw you shoot the impala and thinks it is a great thing."

Xi nodded and clicked affirmatively, then extended his right arm and threw it back in mock recoil.

"Boom! Big ... piss ... tole." He smiled at Kurt with his elfin-like features.

Kurt smiled at the man. He was so small, almost cute, but Kurt knew that Bushmen were the best trackers in the world bar none, as well as formidable hunters. He had always wanted to meet one ever since reading about them, and suddenly here was his chance.

"How did he see that? I would have been aware of ... " Kurt didn't finish his sentence.

"You will only see them if they want you to," Andre interrupted. "Xi and his extended family have been living in this area for a very long time. God only knows how long. By all rights this is their territory. After all, they were here first. All of the newcomers, black and white alike, chose to ignore them. The settlers actually shot them as they would wild animals because they poached an occasional head of livestock. To the Bushmen a domestic and a wild animal were no different. They never domesticated animals. You should feel fortunate; this is the first time he has ever shown himself around a stranger. When I bring other hunters here, the Bushmen stay in the background. I see them but the clients never do."

"You mean like the two hiding in the tree line over there?" Kurt nodded in the general direction, assuming it would be tactless and even threatening to point, as it was in most cultures.

"Good eye," Andre nodded. "See what I mean? They really melt into the bush."

"Definitely, I'd say they've had a bit of practice at the art of concealment. So the little fellow wants to hunt with us, is that it?" Kurt asked.

"No," Andre replied. "He doesn't want to hunt with us. He says he wants to hunt with *you*."

"So to what do I owe this honour? My international reputation, perhaps?"

Kurt strapped on his gun belt and the Bushman's eyes lit up when he saw the handle of the big revolver.

"From my dealings with them, and it's been a lifelong thing with me," Andre continued, "we don't understand them at all. Sometimes they just know things and they can't explain their motives, because they don't understand explanations or motives. He knew you would be friendly to him before he approached you, otherwise he wouldn't have done it. You can't force or coerce them into doing anything they don't want to do. They need and want very little. They carry everything they own. If Xi sees something he needs, he will take it. Personal possessions, like ownership of land, are alien concepts to them. Everything is communal; it's the way they have to live. Sometimes when I watch them it strikes a chord. All of us were like them at one time. We've made our lives so complex and cluttered with things, we've forgotten who and what we are. The Bushmen and the Australian Aboriginals are the only remaining keys to our own past, pure hunter-gatherers."

Xi clicked out a few words. He stood so close to Kurt that the exotic musky smell of this wild man struck him and it, too, recalled things long forgotten.

"What is he saying?" Kurt asked.

"It's hard to translate exactly," Andre said slowly, "but he calls you his brother from the cold forest, I think. And he wants to go hunting with you, to kill a sacred animal."

Kurt pointed to himself and the other members of the party, who were now sitting by the campfire which had been stoked up again for breakfast with smoky green acacia wood.

"You mean us? He wants to hunt with us?" Kurt asked, hoping for clarification.

Andre shook his head emphatically. All Andre wore was a pair of faded green shorts, a t-shirt and a wide-brimmed bush hat cocked to one side. In his right hand he held a blue enamel mug of steaming tea.

"No," Andre reiterated. "He wants to take *you* hunting, that's what he said." He sipped his tea and grimaced as the hot liquid scalded his lips.

"I wouldn't argue with him," Andre stated. "He doesn't understand what the word no means. Besides, Xi will probably get you close to a nice trophy. They can track animals like no one else. Have some breakfast and head out with him. I'll tell him to have you back by dark; we'll wait for you."

⌘

Kurt was amazed at the speed at which Xi was moving; it looked so effortless. The spindly little legs and bare feet sticking out of the ragged holey pair of faded shorts seemed to float over the rough ground. He could barely keep up; after two hours of solid walking they must have covered sixteen or seventeen kilometres over rough terrain. Kurt began to curse. The gear he was carrying; rifle, pistol belt, water and ammo felt like lead bricks now that the sun had vaporized the mist and began to pound down relentlessly.

Was this a test of some sort? Maybe it was a snipe hunt on a grand African scale and Xi would lead him back to camp tonight, half dead, to the ridicule of the others. He pictured Diana laughing at him, but banished that image immediately. Anger, provoked by his own irrational thoughts, boosted his flagging energy and suddenly he seemed less tired.

Xi had been travelling in a more or less straight, fixed course until a moment ago, when he broke and began to cast to the right. They were approaching the end of a broken chain of irregular hills that were tapering off into the true sand dunes so distinctive to the Namibian coast. They had already spooked several head of duiker and impala, grazing on the sparse vegetative cover, but the Bushman seemed to ignore them. He was intent on another quarry. What that was Kurt didn't know.

For the next hour they moved in a gradual arc that paralleled the interface between dunes and brush-covered hills. To some relief, Xi was walking slower now, head bent to the ground. He was not travelling on a straight course anymore but moved in a zigzag pattern, first thirty degrees to the left and then thirty degrees to the right. This allowed the tracker to 'cast a net' so spoor would not be missed if he cut across it. Without being taught, Kurt had developed this same technique while living ten thousand miles away.

Xi slowed and stuck his left arm out behind him, palm down. Although their cultures had never met for at least a hundred thousand years, Kurt knew immediately what the Bushman was saying with the gesture. He had found the spoor he was after. Xi stopped, squatted down, glanced at the ground and then looked up and swept the area in panorama. Kurt walked up quietly behind him and knelt down. He saw spoor just to Xi's front. Unlike tracks in soft earth, snow, or river bottom clay, dry sand was a very poor medium for preserving impressions. Fuzzy collapsed indentations were the only evidence of the passage of a small group of animals some hours before. Kurt knew he would be hard pressed to read the exact number and type of animal. Xi held one hand up in front of him and folded his thumb down.

Four he was saying, but four what? Xi, sensing Kurt's confusion, took the flat of his hand and levelled an area of sand. With his forefinger the Bushman began to draw what looked like a generic four legged animal, a dog or antelope, maybe. Then starting at the head of the figure, he traced a large smooth curve upwards and rearwards until it almost touched the animal's rear end. The drawing looked out of proportion, exaggerated to the point of absurdity. When he finished his sketch, Xi looked up and smiled. His small, yellowish pointed teeth seemed predatory, like a cat or shark, a strange and frightening contrast to the elfish, childlike face.

Kurt studied the sand drawing and nodded. It seemed to be a caricature of an animal he'd seen before only in books; sable came to mind. He remembered reading that they were rare, and their horns were very long, but surely ...? He'd also read that as beautiful and graceful as the horns were, their function was deadly serious. If cornered, a sable would run head first into thick cover and when the predator, usually a lion, pressed the attack from the rear, the sable would flex its massive neck and skewer the cat with its scimitar-like horns. To survive on this continent, an animal must have potent defensive adaptations. But Kurt wondered what force of nature is able to merge the most graceful and beautiful with the most lethal?

There was no time to ponder philosophy because Xi was on the move again. Now directly following the spoor, he bent down after one-hundred metres and picked up some fresh droppings. They were still moist on the underside and he smelled them carefully. He tossed them down and moved on, heading directly towards the massive sand dunes bordering the coast.

Nearly an hour later Xi squatted again and Kurt perched next to him. They sat quietly for a minute. The air was perfectly still and the heat was building in intensity.

The Bushman hadn't consumed any water since leaving that morning. Xi slowly moved his body sideways and sipped from the capped drinking gourd that was slung over his shoulder with hemp twine. Kurt was waiting for this cue and drank heavily from his four-litre bladder canteen. The water was hot and tasted of plastic but wonderful nonetheless.

Xi straightened up and looked directly at the mountainous dunes that rolled away to their front. The sun's angle seemed to set the sand on fire; and it was like looking into the door of a great blast furnace. Xi nodded almost imperceptibly. Kurt thought it was a twitch but he followed the Bushman's line of vision and then saw the animals, small dark spots on the crest of a distant sand dune. The strong mirage caused by the heat coming off the blistering sand blurred their shape, so their forms appeared shimmering and indistinct as they made their way down the slope in their direction. It looked like five or maybe six animals, with the lead animal appearing much larger than the rest. Kurt started to raise the Weatherby up to look through its scope but Xi immediately gave the palm down signal, so Kurt stopped.

The fuzzy apparitions continued to descend the slope of the distant dune and finally, one by one, they began to cross the line where they became obscured by a nearer, overlapping dune. When the last animal was blocked from view, Xi gave the palms up and was on his feet in a crouch, moving forward, signalling Kurt to follow without glancing back at him. Grabbing the rifle, Kurt tried to follow the Bushman using the same bent posture. Xi was as quick as a jackrabbit, and although Kurt considered himself physically fit, he felt like a lumbering sow in comparison.

They moved out of the line of sparse vegetation toward the first dune, but instead of climbing it, Xi turned and skirted its base. Keeping low, he led them on a course that snaked between the ever-shifting dune bases. It was difficult going. Kurt felt his feet sink and move in the soft sand. Xi seemed to glide over the top like the roadrunner he'd seen in New Mexico months before. The Bushman kept his toes pointed level with the ground and landed on the balls of his feet, distributing weight evenly across the foot. Heat from the sand was beginning to soak through Kurt's boot material, making his feet uncomfortably hot. Xi didn't seem to notice. The soles of his feet must be as thick as elephant hide, Kurt thought.

Moving rapidly on a winding course through the dunes, Xi slowed and began to cast back and forth as if he was searching for spoor, but he was not looking at the ground. Just ahead of them was a long dune with an undulating top that formed a bridge between two other dunes. It looked like the wall of a small earthen dam, a strange analogy in this dry place. Xi moved directly up to this wall of sand and indicated for Kurt to follow. Walking directly up the steep dune, Xi was bent almost parallel to the slope for balance, and to prevent being silhouetted from the other side. Just below the crest Xi stopped and slowly elevated his head to just break the top with his eyes. Scanning intently for a few moments, his head was stationary; only his roving eyes traversed the terrain. Then he froze for a few seconds, staring intently in one place. Seemingly satisfied, he stood up and with his feet and hands began to dig a trench starting at the top of the crest and extending down the side they'd just walked up.

Kurt watched but didn't offer to help because he didn't know what the Bushman was doing. After completing the excavation, Xi began kicking sand away on the down slope of the dune just below the trench. Then a light went on; Xi was making a recessed firing position for him to lie in. Kurt lowered himself into the trench and immediately knew why this was done. Instead of scorching hot as he anticipated, the sand in the excavation was almost cool to the touch. Dry sand must be a good insulator, and only the top layer is very hot. He manoeuvred the Weatherby rifle into the position, and laid the fore end on the very crest of the dune so the scope could look over the top.

His view of a large dune to their front was nearly unrestricted. To their front left, another longer, lower dune feathered into a large one. Between them was a draw, and immediately it became apparent what Xi was thinking when he chose this position. Any animal moving inland would most likely follow the draw as the path of least resistance. The position Xi set up would only expose the rifle barrel and maybe a bit of scope lens to animals on the other side. Also, the quarry would be looking into the high morning sun. Xi's tactics seemed spot on; now Kurt thought, "Let's see if he's right."

The sun beat directly on Kurt's back, and he knew in this still air he could not tolerate it for very long. Xi, squatting nearby, seemed oblivious to the heat. Not positioned to see over the crest, the Bushman remained still, silently staring into space … lost in his thoughts, or so it seemed.

Suddenly his head jerked and his eyes transformed in a heartbeat from blank and listless, to sharp and incisive. He rose slightly and pointed in the direction the rifle was aligned. Kurt looked at the far dune and saw that the continuum of sand and sky was broken by the dark shimmering forms, seen earlier, coming over the crest, except they were larger now. Going to his scope, he glassed the forms under nine power magnification, which made the animals clearly visible. Yes, they were sable! His recalled the picture of this most beautiful of antelope. Xi's crude sand image did not seem an exaggeration as he watched the huge buck crest the dune and stop. Its scimitar horns arched and swept almost to the rump. His neck seemed almost a caricature, its sole purpose to support the heavy horns growing from his skull.

Mid-day heat was causing the mirage haze to worsen. Kurt estimated the distance to the big buck at between around four-hundred yards, a range the Weatherby rifle could easily handle. About forty inches of drop would put the point of aim at a foot above the animal's forequarter. But the mirage was running right to left at least ten feet per second due to air movement and temperature differences through the dunes. That would put the crosshairs just above the rear haunches, but the rear of this animal was sloped down unlike other antelope, so that would …?

The massive sable swivelled slightly and turned his head. He'd seen something, the rifle barrel or scope. Those incredible eyes had picked up a slight irregularity in the smooth sand. Kurt instantly knew that he would have to go with his gut instincts on this one, or lose the animal. The sable would bolt momentarily; two bounds and he would be back over the crest, never to be seen again. Kurt picked his aiming point and the Weatherby bucked, throwing a cone of sand up from in front of the muzzle. By the time he recovered from the recoil and the scope was back on target, the sable was gone. When the shot was fired, the remaining sable scattered, kicking up puffs of sand each time their hooves hit the ground. In a few moments the dune before them was deserted once more.

Kurt looked down at Xi. The burnished copper face looking up at his seemed stricken, although no words or even sounds had passed. Kurt shrugged his shoulders and said, "Did the best I could, the mirage was bad, and he was going to bolt. I ... " he stopped speaking, realizing he was talking to himself; the Bushman understood none of it.

"Well, hell, let's go check. Maybe we got lucky and there is a blood trail or something," he mumbled, thinking that action, any action, at a time like this was better than silence.

Kurt slung the Weatherby, turned and started down the opposite face of the dune they were on, heading for the crest where the sable had been standing. The walking was hard. They were in the true coastal sands now, their feet sinking deep in the scorching yellow powder. Xi followed a few feet behind, now taking a subservient role. Kurt felt as though Xi had set him up to make the impossible shot, to make him look the fool, whilst knowing it was doubtful that a Bushman would be party to such planned deception. How could he know the effective range of the rifle?

They approached the point where the giant sable had been standing when Kurt fired at him, the spoor clearly visible and, behind the spoor, was a fan shaped area in the sand composed of small dark spots. Kurt immediately knew what it was. He'd seen similar patterns in the snow in Maine when a deer was heart shot with a rifle. Following the spoor, they crested the rise and simultaneously saw the dead animal sprawled twenty metres down the opposite slope. A dark trail of blood followed the sable to its final resting place.

⌘

At the moment they spotted the dead antelope, Kurt was startled by a high-pitched whistle from the usually silent Bushman. The intensity of the sound was amazing, almost head splitting. It then changed frequency, running up and down the scale and warbling at the same time.

"What the hell!" was all he could get out, but that was lost in the blast coming from

Xi. Then the whistling stopped and there was nothing but silence again. Glancing back Kurt saw movement. Instinctively he began to shoulder the rifle but Xi put up his arm to stop him. A group of Bushmen and women, grossly distorted by mirage, emerged across the crest of the dune behind them.

Kurt shook his head in amazement. This group, numbering at least fifteen individuals, must have been on their trail since they left but he hadn't heard or seen a thing. A pair of NVA soldiers following him that closely would have triggered alarm bells, but over a dozen Bushmen, a couple even carrying infants on their backs, hadn't. Either he was losing his instincts or …

The Bushmen were carrying loads with them. Several were toting rather stout poles balanced on their heads. Others had what looked like large baskets woven from bark. When they got into range Xi began exchanging talk with the group in the 'click language' that was peculiar to these people. Its intensity increased as the group grew near, until it sounded like a swarm of crickets chirping.

Kurt assumed that the group was Xi's extended family. He remembered reading that this was how they lived, truly nomadic, in extended family units. In ancient times this was how all hunter-gatherer cultures lived. Unlike modern man, Bushmen saw no need to change.

There was no formality or greeting when the group arrived. They went straight to the sable and bent, began touching it, feeling the length of the sweeping horns and fingering the jet black hair on its chest and back. As suspected, the .300 Weatherby slug had entered low in the animals left chest, shattering its heart, blowing out pieces from a fist-sized hole in the opposite side. The fact that it moved so far, after taking the hit, was testimony to the incredible strength of this beautiful animal.

The Bushmen began assembling a frame with the poles they carried, tying the pieces together with thin strips of leather and hemp or dried plant fibre of some kind. Kurt squatted by the sable while they worked, wanting to help but knowing that he would only interfere with the ancient choreography he was witnessing.

In a short time a crude sledge took shape. It looked similar to pictures he'd seen of sledges that the Inuit used in the far north. The sledge assembled, several lines of coarse hemp fibre were attached to one end to pull it. In unison the team of Bushmen took hold of the sable and, a little at a time, positioned it on the makeshift wooden frame. Though the individual Bushmen were small in size their combined efforts were co-ordinated and they successfully moved the heavy animal. Kurt helped them to lift it onto the sledge and then secure the limbs to the wooden members with ties. Six of the men grabbed hold of the ropes and began to pull. The sledge, laden with several hundred pounds of sable, started to move, the two runner beams of the primitive sledge digging furrows into the soft sand.

They made their way around the dunes skirting the steep slopes. That made the journey back longer but there was no way of pulling the loaded sledge up the steep dunes. Kurt followed behind the procession but he felt like a slacker watching people who weighed less than half of what he did perform such heavy work. Finally, he unslung the rifle and removed his jungle shirt, and tied the arms around his neck letting it hang down his back to block the sun. Dressed only in shorts and boots he moved to the front and grabbed one of the ropes. Leaning into the load, the sledge began to move more rapidly.

The half dozen Bushmen pulling with him were surprised by the power of this one man, who was easily as strong as all of them combined. Two children, whom Kurt assumed were Xi's family walked up beside him and with their delicate yellow hands reached up and touched his arm and back muscles which bulged under the load. This startled Kurt but he recognized it as a gesture of curiosity, and just smiled at them.

The women in the party were demure and kept their distance, never meeting his eyes directly. The physical structure of the women and older girls was curious to say the least. Being generally diminutive in size, their buttocks were huge in comparison. Only partially covered under tattered skirts, their mounds swayed and wiggled like jelly as they traversed the rough terrain. Kurt thought that the fat in their posteriors must store energy and water just like a camel's hump. Their bare breasts were small and drooped like half empty sacks, even on the young women.

After nearly an hour of pulling, Kurt was approaching exhaustion. He felt shaky and knew he had to stop and re-hydrate soon, or risk collapse. Just over the next small rise he saw the end of the deep sands. The ground firmed up considerably and sporadic grasses and hardy plants were again underfoot. Looking at them, the Bushmen didn't seem tired at all. He noticed they never used maximum physical effort when doing anything, they just steadily plugged along. Endurance was their game. European people always seemed to want to muscle and rush their way through everything. Such an attitude would be fatal in the desert. One had to learn to go with the flow of things.

Dropping his rope, Kurt sat on the ground cross-legged, took out his remaining water bottle and drank the warm diluted saline mixture with small sips. A few minutes later the roar of a Land Rover engine could be heard as it struggled with the sand hills. He took his revolver from its holster and fired two shots in the air to signal to the vehicle. The Bushmen instantly scattered and he knew that it had been a mistake to frighten them. However, when they sensed there was no immediate danger they stopped, turned around, and slowly returned to what they were doing. One of the babies carried on the back of a woman began crying with a thin, reedy wail. A minute later, the straining Land Rover burst into view over a hill and pulled up beside them.

"What in God's name have you shot here, bro?" Andre said, standing next to the huge bull sable bound to the sledge. Diana and Reinhardt stood a little further off, slowly circling the animal. Both of them looked incredulous.

"Is it a big one?" Kurt asked.

All three of them looked at him as though he had lost his mind.

"I really don't know. I've only seen pictures of these animals before," Kurt explained. "But the horns seem much bigger than the others ... " his voice trailed off, knowing he sounded ignorant.

Andre slowly shook his head and let a low airy whistle out of his parched pursed mouth. The dry hot air dried out all exposed skin, including lips.

"Big is not the word for this sable. He's the largest I've ever seen, and believe me I've seen plenty. I believe I glassed him from a distance once, but he spooked and I never saw him again. This one is definitely worth measuring and mounting. Let's get him off of this thing and on the back of the Land Rover so we can take him to camp and skin him out. We need to get moving so we can finish before dark".

"What about them?" Kurt nodded towards Xi and his family standing clustered to one side.

"Oh, they'll follow," Andre said. "They want their share of the meat. They will salt and dry it into 'tong'. There is quite a lot of meat on this animal; it should make several hundred pounds. We'll keep the loins and a haunch. They can strip off, salt and dry the rest."

The sable was untied from the skid and using the winch on the front of the Land Rover a line was run over the top and the animal was awkwardly pulled up, positioned, and then tied to the back. After they'd finished, Andre made a remark about not being sure of 'what was tied to what', such was the size of the sable. Xi rode with them back to camp perched on top of the trophy, pointed teeth grinning in his pinched wrinkled face. The other Bushmen would walk back; they seemed to have no interest in a ride.

⌘

The carcass of the sable was winched up by the back legs to the gnarled limb of an ancient leadwood tree that grew at the very edge of their temporary camp. The Land Rover was pulled up next to the suspended animal and used as an improvised ladder to access the upper parts. By standing on the cab of the vehicle, Kurt could just reach the hind legs which were about fifteen feet off the ground. He used his puukko and circumscribed the hide of both hind legs just above the hooves, then split the hide down the inner aspects of the legs to the creamy pale skin of the abdomen. The small birch-handled blade cut with no effort and the hide began to peel off in a sheet, revealing the bright pink still-moist bands of muscle that had powered the magnificent antelope. Almost immediately on exposure to the hot dry air, the delicate connective tissues and fatty layers turned a light brown.

Xi and Andre worked on the mid and lower sections. Xi wheeled a rusty red instrument that resembled an Eskimo ulu, but was smaller. The blade was hemispherical in shape, almost like the lid of a tin can cut in half but thicker, and had a very keen edge. This crude but effective tool was mounted on a piece of wood used to grasp it, and Xi moved his arm with a smooth sweeping motion, separating hide from flesh at a rapid rate. Andre used a small pointed pocket knife, working around the neck and head, to cape the sable. When this was finished, the hide, horns and skull would be taken to the taxidermist in Windhoek for mounting.

The three of them worked continuously for nearly two hours, with only an occasional water break when lengthening shadows indicated day's end and respite from the ferocious heat. Xi seemed happy. He cut a large quantity of meat strips off the carcass and handed them to other Bushmen in his group who had arrived back at camp. The strips of meat were placed in wicker baskets and carried out into the bush, where Kurt assumed they were being salted and dried into the jerky-like food the Afrikaners called biltong.

When the hide had been nearly removed, Xi indicated that he wanted the soft thin scrotum of the animal. Kurt thought this a strange request. His puukko was not really a skinning knife. It had too much point. He was careful not to penetrate the skin by using the curve of the blade just behind the point. He carefully divided the animal's scrotum from the rest of the hide and threw it to Xi, who held it up for the others to see while emitting a soft cooing sound interspersed with clicks. Kurt imagined the Bushman would make the scrotum into a pouch or bag of some kind. A trophy such as the huge set of horns would be of no use to a Bushman with their nomadic way of life. A scrotum pouch on the other hand could serve a useful purpose, and would be light enough to carry around. He would ask Andre about the scrotum later, if he remembered.

Before dark the sable was only a memory. With Kurt's help, Andre had carefully dissected the head and neck as much as was possible in the field. They also heavily salted the hide and parts of the skull that remained, with the horns, to prevent putrefaction. The taxidermist in Windhoek would do the rest. The loins of meat on either side of the spine were lifted out and placed into cool salted water. It was ideal to soak them for six or eight hours, but after only an hour in the solution, one of the loins was removed and sliced into steaks an inch and a half thick and grilled on the red coals of the campfire that had been burning down since morning.

Before the sun set, the Bushmen departed just as quickly and quietly as they had arrived early that morning. Hundreds of generations living in this land had bred into them a sense of caution, and they would no more wander around at night than a leopard would stalk its prey in midday. Though still faintly tasting of blood, Kurt thought the steaks were heavenly. Nothing he had ever hunted could compare with this meat. Andre approached him after dark and handed him two items. They were Xi's half-moon skinning knife, and the incisor tooth of a large cat suspended on a rawhide string. Unconsciously, he reached up just below his throat and felt the Indian talisman and bear claw he wore all the time. It would now have company.

"He told me to give these to you after they left," Andre told him. "He thought they would be useful on your journey with the spirit, or the great father. It's difficult to translate their language."

"What did he mean by that?" Kurt asked as he rolled the crude skinning knife in his hand.

"I wish I could tell you," Andre replied. "They are such mysterious people. Evidently he thinks you are on a journey of some kind."

"I feel bad that I didn't give him anything," Kurt said.

"That's not true," Andre replied. "Talking to Xi, I get the impression that you fulfilled a Bushman prophesy of sorts. He wouldn't, or couldn't, tell me what it was all about. It was regarding the hunter from the cold forest, killing the sacred sable. The event marks some transition point for the Bushmen. Not just for Xi and his clan, but for all of them. That's all he would say about it before he closed up. It's amazing he told me that much. So, you see, you did give them a great deal, more than either of us will ever know."

"It does seem strange how he just showed up, like he knew who I was," Kurt said.

"Does 'cold forest' have any significance?" Andre asked.

"It might; I'm from Maine, and it's a land of cold forests."

Andre nodded deeply like he understood, but wasn't entirely convinced. What Kurt didn't tell Andre was that just above the threshold of his grandfather's old cabin were those exact words ... Cold Forest ... carved in ancient Norse runes.

⌘

The night was exceptionally clear. In spite of the intense heat of the day, the air cooled rapidly once the sun disappeared. Pockets of warm and cool air mixed and, in their conflict, stirred leaves and grass with soft rustling and lofted the scents of the African bush to his nose, tantalizingly. Jackals and hyenas were heard fighting over the remains of the sable carcass that had been dragged into the bush. Nothing is wasted in Africa, Even the spirits are recycled, Kurt mused. He didn't know where the thought came from, nor did he want to dwell on it, not now. The lyrics of a song, popular a few years before crossed his mind; *we shall never pass this way again.*

That was prophetic he thought and, much as he would like to, he might never pass this way again. He thought of Diana, such a vibrant attractive woman, so full of life and adventure. He tried to picture himself with her living on the ranch, or even in Windhoek but those images wouldn't form. There was too much journey that lay ahead and no ability, or will, to stop. Yet there was a conflicting primal call from deep within saying 'grab on to what is good, what is real, and stop running headlong into the unknown'.

She was probably waiting for him at the edge of camp at this moment. He knew the game. She had made the first move, showed interest; the next move was his, but they would spend the night apart. He was in no mood to chase dreams that wouldn't materialize and make commitments he couldn't keep. What did Xi say? He was too busy trying to find the spirits. Time would tell. He could always return here once the restlessness was satisfied and then maybe ...

Falling asleep beneath the stars, he wondered if the same God looked after Bushmen as the rest of man. If so, why would he leave the purest of his children so vulnerable? Nothing really made sense. He looked up and found the Southern Cross beaming down with profound intensity. Maybe there were some things that could never be understood no matter how hard we thought about them.

"Cold Forest," he whispered. "How could he know?" That was the last thing to grace his mind before the Cross blurred and the night sounds of Africa faded ... even the faint clicking sounds of Bushmen talking in their sleep.

# CHAPTER 14
## RHODESIA

**January 11, 1976**

The big DC-8 flattened out on its approach to Salisbury International, which because of the high elevation had one of the longest runways in the world. From the co-pilot's window Kurt saw a vast expanse of broken forests and grassland. A low line of mountains could be seen to the north, splitting the land as if a giant knife had sliced into the earth, allowing the interior to burst forth. Laced with rivers, streams and occasional lakes, little sign of man's presence was visible except for occasional dusty trails, small irregular clearings, and patches of crops.

"My grandfather was right," Kurt thought. "If people left here everything would revert to a natural state in just a few years."

On the final approach, specks were visible in the sky at the far end of the runway, near a cluster of buildings resembling military barracks. After the DC-8 touched down and was rolling in, the specks in the sky became parachutes. A small group of men must have jumped at high altitude in a free-fall drop. Jack saw Kurt staring at the shapes in the sky.

"Parachute school. They train all of the military jumpers over there. I recall a Yank like you works over there. You may know him, John something I believe."

"Maybe," Kurt said. "There are a lot of Johns around though."

Jack laughed.

"Get your luggage ready, we're just about there. I have to get you through customs but that's just a formality."

"What about the weapons?" Kurt asked.

"Don't worry," Jack replied. "Remember what I do for a living."

The customs desk at the terminal was manned by an attractive but thin white girl of about nineteen, Kurt estimated. As he filled out the immigration forms, she glanced at him and made solid eye contact. She obviously wasn't the shy type.

Kurt handed over the completed form.

"It says here you have a handgun that you are bringing into the country," the girl said in a businesslike manner.

"Yes, I do," Kurt replied with a little hesitation. He didn't want to lose his personal Smith & Wesson; it couldn't be replaced. He looked at her; she just stared back.

"Well, would you get it for me, please? I need to see it," she said, with not a little asperity.

"Sure."

He opened the duffel bag and found the rolled-up gun belt which was wedged between some clothes. Kurt unsnapped the moulded leather holster and removed the revolver, swinging open the cylinder before handing it over. The girl picked up the gun with her fingertips, as she would a poisonous snake ready to bite, and almost dropped it. She then held it firmly at an awkward angle and studied it at arms length for a few seconds.

"This isn't a .38 is it?" she asked.

"No, it's a .44 magnum. It's been modified though," Kurt replied.

"I see," she said, handing it back gingerly.

"How does it work?" she asked looking at him, not the gun.

Kurt opened and closed the cylinder using the thumb latch and with a blur of motion, dry fired the piece by pulling through the double-action trigger and cycling the revolver six times in just over a second.

"Well, that is impressive, Mr ..." she looked at the customs form in front of her, "Christianson. I hope you use it where it is needed most."

The look on her face, like her statement, was serious. Kurt smiled back. She stamped his paperwork and handed it back.

"Thank you," he said, and walked away.

"Come on, I'll drop you at a hotel," Jack said as he led Kurt out of the airport entrance. "Looks as though you could use some time to unwind. Salisbury is a nice city; I think you will enjoy it here."

⌘

Jack dropped him at the Jameson Hotel on the west side of town. It was a mid-priced establishment and rooms cost ten Rhodesian dollars a day. Kurt found that a Rhodesian dollar was worth about one dollar sixty in American money. All considered not a bad deal, and included an all-you-can-eat breakfast. The city was active, but nothing at all like the third world chaos of Brazzaville. Traffic on the wide Jameson Avenue consisted, for the large part, of tiny Renault taxi cabs and smoky military vehicles.

Salisbury had a sleepy atmosphere, but there definitely was an underlying, almost palpable, element of tension. Perhaps it was seeing the military vehicles, but something was in the air ... a smell, an energy, electricity, something. It was intriguing and mysterious but not definable. Kurt showered, changed clothes and had lunch at a small covered café a block away from the hotel. He ordered a hamburger, fries and a Coke. This was almost like home yet very different. The food was bland and greasy but served promptly by one of the many waiters on duty.

Strolling around town, up and down the avenues, proved informative. In his reading he had learned that this little landlocked country had been subjected to United Nations sponsored sanctions since 1965, when it unilaterally seceded from British control. The British government predicted Rhodesia would collapse within six months but international politicians rarely recognize the resourcefulness of a small, but determined, group of people. The Rhodesians, both black and white, proved resilient and instead of buckling, they stood together and demonstrated their determination to be independent.

From the little he new, it seemed the small nation in the heart of Southern Africa had nearly everything needed to survive except oil. Nature had not endowed this land, perched on an ancient and stable granite shield, with any petroleum whatsoever. Plenty of high quality coal was mined in the northwest, and an abundance of hydroelectric power came from a huge dam built over the Zambezi River at Kariba to the north, but not a drop of oil was to be found.

South Africa also had little or no oil due to a similar geology. But both countries had productive gold mines. Barrels of crude oil could easily be traded on the international market for bars of precious metal, sanctions or no sanctions. Jack and his DC-8s and other 'sanctions' busters' took care of the outbound transportation. As long as the tanker trucks of petroleum products flowed in from the south, Rhodesia couldn't be blackmailed, intimidated or destroyed by economic means alone. By the early 1970s Britain and other socialist leaning players on the world stage came to this realization. Rhodesia had become an embarrassment to her former colonial ruler.

The first incursions of armed guerrilla bands came into Rhodesia from Mozambique in 1974. At first their forays were limited to isolated farms and native villages near the border. At the time the colonial power in both Angola and Mozambique was Portugal, and Portugal was having big problems back home. Fearing political instability in Lisbon, Portugal began bringing home its colonial military forces.

The troops remaining in the neglected colonies were severely under strength for increasingly difficult missions, and morale took a dramatic nosedive. There were reports that soldiers patrolled the bush and jungle with as much noise as possible to let the guerrillas know they were coming, to prevent any surprises. In 1975 Portugal withdrew from her two African colonies completely.

Predictably the vacuum formed by this unilateral withdrawal of military power resulted in an influx of international troublemakers hoping to lay claim to abandoned goods. The Soviet Union immediately began sending 'aid' to the confused populace. This aid consisted of countless crates of AK-47s, rocket-propelled grenades, land mines, ammunition and other assorted instruments of destruction. The initial motivation behind these 'gifts' of war material was not altruistic, even in the revolutionary communist sense.

The only way the Soviet Union could fully exploit a given piece of real estate was to destabilize, fragment and destroy confidence in the prevailing government. The Soviet tactic was to encourage the guard dogs to fight amongst themselves, making it is easier for them to sneak in and steal the chickens. There is nothing that tests a government's mettle as thoroughly as armed guerrillas (or terrorists if you prefer) running freely around the countryside, killing and intimidating the populace at will.

When the Portuguese bailed out of Mozambique it was a big win for the communists. Their occupation forces and proxies had already heavily infiltrated the country, so it seemed a given that they would step into power, and become the dominant force. Also, Mozambique shared an eight hundred mile virtually unguarded border with Rhodesia, which to the Marxists, was one of the last hated enclaves of European capitalism on the African continent. It did not take a lot of intuition to figure out what would happen next. The domino theory, coined by Eisenhower in the 1950s, was really no theory at all, but a pragmatic method common to all strategists when conducting international aggression.

Initially, gangs of armed communist thugs hit kraals (small African villages) and isolated white-owned farms. As the villagers found out, when a hyped-up bunch of teenagers stuck an AK-47 in your face, it was best to comply. And so another 'war of liberation' was started. This communist rhetoric and terminology was accepted without question by the mainstream international press. In truth, the only things people were being liberated from were their property, their security, their limbs, their loved ones and their lives. It infuriated Kurt just to contemplate the current realities for these people.

His thoughts weren't helped by the passing army trucks emitting their pungent exhaust fumes, so reminiscent of turbine-powered helicopters. Even more than rations or ammunition, armies ran on diesel fuel. It was used by jets, trucks, jeeps and generators, everything that made a modern army go. The smell suddenly told him that he was back in the thick of it. He remembered the fly strips his grandfather had in the lobster trap shed, and how once a fly landed on the sticky surface it couldn't extricate itself. A fly was too fast to catch with your hand, but it would always fall for the sticky trap, and didn't realize it until it was too late. Was he the fly, and war his trap?

A shadow of doubt blew through his mind like a summer cloud, darkening the brilliant landscape briefly. He could get on the next flight out. Go back to ... where? What? Avoid murderous people while finishing his degree? Get a job behind a desk, or in an oil field? Collect a cheque and buy stuff at the weekend? The thoughts made him shiver despite the heat. He felt himself being drawn into something that couldn't be defined or explained, like gravity, or how a powerful magnet pulls at iron filings. His mind began to run freely as he walked the streets of this strangely familiar town on the other side of the planet. It was early morning in Maine now and the waves would be turning to white foam as they smashed against the rocks at Port Clyde. Besides the hiss of rushing water, only an occasional distant ship's horn would be heard.

⌘

In Salisbury the shadows were lengthening, and it felt pleasant after the direct sun of midday. A beautiful little green park sat to one side of the city centre. Several Africans were sitting on the wooden benches. Two elderly white men were playing chess. The scene was as peaceful as could be imagined. What could be wrong here? Kurt walked over towards a group of jacaranda trees that were blooming in lavender and purple. The trees were South American transplants but looked as native here as the acacia. He sat on the freshly trimmed grass with his back to the rough bark of one. His legs were tired and he needed to rest.

On a nearby bench sat an old, grizzled black man. Despite the heat he wore a threadbare but presentable tan blazer and a bright green tie. On his head sat a brown fedora, with a small white feather in the band. He turned slowly and looked at Kurt, grinning at him. His teeth were large and yellow but looked intact. It was a pleasant and disarming smile and Kurt nodded to him and grinned back. He had probably been a good-looking man in his day, but time had taken a heavy toll.

Leaning the back of his head on the jacaranda trunk, he tried to listen to earth sounds with the bones in his head as his friend Jerry Schriver had taught him in Vietnam. The technique didn't work well in a city. Vibrations of passing vehicles and the natural hum of buildings produced a lot of background noise which made it hard to pick up small vibrations. He closed his eyes for a moment to concentrate on the sounds. When he opened them again, the old man was gone and the park deserted. Traffic was reduced to an occasional car, usually one of the omnipresent mini taxis. It was late afternoon and nightfall was imminent. He closed his eyes again and felt the vibrations diminish, as the city prepared for sleep.

There was a different quality to the earth sounds here. In Laos the limestone karst formations gave the ground a ringing quality. In the sediments of low areas and river basins sounds were muffled, absorbed by soft, loose material. Here vibrations boomed and echoed as if the skin of a tight drum was being struck. The rock must be lying just below the surface of the park, ancient, deep and impervious.

Almost subconsciously he felt the footsteps through the tree; regular, firm, authoritative and moving closer. Kurt opened his eyes and rose to his feet in a single movement. Twilight was deepening as the figure approached. The man wore a uniform shirt and shorts and a service cap. The colour of his clothing was light brown or grey; it was hard to tell in the shadows of street lights filtering through trees. The most noticeable thing was his skin. Arms, legs and a patch of face glowed like alabaster, even in the muted intermittent illumination. Kurt tried to make eye contact with the approaching man, but his eyes were too vague to be seen.

"What are you doing here, mate?" the approaching man said in a voice that was high pitched, almost juvenile in quality, but still strangely authoritative.

Kurt thought he couldn't be more than nineteen at most.

"I'm just resting," Kurt answered. "I guess I'm tired from travelling, the jet lag and all."

"You'd be safer kipping in a hotel," he told Kurt. "Some of the local rowdies might jump you if they find you here alone. We try to police the town but, because of the situation, most of our forces are in the bush."

Kurt looked at the policeman, whose features were filling in as his eyes adapted to the darkness. His hair was light blond and his complexion was pockmarked by acne scars. His arms sticking out of his short-sleeved uniform jacket looked rail thin. There was no weapon on his belt, except a nightstick. No guns in a time of war? Kurt thought this bizarre. What authority could this represent?

"You here to join the forces?" the policemen asked.

The question caught Kurt off guard. Was this kid reading his mind or just trying to recruit?

"I'm just looking around," he finally replied.

The young policeman stepped closer, trying to meet his eyes directly as he spoke.

"A lot of blokes are coming into the country at the moment. Some are layabouts and slackers trying to find some easy money. There is no easy money here, and they don't last long. There are some good ones too, and you look like one of them. We can use all the good help we can get."

"If I was interested in investigating the opportunities," Kurt asked using his words carefully, "where would I go for information?"

The officer didn't hesitate with his reply. He pointed to an adjacent street that dead ended in the park.

"Follow that street down about five blocks and the army recruiting office is on your left. Ask for a Major Lamprecht. The main police barracks is six kilometres out on Borrowdale Road, north-west of town. See a PO Cranley. It will be eight tomorrow before either is open for business. If you want to talk to some of the troopies tonight you could go to the Coq d'Or."

"Where is that?" Kurt asked.

"See that street?" The officer pointed to a boulevard bordering the north of the park.

Kurt nodded.

"Follow it down four blocks. There is a café at ground level. The Coq d'Or is three floors up. Be careful if you go in there; be polite."

"Why is that officer?"

"A pretty rough crowd hangs out there, SAS, RLI, Scouts and the like; just watch yourself. Good evening."

With that the officer tipped his uniform hat and walked away, polished black boots clicking on the pavement.

⌘

Kurt walked down Manica Boulevard until he came to the army recruiting office.

It was just a small store front with posters taped to the windows. 'Be a man among men', one of the posters proclaimed in bold lettering. The picture below showed a camouflaged soldier with a blackened face and an FN rifle held across his chest. Man? Kurt thought. The soldier looked more like a Boy Scout... dangerous work for youngsters.

Circling north he found the Coq d'Or Bar where the police officer had described it. Bright neon lights bent into the form of a gaudy blue and gold rooster flashed on and off. A sign on the ground floor directed him up two flights of stairs to the first floor where loud music was blaring. Groups of young people, mostly teenagers, were drifting in and out of a dance club. The amplifiers hurt his head even from a distance.

After climbing two more flights of stairs, the music faded, and he entered a dim and strangely quiet place. It was a long room with an old hardwood bar running down the middle. The first things that caught his attention were eyes. Several pairs of eyes were watching him, but none directly. Men were sitting at, and leaning against, the worn dark wood talking in murmurs, which diminished to whispers as he came near.

A small table was vacant at the far end of the room so he walked over and sat down, feeling quite uncomfortable. The officer had warned him, but with his back to the wall at least there would be no surprises.

An African waiter stood against the far wall, tray in hand. He wore a clean white smock, buttoned up to the collar, and stood perfectly erect with an almost regal bearing. Kurt thought he looked like one of King Shaka's Zulu military commanders. Sometimes the job or the clothes don't hide the man underneath, and Kurt wondered what he was doing here. Times were hard but ...

He discarded that thought and ordered a beer, a Lion, or Simba as lion was called in the local Shona dialect. He discovered they made their own beer in Rhodesia, a Lion lager, a brew called Castle and a lighter pilsner ... a choice of three. All probably from the same vat, Kurt mused, they just put different labels on the brown bottles.

Downing half the beer with one swig, he was amazed at how when drinking on an empty stomach, the sensation spread, to one's legs and then the bladder, in a few seconds. A beer or two to relax was enjoyable, but he never saw the point of drunkenness, in public or private. Some people had a weakness or need to fog their brain with alcohol on a regular basis, but he never felt that need or understood the compulsion. Several soldiers at the bar were now talking, or arguing animatedly.

A high, loud voice coming from an adjoining room caught Kurt's ear. The only word he was able to decipher clearly was 'motherfucker', an Americanism if there ever was one. No culture but the truly cultureless would think, let alone voice, such a curse. He doubted the Rhodesians, balanced on a nineteenth-century moral tightrope, would accuse even their enemies of having carnal knowledge of their own mothers. Only Yanks would be so bold. The voice that just said that word matched one in his memory. Some things you just don't or can't forget. Kurt stood up. More bursts of heated words were coming from the room, but it was too dark to see in there. Above the connecting doorway was a sign that said 'Round Bar'. Kurt cautiously moved through the darkened entrance.

"Listen you scumbag, if you open your weasely mouth one more time I'll ... "

The man doing the shouting was standing with his back to the circular bar, with one foot propped up on the rung of a bar stool. His opponent had a heavy black beard and was twice his size. The big man's face looked murderous in the dim light, but he backed off a bit when he noticed Kurt's approach.

"Jesus, John, don't we have enough wars without you starting a new one?" Kurt said in a calm voice.

The smaller man shifted his eyes slightly, just enough to see Kurt with his peripheral vision, lowered his fist and turned only as recognition dawned.

"Well, what the fuck, if it isn't Mister-Stay-Behind. What in living hell are you doing here?" John said in an incredulous voice, eyes unfocused, ignoring for the moment the large angry man beside him.

The bearded man was getting ready to say something and was beginning to raise his right arm when Kurt put up his left palm, in a gesture of peace, and shook his head. The bearded man backed away mumbling, "Bloody Yanks", under his breath, as if he had just created the world's premier curse. Kurt didn't understand why: Mainers were Yanks and proud of the fact. To John E. Earl however, steeped in the tradition of the South, the comment was not appreciated. He turned and shouted at the retreating man,

"I'll deal with you later, asshole."

Kurt involuntarily cringed, but the large bearded man didn't take the bait, and walked out of the bar.

"You know you're going get yourself killed one of these days talking like that?" Kurt said, standing beside John, back to the bar still watching the door, not looking at him.

"Don't worry, partner," John patted beneath his left arm, "I've always got my friend with me."

Pulling aside his loose green jacket, which looked like it was sewn entirely of pieces of old parachute material, the butt of a shoulder-holstered Walther PPK was visible.

"That little three-eighty would probably only piss off that big sucker, John. I'd cool it a little if I were you," Kurt advised.

"Yeah, but you ain't me, goddamn it, and I ain't built like Mr Mutherfuckin' universe like some people ... am I?"

Both of them started laughing at the same time and gently punching each other in the shoulder, in the old Special Forces greeting of friends and peers.

"Things don't change much do they, John?" Kurt asked rhetorically.

"Different continent, the same goddamn war," John replied almost pensively, forgetting about the confrontation of a few moments ago. "But this one is more ... well, civilized in some ways."

"How so?" Kurt asked.

"Look around, damn it. Cheap booze, nice women, beautiful scenery, hell, what more could you want? Here, let me buy you a drink."

John flagged the waitress who saw them and smiled, then came quickly over to their side of the bar. She was a fairly attractive pale-skinned girl and she smiled at them coyly, but to Kurt her act looked practiced, belying hardness underneath. When she spoke her accent seemed very British, subtly different from the mysterious Rhodesian dialect. The accents were close enough to be cousins but ... She then cast her eyes over Kurt, gave him a brief but thorough scan, then met his eyes directly, like a lioness would her prey.

"Simba, please," Kurt said to her, feeling a little foolish saying the African word for the first time. She immediately thrust him a brown sweaty bottle and no glass. When she walked off to serve another customer John nodded in her direction.

"Watch that one. She goes through men like tampons; she'll use you up and throw you out."

"Been tossed out already, hey, lover boy? You always were the hopeless romantic," Kurt said, then they both broke out in laughter.

"Maybe, but I am not concerned at all, because there are plenty more around here partner. And that ain't no bullshit."

A few seconds later John's levity evaporated, and he spoke to Kurt in a more serious tone.

"I heard that old George bought the farm."

"Yeah, he did," Kurt replied, his eyes dropping to the floor.

"Were you with him?" John's voice was even and non-accusatory.

"Not when it happened. I was too late. I got to him just after ... I managed to get his body back to the embassy at Brazzaville, and they shipped it home to his family. I wish ... " Kurt halted his train of thought, still staring at the floor.

"Don't do that," John said in a serious tone, devoid of alcohol slur. "We all know the risks. In this business you can't be responsible for everything bad that happens. The fact that you got him back home speaks volumes for you, partner."

"Thanks, John. I appreciate that."

"That's okay. I also heard about a punch up with some Cubans and MPLA in Vista del Sol, I think it was. Were you involved in that?" John asked.

Kurt knew John was Agency and had been for a long time. Inside that little hell-raising exterior, was housed an information-gathering machine second to none. What Kurt didn't know was whether the wild man role was fabricated as a cover or real, that's how good the man was. If it was real, he must be a mixed blessing to his handlers. The disadvantage was that Kurt couldn't lie to John; they knew each other too well. If John asked you something, he probably already knew the answer. He was just checking your reaction.

"Well, kind of," Kurt replied hesitantly.

John looked at him with surprise, like he'd just dropped his pants in church. "Kind of? Kind of? What the fuck is that? You were either there or you weren't."

"I was there all right. I think you know that already," Kurt snapped.

John's smile was vaguely visible, even under his bushy moustache.

"Did you lead the assault team?"

"No," Kurt replied. "George was assigned that. He never made it. The assault team was ambushed as they approached the first rally point." Kurt spoke in a laconic manner, not wanting to relive the incident in his mind.

John looked confused and fully sober now. It was rare for John to be confused by events, and he didn't like it when it happened.

"Then if the assault element didn't get there," John asked, "who hit the Cubans and MPLA at Vista del Sol? Did you have a backup team in place?"

"No, we weren't that organized. This was a half-assed, bullshit operation if ever there was one."

"For fuck's sake, what happened then? I heard between sixty and eighty of their troops were taken out."

John knew he'd made a mistake. He'd just let out some numbers he'd been fed from his 'source', and he wasn't supposed to do that. He glanced at Kurt, but the slip seemed to provoke no interest.

"I went in by air to reconnoitre the target," Kurt explained. "Jack Malloy dropped me from a DC-8 and I was compromised when I hit the ground. I think there was a leak because it should have been a clean insert. Anyway, I had to outmanoeuvre a tracking team that was on to me, and there was a shoot out. My operational security had been blown, so I had no option but to exfiltrate. I figured my best chance was to cause some chaos and confusion and then run for the border, so that's what I did."

John was reaching for his drink, but stopped before his hand touched it. He looked at Kurt with a squint that was partially hidden behind the light purple teardrop lenses of his glasses.

"You did what? By *yourself*? You took out Vista del Sol? Is that what you are telling me?"

"It really wasn't a big deal," Kurt said almost apologetically. "It was an easy target, the Cubans and MPLA were very fucked up, disorganized."

John slowly shook his head.

"So the tall tales we heard about you in Laos weren't just bar stories ... were they? To tell you the truth I thought most of it was bullshit. I guess I was wrong. How about that?"

"What people want to believe is up to them. I've always called things as I saw them, and if people don't believe it, well ... " Kurt shrugged.

They both laughed again and John ordered two more drinks from the sloe-eyed waitress who again looked at Kurt as thought he were naked, and he didn't mind the attention a bit.

"Well, you're coming with me tomorrow, partner. I'd like to show you a few things."

The rest of the evening there was no more talk of war, only of mutual friends, living, lost, and dead. In the final analysis, that's what was most important to both of them.

# CHAPTER 15
## MTOKO

John and Kurt passed through the gate into New Sarum Air Force Base before first light. Despite the early hour there was plenty of activity. Air Force people were usually the early risers of the military. The complex of buildings was only about three miles as the crow flies from the main runway at Salisbury International, but the circular road made the trip by vehicle much longer.

Outside one of the buildings a pair of technicians was spooling up the engine of an old DeHavilland Vampire, a first generation jet fighter with a fuselage and tail boom constructed of wood. The little under-powered but noisy turbojet began to emit a shriek that drowned out most other sounds.

When they got out of John's car and walked toward the building, a voice yelled at them which temporarily exceeded the whine of the jet engine.

"Oh, shit, it's the senior warrant officer of the parachute school," John said to Kurt. "He usually doesn't get here until a little later."

"And who the bloody hell is this?" A small wiry man with a dark complexion walked briskly towards them. He caught up and stood in front of Kurt, intentionally blocking his way to the hanger. The new, neatly pressed Rhodesian camouflage uniform was tailored to fit his petite body tightly, and on his right wrist he wore a wide black leather band with a large metal regimental insignia riveted to it.

"Don't worry, Mr Ellis, he's with me," John said to the man, but the response didn't seem to quell the irritation Ellis was showing.

"What bloody difference does that make? You have been known to associate with all sorts of questionable characters. What makes *him* different?" Ellis screamed.

As he shouted, Ellis thrust at Kurt a decorated swagger stick normally tucked under his right arm, like a riding crop. What followed was a blur of movement, which ended with Kurt holding the stick to the man's nose. No words had been exchanged. The diminutive man looked paralyzed with fright. John quickly reached up and grabbed the swagger stick.

"Let's give the SWO back his stick, Kurt," John said calmly. "He didn't mean anything by it, Mr Ellis."

John then leaned over to Ellis who was still speechless, and said softly, "You'll have to forgive him, Mr Ellis, he was just in a punch up with a bunch of Cubans and he's still a little jumpy."

Ellis seized his stick, turned about, and walked gingerly toward the buildings mumbling something about bloody Yanks, wankers and other colourful curses, before his voice was drowned out by the Vampire's engine.

"Well, now that we have thoroughly pissed off the head of the parachute school, I guess we'd better grab some equipment and get the hell out of here," John said, as they walked the rest of the way into the hanger.

John unlocked the door to a room situated in the corner of the hanger. Inside there were static-line parachutes, free-fall parachutes and reserve chutes displayed on wooden racks. Different sizes of canvas and nylon one-piece jumpsuits hung on pegs on a wall. Both of them selected equipment, then stowed the gear in grey canvas kitbags.

They were joined a few minutes later by a another man who introduced himself as Chris Patterson, an American originally, who enlisted in the US Marines at age seventeen and spent time in the elite Force Recon Unit. When Chris got out of the Marines, instead of re-enlisting, he made his way to Marseilles and joined the French Foreign Legion. After training in Corsica, he spent most of a five-year enlistment fighting in bush wars in Northern and Central Africa, with quite a bit of operational airborne experience in the process. Like John, Chris was also an instructor for the Rhodesian Parachute School and, as John told Kurt later, 'One strange character'.

"Someone crapped in Ellis's cereal bowl this morning," Chris mumbled. "That wouldn't be you, would it?" Despite the years in the Legion, his accent was pure Louisiana drawl, having grown up near Baton Rouge.

"Well, the SWO tried to jam his swagger stick in Kurt's chest this morning, and he took exception to it," John explained.

Only then did Chris turn and look directly at Kurt, his grey-green eyes as cold as two ball bearings.

"You should have shoved it up his Limey ass," Chris said. "There would have been plenty of room to spare."

Chris grabbed his bag and headed off, turning and saying, "The Dak's ready, let's get our butts on board."

John and Kurt followed Chris to the DC-3 or Dak for Dakota as the Rhodesian's called them. The aircraft's two radial engines were already turning over.

"The Dak makes a milk run to JOC Mtoko every morning, or nearly," John shouted to Kurt as they walked across the tarmac towards the aircraft. "We talked the pilots into making a high altitude pass at twelve thousand feet so we can stay current with our free-fall qualification jumps. They usually don't mind, and the winds are generally calm at this time of day. We fly out fresh parachutes and other supplies, and bring back used parachutes and sometimes wounded troops as well as bodies; if there have been recent Fireforce callouts. Three Commando RLI is on rotation at Mtoko now. Kicking some ass from what I hear."

The three men assisted the flight crew and ground technicians in loading and tying down crates of supplies and twenty static-line parachute rigs and reserves. Once everything was lashed down they took their seats along the side of the fuselage and a crewman gave the pilot thumbs up. The DC-3 surged ahead as full power was applied, making any further discussion futile until the aircraft reached cruising altitude.

The nose of the old transport flew directly into the rising sun of a perfect African morning. Rugged terrain and vegetation were abundant once the central highveld was left behind. Oblique sunlight made rock formations, hills and granite outcrops on the ground cast deep shadows in the early morning light.

⌘

Mtoko was the Joint Operations Centre for the 'Hurricane' Area of Operations located in the north-east quadrant of Rhodesia. The base was in the centre of the primary infiltration route guerrillas followed when they came across the border from their Mozambique base camps. John notified Kurt and Chris to suit up when they were twenty minutes out. All three of them were experienced free-fall jumpers and donned the gear quickly, then formally checked one another to ensure that all of the webbing, straps and harnesses were correct.

Kurt yelled in John's ear, "What kind of canopy do I have?"

John grinned in embarrassment, because he had forgotten to tell him earlier.

"A Para Commander," he yelled back. "Trying to get some squares but we haven't got them yet."

Kurt nodded. He preferred to jump a round canopy Para Commander parachute on unknown drop zones anyway. Previous experience indicated they were usually more reliable than the newer and more temperamental square canopies.

"I jumped a Cloud XL into Angola," Kurt shouted back at John.

John lifted his bushy eyebrows in exaggerated surprise.

"Where the hell did you get that, they just came out?" John asked.

"SEALS left it behind," Kurt replied.

"Oh, that figures," John said while bobbing his head. "Those bastards have so much good shit they can just leave it lying around. How did it jump?"

"It was slick as owl shit," Kurt told him.

"I bet ... okay, we're six minutes out," John shouted, holding up the same number of fingers for them to see.

The engines of the Dak changed pitch and the nose of the aircraft picked up slightly. John put his thumb up indicating they were going to altitude. The altimeters lashed to the tops of their reserves with bungee cords indicated six, seven and then just under eight thousand feet above ground level. Their actual above sea level altitude was more like twelve or thirteen thousand feet, due to the relatively high altitude in that part of Africa.

John stuck his head out of the port side door which had been left open for the duration of the flight. Kurt moved in tight behind him and saw the Mtoko runway to their front through some wispy clouds that were just beginning to form. The tarmac runway was a mile in length, but it looked like a narrow ribbon from that altitude.

"Go!" John shouted.

At the command, all three jumpers exited the door together. Kurt arched and looked up, watching the Dak roll over and dive for the ground. The DC-3 would be on the runway before they would touch down, even though they were free falling at one hundred and thirty miles per hour. Kurt looked over and saw John flying about two metres away. John was much lighter than Kurt, so he kept his arms close and partially folded his legs into what was called a frog position to create less resistance. Because he was heavier, Kurt put himself in a classical spread-eagle position to slow his descent a bit. As a result, they matched speeds almost exactly. Kurt then pushed slightly with his right arm so he turned a quarter of a rotation to face John, then looked for Chris but didn't see him. John saw what he was doing, and indicated 'down and over' with a head gesture.

Chris was well below them and 'flying' toward a row of structures situated along the western side of the airfield. His body was in a delta track, with his knees bent and arms back touching his thighs. This made his body front heavy and gave him angular momentum so he could cover ground laterally, instead of falling straight down. This position also accelerated Chris to one hundred and seventy miles per hour because of the reduced air resistance. Kurt looked back to John who shrugged his shoulders then made several loops around his right ear with an index finger.

Their altitude was approaching two thousand feet above ground level, and John waved off by crossing his arms twice, then tucked his heels up and backslid away. Kurt let him pull first. When he saw John's deployment bag extending, Kurt released his own main canopy. The loud crackling sound of unfurling nylon taffeta and the hefty tug was followed by a total silence. They were dropping toward a field adjacent to the Mtoko airfield tarmac. A circular dirt track formed an oval completely encircling the runway. At the far end, just inside the track, smoke emanated from a burn pit. The wind was nearly calm and a tendril of whitish-grey smoke rose up to meet them. Kurt could smell an unusual, pungent odour in the smoke that startled him.

Looking towards the tents and wooden structures along the western portion of the gravel track, Kurt saw Chris's canopy below, heading towards a strange open structure that looked like a windowless log cabin enclosing a central courtyard. John's words were heard easily over the slight wind caused by the forward speed of their parachutes.

"That stupid bastard's heading for the fort again."

"What's that about?" Kurt asked.

"I'll tell you when we get to the ground," John replied.

The ground was coming up quickly. Despite the early hour the upturned faces of fifteen or so people watched their descent. The accurate spotting and calm winds allowed them to position their landings just inside the oval track. John performed a stand-up landing, but Kurt, concerned about his weight and the high altitude, performed a classical military parachute landing fall and roll out. Upon landing, he quickly unclipped his harness, rolled up his main chute, and put all the equipment into the kit bag removed from the front of his jumpsuit.

Shouting could be heard in the distance and the small audience quickly lost interest in them and turned towards the disturbance. Chris's loud southern drawl was heard distinctly over the other voices.

"You don't have to be such a goddamn prick about it! The motherfuckin' wind blew me over here and I can't do anything about that now can I?"

Chris was standing just outside the barricaded entrance to the log building they spotted from the air. Two bearded, long-haired, large men stood with their arms crossed just outside the entrance. One of the pair was talking to Chris in softer tones that couldn't be heard from that distance.

"What the hell ...?" Kurt asked, hoping John would explain the situation.

"That facility is called the Selous Scouts Fort," John said as they walked. "They stage classified operations from there and it's strictly off-limits to anyone not directly involved. Because it's open from the top, Chris thinks it's funny as hell to drop in unannounced. This is the third time he's done it, but he's going to get his ass shot if he keeps it up."

"What's his story anyway?" Kurt asked.

"Oh, he's just your typical US Marine, French Foreign Legion, Rhodesian Air Force parachute instructor type of guy," John chuckled at his own satire. "But seriously, watch him. He fakes being crazy really well. He had me fooled for awhile, but there is something else going on. When you really get to know him, and I hope you don't, he's almost reptilian. They say the Foreign Legion fucked him up, but I think he was fucked up long before that. It takes a special kind of man to be thrown out of their ranks."

"He was thrown out of the French Foreign Legion for bad conduct?" Kurt said in amazement. "That's like being expelled from a biker bar for drinking too much."

"Keep this to yourself but I heard from a contact that when Chris was in Chad restoring order or some nonsense, he liked it too much, if you know what I mean. Martial Law is a dangerous state when the wrong people have the tin badges. It gives them license to ... well, lets just say take advantage of the situation."

"Okay, thanks for the warning," Kurt said quietly as they came up to the Operations building. An older stern-faced Air Force officer stood in front, watching them approach.

"Nice jump, you two," the officer said. "It is unfortunate that your friend there can't control his parachute." He jerked his thumb towards Chris who was approaching from the direction of the fort, carrying his kitbag over his shoulders. John just shook his head in mock dismay before introducing Kurt.

"Wing Commander Fleming, this is Kurt Christianson; he served with me in the US Special Forces."

Kurt and the officer shook hands.

"I'm happy to make your acquaintance, soldier. Are you going to be joining us?"

Kurt hesitated. He wasn't sure what 'joining us' meant: the Air Force? The Rhodesian Army? Breakfast?

"I'm exploring my options," he finally said, hoping that didn't sound too stilted or arrogant.

"Good, we need all the help we can get," Fleming gave John and Chris a glaring look, and motioned them to come inside.

"I'm sure Mr Christianson could use some breakfast. The mess tent is directly across there," he pointed to the largest green wall tent in the compound.

"I need to talk to you two inside," Fleming said.

"Yes, sir," John replied. "We'll catch up with you later, Kurt. Get something to eat and have a look around, just stay away from … "

Chris grinned, and Kurt nodded and walked off.

⌘

There were maybe a dozen soldiers and airmen in the mess tent. Each looked at Kurt discreetly and then looked away again, continuing to chat and swig tea out of large tin mugs. Dishes of eggs, meaty bacon and thick slices of dark toast cluttered one of the tables. Each dish was covered with white cheesecloth to keep away flies, not yet in evidence in the cool morning air.

Kurt loaded up his plate and siphoned off a mug of tea from a large metal urn at the end of the table. The tea was only lukewarm, but so sweet it tasted like thin syrup, and made his lip curl when he sipped it. The food was edible and filling and he washed it down sparingly with the over-sweet tea. He ate alone at the end of a long table. Several soldiers nodded in greeting but none attempted to engage him in conversation. When he finished, an efficient mess attendant dressed in white cleared the table and Kurt stepped back outside.

The morning sun blanketed the spectacular scenery with a rich golden light. Steep granite cliffs, still in shadow across the valley, were turning red. Spindly acacia and blackthorn trees spun fine gossamer green leaves against a background of pale-yellow grass. A pair of Bateleur eagles glided directly above the steep face of the nearest slope, seeking thermals yet to form.

"What a beautiful sight," Kurt thought. It was hard to believe this was the front and centre of a vicious guerrilla war, but then Laos was beautiful too. Maybe if we only looked more deeply at nature we wouldn't fight Kurt mused, but that stray thought was immediately shelved like so many others.

It was apparent there was little or no security on the boundary of the JOC. The perimeter looked wide open. Across from the gravel track there was a low permanent building housing the JOC Mtoko hospital. A raised berm of earth had been pushed up around the circumference of the building, protecting it from low incoming small arms fire or rockets, but leaving it wide open to the arched trajectories of mortars or perhaps recoilless rifles. A trench had been dug on the inner side of the berm to a depth of four or five feet, no doubt for the hospital personnel and patients to take cover in, if they came under attack.

This defensive trench was tied into others that ran like a maze around the JOC. It didn't look like a good place to run across at night unless you knew where you were going. Kurt stepped down into a trench that paralleled the hospital and followed it, both to see where it went and to check for defensive positions along its course. He walked around the first bend in the trench and straight into a frightening animal. The creature looked like a hideous pig with visible tusks and lumps over its head and face. It headed straight for Kurt when it saw him, grunting loudly. The trench was narrow, allowing little room for manoeuvre, so Kurt back-pedalled and drew his revolver from his hip holster and brought it to bear on the animal. It was then a voice came from above.

"Shoot my warthog and you're dead meat!"

Kurt partly turned around, still trying to point the revolver in the direction of the oncoming animal and saw a figure standing beside the trench, his features blurred by the rising sun behind him. The man leapt into the trench just in front of the animal, which gave Kurt a chance to vault out of the trench and view the scene of a bristly hog lying on its back grunting, passionately, while the man scratched its belly and neck. Kurt put the revolver away, thankful he hadn't shot the man's pet.

The man slowly turned his head and looked up at Kurt. His skin was ghostly pale, and he had only short stubble for hair. A distinct scar ran from the top of his head passing in front of his right ear, stopping under his chin. It was an old scar, brown with age. One of the man's eyes was slightly out of alignment, making his gaze unfocused and disconcerting.

"I raised him from a piglet. His mother and siblings were blown up in the minefield near Mukambura." The man looked down at the warthog and smiled, "Lucky little shit, ain't ya?" The pig grunted with bliss.

"You're American too, aren't you?" Kurt felt awkward asking the question.

"At one time perhaps, friend, but this place is my home now." The man swept the horizon with his left arm which also bore scars and a missing finger.

At that moment the speaker in front of the Operations shack crackled to life, immediately followed by a voice over the intercom.

"Fireforce commanders please come to the Operations building immediately."

"They got a hot one going on," the man in the trench said.

"You stay here," he shouted at the warthog and pointed his finger accusingly. "And stay out of the burn pit, goddamn it."

He saw Kurt's look and said, "I don't wanting him eating those burned terrorist bodies; it makes him antisocial. He'll lose all respect for people if he keeps doing it."

Kurt saw John, Chris and several other Air Force personnel moving rapidly from the operations building to the airfield. He nodded to the man and his pig and jogged to catch up.

"What's up?" he asked John.

"The Scouts located a fairly large guerrilla base camp," John replied. "They're going to drop 3 Commando RLI Fireforce on top of them, should be interesting."

"Is there any way I can catch a ride?" Kurt asked, "I'd really like to see this."

After a moment of hesitation, John relented.

"Well, I suppose so, you can help me jumpmaster-check the sticks. If there's room you can get in the Dak and observe. Nobody knows who the hell you are anyway; just stay out of the way."

"Wilco el Kapitan," Kurt said with a grin.

"Knock that shit off. I'm just a sergeant here, remember?"

⌘

The 3 Commando Fireforce sticks were assembling in the airfield next to the parked Dak. A Mercedes Unimog two-and-a-half ton truck drove over, loaded with parachutes, ammunition and other equipment. A pair of troopers jumped into the back and began passing chutes down. The paratroopers seemed so young, averaging around eighteen years of age, but despite their youth they looked like a tough bunch. To a man they were physically fit, with deeply tanned skins and bleached hair from almost continuous exposure to the high-altitude tropical sun. Most of them wore only green shorts, camouflaged T-shirts and black takkies (as they called tennis shoes) with smooth, trackless soles.

In contrast to their minimal uniforms, weapons were in abundance. Most paratroopers carried FN FAL battle rifles that had been adopted by most European NATO countries in the late fifties and early sixties. Most of the rifles had their plastic stocks and metal work painted with camouflage colours. The FN fired a relatively large 30-calibre round also used by the old American M-14. Their 20-round box magazines were bulky and heavy, to accommodate them. Many of the troopers wore canvas vests that were custom made by a company in Salisbury. The vests had multiple pockets for magazines and smaller ones for grenades and other gear. The rigs were a simple, no-nonsense way to carry a basic load of two hundred rounds of rifle ammo, grenades and other equipment with relative efficiency.

Several of the paratroopers were toting FN MAG belt-fed machine guns. The MAG was heavier and bulkier than the American M-60 counterpart but, unlike the M-60, the MAG had a reputation for being very reliable and rugged. The troopers assigned to carry heavy MAGs were easy to pick out. They were usually larger than the average RLI soldier and wore linked belts of 30-calibre ammo over their necks and shoulders. The practice of wearing ammunition was not a good one because it could pick up dirt and debris which could jam the gun, but the distinctive look was evidently worth the risk. It was readily apparent to Kurt why they called this operation 'Fireforce'. These kids looked as aggressive, well armed and dangerous as any soldiers he'd ever seen.

John waved him over and they began jumpmaster checking the paratroopers once they were suited up. The straps and rigging were almost identical to the U.S. military system, but the tie-downs and equipment were arranged a little differently. Kurt had never seen an American paratrooper jump with an M-60 but the bulky MAGs were strapped to the sides of the Fireforce jumpers. Jumping with the big guns was no doubt hazardous but a hot contact without them was probably worse.

Everyone on the mission was assembled for a quick briefing by a tall, young, very thin staff lieutenant who walked out with a marker board tucked under his arm. He set it up in front of the kneeling and seated paratroopers and began to give his briefing with a wooden pointer, looking more like a school teacher than an intelligence officer as he spoke.

"The Selous Scouts report an encampment of ZANLA located here just north of the Mount Darwin Road. Estimated enemy strength is sixty to seventy. No anti-aircraft positions have been reported but the camp does have two 12.7 heavy machine guns that could be used in that role. We are fortunate to have two Hawker Hunter ground attack jets available. They have been scheduled to orbit at altitude then make bombing and strafing runs just prior to our Fireforce drop. Co-ordination will be critical, so Dak pilots stay in constant communication with Operations and wait for their clearance before making your drops. If communications are lost for any reason, abort the mission. Understood?"

The lieutenant looked at the pilots for confirmation.

The two pilots stood in the background and nodded their agreement. Both men had distinguished grey hair, wore sunglasses and were dressed casually in shorts and khaki shirts. Kurt would later find out that they had piloted DC-3s in WWII. In fact, the aircraft they were about to go up in was a veteran of the Arnem drop.

"Any questions?" the staff officer asked, looking around at the young stoic faces. Surprisingly there were none.

From the demeanour of the troops, it seemed the briefing the young officer had just given was superfluous. Their expressions indicated that they could figure it out once on the ground.

The heavily laden paratroopers were given a final equipment check and assisted up the short ladder into the port door of the Dak and into its darkened belly. The old radial engines caught fire; first one then the other spewed heavy smoke until their RPMs increased. Inside the aircraft, two fibreglass bench seats ran down either side from door to forward bulkhead. The paratroopers sat, or squatted, in them as best they could whilst wearing their bulky gear. By the time the last troop was loaded, all of them looked hot and anxious to depart. The late morning sun baked down intensely on the thin metal shell of the aircraft fuselage, with only a little ventilation provided through the open port door.

John was speaking through his headset, telling the pilot that all were aboard and buckled in. The engines were slapped to maximum power and the old 'gooney bird' meandered and kicked up a plume of dust until it reached the paved runway in the middle of the airfield. From his jump seat, positioned directly across from the open door, Kurt saw the cluster of buildings recede as the aircraft rotated skyward and, looking down, at the very end of the runway was the dark still-smouldering burn pit, and a lone grey pig rooting around its edge.

⌘

The enemy base camp was close, only twenty minutes flight time from Mtoko, so John stood everyone up and indicated by clawing of his right index finger to 'hook up'. The paratroopers all reached for the single woven steel cable that ran from the front to the back of the aircraft bay and clipped the metal end of their yellow nylon static lines to it. Everyone then turned 180 degrees and checked one another's static line and other equipment. John put his cupped hands to his ears in exaggerated fashion, and yelled, "Sound off for equipment check!"

One at a time from the front of the aircraft to the rear, each soldier shouted 'okay' then tapped the next man in line on his shoulder. When the paratrooper nearest the door sounded off, John positioned him directly in front of the open door, at the same time shouting, "Stand in the door!"

John leaned out of the open port door while holding onto the edges with his hands, then looked over at Kurt and pointed towards the horizon. A pair of fast-moving aircraft was skimming the treetops about a click away. At that moment they simultaneously released metallic cylinders attached to pylons on their wings. The cylinders were quickly lost from sight as they dropped below the tree line. Several flashes were then seen and smoke began to curl above the trees.

The Dak banked sharply right. They were going to have to wait until the Hunters finished their work before the Fireforce paratroopers could drop in. The Dak then banked right again and proceeded to orbit at an altitude of about one thousand feet several clicks south of their target.

Kurt turned and looked out of the scratched Plexiglas window to his rear and picked up the Hunters as they set up for another run. This time tracers from an automatic weapon emerged from the trees to streak up in attempt to tag the pair of low flying jets. The noses of the Hawker Hunters twinkled intermittently as their 30mm internal cannon went into action. A second later, chunks of trees and vegetation blew skyward. Kurt guessed that one of the explosive 30mm cannon rounds had found an ammo dump, or a stockpile of mines.

The Dak dipped sharply to port and rapidly lost altitude. The paratroopers clung to the overhead cable for balance, while John had his head and shoulders thrust out of the door trying to decide where best to release them. The aircraft stabilized at three-hundred feet, low enough to make out birds' nests in the tall gum trees surrounding the guerrilla encampment.

John saw the ground blast of an RPG-7 rocket launching from the outer perimeter of the camp. The red burn of the solid rocket motor arced skyward towards the Dak. If the shaped-charge warhead touched the aircraft anywhere, it would mean disaster. The Dak's thin aluminium skin offered no resistance to a weapon designed to blow through a foot of armoured plate.

John thought the rocket might strike the port wing, igniting its internal fuel tanks but it missed by six or seven feet, screamed by, and exploded safely above the aircraft when its four-second delay default fuse tripped the warhead. The young, muscular tow-headed paratrooper standing in the door and next to John turned to John with his jaw agape and said, "Are they shooting at us, Sarge?"

John turned to him, face only inches away from his ear and said with as much contrived compassion as he could muster for such a question, "No, they aren't shooting at us, son, don't worry."

Then he screamed at the top of his lungs, "Of course they're shooting at us! Now go and get them!"

With that, John shoved the young paratrooper out of the door.

"Go ... Go ... Go!"

The chant was taken up by all, and the mass of jumpers exited the side door of the Dak as one sinuous column, with no gaps between the parachute of one man and the chest of the next.

Kurt saw green tracers flick by the aircraft and heard one *dink* as a pinhole of light appeared in the forward fuselage. Hopefully the Hunters had put the heavy 12.7mm machine gun or guns out of commission. A good 12.7 gunner could down a slow-flying gooney bird with little problem. It took only seconds for all of the jumpers to clear the plane. Kurt unbuckled and helped John pull in the static lines and deployment bags that were hanging out of the door, flapping against the side of the aircraft.

"Good jump," John said. "We put them smack in the middle. Most of the bad guys will have run for the bush when the Hunters fired them up, but they'll get some."

Now relieved of most of its load, the Dak gained altitude again and flew a wide orbit around the target. The second Dak had just dropped its Fireforce stick. Groundfire directed at the aircraft had ceased. Black smoke billowed up from the burning munitions and white phosphorus grenades the troops were using to root out the guerrillas. The smoke caused visibility from air to ground to be obscured in places. Red and green tracers streaked along the ground, ricocheting off rocks and looping into the air. On their flight back to JOC Mtoko, two Alouette helicopters passed in tandem beneath them, heading to the contact loaded with heliborne troops.

When the empty aircraft landed and taxied in, the JOC was very quiet. Most people in camp were either in the field or listening to radio traffic in the Operations shed. As they bundled up the static lines and deployment bags for unloading, Kurt asked John, "I met a rather strange American just before the callout, had a lot of scars and a pet warthog and he wears black," Kurt said.

John looked at him strangely, "You mean the Mad Medic?"

Fragments of conversation with George about the medic and the helicopter pilot flashed through Kurt's mind.

"That's right; someone told me about him, I remember now," Kurt said.

"He's not an easy guy to forget," John continued.

"What's his story, anyway?" Kurt asked.

"He was a medic with the US Army Rangers. After An Loc was overrun in '72 they found him barely alive under a pile of bodies. The NVA bayoneted him and left him for dead with the others. He eventually recovered and went to school and studied philosophy I think, and by all accounts he did well. He was finishing a doctorate and dropped out to come back to the war. He always talks about redemption and other weird things. I can't figure him at all, don't really want to. I think he has a terminal guilt trip and is trying to play catch up."

"How is he going to redeem himself here?" Kurt asked.

"You'd have to talk to him about that," John replied. "I think he is as nutty as a pecan tree but he is one hell of a good medic. The troops think he has some strange power because he never lost a man who was brought to him alive. That's why they let him stay."

"What's his name?" Kurt asked.

"Just call him Doc or Medic," John told him. "He doesn't want anyone using his name, says he isn't worthy of a real name yet."

⌘

As they spoke the second Dak landed and taxied towards them. Chris jumped off when it stopped rolling and ran up to them in a state of excitement.

"Hot damn, good scene, really good scene. I haven't had so much fun in a long time." Chris sounded ecstatic, though he had only watched the action from the air.

"What reports?" John asked, knowing Chris had been listening to radio traffic on his headset.

"Seven or eight kills so far. One of ours was wounded, but not real bad. Caught some shrapnel, I think. Doc went out to pick him up."

They listened to the reports on a field radio all afternoon until the contact was over and the troops began to arrive back. The battle weary Fireforce soldiers were brought back in lifts, four at a time in the Alouettes. When they landed, troops on the ground ran out to the airfield with bottles of cold beer for those returning. The helicopters refuelled and headed back to pick up the remaining soldiers.

On their return there was the usual back slapping, roaring and boisterous conduct. It was the way combat soldiers relieved stress. Besides drums of diesel fuel, bottles of beer were the other vital liquid that made running an army possible. The amber fluid was a magic elixir that took the edge off self doubt and tension that plagued combat troops. After three beers, Kurt felt the world begin to soften. The sounds, smells and buzzing voices all merged together into a buoyant ball of good feeling ... all it took was war and beer. Without waiting for all the last soldiers to return, the party began.

Just at dusk the hacking sound of the last flight of helicopters echoed around the buildings and rocky landscape. Silhouetted by the sun, now touching the horizon, the first chopper sat down. The Mad Medic helped the chopper crew lift a stretcher out of the open door and lay it on the ground. The party nearly stopped. Besides his own life, nothing was more important to a combat soldier than the welfare of a buddy.

The man lying on the stretcher sat up, then slowly stood, waving weakly at the crowd. The men began to cheer and shake their fists and beer bottles in the air, as the wounded soldier began to walk unsteadily towards them. The Medic heard the commotion and stuck his head out of the chopper door, to see his patient walking away. With a flurry, he jumped down and ran over to the wounded man, grabbed him by the back of the shirt and hauled him back to the stretcher while cursing.

"Goddamn it! You only fucking walk when I say you can!" he screamed, and the rest of his words were lost in the cheers.

Another helicopter arrived. It was heavily burdened with jumbled objects in a dark mesh net attached to a belly hook. Kurt could see in the diminishing ground light the objects were enemy bodies, arms and legs askew, looking like trash or unneeded spare parts.

Picking an empty spot fifty metres down the airfield from the first chopper, the pilot set the load down, then released the hook. The bodies lay in a dark tangled heap in the growing darkness, covered with netting. High above, the pink granite of the hills caught the last traces of sunlight. The pair of eagles began to flap, the heat supporting their heavy predacious bodies now gone.

Two large metal grates were placed over rocks positioned around a fire pit after sawn acacia logs and kindling were stacked inside. The yellow flames replaced the dying sun as a source of illumination for the clustered men. The beer continued to flow freely, the clink of bottles and swoosh of caps flying punctuating the boisterous chatter and strained laughter.

Unnoticed by all but Kurt, were two bearded men who quietly left the log fort and walked towards the pile of bodies lying on the darkened grassy airfield. None of the Fireforce soldiers had beards.

Who were these bearded men who didn't mix with the others and sought out the dead?

⌘

When the fire had burned down to mostly red embers and spits of blue flame, the African cooks began throwing steaks, chops and sausages on the hot grills. Bright yellow flames sprang to life and hissed as hot fat ran out of the meat and flared. One of the cooks also began vigorously stirring a large pot of boiling water into which he was pouring a sack of white corn meal, a little at a time, making sudza, African corn porridge. Another dumped raw ears of corn and other vegetables into a pot. The smells from the cooking were becoming intense.

Kurt realized he hadn't eaten since early that morning and his stomach began contracting in anticipation. Everyone ate their fill. The beer and large quantities of food acted as a narcotic to the soldiers who now became subdued, the horrors of recent combat forgotten for the evening.

Kurt sat on a granite rock that was far enough from the fire so he was on the fringes of the flickering light. His plate was heaped with meat, sudza and some boiled vegetables he didn't recognize. Only half finished with the food, the gnawing hunger subsided, leaving him both relaxed but still alert. Staring into the dying fire, he became mesmerized by the glowing coals and dying flames. A vaguely familiar voice came from behind his right shoulder.

"So, are you going to join this circus, brother?"

He didn't turn around. He knew it was the Mad Medic. The question was meant to be rhetorical but Kurt felt compelled to answer.

"Probably, haven't given it too much thought though."

The voice laughed, but sounded more like a low chuckle.

"You're not fooling me, man. You love this shit, I could see it in your eyes this morning."

"Then why are you asking me, if you already know?" Kurt snapped back. His relaxed state of mind had changed to irritation within seconds of talking to the man behind him.

A scarred arm extended next to Kurt's face. A finger pointed toward soldiers eating, drinking and laughing in the firelight.

"You see them over there? Despite my best efforts half of them will be dead before this shit is over."

"And how do you know that? Have you got ESP or something?" Kurt asked the voice behind him.

"I don't know … but I do. I've seen so many who are going to die that I can tell. They have a look that's different. But if you went right now and asked any of them, they would say it's not going to be me ... you know what I mean?"

"Of course, everyone wants to live. That's just human nature; that's just the way it is, you know that," Kurt countered.

"Yeah, but some of them do know. They know they won't make it, but they pretend. They are in major denial."

"Then what do you recommend?" Kurt questioned. "Going out there and sucking up the first bullet so that your greatest fear will come true? I think you're off base, Medic. Everyone wants to survive. They want to live through this so they can have a wife and kids and a house and all that. It's the human condition, as old as man."

"If they really wanted to live, to survive like you said, they wouldn't be here. They certainly wouldn't be doing this. They'd be somewhere much safer. No one needs to be here. They are all volunteers, here by choice."

"So what is your point then?" Kurt rubbed his eyes. "I've had too much beer, you're making my head hurt."

"The point is that if you are going to play this game, you have to consider yourself dead already. Then you can go out and do the job the right way, with no hesitation, no fear. See, this is what hesitation and fear does."

The Mad Medic stepped out in front of Kurt and squatted down. He had taken his shirt off and Kurt could see the full extent of his scars that ran across his face, arms and chest. He'd been sewn back together like a bad patchwork quilt.

"I lay on the ground and let them do this to me because I wanted to live. I was afraid to die. They let me live all right ... like this. But you can't go back to the world looking like this can you? You aren't accepted and the whole thing becomes a nightmare, worse than a nightmare, you wake up from a nightmare."

"I think you're being too hard on yourself," Kurt said. "I look at you and know what you've been through and respect you for it. You are a survivor, be proud of that."

The Medic shook his head slowly.

"Words ... just words. They're well-meaning words but they have a hollow ring. You see, I was a coward and I didn't fight back and every moment of every day, I'm reminded of that." With his fingertips the Mad Medic traced his scars beginning on his scalp, down his neck and chest, and along his opposite arm.

"So, why are you here?" Kurt asked him. "Why would you come back to a war? War did that to you in the first place."

The Medic stared at Kurt, or tried to with his crooked eye, probably a result of the bayonet scar right next to it. This gave his gaze an unsettling quality, as if he was looking through you or past you, but not at you.

"Redemption."

"Redemption?" Kurt asked, "In whose eyes do you have to redeem yourself? No one would ever question your courage. How long does this have to go on?"

The Mad Medic was silent for a few seconds, then his right eye rolled slightly skyward; the other eye stayed fixed.

"The only reason I'm alive is to redeem my flawed character, to prove to the world and myself that I'm not a coward. You see, with every life I save, with every good act I perform, the gap closes a little."

The Medic put his two forefingers in the air about a foot apart in front of his face and moved them together slightly.

"The gap will never disappear totally," he said, "that's not the way it works. But I figure I can reduce it, then maybe when I die it will be close enough to call it a draw, to break even, and that will be acceptable."

"So your life will be a break-even thing," Kurt interjected. "It will amount to zero."

"Exactly!" the Medic said. "That's the beauty of the plan. There will be no cowardice, no fear, no denial, no ego, nothing of a negative nature, just oneness with all of this." He extended his arms to the heavens and gazed upwards at the stars that had just made an appearance.

Kurt didn't know what to say to the Mad Medic. There seemed to be no appropriate response. His spoken philosophy, though strange, had strong elements of logic woven through it. Maybe he was right, maybe that's all there was, achieving a sum of zero at the end of life so your passing would not upset the balance of the universe. Was he really mad, or was he seeing things others didn't see, or couldn't see?

The Mad Medic rose like a scarred phoenix from the ashes of the fire, and looked down at Kurt.

"Remember ... keep your tally sheet balanced, lest they judge you."

With that he walked away toward the hospital. Halfway there the warthog scrambled out of the trench to follow at his heels. The Mad Medic gave the pig only a cursory scratch on the ears. The creature had been eating burned bodies again and, until the animal altered his ways, he would receive no praise.

The flames of the cooking fire had died. As Kurt sat on the rock and watched, the darkness of the camp seemed overwhelming.

# CHAPTER 16
## THE RLI

It was a bright blue spring day in Salisbury, a million miles and one-hundred and twenty kilometres from JOC Mtoko. The Dak had flown back to New Sarum the morning after the Fireforce attack on the ZANLA camp. Kurt took one of the mini-cabs into town where he checked in and ate breakfast at the Ambassador Hotel, a popular hangout for troops when in town.

He stood in front of the recruiting office he'd passed by two days before. Inside, there was a single wooden desk with a tall, almost skeletal girl diligently working behind it. Papers cluttering the desk and cheap plastic moulded chairs along the walls were the office's only furnishings. No money wasted here. The girl wore a pale-green uniform. Sewn on her right shoulder was a patch with a dark-green background with a stark white rhinoceros head embroidered in the middle. A single small multi-coloured ribbon was pinned to her hopeless chest.

Kurt tried to convince himself that all things worthwhile had inauspicious beginnings, but this was pushing the concept a little. When he finally walked through the door, the girl looked up from her papers, her face completely expressionless.

"Ken ah help you?" she asked in a voice that was a guttural mixture of Rhodesian and rural Afrikaner.

"This is the Army recruiting office, isn't it?" Kurt asked the obvious question with the hope of starting a dialogue with the girl, but it didn't work.

"Yeasss ... ken ah help you?" she repeated, staring at him. He may as well be talking to a store mannequin; the ball was definitely in his court.

"Who do I speak to about ahhh ... joining up?"

"Oh, that would be Major Lamprecht, but he is busy now. You can sit down if you like."

She stood up. The girl was over six feet tall and her legs were no thicker than Kurt's wrists. She walked over to a staircase at the back of the room and made her way up. In less than a minute she came back down again.

"You can see Major Lamprecht at half past nine," she said.

Since it was already after nine there was no reason to go elsewhere. Kurt wished there was a magazine or reading material of any kind in the reception, but there wasn't.

Twenty minutes later a voice shouted down the stairwell.

"You can send him up now, Marjorie."

Kurt walked toward the stairs and at the bottom he could smell the stale odour of hard liquor. It permeated the stagnant air in the office like a box of bad fruit. Major Lamprecht sat at his desk, wearing a uniform that looked wrinkled and somewhat dishevelled. His face and hair were still moist from a cursory splash and comb. The man stood up and extended a pale, moist, shaky hand to him.

"Major Nick Lamprecht," he said with minimal authority, "and you might be?"

"Name is Kurt Christianson, sir," Kurt extended his hand and felt Lamprecht's clammy palm. He nearly pulled away.

"I take it you are interested in joining our security forces?" Lamprecht stared at him. Despite his physical condition his eyes were sharp and steady. Kurt speculated that the man had probably been a good soldier for most of his career, until the drinking caught up with him.

"Before we start, I want to make a few things perfectly clear." From a dubious start Lamprecht quickly settled into a well-practiced routine. "It's no secret that we need good soldiers. Our national manpower is being depleted by the war. For every citizen serving in the forces, there is one less to pay taxes and support the economy. Yet, despite what the foreign press may say, we do not hire mercenaries, Mr Christianson. Every volunteer comes in with the same pay, under the same terms, and is treated the same as any other soldier. Is that understood?"

"Yes, sir," Kurt replied. "You have made that point very clear and I didn't really expect anything else."

"What branch of the Army did you have in mind? I could explain the various units." Lamprecht said.

"What ... or who are the men with beards?" Kurt asked. "I saw some of them at Mtoko when I was there yesterday."

Lamprecht looked surprised and narrowed his eyes into a squint.

"I think you are referring to a unit called the Selous Scouts, but you would not be eligible to join them. You would have to be a member of the regular Army for a time and then pass a selection course."

"What is their mission?" Kurt asked.

Lamprecht was again taken by surprise but after thinking for a few seconds, he responded.

"Their mission and all of their work falls under the Official Secrets Act, and it would be in your best interests if you didn't ask or speak about them. If the time comes when they are interested in your services, they will contact you."

"I understand, sir. Then what about the RLI? The Fireforce paratroopers?" Kurt asked.

Major Lamprecht smiled immediately.

"Well, as you may know already, the Rhodesian Light Infantry is the only unit that wears our national colours. It was formed in 1961 and was the first to engage the terrorists in 1974. Many consider the RLI to be one of the best, if not the very best, regular army unit in the world. But then I am a bit biased on that point, because I was one of the first officers assigned to the RLI when it was formed."

Lamprecht pointed to a group photograph on the wall behind his desk. It showed a dozen young men posed in rigid military posture, two officers and ten enlisted men wearing new RLI bright green dress uniforms. A much younger and more vital Nick Lamprecht sported the single shoulder pips of a subaltern (the British equivalent of a second lieutenant) on his epaulettes.

"I think the RLI would be a good fit for you," Lamprecht continued. "I assume you have a military background of some sort?"

"Yes, sir," Kurt said. "I was in the US Army Special Forces for several years."

Lamprecht's eyes perked.

"Vietnam?" he asked.

"Yes, I worked in that theatre."

Lamprecht rubbed his chin with the knuckles of his right hand, as if contemplating some important decision.

"I see, I see. If you are interested, I will need you to fill in some forms for us and we can get you booked for a physical today. If everything checks out we can swear you in the day after tomorrow."

The major shuffled some papers on his desk and selected one, squinting closely at it before saying, "It looks as though there is an RLI training course about halfway through their cycle. Since you have a good deal of military background, I will see if you can join them. You can test out of the preliminary material, and that will halve your training to eight weeks."

Kurt nodded his head with the realization that this small sign of affirmation would result in a major commitment of as yet unknown proportions. He'd received a small taste of what was going on in Mtoko the previous day, but words like 'voluntary' and 'committed' were momentous concepts, too big to comprehend completely in so short a time. Suddenly Kurt felt like a small piece of driftwood, afloat on the wild surf. The ride could be exhilarating but the destination was anyone's guess. Why he always sought out these situations was confusing to him. Yet here he was again, a world away from the fishing boats of Maine but deep down, he knew he couldn't do it any other way.

Lamprecht interjected, pushing aside Kurt's pensive thoughts.

"I'll get your forms. And by the way, do you know another American by the name of Holliday? I believe that's his name. He said he was an ex-Green Beret also."

Kurt's jaw involuntarily slackened as he looked at Lamprecht.

"You have to be kidding. If that's the same guy I think it is, he's more trouble than a sack full of Texas rattlesnakes." Lamprecht rubbed his chin, and then nodded in agreement and asked, "Fellow that talks like Huckleberry Hound?"

"Yes, that's him I'm afraid. What is he doing here?" Kurt asked.

"Well, like you, he has expressed an interest in joining the security forces. Is there something we should know about him?" Lamprecht sounded concerned.

Kurt shook his head and laughed.

"Not really, but he is a Texan and Bob ... well, he's pretty wild even by Texas standards."

Lamprecht looked stricken, the sweating had returned and his brow was beaded.

"I see," he said. "I imagine it will work out one way or the other. These things usually do. I will get you your forms."

Kurt filled out the paperwork quickly and handed it back to Lamprecht. He didn't want to keep the man from his bottle.

⌘

After eating lunch at another of the many sidewalk cafés on the avenues, Kurt walked the mile or so up the shaded residential streets to the sparkling new Andrew Fleming Hospital located north of town. Walking inside, the corridors were nearly deserted so he asked a young nurse for the X-ray Department. Heading for X-ray, Kurt saw the white trunk and tan arms of Bob Holliday from the opposite end of the long corridor. Bob was leaning on a green tiled wall, shirtless and motionless.

"He's like a horse," Kurt thought, "sleeping standing up." Kurt tried to approach him quietly but even when nodding off, Bob was too alert to let anyone get close. While still leaning motionless he said, "Jesus Christ, if it ain't George of the Fucking Jungle! What you doing over in these parts, boy? There ain't as many trees to hide behind over here. Those terrs are gonna catch you and boil you in a big pot, missionary style."

Kurt stuck his hand out, which finally coaxed Bob to come off the wall.

"Long time no see, Bob. Where was it? I think the last time I ran into you ... you were training a motley pack of RVN snipers in Da Nang."

"Yeah, I never could get that bunch to shoot very well. Trained up a couple to be fair spotters but when it came down to it, their shootin' sucked. I ended up taking most of the missions myself."

"What did you finally end up with, you know ... confirmed?" Kurt asked.

"Oh, last count was fifty-seven I think. Twice as many probables, but that's like fish stories so we won't go there. Then the war ended and they wouldn't let me shoot NVA anymore. I hung around for another six months or so and everything got really fucked up. I went back to Fort Worth and worked construction for awhile but that was even worse, so here I am."

A female X-ray technician came out holding an aluminium clipboard. She was older and quite a bit larger than the young nurse Kurt spoke to earlier.

"Mr Holliday?" she asked.

"Yes, ma'am," Bob said. attempting to suck in his slightly bulging white midsection.

Kurt remembered Bob would flirt with nearly any female, given the opportunity.

"Would you come with me please?" she asked.

"Why most certainly, mademoiselle," Bob said.

Kurt winced. The technician looked strangely at Kurt and he subtly shrugged at her.

"Are you also here for an armed forces entrance physical?" she asked Kurt, ignoring Bob's stares at her starched white chest. Kurt handed her the folder he was given at the recruiting office.

A few minutes later, both had received their chest X-rays and were sitting near an examination room with several other prospective inductees. The door to the exam room was open and a podgy, ill-dressed young resident doctor could be seen performing the induction physicals. Kurt nudged Holliday and said quietly, "Draftee docs are the same the world over."

"Useless fucks if you ask me," Bob mumbled.

The doctor walked out of the exam room as his previous patient was leaving.

"Mr de Koch, you're next," he shouted. "Come in please."

The buttons of the doctor's new camouflaged army shirt were strained in an attempt to hold in his protruding stomach. A hairy navel was visible through one of the gaps. Prospective inductee De Koch had an obviously damaged right hand. Looking like an Afrikaner farm boy, he may have injured it in machinery or something. Kurt wondered what the hell he was doing at an induction physical with a missing index finger and damage to a couple of others.

The doctor and the draftee went into the room but the door was left wide open. Kurt listened closely as they went through the standard routine of an induction physical, but the examination seemed to be brief and cursory even by military standards. Height, weight, chest sounds and reflexes were noted, and then some questions were asked by the doctor.

"Do you have any physical disabilities or abnormalities that would interfere with performing your duties as a soldier?" the doctor rapidly asked the question looking at the paperwork in front of him, not at the patient.

"What do you mean, sir?" De Koch asked.

The doctor finally looked up, his eyes emanating a blend of boredom and irritation.

"Damn it man, can you pull the trigger of a rifle?" he snapped.

"Well ... yes, sir, I can use the middle finger here, I suppose."

"Good enough ... you pass," the doctor said. "Sign here if you will."

De Koch grasped the pen with difficulty but he signed the form.

Kurt turned and looked at Holliday.

"Christ, Bob, they are damn serious here. If they don't give a psychiatric exam they may even take Texans."

"Fuck you, Yankee," Bob retorted. "Hell, I would watch it if I were you, boy."

"Why is that, Bob?"

"I think that doc in there is a little funny, if you know what I mean. He might get excited when he makes you cough an' all."

Kurt faked a look of dismay.

"You know Bob, if I don't meet a girl real soon, I may take him up on it."

Bob leaned close to him and talked in his softest voice, which could still be heard by everyone else in the waiting area.

"From what I've seen there should be no problem here. Hell, there is more nice tail round here than you can shake your pecker at, and I mean fiiiiiine! And since most of the men have gone out in the bush, there should be plenty of nubile young nymphets out there just lookin' for some steely-eyed warriors."

"That would be nice, Bob," Kurt replied. "But I wouldn't get your hopes up. What attractive young woman raised in this respectable British culture, would want to associate with the likes of us?"

"That's the trouble with you Yankees," Bob replied. "Y'all have a tendency to underestimate your own potential. They'll love us man, you'll see." Bob seemed to have totally convinced himself on the point, and with a nod and a crossing of his arms, the issue was closed.

"Next!" the doctor yelled.

⌘

By the time they both finished the induction examination, it was late afternoon and they headed to town on foot. The blooming jacarandas and flamboyants lined the avenues with vivid hues. The non-indigenous trees had been planted many years before, and now their bright lavender and red colours were breathtaking. People taking photographs of the trees were always disappointed, because the colour of the film did not do justice to the real life image. Walking in their shade, as they arched over the streets and walkways, was like passing through a kaleidoscopic tunnel.

The men slowly ambled back toward the centre of town, enjoying the clear sweet air and serenity that Salisbury emanated. Groups of uniformed school children scampered down the streets, either going home or towards one of the many recreational fields to play soccer, rugby or field hockey. Africans, mostly travelling alone, peddled their bicycles in slow motion down the verges of the wide streets. Several others walked by, not meeting the eyes of the foreigners directly, quickly heading somewhere.

"Sure is a beautiful place," Bob exclaimed. "I'd say it's worth fighting for, wouldn't you?"

"Jesus, Bob," Kurt countered. "You would fight on the goddamn South Pole to put down a penguin revolt if you got the chance. You don't have to retrofit your motives for me. We're both over here because we can't help ourselves. When we got back to the world after the first go around, we couldn't stand being a tiny cog in that huge machine. Here it's different, or we hope it'll be different. Over here we can play king of the hill for awhile. We've been trained like a pack of hunting dogs. Having chased real game, we aren't happy chasing sticks any more."

"Maybe you're right," Bob said almost wistfully, "but this sure is a pretty place."

"Yes, it is now," Kurt replied. "It's really a shame. A hundred miles away there is a lot of shooting and dying going on. I wouldn't have believed it if I hadn't seen it yesterday. No matter what we do, it will be right here before too long."

Bob pointed to a massive grey curved building only a couple of blocks away.

"Do ya see that hotel?" Bob asked. "God, it looks like a giant claymore mine."

"It sure does, I bet they don't even have a claymore that big in Texas."

"Well, if we had a mind to, I'm sure we could make a bigger one," Bob said seriously. "You suppose they got any good chow in that place? I'm so hungry I would chase a hyena away from a week-old kill."

Bob picked up his walking pace, now that food was on his mind.

"I'm sure they do, and I'm sure it won't take you too long to sniff it out. You're on point."

⌘

They entered one of the largest and newest hotels in Salisbury, the Monomatapa. The hotel was named after an ancient king of the Mashona tribe, who in his lifetime never witnessed anything grander than a mud and straw hut. Like most modern hotels the Mono, as it was referred to, had a large lounge as well as several bars and restaurants in the building. Unlike most modern hotels, the place was literally swarming with security forces. Most soldiers were wearing camouflaged field uniforms with a variety of different patches, headgear and coloured belts representing army, air force, police, internal affairs and reserve units. The hotel management, concerned that the establishment might be an attractive target for terrorism, reduced the room rate for uniformed security forces to $10 per night, making it the best luxury hotel deal in the world. The management lost some revenue, but it bought them around the clock security, akin to being on a military base.

Holliday was locked on to the scent of cooking food. In a cruel twist of fate however, the restaurant, in an attempt to maintain its four-star rating, demanded that patrons wear a jacket and tie while dining there. They were politely told by the doorman that they couldn't enter, unless they were wearing proper attire. A menu was posted outside the entrance, which despite the rejection, Bob read from top to bottom, before commenting, "It's a good thing they won't let us eat in this place, because I wouldn't eat here anyhow!"

"Why's that, Bob?" Kurt asked, reading the menu over his shoulder. "You just said you'd eat week-old jungle kill, remember?"

"That may be so," Bob snorted in a disgusted manner, "but there are limits even for me. Look at this will ya!"

Bob pointed to a menu item which read, *Monkeygland Steak.*

"I don't know about you Yankees, you eat those big red sea bug things and all ... "

"You mean lobsters?" Kurt interjected. "I don't think they have those in Rhodesia, the country is landlocked."

"Well, thank God for that," Bob continued. "But one thing is for sure, I ain't eatin' no gland of no monkey. In fact I ain't eatin' no monkey meat a' tall, and ya can take that one to the bank." Bob crossed his arms over his chest again, closing the issue.

"I don't think it's really monkey meat," Kurt said. "It's probably some quirky name, you know, a regional specialty of some sort."

Bob kept his arms crossed, looking unconvinced, then added, "If that were the case, there should be Salisbury steak on the menu, this is Salisbury ain't it? And look ..."

Bob again pointed to the menu on the wall.

"It ain't there. That proves my point."

"What point?" Kurt sighed.

"The point is," Bob said with obvious frustration, and moved his face closer to Kurt's, "my point is, if they say it's monkey meat then I'm gonna take them at their word ... it's monkey meat!"

"I'm not going to argue this with you," Kurt said in exasperation. "This place is too snooty for me anyway. I'm sure we can find some other place in town."

Dusk was just beginning to settle when the pair left the Mono and began to wander the streets.

"Man this place sure does shut down at sunset, don't it?" Bob observed.

They gazed up and down the rows of now closed shops. The bustling traffic of midday was reduced to a trickle. They approached the end of a cross street named Kingsway and Bob pointed to a small blue neon sign, two blocks further down.

"Looky there!" Bob nearly shouted. "Well, I'll be. I think we found us an Eye-talian restaurant ... and it's open. I bet they have some real food over yonder, and I bet they don't serve no monkey meat, neither." Bob picked up his pace now his target was within range.

"Okay Bob," Kurt said in resignation. "Until we feed that ravenous stomach of yours, you'll make my life miserable."

Bob turned around to face Kurt, "Well, goddamn, a man's gotta eat, don't he?"

⌘

Guido's Italian restaurant was in an old building, which looked friendly enough and wasn't crowded, which was just as well. Bob was beyond waiting for food. They sat at a small Formica-covered table with a thick red candle burning in the centre. The restaurant was owned by an Italian couple, but the man was a good fifteen years older than his wife. He was slight, balding and did most of the cooking, and otherwise managed the kitchen. His wife was a dark-haired, attractive, well-fed woman who waited tables and took money at the register.

When the two men sat down, she immediately headed their way. The one thing, or two things, that stood out about her were the enormous pair of breasts stuffed beneath her white blouse. Bob mumbled about looking like the Italian Alps in winter, only sideways.

"Hello, boys, nice to see you," the lady gushed.

She handed them two menus and stood touching the table with the fronts of her thighs, her breasts positioned directly between the two men. They couldn't look at each other or at her without looking at 'them'. In his denied state Kurt noticed immediately that her nipples were prominent and clearly distinguishable beneath the thin material. His mind raced, trying to think of how those things could be suspended and still have the nipples showing. He finally came to the conclusion that she must be wearing a bra with the ends cut off. The mere thought of it made the blood rise up his neck to his head, a reaction that didn't go unnoticed by the woman. She smiled at Kurt and moved closer to him. Bob wasn't watching, his eyes were glued on his tightly clutched menu.

"Let me show you what I recommend." She reached across Kurt, to grab his menu, and in the process swiped the end of her left breast across his cheek.

Kurt smelled the sweet musky odour of female skin and closed his eyes to gain control. Then he heard the laughter. The laughing came from a group of young men sitting at a long table on the other side of the small dining room. Kurt's temper flared at the thought of someone mocking him. Bob was oblivious, still studying the menu intently. Kurt had trouble suppressing his mixed emotions of anger at the laughter, and his response to the provocative woman. Bob had trouble deciding which selection he wanted most, so he ended up ordering two. When the waitress left, Kurt rose and walked over to the offending table.

"You guys think something is funny?" he asked no one person in particular.

The spokesman for the four was obviously well oiled and looked at Kurt with mirth. He was nineteen or twenty, had short military hair and was in good physical condition. He briefly looked around the room, as though he didn't want to be overheard, then motioned for Kurt to come closer. Kurt warily lowered his head.

"Don't take it personal, mate," he almost whispered. "She gives that routine to all the new guys who come in here." He motioned for Kurt to sit at an empty chair next to him. For a man with many beers under his belt, he spoke clearly.

"It seems her old man can't do the business anymore. Trouble is he is jealous as hell and won't let her out of his sight, so she gets frustrated and teases. If someone gave it to her in a regular way, she probably wouldn't do it. We meant no offence by laughing."

It's just that it happened to us and was just so predictable."

"That's okay," Kurt smiled at him. "Hell, if one of you guys will hold the impotent old bastard down, I'll give it to her right here." He patted the table top with the flat of his hand.

The speaker and two of his companions who were listening roared with laughter.

"You're a Yank, aren't you? Mind if I ask why you are in Rhodesia?"

Kurt shrugged, "No, that's okay. My friend Bob over there and I are over here to help you out ... in the forces. We swear in tomorrow."

"I thought so," the young man responded. "By the looks of you two, I wouldn't think anything else. What unit are you two going to join?"

"RLI, we will be training at New Cranborne."

The man immediately stuck his hand out to Kurt.

"Dick Wilkins, Three Commando RLI, and you are?"

Kurt gripped his hand firmly, "Name is Kurt Christianson, formerly US Special Forces, as is my friend Bob Holliday." Kurt motioned to Bob, who was now looking at them. "You were in the Fireforce callout the other day weren't you, Dick?"

"And you helped the jumpmaster, I remember you now!" Dick slapped Kurt on the back. "Well, this is good. Tell your friend to come over and we we'll buy you a beer."

Kurt and Bob talked with Dick and the other RLI soldiers over drinks and dinner. Although all the men were young, they displayed the unique maturity that comes to warriors who risk their lives on a daily basis. The food was good and of sufficient quantity to satisfy even Bob's cavernous spaces. Dick and the others provided some detail about the firefight they were in. ZANLA was starting to construct base camps within Rhodesia, instead of just sending teams in from Mozambique. This meant an escalation and a commitment on the part of the enemy to broaden the war. This was bad for the country, but Kurt knew it also meant they would see plenty of action.

⌘

Later, Dick and the others wanted to go to one of the bars but Kurt and Bob were very tired, and only wanted to go back to their hotel and sleep. Exhausted as he was, Kurt had a disturbed night and got up several times and looked out the window. He didn't know why he bothered. Aside from a few fluorescent signs and street lights, the town was quiet. On top of the building across the road was a bright neon sign advertising Air Rhodesia, representing a former hope of the country to join the world economic community, now dashed by sanctions and international castigation.

The city was peaceful but this was deceptive. A hundred miles away and probably much closer, lay the real truth. A storm was brewing and he was preparing to leap into the whirling maw. He'd been lucky thus far, very lucky. No major wounds or injuries, quite remarkable after dozens of engagements. Was this a sign of invincibility, or just a fluke? Why did he keep testing the odds when it was obvious what the eventual outcome would be? He couldn't answer the questions. He didn't even want to think about them. But they rose to the surface of his thoughts like bloated corpses, refusing to stay hidden in dark recesses.

Questions about his future also bubbled up. What would he be doing ten or even thirty years from now? Feeble attempts at peering into the crystal ball failed. It was hard to predict or even imagine events that far away; the screen was blank. What did this mean? He went back to bed and slept fitfully for the next few hours, dreaming about an elusive enemy with no face, running from soldiers with beards.

⌘

The following morning, Kurt met Bob for breakfast in the dining room of the Ambassador. An English-style breakfast was a great way to start the day. Eggs cooked to order, bacon, ham, toast, sweet rolls, juices, coffee, all included in the price of the room. With a mountain of pasta only hours old in his system, Bob ate like he had just spent five years on Devil's Island. When asked why he ate like that, he always answered, "Ya just never know."

After breakfast, they walked several blocks to the sporting goods shop which was recommended by one of the RLI soldiers they'd met the previous evening. Fernando and Son had been in business for many years. The people who founded, and still owned and operated the store, were a Portuguese family originally from Mozambique. Unsurprisingly, business was more lucrative in Rhodesia than in their former country. Currently a large part of their trade was supplying equipment to the security forces, including custom-made web gear and vests, designed for the unique requirements of bush warfare. Most military forces, even those in Rhodesia, hadn't managed to design, procure and issue equipment that was practical and appropriate for guerrilla warfare, or long-range operations.

Fernando and Son would measure the client and sew a combat vest, made of heavy canvas and nylon, to the soldier's exact size and specifications, just as a bespoke tailor would construct a jacket. An assortment of ammunition pouches and straps to hold magazines, grenades and other accessories could be selected and integrated into the vest. The advantage of the combat vest was that you could drop your heavy backpack and still have enough equipment tied to your person to fight effectively.

Bob and Kurt designed their vests a little differently according to their individual preferences. Kurt had individual grenade pouches sewn high up on each shoulder strap, so they could be reached even when lying flat. He also chose ammunition pouches to accommodate his smaller FNC .223 magazines. Bob carried grenades in a large utility pouch, and chose larger ammunition pouches designed for the FN 7.62 box magazines. The clerk told them their vests would be ready in two to three days. Both paid in advance and told the proprietor to hold them until they could get back into town to pick them up.

Their swearing in was scheduled for one that afternoon, so they went back to the Ambassador Hotel again and checked out. They ate an early lunch there and talked until twelve-thirty then, with their luggage in hand, walked to the recruiting office. The tall, thin girl looked up from her paperwork and watched them enter, her eyes expressionless.

"Major Lamprecht is out at the moment," she told them in monotone. "You can wait over there." She pointed at the plastic chairs along the wall then went back to her paperwork.

Three more people came in to the office over the next twenty minutes, including a Brit, an Australian and a South African. They silently eyed one another until the Aussie broke the ice. He was a tall, lean, physically fit man in his mid-twenties with flaming red hair and pink, sunburned skin. He stuck his hand out to Kurt and Bob with enthusiasm.

"Ronnie Robertson's the name, but just call me Bluie," he said.

They both shook his hand but Bob looked perplexed and Bluie saw his look.

"What's the matta, mate, ya neva seen an Aussie befoah?"

"Ah, yes I have," Bob stuttered. "But I was just wonderin' why, if your name is Ronnie, do they call you Bluie? Ya don't look blue to me."

Bluie laughed hard enough to rattle the windows. The stick-like uniformed girl looked over at him with an expression of irritation.

"Blue is Aussie for red, mate!" Robinson shouted. "And as ya can see, I've got a bit a red up top."

Bob nodded, but if anything looked more confused than before.

"Were you in the Australian military, Bluie?" Kurt asked the Aussie.

"You got it, mate," Bluie replied. "Was in Aussie SAS and served in Nam, and I'll show ya something."

Bluie glanced in the direction of the thin female soldier who was now pretending to totally ignore the suddenly raucous group. He stood up and hiked up his left trouser leg, revealing shockingly white skin and sparse red hair. In the middle of his calf muscle was a healed but still slightly pink pit, about half an inch across. He turned around exposing the other side of his leg showing a healed vertical incision about four inches in length and several ladder-like suture scars.

"Goddamn Yank shot me in my leg here!" he said.

"An American shot you?" Kurt asked with surprise. "How the hell did that happen?"

"Well, I was mindin' my own business, pullin' sentry duty in a tower outside of Chu Lai, and a bloody yank thinks the tower is empty and decides to take a little target practice. Shoots me in my goddamn leg with his bloody M-16 ...he did!"

"What unit was he with?" Bob asked.

"Third Marines, I found out," Bluie replied. "Some bloody seventeen-year-old."

"That figures," Bob said shaking his head.

"How's that?" Bluie questioned.

"Leave it to a Marine to shoot a friendly and miss the enemy," Bob said.

Bluie laughed loudly.

"No love lost I see," Bluie said. "You two must have been army then?"

"Special forces ... close enough," Kurt responded.

"Good show," Bluie said, pulling his trouser leg down and sitting. "We're gonna make one hell of a team, ain't we?"

⌘

When Lamprecht arrived, he called them up to his office individually swore them in and made them sign enlistment contracts for three years. In the Rhodesian military, like its British parent, you could actually buy your way out of your commitment by forfeiting approximately one month's pay. This was entirely different from the American system, where an enlistment contract was written in blood.

In less then an hour all the swearing in was completed and contracts were signed. A two and a half ton Mercedes Unimog arrived and the five recruits and their gear were loaded in the back for the brief trip out to New Cranborne Barracks, some miles from the centre of town on Airport Road. The ride was uneventful but had an air of finality about it. Kurt looked forward to the new experience but the progressive gravity of it all crept into his thinking.

The five men were met by an enlisted administrative soldier, who assigned them bunks on the top floor of the 1-Commando Barracks, located at the far end of the New Cranborne complex. Rumour had it that the 156 Regular Training Detachment they were joining had a large number of foreign volunteers, though at least half their number were young local Rhodesian inductees. This made for a strange mix indeed.

"Ya think we're gonna corrupt the fragile minds of these little schoolboys?" Bluie asked when he heard the information. "We probably will ya know."

All of them laughed. Bluie was shaping up to be the joker of the bunch. As if fate had fulfilled some natural cosmic requirement: there had to be one in every group.

"I tell ya, Kurt," Bluie said as he was unpacking his gear, "as soon as we get settled in, you and me is goin' over to the drinkin' club down the road and get us a few wet ones. I'm gettin' bloody thirsty ... I am!"

"You damn Aussies," Kurt responded. "You go through beer like fish suck water. I don't know, Bluie. I don't think we are supposed to drink on the base while we are in training. That club is off limits to us ... I'm sure."

"HA! What the hell are you talking about, mate?" Bluie chortled. "I suppose elephants don't faat 'cause there is some rule against faatin in the jungle. I neva seen no man big or mean enough to stand between me and a beer when I'm thirsty!

"Tell you what Bluie," Kurt said. "If you want to go get beer I'll go with you, but we have to bring some back for anyone in the barracks who wants it."

Blue turned to Kurt in mock surprise.

"Spoken like a true fuckin leedah if evehh there was one," Bluie said, then he turned toward the door, when they heard footsteps on the stairway.

The two assigned RLI training cadre made their presence known to the men in the squad room by marching up the stairs with regular steady steps, intended to denote authority. They walked into the bay one after the other, then stopped just inside the door, standing side by side with crossed arms.

Bluie looked at the two of them and a grin broke out on his face.

"Well, if it ain't Laurel and fuckin Haady," Bluie exclaimed. "How ya doing today, fellas?"

The two corporals assigned as training staff turned to look at each other, their faces flushed red. The funny part was that the two looked just as Bluie described them. Corporal Mathis was small wiry, dark and intense. His partner Ceotzee was large, round and placid. Neither man was over twenty-one years of age. Their attempt to impress the men by visual means had failed miserably. They knew they would have to recoup somehow.

Facing the two instructors was the worst nightmare of any military training NCO. Mixed with the normal Rhodesian inductees was a confusing melange of former British and Australian SAS, Royal Marines, South African paratroopers, Portuguese Army Commandos, American Green Berets and even two Canadians who served with UN Forces. Many had seen real action in one form or another and were here as volunteers, mostly against the wishes of their respective governments. They were here for only one purpose, to engage in armed combat, the one thing at which they excelled.

Corporal Mathis, being the smarter of the two instructors, realized that attempting to control this bunch by fear was useless and would only bring ridicule if they attempted to intimidate them. He put up his arms and informally signalled everyone to come closer and gather around.

"All right, you ouens," Mathis said in a loud but rather high-pitched voice. "RLI has decided to run an abbreviated training course for this class, due to your unique backgrounds. This doesn't mean you can be slackers for the next two months. We do need soldiers in the field but we need good soldiers, trained to our system, not a bunch of international vagabonds."

Bluie let out a raucous laugh, but brought it up short when no one else joined in. Mathis eyed him down.

"And that includes you Australians as well," Mathis added. "We have no kangaroos or dingos, but we do have a lot of beer and even more terrorists. So if that's what you've come here for, you're in the right place."

The whole group let out a simultaneous cheer and Mathis felt a wave of relief. The first step in the battle was won, but he knew there would be many more skirmishes with this bunch. He told all of them to store their civilian clothes and other gear in suitcases or duffel bags, which would be locked in an adjoining unused bay room.

After their things were put away, the group went down to the mess hall, not to eat but to 'graze' as the RLI called eating. Cutlery was even called 'grazing irons'. As they stood in the long mess hall line, two Regimental Police (the Rhodesian Army's equivalent of American MPs), hustled a prisoner into the mess hall, bypassing the line. The man being escorted was dressed in baggy tan prison clothes and wore heavy wrist and leg irons. Far from subdued, the young prisoner was wild eyed and talking loudly to no one in particular.

"I showed the bastard, I shot that damn Kaffir!"

Then he raised his manacled hands like a victorious prize fighter who had just won a belt. A few of the recruits were taken by his spirit and cheered with him, but most just stared.

"What the fuck did he do, for chrisake?" Bluie asked aloud.

One of the more senior Rhodesian recruits standing in the front of the line turned around.

"He's the South African that got drunk and killed a taxi driver last month."

"Why the hell did he do that?" Bluie asked.

The recruit shrugged at the question.

"Didn't want to pay the fare I suppose. He probably figured that it was easier to shoot him with his 9mm than pay, and being an African, it didn't matter."

"The fuck you say?" Bluie said. "What are they gonna do with the little shit fer brains?"

"A statement of charges will be read to him today by his commanding officer," the recruit said. "Then in two weeks or thereabouts, they'll hang him."

"They don't fuck around, do they?" Kurt said. "I can't understand that sort of behaviour anyway. You come here trying to defend the right of a peaceful country to exist, then some asshole pulls this. He's no better than the terrorists we're fighting."

Bluie nodded, "There ain't no accountin' fer idiots mate, they are every-fuckin-whehh."

The mess hall was crowded and the food didn't look very appealing. Kurt had never heard of baked beans on toast for dinner. He figured it must be a British thing. The good news was that if you would eat it, there was plenty for the asking. Bob seemed to be taking full advantage of the situation. His tray was piled high with legumes and bread. Just outside the mess hall was a small white wooden kiosk that sold candy bars and cokes. Recruits were walking around with genuine hourglass-shaped Coke bottles. Kurt thought with some amusement that there probably wasn't a single mud-floored, grass-roofed, single-shelved shop in Africa that didn't sell Cokes.

They were standing outside the mess hall in small groups talking, when Bluie approached Kurt.

"Well, whatdaya think, mate?"

"About what?" Kurt responded. "The food really sucks, I know that."

"Naww, that's the same 'ol story," Bluie said. "I mean this place in general. Whatdaya think about it so faaa?"

Kurt turned his head around and saw the milling unorganized chaos of RLI Training Troop.

"Too early to say Bluie, but it looks like any other military training gang-bang at the moment. Time will tell I suppose."

"Ain't got a whole lot of time, mate," Bluie stated. "We'll be lookin' at the shaaap end of the stick in a blink, and these folks haven't impressed the hell out of me."

"Both of us are in the same situation, Bluie," Kurt told him. "We're combat veterans who've been through the best military training the world has to offer. All we are doing here is getting a little add-on knowledge, just going through the motions."

"I s'pose you are right about that, mate," Bluie said. "But we are gonna be fightin' with these guys and survival ain't an individual thing, it's a unit thing. I guess we could change units after we get done training heah."

"You mean go to the Selous Scouts?" Kurt asked.

Bluie stopped talking, and slowly turned his head toward Kurt.

"Yeah … I've heard rumours about them. Ya think they're true?"

⌘

That evening, on the prompting of the others in the RLI barracks, Kurt and Bluie put on civilian clothes and covertly walked to the Corporal's Club located near the entrance to New Cranborne. Bluie carried a green roll of cloth with him, which he tossed outside by some bushes before they entered the building. They went in and ordered beers, which slid down their throats like nectar. Luckily only a couple of other men were there playing pool, so no one recognized them as lowly trainees who would be banned from even entering the building.

When they finished their beers they informed the bartender, who was an army retiree, that they wanted to buy two cases. He eyed them a little suspiciously, but partying in Rhodesia was as common as breathing, so he went into the back room and came out with two wooden cases of brown bottles. There was a deposit charge of ten cents a piece on the bottles, which increased the anticipated cost significantly. Fortunately the men in the barracks had given them enough money, so they each lugged a full crate of beer outside.

"Now what?" Kurt asked. "We're supposed to carry these back to the barracks? Kind of obvious isn't it?"

"Naww mate," Bluie said, "that's what I brought these foah."

Bluie retrieved the green bundle which consisted of two duffel bags tightly rolled together. They moved to the side of the building that wasn't lit by an illumination pole, and carefully transferred the full beer bottles into the two duffel bags, placing the empty wooden crates along side the building.

"This sucks, Bluie," Kurt said. "If we drop these things or even ... "

"Don't think such horrible thoughts, mate," Bluie cut him off. "It's beer we are talking about here. Just pretend it's nitroglycerine or something, so you'll be bloody careful carryin' it. Now let's go."

They each gingerly shouldered a heavy duffel bag full of bottles of local brew. Their attempts at moving silently were futile. The sharp clink, clink of the bottles knocking together carried across the silent landscape. They were halfway back to the barracks when Kurt sensed movement behind them.

"I think we got company," Kurt said quietly. "We certainly set ourselves up. We got nowhere to run and nowhere to hide."

"Oh, it's probably just another trainee or troopie or something, mate," Bluie replied with little confidence. "Nothin' to worry about I reckon."

"You two there, stop!" an immature male voice shouted at them from behind.

"Oh shit," Kurt whispered. "We really should be smarter than this."

Both men stopped walking and slowly turned around, bottles clinking in mockery of their efforts to be clandestine. Quickly approaching them was a gawky man in uniform wearing a distinctive 'bus driver' hat with a broad red band, visible even by the distant barracks' lights. Both men knew that this was a member of the RPs, or Regimental Police. He took purposeful strides with black polished boots and stopped directly in front of them, less than an arm's length away.

"What have you ouens got in those duffel bags?" the RP squeaked. "Beer would be my guess. Put those bags on the ground ... now!"

Kurt and Bluie glanced at each other and simultaneously rolled their eyes with the universal 'I can't believe this shit' look, then laid their bags on the grass carefully.

The RP continued, "I know you two. I saw you come in on the truck this afternoon. Recruits are forbidden to have alcohol. It looks like you two fucked up early in the game. You will get ten days DB for this."

Kurt and Bluie looked at each other again. This time it was a questioning glance.

"In case you wankers don't know what DB is," the RP shouted, "it means detention barracks, a military prison where they put fuck-ups like you two to get straightened out. I guarantee you will enjoy your stay tremendously."

With that the RP smiled; he had captured a big quarry ... or so he thought.

Kurt turned to Bluie with teeth gritted, "Are you gonna hit this little fuck, or am I?"

Bluie quickly shrugged his shoulders and said almost with resignation, "I will."

With that, a white arm snapped out with the speed of a cobra strike. A crack sounded and the RP fell backwards in slow motion and made a dull thud on the soft grass.

"Jesus, Bluie," Kurt gasped, "you didn't have to kill him."

"Naaa, I didn't hit em that haaahd," Bluie said. "I did snap his head back a bit though. It gives 'em amnesia so he won't rememba much about this tomorrra. Just make sure he's breathin', okay mate?"

Kurt kneeled down and felt the man's breath, then laid him on his side to keep his airway clear.

"Are we just going to leave him here?" Kurt asked.

"Oh, he'll be okay," Bluie replied. "I tell ya mate, someone had to educate this little piece of crap. If we didn't, someone else would and he wouldn't be wakin' up in the morning."

"It's a hard lesson, Bluie."

"Well, it's a haaad world mate," Bluie sighed. "Like Jim Morrison said, ridaahs on the storm."

⌘

There was plenty of beer to go around that night. They stashed the empty bottles in their suitcases stored in the spare room. The next morning they were woken up at four-thirty and ran fourteen miles to the rifle range. None of them felt very good but two of the recruits, both smokers, stopped to puke in the ditch. The column didn't halt for them and they had to run hard to catch up, which worsened their condition. They were all experiencing their first taste of what was expected of the RLI.

They arrived at the rifle range when it was still cool. They practiced with the standard issue 7.62mm FN auto loading rifles. Some of the weapons were manufactured in Belgium by Fabrique Nationale and others called R1s were made in South Africa under licence. Kurt considered the rifle powerful but of mediocre quality, reliability and accuracy. It was designed in the 1950s for a war in the open country of Europe. Firing at a bull's-eye at one hundred yards, the best Kurt could do with his issued FN was a four and a half inch group. This was considered good for an FN, but Kurt considered the performance substandard for a large battle rifle.

The smaller compact FNC he had brought from Angola, shot the smaller .223 (or 5.56mm) cartridge as did the American M-16, and was superior for close-in bush fighting. He would use the smaller rifle in combat operations. Ammunition could be a problem, but the South Africans were starting to use the smaller ammunition, and Jack should be able to help.

They were trucked back to the barracks from the range late that afternoon. Compared with running that distance the rough truck ride felt like a magic carpet. RLI training was intense physically but fairly basic in the academic sense, which was no surprise to any of the experienced soldiers.

The days went by quickly and everyone was so tired, they had little desire to get up to mischief. On Bluie's insistence, they procured beer on a regular basis, and were never bothered again by the wary RPs. The hundreds of empties would make the African janitors very happy when they eventually discovered this hidden treasure trove, after the departure of Class 156.

On top of the physical and academic training there was heaped a generous portion of plain old 'fuck you' harassment. One form of torment that Kurt decided to end to early on, was 'change parades'. Their two training cadre delighted in ordering the recruits to dress in various uniforms, different every time, then make them fall out in the parade square for 'inspection'. When the inspection was complete they would give them another change of uniform and they had five minutes to run to the barracks, dress and be back for another inspection. Stragglers, or anyone not conforming exactly to the uniform, would be made to do push-ups or run around the parade square with their rifles at port arms. The trainers delighted in this senseless activity because it demeaned the trainees, and thus was thought to instil discipline.

After the second day of this, Kurt, Bluie and Holliday conspired to institute a rebellion before they had to hurt anyone. They called everyone together one afternoon after lunch and Kurt spoke to them, "When they give us a change parade today we are going to wear helmets, pistol belts and rubber flip flops, that's it."

One of the young Rhodesians looked at him with a mixture of shock and curiosity, and asked, "You mean naked ... starkers? We can't do that; they'll throw us in the box for sure!"

Kurt looked at all the young expectant faces and shook his head.

"I'm going to teach all of you an important lesson today," Kurt told them. "If we all stick closely together they can't and won't touch us. The whole point of this gang-bang is to get us to work together as a unit, not like a bunch of individuals. Many of us have been through this crap before. We'll show them unity, mixed with a bit of defiance maybe but, after we do this, we won't have to play this stupid game any more."

"How do you know what they'll do?" one of the other young recruits asked.

"Because Laurel and Hardy out there aren't very hard to figure out, that's why," Kurt replied. "Bluie and I had their number the first time they walked in. Look, if this thing goes bad, I'll take the heat. But in order to work *everyone* has to do it."

Corporals Coetzee and Mathis were aghast when they saw their charges standing naked on the parade square, in two perfect ranks, at attention.

"Whose bloody idea was this?" Mathis said, arms crossed in front of him, his dark face flushing red. His overweight and less articulate partner stood behind him with his mouth open.

Bluie began to snigger and Kurt elbowed him surreptitiously. None of the troops said anything, just kept looking straight ahead. Mathis was at a loss for words, his face darkening even more and veins standing out on his neck.

"Fall out!" Mathis yelled, and then added in a hoarse almost inaudible voice, "you bloody wankers."

The ruse worked, but it resulted in a more adversarial role for the instructors towards Class 156. It also resulted in more cohesion among the members of the class. Both changes were positive in Kurt's mind. From that point on, Kurt was the de facto leader of the class and Bluie moved in as his second. Despite the normal teething problems associated with any group of new recruits, the mixture of experienced soldiers and novices had a galvanizing effect, and the group began to mature quickly as soldiers.

The class was also introduced to Sgt Major Erastmus who would be conducting their field exercises. Erastmus was a character of a totally different nature from Mathis and Coetzee. An ex-member of the Wild Geese who had served with the famous Mike Hoare in the then Belgian Congo, he had also fought as a professional wrestler and had a cauliflower ear to show for it. Erastmus was now overweight and drank a case of beer daily, but showed few effects. Kurt liked the man immediately, even though he was way over the hill as a soldier. Erastmus also liked Kurt and saw in him a reflection of his own youth and fearless nature.

A rumour began to circulate that Class 156 was the best ever to go through RLI training, and Kurt was hell bent on making the rumour a fact. He held informal chat sessions with the recruits teaching them about topics like combat tactics, patrolling, tracking and avoiding detection during cross-border operations. No book or classroom could teach these subjects with the clarity and practical focus with which Kurt presented them. The young recruits listened as if their lives depended on this information, because they knew they soon would.

⌘

At the end of six weeks of intense training, Class 156 was ready for its first field exercise that was to be conducted in the Mazoe range located sixty kilometres north-west of Salisbury. The area was picturesque, hilly, green and sparsely occupied with farms. Erastmus told the class that only a short time prior to this, training exercises were conducted throughout the country, but the war had limited the choices to 'relatively safe' areas.

"It's like teaching people to swim with no water in the pool, Bluie," Kurt said.

"I prefer shaaks in the pool myself," Bluie replied. "Keeps swimmin' interestin'."

⌘

The geology of the Mazoe Range was unique. A very ancient fault, or crack, formed in the floor of the granite shield that makes up the floor of most of Southern and Eastern Africa. This 'Great Rift Valley', was made famous by fossil discoveries in the northern part by the Leakeys and others. This fissure in the planet's surface allowed molten rock, rich in minerals, to well out of the young earth and then harden. Iron, chromium, cobalt, copper, vanadium, gold and other valuable and rare minerals were found in the ore, sometimes in abundance. A 'leader' or side channel off of the Rift Valley formed the Mazoe range. Lush green grasses and acacia trees hid a base material of mineral-rich decomposing black rock.

When the class arrived at the Mazoe training site, they hurriedly set up tents and unloaded supplies. Afterwards, Kurt quickly surveyed the terrain and recognized some of the geology. One of the classes he had taken in college briefly discussed its unique nature.

"Jesus, Bluie," Kurt exclaimed, "you know what we're standing on?"

Bluie was squatting on the ground trying to get into a green can of rations with a small metal P38 can opener, sniffing it as he pried and making a concerned face.

"A shit load of dirt and rocks probably," Bluie replied without looking up, "Do you Yanks have to be told every bloody thing?"

"Okay, wise ass," Kurt said, "Just pull out your compass and tell me which way north is."

Bluie shook his head in mock resignation, "Like I told ya, mate. Oh, nevah mind."

Bluie withdrew his military compass from his belt pouch, opened the bezel, let it settle down and pointed.

"It's that way, mate."

"Now turn it one hundred and eighty and tell me again," Kurt ordered. Bluie rotated his compass and watched as the bezel turned with the body.

"Bloody hell, this thing is broke," Bluie said angrily. "How'd ya know my compass was buggered, mate? Did ya break it?"

"No, your compass is fine," Kurt explained. "It's just that we are standing on billions of tons of hematite and magnetite; they're forms of iron ore."

Kurt reached down and picked up a heavy black chunk of rock and threw it towards Bluie's feet.

"That stuff," Kurt said, "really screws up a compass needle."

"If there's so much of that stuff here," Bluie asked, "how come no one's mined it then? It must be worth a fortune."

Bluie tossed the rock which went scurrying down the slope to be lost among the countless others.

"Oh, they probably will in time," Kurt answered. "Right now politics stand in the way. Most of the African interior is undeveloped. Makes you feel good in some ways. This country is not much different now from when Stanley, Livingston and Selous explored it a century ago. At least we are able to see it before people completely ruin it."

"I suppose you're right, mate," Bluie rose to his feet and looked around. "It sure is a beautiful place."

"All right, you lazy buggers," Erastmus yelled, "fall in!"

Erastmus emerged from his tent. From the time the tent had been erected an hour ago and when he emerged, he had downed eight beers. Beer was both fuel and lubrication for his worn body. Take his beer away and the hard old man would certainly perish. His limp was more pronounced today. Word had it that when was serving with Mike Hoare in the Belgium Congo uprising in 1964 and '65, he caught a round in the leg fired by a Simba tribesman armed with an old Enfield 303.

Erastmus looked as mean as a man could be packaged, but when Kurt met him for the first time he knew it was a facade. The grizzly old alcoholic was really a nice man who loved his troops but, in the tradition of the old British Army, could not afford to show it. He was really a sentimental old guy who often worried about his 'kids' some of whom were only sixteen years old. He shed tears when the young ones were killed, but only in private.

It was different for the likes of Kurt, Bluie and Holliday. Although they were all much younger than him, Erastmus saw in their eyes the seasoned warriors so prized by any army. Long gone were the signs of innocence and fear so prevalent on the faces of the new recruits. What he saw was the steel and ice of determination that can only be forged on the hot anvil of combat. These men were his field leaders. He separated them out, and called them into his tent for a talk.

"This war here is changing," Erastmus told the three men standing before him while he opened another bottle of beer, but not offering them one. "Unless we can train these lads properly, they will wander around the bush clueless and be wounded or killed on their first operation. It's up to us to do what we can for them. We are all combat veterans and it is our duty to pass on what we have learned."

Kurt spoke first, "I agree with you, Sergeant Major, but in order to do that we have to get away from the standard RLI training plan. I've seen it and it's not bad for training conventional army troops, but it's pretty weak in the type of fighting we will be involved in."

Erastmus cast a rheumy eye in Kurt's direction.

"Well, soldier, what do you recommend?" he asked. "I am given quite a bit of flexibility, all you have to do is convince me."

"For a start," Kurt said, "let's split Class 156 into two groups. Bob will take one and I will take the other. To start, Bob's group will be an insurgent force, and mine will be the counter-insurgent, or COIN, force. We did a similar thing in US Special Forces training. At the time I thought it was good, but we can improve it."

Kurt looked into Erastmus's eyes but they revealed no indication of his thinking. He took another swig of beer, which was for him half a bottle.

"That all sounds reasonable," Erastmus said. "You all go off and put your proposal on paper and we will come up with a game plan. I don't want this training to turn into a fuck-up because it will be my backside on the fire, not yours."

"Understood, Sergeant Major," Kurt looked at his watch and it said just before two o'clock. "Bob and I will have something to you by say, seven-hundred hours?"

Erastmus nodded his head and dismissed the three of them with a wave. The talk was starting to interfere with his drinking, which made him impatient.

⌘

Both Bob and Kurt were surprised at how quickly the training plan came together. Both had in their minds how they would train Special Operations troops if they ever had the chance, so the information flowed easily. They only argued over minor details. Bluie contributed some valuable lessons learned from his years with the Australian SAS. They were finished an hour before the plan was due, so Kurt decided to rewrite a clean copy.

Bob figured it was past meal time and went off to find some food, and shortly came back with a couple of boxes of Rhodesian Army rations. He opened one of the large green tins with a P38 can opener, and then let out a noise that sounded like a groan of a dying man.

"What the hell's wrong, Holliday?" Kurt questioned. "You get snake bite or something?"

Bob was shaking his head in dismay, as he would if his favourite dog was hit by a car.

"Can you believe they feed this shit to their own troops?" he lamented.

"What is it?" Kurt asked. "I can smell it from here, it must have gone off."

"I don't think so." Bob was only beginning to appreciate the full magnitude of the tragedy. "It's fucking fish. Can you believe they would feed us fish ... in a can?"

"Like sardines?" Kurt said, not looking up from his writing. "Sardines aren't bad."

"No way, man!" Bob moaned. "We ain't talking sardines here, but I wish we were ... I sure wish we were. No, we are talking big fish in tomato sauce. If they fed this crap to prisoners it would be cruel and unusual, for sure. It would be a war crime, that's what it would be."

"Well, open another can and maybe you'll get beans or something," Kurt said.

"Anything would have to be better than this," Bob held the open can of fish at arm's length, like it was old road kill.

"Goddamn it, Bob," Kurt looked up from his paper, "we are going on a survival exercise tomorrow; by the end of the week you'll wish you had that can of fish."

Kurt completed the last sentence of their proposal, and slammed his pencil down.

"Nope," Bob shook his head with firm insistence. "I'd be skin and bones but I'd never eat *that!*"

"Okay, Bob, you've made your point, now let's go see Erastmus."

# CHAPTER 17
## NEXUS

The small group of men ascended the face of the Iron Mask Range. The base of the slope was strewn with loose rocks that varied in size from pebbles to boulders. Their footing was precarious until they were above the loose material, broken away by the millennia of expansion and contraction, and plant roots trying to gain a foothold in the sterile surface. Though the day was grey, enough sun broke through for thermals to spring from the black rock face, distorting images as they looked upwards.

In the lead was a seventeen-year-old Rhodesian RLI trainee, with a stocky build and muscular legs that were ideal for climbing. It was his turn to lead the group. His plan was to set up an observation post near the crest of the ridge line in order to spot the opposing team, which was expected to move through the valley below. Kurt knew the trainee's plan had some drawbacks but he let him go ahead in order to demonstrate the faults, once they became apparent.

When the group was about a hundred metres from the crest, an unusual sound was heard and everyone dropped to a kneeling position with their rifles to the ready. Movement on the crest of the hill was distorted by the thermals.

Another local trainee to Kurt's left flank said, "*Bobo.*"

Kurt shook his head in an 'I don't know' gesture.

"Baboon," the trainee said. "Big male baboon, doesn't want us on his mountain."

Kurt nodded. He gave the others in the group hand signals to stay put while he moved up with the point man.

"Now what's your plan, Trevor?" Kurt asked the young soldier, who was looking confused. "That big baboon is not rolling out a red carpet for us, is he?"

"I dunno," he replied. "That bloody thing. I guess we're gonna have to take him out."

Kurt unsnapped his combat knife and placed it butt first in the youth's hand. The blade glistened as it turned.

"Are you fucking looney? That bastard will have my arm off before I can stab him to death."

"Then how do you propose we take him out?" Kurt asked.

"Shoot him of course. How the hell else would you do it?"

"We're tactical," Kurt told him sternly. "One shot would alert the whole valley and compromise our location. It's pretty stupid to risk that for a fucking monkey. I'll give you a clue. Animals are territorial just like people so ... "

The young trainee looked both angry and confused, but he finally replied, "We should move down the crest a little and try there?"

Kurt nodded and took his knife back.

"This is a real fuck-up here," Kurt told the youth. "I let you continue to prove a point.

If that baboon had been the enemy this group would be dead. When you approach a ridge line you never walk straight into it, especially if you have no cover. You approach from the side or at a steep oblique angle and cross the crest low, then parallel the crest with your point element zigzagging to spot any ambushes. Understood?"

The trainee nodded his head reluctantly.

"Okay," Kurt said. "Now, let's go down and do it the right way."

"You mean go back down the mountain? Hell, we are already here!"

"Doing it wrong is never good training for doing it right," Kurt said. "Let's move out."

⌘

The group began descending the face of the ridge when the wind suddenly shifted and the sky went from grey to black in minutes. The clouds were ominous, promising unrestrained mounting energy. With darkness underfoot and darkness above, the men felt like they had just fallen deep into a dark well.

The air cooled and the sky closed in. Without warning a blinding flash illuminated the scene, followed rapidly by a concussive boom and crash that stunned their senses. They were caught in the open, in a tropical lightning storm, standing on the Iron Mask Range. The metal-rich rock beneath their feet was an excellent conductor of electricity. There was nowhere to hide and the storm was moving fast and would sweep over them before shelter could be reached.

Trevor tugged at Kurt's sleeve and yelled at him trying to be heard over the approaching wind and rain.

"Can't we go somewhere? We are gonna die if we stay here."

Kurt did a quick three-sixty degree and the only relief he saw was a slight depression in the rock face about fifty metres directly down hill. He motioned with his head for the others to follow.

The men dashed to the hollow and were nearly there when low electrically charged clouds made their hair stand on end. Kurt attempted to herd them into the depression when a bolt of lightning struck nearby. There was no sound, but the searing heat and pressure wave stunned them, and they dived to the ground. Small shards of rock were thrown from the point of impact, cutting two of the men. A jumbled collection of limbs, bodies and equipment lay on the rocks.

Kurt extricated himself from the pile and sat up as the wall of rain ran over them like an express train. For half a minute he couldn't see the men next to him. Then as suddenly as it came, the storm departed. Totally soaked, they sat silently and watched the squall blow off the ridge and into the valley below. Lightning flashed in jagged spears and thunder boomed and echoed, rolling around the surrounding slopes.

"That's a fine how-do-you-do, ain't it?" Bluie said wringing out his jungle hat like a soaked dish rag.

"What do you mean, Bluie?" Kurt asked with a little irritation in his voice. "Just caught in a damn thunderstorm, happens all the time."

"Almost kilt by a bloody lightnin' bolt I was ... Lookit."

Bluie pulled up his trouser leg and revealed a trickle of crimson blood running down his alabaster leg.

"A little nick, quit whining." Kurt said. "Let's move up to one of those caves we spotted higher up to dry out and patch up injuries. We will stay tactical until we're in position. I'm point. Grab your equipment and let's move."

⌘

Kurt led the wet and bedraggled group diagonally up the mountain face until they approached the entrance of a cave located just below the crest. He'd spotted the cave while descending the parallel slope from across the valley, but because it was recessed, it couldn't be seen from below until they were only a few metres away. The group halted just short of the entrance.

"Bluie," Kurt said, "take Trevor and check it out. Something nasty may live in there. Caves are attractive to all kinds of wildlife, so be careful."

"Got ya," Bluie responded. "If it moves I'm gonna shoot it."

Bluie and Trevor approached the cave entrance cautiously with their rifles at the ready. They were out of sight for about five minutes and without drama returned by the same route.

"Looks clear," Bluie said. "No recent tracks. Someone was up there quite a while back, there're old campfire ashes and drawings on the walls."

"Drawings?" Kurt questioned.

Bluie nodded, and motioned for the others to follow.

The entrance to the cave was inset into the face of the slope fifty feet below the crest. Loose rocks and boulders that had fallen from the peak cluttered the narrow shelf in front of the entrance, nearly obscuring it. Charred remnants lay at the threshold to the cave, but the ash was totally flat, and mixed in with clay and silica. The fire was old, but how old was impossible to tell. Little light fell beyond the entrance of the cave due to a rock overhang which shielded the depths.

Kurt stepped inside the entrance and in seconds vague forms began to appear, as if shapes were floating in the cave's darkened recesses. As his vision began to adjust, drawings of animals and stick men covering the surfaces of the inner walls came into focus. Although crude in comparison with modern art and frozen on stone for centuries, the figures seemed to be moving.

The drawings nearer to the entrance were faded. Some were nearly gone, with only fragments remaining. Walking further inside Kurt found clearer figures, some with the hint of colour, but that was hard to determine in the dim light. Unclipping the green angle head flashlight from the side of the ALICE rig, he flicked on the beam.

When the electric light hit the figures, Kurt gasped with surprise. Elephants, rhinos, giraffe, wildebeest, kudu and other game animals swarmed over the rocky landscape. The animals were clear and almost lifelike. Some were drawn around natural projections in the rock wall, which gave the figures a three dimensional appearance.

Bluie, who was standing just to Kurt's left, reached out to touch one of the figures.

"No!" Kurt said, and his hand reached out to stop him.

"What the hell?" Bluie said loudly, his words echoing off the rock walls.

"This stuff is very old, Bluie," Kurt told him. "One touch may ruin it."

"Who the fuck cares?" Bluie asked indignantly. "It's been sittin 'ere who the hell knows how long and no one gives a rat's ass about it."

"I wonder who painted these," Kurt said aloud. He thought of the runic figures on the front of the house in Maine and on his grandfather's grave, inscriptions that were meant to say something to others long after the artist was gone. What were they saying to us?

"Bushman," a voice said. Trevor was standing behind Kurt and Bluie looking at the pictures, but he seemed disinterested.

"Bushmen?" Kurt asked. "How do you know that?"

"There are paintings all over the place from the northern hills here to down south by Bulawayo," Trevor said. "There are even some on my dad's farm near Shamva."

Kurt nodded his head in agreement.

"When I was on the Namibian coast a few weeks ago, I went hunting with some Bushmen, but there can't be any around here now. Can there?" Kurt asked.

Trevor shrugged, "Don't think so. When the Mashona tribe moved into this area a couple of hundred years ago they probably killed them off ... or ran them out."

"I wonder how old these drawings are then," Kurt pondered aloud.

Trevor, thinking he was being addressed, responded, "There's no telling. In school we learned that the Bushmen were the oldest people on earth. I don't know if that's true or not, I've never seen any myself."

Kurt scanned the rest of the wall with his flashlight and stopped in front of a figure that was different from the others. He moved closer.

"Bluie... look at this one."

"What, the big dude?" Bluie asked as he moved closer.

"Yes, look at him."

Most of the human figures portrayed in the drawings were crude stick figures dominated by their huge spears and bows, except for this one. His position on the rock canvas was central, and his body was well defined and anatomical. He was poised with a spear extended and ready to throw in his right arm. The figure had large bulging arms and chest muscles, and legs with the grace of impala limbs supported him.

"That ain't no Bushman, mate," Bluie said. "Looks like a white man, don't he? But naaah, there weren't no spear-throwing white men in these parts. Maybe he's ... like a god or something."

Bluie drew closer to the mysterious figure, squinted and said, "He *must* be a god or a king, look at the size of that thing would ya!"

Kurt stared closer at the wall.

"Oh, you mean his phallus? Primitive peoples always exaggerate that part. I guess at that time they were worried about their fertility keeping up with the mortality rate what with all the disease, lions, crocs, wars and things.

Bluie shook his head, "I didn't know a big dick was a survival tool, mate." With that he laughed and turned and left the cave, leaving Kurt standing there alone.

For several minutes he studied the incredible art, recalling the hunt with the Bushmen in Namibia. Unconsciously he reached up and touched the bear's claw, cat's tooth and Navaho charm that hung on the braided elephant hair rope along with his fibreboard dog tag disks.

The ancient drawings and pieces of long dead animals spoke, not with words but with powerful, surging emotion that crashed down like a wave of dark, warm water. A land, a world once theirs, was gone. All that was left of their universe were faded rock paintings of man and beast poised on the brink of survival, or extinction. For the first time in his life Kurt was engulfed by a sense of mortality. He thought of the Mad Medic and his bizarre views. What did he say? In the end we are doing well if we break even, or something to that effect. Maybe he was on to something.

We are all like the Bushmen, he thought. Just here for a brief time. Nothing in this life has any permanence.

With that thought he left the depths of the cave and joined the other men who had started a brisk fire outside the entrance.

# CHAPTER 18

## THE MISSION

**Combined Operations—Rhodesian Security Forces**
**Intelligence Section**
**October 13, 1976**

The trio of officers sat behind a beaten-up light-green table in the small and airless briefing room. Stacks of maps and files obscured the table top and spilled on to the floor. The windows, or where windows had been, were blacked out. Not with curtains or sheeting but with pieces of plywood, painted black, nailed over the inside of the window frames. Lighting in the room was provided by an antiquated bank of overhead fluorescent bulbs that gave off a sickly yellow and orange tinted hue. Large detailed topographical maps full of coloured pins covered most of the wall space.

Kurt was escorted into the room by an SAS corporal of medium height, with a build like a rugby player, who carried an UZI slung over his shoulder. The corporal didn't show any emotion. After accompanying Kurt inside the room, he saluted the officers and marched out, followed by a heavy *click* as the bolt was thrown on the door.

"Good morning, Sergeant Christianson."

The youngest of the three men stood up while he spoke, the other two remained seated.

"Good morning, sir." Kurt wasn't sure if he should also address the seated men, so he made brief eye contact with each of them.

"Please have a seat," the young officer said and indicated a wooden chair facing them on the opposite side of the table, painted the same pale green as the desk. Kurt pulled out the chair and sat down, resting his forearms on the table. All three of the men unconsciously glanced at his arms, in an unacknowledged but ancient ritual of sizing up a new man.

"I am Lieutenant Blythe, and this is Major Moore and Colonel Ainsley. We are all staff officers from the Combined Operations Intelligence Section. Sergeant, on reviewing your records we have seen that you may possess some special skills that may be of interest to us."

Major Moore, a burly and balding man in his mid-forties cleared his throat. The younger lieutenant stopped talking and sat down.

"Let's get to the point," Moore said.

"Sergeant Christianson; first, I'd like to thank you for coming today on such short notice."

Kurt was inclined to mention something about following orders but thought better of it and just nodded.

"We have reviewed your performance since joining the ranks of the RLI," Major

Moore continued, "and I have to say all of us are impressed, very impressed."

Major Moore opened a tan file in front of him but first put on a pair of half-frame reading glasses before leafing through the paperwork silently for a full minute before speaking again.

"Yes, outstanding. You have been promoted from corporal to sergeant, and been awarded the bronze cross and nominated for the silver cross in a period of seven months. The nomination for the silver cross says, ... Awarded for actions during an armed contact with ZANLA guerrillas in the vicinity of Merawa, You entered a cave and killed nine armed combatants using only a pistol. How did you accomplish that, Sergeant?"

"Truthfully, sir, I underestimated the number of enemy holed up in the cave, and wouldn't have gone in so lightly armed if I had known."

"Tell us what happened, Sergeant?" Moore asked.

"Sir, the revolver only holds six rounds, and it's difficult to reload when someone is firing an AK at you in an enclosed space. I was just lucky that they were bad shots, sir."

"This report also says that the troop you led was responsible for killing one hundred and fifteen guerrillas in a period of three months while suffering no casualties or serious wounds."

"Yes, sir, they are a great bunch of kids."

"Also, Sergeant, there is something else in your file we would like to ask you about."

"What is that, sir?"

"Did you parachute into Angola prior to coming here and inflict considerable damage on the Cuban contingent at Vista del Sol?" Moore asked directly while looking at him.

Kurt was caught off guard. The man obviously knew about the abortive Angola operation, to deny it would only make him look deceitful. He was in their employ now and, despite the momentary hesitation to collect his thoughts, he would have to answer truthfully.

"Yes, sir."

The major was a bull of a man with salt-and-pepper close-cropped hair. His bushy eyebrows went up almost comically when he heard Kurt's reply.

"You did this alone?" Moore asked in a puzzled tone.

"Well, sir," Kurt replied, "I was supposed to tie up with our FNLA assault team but they were ambushed so I had to fight my way out. I had little choice."

"You had no choice but to attack the garrison yourself?" Moore stood up and began pacing the room with his hands behind his back, like a trial lawyer.

"They had trackers on me, sir, so I had to attack or be captured," Kurt explained.

Moore nodded, his face only a short distance from Kurt's.

"And that is precisely why we brought you here, Sergeant," he said in almost a whisper.

"That was luck, sir, by rights I should have never made it out of that mess."

"But you did get out," Moore said emphatically, "and you are sitting right here in front of us aren't you? I've been in the military since World War Two. I've retired twice and for some reason unknown to me I'm still at this game. In all of my experience I've never heard of luck of this magnitude. Luck happens once or twice, Sergeant, but it seems to follow you around."

Major Moore sat down on the corner of the table and looked directly at Kurt.

"We have an important mission, sergeant, and we would like to ask if you are interested."

The room became very silent and suddenly hot. The black plywood over the windows radiated heat as the unseen sun struck it.

"I am only an enlisted man in this army, sir," Kurt said. "If I am given a mission by my superiors I will do my best to carry it out."

Moore nodded in agreement. "This is not a mission we can just assign to any individual, sergeant. This mission is inherently risky and we would not give it to … let's say a less than enthusiastic soldier."

"Sir," Kurt said, "in that case I will evaluate this mission and, if I think it's feasible, I will accept without hesitation."

Moore then nodded to Lieutenant Blythe who stood and walked to a large map hanging on the far wall. Kurt turned and sat backwards in his chair in order to face the map.

"Sergeant Christianson you are now subject to the Official Secrets Act and unless authorized, anything you hear in this room will not be discussed with any other party, under penalty of imprisonment. Is that understood?" The lieutenant stopped moving, waiting for a reply before proceeding.

"Yes, sir, understood," Kurt said.

Blythe grabbed a pointer and tapped an area on the map and began;

"Last week an over flight by one of our Vampire reconnaissance aircraft detected a large ZANLA terrorist base camp located in the vicinity of the Pungwe Gorge in south-western Mozambique, about seventy kilometres from the Rhodesian border." Lt Blythe took an opaque covering off a smaller picture positioned on the wall next to the larger map, and used his pointer.

"The camp is situated in extremely inaccessible terrain and nearly covered by thick forest canopy. Because it is winter, the trees are partially defoliated and from the photograph we can just make out the camp layout, including a defensive perimeter with medium to heavy weapons emplacements. Interrogation of captured ZANLA guerrillas indicates there is a major training and supply base in this area and we think this is it. There are two other bases of this size that we know of but they are located hundreds of kilometres from us straddling the Tanzanian Border."

Lt Blythe moved back to the larger map and continued, "We think that this is an aggressive move by ZANLA to shift their operational infrastructure to within easy striking distance of Rhodesia. In this way they will be able to train recruits, deploy and re-supply guerrilla teams more easily. Up to this point we have been playing a defensive war: forays by our security forces into sanctuary states like Mozambique have been limited to brief hot-pursuit missions. This Pungwe camp is especially dangerous because it is located close to our eastern flank and terrorist detachments will be able to infiltrate all along here."

On the large map Lt Blythe swept his pointer along the hundreds of miles of border thus affected.

"To be succinct, Sergeant," Blythe continued, "we need to know more information about the camp and we need to know it quickly. Information such as layout details, defensive positions, routes of access and manpower are all vital pieces of the puzzle. The enemy placed this camp in Pungwe Gorge to take advantage of the heavy cover and natural defences provided by vegetation and terrain. Our initial thoughts are that we may be able to use those same features to our advantage if we know the camp well, and plan our attack accordingly."

Lieutenant Blythe lowered his pointer and turned directly towards Kurt.

"Last week the Selous Scouts attempted a ground reconnaissance probe, but the approaches were guarded and they couldn't get close enough, undetected. If Rhodesian forces are seen on the ground in the vicinity of the camp, ZANLA will know we are up to something and will strengthen their defences or move, making it much more difficult for us to attack."

"So you want to take this camp out fairly quickly then?" Kurt asked.

"We'd like to hit Pungwe before their security becomes too formidable," Blythe continued, "but we are afraid if we go in with bad intelligence, our men could be trapped by terrain and heavy weapons crossfire. That scenario would entail significant casualties and that possibility is unacceptable because of our severe manpower restrictions. We need someone who can go in and come out, undetected, with the information needed to plan the offensive."

"And someone who is deniable," Kurt added.

"Excuse me, Sergeant? Blythe said.

"Respectfully, sir, let's cut through the crap," Kurt interjected.

All three officers looked at him with rather stunned expressions.

"I am an American and if I was captured, there could be legitimate denial that I was a member of the Rhodesian military."

"Well, I ... " Blythe stuttered.

"Don't get me wrong, that's okay," Kurt injected. "Let's just not play games here, my life is on the line and I take that pretty seriously. All I request is for you to be honest with me and not try to sell me dog crap and say it's sirloin steak."

Kurt stood up without prompting and walked toward the map like a cat drawn to a rat. The officers were silent but looked at one another with a dry quizzical expression only the British can master. Standing in front of the map he felt the contour lines with the tips of his fingers. Even though the map was plain paper and smooth, he touched the map as though receiving tactile feedback. Kurt stared at the contour lines intensely for a few minutes, while the three officers individually pondered the magnitude of the mistake they'd just made.

Without warning Kurt suddenly turned around and eyed each man briefly.

"Sirs, How do you propose for me to get in and out?"

Major Moore again stood up and Blythe tried to blend in with the wall, still holding his pointer awkwardly. Moore was sweating profusely now as the enclosed room grew increasingly hot, perspiration staining the armpits and neckline of his uniform.

"There are a variety of means at our disposal, Sergeant," Moore said. "We haven't decided on the method or methods at this time. Since you would be the one going in, your input is vital before any decision is made."

Kurt nodded. Good ... at least they are considering my opinion, he thought.

"Have you ever dropped a parachutist from one of your Canberras?" Kurt asked.

The officers glanced at one another before Colonel Ainsley answered, speaking for the first time.

"The Canberra as you must know, Sergeant, is a bomber. We normally drop parachutists from Dakotas, the old trusty DC-3s. They are set up for that type of thing."

"Yes, sir, I realize that," Kurt replied. "Let me restate the question. In its current configuration is it possible to jump out of the bomb bay of a Canberra?"

"I think that might be feasible, Sergeant," Major Moore replied. "We would have to look at the bomb bay clearance, airspeed, altitude and other factors, but let's say it's hypothetically possible. What would be your plan?"

"A single high altitude over-flight would draw little attention from the ground or any radar sites," Kurt said, "especially if the pass is not directly over the target. Depending on the prevailing winds and other factors we can offset the flight twenty to twenty-five kilometres. If I can use one of the new square parachutes the Parachute School just received from South Africa, I could fly it close to the target as I did in Angola."

"Where would you attempt to land, sergeant?" Colonel Ainsley asked.

Kurt scrutinized the Colonel, thinking that it was a premature question for a senior officer to ask.

"Looking at the map on the wall here there are several possibilities," Kurt replied. "But I'd like to study some more aerial photos if they are available," Kurt told Ainsley, purposely skirting the question.

Lieutenant Blythe nodded.

"That is possible, Sergeant. After we are done here I can escort you down to the intelligence shop where those photos are kept."

"I will insist, however," Kurt said, "that the LZ I finally select will be known to no one but myself."

Colonel Ainsley spoke again with the classic British harrumph that Kurt found humorous, but he tried not to smile or laugh.

"That is very irregular, Sergeant ahhh Christianson, is it? What if something were to happen, go wrong as it were, we should know your location."

Kurt turned to Ainsley, "Sir, I don't doubt the integrity of anyone in this organization, but I have been caught in similar situations before. I work alone. On this type of mission I trust no one. The only advantage I have out there is total surprise. If anyone knows I'm coming my survival is in extreme jeopardy. If you insisted on knowing where I would make an infiltration, I would have no choice except to mislead you."

"Understood, Sergeant," Moore said intercepting any argument from Colonel Ainsley. "What about getting out of the area, exfiltrating? Do you have any thoughts at this point?"

"Sir, obviously I haven't had time to think any of this through," Kurt replied. "But my first thoughts are walking out and meeting up with a team of your Selous Scouts at a pre-determined location some distance from the target. We could designate primary and alternate locations and times. I could work with Lieutenant Blythe on this."

"So based on what we have told you thus far are you accepting the mission?" Moore asked.

"Yes, sir," Kurt responded. "It sounds reasonable, count me in."

"Thank you, Sergeant," Moore said as he stood up again and moved towards Kurt. "Do you have any further questions for us?"

"This probably isn't the time or the place, sir," Kurt told him, "but if I carry out this operation successfully I would like to be considered for the Selous Scouts."

Colonel Ainsley raised his eyebrows and attempted to say something but was cut short by Major Moore.

"If you pull this off as you say, soldier, I'd say that you could have your choice of units."

"I appreciate that, sir," Kurt said.

"Then you are dismissed," Moore said, "and I'd like to add that you are a courageous soldier for volunteering for this important mission. God speed to you."

Moore shook Kurt's hand and Blythe led him out of the room after knocking for the SAS guard to open it. Ainsley stood up, smiled and shook his hand. Kurt noticed his hand was unusually cool and moist on such a hot day.

⌘

The Canberra Bomber, designated RB-57 for Reconnaissance Bomber by the United States, was designed in Britain as a strategic strike aircraft in the early 1950s to carry nuclear weapons into the European theatre. By the 1970s these aircraft were obsolete by Western standards, but serendipitously, they were found to be ideally suited for covert or small-scale conventional operations. Rhodesia had half a dozen of these antiquated planes in its inventory, and managed to keep them flying by scrounging parts from the international market. The bat-winged Canberra was very quiet by jet aircraft standards, with a service ceiling of thirty five thousand feet and a relatively long range. These characteristics also made it a nearly ideal high altitude reconnaissance platform.

Kurt was crammed into the bomb bay next to an air force technician assigned to assist him. The tech wore a pilot's pressure suit and was hooked up with pneumatic lines to couplers to the bulkhead. Kurt only had on a parachute and his combat gear, which had been put on before climbing aboard due to the cramped quarters. Both men breathed pure oxygen from the masks fed from overhead tanks. Kurt also had a small three cubic foot 'pony bottle' of oxygen strapped to the top of his front-mounted reserve chute, to which he would switch over just before he left the aircraft. Without oxygen at this altitude, a man would lose consciousness in a short time.

It was just before dusk. Like the jump into Angola months before, inserting at this time would allow movement away from the landing area before daylight set in. There were no warning lights in the bomb bay, and it was cramped and extremely cold. The space was designed to hold racks of free-fall bombs, in a rotary bomb bay which had been removed, not to carry cargo or people. Both men perched uncomfortably on their knees facing the closed bomb bay doors. A single twenty four-volt overhead bulb was their only light, and it cast eerie shadows on the flat grey metal interior.

The technician suddenly waved at Kurt and with a dramatic gesture pointed down at the bomb bays, then grabbed hold of a metal cross brace tightly. Seconds later the bay doors dropped and freezing wind swirled around the compartment with cyclonic force. Kurt squatted and grabbed the lip of the opening to help stabilize him in the wind. He was wearing leather gloves but even through the padding, his fingers went numb instantly.

The technician was talking to the pilot through an intercom link. Just before departure the pilot was informed of the release point, and the technician was waiting for confirmation. There was no choice but to trust the pilot; they were too high to spot the release point from the limited aperture of the open bomb bay. Both men watched as thin wisps of cirrus cloud shot beneath the aircraft. The clouds did not obscure the ground entirely, but did give a three-dimensional perspective to their extreme altitude.

The technician suddenly pointed at Kurt, which was his signal to exit. Kurt looked through the open metal rectangle, knowing he would have to drop cleanly through the hole into the rarefied air beneath. Their air speed alone made the exit hazardous. Impact with any part of the aircraft could prove disastrous. Releasing the grip on the edge of the bomb bay, he sprang from his position like a leaping rabbit and seemed to hang suspended for a moment above the opening before disappearing from the technician's sight.

Hitting the slip-stream at five hundred and fifty kilometres per hour his legs instantly bent, but there was no other sensation before temporary blackness overtook him. Later he was vaguely aware of spinning, pin wheeling, feeling like ropes and horses were pulling at all four limbs. The oxygen mask flopped wildly against his face and upper chest. These events were distant, experienced like an outsider looking at this cataclysmic scene from some other place. Only a single hot spark still burned within, which had to be grasped, or death would be the only outcome.

With every scrap of strength he could commandeer, he pulled in his arms and legs to make his body into a ball. At first this proved impossible, but slowly his limbs came to the centre, defying centrifugal forces to regain control of his limbs. Trying to maintain the ball but still spinning, the air rapidly grew warmer and more breathable. After holding this foetal position a few seconds longer, he flared out and reached for the ripcord.

With the opening shock, white pain shot through his back and neck. The twisted lines rotated for a few revolutions then the square canopy cracked and flapped above. Consciousness was again fading and Kurt had no idea where he was.

The ground loomed, rushing up to smite the intruder like a brown wall. At the last moment he flared the canopy to slow airspeed, but his depth perception was off and he and the parachute crashed and tumbled into the low bush. All was still and the blackness now rushed in like an inky cloud of narcosis. For the next few hours there were no dreams, no hallucinations, and no thoughts.

Kurt came around slowly, in stages. Large red ants raced inches below his face, ignoring the intrusion. The next conscious memory was of twilight, and the thought of lying helpless in the African bush at night triggered primal fears that were deeper than conscious thought. In some buried part of the brain he knew he must awaken now, or risk being taken by a predator come nightfall.

His right arm was numb and trapped underneath his body. Removing the left leather glove with his teeth, he reached up and felt the hard shell of the motorcycle helmet which was still strapped on. The helmet was uncomfortable and horribly hot. Running his fingers along the surface, he found a large jagged crack on back of the helmet, with smaller ones branching off. The helmet must have struck the rear of the bomb bay. Exiting the aircraft in the extended position had been a mistake, the speed had been too high.

The chin strap released, he eased off the shattered helmet. Fresh air struck his sweat-soaked hair and skin, affording him relief. He began checking to see if all parts moved. His right arm began to tingle when he shifted his weight. His neck and upper back hurt but there was no sharp or focused pain, just severe soreness.

With effort, he rose to his knees and unclipped the parachute harness that felt so constricting. The large equipment bag was gone, but the body pouch containing essentials like map, compass, knife and revolver was still attached. When planning for the mission he decided not to take the FNC but instead packed a folding stock AK-47, though this too had been ripped away and lost during the jump. Deliberately, stiffly and painfully, he rolled the parachute and harness into a bundle and stashed it beneath some nearby thick bush, and covered it with loose grass and fallen branches.

Slowly but steadily Kurt began to move away from the landing area. Not knowing where he was meant there was no point plotting an azimuth, but he knew the general topography would run toward the lower elevation of the Pungwe River Valley. The early evening was quiet and strangely cool. Winter, or what passed for winter in this part of the world, was beginning. Winter was also the dry season. The dry ground cover made walking noisy, so he slowed the pace and used the toe forward technique of the Indian hunter.

After an hour and a half of walking through ever increasing darkness, Kurt stopped and found a hide. Nearby some giant tropical hardwood trees threw wide buttresses that ran like angled shadowy shark fins along the ground. He sat propped against one of them. There was only one pint of water in a sealed emergency packet, and one food ration pack in his vest. The rest had been lost with the rucksack that ripped free when he jumped.

He drank half the water and re-sealed the packet, then took out a pack of 'dog biscuits', hard crackers, in the ration pack. The crackers had been crushed and were now just fragments. The water and cracker bits mixed in his mouth into a sticky paste, but in seconds it began to taste sweet as starch converted to sugar.

What to do now? He had most of the night to think about it, and his mind worked on the problem between brief periods of light sleep. He visualized the large map on the wall of the briefing room, along with the plotted release point. The altitude was fairly low when he pulled the ripcord so the parachute shouldn't have drifted very far. Heading east-south-east should take him to the feeder tributaries which eventually funnelled into Pungwe Gorge. As for food, water and a main weapon, that would have to be worked on.

⌘

Kurt stood up several times during the night to flex his back, neck and limbs, for fear that the injuries would stiffen and freeze his body by morning. As the false dawn broke he began to move to the east-south-east using compass bearings. Gathering some dry baobab pods lying on the ground, he split them open with the knife and sucked the seeds. The furry seeds released a tangy, sour flavour that immediately made his mouth water, somewhat relieving his ever-increasing thirst.

Kurt sensed movement and froze. A grey shape loomed very close ahead. Were it not for the reflection of a small glistening eye, he might have stumbled right into it. The shiny eye gazed back with intelligence but no hostility. Around the lone eye the huge contour of a bull elephant began to form. Sweeping tusks glowed softly in the faint starlight, contrasting with the nearly perfect camouflage of dull grey, wrinkled skin. Kurt recalled that big bulls usually led solitary lives; he was probably also after the baobab pods.

"Hey there, big fella," Kurt voiced softly, unconsciously breaking the self-imposed noise discipline for the first time since landing.

The bull lifted his trunk gracefully, taking in the scent. Kurt slowly moved off at an angle, still maintaining eye contact with the bull using peripheral vision. They went their separate ways, one a prehistoric giant intent only on survival, the other also a long-absent African, transformed by the ice ages in the far north, now returned.

⌘

By mid-morning he found himself in denser vegetation which led into a now dry stream bed. Following the stream bed down gradient, it grew larger and ran towards the south-west. Not wanting to be trapped and risk an ambush, Kurt paralleled the dry channel until he crossed a trail. Originally the trail must have been a game track leading up to a seasonal water source but, on closer inspection, there were signs of recent use. The ground was hard and packed but faint scuff marks and boot tread impressions were discernable.

Employing even more caution, Kurt paralleled the trail for another half hour until a crater came into view. Ten metres to the front a fresh ragged hole, almost a metre in diameter, bisected the trail. Cloth and pieces of metal and green debris were scattered around. Kurt dropped to his knees and quietly observed the site. For several minutes he watched and listened intently, but nothing moved except a lone tsetse fly trying for a blood meal with its needle-sharp mouth.

Slowly moving closer to the small crater, he realized what he was seeing was the result of a land mine. Most likely a group of guerrillas had been moving down the path when one of them triggered a buried anti-personnel mine, which was a large one, by the looks of it. The man had either been killed or mortally injured by the blast. His companions had probably taken off when they heard the explosion, leaving him behind.

The body would have soon been discovered by predators. That first night, cats or hyenas would have pulled it to pieces. Bones, hair and bits of sinew lay scatted randomly around the scene. Predators had no use for the man's equipment and most of it was lying near the crater including a pack, a canteen, canned rations, an AK-47 and loaded magazines. If the gear could be safely retrieved, one of his problems would be resolved.

Crawling on hands and knees Kurt began to probe the pathway to the needed equipment with his knife blade. Often those laying the devilish mines placed them in clusters so that those running from the first explosion, or those trying to rescue victims, would suffer the same fate. A newly laid mine would cause a soft spot in the normal soil consistency but with time, the soil packed down making their location more difficult to determine. This mine may have been placed by any of several military forces or guerrilla groups operating in the area. It was usually impossible to tell where they originated. The probing process took an hour, but Kurt finally reached the equipment without finding any other mines.

The recovered AK-47 seemed mechanically functional but he dared not test fire it here for fear of revealing his presence. The rifle was a newly manufactured Hungarian AKM which looked unused except for pitting on one side of the receiver as a result of the mine explosion. The dead man's pack also contained three ration meals made in East Germany. Had the whole Warsaw Pact supplied this guy? Kurt sat down a couple of hundred yards away from the mine crater, ate one of the recovered meals, and felt immeasurably better. The bruising and stiffness were still painful, but the more he moved, the less uncomfortable the injuries felt.

⌘

Later that day, Kurt sensed the presence of the Pungwe camp before he could see or hear it. The ZANLA High Command believed they would have sanctuary here, just like the NVA had in Laos. This over-confidence on their part would make reconnoitring the camp easier, but just one alarm raised and the game would change drastically. There was no backup, no air support and the terrain was alien. In this situation the only means of survival was effective concealment and total stealth. Even if they knew someone was in the area, he was just one man in a very large forest.

The Pungwe ZANLA guerrilla camp was in the valley formed between two major branches of the river of the same name, which merged and then ran through the cliffs of a gorge. Defence included several 12.7mm and 14.5mm heavy machine guns, dug into sandbagged bunkers in the walls of the steep ravines on the perimeter of the camp. This location had both advantages and disadvantages. A major portion of the camp was virtually hidden from the air due to the lush vegetation growing near the water source. If the camp was attacked, the occupants could jump into the river channels and run, their retreat covered by defensive fire from the elevated heavy machine gun positions. This type of defensive plan would serve well from both aerial attack and fire from a ground assault.

A kilometre from where he expected to encounter the outermost defensive positions, Kurt found another temporary hide until nightfall, when he would begin to probe the camp's defences. He rested there, drinking a small amount of water and eating half of a meal recovered earlier. His back and neck were still sore but had become tolerable. With darkness complete, he moved out and made his way directly toward the camp perimeter.

Fifty metres from the bunkers that made up the outer circle of defences he could clearly hear talking. Culturally, Africans thought it rude to whisper to one another because it hinted of conspiracy. When his night vision kicked in, he was able to manoeuvre around several of the outer defensive positions without being detected.

The men occupying the perimeter gun positions were on a low level of alert, which made penetration easier. For each of the fixed weapons in the outer ring of positions, he took mental notes of their locations and estimated fields of fire. Water bottles, ration boxes, ammo crates as well as other equipment and debris were lying around randomly, so Kurt quietly took what he needed, figuring no one would miss it.

Late that night, after making a complete circle of the outer perimeter, Kurt walked into the centre of the Pungwe Gorge camp. The moon had risen, casting a faint light on the target. A cluster of single-story barracks-type buildings were interconnected with crude pathways made from dirt and river rock. To the north of the buildings was an assembly area, or parade square, that was at least half an acre in size. Surrounding the buildings were tents that probably held six to ten men each. It looked as though most of the troops were housed in the tents, which were scattered irregularly over two to three acres surrounding the central parade square.

The camp was very quiet at this hour with only the occasional sound of a voice, snoring or cough breaking the calm. He crossed through and around the inner perimeter of the camp to gain perspective on the permanent structures, defences and approaches. Before morning Kurt felt he understood the physical layout and detail of the camp fairly well, but the next stage of the reconnaissance mission would prove more difficult.

To complete the intelligence assessment, observation of at least one daily cycle of activities in the camp was essential. Before daybreak he had to find a hide from which most of the camp would be visible. A few hundred yards north of the base camp, the Pungwe Gorge rose in sheer walls of fissured granite on both sides of the river. By the faint light of the crescent moon, Kurt could see a ledge protruding from the top of the northern wall. Come daylight, from that lofty location and angle, most of the Pungwe camp should be visible. The position also looked far enough away to ensure he could not be seen without a telescope or field glasses.

Kurt moved out from the camp and followed the river, then laboriously climbed the steep hill on the back side of the gorge. Estimating where the ledge was located proved difficult in the dark. Standing on the precipice of the cliff, the ledge was thirty metres further north. Carefully climbing down the steep face of the cliff for fifteen metres, he finally stood on the ledge overlooking the blackness of the Pungwe Gorge below. Skilfully and quickly, he worked to create sufficient cover on the ledge before daylight broke.

Satisfied, he climbed back up the cliff to the hilltop and defecated and urinated some distance from the approach to the ledge. This prevented smell from giving the position away if anyone came into the area. Moving back to the hide, he erased prints and signs with leaves and twigs before descending on to the ledge. He crawled forward to the very edge which projected out over the Pungwe River Gorge, hoping the rock was strong enough to bear his weight. He adjusted the vegetation growing on the ledge for maximum concealment from anyone looking from the direction of the camp, then settled to study the target situated five hundred metres south and one hundred and fifty metres below his position. In minutes, the eastern sky began to soften and turn deep lavender.

He'd been in the observation point only a short time when the camp sprang to life. A pair of compact Zeiss 8 power field glasses that thankfully were in the chest pouch and not the missing rucksack, brought the scene closer. Before the sun rose, men began to emerge from field tents and move around the camp with the meandering aimlessness of soldiers forced to rise at an early hour. A short time later an officer emerged from the wooden barracks and yelled something at the top of his voice that reverberated around the cliff walls. The shuffling men suddenly came to life and quickly assembled in the parade square. Kurt looked at his watch. It was exactly seven hundred hours.

Kurt estimated nearly one thousand troops were assembled in rank and file, about fifty abreast and twenty deep. While they stood at attention the bellicose officer positioned himself to the centre front and conducted a roll call by sections. After this was completed, the troops spread out and performed some exercises, including push-ups, jumping-jacks and toe-touches. Twenty minutes after this was finished they reassembled in formation, came to attention, and the officer dismissed them. The soldiers then made their way to the mess tent for breakfast. It was zero-seven-forty-five.

An hour later, a convoy of vehicles made its way in a slow procession over the rutted path that served as the only vehicular access to the camp. Two ZANLA soldiers posted as security guards at the gate watched impassively as the vehicles rolled through, not stopping or challenging them. Using the binoculars Kurt carefully studied the vehicles that had just entered.

The convoy consisted of five beige Land Rovers with two camouflaged cargo trucks bringing up the rear. He made out what looked like Portuguese military markings on all the vehicles. Both drivers and passengers wore camouflage uniforms. By the markings and uniforms Kurt assumed that the trucks and troops belonged to FRELIMO, the Mozambican National Army, who actively supported ZANLA. Several pedestal-mounted machine guns were fitted on the backs of the open trucks. The gunners were sitting on the edge of the beds, not manning their weapons but holding the barrels to prevent them from flopping in their mounts while driving over the rough terrain.

The convoy of Land Rovers and trucks pulled up in a loose semi-circle in front of the main barracks and parade square. The drivers and soldiers jumped out of the Land Rovers and walked back to the trucks where they began to unload boxes from the cargo beds. The convoy stayed for about an hour and then left by the same route.

In the early afternoon two groups of a dozen guerrillas each gathered on the parade square. The team leaders or senior cadre of each group conducted an inspection of the equipment they would be carrying. After repacking some of the gear, both groups headed out of the camp towards the west. Kurt assumed that these groups were heading toward Rhodesia. Mid-afternoon weapons firing could be heard, the sound bouncing off the walls of Pungwe Gorge in a confusing staccato. Kurt reasoned that ZANLA was conducting firearms training nearby.

Kurt was tempted to stay in position and observe the camp for at least another day, but his back and limbs were becoming very stiff and painful from injuries and inactivity, and another day might lock them up. An hour after sundown he left the ledge, circled around the camp, and headed for the Rhodesian border. The primary contact point that had been arranged was just on the other side of the border minefield. After a day of immobility, it took a couple of hours for his stiff neck and back muscles to loosen up and move efficiently again. He stopped for breaks only for a few minutes at a time and filled his canteens from a small artesian course, which was flowing even in the dry season.

That night something stalked his trail, either a leopard or lioness. The animal was being stealthy but still emitted a few low growls. The zone near the border was a barren scrubland. The indigenous people had evacuated the area due to the war and there was little sign of game or animal life. Conditions like this would make the big cats desperate and hungry. Stopping near a tree matted with a strangling fig vine, Kurt urinated on the trunk. Humans were predators and also ate meat, which caused strong chemicals to be excreted in the urine. Marking a tree like this might confuse the cat, making it hesitate to stalk and attack.

Through the heat of the next day he kept moving. This featureless bush had few landmarks for navigation. Late that afternoon the Rhodesian border came into view. Beside the dirt boundary path, intermittently patrolled by vehicles during the Portuguese occupation, there were scraps of barbed wire and rusted metal signs nailed to trees. For several years, much of the one thousand two hundred kilometre long border had been mined to prevent crossings by guerrillas. Mines and booby traps not only proved lethal to guerrillas infiltrating from Mozambique, but also to villagers, visitors and wildlife.

Crossing the field or even being in the vicinity was dangerous. Rain and settling soil had a tendency to drift the mines from their original locations. Before Kurt left on this mission, intelligence provided a map indicating two 'safe passage' corridors through the border mine fields. These were routes that friendly troops could use to cross into Mozambique and come back again with safety. To keep the enemy from learning where these corridors were, and also to guard against 'wandering mines', they were changed and maintained at regular intervals by Rhodesian Army engineer units.

According to an azimuth shot with the compass and compared with an intelligence map, he was just north of the Whiskey Corridor, as it was designated. Alongside the border just outside this 'no man's land', the carnage caused by the mines was evident. Animals travelling on their normal migratory patterns would trigger antipersonnel mines which would either kill them or, more commonly, blow off a limb. Predators would go in after the wounded animals, also triggering mines. Difficult to tell apart from a distance, bleached human and animal bones lay scattered in the dust and weeds. Circling black carrion vultures feasted on all of it. They were too light to set off mines so the strip became a huge dining table for their insatiable appetites. The scene was straight from the gates of hell and smelled even worse.

A stony hill was the landmark Kurt was looking for and it abruptly appeared ahead, swathed in lacy acacias. At the base of the hill was a pair of ancient baobab trees standing like sentinel markers. According to the map, the baobabs marked the Mozambique side of the safe corridor, which was only ten metres in width. The instructions said to take an azimuth of two hundred and seventy degrees from between the tree markers, and follow that for exactly two hundred metres. Then it became tricky. The safe corridor wasn't a straight line; that would be too easy for the enemy to follow. At two hundred metres inside the minefield the azimuth changed to two hundred degrees and this direction was to be followed for another three hundred metres, before reaching the other side ... and safety.

Kurt sat down against one of the giant baobab trunks, drank warm water from his canteen and studied the crossing. There was little movement in the late afternoon just before sunset, except for the wheeling and gliding dark spectres overhead and all along the deadly strip. Waiting until morning and crossing at first light made sense, but the thought of spending another night on this side was too ominous, so he decided to cross the minefield before dark. During the crossing there would be virtually no cover, making speed and decisiveness imperative.

He was confident no one had followed his route from the camp and he hadn't heard the cat lately, but there was no certainty of anything in this wasteland. Twice during the walk from the camp he performed switchback manoeuvres. Glassing the Rhodesian side revealed only a pair of tiny duiker antelope grazing on the verge of the minefield, indicating that, for the moment anyway, all was peaceful over there.

Starting the crossing midway between the bulbous trees he walked directly to a pale coloured rock the engineers had laid, that marked the turning point where the course had to be altered to two hundred degrees. Sighting through the wire on the lensatic compass, he noted a pair of light coloured stakes which evidently marked the lane on the Rhodesian side. The engineers had done a good job, placing inconspicuous but visible markers along the way.

Several metres away from where he stood at the midway point lay a human skeleton, intact except for splintered leg bones. Pieces of denim uniform favoured by ZANLA guerrillas lay scattered around the bleaching white sticks. The guerrilla's pack, weapon and equipment lay where it fell. The dead man had crossed the first piece of the corridor correctly, probably following footprints, but had unknowingly blown the subtle turn, a heavy price to pay for a slight navigation error.

Kurt made the adjustment to two hundred degrees and followed the second leg of the corridor carefully, heading directly for the guiding stakes, breathing a deep sigh of relief when he reached them. It was just getting dark, and the shadows were merging into twilight.

A voice called out just as he reached the other side of the minefield.

"Good show, soldier, you crossed dead centre."

Kurt spun with the AK and saw a man with his arms crossed standing a few metres away.

"Don't shoot, I'm a good guy," the voice laughed. "I told those uptight assholes that you'd be alright, but they said, 'Nooooo ... The cocky bastard was knocked out jumping from the jet and he's dead.'

"But I told them that they didn't know this dude like I knew him. He's one tough SOB, I said; he's really hard to kill. I couldn't convince them to come down to meet you, so I came myself. How are you doing, bro?"

"Okay I guess, Medic, all the better for seeing your smiling face again ... "

# CHAPTER 19
## HAMMER TIME

For two days after his return from the reconnaissance mission of the ZANLA camp at Pungwe Gorge, Kurt underwent intense debriefing by Army Intelligence. Afterwards, he was assigned to a building at Cranborne Barracks working with a husband and wife team to construct a scale model of the Pungwe camp. The intelligence officers were initially dismayed that he had not brought back drawings or photos of the target, but the notebook and camera were lost on the nearly fatal drop. Their concern was mollified a little when he was able to draw very detailed maps of Pungwe from memory, including distances and elevation lines. The maps were then converted into a detailed three-dimensional scale mode.

Against his wishes he was sent to Andrew Fleming hospital in Salisbury for a medical examination and X-ray of his back and neck. He had some serious contusions of the occipital and cervical areas but no fractures, or other irregularities.

After leaving the hospital, he was driven to the airfield to view the damaged Canberra. Beneath the low fuselage, a shallow depression adorned the aluminium skin at the rear edge of the bomb bay. Fortunately the doors of the bay closed after the jump, and the aircraft had landed safely. Even while looking at the evidence, Kurt couldn't picture exactly how the accident happened, only that it nearly cost him his life. He realized that these close calls were becoming too frequent.

⌘

Working on a sheet of plywood atop a large table with coloured clay, and pre-made toy buildings, trees and tents, a fairly accurate representation of the Pungwe camp was completed by the three of them after four days of intense work. Kurt was exhausted at the end of the session but agreed to a de-briefing with the intelligence officers and field commanders immediately, rather than allowing details to grow stale with time.

The formal mission de-briefing was held at zero eight hundred hours the following Saturday morning in a more spacious briefing room on the base where the covered scale model had been assembled. In addition to the same three intelligence officers who conducted his initial orientation, four military operational commanders were also in attendance.

Kurt was introduced to the four operations officers, all of whom he had either met or was familiar with by reputation. They all had the shoulder pips of captain or major, and represented the Rhodesian Light Infantry, C Squadron SAS and the Selous Scouts. Also present and representing the air force was Wing Commander Fleming, whom Kurt had met at Mtoko on his first day in the country. These military units were responsible for all major internal and external defensive and offensive military operations. Fleming looked rather surprised when he saw who was giving the presentation.

Major Moore stepped to the front of the room and everyone took their seats.

"Gentlemen, a fortnight ago," Moore began, "Sergeant Christianson agreed to carry out a dangerous and important mission. He was charged with infiltrating and collecting field information on a recently identified ZANLA camp located near the Pungwe Gorge, seventy kilometres across our eastern border in Mozambique. Against all odds, it seems he was successful: on the table before you is proof of that. Our goal today is to receive a detailed briefing of the layout and defensive capabilities of the Pungwe camp, then make a preliminary assessment of the man and material resources it would take on our part to attack and destroy it. I will now turn the briefing over to Sergeant Christianson."

Kurt rose and walked to the front of the room while Major Moore took a seat. He felt uncomfortable talking in front of a group of officers when all eyes would be on him. Talking was never his forte. He always felt he was more of a doer than a talker. He wished George was here; George was so good at this sort of thing.

Walking to the front he looked at every man in the room, seeing something in their eyes that he hadn't experienced before. Every one of them was looking at him with both expectation and deference. This respect began to wash away his uncertainty, replacing it with a tentative, calm confidence.

The briefing lasted less than an hour and Kurt thought he had effectively summarized his observations and findings. After that there were questions, primarily from the three army operations officers. Their questions were specific and reflected a tactical knowledge understood only by experienced combat soldiers. Questions regarding terrain, manpower, defensive positions and level of alertness were all posed, which Kurt answered to the best of his ability. Finally Major Patrick Allen, the RLI operations representative, stood and walked toward the model. The other officers followed suit.

The officers walked around the table on which sat the newly constructed mock-up of Pungwe, viewing it from different directions and then kneeling to look at it from ground level. The composite map and aerial photographs that Kurt studied before the mission were also taped to the wall for their review. All four operations' officers walked from the model to the wall trying to develop a detailed picture of the target.

Colonel Ainsley finally broke the silence.

"What are your impressions, gentlemen?"

Major Allen of the RLI was the first to speak. Kurt knew of the man from several joint RLI missions, but had never served under him directly.

"It looks like we could place stop groups here, here and here," Major Allen said as he pointed to the three tributaries feeding in to the Pungwe River before they came together, "and then drop a parachute assault force just to the east of the camp."

Major Allen then stopped and rubbed his chin in contemplation.

"But by the looks of it there are no good landing zones. We'll have a lot of the blokes landing in the trees or on large rocks, and with a thousand defenders … "

Captain McKenzie, the SAS representative interjected, "We could chopper in six sticks from C Squadron and … "

The discussion went back and forth between the officers for half an hour. During this time Kurt leaned against the far wall. Now he had provided the information they wanted, he'd ceased to be of any interest to them. The tactical planning session seemed to be stagnating. The RLI, SAS, and air force commanders were all vying for a big piece of the action on such a dramatic and high-profile mission. The only one not involved in the argument was the Selous Scouts representative Major Clive Murphy. Kurt looked at him and Murphy smiled and shook his head.

Becoming concerned, Kurt stepped away from the wall and toward the table.

"Sirs, I know I'm probably out of line on this, but may I make a suggestion?"

The discussion between the officers stopped and all eyes again turned to him.

"Go ahead, Sergeant Christianson," Major Moore allowed.

"I mentioned in the briefing that a column of FRELIMO vehicles pulled into the camp the morning of the day I was observing. At the time I had an idea. If we could put together a convoy of vehicles that look like FRELIMO, we could pull right up to the camp, ideally while the ZANLA troops are having their morning parade. The vehicles could be positioned in a semi-circle around the parade square and, with enough firepower … "

Colonel Ainsley interrupted.

"That plan sounds far too simplistic, Sergeant. There are other things to consider. Attacking this camp will require an initial air strike, followed by a ground assault force, working with stop groups and that sort of thing."

Kurt walked around the table with his eyes on the model. He didn't want to make eye contact with the officers because that might disturb his train of thought. After a few seconds he spoke again, "The first bomb that drops on that camp will scatter ZANLA up and down the Pungwe Gorge and its tributaries, which is exactly why they placed the camp there. The same thing will happen if the assault is initiated by a conventional ground attack. There will be enemy all over the place very quickly, without a decisive victory. The only way we will ever be able to carry this off is with complete surprise and overwhelming firepower. In order to achieve this level of firepower using conventional forces there will have to be a lot of rifles, with a man attached to each one."

Kurt paused and looked at the officers, but they remained silent.

"When too many men are involved, the surprise is gone. However, military vehicles are by nature designed to carry a great deal of weight. We could mount several heavy and light machine guns on every vehicle in a small convoy and carry all the ammo we could possibly need for the mission. If we can have those vehicles in position at the right time, the show is over. The enemy's defences are positioned to guard against an external attack. They would never expect the enemy to roll inside their perimeter."

The room became totally silent; no one knew how to respond to Kurt's proposal, it seemed too revolutionary, but was in fact just a modern rendition of the Trojan Horse. The bearded Major Murphy finally stepped forward. His face and nose were sunburned and peeling. His hands were callused and nails broken. A long jagged white scar ran down the length of his left forearm, and a smaller one discoloured his cheek.

"Gentlemen, I think the sergeant may have hit on something. We have been planning to put together an armed vehicular unit, and this may provide that justification. The Pungwe raid may just be the right operation to test the theory."

Major Moore broke in, "The idea is interesting because it would mean a minimal commitment of both men and resources. The Portuguese left behind all the necessary vehicles, and there is no shortage of captured weapons. I believe at a minimum, the concept deserves further investigation."

Colonel Ainsley remained impassive and non-committal during the discussions regarding strategy and tactics. His eyes shifted from person to person, attempting to get an estimation of which officer would carry the day and dominate. Like a good staff officer, he would document everything and if things turned disastrous those responsible would take the heat, but it would not be him. If however the operation was successful it was easy enough to intervene and take credit. This was how Ainsley had learned to play the game, and so far it worked.

"I believe there has been enough discussion on this matter today, gentlemen," Major Moore finally said when everyone was about talked out. "I recommend we go forward with the planning for the attack on the Pungwe camp. My opinion is that this operation warrants more study before a firm commitment is made regarding implementation. Colonel Ainsley and I will inform General Wallis about the results of this meeting when he gets back from Mt. Darwin this afternoon. I would like Major Allen, Captain McKenzie and Commander Fleming to also put together a plan for a joint airborne and ground operation. I think we all agree that this target is of highest priority, but we want to make certain it is planned and conducted with the utmost care."

With that, the group began to file out of the briefing room. Major Murphy, the bearded Selous Scout officer, stopped and spoke to Kurt.

"It looks like we will be working together, Sergeant."

"Call me Kurt if you don't mind, sir."

"That's fine with me. Formalities aren't necessary unless there is brass around."

"Sir," Kurt said, "is it coincidental that the Scouts are putting together a plan for a unit of armed vehicles? I didn't know anything about it."

Murphy laughed, "Maybe that's because there isn't one. When you described your concept I liked it and thought it was viable. Because of our mission, the others have no idea what we're up to most of the time so they couldn't call me out on it."

There was a moment of silence as Murphy was thinking; scheming was probably a better word.

"Kurt, meet me here tomorrow at zero-seven-hundred. I'll arrange your temporary transfer to the Selous Scouts."

"Sir, it would be a pleasure," Kurt smiled openly, a rare event.

Major Murphy got into an unmarked brown Land Rover and drove off. Kurt felt as if a huge weight had been lifted off his shoulders. What he had set out to do was working better than could have been imagined and the wheels were really starting to turn. It felt like setting out on a voyage with a new fleet of ships, not knowing the destination but realizing it was going to be an exciting trip. For the first time since George's death he felt like celebrating. He wished George was here with him to share this and not in a wooden box in Virginia.

⌘

Inkomo Barracks were located about fifteen miles north-east of Salisbury on Lomagundi Road, which if followed further, headed towards the Zambezi River and Lake Kariba. The base was very isolated despite its relative proximity to town, making it an ideal location for the secretive Selous Scouts.

The unit was named after a legendary hunter, explorer and tracker, Fredrick Courtney Selous, who roamed and hunted east and southern Africa in the late 1800s. The concept for such a unit originated with Reed Donovan, a crusty British/Rhodesian sergeant major who served with the British SAS during the Malayan Emergency in the early 1950s. Donovan thought that a unit was needed that was capable of both infiltrating and tracking down guerrilla groups that began to invade Rhodesia in the early 1970s.

The Selous Scouts were unlike anything ever attempted in Africa or for that matter, anywhere else. The unit was composed of both black and white soldiers who were mixed into flexible operational teams. White members were primarily drawn from Rhodesian farms because they usually spoke African languages fluently. The primary mission of the Selous Scouts was to fool the enemy guerrilla forces into believing they were guerrillas also, at least for long enough to locate the positions of their base camps. When this was accomplished, a hidden radio signalled other military units such as the RLI Fireforce, which would then attack and destroy them.

By nature, the work was extremely hazardous for two reasons. Because the Scouts were usually greatly outnumbered in the field, if the guerrillas found out who they were, their only options were to escape or die. Also, when the attacking Rhodesian troops and aircraft showed up, their appearance was so similar to the enemy's they could be easily mistaken for them and targeted. The operations of the Selous Scouts were so sensitive and classified that details of all their missions were on a 'need to know' basis. It was into this peculiar lair that Kurt entered with Major Murphy on a clear spring day in 1976.

Unlike the American military, where a new or even modified piece of equipment might take years to see the light of day, the little beleaguered Rhodesian forces had no such bureaucratic obstacles. The very morning of Kurt's arrival, several Land Rovers and two Mercedes Benz Unimog six-by-six trucks were driven into a fenced enclosure situated between two equipment storage buildings in the back lot of the isolated facility. Inkomo, being a centre of special operations, was also a repository for purchased, captured, acquired and otherwise requisitioned weapons of all types. Murphy and Kurt toured through the makeshift armoury, selecting weapons they considered appropriate to mount on vehicles.

A favourite of both sides in the guerrilla war was the 12.7mm Chi Com heavy machine gun. At over seventy pounds, it was too large to be transported in the field by guerrilla units, but it was first choice to use as perimeter defence and, with the appropriate mount, air defence of base camps. Several dozen of these guns were captured in cross-border raids on small ZANLA camps; some had also been found in guerrilla weapons caches.

A number of lighter drum-fed RPD light machine guns were also in the inventory. At only fourteen pounds in weight, these were popular as squad support weapons by the guerrilla bands because they were portable, mobile and packed a lot of firepower. Kurt dismissed these for mounting on vehicles because of their light weight, relatively weak cartridge and their tendency to overheat quickly, which made them unsuitable for sustained fire.

"Murph, do you have any 1919 Browning air-cooled guns?" Kurt asked.

"I don't think we have any at Inkomo," Murphy replied. "The Air Force may have some spares for their choppers. They had them all converted to short barrelled twin mounts for the doors of the Alouettes."

"Can we get any?" Kurt asked.

"That's like asking for gold," Murphy replied, scratching his heavy brown beard. "The Air Force tends to hoard their hardware; if I ask them outright I know what they'll say."

"We would just be borrowing them for the mission: then we can give them back," Kurt pressed.

"Let me run the idea by Colonel Donovan. He has more clout than you'd think with the big guys ... including General Wallis."

Kurt walked around the Selous Scouts' cluttered armoury storage room, digging through the racks and boxes of equipment.

"I see you have quite a few 82mm mortar tubes," Kurt said.

"We have a lot of those," Murphy replied. "As heavy as they are, the guerrillas like to haul them around, but when they make contact they usually drop them and run, so we've recovered quite a few."

"You have mortar bombs, too?"

"Plenty, but what do you have in mind? You aren't going to mount them on vehicles, are you?"

Kurt just grinned at Murphy.

⌘

Within days the Land Rovers and trucks began to take shape. Vehicles that were designed and constructed as people and cargo transporters began a transformation into lethal weapons platforms like none ever built. In the fore and aft beds of one of the Unimogs, two steel pedestal mounts were welded to the floor to support 12.7mm heavy machine guns that could be rotated full circle. On the truck bed between the guns large feed trays for the looped ammunition belts were welded from sheet metal. On the starboard side of the vehicle six 82mm direct fire mortar tubes were mounted on angled pivots.

When training with SEAL Team two in Norfolk VA, Kurt had seen 81mm direct-fire mortars mounted on PT boats. Instead of dropping the mortar bomb down the tube and striking a fixed firing pin at the bottom, the direct fire tube was shorter and had a pull-type firing device mounted on its base. Mortar bombs were pre-loaded into the tube and were fired when the lanyard was pulled. The distances they would be firing were known, so the angle of each mortar tube could be set by using pre-adjusted stops. After each mortar tube was fired, it could be pivoted up and reloaded. The short distance to the targets should allow a relatively flat trajectory using light powder charges to propel the mortar bombs.

This first converted Unimog was named the 'Centre Truck' because of its massive firepower. The plan was to pull this vehicle directly in front of the heaviest troop concentrations. The second Unimog to undergo modification was termed the 'Flex Truck'. It had a single 12.7mm HMG mounted in the middle of the bed, with reluctantly-loaned 1919 Browning aircraft twin 30 calibre guns fixed at either end. The Flex Truck would be positioned at an oblique angle to the troop formation, and would engage targets with cross fire. This vehicle would also look for any return fire and engage it.

Two of the three Land Rovers would have belt-fed FN MAG 7.62mm light machine guns mounted on welded roll bars. These Land Rovers would be positioned on either end of the convoy and be pulled up at the flanks of the troop formation. Their role would be to take out fleeing troops and to engage targets of opportunity, for this mission meaning 'anything that moved'.

The third Land Rover was to be used by the mission commander Major Murphy. The original plans had no guns mounted on this vehicle, but Kurt thought that wasteful, and successfully lobbied to have a 20mm Hispano shortened cannon mounted on beefed-up roll bars. Luckily the Air Force had several of these guns as spares in inventory, and let the Scouts borrow one of them for the operation. The 20mm high explosive fragmentation projectiles were lethal on ground targets as well as aircraft. With this gun mounted on his Land Rover and at his command, Murphy could engage any target on the larger battle zone if he chose to.

Kurt was impressed by the small crew of armourers and artisans who took his concepts and paper sketches and made them into functioning systems. The cutting, grinding and welding went on around the clock. When working with any prototype, changes always had to be made but the workmen always took it in their stride, never protesting about the added work and inconvenience.

The firing mechanism for the 82mm direct-fire mortar tubes was totally designed and manufactured at the Inkomo Barracks maintenance shop. After several false starts, they finally settled on a configuration built around the firing mechanism of a Hawker Hunter 30mm aircraft cannon, of which oddly enough there were also several spares. The final design allowed them to fire each mortar tube independently, or it could be rigged so one pull of a lanyard would fire all six mortar tubes simultaneously.

Before final assembly and painting of the converted vehicles, the Land Rovers and Unimog trucks were taken out to the back firing range at Inkomo and the gun systems tested. A large part of the range was roped off in the approximate dimensions of the Pungwe Camp parade square, and the vehicles positioned optimally for the attack. The guns were then fired singly, then in salvo.

The direct-fire mortar tubes proved somewhat fickle to adjust. With weak propellant charges of one and two, the tubes had to be elevated dramatically. Slight inconsistencies in the charges and the bombs resulted in the inability to place the projectiles precisely. Experimentation showed that increasing to a stouter charge of three and then to four allowed the tubes to be aimed nearly horizontally like a rifle barrel, and the bombs followed nigh on horizontal paths to their targets. Kurt took measurements of the final angles of the tubes to have the artisans craft some rudimentary sights that would allow for quicker targeting.

As a final test, all of the guns were fired together. The noise and devastation to the impact zone impressed everyone, but there was no way of simulating the intended targets. It was found that the mortar bombs were landing close enough for the fragmentation to strike those firing the guns; two minor flesh wounds and some dings in the vehicle bodies verified this. Based on this observation, a thin armour plate in a V-shape was mounted around the gun pedestals and the guns themselves to protect those firing them from injury. The mortar operator would also be given a layer of hardened steel plate to use as a shield when the tubes were fired.

After the initial testing was completed, the convoy rolled back to the equipment yard. The entire crew was in a state of exhausted jubilation. With some additional work and modifications their design goals would be achieved, and then some. All the team members could imagine the shock and devastation these vehicles would wreak on the enemy, assuming the targets could be infiltrated as planned. This kind of mission is what a special operations soldier lived for, and dreamt about. All they had to do now was to reach the target undetected. Not a simple task.

⌘

After this success, every member of the team thought it was time to wind down a little, not that any soldier needed encouragement to do that. Several cases of locally brewed Lion and Castle beer were pulled out of the mess storage building and the bottles were thrown into buckets of ice. Major Murphy also brought out a bottle of single malt scotch, a rare and valuable commodity in a country with restricted importation of foreign made goods.

Kurt hadn't bothered to shave or even cut his hair during these weeks of intense work and he looked ragged but he was beginning to feel incredibly comfortable with the Scouts and hoped they did with him.

Walking around the vehicles that were first designed in his imagination, Kurt thought briefly that the ancient war god Thor would no doubt smile at this creation. If the Viking raiders had these … his thoughts drifted off. That was all a fantasy and foolishness, God or Gods were just abstractions to pacify the needy. The gun trucks before him came into existence through his own ideas and perseverance. The still-hot barrels gave off waves of heat that made passing air boil. And now these machines were real, very real. He walked up to the centre truck and traced an outline of Thor's Hammer on the dusty driver's door. 'Operation Hammer' was a good name and there would be no denying it was appropriate.

⌘

Team selection for the Pungwe Raid, or Operation Hammer, as it was now known, was conducted with great care. Those participating had to meet two criteria. First they had to be believable as either FRELIMO or ZANLA troops. The convoy had to get by the camp security checkpoint and into their pre-selected positions without arousing suspicion. If one thousand ZANLA guerrillas were prematurely alerted and began to return fire, the raid would degenerate into a slug fest, their vehicles disabled, and their advantage would evaporate. To prepare for this contingency, an RLI Fireforce with helicopters would be on standby for a rescue mission at a launch site just across the border.

The second requirement of the team members was demonstrated skill with weapons and the ability to work together, as a cohesive group, while under fire. Personnel selections were made based on demonstrated combat experience and personal knowledge by Major Murphy and other officers. After the final cut was made, the team consisted of five drivers, eight gun operators, and three loaders and alternates, with the command element consisting of Murphy, his second-in-command Lieutenant Costas and Kurt. Kurt convinced Murphy to put him on the 20mm cannon mounted on the command Land Rover. Nineteen men would be going into battle against approximately one thousand enemy.

Concern was also expressed about the possibility of FRELIMO or ZANLA reinforcements arriving at the camp during the time the assault team was vulnerable. Since the only vehicular access to the camp was via the single entrance road, two sticks of SAS would be infiltrated the night before the raid and set up command-detonated mines and an ambush position several clicks up the road. They would let the assault convoy pass, but then would shut the door to any other traffic until the job was completed. When the mission terminated, the SAS troops would depart in the raider's vehicles.

One of the drivers selected for the mission was Calo, an ex-Portuguese soldier who was a professional hunter in Mozambique during the recent colonial occupation. Calo knew all of the roads, trails, even game routes in the area they would be travelling through. In the days leading up to the raid, Calo made a series of covert border crossings with a specially selected SAS stick. They surveyed the back trails that would tie into the Pungwe Camp road. Some minor brush and obstacle clearing was necessary, but the primary route and two alternative routes were successfully identified and mapped.

To avoid suspicion, one vehicle at a time was moved to a selected location on the Rhodesian/Mozambique border outpost of Villa Salazar. The pedestal mounts, machine guns and mortar tubes were disassembled, and stored beneath covers in the back of the Unimogs for the trip. An old, currently unused vehicle maintenance building just North of Villa Salazar was used to reassemble the vehicles behind closed doors. Team members were also put into isolation in the same building. It was here they packed up and checked their personal gear, and waited for the pre-mission briefing by Army Intelligence.

Because of his past experiences, Kurt expressed concern privately to Major Murphy about operational security. Murphy tried to ease his fears by telling him that this had never been a problem in the past, and details of the mission were on a strictly 'need to know' basis. Murphy also told Kurt that this mission had the blessing of none other than the Rhodesian Prime Minister himself. The PM's rationale for approving this raid was that the Entebbe raid recently carried out by the Israelis in Uganda set a precedent to publicly attack terrorists wherever they were, and Operation Hammer was no different in his eyes.

The pre-mission briefing consisted of information the team already knew, plus additional aerial photos taken by Vampire over flights in the past weeks. Details of the route they would take to the target and back were also discussed. Except for new recruits coming in to the Pungwe camp for training and bands of guerrillas leaving, there were no notable changes in the camp's status.

A rumour picked up by intelligence indicated that the deputy military commander of the ZANLA forces, General Josiah Taderera, might be visiting the camp on the day of the planned attack. His presence would be a big bonus if the rumour was true. The big brass of the ZANLA leadership generally didn't spend much time in the forward areas because it put them at personal risk. Taderera was said to be an exception. He reportedly went on patrols with guerrilla bands and was believed to be skilled in the use of the RPG shoulder-fired missile, which resulted in the death of at least two farmers. When Kurt heard the name Taderera in the intelligence briefing, his attention perked. Battling a wily and skilled adversary was always good. It made this game more interesting.

The night before the raid there was a distinct absence of the traditional partying and pre-mission hype. All the members of the team were subdued and spent the time checking and re-checking the vehicles, guns and other equipment. The armourers, who were brought down for the preparation, stripped, detail cleaned, and lubricated all of the heavy weapons. Everyone knew that the lives of the outnumbered assault force depended on their flawless functioning. Several spare tyres were also put into the vehicles in case of blowouts or punctures.

Kurt checked his 20mm Hispano cannon and belted high explosive ammunition, but let the armourer disassemble and lube it because he was not totally familiar with the gun's mechanism. The cannon had been obtained from France, thanks to the eagerness of the French to sell anything to anyone if the price was right. This interfaced nicely with Jack Malloy's ability and willingness to carry sensitive cargo anywhere, anytime.

None of the men slept much that night. Kurt dreamt of Maine for the first time in weeks. He was hauling up a lobster trap for his grandfather. The more he pulled in the line the heavier the trap became, until he saw something hovering just below the surface. The trap couldn't be released or the catch would be lost, but there wasn't any way to pull it out of the water. There may not be lobsters in the trap but something else, something far more terrifying. A monster from the deep reaches was on his line, and he could do nothing but hang on.

He awoke with a start at quarter to three in the morning, his neck and hair soaked in cold sweat. The men were beginning to stir. It was time.

⌘

The convoy crossed the Mozambique border at zero four hundred hours. The Camp was approximately seventy-five kilometres distant following their mapped route. The goal was to arrive just in time to catch the ZANLA troops standing on the parade square at the Pungwe Camp during their zero seven hundred formation. Any excess time spent on the hostile side of the border would only increase the risk of detection.

In the lead Land Rover was Calo, the Portuguese big game hunter who, along with a few SAS escorts, had selected the route to the camp. In a few weeks the rainy season would begin, and the now firm dirt trails would become impassable to vehicles. In spite of bone-jarring ruts which tested the suspension of the vehicles, as well as the backs of the occupants, progress toward the target was slow and steady.

They hit their first milestone, a small bend in a stream, at zero five thirty hours when the eastern sky began to turn from black to dark blue. They saw no people along the route, but encountered abandoned and overgrown kraals every few kilometres. The war had left the area devoid of occupants, leaving a strangely silent and eerie land to cross.

The convoy swung on the vehicle trail leading to Pungwe twenty minutes early. They reduced speed and began looking for the SAS stop group that infiltrated the previous night. Just around the curve a lone figure stood in the middle of the dirt track. Guns in the convoy swung in unison on the man who now had his hand up in the universal sign of 'halt'. It was SAS commander Captain McKenzie, who decided the mission was important enough to come himself. McKenzie was confident the convoy would not fire at him because it would blow the mission and put everyone in peril.

The vehicles halted with their engines idling. Murphy jumped out of the command Land Rover and went to confer with McKenzie. Several heavily camouflaged SAS soldiers appeared out of nowhere. Two of them had camouflage-painted MAG machine guns slung over their shoulders and belts of ammo loosely draped across their upper bodies. The ammo belts shone soft gold in the breaking light. McKenzie pointed out to Murphy the positions of his troops, and where the command-detonated mines and claymores were positioned.

The men on the vehicles were growing edgy; now they'd arrived they wanted to get on with the mission. Sitting still in the idling vehicles several kilometres from the target made them feel vulnerable, even with the awesome firepower at hand, and the well-armed SAS surrounding them. Kurt looked at his watch. They needed to stay here for another five minutes. The dark camo cream smeared on his hands arms and face began to itch, and the brief wait seemed like an eternity. Diesel fumes grew thick in the still-moist morning air.

Murphy climbed back into the command Land Rover and signalled for the vehicle crews to cover their guns. Canvas tarps were thrown over the truck beds and the machine guns mounted on the Land Rovers. The effect looked sloppy and haphazard, but hopefully it would confuse the camp security guards for the few seconds it would take to move into position. The task completed, Murphy motioned for the convoy to move out.

⌘

The Pungwe ZANLA camp awoke to another day. Several roosters men had brought with them from their home villages began to crow just before sun-up. The rooster was the symbol of the ZANLA political movement because of the pride, bravery and colour it exhibited. The RLI Commandos had a cheetah, an eagle and a lion as team mascots. The native Africans did not worship predators; for thousands of years their ancestors had been prey for these animals, and their presence or images were not seen as inspiring.

At the camp, newly recruited villagers and young men from the urban townships were put through a course in weapons training and tactics before they were sent into combat. There was no fixed length of a training course for ZANLA guerrillas. Every recruit was evaluated by veteran cadre and were sent over the border when they were determined to be ready. Casualty rates were high. Two out of three men sent across the border were never heard from again. Some gave up the fight and headed back to their homes. The rest were killed, captured or seriously wounded.

The captured were usually interrogated and then quickly sent to their deaths on the well-used gallows at Salisbury Central Prison. The wounded often died of infection because their injuries could not be treated properly in the field. Despite the apparent slaughter of poorly trained troops, the ZANLA commanders were under political pressure to send more combatants across the border and accelerate the war, which is what they were doing at the Pungwe camp.

Immediately following ablutions and dressing that morning, the soldiers in training assembled in the camp's parade square for roll call, a short political speech by the camp commander and some callisthenics. After this routine was completed they would be allowed an hour for breakfast and the cleaning of equipment prior to the commencement of the day's training. On that warm morning in the spring of 1976, some nine hunded and fifty men stood at attention, bathed in the uneven light filtering through the trees surrounding the craggy, picturesque Pungwe Gorge.

That morning the camp commander positioned himself in front of the ranks of troops and began to talk about the importance of the struggle, when he heard the sound of an approaching convoy. He stopped talking and turned to see several tan vehicles with familiar black-and-yellow markings roll into camp. The FRELIMO convoy was early, he thought. He would ask them the reason when he was finished. He turned back and continued addressing the recruits.

Two ZANLA trainees were assigned to sentry duty at the rudimentary wooden gate at the camp entrance. They'd been given no specific orders regarding who was to enter and who wasn't. They did know that on some days a convoy of their FRELIMO comrades would come in to unload boxes of food, ammunition and other supplies. Usually such a visit meant fresh fruit like mangoes and papaya so they looked forward to it. On some occasions the convoy stopped next to the gate, and other times they just drove straight through. Today they drove right on by, but the two guards didn't want to offend the FRELIMO in any way. Both guards thought it was odd the way that the FRELIMO in the last Land Rover kept his eyes on them, a look that was anything but friendly. But even at this, they didn't raise their AKs, or sound the alarm.

The camp was laid out exactly as the detailed model indicated, to the point where the Scouts thought they had been there before. The drivers positioned their vehicles in pre-determined locations as planned. The gunners threw off the loose canvas covers and the weapons were charged almost simultaneously.

One of the 12.7 HMG gunners on the centre truck took a sighting between the shoulders of the man addressing the group of troops packing the parade square. On Murphy's radio command he touched off a single round with his thumb button. The massive ounce and a half steel-core slug, which was designed to disable military vehicles, flew through the ZANLA commander, barely reducing its velocity. The single bullet then passed through eleven more soldiers before coming to a stop in another. Thirteen men dropped like dominoes. The raid had begun.

Fire from the combined vehicle-mounted machine guns roared with an unearthly din. The 82mm mortar bombs seemed to leave their tubes in slow motion, detonating in the midst of the tightly packed soldiers crowding the parade square. Whole bodies and body parts flew into the air, like debris lofted by a sudden windstorm. A stream of 12.7mm bullets ploughed down the rows of men like a sharp scythe, leaving clouds of pink mist in the still morning air, as flesh was vaporized.

Weaponless and defenceless, the men caught in the parade square tried to turn and run, their way blocked by the already fallen. Stumbling, they tried to claw their way out of the killing field, but the rapid-firing machine guns were merciless, and left no patch of ground untouched. Several dozen men standing in the rear ranks managed to break free after the firing began, only to be cut down by intersecting fire from the rapid-firing twin 30 calibre Brownings, positioned precisely for this purpose.

For twenty seconds Kurt sat mesmerized by the scene until incoming rounds began impacting the dirt around the gun trucks and Land Rovers. The main barracks building some sixty metres away and at right angles to the parade square was not initially targeted by the convoy. Troops inside the building when the attack began had taken cover and were now firing back. Flashes could be seen coming from the two windows facing the raiders.

Kurt swung the firing handles of his 20mm cannon towards the building, found one of the windows in his circular sight, and fired a single round. *Whump!* A patch of material just beneath a window frame came away as the high explosive fragmentation round struck. Too low, correct the sight, *whump! whump!* The burning base of the cannon rounds passed through the window and debris flew out as they exploded. He sighted at the other window and squeezed the firing lever, *whump!*, *whump!* There was a larger explosion this time. Then a huge blast took the building apart and rocked the camp, temporarily drowning out the still-blazing machine guns. Kurt knew that one of the cannon rounds had hit an ammunition cache.

On the periphery, two ZANLA troops escaped the camp and ran towards the gorge one hundred and fifty metres away. The men were running an arm's length apart and appeared and disappeared between clumps of bush. Kurt swung the cannon barrel around and led the pair, picking out a gap in the vegetation they would pass and fired just before they got there. *Whump!* ... the 20mm round exploded at their feet. The two bodies spiralled in different directions, disappearing into the bush.

The intensity of the gunfire dropped off. From the continuous firing initially, the gunners used short bursts now, mainly from the twin Brownings. All of the guns were very hot from the sustained shooting, and they would be destroyed if that rate was maintained any longer.

In any event, further firing wasn't necessary. The once orderly camp was now a nightmare vision of carnage. The entire parade square and surrounding ground was carpeted with pieces of cloth, body fragments, and entrails. The barracks were burning fiercely and rounds of ammunition cooked off ... popping and banging. Nothing moved in the camp but the rising smoke and settling dust.

Kurt looked up. The sun was cresting over the horizon in a beautiful display. Shafts of breaking light illuminated the particles suspended in the air like curtains in a stage production, but for this one there would be no encore. The great dark scavengers of the sky were already beginning to gather, circling and wheeling at the prospect of the decadent feast to come.

Kurt shuddered as their cold shadows swept across the sun.

Major Murphy slowly climbed out of the Land Rover and walked forward to the edge of the parade square. Kurt followed him silently. Murphy looked both shocked and thrilled as he witnessed the scene.

"Oh, mother of God ... Look at this!"

Kurt stood silently beside Murphy for a moment.

"Violence begets violence, sir," Kurt said. "We just got them before they got us. It just happened here all at once."

"This isn't combat, Kurt; it's a massacre." Murphy stopped and looked at him, as if waiting for some reply.

Kurt could see Murphy was trembling slightly with emotion. Whether it was joy or horror wasn't clear; they were often expressed in the same way. Perhaps the fair play and honour of his upbringing had been violated, and this scene was far beyond that.

"This is what it always comes down to," Kurt said. "People dying. Whether it's one or a hundred or ... " He gestured toward the carnage on the parade square, "A thousand, it's the same thing. Our job is to kill the enemy before they can kill us and by the looks of it, we've done a good job here."

Kurt left Murphy standing at the edge of the devastation and walked towards the centre gun truck. The gunners were jumping up and down in the bed, shouting with joy, high on what they'd just done. As Kurt approached, they began clapping. This response was unexpected and brought an involuntary smile, which masked by an underlying numbness at what he'd just witnessed.

# CHAPTER 20
## ON THE ROAD

The mission briefing for the Pungwe raid was held two days later in the main conference room in Cranborne Barracks. The intelligence briefing room where the mission started weeks before was far too small to hold the crowd of nearly every senior officer in the Rhodesian military. The detailed clay model, constructed prior to the raid, was carefully moved to this new venue and displayed prominently. Aerial photographs of 'before' and 'after' scenes of the destroyed camp were blown up to mural size and tacked to the walls. Colonel Reed Donovan of the Selous Scouts, who made the operation possible through his behind-the-scenes support, took the front chair. Medals and decorations on Donovan's dress uniform, accumulated through participation in three wars, fought for room on his chest.

Before the briefing began, Major Murphy called Kurt, who was hovering in the back of the room keeping out of the way of the brass, up front and told him to stand at attention. Kurt froze in position, not knowing what to expect and feeling very uncomfortable. General Kenneth Wallis stood up and strode briskly forward and stood in front of him. Imposing by rank and reputation, Wallis surprisingly had the kind face and pleasant demeanour of a middle-aged farmer.

"Sergeant Kurt Christianson, by direct order of the office of the prime minister, I hereby promote you to the rank of lieutenant and also award you the Silver Cross for gallantry in battle with the enemy."

Kurt remained rigid as General Wallis pinned a silver pip on each epaulette and also placed the multicoloured ribbon with the heavy polished metal cross around his neck.

"Congratulations and well earned, Lieutenant," Wallis said as he saluted. Kurt spontaneously returned the salute, attempting to imitate the British flair.

After the surprise presentation Kurt walked back to the rear of the gathering, proud of what just occurred but very conscious of all the eyes following him.

Major Murphy proceeded with the briefing, first by describing the operation in a much summarized form, then by passing around photographs of the modified vehicles used in the raid while detailing how they were employed. For security reasons he did not mention or describe Kurt's initial reconnaissance mission, the assistance received by the Mozambican national Calo, or the exact routes followed when infiltrating and exfiltrating the camp. Murphy walked over to the wall and pointed to a large photo of the Pungwe Camp taken approximately one hour after the attack. The high altitude image showed a plume of smoke drifting east from the burnt-out buildings, away from the littered parade square.

"Our photo interpreters estimate that over nine hundred ZANLA troops were killed in the raid," Murphy told the hushed audience. "We have no idea of the number of wounded since any survivors would have fled into the bush. This camp was used as a centre for military training as well a staging area for the infiltration of guerrilla units into eastern Rhodesia. For all practical purposes the Pungwe ZANLA camp has been totally destroyed. We seriously doubt that it will be rebuilt, at least in this location. This military action will seriously degrade the morale of the ZANLA forces, along with their ability to cross into our eastern provinces."

Murphy moved away from the maps and walked directly to the front of the seated audience.

"I must caution everyone, however, that although we have undoubtedly dealt a serious blow to the enemy, this raid by itself does not by any means represent their defeat. Intelligence has determined that other training camps are being set up in Mozambique and Tanzania that are beyond the reach of vehicular or helicopter operations. We in the security forces must remain vigilant and new methods and tactics of reaching and destroying our enemies must be developed. Are there any questions?"

A balding colonel stood up and Murphy nodded to him.

"Major, you described the enemy casualties, what casualties did we suffer on this operation?"

"None, sir," Murphy replied.

The colonel cast his eyes around the room as if confused, looking for confirmation of the statement.

"Major, none of our men were even wounded when nearly a thousand enemy were killed?" the Colonel asked.

"Yes, sir, that's what I'm saying," Murphy said.

"Amazing, Major Murphy, I believe this is unprecedented. With kill-to-loss ratios like that we can win this war."

Murphy stepped closer to the balding colonel.

"I must express caution that this raid was a one-off situation. In many ways we were very lucky. The total surprise on our part and the lack of preparedness on theirs resulted in this total victory. They won't make the same mistake again."

General Wallis stood up unexpectedly and walked to the front of the room. Murphy stepped aside, turning over the floor to the Rhodesian military commander.

"I'd like to thank Colonel Donovan, Major Clive Murphy and all those who planned and took part in the very successful Pungwe raid. I've been a soldier for over thirty years now and I have never witnessed a military operation that was this daring, innovative or successful. Like the pilots who saved England in those dark days during the Battle of Britain, our own young soldiers have stepped forward and have taken the fight to the enemy. England was fighting an air war and countered the enemy with Hurricanes and Spitfires. Ours is a ground war and we countered the enemy with these amazing vehicles built and manned by the Selous Scouts. We will do whatever it takes to be victorious in this fight against those who would inflict terror on our people. Thank you and God bless you all."

⌘

After the brass left, Colonel Donovan, Murphy, Kurt and a few others remained in the conference room. The men were still glowing from the victory but they were also concerned about the future of the gun truck unit they had just created and used in battle. Donovan spoke to Murphy. Kurt listened to the conversation at a discreet distance.

"Major Murphy, we definitely need to capitalize on our success, an opportunity like this doesn't come around very often. As you are aware, units like the SAS and Scouts have to fight for everything we need to stay operational. The Air Force hates us. They expend a million dollars every time a couple of aircraft leave the ground on a combat mission. We have just destroyed more enemy in one cross-border incursion than they have in their entire history, and we pulled it off with nineteen men plus a few captured vehicles and weapons. What I'm saying is that we have to maintain this momentum, before we are out-politicked again. In warfare, like in any other business, nothing speaks like success."

"How would you like us to proceed, sir?" Murphy asked.

"I want you to expand and enlarge the unit beyond its current strength," Donovan said. "We have more trucks and weapons at our immediate disposal. What I picture is a mobile flying column we can use to take out fixed sites as well as targets of opportunity. With this massive firepower we have no fear of ambushes or counter strikes. The project is still classified, but we are developing a mine detection vehicle that is better than any yet fielded. With one of these and a squad of engineers paving the way, we can go virtually anywhere in western Mozambique. Of course most of the vehicular operations will have to take place in the dry season, but that is just a fact of life."

"Sir, should we begin work on this proposed expansion immediately?" Murphy asked.

"Yes," Donovan responded. "Unless I hear otherwise from the prime minister's office, I give my tentative order to proceed. Send all requisitions directly through me and I will keep the entire project in covert channels. Not a word to anyone about this, you understand?"

"Yes, sir ... as always," Murphy replied.

Donovan then turned to Kurt, "We haven't had an opportunity to talk much, Lieutenant Christianson. Welcome to the team."

"Thank you, sir, it's a pleasure to be a part of it," Kurt said.

"I read a briefing about your exploits in Angola," Donovan said. "You seem to be quite a soldier. Jack Malloy is an old friend of mine also. I am sorry for the loss of Mr Barlow, I had the pleasure of meeting him once and he struck me as a fine man."

"He was the best, sir," Kurt said. "I think about him often."

"We all have to die sometime, son; as long as it's an honourable death and we are doing what we love, its all we can really ask for. I know he'd be proud of you, Lieutenant. Keep up the tremendous work."

Kurt nodded to his commander and said nothing more.

After Colonel Donovan left, Murphy turned to Kurt, "Well, Lieutenant, it's Friday just before noon. You've just been promoted and been given a plum assignment. So what say we go into town for a few, and not worry about any of this crap until Monday morning?"

"That sounds like a plan, sir ... a real fine plan," Kurt said.

"I thought you would agree with me, and knock off that 'sir' stuff in private, will you? My car is over there."

⌘

Activity in the bars and hotel lounges in Salisbury began at noon, in earnest. Because of the discounts they received, the hotels were full of troops. The prevailing philosophy was that no terrorist with any sense would attack a hotel full of soldiers. This theory of deterrence by armed guests was in fact never tested, and this was probably fortunate. It was anyone's guess what sort of defence could be mounted by a hotel full of soldiers who had been drinking uninterrupted for several days. Also, the degree of mental comfort gained was more than offset by groups of loud, drunken, camouflaged men sprawled all over the place like occupation forces.

For security reasons, the Selous Scouts were encouraged not to wear their uniforms in public. Compliance with this informal directive was variable. While most of the members followed this guidance, it wasn't difficult to pick out the long-haired, mostly bearded, sunburned men anyway. Kurt and Murphy began their long weekend at the Monomatopa lounge, where the off-duty RLI, SAS and Grey Scouts, who were horse-mounted troops, usually hung out.

Several of the young troops from Kurt's training class greeted him with much exuberance. They ribbed him, with little mercy, about his ragged appearance but seemed awed by the rumours just reaching them about Pungwe. Several soldiers asked about the operation, but Kurt put a finger to his lips and subtly pointed at a waiter clearing glasses at a nearby table. Intelligence had informed the unit commanders that ZANLA had infiltrated agents into hotels and bars for the purpose of eavesdropping on loose-lipped soldiers.

That afternoon Kurt bought not one drink. He seemed to be the centre of attention which was enjoyable, but being that high-profile bothered one who preferred, and depended on, a covert existence. Kurt asked one of the RLI troops where Bluie and Holliday were, and the soldier said they both would be back from the bush that evening. Without asking, Kurt knew where they could be found, and at five-thirty he walked the several blocks to the Coq d'Or and waited for his old buddies to make their entrance a short time later.

⌘

Night life in Salisbury was a rather strange dichotomy of young teens and off-duty military. There were several nightclubs and dance clubs around town that played loud disco music to the accompaniment of flashing lights, glittering balls and sweaty gyrating bodies and despite the outward appearance of normality, these clubs were primarily an essential outlet for tension brought on by a war of ever-increasing tempo.

Most of the males in the country above the age of sixteen were either in the military, or about to join-up or get drafted. Those not wishing to heed the call left the country to attend university or pursue some career, usually never to return. Many of the older men had families or jobs they couldn't leave for long periods, so they enlisted in the Territorial Units, the Rhodesian equivalent of the National Guard or Reserves. In this way, they could participate as part-time soldiers and still be a member of the work force which kept the country's economy afloat.

The full-time professional soldiers comprised the Rhodesian Light Infantry, Special Air Service, Rhodesian African Rifles and Grey Scouts, the wildcard Selous Scouts and other less flamboyant units. On a nightly basis, all of these factions mingled in the nightclubs, bars and restaurants. There was some fighting among them but it was surprisingly minimal, considering the number of aggressive young men and the huge egos involved. They all knew that the real fight was only a short helicopter flight away. As much as one soldier could dislike another for whatever reason, they were all still allies in the face of a common enemy.

Kurt, Bluie and Holliday drank several beers at the Coq d'Or and decided to go 'clubbing', although all felt too old to fit into that scene. At the Balancing Rocks Motel Bar they met three girls in their early twenties who were on their own, and the six of them became quickly acquainted thanks to the alcohol-fuelled casual atmosphere. All Kurt remembered of the rest of evening was a series of taxi rides, more drinking at other places, then nothing more.

He awoke at first light lying on a wooden bedroom floor with a splitting headache. The rest of the group all lay fully clothed on a large bed in a strange apartment. The faces of the girls had looked enchanting enough the night before but were now streaked and caked with makeup that was never meant to see the light of day. The need for fresh air was paramount. On a piece of blank paper in the small kitchen he scrawled: 'See you guys later, Kurt', and placed it on the table.

Outside, the morning air was brisk and refreshing and began to clear the cobwebs from his throbbing head. An African vendor with a push cart was selling bottles of milk and juice. Kurt gratefully bought two bottles of fresh orange juice and drank them rapidly. The fresh air, fluids and exercise made the throbbing recede somewhat.

In the flower gardens, there were vibrant tropical blooms; numerous brightly coloured birds fluttered, chattered and skipped from patch to patch. This town was a major contradiction. By all indications it seemed like paradise, somewhere you would go as a reward in the next life, not a staging area for a brutal war in this one.

Back at the Ambassador Hotel, Kurt had breakfast in the dining room, then went and slept for a couple of hours before going back on the streets to pick up some supplies in the shops. He linked up with Bluie and Holliday when the stores closed at noon, and for the rest of the day they accompanied other soldiers making the circuit of hotel bars, which was a weekend ritual. After two days in town Kurt was agitated and impatient. The war wouldn't be won sitting on a stool with a drink in hand. At eight o'clock he decided to call it a day and head back to Inkomo the next morning, even though it was Sunday. There were some new ideas he wanted to discuss with the armourers and mechanics.

Going to bed too early caused Kurt to wake up in the small hours of Sunday morning. He was unable to go back to sleep because of the tension that inhibited much-needed rest. He dressed quickly for the silent streets beckoned; walking was better than staring at the ceiling. Like most nights, the only movement on the streets was from an occasional mini taxi. The darkened park he remembered from his first night in town was only a few blocks away so he wandered in that direction, for no reason in particular.

There was perhaps a secret wish for a mugger to jump out from the bushes and try to rob him. A good fight and the attendant adrenaline surge might dispel the mounting tension of the weekend in town, but there were no muggers apparent, no people at all.

From the mixed shadow and patches of street light in the middle of the park, a voice called his name. Turning, he saw no one, the voice must have been imagined ... too tired. Again ... his name, louder and clearer now. He turned a second time and saw a familiar figure standing on the grass, recognizable even in the dim light, his black shirt and shorts contrasting with almost luminous skin.

"Medic," Kurt said. "We meet in the strangest places. What are you doing here?"

"Can't sleep, you?"

"Same," Kurt replied. "It seems we both have insomnia."

"An occupational hazard," the Mad Medic laughed. "When you are out there," he pointed his finger to the horizon, "you're too preoccupied with the job to worry about it. But when you are in here," he pointed to the ground beside his feet, "then the little demons come out, don't they?"

Kurt shook his head as if dismissing the statement.

"No, Medic, not me," Kurt said. "I just get too charged up in anticipation of what I'm going to do next. My brain can't seem to calm down."

"So it's not the regrets, remorse, guilt, that sort of thing bothering you, keeping you awake at night?" the Medic asked, grinning oddly in the irregular broken light.

"So you're a psychiatrist now, Medic? Expanding our horizons a bit, are we?" Kurt asked, his voice heavy with sarcasm.

The Mad Medic laughed again, more coarsely this time.

"Oh, it's part of being a healer, believe me, a major part. There are more mental casualties in war than there are physical ones. In fact if we could heal the mind there wouldn't be any war, would there? It's self-perpetuating, you see."

"Then we would both be out of jobs, wouldn't we, Medic?" Kurt replied. "Anyway, you're talking crap. As long as there are people on this planet there will be conflicts over territory, religion, resources, politics, or whatever. There always has been and always will be conflict, and we are both caught up in it. It's been said that prostitution is the world's oldest profession; but that's wrong, soldiering is."

The Mad Medic listened thoughtfully, contemplating Kurt's words before he spoke again.

"I don't disagree with you at all, and that wasn't my point. My question wasn't directed at the without ... but at the within." The Mad Medic drew close and looked at Kurt, but the gaze was misdirected because of his bad eye. Kurt was uncomfortable being this close to the madman, but he felt strangely powerless to back away or resist him.

"I really don't know what you are talking about, Medic, and besides, I'm very tired now, too tired for this sort of banter."

"It's important," the Medic insisted. "I'll just leave you with one thought to mull over. Shouldn't everyone reach a point in their lives when violence and its offspring, war, doesn't make sense to them anymore? That's what I mean by the battle within. It's a fight for the heart and soul of each person, and if we win this battle then everything will change, won't it? You see, I've spent my life patching up the results, and it's the only answer I've come up with. It's got to end you know ... it's got to."

With that, the Mad Medic turned and strode away, not down the walkway but across the grass into the surrounding trees and bushes. Kurt listened carefully for his footsteps in the dry undergrowth but heard none. The man was obviously mad and should be locked up. Worse than that, his words were always disturbing, more so than anyone he had ever talked to. That was the last thing he needed at this point; he had to concentrate, not be distracted. At any rate, it was pretty obvious how the Mad Medic got his name.

Kurt walked back to his hotel. He was weary now ... very weary.

⌘

Kurt was eating breakfast with Major Murphy and the armourers and technicians in the mess hall at Inkomo Barracks early Monday morning. The mess hall was an 'all ranks' consolidated facility, which was rare in the Rhodesian Army; in fact it was unique. According to the old British Army system, facilities were strictly segregated, based on rank. Troopers, NCOs, and officers were all divided into separate mess facilities, and this separate and unequal treatment was strictly enforced, sometimes to the point of absurdity. The quality of the food, furnishings and utensils also reflected this distinction in rank. Officers ate on fine china, used polished silver and drank from crystal glasses. NCOs were allowed lower grade glassware and steel utensils, while troopers gobbled their carelessly prepared food from tin trays, sometimes in the rain.

Special operations soldiers learned quickly that such arbitrary and discriminatory practices did not work in their units. When in the field, operator experience counted much more than rank, and respect among your peers was not conferred, but earned. Every time a special operations soldier was employed, he was running on the razor's edge of success or catastrophe; there was no neutral ground. In order to stay alive, team members had to trust one another implicitly, and it was this trust upon which all else depended.

Kurt was not really concerned about his official status or rank, it was just the means to an end. His personal goal was to position himself where he could do his job in the most efficient and direct manner. The rest was just cosmetics and appeasement of personal ego, something for which he had little time or thought. Unlike other military units that relied heavily on custom and inflexible regulations, special operations units didn't operate that way. They couldn't afford to be that rigid, and this unconventional environment attracted a different sort of man ... and soldier.

⌘

After breakfast the small group of men went out to inspect the vehicles and equipment. In the vehicle yard there were a variety of military and civilian trucks with Portuguese markings and tags and, almost hidden behind them, sat a few well-used buses. The people transporters were in relatively poor condition, but on the whole they looked functional. Kurt's curiosity was piqued enough to ask the chief of maintenance section about them.

"What's the story on these vehicles, Chief?"

"When the Portuguese left Mozambique in 1975 the whole country was in a mess," the chief responded, "so our soldiers went across the border and took every vehicle they could drive back. We figured it was either that or the FRELIMO would get them and use them against us, because they were starting to rattle their swords. We didn't even have enough drivers for all of them, so we burned or blew up a lot of what we couldn't bring back."

"And what about those buses?" Kurt asked, pointing to the dirty forgotten vehicles.

"Buses could easily move FRELIMO or ZANLA troops, so we got some of those as well," he said. "Most we gave to the African bus lines that serve the tribal areas to help out their businesses but lately, most of the bus companies have been shut down out there because of terrorist ambushes. These here weren't serviceable enough to release."

"Can they be fixed?" Kurt asked.

The chief shrugged.

"Some of them probably could, with a little work. What are you thinking of doing with them, sir?"

"I think we could turn those old clunkers into something useful," Kurt replied.

⌘

With Murphy's permission, Kurt gathered together a group of armourers and craftspeople to brainstorm the problem. As part of their campaign to lay siege to Rhodesia, groups of guerrillas were operating in the African tribal lands, stopping buses and other vehicles on rural roads, robbing and terrorizing the occupants. Sometimes the buses were burned and destroyed and the passengers assaulted and sometimes murdered. The problem was so prevalent in some areas that the bus service was disrupted or halted altogether. This was bad for the morale of the population and bad for the economy because people couldn't get to work or to the towns.

The guerrilla groups usually followed a standard pattern. A group would lie in wait along a remote rural road. When a bus came along, the group commander and several other members would stand in the middle of the roadway and the rest of the armed force would be in hidden in the verges. Usually old tyres or trees were placed in the road to act as barriers. The driver had no option but to comply with the demands of the ambushers, or the lumbering vehicle would be riddled by gunfire and many of the passengers would be killed or wounded.

After discussing the problem at length and arriving at some agreement, the Selous Scouts under Kurt's direction decided to assemble a prototype anti-ambush vehicle. Rural African buses had a particular and unmistakable look about them. In most instances, luggage and boxes of assorted sizes and shapes were stacked on the roof rack, sometimes to an absurd degree. The buses were invariably crowded with people because they were the only reasonable transportation serving the vast and often remote tribal areas. Without these hallmarks, a band of guerrillas intent on ambush would be suspicious of any bus traversing the rural roads, and would probably let it pass.

Kurt and his team looked at this problem and came up with some novel ideas. Old luggage was procured at several African markets and brought to Inkomo. A framework was welded out of tubular steel and the luggage was chopped into pieces. These luggage pieces were then assembled over the steel frame to resemble a pile of suitcases and boxes. While this was being constructed, reinforcing bars were welded to the side frames of the bus forming a strong support running parallel to, and just beneath, the roof. A hole was cut in the sheet metal roof and a 12.7mm HMG supported by a swivel mount was bolted to the tubular framework. The 'luggage cover' was then placed over the assembly, which from the outside looked like a haphazard pile of suitcases and boxes tied on the roof rack. A pull of a lever would allow two powerful springs to throw off the cover, giving the machine gun operator beneath a 360-degree swing at any target he chose.

The 'occupants' of this rural bus took a bit of ingenuity, but Kurt noted that the Inkomo Armoury had a surplus of RPD machine guns in inventory. The effective light fully automatic weapons used the same cartridge as the AK-47 and featured a longer, heavier barrel, a folding bipod for support, and a high cheek piece on the stock. Their standard magazine was a 100-round drum containing a linked steel belt of ammunition. The long barrel and stock made the gun somewhat difficult to manoeuvre in tight quarters. As an experiment Kurt and the armourers cut off the barrel progressively on one gun until the gas system failed to function. The gas port was then enlarged and the barrel trimmed back even further until it was only a few inches forward of the gas port. When fired, the shortened machine gun had a blinding muzzle flash that was two feet long with a deafening report.

"We'll have to use earplugs to fire these babies, huh?" Kurt said to one of the armourers. "Let's cut the stocks down so they can still be shoulder fired if needed, but mostly they will just be pointed out of the windows."

The plan was to put six or eight Selous Scouts in each side of the bus dressed like and pretending to be normal rural passengers. White soldiers would be made up with black camouflage paint. In the rest of the seats would be placed African mannequins discarded from department stores. Each Selous Scout 'passenger' would sit next to an open window and have a shortened RPD and a stack of loaded ammunition drums on the seat next to him. The shooters would also wear earplugs.

As a finishing touch, several aircraft 70mm rocket tubes were obtained that were designed to be mounted on aircraft and helicopters for air-to-ground use. With modifications to the rocket warhead to make it arm more quickly, the armourer didn't see any reason the weapon couldn't be used in a ground-to-ground role, but to their knowledge this hadn't been done previously. Clusters of four rocket tubes were mounted on either side of the front frame of the bus, just in front of the wheel wells pointing forward. Minimal cut-outs of the body were done to allow clearance for the fired projectiles, and the openings were covered with very thin plastic covers that would pop off easily. The rockets were aimed at a point on the ground fifty feet ahead of the bus. The bus driver had two firing buttons mounted on the dash board, one for the right bank of four tubes and one for the left bank.

Initially, the rocket clusters were tested by remote control and the effect was devastating. It was quickly found that the front windscreen of the bus had to be lined with clear Plexiglas to prevent shrapnel from the exploding warheads and ground clutter from flying back through the windscreen. A piece of armour plate was also welded directly in front of the bus driver. Just before firing the rockets, the driver was to dive behind the armour shield. When all the modifications had been completed and range tested, everyone agreed to a live field exercise to validate the design.

⌘

The ZANLA gang had been operating in the Merawa tribal land for several months. Their overall mission was to destabilize the Rhodesian government by whatever means possible. This meant attacking 'soft' targets such as remote farms and villages and any people or organizations that recognized the government's authority. The gang lay low initially, and depended on sympathetic villagers for food, clothing and other supplies.

If villagers weren't sympathetic to the cause, they were soon converted by the muzzle of an AK-47 or bayonet thrust in their face. Any further resistance would result in a trigger being pulled. This group, as of yet, hadn't killed any villagers because the locals were sympathetic, or at least pretended to be. The overwhelming concern of every member of the guerrilla group was to avoid contact with the Rhodesian military forces at all costs. Operating units that had a serious encounter with their opponents were usually killed or captured, or at least shot-up and scattered.

Robbing rural buses was an idea that came to Simon Mangazi, who was the commander of this group of ZANLA guerrillas. While Simon and his men were on patrol near Merawa several months before, a bus had passed by them on a dusty road. This was a normal occurrence in this remote part of the country but when Simon saw this bus he didn't see just a form of transportation, but a treasure trove of basic goods desperately needed by the group. All they would have to do was stop the bus and at gunpoint take whatever they wanted from the unarmed passengers. It would be too easy, and Simon was angry with himself for not thinking of it earlier. Being an enterprising man, as well as an up-and-coming leader of the ZANLA military arm, Simon had one of the friendly villagers obtain a bus schedule of the local area. By studying the schedule, they could select when and where his group would stage their ambush.

Their first bus robbery took place at the bend of a road in a remote hilly area. Small boulders were positioned near the edge of the roadway and when they heard the bus coming, the men rolled the rocks into the middle of the road blocking the vehicle's passage. Simon and two other combatants stood twenty feet beyond the obstruction and waved their AKs over their heads as the bus approached; the others in the group hid out of sight in the bush, on the verges.

As planned, the bus stopped on demand and the ambushers stormed aboard, forcing all of the passengers and the driver off into the bush where they were relieved of money, jewellery, clothing and anything else of value. An athletic member of the gang jumped on the roof of the bus and threw down the luggage, which was then ransacked. The whole event would have only taken a few minutes except that several of the group were feeling the deprivations of too long in the bush, and forced several of the younger women to a nearby ravine and raped them. Simon didn't encourage or condone such behaviour, but he accepted these actions as necessary and important to maintain the morale of his men.

Simon was in two minds. His first thought was to burn the bus, thus denying a piece of transportation to the Rhodesian government. On the other hand, that was like killing the golden goose. The buses proved to be a great source of needed cash and supplies which were theirs for the taking. Why destroy good fortune? After taking everything of value Simon decided to let the bus go.

Several months and a dozen bus robberies later, Simon's gang was practiced and proficient at the task and, as a result of their successes, had caches of pilfered goods all over the countryside. The ZANLA gang no longer had to rely on the largesse of the villagers to obtain these things. All it needed was one turncoat in a village to open his mouth and the Rhodesian forces would be on them.

As it turned out, Bus Number 13 was Simon's unlucky number, but not being a superstitious sort, the number meant nothing to him. This time the rural road was barricaded with fallen tree trunks dragged into place, and according to their usual routine the bus was waved to a stop. The man standing next to the commander held an RPG-7 at the ready. Any attempt to run the blockade or reverse, would result in an armour penetrating missile through the vehicle's windscreen with horrible results. Simon smiled when he saw the driver disappear to the floor when the bus stopped. The driver would have to be slapped around for being such a coward and resisting. After all, where was he going to hide?

Simon suddenly sensed rather than saw that something was terribly wrong, but had no time to react. As the thought crossed his mind, his vision picked up a red flash coming from the right side of the bus, just in front of the right wheel. One of the 70mm aircraft rockets fired from the right pod skipped over the top of a log in the road and exploded near his feet. He was blown apart so fast that his brain had no time to register the pain. The other two soldiers standing with him in the road were also dealt fatal wounds by the fragmentation warheads.

After the explosions in front of the bus, gun barrels extended from open side windows and spewed massive fire, the flashes from the shortened barrels visible even at midday. As if blown off, the fake hollow luggage shell on the roof fell into the road. The booming 12.7mm HMG dominated the din as the heavy slugs churned up the ditches. In twenty seconds calm returned, only the smoke and dust gave evidence to what had just happened.

Kurt climbed out of the bus and walked forward. Murphy followed him shaking his head side to side as though his ears were plugged with water.

"Goddamn, I think we got the big guy Mangazi," Murphy said. "I recognized him just before the rockets fired. According to Intel he's been very troublesome in this area."

Kurt looked at the bodies in the roadway.

"I'm glad you recognized him before the rockets hit, Murph, there isn't much left to identify now. I think his hijacking days have come to an end. What do you think?"

Two rapid shots came from behind the bus. Both men ducked and pointed their weapons toward the sound. A moment later, one of the Selous Scouts emerged from the ditch.

"One was badly hit but still moving, sir, so I finished him," the Scout said.

"How many total?" Murphy asked him.

"I counted fourteen, sir," the Scout answered. "A few may have bolted; we can't be sure."

"Damned effective, Kurt," Murphy said. "But no doubt they will catch on quickly and leave the rural buses alone."

"Maybe," Kurt scratched his beard. "That's not all bad, it will cut them off from a source of money and supplies, but we don't need to limit this jack-in-the-box trick to buses. It can be used on any large vehicle that would make a tempting target."

"I'll make the recommendation that we add this to the existing armed vehicle programme, Kurt," Murphy said, "and that you be put in charge."

"We'll talk about that, Murph," Kurt said hesitantly. "I have another idea I've been working on that is ... well, on a broader scale."

"Oh, is that so? What ideas are brewing this time?" Murphy asked, rolling his eyes to the sky.

"Once this programme is up and running, one of the other troop commanders can head it up," Kurt replied. "Someone like Sergeant Nkomo will do well, he's got what it takes."

"And you?" Murphy enquired.

Kurt turned to Murphy and looked at him directly.

"As I've said before, Murph, if we are to have any chance of winning this war, we have to take it directly to the enemy."

"You mean Mozambique?" Murphy asked. "We already did that at Pungwe and did it well."

Kurt shook his head.

"That's just the tip of the iceberg and you know it. We have to eliminate the enemy's administrative and military headquarters. Go right to the heart of the beast."

Murphy looked at the ground and nodded his head in agreement.

"Of course we've talked about that, Kurt, but those locations are out of our reach and besides, some are in places that are off limits politically. We just can't go in there with guns blazing. The international repercussions would be too severe."

Kurt looked Murphy steadily in the eyes.

"This may surprise most people, Murph, but there isn't an individual in the world that doesn't understand the right to defend oneself. Our enemies will no doubt whine and moan, but they still understand it. Where there is a will there is a way, the only question is. Do *we* have the will to survive?"

# CHAPTER 21
## ATROCITY

In order to more efficiently pursue the war effort, the Rhodesian military appointed General Kenneth Wallis as Commander of Combined Operations. This reorganization put the air force, army, police and all auxiliary units under a single central command structure. It was thought that this consolidation would result in a more co-ordinated and effective use of Rhodesia's overtaxed military resources, which were combating an enemy of ever-increasing numbers.

The Selous Scout officers and several field commanders from other army operational units, including RLI and SAS, met at Joint Operational Centre (JOC), Mtoko to discuss forthcoming operational plans. Kurt recalled his initial visit to Mtoko when he'd seen the men with the beards for the first time. Now as if by some sorcerer's magic he was one of them.

Discussions at the JOC conference room focused on future planning; in particular, how to inflict the most damage on the enemy with the limited military resources available. The group received a lengthy intelligence briefing outlining the latest enemy numbers and capabilities. It was obvious to all that there was an increasing effort on the part of ZANLA to expand both their external infrastructure, and also the number of guerrilla groups operating within Rhodesia's borders. Comments by the other officers were predictable, and mainly addressed how to deal with the guerrilla groups once they were operating in the country.

As the lowest ranking officer present at the conference, Kurt attempted to stay in the background, alternately studying the maps tacked on the walls and listening to the briefings and questions by others. For weeks now he'd been mulling over ideas that were just beginning to gel, but wasn't sure if now was the time or place to present them. Finally, unable to contain himself any longer in the face of the uninspired discussions taking place, he stood and moved in front of the wall maps. Everyone became quiet, and regarded the most junior member of the group. .

"Gentlemen, we need to look at the big picture rather more than we have done. Unless we organize our combined efforts into an intelligent offensive campaign, we are stuck in a no-win loop of just reacting to enemy aggression. This allows them to take both the lead and the initiative in this conflict. As I've stated before, we need to take the war to them if we are to have any chance of victory."

"I don't think anyone here disagrees with that, Lieutenant," Major Allen interrupted. "It's just a matter of how best to accomplish this within our capabilities. What are you thinking?"

Kurt nodded and picked up a whittled acacia branch that was used as a pointer. "Our current intelligence indicates we can basically divide the ZANLA infrastructure into two groups." Kurt indicated on one of the wall maps. "Firstly, there are the field operational bases and launch sites in close proximity to our eastern border. However, since the Pungwe raid we have seen a substantial withdrawal of troops and support personnel from these forward areas.

"Secondly, there are the large camps that have been recently constructed in northern Mozambique and southern Tanzania that are located hundreds of kilometres from our border. Most of ZANLA's training, administration and support have been relocated in or near these safe complexes. This means a longer transit time for guerrilla groups crossing into this country, but evidently ZANLA high command thinks this security is worth the logistical trouble.

"As everyone is aware, it is difficult for us to detect small groups of mobile guerrillas once they have arrived. For every insurgent in the field it takes five or more troops to find and destroy them by conventional means. This requires manpower we just don't have. Our only effective option is to attack fixed facilities and troop concentrations. Once ZANLA detachments arrive and spread out as small operational groups in the field, we just can't deal with them effectively with our limited manpower."

On a large map pinned to the wall of the conference room, Kurt pointed to an area nearly four hundred and fifty kilometres from the north-east corner of Rhodesia on the junction of the northern border of Mozambique and southern Tanzania. The site was only a short distance from the Indian ocean.

"As briefed by intelligence, the Atibo camp currently serves as both operational and logistical headquarters of the ZANLA Army," Kurt continued. "Just nine kilometres to the north and east of Atibo in Tanzania is Kitaya, which is an administrative support centre. Currently, information on both camps is admittedly sketchy, but places personnel strength at four to five thousand. Both camps are located a great distance from our borders. Even sorties with Canberra and Vampire reconnaissance aircraft aren't possible due to radar coverage at nearby Dar es Salaam, and the possibility of MIGs reacting to such an intrusion.

"Closer to our border," Kurt continued, "reconnaissance indicates smaller ZANLA facilities are becoming operational at Mapai and Chioco and possibly several other locations. These are strictly launch sites for combat-ready teams trained and equipped at the larger complexes. These launch sites make use of existing abandoned Portuguese military structures in order to minimize the identification of new construction by our aerial photography.

"Due to their proximity, ZANLA knows full well that we will make cross-border incursions and attack their border launch sites as we did at Pungwe. They also know that we will do our best to detect and eliminate insurgent groups deployed within our borders, but as I've said, this is a losing battle. They are playing a numbers game with us the same as North Vietnam did with the United States. Winning this type of unconventional war by attrition is a fool's dream. We can never hope to eliminate the enemy by destroying them once they are in the country, or even in their staging areas.

They will just keep sending more insurgents in, and eventually overwhelm our ability to stop them. The situation seems hopeless, unless we truly understand the problem and deal with it directly, on our terms. If we fight them on their terms we will lose, there is no doubt about it."

"And how do you propose we accomplish these grandiose plans Leff-ten-ant?" Ainsley asked, drawing out Kurt's rank as if to emphasize its lack of importance as well as to throw a bit of cultural intimidation his way.

"Sir," Kurt replied directly, "we hit them hard where and when they don't expect it. We must destroy their core infrastructure to neutralize their ability to send armed men into this country. An insurgency like this is like a cancerous tumour. We must cut it out at its source to destroy it. There is no other way to win this war. However, to accomplish this successfully with the limited manpower available we must know these targets intimately, like the backs of our own hands.

"You mean better intelligence, Lieutenant?" Major Armstrong asked. "Our aerial photos and the information obtained from captured guerrillas have been substantial. I fail to see your point."

Kurt turned from the map to face Armstrong directly.

"My point, sir, is that any attack on these base camps will have to be done with absolute and surgical precision. Given the difficulty of transporting our forces to the targets and back with the limited resources available to us, we will be extended far beyond normal operational parameters. There can be no mistakes or bad calls on an operation of this nature, or the whole effort could wind up being a catastrophe."

"That is precisely why we think such an attack is not wise, at this time anyway," Ainsley said.

"Colonel," Kurt replied, "at this time I agree with you. However, if it were possible to obtain additional precise ground information, there is a real possibility of taking out both camp complexes in one fell swoop."

"Lieutenant, are you referring the Atibo and Kitaya camps?" Ainsley asked.

"Yes, sir, and their launch sites near our border." Kurt again pointed to the map with the whittled branch and pointed to the twin ZANLA camps hundreds of kilometres distant, then to a series of points marked by red stickers just across the border.

"You are proposing to attack them all at the same time, Lieutenant?" Armstrong asked as he stood up and walked to the front of the room with Kurt. "Won't that stretch our manpower and logistics too far?"

"I don't think so, sir," Kurt replied. "If we continue piecemeal operations as we have in the past, it gives ZANLA too much time to recover. They just spread their resources around and in that way we will never be able to strike a fatal blow; they will always pop back up. The proposed attack on Atibo and Kitaya will have to be conducted with air bombardment, followed by parachute and ground assaults. All of the RLI, SAS and Scouts plus most of the reserve units will be necessary. We will also have to secure at least two staging and refuelling areas for helicopters in the northern sector of Mozambique but, according to some initial assessments, that should not be a problem."

"What about the staging areas near our border?" Allen asked as he studied the map. "If we have committed all of our resources to the combined Atibo/ Kitaya attack, what manpower would be left to deal with these launch sites?"

"We can use the gun trucks, sir," Kurt stated. "We can't take them with us on the big raid so we use them as a diversion. Major Murphy and a skeleton crew of Selous Scouts could go across and fire up their staging areas. This action will put pressure on ZANLA to react to our aggression, and it would also be a sensible diversion to our true intentions. Temporarily, the big camps in the north will have a false sense of security. ZANLA would think that our resources are being focused on the south-east Rhodesian border, when in fact the big lion will spring at them in the north."

The room was quiet, but this did not indicate unanimous agreement. The plan was so bold and on such a large scale that none of the officers yet had grasped the full implications.

"I estimate," Kurt continued, "that in one perfectly executed attack we can destroy maybe ninety percent of ZANLA's external infrastructure. Once their consolidated headquarters and support groups have been eliminated there will be no more replacements, and the guerrilla teams remaining in the field can be tracked down and destroyed. This war is winnable, but success will depend on our ability to conduct a broad, well-coordinated strike on an unsuspecting enemy. Even if it doesn't work exactly as planned, the damage inflicted will buy much-needed time."

Kurt looked into the eyes of his audience. By their expressions, most of them wanted to believe his plan possible, even if they had doubts. Several in the group, particularly staff officers, had their arms crossed, signalling resistance. Surprisingly, even Colonel Ainsley looked as though he was seriously contemplating what had just been said. "Perhaps even that old fossil can be brought around," Kurt mused.

What had just been proposed was unprecedented. A junior and an outsider was venturing into territory that was clearly the domain of others. Successes in the field aside, Kurt realized that his biggest opponents were not the enemy but supposed allies. To overcome that obstruction, with such an audacious plan, was a formidable task. Something else was needed, something to sway the ambivalent over to his side, but he couldn't put his finger on it. He had the feeling that his plan could be headed for ridicule, and the scrap heap.

Colonel Ainsley stood and walked to the front of the briefing room.

"Thank you, Lieutenant, your presentation is very thought-provoking and will be given due consideration by the senior staff. Please write up the details of your proposal and submit it to me by week's end."

"Yes, sir, I will be glad to," Kurt said as he returned to his seat.

"Gentlemen, it is ten minutes to one," Colonel Ainsley said, looking at his watch with an oddly quizzical expression. "I propose we break until two-thirty, at which time we will resume these discussions.

⌘

Kurt didn't feel like eating. It was very hot, and being cooped up in a stale briefing room all day made his head hurt. Staff meetings he hated with a passion, but in reality the only way to sell his ideas was to talk to the staff officers. He walked across the scorched gravel and parched earth of JOC Mtoko with no actual destination in mind. The only cool spot on the JOC was the hospital building that was inset between protective earthen mounds and was situated slightly below ground level.

Large double doors on the front of the hospital were wide open to allow the passage of casualties on rolling gurneys. Some comedian had nailed a green sign above the entrance that said, 'ABANDON HOPE ALL YE WHO ENTER HERE.' Below the words were two bored buzzards sitting in a dead tree. You had to admire the human spirit, Kurt thought, even at times like this there was an attempt to rise above it. The sign was no doubt the work of the Mad Medic. Maybe he was here.

When Kurt entered the double doors, a scholarly looking man in green shorts and a camouflage T-shirt quietly appeared from around the corridor.

"Can I help you, sir?" the man asked.

"I'm looking for someone," Kurt said hesitantly, realizing he didn't know the Mad Medic's name.

"Well, I'm the only one here now, Lieutenant, everyone else is out in the bush, but you are welcome to some tea, I've just brewed up a new pot."

"Sure," Kurt said without hesitation. He felt like talking to someone removed from what he was doing, to clear his mind.

The two sat at a table in the supply room, next to the industrial-sized tea urn where the hospital supervisor had his desk, and talked. Kurt found out he was Jim Nichols and he was planning to attend the local medical school, once his compulsory military service was completed the following year. He talked with enthusiasm about a good future in Rhodesia after the war was over, and the role he wanted to play in it. Jim's attitude seemed refreshing and it gave Kurt a positive feeling. This just wasn't just a war *against* something, he thought, but *for* something, something tangible. In those few minutes of talking with this man, Kurt felt his flagging commitment strengthen.

⌘

The early afternoon was quiet. Only the distant hum of the camp diesel generator provided background sound. While the midday sun baked the dusty camp, the hospital remained comfortable. A vehicle pulled up to the hospital entrance. Jim, a thin nervous man, jumped to his feet, and Kurt followed. The vehicle wasn't military as expected, but a civilian Peugeot station wagon. A man, a woman and a small girl got out. Jim knew the family and greeted them by name, then introduced Kurt.

"Lieutenant Christianson, this is Mr and Mrs van Ryl. They farm just out of Mtoko. If my memory serves me right, there are some stitches to remove from your arm, aren't there, Johan?"

The man held up his left arm which had a dirty bandage wrapped just below the elbow.

"And its about bloody time you took them out, doc, it's been itching like mad."

Of medium height, Johan was stocky and two decades of farm labour was evident in his burly physique. His hair was dark and slightly curly as if it spoke of some Malay or Hottentot blood many generations back. His wife Eileen was blonde and fair skinned to the point of almost hurting the eyes to look at her in the bright sun. She wore a large straw hat for protection, but her skin was red and freckled where it was exposed. She was waif thin, quiet, with gentle eyes and an appealing manner. The hard existence of a farm wife on the African frontier hadn't compromised her femininity.

Close by the woman's knees was their only child, a daughter named Cassie. The little girl was three or four years old and Kurt had never seen a more beautiful child. She had her mother's hair but the darker more easily tanned skin of her father. Kurt looked at her and smiled involuntarily, when she smiled back at him and tried to hide her face in her mother's skirts, but peeked out a second later. She clung tightly to a cloth doll that wore a pink dress and had yellow hair.

"I think she is frightened of your beard," Eileen said. "I don't think she has ever seen a man with one."

"Come here, little one," Kurt said to the girl, and knelt down and put out his arms.

Cassie looked up at her mother quizzically. Eileen nodded to her and the little girl bravely walked over to Kurt who lifted her up in his arms. Kurt had never been around children, and the little girl felt whisper light. Cassie reached out slowly with her left hand and touched his coarse beard which shone like burnished copper in the sunlight. Kurt laughed and took his own hand and pulled at it.

"You see, it won't hurt you, little one. Let's go inside and see if we can find a cold soda for you, and maybe a biscuit.

Kurt talked to Eileen and played with Cassie for a few minutes while Mr van Ryl had his stitches removed by Jim. They seemed to be friendly, sincere people. Both of their families had been farming for generations in Southern Africa, and they truly loved the life. As with everyone, the recent advent of terrorism was causing them great concern. They decided to use the military camp hospital near their farm in preference to the larger facility at Marandellas because they feared an ambush on the road.

Kurt noticed that Eileen was pregnant. Her condition wasn't noticeable under the loose-fitting dress, but was apparent when she was seated. When Kurt asked about her condition, she indicated that her second child was due in three months, and they were hoping for a boy, to take over their farm eventually. This struck a melancholy chord in Kurt's mind. His grandfather had talked of him taking over the lobster business, but it was never really a business, only a continuing and impossible struggle. When his grandfather had spoken those words, both recognized the futility of such a hope. Kurt trusted fate would treat the van Ryls and their unborn child better.

Eileen asked Kurt if he would like to come and have dinner with them on their farm. Kurt readily agreed and told her that he had to go back to Inkomo later that day but he would be back in a week or two and would call them.

Cassie was totally enamoured with Kurt. He father was a kind, strong man and she loved him as most little girls do, but for her being held by Kurt was like being encased by the limbs of a giant tree. Even little girls are conscious of masculine strength, and the security it afforded them throughout their lives. Kurt radiated that strength like a beacon. A defender who would never harm his own, he would fearlessly and ruthlessly protect them at any cost. The little girl had no idea of his exploits but she felt the force anyway. Her instincts for safety and security were not clouded by the deceptions often practiced by adults.

Kurt gently kissed Cassie on the forehead in parting and brushed his beard on her pink cheek. She giggled and smiled. The affections of this child were so pure and unconditional and unlike anything he'd ever experienced.

At that moment a new feeling engulfed him, both disturbing and pleasant. His thoughts wandered to Diana and the ranch on the remote Namibian desert. He'd recently written several letters to her and, to his surprise, she had replied. He subconsciously patted the left packet of his uniform shirt where he kept the letters she had written. When they first met, he'd thought her aloof but first impressions are often confusing. It takes time to get to know someone well enough to make a judgment, and they'd had so little time. The letters seemed to be serving that purpose and, by her tone in the most recent correspondence, she was interested.

Combining the thoughts of Diana and the child resulted in a powerful wave of feeling that swept over him. The concept of giving life back when he had witnessed so much destruction was like a magical gift, an elixir that could repair the damage done, or at least some of it. Images appeared of their barefoot children running in the desert sands, learning the clicking language of the Bushmen. The pureness of it all was far removed from the foulness and pain of war. The pictures played through his mind rapidly like a kaleidoscope, then faded. He hoped they would return soon.

He put the girl down and she scampered to the dusty Peugeot, trailing her worn and dusty doll. When he visited the family he would remember to bring something for Cassie, but what? He knew nothing about what children liked, he would have to ask someone, maybe Murphy's wife or better yet ask Diana. Kurt said goodbye and thank you to Jim and walked back to the TAC conference room. He thought it funny that you could live years at a time and nothing important changes but in minutes, unexpectedly, everything can metamorphose.

⌘

Little more of substance was said that afternoon. The planning discussions were concluded for the day and the men moved to the officers' mess tent to drink tea and relax until the sun was low on the horizon, when the drinks changed to beer. A DC-3 was scheduled to arrive and give the officers a lift back to New Sarum, but the word arrived that it was cancelled due to a higher priority mission, and their ride wouldn't arrive until the next morning. Nothing concrete had been decided at the meeting, but Kurt was confident that a seed had been planted in the minds of the decision makers. In his gut he knew the plan was workable; if successful, it would dramatically change the outcome of the war.

The shadows lengthened and the air cooled as the sun was lost behind granite hills. Two of the African workers started a bonfire with dried acacia branches and broken-up wooden pallets. Kurt almost forgot that Saturday was braai night, and suddenly he was glad the DC-3 wasn't able to make it. The yellow flames of burning wood cast the JOC in shadow, transforming the camp into its netherworld counterpart. Animated figures in this shadow land lost human form, and appeared as puppets and marionettes, not moving of their own accord but manipulated by unseen hands and strings. Eating and drinking filled a primitive void, but also encouraged his mind to ponder the surreal scene.

"Humans are such simple creatures," Kurt thought. "Give them some hot food and beer and hell becomes heaven, even if it's just for awhile."

Kurt unconsciously searched the shadows for the Mad Medic, who usually seemed to make his appearances at night, but he was nowhere to be seen. Not that he really wanted to talk to the Medic. The Medic was disturbing, more than anyone else he'd ever met, but the crazy man did help in understanding this complex situation. For the first time in quite a while Kurt was thinking of peaceful things. Holding the child today triggered some latent feelings that began to well up within. The thoughts were unexpected and even unwelcome, but they couldn't be denied. How could peaceful thoughts and good feelings be frightening? Maybe that was the true definition of fear … change.

The beer and food made him very sleepy and his thoughts were no longer logical or coherent, but jumbled. Slowly he wandered back to an assigned room in the air force officers' quarters and, through the room's window, watched the flames of the cooking fire diminish to a dull red, then to near blackness. An anonymous verse came to mind: 'All light is followed by darkness, and all darkness is followed by light.' It was simplistic, but truth was always simple, and hidden. What about man? Kurt thought. Will we awaken from this darkness of our own creation to find a great light, and understanding? Or is this period of darkness never ending, a hole we ambitiously dug from which we will never emerge, a terminal punishment for our collective arrogance? There were no other thoughts before he drifted to sleep, eyes closing on the fire, now cooling to ashes, which he could see through the window.

Only dying embers of the once bright fire remained and everyone was asleep, except for two guards on the far perimeter of the camp. A solitary figure wandered towards the abandoned fire pit. Squatting down, he poked at the red ashes with a stick, making them change colour and flame again, then extinguish with a pulse. He enjoyed this deep quiet time that most people shunned or even feared. It provided opportunity for thought. Thinking was what he did best, although everyone who knew him would probably disagree. Dramatic changes were afoot. He was able to sense the subtleties as a hawk senses an air current, could feel it, even see things before they happened. For now it was his secret, but everyone would know soon enough.

He wandered off, his special shoes leaving no tracks in the dust, black clothing rendering him nigh on invisible. In this deepest of night, in the darkest of dark, the world became very clear. It was man who clouded the water of life with artificial complexities, pretence and self-deception. No, the world was a simple place, where two giant forces of good and evil battled for dominance within ... simple indeed. And they called him mad!

⌘

After a fitful sleep, Kurt awoke just before dawn and wandered around the compound. The African civilian employees were already up and busy cooking food, hauling supplies and preparing for another day. It was Sunday morning. That fact meant little in a combat area, but everyone tried to take things a little easier on Sunday even if it wasn't official policy. He begged a large mug of hot sweet tea from a smiling mess steward, then holding it carefully so not to spill any, wandered to the edge of the airfield to watch the sun rise on the granite cliffs.

It was just before eight when the JOC alarm sounded. Kurt was eating breakfast in the officers' mess tent with Murphy and several others. The alarm took them all by surprise. Usually there was some warning before the callout alarm. No Fireforce troops were on standby this morning, and there were no Daks on station.

"What the fuck, Murph?" Kurt said.

"I don't know," Murphy shrugged. "Maybe it's a local thing, some incident nearby."

"Let's see if they need us," Kurt said to all of the men at the table.

Kurt, Murphy, and the others walked quickly to the front of the TAC building.

The men were told to get their gear and reassemble next to the trucks. They would be transported by two Unimogs that were parked nearby. It was early and a rapid response was needed, so it was decided just to take who showed up first without regard to rank or unit assignment. Nobody seemed to know what the alert was about, but a local policeman had radioed the JOC minutes before in a panicked voice saying he needed backup, urgently.

The ride was short, only six kilometres from JOC Mtoko. Kurt had an instantly ominous feeling when they pulled off the road near a parked police Land Rover. In the road, the frame of a destroyed passenger vehicle lay on its side, still smoking. Twisted tan sheet-metal parts lay scattered in the roadway and ditches. A three foot diameter crater to one side of the gravel road marked the detonation of a vehicle mine. The rest of the details hit Kurt like a fall from great height. The horrific sight was impossible to assimilate or comprehend at once, and pall of unreality hung over the scene like a choking cloud of poisonous gas.

Kurt leapt off the truck and wandered through the debris that lay helter skelter. Human remains were scattered in bloody bits. It became clear what had happened. A group of guerrillas had lain in ambush, with a command-detonated mine, and blew up the vehicle as it passed over. The stunned and injured occupants were pulled out, and the unspeakable committed.

The woman lay naked and spread eagled in the centre of the road, by intent. Her abdomen had been slit open with a bayonet, and a boy child ripped out and dashed to the ground beside her, where it lay lifeless. Next to them was a splash of what looked and smelled like vomit. A tattered and bloody piece of pink cloth lay next to the woman's body, Cassie's doll. Kurt picked it up and held it. There was nothing recognizable left of the husband, Johan, only small pieces strewn about. The limbless and headless torso of the delicate little girl had been tossed up in a nearby acacia, her other parts lay around her mother. Reconstructing the scene, the little girl had likely been dismembered in front of her mother before she was killed by having her womb slit open, and her unborn child ripped from her.

The soldiers and police responding to the incident mostly stood in stunned silence; two or three wept openly. Nobody talked or moved except Kurt who slowly moved about the scene, head bent to the ground. To the others it looked like he was indifferent to the horror. Several times Kurt knelt down and felt the soil with his fingertips. What appeared to the others like impassive, almost casual interest was in reality the equivalent of giving a bloodhound a swatch of clothing belonging to a missing person. Within minutes Kurt knew how many perpetrators there had been, and who had done what. The information was programmed into his brain, like data flowing into the guidance system of a ballistic missile prior to launch.

When Kurt had finished he began to take his equipment off and lay it on the ground.

"Water bottles, I need water bottles," he said to no one in particular, his voice flat and lifeless.

Major Murphy turned to the assembled group of men.

"You heard him damn it, get water bottles!"

The order cured their paralysis and men scrambled to give Murphy several full canteens which Murphy carried to Kurt, and set them near his feet. Kurt nodded to him. Murphy avoided looking into Kurt's eyes; he feared what he would find.

A lieutenant colonel in the territorial reserve force, who happened to be the ranking officer in the hastily assembled group, decided to take charge of the situation. He walked towards Kurt, with a practiced authoritative air in his step. Murphy grabbed at the officer's shoulder.

"Don't go near him, sir!" Murphy said desperately.

The lieutenant colonel, a corporate executive for a large chemical company in civilian life, was one of the elite of society who was used to the world following his rules.

"You don't tell me what to do, Major!" he turned and spat at Murphy. "I am the senior officer here, and this will be run like a military operation!"

He then walked directly to Kurt who was putting his webbing back on, after he had added the water bottles to his vest and reconfigured it.

"Lieutenant, I order you to ... "

The officer never finished the sentence. Kurt was bent over, picking up his rifle; he straightened up and, like swatting an insect, he flicked the stock with a blur, striking the man in the jaw. There was a sharp 'crack' and the reservist officer flew backwards with the force, his jaw shattered and temporarily unconscious.

For the first time since their arrival, Kurt lifted his head and looked directly at the group of soldiers standing by the scene. To a man, it made them cold with fear.

"Major Murphy," said a disembodied voice, which cut through the silent men like a circular saw. "Get the team of Scout trackers here and tell them to follow my spoor. I will make my trail obvious. Tell them not to get closer than five-hundred metres. Their job will be to identify and log my kills. I will be moving too fast to do it."

With that, Kurt disengaged from the group and began to circle the site at a trot, head bent to the ground. He turned two complete circles, before disappearing into the bush.

"What the hell is he going to do by himself?" a sergeant from the group said aloud. "Do you think he can catch them?"

"God help anyone he catches," said another soldier softly.

"Those who did this have no God," Murphy said, his attitude suddenly that of the minister he never became. "Their reward for this bestial crime is to have a very dangerous man hot on their trail. Those vermin are dead already. They just don't know it yet."

# CHAPTER 22
## PURSUIT

The men were moving fast and had at least a two hour lead. The group wasn't even masking their tracks, just running straight for the Mozambique border. This wasn't unusual. In most cases the quarry would run very fast after leaving a scene to put precious distance between themselves and their pursuers. After gaining the separation needed to feel a little more secure, they would slow down. A tracking team normally took several hours to mobilize, and the group of insurgents were taking advantage of this. Distance was everything in this game, the further you were from your pursuers the better. In these early stages Kurt had to close as rapidly as possible; fresh spoor was much easier to follow.

A major risk to the tracker is to run headlong into the quarry. Some of the best trackers had been killed in this way. Kurt was trained as a child to track bear. Bears were smart animals that would ambush their pursuers if wounded and desperate. When being chased, a man would behave in a similar manner. When tracking dangerous quarry it was important to get close but not too close, or as his grandfather used to say, "Close enough to read, but not close enough to bleed." The saying seemed corny and simplistic, but it held a truth that might keep a tracker alive.

Before leaving the scene, Kurt assessed that there were seven people in the guerrilla unit he was pursuing. Based on the way they were travelling, there was a group of four, with a separate group of three. Those in the group of four were trainees, juveniles or beginners. Their spoor indicated that they were keeping an irregular pace. They would make a fast dash then slow down as they turned to look back over their shoulder. This was marked by a blurred print as a boot pivoted. The four ran in a cluster a short distance behind the other three.

The members in the group of three were pros. Their pace was rapid but even, and they didn't stop to look behind like the novices. In the early stages there was no need for them to check their back trail. This manoeuvre just slowed them down and diverted attention from obstacles and threats to the front, and on the flanks. Of the three experienced guerrillas, one stood apart from the other two. At first sight of the man's spoor Kurt feared he was imagining things. Trackless soles, a forward bearing thrust, a slight turn-in of the left foot ... the spoor were familiar. Every set of tracks was distinctive, like a fingerprint that couldn't be duplicated. He first recalled these same impressions in Angola, and now here. Who was it? Thinking about it would consume too much mental energy now; energy was precious and had to be conserved. At any rate he'd find out soon enough.

The morning was still cool in shadow but warming rapidly. Soon the overhead sun would begin to suck out moisture and overheat his body. Kurt forced down a canteen of water a couple of ounces at a time, even though he had no craving for it yet. It was better to load up on water early, even to over-hydrate a little than be pushed into deficit later. The human body, as well designed as it was, reacted slowly when subjected to extreme demands. When this happened, it could shut down unexpectedly and precipitously. Kurt tried to pace himself by setting a state of physical and mental exertion that could be sustained for many hours. Push too hard and fatigue and collapse would result, too little and the quarry would escape. Either option was unacceptable.

The seven men were still running together, but signs of growing fatigue could be detected in the four beginners. These signs included unsteadiness, temporary resting and speeding up to catch the others. These four were quickly becoming a liability to the group leaders, and Kurt anticipated they would be split off soon.

A large part of a tracker's job was being able to get inside the minds of the quarry. This was done by melding the physical signs with projected thought. It was a talent few could master. Kurt's grandfather told him that it was a trait that could only be developed by those born of 'hunting blood'. The talent was not science nor an acquired skill, but pure animal instinct.

Kurt tried consciously to 'project himself' into the minds of the quarry by asking what he would do in these circumstances. Initially this didn't work, and he sensed and saw nothing. Then he remembered his grandfather's advice on 'shadowing' game, getting inside their hot zone, tapping onto their energy. He allowed his mind to open up by letting it relax and go blank and he quickly scored a 'hit' ... a flow of warm energy that could only be coming from the pursued.

An image of the group of men formed, faded out and then reformed. This time the picture was in better focus, like a vivid dream. The leader of this group was the most distinct. He had dark hair and was Eastern European or Russian probably. There had been a similar but less definite image when playing cat and mouse in both Laos and Angola. This was the same man ... it had to be. By concentrating intensely on the picture, Kurt could almost feel what he was thinking, what he would do next.

A connection had formed. Two people were on the opposite ends of a live wire, the pursuer and pursued were now linked. Kurt could sense he was going to split the group, but where would the split take place? Vaguely he remembered a geological map of the area, with a low ridge line branching off towards the north-east. That would be the perfect place. It would happen there.

Just after midday the group leader would break off the four struggling novices, and tell them to head toward the north-east following the base of the ridge line. The other three, the leader and the two senior members, would then head straight for the Mozambique border ... and safety. This tactic presented Kurt with a dilemma. Did he stay on the spoor of the leadership and let the others go? Or did he go after the novices when the split took place, at the risk of losing the big three? It was an intentionally confounding situation.

There was a visceral need to bring down all of the perpetrators, and he knew that's what he would do. Defying all logic, he would try to make a clean sweep. An emotional part of the brain, over which there is little control, guided him to his decision leaving no doubt or room for further analysis. Pulling this off, however, would take every tracking skill he could muster, coupled with more than a little luck. The plan was now in place, whatever the outcome.

It was fortunate there was no need for Kurt to be covert and cover his spoor. This would have taken too much time while engaged in hot pursuit. The best of the Scout Trackers would be following in a few hours; they would have to be counted on to cover his back trail, if necessary. All his attention needed to be focused forward, towards the fleeing enemy. Kurt ran on with his pace adjusted for a long chase, eyes cast ten to twenty feet ahead. It was no technical challenge following seven men who were moving fast, especially with four novices who knew nothing about stealthy movement.

The group had halted so Kurt slowed. They'd stopped for a rest. For how long wasn't clear but even a few minutes would help close the gap. Food wrappers had been discarded and there was the strong smell of urine from men who were dehydrated and under stress. The first pungent smell of the quarry gave Kurt a rush, a prickly sensation and light-headedness that was unexpected. He felt something new happening to his mind and senses, a sensation that was both exhilarating and frightening.

⌘

The sun was high, and the shadow cast by his lone figure on the brown grass was short. Sweat saturated his clothes, hair and beard. Slowing the pace only slightly, he used the razor edge of the knife Joe had made to cut slits in his pants and shirt. The ventilation holes would help to cool his skin from the building heat. If he removed his clothing entirely, the sun would fry his exposed skin and thorns in the bush would shred it. Unfastening a water bottle he took frequent small sips of the contents so the water would be absorbed more efficiently, and discarded it when empty to save weight. He'd passed no urine since leaving that morning. This indicated inadequate hydration, but there was little more he could do.

Though there were a couple of cans of rations in his pack, eating was not an option. Food in the stomach would only redirect blood that could be better used by muscles and brain. For the next few hours he would run on reserves; as long as there was enough moisture in his body, he would manage. After running hard for another hour, the spoor appeared cleaner and more distinct. This meant Kurt was gaining on the group. Only an hour and very few kilometres separated them now, and the gap was rapidly closing. The quarry was tiring. The footprints of the four novices showed clumsy gait, stumbling, shuffling and staggering. Even the three leaders were showing signs of fatigue. The leader would soon have to split the up the group; otherwise they would not be able to keep ahead of their pursuer much longer.

The four beginners would be broken off and sent in a different direction. Their leader would know that the trackers would see this larger group as a sure kill, and would be tempted to follow them. The three pros would continue on a straight line towards the Mozambique border. At some point further on, the leader would set his two experienced partners up in an ambush to intercept any pursuers and then the leader alone, unencumbered by the others, could make his cross-border escape. At least that is what Kurt reasoned he'd do. This meant the group leader was prepared to sacrifice the rest of his team members in order to save himself. Kurt could also sense his target was somehow aware of his presence. He didn't know how or why, and there was no time to dwell on it now.

As on so many other occasions, there was only gut instinct to rely on. Neither Kurt nor the guerrilla leader realized that although on opposite sides of this conflict, they had much in common. Of the billions of people on the planet, in some ways no two men were more alike. Both had relinquished the comforts of modern civilization and regressed into a primal state, the hunter, the killer, the survivor. This bond linked them in ways that defied conventional explanation or human experience. At this moment they could sense one another through opposite sides of a looking glass. Fate had put them on a collision course twice before, but both knew this time would be the last.

The separation was approaching. In fact Kurt knew the split had already occurred. The seven men were now only around thirty-five minutes ahead of him. Crossing over a small rise the anticipated topography suddenly came into view. The four novices would be split there, and would follow the base of the hills towards the north-east. The leader would tell the four novices that if they moved hard and fast they would be safe. However, a bunch of tired beginners not pushed by experienced superiors would certainly stop to rest, almost immediately.

Without hesitation, Kurt headed forty degrees to the north to follow the group of beginners. A wrong guess would mean with near certainty he would lose the others permanently, but there was no other choice. Continuing to follow the existing spoor would end in a surprise ambush at worst. At best, only some of the perpetrators could be caught. This mission was an all or nothing proposition from the outset, with no compromise. Relying on blind faith in ancient instincts, he headed across the open, trackless bush.

⌘

Vladimir Cochican felt a presence now like he had never felt in his life; what was worse, he didn't know who or what it was. Maybe it was paranoia caused by age, bad nerves and so many close calls. His vision and hearing weren't what they used to be and he tired more easily. After this mission he would give it up and go back to Patrice

Lumumba University as an instructor. He had been offered that position years before but had turned it down; he far preferred the field, but there were too many ghosts lately.

As an ex-Spetnatz and KGB operative nothing in this life had truly frightened him, until now. In 1969, almost a decade before, Moscow sent him to Laos. It seemed that their allies, the Paphet Lao, and troops from the People's Republic of North Vietnam, who were in the country covertly, were having morale problems. People were dying strangely, ammunition and munitions stockpiles were blowing up and troops were in a state of panic. Some of the comrades were running away from their posts, while others refused to go into the jungle and fight, claiming ghosts and spirits were responsible. Vlad's assigned task was to locate the source of this trouble and eliminate it.

Born in a remote corner of Siberia just before the Great Patriotic War, his father was one of the anonymous bodies that littered the frozen landscape around Stalingrad. Like millions of others, his family had nearly starved and probably would have, except for young Vlad who had a talent for tracking and hunting animals in the stark barren landscape. He trapped, hunted and even stole, to keep his mother and five younger siblings fed. Once he even had to kill a man with a knife after he was caught stealing potatoes out of a garden. Vlad regretted nothing; life was about survival and he was a survivor. He did not enjoy butchering women and children, but the constant hardship in his formative years left his soul bleak; if the mission called for that sort of thing, he didn't argue. The dead had been exploitative capitalists at any rate, enemies of the people.

Vlad never found the source of the problem in Laos; he went into the jungle and tried to track the enemy but found only a ghost that never took form. Soon the strangeness stopped altogether and he stayed on until the great people's victory in Vietnam, two years ago.

He was back in Moscow less than a year when orders come through for Angola. Cuban comrades were supporting a people's revolution, and imperialist forces in the countries to the north were ambushing and killing the Cubans and their MPLA allies. Moscow received word that an attack was imminent at the base located at Vista del Sol. On the day that Vlad arrived there, he was told of the impending invasion and that a lone enemy soldier would be parachuting into an area south of the military base. The story sounded like someone's crazy imagination, but Vlad took several men and went to investigate. That is when things started to become very strange ... again.

Vlad was hit by a pistol bullet in the right side, his men were killed, the base was attacked and destroyed, a main bridge was blown up and his Cuban counterpart, Major Reyes, was shot and burned to death. The liberation forces had ambushed and destroyed the entire capitalist convoy of attackers, so who had done all of this? Vlad didn't know and was unable to find out. Moscow wasn't at all pleased with his performance and he was assigned to this God-forsaken place to redress his failure.

Moscow had allowed one last chance, more generous then usual when a disaster of this nature occurs. This time he must not fail.

Now the strange presence was back; stronger than before, much stronger. Vlad tried to suppress panicky thoughts, the normal gut reaction to a frightening unseen menace. Paranoia was an end result of living such a thankless and stressful life. It happened to others, good men whose minds crumbled from experiencing too much pressure for too long. He'd held up well ... until now.

Was there actually someone or something out there coming for him? Could the terrifying nightmares that had secretly plagued him since childhood have finally taken form and come to life? At the end of one's existence, did the real and dream worlds merge?

Vlad didn't know the answer to these questions; he doubted if anyone did. The thought of the answer terrified him more than any man or men ever had. Like most communists, he had no real religious upbringing, but superstition played a large part in rural Siberian life. Similar to all superstitions in all peoples, the stories and fables heard as a child centred on redemption, retribution, revenge and the righting of wrongs. Vlad knew both consciously and subconsciously that there were many wrongs to account for; he knew that sooner or later he would have to face the redeemer.

⌘

Kurt saw where he needed to go. The line of low hills that made up the ridge ran towards the north-east and then flattened out for a short distance before starting again. The gap formed was probably an ancient river valley that cut through the granite hills. The only logical route for the four novices would be to go through that pass and then head straight towards Mozambique.

He needed to reach the pass to determine if the group had arrived yet. If they were travelling quickly they would reach it first, but that was doubtful. Soon after the exhausted men split, they would rest for at least half an hour and maybe longer to get their wind back. In which case, Kurt planned to head directly into their predicted route and hit them head on. This was a risky tactic, but there really was no alternative. This strategy would save precious time and allow him to get back on the spoor of the big three, as quickly as possible.

Kurt took a compass bearing on the gap in the ridge line to establish navigation landmarks, and headed to his destination with as much speed as possible. Arriving at the pass just as the sun passed its zenith he rapidly cast for spoor but ascertained that no one had passed through recently. There were some animal tracks and two barefoot human prints but both were more than a day old. Convinced that his quarry hadn't made it this far, Kurt began to move south-west down the base of the ridgeline, in their anticipated direction. Slowing the pace slightly, he now tried to heighten his awareness using every physical sense. The only warning would be when the enemy suddenly appeared to his front, and then he would have only seconds to react.

The only advantage Kurt had over his quarry was surprise, but any surprise would be momentary. The guerrillas would suspect that they were being tracked, but had no way of knowing that their pursuer would be able to predict their course and approach them from the opposite direction. He could lay in wait and ambush the party as they moved towards him, but that would cost too much in the way of time. After dealing with the four novices, there were still the others, and come nightfall it would become nearly impossible to follow their trail.

An old game track skirted the southern base of the ridge line. For millennia, animals had followed this path of least resistance on their seasonal migrations, so the walking was easiest there. An experienced soldier would never move on such an obvious path, especially in daylight. These four, devoid of leadership, would take the easiest route and follow the game trail. Kurt paralleled the trail, walking in the bush about five metres to the south. Close enough to see anyone on the trail, but also far enough away to use the intervening bush as cover. Half an hour later, obvious movement was heading his way.

Kurt froze. A solitary man was walking tactically, the muzzle of his rifle held to the left as he scanned both sides of the trail. Kurt's hope had been that the group would be moving together in a disorganized cluster. That would have made things easier but, unfortunately, that was not the case. The other three soldiers weren't visible but they were most likely following behind, checking their back trail. Unfortunately the bush was too thick to see any distance in that direction. Making a spontaneous decision, Kurt headed straight towards the man on the trail.

The point at which the man became aware of Kurt's approach was when he was less than two metres away. When the guerrilla began to raise the AK-47 to his shoulder, Kurt fired one shot from the FNC that caught the point man in the upper chest. This shot was followed by a rapid second bullet that blew the man's skull apart. The soldier reeled backwards and fell sprawling across the dirt trail. Kurt kept his momentum and stepped on to the trail breaking into a full run down the path he hoped would lead to the other three. Seconds later, he encountered two men standing astride the path looking stunned, rifles still pointed sideways into the bush.

Both of the guerrillas saw Kurt coming, albeit too late. Each man was double tapped with two shots to the midsection and they spun from the impacts. The man on the right automatically pulled the trigger of his AK with the barrel still pointed into the bush beside the trail. Bark and dirt exploded and rained down on the scene from the impact of the wild full-auto fire. Releasing the rifle, the soldier slumped to the ground.

He didn't stop to check the two kills. The shots seemed like solid hits, he would have to trust his aim. There was still a fourth man somewhere; finding him was essential. Kurt ran up the trail for another thirty metres scanning furiously in all directions, but saw nothing. The trail was still and quiet. The recent shots made his ears ring, which masked soft sounds. His vision would have to suffice. Maybe there were only three? Maybe the other man went with ...

A small sharp metallic click found his ears, a magazine or safety catch. It was on the north side of the trail ... behind him. Kurt turned just as an AK-47 flashed a few metres away. The first bullet in the string dug a furrow on his left side, catching and fracturing the floating rib. Fortunately, a major flaw with the AK on full auto is its tendency to go high and right if the rifle wasn't held down firmly. The second round nicked his left upper arm and the remaining ten or twelve rounds all went high into the trees. He dived into cover towards the sound of the shots. The first instinct was to close with the attacker as quickly as possible, but colliding with the ground made his side scream with pain.

Seriously injured men behave in different ways dictated by their character. Some cry out, some want to quit, some carry on but seek cover. Kurt's reaction was to eliminate his opponent before his wounds killed him or made him too weak to fight. The thought raced through his mind, "If this was the last play in the last game of your life, then make it a winning one."

Kurt raised his head above the low ground cover in a blatant game of chicken, and detected his quarry immediately. An inexperienced soldier would be rattled by a contact of this nature, and the adrenaline rush would make it difficult to re-acquire a target quickly. An AK barrel twitched above the low vegetation and with the sights of the FNC placed slightly to the right ... *bang*! Kurt then rolled rapidly three or four times in spite of the searing pain, and came to rest with his rifle pointing in the direction of his opponent, and waited.

A low moaning, that could only mean a hit, came from that direction followed by thrashing in the undergrowth. The gun barrel was no longer visible. Kurt threw himself to his feet and crouching low, bounded directly at his opponent, despite the agony, with the FNC shouldered and thrust forward. A few seconds later he was standing over the man who had shot him.

The soldier wasn't really a man at all but a boy sixteen or seventeen at most. He lay on his back looking up at Kurt with wild and fearful eyes; the AK lay beside him. The single FNC round had chipped the AK's butt stock and gone into the soldier's shoulder, shattering the ball joint and breaking the right clavicle. The soldier made no attempt to resist or fight when Kurt knelt beside him.

"Do you understand me?"

"Yes, suh," the injured boy sputtered.

"Then listen to me closely and answer me truthfully. Why did you do that to those people?" Kurt asked, his voice flat and toneless.

"Suh, it was a terrible thing. I did not want to do that, but they made me do it."

To Kurt's ear this boy obviously was educated and intelligent. He should still be in school. What was he doing here? Was he doing this against his will?

"Who made you?" Kurt asked him.

"The others, suh, the one they call Comrade Vlad," the boy replied.

"Comrade Vlad?" Kurt asked with some surprise. "Is he a Russian, a foreigner?

"Yes, I think so, suh. He is the one who made us do those terrible things. I threw up, suh, I was sick, they laughed at me."

Kurt remembered the stain on the road near the woman's body that smelled of vomit.

"My arm hurts, suh, so much."

"I know it does, and if you answer a few questions for me I will give you some medicine that will take the pain away."

"Yes, suh."

"Where were the others going when they split off from your group?" Kurt asked.

"To Mozambique, suh. I heard them talking."

"What did they say exactly, do you remember?"

"Comrade Vlad was worried, suh. He knew someone was coming."

"He knew I was coming? How did he know that?" Kurt asked, sounding confused.

"I ... I don't know, suh. But he knew, he acted very strange, the others speak of the tokoloshe."

"The tokoloshe?" Kurt asked. "I've never heard of it, what is it?"

The wounded boy thought for a second before replying.

"It is what you call in English a spirit, suh, an evil spirit that comes at night to people who do bad things."

"A ghost then?" Kurt asked. "That redeems for evil?"

The boy shook his head but stopped quickly when it caused pain in his arm.

"Not a ghost, suh, it is a real thing," the boy said grimacing in pain. "Are you a tokoloshe, suh?"

Kurt pulled up the left side of his jacket and showed the wounded boy the evil purple ravine that was weeping blood, and had stained the left side of his shirt and trousers.

"Do spirits bleed, son?"

"I ... I don't know, suh ... I never seen one before."

Kurt took an ampoule of morphine sulphate out of his medical pouch and injected the fifteen grain contents into the boy's good arm. Kurt then withdrew his ivory-handled knife causing the boy to cringe with fear, but only used it to cut away the shirt around the boy's wound. The small entrance the bullet had made was no indication of the trauma it caused inside. Sprinkling a packet of sulfur powder on the open areas of the wound, Kurt tied a pressure bandage in place, and with a green cloth cravat stowed in the leg of his trouser pocket, bound the boy's arm across his chest.

"Son, in a couple of hours a team of Scout trackers will come this way. I'm going to move you onto the trail, and I want you to stay there. When you see them don't fight them or try to escape, because they will shoot you. Co-operate with them and answer all of their questions honestly and they will treat you well and take you to a hospital. When I get back, I will let them know that you helped me."

"Yes, suh," the boy said, now starting to breathe deeply and heavily as the narcotic took effect.

"Here, wear this," Kurt said as he took off the leather necklace with the bear claw, warthog tooth and Navaho charm. He put it around the wounded boy's neck so it could easily be seen.

"The trackers know that this belongs to me. Tell them I gave it to you and it will help convince them. If you survive, I want you to promise to go to school and study very hard. You are a smart young man, and can do much more for your people and country as an educated person than as a thug with a gun ... alright? Think of all of this as a lesson, as hard as that seems."

"Yes, suh, and thank you for not killing me. But, suh ... "

"Yes?"

"What will you do?" the young soldier asked.

He looked away from the boy who was sitting on the trail propped up against a tree. Kurt knew what he meant, but he couldn't answer him to his face.

"Comrade Vlad is expecting me, and I wouldn't want to disappoint him."

The boy looked up at Kurt to ask another question, but he was gone.

⌘

Kurt's side alternated between throbbing and scalding pain, so he stopped briefly to cleanse the wound with an alcohol swab and put some sulpha powder on it. The bleeding had almost stopped. He dared not use morphine because it would dull his senses. Taking the game trail, he followed it to within two hundred metres of where the group had split up, looped east for approximately one kilometre, then turned south, hoping to intersect with the spoor of the remaining guerrillas who were heading for Mozambique. This was the difficult part, requiring both luck and skill to pick up the trail again, especially when cutting across their tracks at a right angle.

The leader, now identified as Comrade Vlad, would try to move covertly from this point on, especially if he had dumped his other companions and was now travelling alone. Just prior to reaching the anticipated point of picking up the enemy spoor, Kurt began to cast. Locking his eyes to the ground he knew that if an enemy saw him now, he would be vulnerable. It took nearly half an hour of intense study of the earth and zig-zagging, but finally he discovered faint impressions made by smooth anti-tracking soles. Vlad was indeed alone.

Kurt wanted to close with Vlad first and then come back for the other two. However, doing that would expose him, and the two remaining soldiers could come from behind while he was closing with the Russian. The Scout trackers were still hours away and wouldn't be there to cover his rear.

Vlad must have set up the other two soldiers in an ambush position and told them to wait for him after the two groups split. They would be told to stay in position for a certain number of hours before following Vlad into Mozambique. Vlad was wily and totally ruthless. He'd just constructed a two-sided trap that would allow him to escape while probably sacrificing his men.

Kurt took out his knife and notched a sapling near one of Vlad's prints, then turned and followed his trail in reverse. The two soldiers, lying in ambush, would not suspect someone approaching from the east, but they would be on high alert anyway. Moving quickly for five hundred metres, Kurt slowed and then began to scan the terrain for possible ambush locations which Vlad would have chosen. Dealing with professionals was always easier than dealing with novices. The actions of pros could be predicted with a high degree of certainty, while those of amateurs could not. Kurt had a bullet groove on his left side as proof of that.

At a point he estimated to be around two-hundred metres past where the split occurred, Kurt saw the ideal ambush position located in a small clump of trees on a slight hill that was overlooking the trail. Circling slowly and quietly, he wanted to get behind it, where there was less cover. Kurt heard low voices, and stealthily moved closer. The two guerrillas were sitting in the trees eating rations and talking quietly. They glanced to their front regularly, but seemed more absorbed in their discussion than in maintaining security.

Taking out these two was like shooting fish in a barrel, but with the horror on the road that morning still fresh in Kurt's mind, he had no compunction. Sighting behind the ear of the nearest guerrilla, he squeezed the trigger of the FNC. A halo of red mist formed when the bullet struck. The second man tried to dive away, but had no time to respond before a bullet entered the back of his neck and went out through his throat. The second man was still alive when Kurt stood over him. He was paralyzed from the neck down, and gasped as a mixture of air and arterial blood spurted from the wound. The soldier's eyes blinked rapidly at the figure that towered above. His last thought was that the face had no anger, no pity, no solace, nothing at all.

⌘

Vlad heard the shots, but because of the distance and the echo it was difficult to tell if there were one or two. The reports sounded lighter and higher-pitched than an AK. Rhodesians used the FN battle rifle, which fired a larger cartridge, which was even louder but then again, with distance, the terrain can play tricks with the sound. These shots sounded like those from an M-16, which Vlad had heard on many occasions. But there were no Americans here.

As it was explained to him, his mission was to ambush and kill a renegade soldier of the Rhodesian Army who was causing the KGB problems. Like a splash of cold water, it all suddenly came together. Laos, Angola, this mission, all with the same strange feeling. Vlad involuntarily shivered and began to move more rapidly. His original intent had been to circle back and take out the man or men on his trail, but he quickly discarded that idea. Now his only thought was to get away. He could afford to be stealthy no longer. He needed distance, distance to escape from what was coming.

⌘

Kurt ran back to the marked tree and began to follow Vlad's spoor towards the Mozambique border. The dead guerrillas had some water which he'd consumed. He didn't need any extra weight. Following the Russian's tracks was hard in the diminishing light. Vlad was being careful and minimized his trail. Several times he almost lost the spoor, but by slowing down and casting, he found the tracks and continued the pursuit. The sun was on the descent and only two hours of daylight remained, with only an hour of good tracking light. At this pace Vlad would outrun him. The thought of him escaping stuck in Kurt's throat overriding the fatigue and the pain of the wound.

Thirty minutes later the tracks suddenly changed. A blurred print indicated Vlad had turned there and stood to watch or listen. This was out of character for someone trying to move covertly. Had he heard the shots, the shots that told him that his back trail was now exposed and he was on his own? From that point on the spoor was obvious: Vlad had decided to run for his life. Kurt knew that this turn of events was both good and bad. There wouldn't be a problem following the trail, but now it would definitely be a race against time.

Slowing his pace only slightly, he emptied what remained in the last water bottle and discarded it. Spare ammunition and some other non-essentials he also dropped. The Scout trackers would pick them up. Kurt set his eyes ten feet ahead and began to run.

⌘

Vlad reached the border just as the setting sun was casting long shadows in the dense tropical hardwoods. One of the safe corridors across the border minefield was only a jog of one kilometre north, according to information provided by the 'source'. The crossing proved uneventful thanks to this information. Without it, there would have likely been one more legless skeleton littering this no man's land.

When he reached Mozambique, Vlad felt a wave of relief. The exhaustion and tension of the day caught up all at once. It was growing dark, and the pursuer would have to wait until next light before following his spoor. With the border minefield behind him, it felt like he was now on the other side of an impenetrable wall. No-one would cross a minefield in the dark.

Vlad pushed himself for several kilometres before he would let himself rest. He knew when he sat down that he would not get up again soon. The ZANLA base at Chioco on the Luia River was still another half day's heavy walking, and he did not want to navigate at night in his present state of exhaustion. A rocky outcrop with an overhang that afforded protection from three sides looked inviting, so he sat down in the natural alcove. Any animal attacking from his front could be easily dispatched with his AK. Once sitting down, his legs turned to lead. Vlad reached into his pack for some ration bars and water but, before he found them, he collapsed into a deep dreamless sleep.

The forest was in total darkness and deathly silent when Vlad awoke. Somewhere in the distance a big cat roared. He reached for his AK, which he'd left propped up on the rocky wall, but his grasping hand struck nothing. Reaching again he felt something soft, like a small animal. He recoiled expecting to be bitten or for the animal to scurry away, but nothing happened. Vlad reached out again, slowly grasped the object and brought it closer. It was light and inanimate, like a toy, a child's toy, a doll. As he realized what it was it began to burn in his hand like hot acid. He flung it away and screamed out loud.

Vlad was having a nightmare. So many others had disturbed his peace through the years. Vivid hallucinations like this were caused by lack of sleep and stress. The dreams when you seemed awake, but you were helpless and unable to move. But he could move, and he reached out again and touched the AK, just a little farther away than expected. It was all just a nightmare. He would stay put until first light holding the rifle, then at dawn would walk to the safety of Chioco.

In the dim starlight a new object appeared. It was directly in front, like a tree stump or a rock, but it moved. Vlad rubbed his eyes and the form slowly took shape, a trunk and a head ... then a voice.

"It's time to pay for your sins, Comrade."

Vlad swung the muzzle of his AK-47 on to the form and pulled the trigger in one swift move ... *CLICK*. The impotent sound echoed off the rocks and trees, like metallic death.

Vlad manually cycled the action again, chambering a new round to replace the dud or empty chamber. *CLICK*. The sound seemed louder this time.

"It works better with this, comrade," the voice in the darkness said.

*Ding,... Ding,... Ding*, an AK-47 firing pin bounced off the rocks next to Vlad.

Vlad let out an animal sound, hate coupled with terror, and leapt up to swing at the form with the butt of the rifle.

Kurt had anticipated this reaction and stepped aside, grabbed Vlad's arm, and used the Russian's own momentum to smash him into the rocks face first. Vlad lay on the ground stunned and moaning. Kurt unsheathed the razor-edged combat knife and made several precise cuts. Triceps, tendons, Achilles' tendons and the hamstring group on both sides, being careful not to sever the large arteries than ran close by. The knife was so sharp and the cuts were so rapid that the stunned Vlad felt little pain. When he recovered slightly and tried to move, his limbs were useless. He cried out in gurgling agony, and an unimagined fear.

Kurt grabbed the Russian and rolled him over on his back, then squatted down so their faces were only a foot apart.

"You are such a brave soldier, Comrade Vlad," Kurt almost whispered. "You butcher women and children and condemn your fellow soldiers to death, so you can escape. Yes, what a truly brave man you are. Now, Comrade, we will see how brave you *really* are."

"How do you know me?" Vlad screamed, his lips frothing. "You are not a man, you cannot be. I don't know you!"

"I am grateful that your terrorist training included English, Comrade," Kurt said. "I don't know Russian, nor do I care to learn it. But you know me alright ... you do know me."

Kurt cut the front of Vlad's combat shirt and laid bare his chest. The light was insufficient to see any detail so Kurt felt Vlad's chest with his fingertips and quickly found the healed welt on his left chest wall.

"I thought so ... that wasn't a good shot, was it?"

"You are American," Vlad screamed with a voice that was growing raw and hoarse. "You imperialist pig!"

"Isn't that a coincidence?" Kurt replied. "That was exactly what that Cuban officer said in Angola just before he was roasted. What was his name ... Reyes? Was he a friend of yours, Comrade Vlad?"

Vlad tried to swing his arm at Kurt but it was a sluggish club, and he screamed in agony at the effort.

"Are you going to burn me too, you Yankee pig?"

"No, Comrade, "Kurt said almost indifferently. "That would be a waste of my time, starting a fire. Like all good soldiers, I believe in using the resources at hand. There is a female leopard close by. She's probably desperate to feed her cubs, since the war has run off most of the game. I thought you would do nicely, and I can't think of a better fate for your evil self than to become cat shit in the jungle."

Vlad shook and foamed and tried to spit at Kurt but due to the strategically placed wounds, he couldn't move.

"And one more thing, Comrade," Kurt said his voice changing from detachment to pure menace. "Since you didn't live your life as a man, I don't think you should die as one."

Kurt took the knife and slit open the top of Vlad's trousers and ripped them down to the knees, exposing Vlad's bulky uncircumcised penis and scrotum nearly buried in coarse back hair. Kurt grasped both and with one stroke of the blade they came away in a welling of blood. Kurt flung the tissue into Vlad's face as the Russian howled with a final curdling agony.

"Leopards are used to eating primates," Kurt said, almost academically. "They have done it for millions of years. If you're lucky she won't leave you waiting long, and I hope she doesn't choke on your foul carcass."

Kurt was gone. Twenty minutes later, Vladimir Cochican, weak from blood loss and terrible pain, smelled fetid breath and looked up to see a pair of huge round eyes that glowed brilliant yellow, even on the darkest night.

# CHAPTER 23
## REVELATION

"We are very lucky to have found him alive, sir. In another few hours he would have been dead."

The Scout tracker team leader was talking to Major Murphy. They had located Kurt and called in the Casevac chopper that morning. Murphy nodded glumly.

"Good job, Sergeant, where exactly did you find him?"

"Just on this side of Corridor Kilo, sir," the tracker said. "We believe he positioned himself there because he knew that's where we would have to go through the minefield. He was unconscious, a real mess. He had lost a lot of blood and was so dehydrated that his skin felt like dry paper."

"What else did you find?" Murphy asked.

"We found five bodies and one wounded ZANLA terrorist, sir."

"Wounded?" Murphy asked, quizzically.

"Yes sir," the tracker replied. "It looked as though Lieutenant Christianson shot him in an exchange of gunfire and then patched him up. He's a young man. Says he was abducted from a school in the Umtali area last year by ZANLA. So far he has been very helpful. We moved him to Marandellas Hospital for surgery. He had a badly damaged shoulder."

"What information has the wounded man provided?" Murphy asked.

"It was jumbled and mostly nonsense at first, sir. He was in a lot of pain and on morphine. There was talk of the Tokaloshe and a Comrade Vlad or something."

"Comrade Vlad!" Murphy's voice rose in intensity. "Did he mean Vladimir Corinchin?"

I don't know, sir. Maybe we can drive over there and ask him."

"We heard that bastard was operating here," Murphy said. "Was he one of the bodies?"

"No sir, the bodies were all ZANLA; we are trying to ID them now."

"Sergeant, you said that you found Christianson near the Mozambique border before he crossed over?" Murphy asked.

"No, sir, it looks like he went over and then returned by the same route."

"He got him then," Murphy mumbled.

"Sir?"

"Christianson would have never come back if he hadn't found him. Corinchin is dead. How is Kurt doing?" Murphy nodded in the direction of the Mtoko hospital.

"You can check with the doc, sir, but I think he'll be alright with some more blood, fluids and rest. The doc doesn't want anyone to disturb him right now. As soon as he is stabilized, he will be moved to Salisbury."

⌘

Kurt was only vaguely aware of being lifted and of movement, like glimpses from a vague dream. Every time he surfaced even slightly, the pain returned, so he submerged again, to where there was no pain and no dreams. It was evening when his eyes finally opened, but little other movement was possible. He was alone, lying in the side ward with only dimmed lights. An IV bag hung on a pole stand to the right, with a see-through drip chamber beneath, *drip ... drip ... drip*. A drop fell every three seconds, mesmerizing him.

Then footsteps ... not the purposeful foot falls of a soldier but measured, hushed and incredibly even-paced footsteps that took longer to arrive than they should have. The steps ceased and Kurt felt the presence. Then the voice, that cut like a knife and left his insides exposed. Barely being able to move, Kurt had no choice but to listen.

"Have you had enough yet, Kurt?" the voice said. "You can't win this war by yourself, you know."

Kurt tried to speak, but his tongue was thick and clumsy, and his throat raw and inflamed.

"I missed your smiling face, Medic. Where have you been?" Kurt managed.

"I've been around, Lieutenant. I try not to get in the way ... mostly," the Mad Medic said.

"I guess I pulled through, didn't I?" Kurt tried to smile but his face felt frozen.

"Just," the Medic said while adjusting the drip rate to flow more slowly. "You were about as close as a person can go to the other side, but you are a remarkable physical specimen."

"Thanks, Medic, but I'd appreciate that comment more if it was coming from a woman." Kurt tried to laugh at his own joke but only coughed weakly.

"Humour has never been one of your strong points, Kurt, I'd try to refrain. By the way, I saw you spared that wounded boy," the Mad Medic said.

"So they found him." Kurt attempted to lift his head off the pillow, but couldn't.

"Yes they did, and he is in pretty good shape. He was cleaned up and went to the regional hospital for surgery. What made you do that?" the Medic asked.

"Do what, Medic?" Kurt asked.

"Save his life ... not kill him."

Kurt was silent for a few seconds. He tried to think about the question but his thoughts were cloudy, he couldn't concentrate.

"I don't know. I thought it was the right thing to do at the time, I suppose."

"The right thing to do." The Medic mulled the words. "Yes, it was the right thing to do. Focus on that, Kurt. Think about it very hard; you may be surprised where it leads you."

Kurt attempted a response but the Mad Medic was already gone. That was odd; he'd heard no footsteps when he left.

⌘

It was the following day before they transferred Kurt to the Andrew Fleming Hospital in Salisbury. Though feeling strong enough to leave, the staff insisted that he stay for several more days of observation. Some of the doctor's comments included concerns about kidney output as a result of blood loss and severe dehydration which had almost resulted in acute renal failure. However, his renal output was now improving daily. When friends from the Scouts and RLI heard about the hospital stay, they came to visit, much to the consternation of the hospital staff.

Their primary motivation was not to lift his spirits, but to check out the abundant nurses in training at the facility. Bluie showed up with a bottle of single malt Scotch that was obvious contraband, because there wasn't any legally imported. To Bluie giving away a bottle of this was equivalent to giving up his first-born son. Since there was no place in the hospital room to hide the booze and it was banned from the building, Kurt thanked Bluie profusely and said to save it until his release. When Bluie smiled, Kurt knew the whole thing was a scam. The Aussie had collected from all of the guys to buy the bottle, and now he intended to keep it.

When released from the hospital several days later, the doctors put Kurt on 'light duty', which meant no field operations or other heavy work for at least a month, maybe longer. He spent some of the time running and using the weight room at the RLI Barracks. These activities were hardly light duty by definition, but his physical condition had deteriorated remarkably in a short time and had to be restored quickly, or it could be lost forever. Kurt also went to Inkomo several days of the week, where details of the massive assault on the twin camps proposed earlier were being formulated. The seeds of that idea planted in the officers' minds were starting to sprout.

In the course of human history original ideas are mostly an inspiration that comes from the mind of a single person, not from collective thinking as commonly assumed. Ideas are thrown to the winds where most evaporate and die. Occasionally an idea takes root and is nourished by others in an environment of need, and timing. Kurt's proposed operation was, at first, considered far-fetched but quickly Operation Valkyrie became the centrepiece of military planning.

A piecemeal defensive approach to insurgency warfare was doomed to fail. Everyone knew this truth, but few would admit it. Many of the senior officers in the Rhodesian military were young soldiers who had cut their teeth during the communist insurgency in Malaya in the early 1950s. Successful techniques developed and practiced there, including the establishment of 'protected villages' for the native population, combined with tracking and small-unit operations, were adopted in Rhodesia. This was done due to the many similarities in the conflicts, and the individual military experiences of the planners.

There were also major differences, however, between the conflicts in Malaya and this one. While Malaya was a localized insurgency and played on a small stage at a time when the world was still reeling from WWII, Rhodesia was a child of the 'cold war' where surrogates of the superpowers vied for dominance globally. Where Malaya was isolated in a small corner of Asia, Rhodesia was right in the middle of a huge expanse of Africa where sanctuary was given to hostiles on three of the four borders. Any hope of victory against such odds would have to be made with a bold and dramatic offensive akin to the 1944 invasion of Normandy, or Macarthur's Inchon invasion. A quid pro quo, politically correct, measured response would guarantee defeat, and that was the approach the Rhodesians had been pursuing.

During the military strategy planning sessions involving Kurt, it became apparent that there were two major shortfalls in the Rhodesian military's conduct of the guerrilla war. Firstly, there was a shortage of accurate and viable intelligence regarding the enemy and secondly, there was the lack of vision regarding immediate and long-term goals. In order to pit a smaller attacking force against a numerically superior and entrenched opponent, accurate and timely intelligence collection and interpretation was crucial.

Not only was good intelligence required, it was vital to act on it quickly and with extreme force. Intelligence lost its value in a very short time and soon became worthless. There was little or no room for error when your forces were outnumbered ten to one. Success would depend on complete surprise and flawless deployment and execution. There would be little time for errors or re-evaluation once the soldiers hit the ground. Battles would be won or lost in minutes or hours, no more.

⌘

The large ZANLA headquarters and administrative support camps at Atibo and Kitaya were beyond flight range of the aging Alouette helicopters. Because of this, staging and fuelling areas would have to be set up deep in Mozambique without enemy knowledge. Some information on the camps was provided by Canberra and Vampire photo-reconnaissance aircraft, but both complexes hugged the Tanzanian border, and further activity risked alerting regional air defences. The two camps were also situated in thick east African bush, and high flying aerial photographs were not able to resolve the detail necessary to support a surgical ground attack. It became apparent that more detailed intelligence of the targets was required, or the proposed raids could not take place.

Interrogation of captured ZANLA prisoners was of some help, but information obtained in this manner was generally inconsistent, contradictory, unverifiable and often too old to be of much value. Kurt privately dwelled on the problem before unexpectedly walking to the front of the planning group during one of their sessions.

"We are going to have to conduct ground reconnaissance, gentlemen; it is the only way," he stated bluntly.

"I agree that this would be preferable," Colonel Ainsley replied, "but I don't think it's possible because of the great distance from our borders. Our boys would be beyond our ability to extract them if things went wrong."

Kurt had lately, and only privately, called Ainsley 'Colonel Negativity' because of his consistently negative attitude.

"Yes, sir, I realize that," Kurt replied. "I considered taking an element of the Scout tracking team in to reconnoitre the Atibo and Kitaya camps, but I thought it would be best if I went in alone."

"I don't think that is such a wise idea, Lieutenant Christianson," Ainsley said. "You've done this sort thing in the past I know but ... there is too much riding on this proposed operation."

"Exactly, sir," Kurt responded. "That is why we need the best intelligence for this plan to succeed. "The highest quality information generally comes from a single source. I've found that when you start pooling information, it becomes degraded."

"Do you think you are the only one capable of doing this, Lieutenant?" Ainsley questioned. "That seems a little arrogant."

"No, sir, I'm not saying that at all," Kurt said, trying to stay calm and not rising to Ainsely's bait. "I just know what I can do and I am confident I can get the job done correctly. If I didn't think so, I wouldn't be proposing it."

"Well, I ... " Ainsley began but was cut off in mid-sentence by Major Murphy.

"Lieutenant Christianson, would you be kind enough to leave the room while we discuss this?"

"Be glad to, sir," Kurt replied as he walked out of the briefing room, shutting the door behind him.

Murphy was still on his feet and he turned to Ainsley.

"Look, let's stop this arguing among ourselves. Lieutenant Christianson conceived and planned the Pungwe raid which has been by far our largest success to date. None of us in this room including me would have come up with a concept like that. It was a bit too daring and bold for our blood. I say we either have to trust him and go with his ideas, or not do this operation at all. The bunch of us jabbering about details will do nothing to increase our effectiveness, and will very likely just make things worse." Murphy then sat down, and the room was silent.

"Major Murphy," Ainsley rose from his chair, "would you trust the opinion of this young lieutenant more than the combined experience sitting in this room?"

Murphy stared at Ainsley, knowing that he had been set up; no matter how he answered the question it would come out wrong.

"Let me put it this way, Colonel," Murphy replied in a restrained manner, "having worked with Lieutenant Christianson on many occasions in the past months, I would trust his opinions beyond any doubt."

"I agree Lieutenant Christianson has many strengths, Major," Ainsley replied, "But let's not get carried away with this. Developing our entire military strategy around the capabilities of a single junior officer is preposterous. Wars aren't fought in this manner; they never have been and never will be."

"It's just that … well, sir, I worked with Lieutenant Christianson for some time now and there is a feeling I have that is difficult to explain. I've never experienced anything like it before in my life."

"And just what is that exactly, Major?" Ainsley asked.

"As I said, sir, it is hard to define, but Christianson is a very gifted man. Like Mozart was to music or Picasso was to painting, it's beyond our abilities to comprehend. All we see is the end product after the fact, like the Pungwe raid. He is able to see the best solution to a military problem without analysis, without discussion and without argument, debating, or input from others. Christianson just *sees* it, and then spends the rest of his time just trying to get *us* to see it."

"Do you really believe that, Major?" Ainsley coughed. "Or have you just succumbed to the influence of this man? I don't see how one very junior officer, an American at that, could be wiser than the whole senior staff of the Rhodesian military. This isn't music and it isn't painting; it is a very complex interaction among experienced military professionals."

"I know what I am saying may sound illogical, sir. Nonetheless, sir, there is no denying the facts, his performance speaks for itself. We military men are trained and schooled to be logical thinkers and use deductive reasoning. When something like this happens, it lies outside the boundaries of our understanding, beyond our comfort zone. We have a natural tendency to reject things we don't understand, but in this case, sir, we do so at our own peril."

"Just what do you mean by that, Major Murphy?" Ainsley responded.

"Sir," Murphy hesitated, "you already know I am a religious man; I studied in a seminary and was taught by Jesuits so that background may colour the way I think. I try not to let that interfere with my decision making, but I believe most of us are spiritual in some way."

"Yes, I follow what you are saying, Major," Ainsley said, "but what does that have to do with Lieutenant Christianson? You're not implying that … "

"I'm afraid I am, sir," Murphy said as he looked Ainsley in the eyes and then turned to make eye contact with all of the officers sitting in the room. "I truly believe, gentlemen, that in the person of Lieutenant Christianson may lie our only hope of defeating our enemies, given the dire circumstances we find ourselves in. I felt it the first time I met him and heard him speak. That's why I supported him on the Pungwe operation, which most of you initially opposed."

"But the Pungwe raid was a combined effort, Major," another senior staff officer said. "I know Lieutenant Christianson participated, but … "

Murphy held up his hand, causing the officer to stop talking in mid-sentence.

"No, sir," Murphy shook his head. "Lieutenant Christianson, conceived and planned the whole operation himself; he just didn't want the credit for it. He was even responsible for the design and construction of the gun trucks. And as you all know, Christianson single-handedly tracked down and eliminated Vladimir Corinchin and his gang that butchered the local farming family. The man is a modern military genius, perhaps another Alexander the Great or Julius Caesar ... and he works for us. Think about it, gentlemen."

There was a pause, and nobody spoke for at least a minute. Murphy knew he had laid himself wide open. The statement he had just made sounded bizarre, almost sacrilegious considering his position and background, but there was no sign of rejection or scoffing from his audience.

Ainsley was scowling and about to say something but Colonel Donovan stood up, which pre-empted him.

"What you are saying may sound a bit extreme, Major, but I suppose we should consider all of our options, especially if we have such a ... great resource in our midst. Do you agree, gentlemen, that we should continue preparations for Operation Valkyrie?

There were murmurs among the officers in the room. The only one not talking was Ainsley, who sat with his arms crossed. After a few moments of discussion, no further objections were voiced.

"Then I will send the plan forward to General Wallis," Donovan said. "I think he will buy into the idea. Unless you hear otherwise through official channels, let's consider the plan tentatively a go."

Unknown to the assembled officers, Ainsley, as chief of intelligence, had had a meeting with General Wallis the day before and attempted to protest the proposed operation. To Ainsley's chagrin, Wallis was strongly in favour of it, and could not be dissuaded. It was a defeat for Ainsley but by manoeuvring as he did, he would manage to save face by making it look as though he sold the difficult plan to General Wallis, even if he was personally opposed to it. That still didn't placate his annoyance over the whole affair. He felt excluded from the decision-making process, and the whole venture seemed to be spinning out of control.

⌘

When Kurt walked back into the meeting room half an hour later, the atmosphere was decidedly different from only a few minutes before. Speaking of the plan now, all eyes were glued to him and all ears listened intently. He wasn't aware of what was said in his absence, but something had happened. From this point forward it would no longer be a struggle to convince the senior officers of Operation Valkyrie, or other ideas.

Conflict is always expected in warfare, not only from the stated enemy but also from allies who oppose you. Kurt intuitively felt that things would be much smoother from this point forward. Prior to the change, he was always the little tail wagging the big dog, but the dog had suddenly become compliant. Now every word spoken was taken seriously. While this strange turn of events could result in heady egoism and identity problems, Kurt saw the situation only as a fortunate opportunity to fulfil a mission, which was to combat and defeat the forces that threatened the world he knew and understood.

⌘

For several weeks Kurt worked with Rhodesian military intelligence and operational commanders to lay out the battle plan for Operation Valkyrie, as it was now officially known. To gather essential ground intelligence the best reconnaissance and tracking soldiers from all branches of the Rhodesian military were identified. Kurt's initial idea was to employ several small independent teams to reconnoitre critical target areas just prior to Operation Valkyrie. In this way, current ground intelligence could be collected and fed back to the planners, so that details of the operation could be fine-tuned with this last-minute information.

It soon became apparent that there were large tactical and logistical problems with deploying that number of reconnaissance people in and out of the target, undetected. After running several scenarios, Kurt finally decided to go alone. This seemed illogical to everyone he discussed it with, because the success of the operation became dependent on the performance of a single individual. If he failed or was captured or killed, the operation might not be viable.

What became obvious was that a larger force of people put into that area would stand a much greater chance of compromise. As it stood, ZANLA had no idea that the Rhodesians could or would cover that great a distance, or risk international political fallout as a result of attacking their main base camps. Any warning in the form of ground reconnaissance teams would surely alert them to this possibility, making the mission much more hazardous for the assault force. He would go in alone, as he had done in the past, and collect the information by himself. One skilled person would still stand the best chance of being undetected.

The other trackers, reconnaissance personnel and SAS teams would concentrate on locating and scoping out the forward launch sites, the cross-border landing and refuelling sites that would be needed by the helicopters. Even if spotted, the presence of Rhodesian troops in the border area would be no surprise to ZANLA, and would not give warning of the large raid to come on the distant twin camps.

Kurt's new unofficial status seemed to confer tacit immunity from the normal process of review and criticism of his ideas and plans. The senior officers had looks of concern on their faces when briefed, but there were no difficult questions, objections or reprimands as experienced previously. This carte blanche acceptance, however, was a double-edged sword. Success was demanded, and the burden of responsibility would be very heavy.

There would be no sharing or passing the guilt if things went sour. But the situation did eliminate tiresome, redundant questions and the buckets full of two-cent contributions that normally had to be considered, sifted through and eliminated. In a matter of six weeks from when it began, the baseline planning for Operation Valkyrie was complete. The only thing remaining was the final reconnaissance mission and fine-tuning, based on detailed ground information.

One potentially weak point was the operational security so vital to a mission of this type. There could be no leaks prior to the raid. To maintain this level of stringent confidentiality, only carefully selected senior officers and the prime minister would be told of the plan. There would be only two days to brief the troops after they had been confined to camp, with no provision at all to actually rehearse the raid.

After spending time on the ground, Kurt would have more first-hand knowledge of the targets than any other individual. For this reason, and the fact that the plan was his from the start, it was assumed he would direct the attack from a command Alouette helicopter, or K-Car, a function usually reserved for a field-grade officer.

⌘

With his responsibilities increased many fold, there was less time to socialize with friends and fellow soldiers. Promotion to the rank of officer also created a barrier that made socializing more difficult. Although never a heavy drinker anyway, the pips on his shoulder epaulettes prevented the carefree relaxation of the past. After a rare weekend of leave in town, Kurt grew increasingly tense with every passing hour. It was time to go back to the bush, or he would suffer from paralysis caused by tension and anticipation.

Early the following Monday morning, he was sitting in the briefing room at Inkomo barracks, surrounded by the commanders who would participate in Operation Valkyrie. They included Reed Donovan, Major Murphy, Major Allen, Colonel Ainsley and several others. When Kurt stood up, the lack of sleep showed in his bloodshot eyes and slightly haggard look. This was very unusual and surprised everyone in the room. In the past he had always seemed in perfect mental and physical condition. It didn't occur to any of the officers that the reason for his dishevelled appearance was that he had been away from the field too long. The life of a garrison soldier, especially a staff officer, was anathema to Kurt. Now that he had regained his health, it was imperative he go out again, if not for the sake of the mission, then for the sake of his sanity.

"Gentlemen," Kurt addressed the officers, "as you probably have heard by now, I've decided to personally go to the Atiba and Kitaya camps in preparation for Operation Valkyrie."

"I was hoping you had changed your mind, Lieutenant, and were planning on taking other team members with you," Ainsley responded.

"No sir, I plan to go in alone," Kurt replied. "As we discussed earlier, more people on the ground would only increase the chances of compromise. I know what information is needed in order to complete the mission planning, so there really is no need for additional personnel. This will also allow the other reconnaissance teams to be deployed simultaneously to scout the refuelling and staging areas."

"Well, nobody can accuse you of not being a hands-on leader, Lieutenant," Major Allen interjected. "We all wish you the best of luck on this mission, and God's speed."

"Thank you sir," Kurt nodded to him. "I appreciate that and also the confidence in me you have demonstrated. We can achieve a total victory here ... I can feel it."

All eyes in the room were rapt, translucent windows that allowed doubts and resistance to escape, and the cool waters of new found faith to enter. All were concentrated on Kurt and his message: their aspirations fulfilled in the form of a single man in whom to believe, trust and follow without question.

Kurt saw none of this. If he had, he wouldn't have understood it at all. All he saw was a job that had to be done, and the best way to carry it out.

⌘

The planners assumed that Kurt would be jumping into an area near the Atibo and Kitaya camps from an ATA DC-8. Because company aircraft were all registered in Oman, Jack Malloy had occasion to visit the Sultanate for licensing and inspections of his fleet. The regular flight path was near enough to the targets not to arouse suspicion. The presence of a military aircraft would ring alarm bells and put MIG fighters on alert, even though several previous solo, high altitude sorties by Canberra and Vampire photo-reconnaissance aircraft had not been attacked.

Kurt's return after the completion of the reconnaissance mission was to be more difficult. The targets were too far into hostile territory to walk out on foot or be picked up by vehicle. Several options for his return were discussed, and the best seemed to be the utilization of a mostly abandoned safari camp located in Tanzania, about forty kilometres north of the targets. Because they made a lot of foreign currency for the governments, a few big game hunting operations remained active, even during this time of increasing hostilities. Income from foreign hunters was just too attractive for the governments to shut them down, at least for now.

Several of the hunting guides in these camps were ex-Rhodesians and, though professing to be non-political, they were still loyal to their country and could be relied on to help out if needed, even at personal risk. If Kurt was able to make his way to the hunting camp located in the Tanzanian bush, a chartered aircraft could lift him out, hopefully without arousing suspicion.

Equipment to be taken on the reconnaissance mission was assembled, prepared and personally inspected. Instead of the FNC, he would carry a large hunting rifle and wear safari clothing. In the advent of being compromised, he would use a cover story about being a lost American hunter. The deception for the most part was irrelevant. A skilled operator working alone in a hostile area will go to any lengths to avoid human contact. Kurt didn't believe such a simple ruse would work but, in the eyes of the military planners, it gave a touch more credibility to the one man mission. In any event, he planned to do everything his way once he was beyond their oversight.

The lone insertion hundreds of kilometres from friendly lines was a high-risk venture without doubt. It was even more of a risk when others knew about the plan and this bothered Kurt far more than the thought of the physical challenges he would face. A feeling of uneasiness began to develop. This was not just the usual mission jitters but was something he couldn't put his finger on. The only totally trustworthy senior officer was Colonel Donovan, and Kurt felt compelled to express his concerns to the Selous Scout commander. Donovan was sympathetic and willing to discuss an alternative plan for clandestine entry into the Atibo/Kitaya area.

⌘

Two days before the scheduled drop by DC-8, Kurt went into Salisbury, and wandered around the usual military hangouts. Replacing the tenseness and irritability of only two weeks before, was a growing sense of relaxation and elation. There was a dawning realization that his response to stress must be the opposite to that of most people. It was only when a mission was imminent that he felt totally alive, and all his senses heightened with the anticipation.

When he encountered acquaintances at bars and on the streets, he was aware of being viewed and treated differently. Conversations with the old crowd still occurred, but there were no more invitations to wild drinking parties. Unconsciously, friends now held him at arm's length, perhaps thinking that after recent events he was not the same person anymore. This de facto rejection was depressing initially, but he recognized that socializing was a distraction anyway, and he would make better use of his time concentrating on the mission.

When left undisturbed, Kurt's unconscious mind ran free, analyzing tactics and scenarios and arriving at solutions. This processing went on continuously, and resulted in a mental and physical detachment often misinterpreted as aloofness or arrogance. As ever, Kurt wasn't aware of, nor did he care, how he was perceived.

On the last free night before going to Inkomo and preparing for the mission, he dozed off in the evening but was wide awake at two in the morning. This wasn't unusual. His sleep cycle was seldom consistent, or conformed to what was considered normal.

Slowly strolling up the empty quiet avenues suited his purpose perfectly. The quiet allowed relevant thoughts to percolate to the surface, winnowing out much of the accumulated subconscious jumble. This undisturbed time allowed him to consolidate and organize facts and completely focus on the approaching mission.

The process was near completion when there was a voice behind him, with no warning footsteps this time.

"The boy lived, you know. Some damage to the brachial plexus so his right arm will always be weak, but otherwise he's fine."

The Mad Medic was beside Kurt, walking in step, as if both were marching to unheard music.

"Glad to hear that, Medic," Kurt replied, his concentration about the mission now derailed. "But why do you always interrupt me when I'm thinking?"

"These days you're a popular guy ... a big shot. You have these people believing everything you say. It's hard to talk to you," the Medic said, with a smirk on his face.

"You wouldn't want me to charge you with insubordination because of your big mouth," Kurt snapped. "Would you, Medic?"

"It's just you and me," the Mad Medic replied, "and I don't work for you, never have and never will. I guess you'll just have to tolerate me."

Kurt shook his head in resignation.

"I suppose we all have our crosses to bear, Medic," Kurt mumbled, "and you appear to be mine. In spite of everything I've done, you think I'm a fraud, don't you?"

"No, not a fraud," the Medic replied. "I never said that. It's just that you seem to be missing something, something fundamental in the way you view the world."

"Oh, really," Kurt said tersely. "Well, maybe you could enlighten me on just what it is I'm missing."

"Well, sir, it's just an observation on my part, mind you," the Medic said, "but compassion, sympathy, respect for human life, a balanced approach to your place in the world maybe?"

"Medic," Kurt shouted back, "if I had all that crap, there is no way I could do what I do. I would be just like all those other people, afraid of everything and so paralyzed with self doubt that commitment and decision would be impossible. That's the *only* thing that separates me from them, you know."

Both men were quiet for a moment as they continued to walk the deserted street. The Mad Medic finally broke the silence.

"I'm glad that you said that, Kurt, not me. I think you are starting to understand."

"Understand what? That I need to suddenly acquire personality traits that I don't want or need, which will guarantee that I fail at what I do so well?

"That is *your* decision, Kurt," the Medic said softly.

"What decision, Medic?" Kurt snapped.

"Whether you want to be an icon or a man ... that's all."

Without a goodbye, the Mad Medic turned away and hurried down a darkened side street. Kurt stopped and watched him fade into the darkness.

At that moment it began to rain—big warm drops that speckled the pavement, turning the surface from dull to reflective in seconds. The lights on the streets and buildings made a mosaic of shadow and glare. Kurt had a strange feeling that he would never speak to the Mad Medic again, and he felt both relief and sadness. Like Kurt, the Medic was a man of missions, and when he was through with one, he wouldn't look back.

# CHAPTER 24
## IN DEEP

"Sir, as we discussed a few days ago, I have a strange feeling about this operation. I hate to say it, but I fear we may have a leak somewhere in the command structure. If word of my infiltration reaches ZANLA they'll be waiting for me. I won't stand a chance."

Colonel Donovan stared out the window towards the lake in front of his office as Kurt spoke, listening carefully but not reacting.

Kurt continued, "Those aware of the plan are convinced that I will be jumping from one of Jack's ATA DC-8s. If we have been compromised that is what they will be looking for. I need another way of infiltrating. Jack will still make the flight, to confuse them enough so I can operate undetected as planned."

"After our previous discussion I thought about the matter and may have found a possible solution, Lieutenant," Donovan said. "I've been talking to some of our associates in South Africa and as a result we have a possible alternative to consider."

"Well, I'm all ears, sir," Kurt said, "I like the idea of dropping into that area by DC-8 less every time I think about it."

"Lieutenant Christianson, what would you think about the option of sea transportation?"

Kurt looked at Donovan for a few seconds taking stock of what he had just said. The sea was a long way from Rhodesia, but the Atibo and Kitaya camps were located fairly close to the Indian Ocean.

"Hadn't thought of it, sir," Kurt replied. "Not in this situation. We're a hell of a long way from the water."

Of all the senior officers in the Rhodesian military, Kurt liked Reed Donovan the best. He was no politician and because he didn't play that game, it was unlikely he would be promoted beyond Lt Colonel. Donovan was an elite soldier, pure and simple, and looked after and supported his men as a commander should. When the man said something it would generally translate into action. Kurt thought he must have already worked a deal: he wouldn't even mention something he couldn't deliver.

"Lieutenant, be here at seven tomorrow morning and we'll finalize arrangements."

"Yes, sir," Kurt said and walked out. Water? ... hmm ... it had been a long time since the Lil' Katie, he thought.

⌘

The following morning Kurt went to Donovan's office as instructed, and was surprised to see his old friend and fellow ex-Green Beret, John E. Earl. The colonel asked them both to have a seat.

"Gentlemen," Donovan began, "I've managed to come to a tentative ... agreement with our allies in Pretoria, pending finalization of some details of course."

"The South Africans, sir?" Earl interjected. "You'd better watch your ass."

Donovan gave him a stern look, and John said no more and shifted his eyes to the floor.

"As I was saying," Donovan continued, "we are in need of their support to insert Lieutenant Christianson on a reconnaissance mission."

Earl looked at Kurt in a curious manner; until this moment he knew nothing about the big raid, and his intelligence collection wheels began to silently turn.

"What the South Africans need is for someone with expertise in high altitude parachuting to set up a HALO school for their One Rece Unit." Donovan looked directly at John as he said it.

"But sir," John replied, "they've already tried to tap me for that a few months ago, and I told them that some of the information I had on HALO operations was still considered classified by the US government, and I couldn't ... "

John's voice tapered off, and he realized he had been deftly outmanoeuvred.

"I am aware of that, Sergeant Earl," Donovan said patiently, as if talking to a child, "but you really must examine your loyalties and priorities and decide. Lieutenant Christianson's safety is dependent on assistance that only the South Africans can provide. Also, it might also put you in good standing for that promotion you applied for."

John's head picked up in curiosity, and Donovan waited for his response.

"How so, sir?" John asked.

"If you successfully complete this assignment to the satisfaction of our friends to the south, you may be looking at the command of the parachute school."

John's eyes shifted back and forth as he assessed the rapid developments. Kurt knew that John was in a dilemma. As an intelligence operative a commissioned rank was preferable to an enlisted one. It would provide access to more information. The trade-off was giving away some high-altitude parachuting techniques the US government was still holding under wraps, which in fact weren't very sensitive. John wasn't high enough on the food chain to make decisions of this nature: that had to be done in Washington or Langley. However, the decision had to be made now.

"Alright, sir," John exclaimed suddenly. "Tell them they have a deal."

Kurt knew that in all likelihood that Donovan was the one who just got the deal, if the grin on his face was any indication. Information transfer of this sort was worth a lot to the South Africans, especially in the currency of returned favours.

Kurt felt a slight confusion and distaste for such dealings. It was an alien concept but the military was in reality just like any other business. In his eyes dedication and loyalty were not based on favours, deals or profit motives. His calling to the military was like a religious vocation. Would a dedicated man of the cloth think of selling religious artefacts for personal gain?

The planning moved quickly once the agreement was reached. Only two days after their meeting with Donovan, Kurt and John were given orders to report to the ATA offices the following morning with all of their equipment for a flight to South Africa. No further information was provided, except that the entire operation and their destinations were to be discussed with no one.

⌘

The Air Trans Africa flight 728 departed from Salisbury International just after nine in the morning the following day. John and Kurt sat in the cockpit with Jack. Their destination was Jan Smuts Airport near Johannesburg, which was a regular ATA cargo stop. Fifty forty-kilogram bars of raw gold, a product of the Rhodesian mines, were in the hold of the aircraft and would be traded to the South Africans for gasoline, diesel fuel and other petroleum products. South Africa in turn bought oil covertly in the international market, mostly from Iran. The integration of this relatively small quantity of gold into South Africa's huge mining production was not a problem. This clandestine trade in precious metals and petroleum kept Rhodesia alive, thanks to Captain Jack and his winged pirate ships.

They landed just before noon at the main runway at Jan Smuts, but the DC-8 taxied off an access ramp to a secured apron where ATA had an office. Upon deplaning they were met by a group of thinly disguised customs officials, who were actually representatives from South Africa's Bureau of State Security and liaison officers from both the South African Air Force and Navy. They quickly introduced themselves, and the party retreated into another building next to the ATA office.

It was apparent that John and Kurt would be split up to go on their separate assignment.

"Good luck, bud, see you on the flip side," John said to Kurt as he stuck out his hand.

"Thanks, John," Kurt replied. "Take it easy on these guys, don't plant any of them in the ground, I hear they don't grow very well."

"Not me, I like to keep a neat drop zone, you know that." John slapped Kurt on the back, then turned and walked off with the Air Force officer.

Kurt went with the naval liaison officer who was assigned to be his escort. The man introduced himself as Allan Nel, a mid-level officer in his thirties.

The two of them drove to the main terminal at Jan Smuts Airport and took a commercial flight to Durban that afternoon. Durban was the third-largest city in South Africa, located in Natal province on the warm waters of the Indian Ocean. The South African Navy's main base was located at Simon's Town, south-east of Cape Town. But, as Kurt was made aware in the briefing before he left, Durban had submarine support nearest to his target.

Too small to be an actual naval base, the facility consisted of docks, a repair and maintenance complex, and an unpublicized two bay submarine pen. This was adjacent to the large international seaport that was the centre of Durban's bustling commercial sector. After arriving in Durban and eating at the small Navy dining facility, Kurt spent that night in a room in the nearby officers' quarters.

South Africa's Navy was relatively small considering the huge coastline they patrolled. The backbone of their naval forces consisted of several frigates, a fleet of small, fast patrol boats and three French Daphne-class submarines. Although few in numbers the subs did give South Africa an undersea capability which could prove crucial if an international conflict escalated and a threat was posed to the Cape route, around which transited a large portion of the world's oil supplies.

Accompanied by Allan, Kurt was allowed to walk the streets of Durban the next day. The submarine was due in port that evening and there was some time to kill before it arrived. He found a surprising number of Indians and other Asians living in Durban. He discovered that Natal province, where Durban was situated, developed as both a seaport and an agricultural centre. Sugar cane grew exceptionally well in the hot wet lowlands, and thousands of Indians were brought over in the ninteenth century to work in the cane fields. Gandhi himself spent many years in Natal before going back to India to spearhead a revolution that would change much of the world.

Allan, the liaison officer, wanted to have lunch at an Indian restaurant, but Kurt thought that was not a great idea. The last thing he needed in the next few days was what he had heard called 'Delhi Belly'. They compromised and ate at a Wimpy, a place that served American-style hamburgers, or so it claimed. A sports store on Smith Street had some useful items, including waterproof matches, fishing line, hooks, a small mirror and waterproof pouches. He bought the items with a wad of rand notes generously provided by Allan.

When they arrived back at the Durban naval facility that afternoon, the submarine had arrived and was in the maintenance pen. Kurt was given a brief tour of the nearly antique craft. The cramped and dank quarters in the WWII ex-British vessel made him grateful that he wasn't assigned to it on a long-term basis. After spending most of his life in the open spaces, he doubted that he could tolerate such confinement for long. The three-day excursion to his target would be a challenge.

That evening they ate again in the Navy mess and Kurt talked to some of the crew briefly. He did not discuss details of his mission with anyone, and none of the crew asked. Everyone thus far had been extremely security conscious and the 'need to know rule' seemed to apply without question.

The original plan, which included wearing game hunter's clothing and carrying a hunting rifle, had been changed in discussions with Donovan. The pickup point near a safari camp in Tanzania was now the alternative extraction site. If Kurt was compromised for any reason and could not meet the submarine for the ride back, he would move overland and reach this rendezvous site where food, water and weapons would be cached. There he would be contacted for the flight back to Rhodesia. Only a handful of Selous Scouts knew about this option, so with luck, neither he nor the mission would be endangered.

After dinner, he went back to his quarters to organize and pack gear into a waterproof box provided by naval supply. A captured AK-47, several magazines and ammunition were brought to him as per the agreement brokered by Donovan. This was more circumspect than carrying an assault rifle through South African customs from Rhodesia. The weapon had, in all probability, been captured from South Africa's own political opposition group the African National Congress, or ANC.

Originally intended for storing supplies in case of an emergency at sea in a submarine, the waterproof box was about five feet in length and two feet in width and depth and sealed with an O-ring on the lid that made it waterproof and pressure proof to a reasonable depth. The container had British manufacturing marks but was, unfortunately, vivid orange. After informing Allan of the problem, the box was taken down to maintenance where it was given a coat of quick-drying drab green.

The next morning Kurt briefed the submarine commander on the drop off point, but deliberately left out details and the purpose of his mission. If everything went according to plan, he would rendezvous two days later with the same sub, two kilometres south of his drop off point. By tacit agreement, the South Africans were not informed of Kurt's mission. Their part of the deal was to provide covert transportation. It was implicitly understood that should complications arise, Kurt was 'on his own'.

The excursion would take the diesel submarine nearly two thousand, four hundred kilometres from Durban through the Mozambique Channel to the mouth of the Kumva River which divided Mozambique to the south and Tanzania to the north. Approximately thirty kilometres up the river and a short distance from it were the Atibo and Kitaya ZANLA camps, which were his targets.

After being dropped off by the sub, Kurt would move up the Kumva River valley and reconnoitre both camps. The submarine would be at the limits of its range and would refuel at the South African naval depot on the Comoros Islands, which were across the channel from his intended drop-off point. Two days later, on their return to Durban, the sub would be in place for the pick up. If he wasn't at the rendezvous point within a two-hour time frame, it would depart without him.

Kurt, accompanied by his freshly painted box of gear, was loaded on the sub first, followed by four strangers who also had heavy crates of equipment. It was apparent that there was other cargo being transported on this trip, but whatever else was going on was not his business. The four men looked like military types but spoke with strong French accents. French was the main language on the Comoros, but that was about as far as the guessing game could be taken.

That evening just before sunset, the submarine sealed its hatches, started its diesel engines and got underway. Kurt new little about submarines or undersea operations except the limited training he'd received at Key West, locking in and out of stationary subs at the naval base, during scuba training. For the trip to be entirely underwater, would be too slow and much too far for an old diesel boat. The majority of the journey would be spent running fast on the surface. The Mozambique Channel is not known for smooth conditions, and Kurt realized that two days of rough riding in a dark, sweaty steel tube was on the agenda.

The years working on his grandfather's lobster boat conferred a near immunity to motion sickness, but claustrophobia was another matter. To fight this he spent most of the time in his bunk reading and studying detailed maps of the targets, committing to memory the contour lines, streams and vegetation overlays taken by photo-reconnaissance aircraft. By capturing the maps and photos and comparing them to charts of the terrain and natural geology, he created a mental image of the targets and the surrounding area. Kurt's goal was to commit as much of the detailed information as possible to memory and take only a commonly available map with him. Unfolding and reading maps during the mission was not conducive to remaining covert.

According to the plan and scenario agreed with Colonel Donovan prior to departure, Kurt was to move in at night off the southern outfall of the Kumva River and scout the Atibo camp on the Mozambique side first, then cross the river at night and scope out the Kitaya camp on the Tanzanian side. Mission completed, he would move back to the coast to meet the same submarine on its return leg. If things went sour, the alternative, unknown to the South Africans, was to move overland in the opposite direction to a little-used safari camp in southern Tanzania and await pickup by bush plane.

The plan, as it stood, seemed logical and efficient. Kurt decided not to do it that way. The cardinal rule of success was never to trust anyone. Even the most secure establishment could, and probably did, have leaks. In any conflict, the enemy always tried to develop sources of information deep inside the opponent's political or military apparatus. If covert plans fell into enemy hands by way of a leak or traitor, there was no chance of pulling off the mission. However, if some of the details were changed, then even if they were aware of the mission, there was at least a chance of slipping through. The ability of a single person to remain undetected was invariably underestimated.

Because of the cramped space inside the vessel, by necessity Kurt spoke to the mysterious French-speaking passengers. Only one of the four spoke English fluently, and he introduced himself as Robert Denard. The purpose behind four French heavies infiltrating into the Comoros Islands with equipment wasn't very difficult to guess, but Kurt didn't inquire. There had been recent newspaper articles indicating that the Comoros were being threatened by a communist or leftist takeover. Although until recently a French colony, South Africa had interests in the region. It didn't take a lot of insight to assume Mr Denard and his companions in some way represented those interests.

After all the confinement he could stand, late in the afternoon of the third day Kurt was given warning by the submarine's captain to be ready to disembark. Shortly thereafter the sub dived for the first time since they were underway. The transition was miraculous. The constant heaving and movement suddenly stopped, and the ride was smooth and very quiet. Kurt put on a thin neoprene body suit, a black buoyancy compensator, and held on to his dive mask and fins. Two hours after submerging the sub surfaced and Kurt moved up to the conning tower using the ladder. Two of the crew helped him with the gear and hauled up the sealed box.

It was early evening and the waters were relatively calm. A shallow swell bobbed the sub up and down with a slow regular rhythm. Kurt climbed down the external ladder on the conning tower and stood on the steel deck of the sub, only inches from being awash. The vague outline of the African coast could be made out a kilometre or two off the port side of the vessel, against the last embers of sunset. The freshwater outflow of the Kumva River over the millennia had scoured a deep channel in the floor of the sea bed, allowing the submarine to approach this close to the mainland.

Unfortunately, Kurt had to be launched into the middle of the big river's outflow, and swimming directly against the current would be impossible. From the release point he would have to swim ninety degrees to the mainland and evade the river's current before heading in to shore; otherwise there would be a good chance of being swept out to sea. He was supposed to go to the Mozambican side of the river, which seemed the easier swim, but had decided to swim north to the Tanzanian side to confound those who might be waiting if his plans were leaked.

After adjusting the dive mask and fins, with a cursory wave to the crew Kurt slipped over the side of the black steel sub into the dark waters. The green equipment box with an attached twenty foot length of rope was lowered over the side by the two crew members. The floating box he towed by wrapping the rope around his left arm and side stroking with strong fin kicks. The liberation from the cramped quarters of the sub was exhilarating as the tepid water entered under the thin wetsuit and bathed his skin beneath. After several days of enforced idleness, he paced himself with care to prevent cramps and exhaustion.

After clearing the sub, Kurt turned north towards the Tanzanian side of the Kumva. This last minute change in plans was intended to thwart a possible leak, even at Colonel Donovan's level. If no one else knew he was going ashore there, then there was little likelihood of a reception committee waiting on the beach. There were always risks in a mission of this nature: being unpredictable was his only insurance.

The spectre of dark objects under the water crossed his mind for the first time. The Kumva River outflow mixed fresh water nutrients with salt water, which normally meant a proliferation of sea life and attracted predators like sharks. Despite the threat,

Kurt kept swimming with even and steady strokes keeping his fins well below the water's surface to minimize splash, which might attract the marine predators.

Strings of small white lights came into view, seemingly dancing and bobbing on the sea's surface. The lights belonged to a score of tiny fishing boats working the river mouth with nets, dipping into schools of small fish that swarmed there at night. The little lights, like Christmas tree bulbs, were strung on lines decorating the gunwales and masts of the boats. The lights both attracted the fish, and made each boat visible to one another in the dark. The small anchovy or sardine-like fish were an African staple. The night's catch would be salted and then dried whole under the hot sun before being sold.

The current was stronger than he had anticipated, and pushed Kurt towards the arc of fishing boats. The fishermen were busy and the lights would inhibit their night vision somewhat, but being snagged in a net or seen by them was too risky, so he adjusted his course, avoiding the boats. With each fin stroke little fluorescent plankton blinked at the disturbance, like tiny fireflies in the clear water.

As he crossed the main channel, the outbound current diminished, improving his progress towards the coast. Finally, caught by an inbound current, he was driven rapidly towards shore. Kurt had been in the water for nearly three hours before washing up on the rough shoals of the coast. The incoming waves were only two or three feet high, but in his exhausted state they felt like breakers.

Lying in the shallow surf, he didn't attempt to move ashore until he had scanned the beach. Rural Africans usually stayed put at night and seldom wandered around. Hundreds of generations of living on a hostile continent with vicious night-hunting predators made this behaviour understandable. Also, the lack of electricity encouraged an 'early to bed, early to rise' lifestyle. However, there was always a chance of an unexpected surf fisherman or soldier on patrol. Discovery now would be disastrous … there was no way back.

Kurt clung to the tip of a large embedded rock some forty metres offshore. The waves slammed him and the floating box into the sharp and unforgiving edges. After watching the shoreline intently for several minutes, he felt confident he was alone. Letting go of the rock, the incoming surf washed him and the box ashore like driftwood. Only a thin slip of moon hung near the horizon, and a faint golden glow lit the very crests of the incoming waves. Anyone casually observing the scene that dark night would not have noticed anything unusual.

He lay still for several minutes and breathed deeply to restore his depleted energy. Then he rolled over, removed the mask and fins and unzipped the neoprene wetsuit. Even at night the air temperature was over ninety degrees, and though slightly chilled from the ocean, a few minutes in the rubber suit would cause overheating. He also removed the foam boots worn under the fins. Left on they would leave strange tracks, while barefoot prints in the sand were common.

Feeling exposed and keen to put distance between him and the beach before sunrise,

Kurt picked up the box and took cover beneath palm trees and scrub twenty metres from the water line. Opening the equipment box, he removed the military red lens flashlight. Utter disbelief washed over him as he found that the AK-47, provided by the South Africans, was not there, nor the bandolier of magazines or extra boxes of ammo. With something akin to panic, he searched the ALICE rig; it was no small relief that the familiar form of the suppressed Browning High Power pistol was where he had packed it. Who had tampered with the box? How? And why? His mind scanned through the options, but the reality was that he was vulnerable, in hostile territory, with no way out and no main weapon.

Refusing to succumb to panic, he swapped the wetsuit for a set of camouflage fatigues then blackened his face, neck and hands with camo cream. He removed the ALICE rig with the food, water and other equipment from the box. Using the entrenching tool he dug a hole in the soft sand and pushed the box into it. Only the AK-47 and ammo were missing. He threw the wetsuit, mask, fins and tow rope in the box and sealed it before covering it with sand and smoothing the surface. Fallen palm fronds and other plant debris was scattered over the area.

With that out of the way, he began to move inland, travelling west on the escarpment of the Kumva River. The camps were still many kilometres of hard travel away, and there was little time. Perhaps the lack of a main weapon would actually be beneficial. A powerful battle rifle instilled some degree of confidence, unwarranted in a situation such as this. He would stand no chance if he was discovered, no matter how well armed he was. To go in and come out undetected was the goal, hopefully without a shot being fired.

⌘

General Taderera and a dozen ZANLA security troops waited on the Mozambique side of the Kumva River. They had been waiting since late afternoon the previous day, and now it was nearly dawn. Taderera was angry. Usually his source of information was good, but lately the intelligence received was irregular and inaccurate. First there was a warning last week that a lone soldier would be parachuting into the vicinity of ZANLA command. That warning had sounded strange from the outset, but spotters were posted around the clock. No enemy aircraft and no lone parachutist had been spotted, as he had suspected would be the case all along.

Then two days ago there was a report that said to ignore the lone parachutist. Instead a single soldier would be landing on the Mozambique side of the Kumva at night, from the water. This sounded even more unbelievable: and here they were and still no enemy. Someone was making him look a fool, and that was the one thing he hated more than any other.

Why would a single soldier come in from the sea all by himself? What could one man do against several thousand armed troops? At about nine o'clock that night, Taderera thought he'd seen a dark form in the sea, but when others came over with field glasses it was no longer there. He thought it was his imagination wanting to see this ridiculous threat actually materialize.

He would tell his KGB contact of his strong displeasure and might even recommend they withhold payment, until the source provided some useful information, to stop this farce. Security would be increased at both camps as a precaution anyway, but this latest information was no doubt just more time-wasting nonsense.

⌘

Kurt made good time moving inland. The vegetation wasn't as dense as he had anticipated. Keeping between the river and its flood plain was the best route because there were no permanent dwellings. Several kraals and small villages on top of the escarpment he quietly bypassed with no disturbance except for a couple of yapping dogs. Village dogs probably barked a lot at night anyway. Just before daybreak, he took shelter in a thicket of hardwood trees halfway up the escarpment. No obvious human or animal paths led to or near the dense growth, so he settled down in the middle of the thicket and waited for first light.

Exhausted from the hours of swimming and hard walking, sleep overwhelmed him in an instant. The next sound was the soft lowing of cattle, distant voices and the rattling of ox carts rolling on rutted dirt paths as the eastern sky turned pale blue. Morning sounds, pleasant and pastoral as they were, alarmed Kurt. The maps and aerial photos indicated that this area was sparsely inhabited, but there were definitely people moving around.

There was little choice but to spend the day hidden and, hopefully, undetected. Knowing that he wasn't going anywhere soon he allowed himself to relax and sleep. The smell of ocean salt, still thick on his skin and clothes from the night before, invoked vivid dreams of the Maine coast.

It was mid-morning when he opened his eyes again. A gap in the foliage admitted direct sunlight, which struck his bare skin like a flame, shocking him out of a soothing dreamland. Sounds, close this time, little bells, reminded him of a wind chime blowing in the breeze. Kurt froze, not daring to move, barely breathing. There was rustling in the dense leaves only a few feet away. Slowly he reached for the silenced 9mm strapped to the left side of his vest. The subtle unnatural movement in the branches and leaves was mesmerizing, when the vegetation suddenly parted.

His pistol was ready and thrust forward, when the head and neck of a multi-coloured goat burst through the green wall. The animal ignored him as its long ears twitched and mouth moved continuously, biting off and chewing succulent shoots that grew in the thicket. Around the goat's neck was a knotted piece of twine on which hung a miniature copper cow bell, which tinkled as the animal moved. With relief, Kurt nearly laughed at the goat's animated behaviour, but the reality of the situation quickly dawned on him. In Africa, goats were usually not allowed to roam unaccompanied because they made such easy targets for predators. Kurt peered through the greenery around him, and a face appeared.

The boy's face was nearly hidden except for the huge shining dark eyes looking directly at him. The expression was a seamless mixture of curiosity and fear. Kurt's eyes fixed on his for an eternity that lasted a few seconds and then the apparition was gone in a rustle of leaves.

Kurt leapt to his feet, scaring the goat, which bolted back through the thicket braying loudly. Crashing and weaving through the dense growth, he finally broke out to see the boy running up the river escarpment. No one else was around, but the boy was running fast. Kurt saw that he might not catch him until after he'd crested the escarpment and they would be visible to whoever may be there. The boy turned his head around while running and saw Kurt emerging from the trees. Totally silent until now the child began to yell at the sight of the frightening stranger.

The boy would no doubt tell others about his presence and that would be catastrophic. Kurt swung up his silenced Browning High Power and aimed at the departing figure, and was squeezing off the shot when the voice of the Mad Medic was heard "Do the right thing" ... and again ... "Do the right thing."

"Goddamn," Kurt swore in a hoarse raspy voice, and unbuckled the vest, tossing it to the ground.

With every bit of energy he possessed, Kurt sprinted after the running herd boy. Free from excess weight, the gap closed quickly and the boy saw that there was no way to escape. Instead of continuing to run, he stopped and waited for fate to claim him, still yelling at the top of his lungs.

Running like a football tackle with his shoulder level with the ground, Kurt bent down while still running and hit the boy amidships with his lowered shoulder and scooped him off the ground. With the impact the shouting stopped and the thin child, too stunned to resist, flopped on his shoulder like a rag doll. Kurt spun around and ran back to the thicket and cover.

The same goat that stuck its head through the thicket was still grazing nearby, as if nothing had happened. Kurt took off a green bandanna, kept around his neck to catch perspiration, and tore it in half. One half bound the boy's wrists behind the back and the other half went around the boy's mouth to prevent any further shouting or screaming. The child's eyes were huge, like glistening saucers staring steadily and expectantly, even though his thin body was quivering uncontrollably with fear. Collecting his equipment, Kurt picked up the child, slung him over the shoulder like a bag of grain, and left the patchy thicket for heavier cover further down the escarpment.

"I have to take you with me a little way to buy some time, kid," Kurt mumbled.

"Sorry about all this, but you can thank the Mad Medic if you see him."

Kurt knew he was talking to himself. The boy didn't understand English, but the words seemed to relax them both. After moving about half a click along the escarpment Kurt stopped and sat the boy down beside a tree with a small trunk.

"Kid, I'm going to tie you to this tree with some parachute cord. I'm not tying it very tight and you should be able to work yourself loose in an hour or two, at least I hope you can. It's the best I can do I'm afraid."

For the first time in his life Kurt deeply regretted what he had to do, but at least he didn't kill the child. Situations like this were impossible to resolve cleanly. Killing the boy would have been a gross violation of his own ethics, contradicting the reason he was doing this job in the first place. On the other hand, letting him go would in all likelihood mean his own death or capture. What he did was compromise; this way they both had a good chance to make it, but it still didn't sit very well. Innocents are invariably caught up in war, even when you tried your best to keep them out.

Kurt felt physically and emotionally numbed, but the possibility that people might be on his trail once the boy freed himself meant he needed to move quickly. Making his way further down into the escarpment, he pushed upriver through relatively thick undergrowth until just before nightfall, when the cover of darkness allowed travelling higher up, where walking was easier. Pushing hard and continuously, well past dark, he arrived at a point where a prominent tributary fed into the Kumva River. This branch was a key landmark. The Kitaya camp was just four or five kilometres further. Finding another hide, he spent the remaining hours of darkness resting and trying to reclaim some energy.

# CHAPTER 25
## THE GAUNTLET

Unlike the Pungwe camp which resembled a military garrison, Kitaya looked more like a normal village or small town. Wisps of smoke from dozens of cooking fires rose straight up into the still air and drifted thirty feet above the ground, where it pooled like oil poured on a pond. Women balanced bales of laundry and firewood on their heads, gracefully walking the roads and paths leading to and from the centre of the compound in the soft pre-dawn light. A mixed assortment of cattle, sheep and goats grazed nearby, attended by their herd boys. Kurt saw the boys and fleetingly wondered about the child he had tied up.

Kurt tried to focus on what had to be done next. This reconnaissance mission of the Atibo and Kitaya camps was a vital piece in the overall strategy of destroying the enemy's ability to wage war. The next day or two would be a trial, another seemingly impossible challenge poised on a razor's edge of success or catastrophe, but there was no one else to blame because the whole thing was his idea. The moment of reflection complete, he channelled all his attention and energy towards the task at hand.

Manifestly, the ZANLA camp in southern Tanzania was not constructed with defence in mind. Kitaya was a facility that provided the ZANLA military and political organization with logistical and administrative support but, officially, was located in a 'neutral' country; thus considered immune from external aggression. Both Kitaya and Atibo, located nearby but across the river in Mozambique, were hundreds of kilometres from the Rhodesian border and therefore out of the range of troop-carrying helicopters.

The ZANLA leadership must have considered these camps an almost perfect sanctuary, and a haven from attack due to their location. Flying in DC-3s, paratroopers could easily parachute in but then would have no viable way of getting home. Air attacks could inflict serious damage on the camps, but this could be quickly repaired and international sympathy and aid would arrive promptly. Kurt knew that only total destruction of both camps would seriously disrupt ZANLA aggression, but to be successful the attack must be carried out primarily by ground forces.

With all of his senses on full alert, he moved out of the hide and with great stealth, moved from one piece of cover to the next, memorizing details of the camp layout. Even though Kitaya was not a classically fortified military garrison, he treated it as he would any other target. Information collected included buildings, cover, defensive positions for troops and support weapons, fields of fire and movement, roads, footpaths and possible approaches. Everything was committed to memory by looking at the scene, then closing his eyes and burning in the image, and then looking again. By moving around the camp in a circular pattern, he acquired both two and three dimensional perspectives, and a composite image became locked into his permanent memory.

Once the baseline picture was etched in his mind, additional details were added by layering them with virtual sheets of acetate. This technique allowed for absolute precision. Working later with the modellers, an accurate reconstruction of the targets would be created by recalling these mentally stored images. There were only two heavy weapon defensive positions to deal with, and he'd seen only a handful of armed troops. Before the end of the day Kurt was confident that he had sufficient information.

He became anxious to cross the river and begin work on the larger, more strategically important Atibo camp. After resting in the hide for two hours until darkness had set in, he walked down the river escarpment, selected and then monitored a crossing site. The water in this part of the river was shallow but fairly swift, and he had to cross it holding his weapons and gear above the water line. Kurt offered a silent prayer that crocodiles weren't hunting in this part of the river tonight.

Two hours after sunset, Kurt cautiously moved up the Mozambican escarpment on the opposite bank and headed towards Atibo. After several hours of hard marching, and an estimated two to three kilometres from Atibo's anticipated outer perimeter, he heard human voices. He halted and listened carefully. The voices were low, soft and intermittent, like men trying to talk quietly but without any thought of security. Their lack of discipline was a bonus. Without it he might have walked directly into a ZANLA forward defensive position.

After listening intently for fifteen minutes, Kurt identified the position, which was manned by two soldiers. With exaggerated slow motion he moved close enough to hear them speaking and wondered why they were so far from the camp perimeter. It didn't make much sense putting people this far out when an attack wasn't expected. While he couldn't comprehend their Shona dialect, several English words and phrases caught his attention, one of which was 'Selous Scouts'. Why would they be talking about them in the middle of the night? Failing to glean any more from the conversation he moved on, the soldiers unaware that an intruder was in their midst.

Now inside Atibo's outer perimeter, Kurt was again on maximum alert. There was a damp dusky smell of freshly dug earth that permeated the air just prior to encountering several additional recently constructed defensive positions. These formed a series of short trenches that were dug in a circle or semi-circle around the camp centre, creating an inner perimeter. These positions were silent, and perhaps unmanned. However, moving very cautiously and slowly he heard heavy breathing and determined that most of the positions had at least one soldier in them, but they all seemed to be asleep. This was a perfect example of why a single soldier should never be put in a defensive position at night. Either they fall asleep, or panic at a small sound and fire at shadows.

Humans relied primarily on vision, but Kurt had trained himself to use the skills of smell, touch and even skin perception, to compensate in the darkness. A good reconnaissance man took full advantage of these underutilized senses: by using them darkness could be his best friend and daylight the worst enemy. Everyone could see, but it took artistry, cunning and concentration to develop hearing, touch, and smell to a level that substituted for vision. By continuously calling on this alternative intelligence, Kurt was as comfortable walking through an enemy position at night as another person would be walking down a city street during the day.

Kurt decided to lay low for the rest of the night and check out Atibo during daylight hours. Operating during the day was more risky but the amount of information that can be obtained at night from such a large target was insufficient. He found a good hide about three-hundred metres from Atibo's outer defences and dozed intermittently until the eastern sky began to lighten, then he moved out.

Atibo proved to be a much more challenging target than either Kitaya or Pungwe. Kitaya was small and open. At Pungwe he had a bird's eye view from an elevated observation point. Atibo was situated in densely vegetated, flat, river flood plain and was extremely difficult to reconnoitre. The only way it could be managed was to probe the perimeter of the camp from different directions and then compile his observations. He found it necessary to record the distances and physical findings on paper because the terrain was so featureless that he couldn't rely on memory. All day he tediously probed, withdrew and recorded, moving with great stealth in order to avoid being detected.

By late afternoon Kurt had probed three hundred and sixty degrees around the Atibo camp and was satisfied that he had a good grasp of the location of the perimeter as well as the number and positions of outer and inner defences. Unfortunately it wasn't possible to record details of many structures making up the inner camp because they could not be seen from where he was concealed. The only way to do this effectively was to make a 'walk-through' and the only time this was possible was at night when the camp was asleep. He rested in the hide again for a few hours until darkness.

Avoiding the previously observed defensive positions, Kurt worked his way towards the centre of camp, which comprised several two-storey wooden barracks, and low single-storey concrete block buildings with tin roofs. Atibo was a former Portuguese military base; obvious from its construction and layout. Kurt felt a wave of déjà vu, as if he'd been here before, but knew this feeling was probably due to its similarity to Vista del Sol in Angola two years before.

The camp was very quiet at this hour; most of the buildings were in darkness. Only one of the low concrete buildings had a light on inside, and it lay in the centre of the camp. It piqued his curiosity as to why someone would be up this late, so cautiously he approached the illuminated structure using the corner of a darkened building for cover.

Peering around the corner of an adjacent building, Kurt saw a soldier through the illuminated window sitting at a desk studying papers in front of him. From the intelligence briefings there could be little doubt that the soldier he was looking at was

General Josiah Taderera, the military commander of the ZANLA forces. Even seated, the man appeared huge, over six feet five inches in height, with massive shoulders and arms resting on the desk before him. The general looked weary, as one would expect from someone with his responsibilities.

Taderera was an easy target from this range, and with a silenced 9mm there wouldn't be much sound. Kurt's first instinct was to take the shot and eliminate the ZANLA commander. The general's demise would definitely put a crimp in the ZANLA high command, but everyone was replaceable, even Taderera. On the other hand, if he shot the commander he would have to leave Atibo immediately, hotly pursued by hostile forces. His position was too precarious to attempt that. He needed to reach one of the extraction points to get to safety. It was too far from home to walk back.

This big fish would have to live for the time being, with the hope that Taderera would be caught in the net when it was dropped from the sky. As Kurt was preparing to move on and continue to reconnoitre the camp, Taderera stood up, rubbed his eyes, and walked through the inner office door. The door clicked and there was the sound of a lock turning. The office door was locked but the window was left open. The tired general had made a major oversight. Without hesitation, Kurt downed his equipment by the outer wall of the darkened building and running low, crossed to the open window. Grasping the lower sill, he lifted himself soundlessly inside onto the floor of Taderera's office. This spontaneous reaction was extremely risky, but he could not turn down a gift like this. This opportunity was like a flower full of nectar to a bee.

The general's desk was cluttered with papers, and Kurt knew he had very little time. Staying on his hands and knees he sifted through the papers lying on the desk. There were rosters, requisitions, orders and all the expected headquarters paperwork and forms. On the right side of the desk lay a red file. Red always meant something important in a government or military office. At first glance the contents looked like verbal transcripts. Some of the other loose papers on the desk that appeared promising he stuffed into the red file. He wished there was more time to look, but his luck was being pushed to the extreme as it was. Stealing these documents would cause all hell to break loose in the camp when it was discovered, but someone inside the camp would hopefully be blamed.

He crammed the bulging red file down the front of his uniform shirt which was secured by the trouser waistband. Using forearm and shoulder muscles, he flung his body out of the window onto the ground outside. Picking up the gear he'd downed before entering the room, Kurt quickly made for the perimeter of the camp, making mental notes of structures and positions while moving. On reaching the cover of trees he slowed, knowing that the camp's perimeter defensive positions would be well dug in and camouflaged, similar to those on the other side. The goal was to be on the outside of the camp perimeter before an alert sounded.

It almost worked.

The soft dark night was shattered by an horrific noise that sounded like the mix of a lion's roar and a man dropped into boiling water. Kurt ceased moving and a moment later lights began to go on, flooding the camp and casting harsh long shadows into the trees. Seemingly out of nowhere, people appeared and began running around frantically. They streamed out of the buildings, barracks and defensive positions, transforming his cakewalk into a nightmare in seconds.

Kurt continued to ease away from the camp, but in the commotion a half-dressed soldier physically ran into him. Without hesitation, Kurt grabbed the man by the skull and spun his head around in a circle fracturing the soldier's neck vertebrae. Another unarmed soldier scrambled by and witnessed what had happened. Instead of stopping to help his comrade, he bolted toward the centre of camp shouting something in Shona. Kurt let go of the first soldier who jerked spasmodically, pulled out the suppressed 9mm and fired one round at the retreating figure, which stumbled ... and dropped.

At that moment he knew the jig was up. It wouldn't take long for ZANLA to guess what had transpired and send hundreds of soldiers in pursuit. Facing directly away from the camp he began to move as fast as possible. Distance was the key to survival now, not stealth. He had enough information to make a good reconstruction of both camps, besides there was no possibility of remaining any longer. With less than two hours until first light, he had to take full advantage of the remaining darkness.

After clearing the perimeter of the Chimoyo camp, Kurt angled north, down into the river escarpment. Crossing back over the Kumva River into Tanzania as soon as possible would make tracking him more difficult, and prevent him being trapped in Mozambique, which would cut him off from the alternate pickup point. It took more than an hour of hard pushing through unfriendly vegetation to arrive at the banks of the Kumva; this stretch looked different from the one he'd crossed a few kilometres downstream. The sky was lightening in the east, which brought up a faint reflection off the surface of the running water.

Normally Kurt would wait and check out the area for at least half an hour before attempting the crossing, but pursuers and diminishing darkness precluded that. The river here looked narrower and deeper than where he had forded the night before. Before crossing, however, he would have to deal with the bulky red file of papers stuck beneath his shirt. Getting the papers wet would ruin them. Buried in the pack was a clear waterproof bag which contained matches, maps, and a few other accessories. He crammed the file into the bag and resealed it.

He had to move now. When the sky became lighter, he would be clearly silhouetted against the water. Kurt placed the suppressed 9mm, fully charged and cocked, in the top of his shirt with the grip just under his throat ready to access if needed. Holding the backpack containing all the other equipment and the waterproof pouch with the file on top of his head, he stepped into the river. The weight held aloft serving as ballast to increase the downward force, and to counteract the buoyancy of the water.

The water deepened rapidly but then levelled out at chest height. Fortunately the water was not moving too swiftly since the river was fairly wide at this point, but the trackless soled boots had little grip on the stony bottom. In a couple of places the water deepened and rose to the level of his chin. Kurt kept walking, though at times it felt more like floating vertically and bouncing across. The river gradually became shallow again to Kurt's relief, but the euphoria was short lived. Still stomach deep in the river with his feet bogged down in a bank of sticky sand, a rapid movement appeared upstream. A wake in the water in the shape of a V with a black tip at its point was heading directly towards him.

A crocodile was bearing down and would arrive in seconds. Not wanting to lose the contents of the backpack held over his head, Kurt tossed the bundle as hard as he could towards the river bank and, hopefully, solid ground. The pack arced and landed with a splash in the shallow water just shy of the bank, and began to drift slowly down stream. His hands now free, he reached down and withdrew the 9mm. The bulge of the suppressor hung up briefly on his shirt, but brute force ripped it free. The wake was heading directly for his legs so Kurt sidestepped, changing position enough to put both legs parallel to the direction of the animal's approach, and reduce the predator's target.

Aligning the top line of the silencer between the bulging eyes of the crock now only feet away, he fired. The 147-grain subsonic bullet didn't have enough energy to pierce a croc's thick skull, but it crunched directly on top of the rigid case surrounding the brain. The bullet failed to penetrate, but shattered the bone like glass before bouncing off. The impact sent shockwaves into the walnut-sized nerve centre, causing it to malfunction temporarily. Although the beast was out of commission, it still had huge forward momentum. The croc's neck and left foreleg struck Kurt's legs solidly, bowling him over. Flailing in an attempt to recover, he dropped the 9mm into the river. Momentarily submerging and struggling for the surface, he waited for the final grab of razor teeth.

Being taken by a crocodile is a nightmare beyond description. Because of its small throat, this voracious prehistoric reptile is capable of eating large animals only if they have been dead awhile and have decomposed. When a crocodile grabs large prey, they may be killed in the attack … or not. In either case the beast drags the prey to a den located beneath a hollowed-out river bank, and leaves them there with other carrion to rot, before eating them. The thought of finding oneself trapped in a dark, totally enclosed space with rotting animal carcasses and no way out makes most nightmares seem tame. Kurt had heard about this scenario and was truly terrified at the prospect.

After a few seconds of chaotic splashing about in the water near the river bank with the nine-foot long 'flat dog' as Rhodesians called them, Kurt realized that the animal was seriously injured and not on the offensive. After re-orientating himself, he waded to the river bank and clambered up the slippery slope. The pack containing his gear was floating near the bank about thirty metres downriver. He ran down and retrieved the pack before it floated out to deeper water and sank. The croc was still thrashing and rolling in the water, floating down with the current. Shouldering the pack, heavy with water, Kurt headed up the north escarpment, away from the river. There was no time to search for the lost pistol. Angry ZANLA troops might arrive shortly and the 9mm would be of little use against dozens of AKs if they caught up with him.

There was no way to make it back to the submarine pickup point now; that would mean re-crossing very hostile territory where everyone would be looking for him. He had to invoke plan B, which was to reach the other cache of equipment that was supposed to be stashed about fifty kilometres from his current position, or there was little chance of surviving this one.

⌘

Wet, bedraggled and carrying a waterlogged rucksack, Kurt crested the valley and headed on a bearing of two hundred and eighty degrees magnetic. Once away from the river escarpment there were few landmarks in the increasingly dense bush. Moving with the speed of a forced march, there was no time to slow down and go into anti-tracking mode.

Currently, speed and avoiding contact were the only rules. For the first time in memory he was in the forest without a gun, and it was frightening. Without a weapon, man was not at the apex of the food chain anymore but ranked somewhere near the bottom. A human without a gun in the wilds of Africa was nothing more than a two-legged meal. Perhaps it was only his imagination, but he could feel hidden eyes watching as he walked.

For the next few hours Kurt moved without stopping in the direction of the alternate cache. Whenever he heard voices or activity, he stopped to listen and observe where the people were going and then proceeded with caution. Since leaving Atibo, there had been no obvious military activity in the vicinity.

By now the ZANLA troops should be checking the river escarpment and also east of the camp towards the ocean. It made little sense for a lone infiltrator to head inland into the remote and hostile bush or hopefully, that's what they would think. By midday, the single remaining water bottle was dry, and at this time of the year there was no surface water to be found away from the river. He could make it the rest of the way if no other problems developed, but little had gone as planned on this mission.

The bush became hotter by the minute and an eerie silence prevailed; no sane animal would move in this heat except for the infernal and omnipresent bugs. The tsetse flies were out and would dive down like an aircraft, striking with their blood sucking mouths with a bite that felt like a red-hot ice pick. Kurt tried to crush them but they were too fast, the Darwinian descendants of untold generations of survivors, skilled at dodging animal tails.

The dry brush cracked underfoot. The bulbous trunk of a baobab tree lay ahead. Searching for dropped pods, the few he found were pocketed. Cracking one of the brittle shells, he popped a bean in his mouth, the sour flavour making him salivate. Trudging on, he took a compass bearing every twenty minutes or so. His mind drifted back to Maine, as it usually did in times of hardship and stress, and of how the breakers pounded the rocks throwing cold mist into your face. Shivering in spite of the heat, the memory helped to keep exhaustion at bay. His thoughts then wandered to Namibia and Diana, but before the memory of her became palpable he heard something that snapped him back to reality.

The sound was raspy and rumbling. Kurt stopped moving and listened closely. A slight movement caught his eye. The camouflage was nearly perfect. If not for the movement, he would have missed it entirely. He attempted to identify the shape and at first couldn't, but then a subtle form began to emerge. The yellow eyes were the give-away. They were perfectly still and shone with the steady intensity of a predator.

The lioness had been stalking him, probably for some time. She was growing bold; hunger and frustration had made her impatient. Unlike leopards, man was not a normal prey for lions. Lions were hunters of four-legged plains game but any predator, when desperate, will consider alternatives. Kurt could see that the lioness was young, not yet full size and she looked thin and hungry. Her individual ribs could be seen when she breathed in and out. He had no weapons left except the combat knife which was of little use against such a large cat.

Reaching down Kurt unsnapped the keeper on the sheath and withdrew the wide polished blade which reflected the intense early afternoon sunlight. Slowly rolling off the backpack, he lowered it to the ground as he faced the young lioness. The demeanour of the cat changed once she made direct eye contact with her prey. The slow, cautious stalking shifted into direct confrontation. If Kurt had been an antelope or even a baboon, the lioness would have attacked immediately, but this big primate seemed different to the cat. This prey seemed to be stalking the stalker, and that made her uneasy.

Kurt slowly and smoothly sidestepped, trying to keep vertical tree trunks between them. The trees were too small and straight to climb, and at any rate such a young cat would also be a good climber and would grab him by the legs, which would be the end. The only viable tactic was to fight the lioness on her own terms on level ground, pitting his greater intelligence against the stronger and faster cat. Kurt reckoned his odds were at best even, perhaps less. If he could keep manoeuvring, keeping barriers between them, that would prevent the lioness from making a straight run and he would have a chance. If the cat rushed with no obstructions, he would be overwhelmed. Even with a lucky thrust with the blade, it would be too late.

The lioness hissed and bared her fangs, a common technique of intimidation used by cats. Kurt did the same, hissing and growling at his pursuer, in a universal sign in the animal world of the intent to fight, but his throat was dry and a rush of air was what came out. The lioness mock charged and Kurt mirrored her tactic, advancing two steps ahead then slowly backing up. The lioness broke eye contact and backed off, ears flattened. Kurt took the initiative she provided and ran at the cat, waving his knife in front of him and shouting hoarsely. The lioness bolted. Predators live by instinct, and a large part of instinct is expected or anticipated behaviour of their prey. Though hungry, the young cat had no instinct on how to cope with the aggressive moves of a prey that attacked. She fled, snarling once over her shoulder in defiance and then ran off.

Kurt knew that this shot of adrenaline was his last. Out of water, tired beyond description and unarmed, there was still more than twenty kilometres to cover before reaching the cache, if it was there. His eyes fogging from dryness, he took another map reference and a compass bearing. The next few hours were a blur with only trees, scrub, underbrush and the voracious tsetse flies that bit mercilessly. His only thoughts were those of recognizing the vague landmarks on the map, and forcing himself to move, step by step.

Just before dusk he staggered to the spot, one hundred and fifty metres up a small dry ravine. There was the large branch that bent down from a nearby tree, as described. Loose leaves and forest debris covered the area below the limb. Holding on to the branch for balance, Kurt kicked and pushed the debris away, revealing smooth but freshly turned earth beneath. Marshalling the last bit of energy in his body, he cleared the dirt away until the top of a sealed wooden box became visible about thirty centimetres below the loose surface. Kurt pried at the two sealing bands with the blade of his knife, snapping them both before he could lift the lid.

Fumbling through the equipment that was tightly packed into the buried box, he removed two five-litre bladders of clean, fresh water and, not having the patience to unscrew the cap, he slit one of the bags with the knife and poured the contents on to his face and down his throat. As the sweet liquid found its way into his stomach, Kurt knew he would survive.

Packed in the box was a powerful Rigby 416 hunting rifle and ammunition, safari clothes, rations, a compass and area maps. First he loaded the rifle and then ate two of the ration packs, washing the food down with water from the second bladder. An hour later the bush descended into darkness, and sounds of the night hunters appeared from all around. Too exhausted to move any further, he felt a glowing satisfaction at having survived yet again. Backed up against a large tree trunk, he spent the rest of that night in the twilight between sleep and wakefulness with the hunting rifle cradled securely in his arms.

Kurt stayed there until morning, knowing that he could take down any animal on the continent with the rifle. Just as dawn was lighting up the east, giving contrast to the finger like crooks of the tropical tree branches, gentle footsteps crackled the dry brush. He swung up the muzzle of the big rifle towards the sound, which was drawing closer, and a moment later Major Murphy stepped into his sights.

⌘

"Don't shoot, Bwana, I'm a friendly," Murphy said, putting his hands up feigning surrender.

Murphy looked at Kurt and began to laugh, more in relief at finding him alive and safe than ridicule at his ragged appearance. Covering Murphy's flanks were two enlisted Selous Scout trackers, whom Kurt had trained. All three men wore safari garb and were carrying heavy hunting rifles. The men were also clean shaven, in line with their 'wealthy businessman hunter' cover for this operation.

"I really didn't think we would see you again, Kurt," Murphy said as he squatted beside the tree with his rifle butt on the ground. When you missed the sub pickup we thought you'd bitten off too much this time, but I guess we always underestimate you."

"Well, this one was pretty ragged, Murph," Kurt said, his voice still raw and hoarse. "I wouldn't want to do it again."

His exhaustion had eased a little but the lack of sleep and continuous stress over the past few days had put Kurt into a state of disassociation, as though he was looking through someone else's eyes and his own body had ceased to exist. There was no pain, no emotion, just a passing series of images which couldn't be strung together to make any sense.

Murphy saw Kurt's condition and was immediately concerned. His eyes looked vacant. The legendary 'thousand-yard stare' in this case had become infinite.

"We've got a Land Rover just a few clicks from here," Murphy said quietly. "Do you feel up to the walk?"

"Sure, Murph," Kurt replied. "I've come how far? Hell, I don't even know. What are a couple more clicks?"

At Murphy's prompting, Kurt removed his dirty military uniform and put on the clean khaki safari clothes from the cache. The contents of his backpack were transferred to the canvas duffel bag in the bottom of the buried box. Kurt handed Murphy the plastic bag containing the red folder.

"What is this?" Murphy said, holding the sealed bag up to the light.

"Oh, that's just something I picked up at Atibo," Kurt replied, sounding vacant and uninterested.

"Where? Atibo?" Murphy asked, turning the file in his hands.

"Off General Taderera's desk," Kurt told him. "He went to take a piss and left his window open, so I took advantage of the opportunity. You think it's any good?"

Murphy had zipped open the container and was thumbing through the red file when his hands began to shake.

"Holy mother of God, Kurt, do you know what you've got here?"

"No, I didn't have time to look at it with the croc and lion and everything," Kurt replied.

"Croc and lion?" Murphy looked at him with a puzzled expression.

"Never mind, Murph. You wouldn't believe it anyway," Kurt said dismissively.

Looking back to the red file again Murphy seemed incredulous.

"This is the master ZANLA intelligence file by the looks of it; KGB correspondence, sources, codes and methods. It is a gold mine; we've never had anything approaching this, to my knowledge."

"That's nice, Murph," Kurt said as he began to walk. "Let's get the hell out of here before the bastards catch up with us."

One of the Scout trackers grabbed Kurt's gear, and using semi-tactical movement they made their way back to a light brown land rover that had been pulled off the trail and hidden in the bush. On the side was painted 'F.C.S. Safaris, Arusha, Tanzania' in yellow lettering.

"What is the F.C.S. for, Murph?" Kurt asked.

"Fredrick Courtney Selous of course," Murphy replied. "Don't you read your history, boy?"

The ride to the hunting camp was bumpy but uneventful.

As they pulled into the camp, Kurt remembered his grandfather taking him up to Ellsworth Maine once in 1962 to see a movie called Hatari, one of the few movies he ever saw as a child. John Wayne and his crew were chasing animals with cars and jeeps for zoos. He thought that the movie was shot in Tanzania and now he was here. John Wayne also starred in the movie the Green Berets. Kurt wondered what the Duke would think of him.

The rest of the day Kurt, Murphy and the other Scouts stayed out of sight. Late in the afternoon a single-engine bush plane landed on its regular supply run from Arusha. The four-passenger Cessna 182 refuelled and took off immediately with Murphy and Kurt on board. The other two Scouts would fly out the next day. Keeping very low in order to avoid radar, they flew around the huge Caborra Bassa reservoir in northern Mozambique, and an hour and a half later crossed the Rhodesian border near Mukemburra, then returned to altitude vectoring into Salisbury control.

Evidently the word of Kurt's mission success and return had reached the Rhodesian military. As the aircraft taxied up to the hangar at New Sarum, Colonel Donovan and half a dozen other military officers were waiting. When Kurt climbed off the aircraft they began to clap their hands. It was not a noisy, raucous applause but the very measured and polite clapping one would expect from spectators at a British cricket match. This act was a surprise, but strangely compelling to Kurt.

# CHAPTER 26
## CRESCENDO

For nearly a week after returning from the reconnaissance mission at the Atibo and Kitaya camps, Kurt worked with the modellers at the intelligence shop to create scale reconstructions of the two targets. Using aerial photographs combined with his recently acquired ground knowledge, details of the camps were carefully built up until they were all satisfied. When finished, the scale models were accurate enough be used as training aids for the forthcoming raids.

While Kurt was finishing up with the modellers, he received a message that Colonel Donovan needed to speak to him and a jeep would be sent to collect him. Upon arrival at Inkomo, Kurt went directly to Donovan's office, and the two of them were soon behind locked doors.

"First of all I want to thank you, Lieutenant Christianson," Donovan said shaking Kurt's hand. "Your achievements to date have been incredible. Unparalleled is a good word to describe it."

"Thank you, sir," Kurt responded. "I'm just trying to do my job."

"Please have a seat." Donavan waved Kurt to a chair near his desk. "I'd like to ask you a few questions."

"Yes, sir."

Colonel Donavan sat down at his desk, opened a drawer and pulled out a battered red file that Kurt immediately recognized as the one he had carried back from Atibo.

"This is a very interesting file you brought to us, Lieutenant."

"It was just a lucky break, sir. I had an opportunity to snatch it from General Taderera's desk, and I thought it may be of some use."

Donovan looked at him and elevated his thick eyebrows.

"You're correct, Lieutenant. This information is very useful, and unique I might add. Did you look at any of the documents?"

"Not really, sir, I just turned it over to Major Murphy. I didn't have time to study what was in it. I was too busy trying to get back to the rendezvous point. Frankly, sir, it probably would be of little interest to me personally. I leave those things to the intelligence people."

"Have you spoken about this file to anyone?" Donovan asked, his face suddenly serious.

"No, sir. As I said, I just turned it over to Major Murphy. As far as I know Murphy and the two other Scouts that were with him are the only others who know about the file. Why, sir, is there a problem?"

"I've already spoken to the other three," Donovan said. "To answer your question, yes, we do have a problem. It's a problem that shouldn't be discussed with you, but I have little choice."

"Sir?" Kurt looked at Donovan with a puzzled expression.

"To cut to the quick, we have a traitor in our midst, Lieutenant," Donavan said looking down at his desk.

Kurt was silent, there was a pause, and neither man spoke.

"Colonel Ainsley, sir?" Kurt asked.

Donovan looked up at Kurt with surprise in his eyes, which slowly hardened.

"You told me that you did not look at this file, Lieutenant!" Donovan rested his head on his hands and looked at Kurt, waiting for his response.

"I didn't, sir, but I don't trust Ainsley. The first time I met him I saw something in his eyes that troubled me. He is the reason I changed the location of my last insertion."

Although Donovan's face remained expressionless, he was trying to gauge Kurt's response.

"I imagine it's pretty obvious," Donovan said, turning to a more relaxed and open manner again. "Ainsley has always been a bit of a thorn in our side. Everyone has just tolerated him but things have changed now."

"What is this about, sir?" Kurt asked.

Donovan put his hands behind his back and began to pace back and forth in the small office, looking like a big dog confined to a small cage.

"You are an outsider and wouldn't know this, but Colonel Ainsley is very well connected. He is a personal friend of the prime minister, and his brother is a member of parliament in South Africa. That and his access to all of our intelligence files made him one hell of a catch for the KGB. I have to congratulate the Russians on this one; they couldn't have done better."

"But we could have, sir," Kurt interjected. "Traitors are an abomination. I respect the enemy more. At least you know which side they are on."

"I agree," Donovan replied. "But in this situation I feel powerless. This has become a political and military nightmare."

"Is that why you are telling me this, Colonel, because you feel powerless?"

Donovan gave Kurt a stern 'don't go there look', which said more than words.

"I'm not trying to be disrespectful, sir," Kurt replied with unusual force looking the colonel directly in the eyes. "There is only one possible reason you are giving me this information. I know what you are asking me to do."

"It is a very difficult situation, Lieutenant, but as I said my hands are tied on this one. If Ainsley gets wind that we know, he will either bolt to the enemy with all his knowledge, or fight back and take the Scouts down. Either option is unacceptable, and may destroy us. He is a powerful man, and if cornered he will use every resource at his disposal to save himself." "And because I am an outsider," Kurt said, "if things go wrong I am deniable. I would be just a crazy rogue American who is prone to violence, and nobody would be that surprised. I would be strung up in Salisbury Central Prison and that would be the end of it."

"It wouldn't come to that, Lieutenant," Donovan said. "You are a man of exceptional talents, and we have some important friends who would support us."

"I understand, Colonel, but this isn't the sort of thing I do. Assassination isn't in my nature. I am a soldier, not an executioner, and this is a political problem. It should be dealt with by political means."

"Again I agree with you in principle, but you have a stake in this too."

"In what way, sir?"

"The plans for the raid on Atibo and Kitanya that you conceived are in serious jeopardy," Donovan replied. "If Ainsley turns over our detailed plans to the enemy, the raid will be a disaster for us. ZANLA will be waiting and, as outnumbered as we are ... On the other hand, if we don't conduct the raid and take the fight to the enemy, as you stated before, we will lose this war."

Donovan paced the room again before turning back to Kurt.

"If you don't mind me saying so, you have always been a man willing to deal with a difficult problem, and this is a very difficult one indeed."

"I am, sir, but not *this* problem; someone else can deal with it."

Donovan, now seated at his desk again, put his hand on his chin contemplating what he would say next.

"I respect your opinion, Lieutenant, but what if I told you Ainsley was directly responsible for the massacre of the family in Mtoko? In fact he arranged it through the KGB and ZANLA in order to draw you into an ambush."

Kurt was silent but he studied Colonel Donovan's face and saw no trace of deception or connivance. Lying was not natural to the colonel.

"He must have seen me that afternoon," Kurt almost whispered. "We were on a lunch break from discussions at Mtoko and I recall Ainsley walking by the hospital, now that you mention it. There were also dozens of civilian employees working in the camp, including the hospital. Any one of them could have ... "

The information Donovan had just unleashed was shocking but now he dwelled on it, even this level of brutal manipulation was not unexpected. It was beginning to become apparent that war was a total commitment, and far from the 'gentleman's game' it was often portrayed as. There effectively were no rules; there was only defeating the enemy by *any* means. If the enemy chose to be personal and ruthless in order to win he had to be also without regret, without conscience and without hesitation.

"I'd say, sir," Kurt finally whispered hoarsely, "if that information is verifiable, then it would definitely change things."

"It is all in the file that you brought back, Lieutenant," Donovan said. "The request by Colonel Ainsley, and the field orders to the team responsible for the massacre. I can show them to you if you wish."

"That won't be necessary, Colonel; I don't doubt your word."

"I shouldn't be telling you this either, Lieutenant," Donovan added, "but I will anyway.

You have been nominated for the Grand Cross of Valour, the nation's highest military award which has not yet been given to anyone. As I see it, that award could be made to happen. There could also be a promotion in your immediate future, perhaps directly to senior captain, with command of your own assault unit here in the Scouts. We've been thinking about putting such a group together for awhile; maybe now is the right time."

"Sir, you know that I'm not motivated by medals and awards, but I do appreciate the effort on your part. I assume one is not conditional upon the other?"

"I didn't mean it to sound like an enticement, Lieutenant. Everything I mentioned is due to you, regardless."

Donovan was looking out his office window as if in meditation, and spoke into it.

"Sometimes things become very complicated, Lieutenant, and we just have to deal with it. No amount of military training or experience can prepare you for this." Donovan was silent for a few seconds. He scratched his scalp and looked out of his picture window watching two brilliant flycatchers flitting about, their long tail feathers streaming in circles like bright ribbons.

"Sir," Kurt replied, "I recognize that occasionally it may be necessary to do something distasteful for the greater good, but we're really dancing with the devil on this one and the floor may get pretty hot."

Donavan nodded solemnly in agreement.

"I'm glad you see the situation clearly, Lieutenant. Of course, officially this conversation never took place."

"What conversation, sir?"

"Good man." Donovan turned and unlocked the office door.

"Thank you, Colonel," Kurt said as he stood up. "By the way I will need access to the armoury."

"I will tell the armourer, Lieutenant, uh ... I mean Captain Christianson."

Kurt smiled at Donovan and donned and smoothed his brown beret so the silver Osprey was in the left front and straight up and down.

Colonel Donovan watched Kurt leave, but he wasn't smiling.

⌘

Colonel Phinneas D. Ainsley usually enjoyed Sunday morning breakfast on the patio of his spacious and well appointed house in the affluent Salisbury suburb of Borrowdale. He'd met his wife Helen while going to university in Cape Town. Helen came from a once wealthy family, and was an active socialite in the arts and garden clubs. She had not cooked her husband breakfast. In fact she didn't cook at all, or drive for that matter, because African servants did all of the mundane work. That was just as well, for wearing an apron or being up to the elbows in flour wasn't her style.

The lifestyle Helen demanded was in no way supportable on the meagre salary of a military officer, even a senior one. Phinneas, however, was a resourceful man and he did not involve his wife in his 'business interests', nor did he complain about her shopping trips to Europe twice a year. Her needs were understood and provided for. Because Phinneas was able to support Helen in the manner to which she had become accustomed, he was able to attend social functions escorting an attractive and elegant wife. This was a definite plus for a slight, balding, un-athletic man who felt he was never given the degree of respect he deserved.

In the dark recesses of his mind, Ainsley knew he had sold his soul and country for an elevated lifestyle that was beyond his means, but life had its choices and he had little regret. He justified his treason by convincing himself that society had not given due credit to the brilliant and charming person hidden beneath such a nondescript shell. Becoming a spy liberated his trapped soul. It proved beyond all doubt that he was very clever indeed, smarter than those who dismissed him. Sometimes in a mirror the boring administrator wasn't there anymore ... James Bond looked back.

What Ainsley never counted on and couldn't predict, were forces that operated beyond his comfortable, limited world of social and military protocol. The first time he met Kurt at the Pungwe briefing, the crude, insolent, foreign-born enlisted man was regarded as a bad joke. How could a single man of dubious nature be taken seriously? It was so preposterous that he ignored the whole episode. Reporting such foolishness to his KGB handlers would have just invited ridicule.

At that time he was also having a serious argument with his KGB contact. Notoriously cheap, the handler wasn't willing to pay him anywhere near what the information was worth, or at least what Ainsley thought it would be worth. After all, he wasn't doing this out of loyalty to a political belief. Having an elitist upbringing, he could never identify with the communist cause anyway, it was just a means to an end. That 'end' for him was a comfortable retirement elsewhere in a few years, which couldn't be accomplished with a few thousand dollars. He needed at least ten times the amount he was being paid, so he relayed this demand to his contact.

His KGB handler had just laughed at his request for more money. After all the hard work, danger and quality intelligence he had provided, all he received in return was derision from an unsophisticated errand boy! The Pungwe raid proved to be the perfect solution to the dilemma. Ainsley decided to not provide any further information to his contact until they met his demands, and had withheld details about the Pungwe raid. He kept quiet about the whole affair. The KGB needed to be taught a lesson.

Although it resulted in more money as he had predicted, both ZANLA high command and the KGB were furious in the wake of the raid. This action alone put ZANLA at least two years behind schedule for national liberation. The handler informed him that Christianson was a known foe, an elusive enemy of international communism. Ainsley was given the task of engineering Kurt's demise, but initially he baulked at being assigned such a lowly task.

"I am an intelligence operative, not a murdering assassin," he told them. When that response provoked a very cold reaction from his handler, he agreed to do his part, provided he didn't have to personally dirty his hands.

The meeting in Mtoko gave Ainsley the unexpected opportunity. One of the workers at the hospital was a ZANLA undercover agent, and informed him about Kurt's conversation with the farm family. His KGB profile indicated that the American would react impulsively because of his rash and righteous nature. Initially, the plan worked perfectly and Christianson was drawn away from supporting troops so he could be eliminated. The plan would have succeeded, except that most of the ambush team were amateurs and did not live up to expectations. The unfortunate demise of Comrade Vlad marked the end of KGB tolerance, and Ainsley was given the task of eliminating Christianson ... or else.

The arrangements to do just that were already in motion on that breezy, warm Sunday morning. Ainsley sat on his patio finishing his breakfast and outlining the plan on a pad of paper on the table in front of him, when the phone rang in the house.

"Would you take that please, love?" he said to Helen. "It's probably for you anyway."

His wife rose from her patio chair and went inside. A moment later a shadow blocked the warm rays of the morning sun falling on Ainsley's back. The colonel looked up. "Funny, there were no clouds today, what ... "

Instead of the blue morning sky, the last thing Phinneas Ainsley saw was a field of bright stars sweeping across the blackness of space.

⌘

Wearing thin black gloves, a sweat suit that covered most of his body, trackless shoes, and a balaclava over his head, Kurt hid in the hedges near the patio waiting for the phone call that had been arranged. When the call came and the woman disappeared into the house, Kurt quietly moved directly behind the colonel and without any hesitation placed the muzzle of a silenced 9mm behind his right ear and pulled the trigger. The gun shot itself made little sound, more like a fizz than a bang. The silencer on the piece had been externally friction fitted around the end of the barrel, not threaded on the end as was more usual.

Kurt quickly removed the silencer and pocketed it. The pistol was wrapped in Ainsley's drooping hand. He moulded the man's fingers around the grip, and then allowed the pistol to fall to the grass beside the slumped body. The action had taken only a few seconds. Turning to leave, Kurt noticed the legal pad of paper lying on the glass patio table. There was a second's hesitation. The plan didn't call for taking anything from the scene, but the pad of paper looked like an outline of some kind and was covered with fine droplets of blood.

Reaching down he grabbed the pad, put it beneath his sweat suit top, and quickly left the scene. Returning to the thicket of bushes where he'd waited earlier, Kurt removed a second pistol from his belt and fired a single loud shot into the air. He attempted to recover the ejected casing but it flew into some thick underbrush and unable to spot it right away, there was no time left to look. Leaping into a ravine that bordered the property, as he made his escape along a pre-planned route he heard a woman's shriek coming from behind. Sunday mornings were quiet times in Rhodesia; hopefully nobody had seen him come or go.

⌘

The presentation was planned as a small affair, with a limited press release after the fact. Rhodesia was a small, tight-knit country, however, and when the word slipped out that the Grand Cross of Valour was to be awarded for the first time, the news travelled like quicksilver down a hillside. Because of all the newly generated interest, the presentation ceremony was delayed a few days so the much larger Salisbury Fairgrounds could be prepared to host the event.

Kurt was bemused by the publicity that the award was receiving. By nature he was a quiet and secretive person, a fact reflected by his life and military skills. This type of fanfare was something he really didn't enjoy or encourage, but would have to tolerate again. He received orders a week after Ainsley's 'suicide' for promotion to Captain, Senior Grade, with permanent assignment to Selous Scouts Assault Force, Inkomo Barracks. It was a unit that didn't yet exist. Colonel Donovan, it seemed, was a man true to his word.

⌘

Inspector Robert T. Greenfield was a forensics expert for the British South African Police, based in Salisbury. The name of the proud organization went back to early colonial times when the British South African Company was the administrator in what was now Rhodesia.

As a result of the war that had ravaged the land for several years, his expertise in gunshot wounds and homicides was considerable. He was called in occasionally when the municipal police force required technical assistance, or the crime was of high enough visibility to warrant the additional scrutiny. The death of Colonel Ainsley easily qualified and, responding to a Sunday morning phone call, he appeared at the scene shortly after the incident was reported.

On initial inspection, it appeared to be a suicide. His body was slumped in a white wrought-iron patio chair with an entrance wound of a high velocity projectile over the right mastoid bone. The bullet had penetrated the brain and passed out of the left parietal area. On closer examination, Greenfield found a distinct lack of tattooing, or powder burn marks, surrounding the entrance wound. Suicides by handgun to the head were almost always contact wounds, or fired from a very short distance. The gun also looked a little strange. It was a conventional and fairly common Browning 9mm High Power, but instead of the barrel being nearly flush with the front of the slide as was normal, it was about an inch longer.

Greenfield had seen examples of Browning High Powers with longer barrels that were meant to be fitted with silencers or muzzle brakes, but the barrel extension was mostly threaded for this purpose. This one wasn't, but on close inspection the end of the barrel had scratch marks on it, ending precisely at a ring, as though something had been friction fitted on the end.

Even though it was Sunday, Greenfield went to his car and made a call on the radio for his small forensics team to assemble. A painstaking and detailed sweep of the scene and the surroundings was completed by late afternoon, and two items of interest were recovered. Both items were spent 9mm shell casings: one found a few feet from the corpse, and the other fifty feet away in the bushes surrounding the back yard. Both shell casings were recently fired and had the same military head stamp. Even a preliminary look, however, indicated slightly different extractor markings on the cases, suggesting that they had been fired from different guns.

Besides the shell casings, there were a couple of other inconsistencies noted by Greenfield. On the glass-topped table in front of the dead man there was a spray of blood droplets from the head that would be expected in a shooting of this nature. On closer examination however, the droplets were missing on a piece of the table that matched the outline of a book or paper of some kind. After the Colonel was shot, it looked as though something was removed from the table. Helen, the only other person to have access to the area after the incident, denied taking anything, but confirmed that her husband was 'working on something' when she had answered the phone. The other discrepancy was also interesting. Ainsley was ambidextrous ... but primarily left handed.

⌘

Publicly, Colonel Ainsley's demise was treated as a suicide from the outset, although his wife was very vocal in her protests and declared to anyone who would listen that her husband was murdered. The country's sole newspaper, the *Rhodesia Herald*, had heavy editorial censorship due to the war, and none of her opinions saw print. There were also rumours planted by unidentified sources regarding Ainsley's 'financial troubles' and also allegations regarding the smuggling of contraband.

Though unfounded, the rumours explained his high-rolling lifestyle, and unofficially substantiated his suicide. The affair seemed to be an open and shut case, at least in the minds of the press and the public.

⌘

The award ceremony took place on a beautiful Saturday morning near the end of winter before the tropical convergence zone brought rain down from the Congo basin. Kurt put on his full Selous Scout dress uniform for the first time. Army officials allowed his American awards and decorations to be worn along with his Rhodesian medals. It was a juggling act to find room for everything and make the coloured ribbons and metal insignia look balanced.

The British and their Rhodesian descendants had no moral hang-ups as suffered by their more retentive American cousins about serving in a foreign military. Their colonial rule once spanned half of the earth; hence it was only natural to have men serve in foreign armies and foreigners serve in theirs. Because the US was historically isolated, there was little cognizance that soldiering was an occupation like any other and sometimes one had to move around to remain employed.

Due to the high profile nature of the event, Kurt shaved off the beard and had his hair shortened and neatly trimmed. Public scrutiny wasn't something he was used to or liked, but common sense told him to look his best today.

Standing in his room in the officers' quarters just prior to departing for the fairgrounds and the presentation ceremony, Kurt looked in a mirror, something he seldom did. A child raised by a poor fisherman has little chance to ponder self image or appearance. Pure survival was always the predominant challenge in life. Survival meant battling external forces, which was why soldiering came so naturally. Introspection, self reflection and personal ego had played little role until now, but when he saw his image in the mirror on that morning, he was confounded by what he saw.

The man reflected there in no way resembled the ragged youth, a self portrait etched into his consciousness. Though resplendent in a brown tailored uniform and coloured ribbons and metal badges, an entirely different reflection manifested. The man looking back wore scarred metal and leather shoulder plates and a heavy vest of chain mail. Replacing the stylish beret with the silver osprey badge was a smooth steel helmet, designed to deflect blows from heavy swords. In this transmogrified vision that lasted only a moment, all there was to know about him became clear. His Viking warrior blood could not be denied, and he smiled. Occasionally latent truths surfaced. Breaking eye contact with himself, he left for the presentation ceremony.

⌘

Kurt was amazed by the number of people gathered at the fairgrounds. It looked like the whole population of Salisbury and the surrounding communities were there. In times of crisis people rallied around heroes, because heroes personified the righteousness of their cause, and salvation. If heroes didn't come forward on their own merit, they were selected or created by the people or their leadership. Presentation of the first Grand Cross of Valour created this opportunity for this bitter war, and for these people. Kurt had been elevated to the position of 'hero' because a hero was required.

All of the military chiefs and government dignitaries were in attendance. Every officer was competing to outdo the others by wearing awards and decorations that went back to WWII in some instances. The senior officers stood in a loose cluster; their wives, wearing elegant day dresses and hats, kept a discreet distance from their husbands and chatted among themselves. Most of the officers were comfortable with one another, having spent years in the British or colonial armies. Some were Sandhurst graduates, the British equivalent of West Point, and still lived by the etiquette learned at that prestigious institution.

In many ways, the Rhodesian army differed little from the pre-war Colonial army, but the old tactics and protocol were at great odds with the type of war being fought in Africa and elsewhere in the world in the 1970s. The officers of polite society, with their regulated and rigid behaviour, were facing guerrilla fighters who played without a rule book and respected nothing. Time and radical changes had caught up with the old guard. Although loath to admit it, they understood this truth, and in order for their cause to survive they realized that a new breed of soldier and officer had to be forged. Created in the mirror image of the enemy, they would be just as ruthless and aggressive, but superior.

Reed Donovan stood to one side of the social clique of officers, a true outsider amidst this league of gentlemen. Until recently, Donovan was an enlisted man, and only reluctantly made the transition to officer at the insistence of the prime minister. Donovan's uniform was covered with decorations won in all corners of the world when British influence was still paramount. Always a pragmatic and unconventional thinker, he was an old soldier now, but in many ways a perfect template for the 'new' soldier. A rebellious nature and disdain for weak leadership had gained Donovan many serious enemies in his career. He understood that the best hope for promotion of his ideals was to pass his sword to a member of the younger generation, a man forged from the same metal, but without his baggage.

When Kurt walked into the room the hush was immediate. Both the officers and their wives stopped talking. Every pair of eyes pivoted to watch the strapping figure that radiated an animal strength and vitality, rare in the polite world of social graces. Kurt moved directly to Colonel Donovan and stood at attention and nodded in respect to his commander. Donovan nodded to Kurt and immediately began to escort him around, formally introducing him to the officers and their wives. Kurt was polite but did not display deference even to the senior officers, including Generals Wallis and Hicks. He looked all of the men directly in their eyes, as an equal.

When the prime minister arrived, Kurt was ushered to the steps leading up to a newly constructed platform just in front of the reception hall. He stood at the back while the prime minister and his wife, were escorted up the flight of stairs. They were followed by half a dozen military dignitaries, including Colonel Donovan.

To one side of the presentation platform, clearly visible to the crowd below, was an object totally hidden by a large white drape. The assembled crowd looked at the hidden form with curiosity but there was no reference to it when the prime minister began to speak into the microphone to the assembled crowd.

"We are here today, citizens of Rhodesia, for a very special presentation."

The Rhodesian prime minister spoke in a steady monotone. As a farm lad of twenty he volunteered to be a Spitfire pilot in the Battle of Britain where a portion of his face was blown off by an exploding German Me-109 cannon shell. The reconstructive surgeons did a remarkable job at the time, but the extensive injuries meant the left side of his face had little muscular movement. Since all smiles and other facial expressions looked lopsided as a result, he chose to use no expression, and his voice followed suit.

"In the history of armed conflict," the PM continued, "it is seldom we have the opportunity to recognize a single person who has contributed as much to the cause of our country's freedom as the man we are honouring today. Captain Kurt Christianson has not only exhibited unmatched personal bravery while under enemy fire, but has, through the force of his character, brought innovations to our security forces that have resulted in the destruction and defeat of our enemy on a massive scale. Most of his exploits cannot be discussed for reasons of national security, but I would like to say that his courage, talent and boundless spirit give us inspiration and confidence that we will win this terrorist war. For these reasons, the Rhodesian government and the Security Forces have decided to award the first-ever Grand Cross of Valour to Captain Kurt Christianson of the Selous Scouts."

On that practiced cue Kurt ascended the short flight of steps to the platform with an effortless glide. He reached the top and stood to attention, sharply saluted the prime minister and, with that, the crowd roared. The bright morning sun made the polished gold, silver, and chrome decorations glitter and sparkle with metallic radiance, and painted his coloured ribbons with vivid intensity.

Rhodesians were by custom and culture a quiet, confident and stoic people. The last few years of bitter war, however, had brought upon them an uncharacteristic sadness and despair at their personal plight and unknown future. Kurt's presence on that beautiful morning burned through the clouds of defeat, filling their hearts with hope again. Women cheered, men shouted and children, too awestruck to make a sound, had the memorable image permanently engraved in their hearts and minds.

Kurt performed a perfect military half turn and stood to attention in the middle of the platform as he had been instructed. An aide bearing a green velvet presentation box walked stiffly to the side of the prime minister, where they both manoeuvred to stand directly in front of Kurt. The aide raised the lid of the box and the prime minister lifted the solid gold medal attached to a green and white ribbon out of its nest. Kurt bent down slightly, enabling the prime minister to easily place it around his neck. The prime minister then stepped to the side allowing the public and press an unimpeded view of the first Grand Cross of Valour ever awarded. On the face of the medal was carved the image of an attacking lion. The award was heavy, but to Kurt it felt weightless as he looked at the eyes of the ecstatic crowd.

All eyes in the crowd were looking directly at him. In spite of the multitudes of people present in the audience, a single individual stood out clearly and Kurt's eyes were immediately drawn to him. The man's skin looked a sickly pale and his head was shaved revealing stark white scar tissue on his scalp and neck. The Mad Medic hadn't been around for awhile, and seldom made his presence known in public, for he preferred the shadows. Now, the crazy man was here, arms crossed in front of him and a smug look on his face almost as if to ridicule the entire event. Kurt's elation was instantly deflated.

Another man also watched from the crowd, but his presence went unnoticed. His police uniform was neat and pressed and his face was placid and impassive. Inspector Greenfield had been working the Ainsley case tirelessly, despite many other demands on his time. This case was coming together and he was anxious to attend the presentation today, to take a look at a 'person of interest'. The man stood on the platform, resplendent. A highly decorated idol in the eyes of thousands and the best soldier to come out of the long guerrilla war, but to Greenfield he represented something else.

⌘

When the applause and cheering died down, the prime minister held up his hands to quieten the crowd.

"If I could please have your attention," he said into the microphone. "I have a surprise." The crowd quickly became silent.

"In order to commemorate this event," the PM said, "I've commissioned a statue to be made in the image of a soldier in our security forces. It did not take extensive discussion to agree on a model for this statue. When Captain Christianson was serving in the Rhodesian Light Infantry, a photograph was taken of him during a combat operation. This picture was used by the artists to construct this model."

The PM waved his hand and an aide carefully pulled a cord that caused the white drape to fall free from the covered object, revealing a plaster statue that glistened pure white in the brilliant sun. The figure's fine features were lost in the glare, but at seven feet in height and finely sculpted, the crowd collectively gasped and murmured at the stark boldness and beauty. The statue was a perfect portrayal of Kurt with a rifle in his right hand and wet hair clinging to his head. The boots, uniform and web gear were exact and were all in proportion. The figure looked like he was in the midst of an exhausting mission and would pursue it to the end. The image represented a soldier who would never tire in his quest for victory.

The PM spoke again, "An exact duplicate of the statue you see before you will be cast in solid brass made from melted-down rifle cartridge cases. It will then stand in permanent display at the entrance to Cranborne Barracks. The courage of our brave soldiers will never be forgotten. Thank you all for coming today."

A deafening applause followed. Kurt walked down the stairs and was instantly inundated by people. People with kids, people with cameras, reporters with microphones, people's hands were all a blur. Kurt wanted to get back to Inkomo to start preparing for the big raid. All this publicity would not help but he was coming to realize that sometimes you did have to dance with the devil, and everything had a price. Kurt looked for the Mad Medic, he wanted to talk to him ... but he was nowhere to be seen.

⌘

For several weeks there was little sleep as a newly formed assault unit was built from scratch. Requests for manpower were met only reluctantly, and sometimes not at all. Every unit was short of experienced soldiers and to have a junior officer cherry pick the best people raised the hackles of many commanders, but there were exceptions. Bluie was easily pulled from his slot as troop leader in 3 Commando RLI; even though he was very good, he drove everyone in the Commando to distraction. Kurt made Bluie NCO in charge of training for the new assault group where he became a changed man, at least for the moment. His SAS background would be invaluable in establishing the sort of tactics needed for the new unit.

Bob Holliday came over to fill the slot as sergeant major. His maturity and extensive combat experience made him a natural for the job. Bob was released without much argument. The Rhodesians couldn't get used to his strong Texas accent.

The other key person, John E. Earl, was offered the position of deputy commander of the new unit, and he was also put in charge of air operations. John's four thousand personal jumps and wide-ranging experience deploying combat parachutists made this assignment a comfortable fit. Kurt was surprised that Earl was released so easily, but there were rumours of an incident involving heavy drinking, singing rugby songs and shooting up neon signs with a Walther PPK at a tourist resort. This killed his plans for becoming commanding officer of the parachute school, and facilitated the transfer.

Kurt's Scout Assault Force, or SAF, would consist of three main elements. There would be a tracking and ground reconnaissance group that Kurt would train and command personally. This small and elite section would act as the spearhead and also be the eyes and ears in the field. Soldiers assigned to this section would be deployed before an operation took place to gather intelligence but during the combat operation itself, would function as assault co-ordinators and snipers.

The airborne element, headed up by Earl, would consist of light infantry paratroopers and also individuals trained to act as forward air controllers who would liaise with aircraft, including DC-3s, fighter bombers and helicopters that supported the operation.

The third element of the assault force was the gun trucks and heavy weapons section that Major Murphy would continue to lead. Even though Murphy outranked Kurt, there were no concerns with the chain of command. Colonel Donovan was officially listed as the unit commander and he would field all inquiries and represent the unit at the army senior staff functions. This left Kurt free to plan, train and be in the field and not be bothered by staff meetings or politics.

⌘

Training for the raid on the Atibo and Kitaya camps began in earnest at Inkomo Barracks and at other locations around the country. Initially, no one except the senior officers directly involved were given any specific details about the raid for fear of leaks. Ainsley was out of the way, but there were possibly other turncoats buried in the military and political apparatus.

Kurt worked intensively with all members of his new assault force by utilizing the scale models of the targets he had helped construct. He thought that if the soldiers could be intimately familiar with all physical details of the targets, there would be less confusion on the ground and the goal of complete destruction of the camps would be achieved more quickly while incurring minimum friendly causalities. Economics and security issues prevented the construction of full scale mock ups of the camps, so small scale models and taped representations on the ground had to suffice for training purposes.

The raid was scheduled for the first week in November, just before the onset of the rainy season. In addition to the first and second elements of the SAF, nearly every other active and reserve military unit would be called on to provide the needed manpower. The raid would be by far the biggest operation in this war to date.

The goal of the operation was to crush the ZANLA high command by killing as many enemy soldiers as possible, and destroying or confiscating war material. If ZANLA lost the initiative by being dealt such a heavy blow, they might never recover sufficiently to mount a credible threat. Winning or losing wars, especially in low intensity guerrilla insurgencies, was both physical and psychological. Whichever side was on top could capture the momentum and run to victory.

Rhodesia needed a turning point. Guerrilla warfare is by nature a war of attrition, a slow progressive battle to destroy the faith and confidence citizens have in their government and military to keep them out of harm's way. Like cancer, the erosion of confidence is cumulative and insidious and the decline is only noticed in the terminal stages. To correct a life threatening cancer, radical surgery is often performed. In the same manner, when the life of a country is at stake, a bold and radical plan may be attempted to save the nation, and the dream.

Kurt was not aware that he had been collectively chosen to fulfil this role, as saviour of the cause, vanguard of the last hope. As an outsider, a foreigner, he did not carry the stigma of a demoralized and defeated people but was an external force, that came in a time of dire need. In history and in legend, heroes from the outside are commonplace. As an American, Kurt had another advantage. Since the bloody and unprecedented American Revolution two centuries before, the United States had been looked to as a provider of moral force and liberation. This aura still existed, despite the fact that the original firebrand revolutionaries had long since been deposed by self-serving bureaucrats, financial manipulators, and polished 'yes' men.

⌘

On the day before the Atibo and Kitaya raid, the entire combined strike force including Scouts, RLI, Air Force, various reserve units and police assembled at JOC Mtoko. The base was under a state of total lock-down to maintain absolute security. The atmosphere at Mtoko could be described as both enthusiastic and tense. Never before had such a group been assembled in Rhodesia, and the phrase 'It's about time' was on everyone's tongue. Mtoko would be the primary assembly point and marshalling area. The actual launch sites were selected points on the border, but they would not be occupied until just before the attack. The thinking was that this would prevent the enemy from getting wind of the operation before it was underway.

The distance of the targets from the border made it impossible to employ the armoured trucks and heavy guns that had become the Scouts' favourite raiding tools. There was just no way to get them that far into enemy territory and back again safely. In order to optimize their resources, Kurt planned a diversion utilizing those assets.

That morning Major Murphy had taken the armoured column and began attacking several small ZANLA base camps and launch sites located in the southern area of operations, just over the Mozambique border. This action would be publicized in order to distract ZANLA HQ into believing that an offensive was being mounted in the south, hundreds of miles away from the Atibo and Kitaya camps. There was no historical precedent or reason to believe that Rhodesia would or could commit the large numbers of airborne and or ground forces necessary to take on the more than two thousand personnel located in and around the two camps. The beauty of the plan was even if it leaked out, few would believe it.

Kurt made the rounds with the various units and discussed details of the forthcoming attack with commanders, NCOs and troopers alike and to a man, their response was one of respect and enthusiasm. Even senior officers treated him as a contemporary, not an army captain. This held true except for old friends, who were not impressed by his new status.

Kurt walked over to Holliday who was lying out and inspecting all of the equipment to be taken on the operation by the Scout assault group. The gear looked as though it was spread over half of the Mtoko airfield.

"Christ, Bob, it looks like a yard sale," Kurt said from behind Holliday as he was squatting down adjusting straps on a pack.

"Come to spread some holy water over the web gear, have ya?" Bob said in his usual surly manner, without looking up from his task.

"Holliday, you are one impertinent SOB you know that?" Kurt said, with feigned irritation.

"Of course I know that, Boy Wonder," Bob said turning to look up at Kurt. "But that's just me ... love me or leave me."

"Well, I certainly don't love your nasty ass, but I couldn't think of a better person to drop on the ZANLA High Command," Kurt replied.

"Amen to that, brother. I want to get the boss myself, put a bullet between his eyes and bring his scalp back."

"Must be that renegade Comanche blood in you talking, Bob," Kurt said. "It's finally coming out. Sorry to say you won't get a chance at the big guy, he doesn't spend much time with the troops. He will probably be politicking with the Russkies or East Germans. You'll have to settle for some of his military commanders."

"Don't worry my cap-ee-tan, there won't be nothing left in those camps when we get through," Bob said.

"We're counting on it, Bob. Have you seen Bluie? I have to talk to him."

"I've seen that red-headed kangaroo fucker round here someplace, probably over in the mess hall." Bob went back to work on the equipment.

"I'll be in the K-Car, co-ordinating the assault," Kurt told him. "You can talk to me if need be at any time. Just keep your radio close."

Bob nodded but didn't look up from his task or say anything more. Kurt felt genuinely humoured for the first time in weeks. For all that has happened recently, none of it impressed those closest to you. They know you too well, he mused.

A minute later Bluie came walking toward the equipment layout area. He was eating something, but it was hard to determine what it was.

"Hey, cap, getting ready for the biggie, arrrh we?" Bluie asked.

"Hi, Bluie, need to talk to you."

"Yea, what about, Cap?

"Come and walk with me, we have to be out of earshot," Kurt said quietly.

Kurt and Bluie strolled toward the far end of the Mtoko airfield where the white winged crows were circling the smoking burn pits, waiting for another meal to cool.

"I have some information I need to give you but I'm hesitant," Kurt said with a serious, almost conspiratorial inflection.

"You know you can trust me, Cap, except if there is beer or women involved," Bluie chuckled.

"Yes I know I can, Bluie, but I still feel I shouldn't ... involve you."

"Quit the crap and give it to me, will ya. You know you're gonna anyway."

Kurt hesitated for a moment, but finally said; "There are some traitors among us, Bluie. We have two names from a very sensitive source, that can't be discussed. There is one army and one air force that we know about. I think they could pull something when we get on the ground. I can't say much more."

"Can't you have 'em pulled from the mission, cap?" Bluie asked, finally becoming serious.

"That would be too obvious," Kurt replied. "They would know something was not right and, as I said, the source of the information is very sensitive. Since you're going to be on the ground with the first wave of paratroopers, I thought you could ... "

"Not to worry, Cap. I'll keep and eye on the baastaads and I'll switch rifles."

"You'll do what?" Kurt asked.

"I'll carry an AK-47, not an FN. Then if someone was unfortunate enough to get shot ... accidentally that is."

"Deniability," Kurt added.

"That's the word I was lookin' foah!" Bluie said, then turned and smiled.

"Thanks Bluie, it's just between us."

"Of course it is, our little secret," Bluie said, and then he winked at Kurt in an exaggerated manner.

# CHAPTER 27
## PINNACLE

## Joint Operations Centre Mtoko
## November 17, 1977

The night prior to the attack on the two ZANLA camps, few of the soldiers slept. Equipment was cleaned and packed then disassembled and repacked. Hours before dawn, the first wave of troops left the Mtoko airfield in Alouette helicopters for the launch sites on the Mozambique border.

The helicopter-borne soldiers were organized into four-man 'assault sticks' and the choppers were refuelled and checked for mechanical faults before the long flight over enemy territory. The targets were far beyond the operational range of the small aircraft, so refuelling points had been established deep inside Mozambique. On the days prior to the attack, drums of aviation fuel had been flown in and small security detachments with radios remained behind to guard them. Communications with these expedient refuelling sites indicated that the locations chosen in the trackless bush remained undiscovered by the enemy.

Timing and choreography of the raid were the most critical factors in the success of the operation. The first strike would be conducted by Hawker Hunter and Vampire fighter bombers to soften up the defences and panic the defenders of the Atibo military garrison. The air attack was to be followed immediately by Fireforce paratroopers who would jump into Atibo and set up stop positions at key points surrounding the target to intercept guerrillas trying to escape, then they would begin to clear out resistance. In the final stage, helicopter-borne infantry would be inserted to sweep through the camp, neutralizing remaining resistance and seizing anything of military or intelligence value.

The Kitaya camp across the river in Tanzania was a smaller target with minimal defences. Plans called for a single DC-3 loaded with a carefully selected stick of Fireforce paratroopers to jump into the outskirts of Kitaya and bottle up the occupants with rifle and mortar fire until Atibo had been dealt with. Fireforce and helicopter-borne troops would then be airlifted across the river to attack and neutralize Kitaya. This part of the plan was admittedly the weakest, and the result of the limited number of soldiers available and the risk of dividing manpower and air assets below critical levels. This compromise was finally reached, but neither Kurt nor the other operational planners liked it. John E. Earl volunteered to command the Kitaya stick because of its difficult nature.

The DC-3s carrying the paratroopers were faster than the helicopters and could make the round trip without refuelling. Jets were in turn much faster than both of the other aircraft, so departures had to be calculated from the time they were required at the targets. This vital timing of events was checked and rechecked before take off times were assigned to the aircraft.

At zero four fifteen hours the first flights of helicopter troops lifted off from the Kotwa launch site on the Mozambique border, headed towards their refuelling stop two thirds of the distance to the targets. They would be the first to cross the border, but the last to arrive at the target due to their relatively sluggish speed. At zero four twenty-five hours a single DC-3 loaded with Fireforce paratroopers, took off from the Mtoko airfield destined for Kitaya. Two more DC-3s full of paratroopers took off at zero four forty-five hours headed towards Atibo. At zero five zero five hours all of the participating jet aircraft took off from New Sarum Air Force base in Salisbury. Once the jets were airborne, everyone realized that the raid was a go and there could be no turning back.

Kurt had a personal K-Car for the operation. The K-Car was a designation given to a 'Command Helicopter' that acted as an eye in the sky, allowing the battle commander to direct action from above as a composer would oversee an orchestra. This helicopter left at dusk the night before the raid, and spent the night at the refuelling site so it could arrive at the target before the others. The K-Car needed to be over the targets immediately following the air strike but not before, or they risked being blown out of the air when the bombs fell. Helicopters were very vulnerable to blast and fragmentation, so the plan was for the K-Car to orbit several kilometres away from the targets and wait for the aerial bombardment to cease. Then it would sweep in to help co-ordinate the ground assault.

Mounted on the port side of the K-Car was a Hispanu 20mm short cannon, the same weapon Kurt had used attached to the Land Rover on the Pungwe raid. This effective and powerful gun was manned by an Air Force technician and allowed the commander to engage point targets on the ground, and also to mark targets for air or ground attack.

On the morning of the assault, Major Murphy was in his second day of ravaging small ZANLA bases hundreds of kilometres to the south-west. There were few enemy soldiers in these temporary camps, because most of the guerrilla teams had been deployed into Rhodesia. ZANLA had learned a costly lesson at Pungwe and not many troops were kept in these staging areas so close to the border. From a tactical standpoint the vehicular attacks were not very decisive, but they provided an effective diversion for the larger raid.

The senior ZANLA military leaders assigned to Atibo were in a conference in General Taderera's office early that morning. They were heatedly discussing reports from the field that the Rhodesians were on the offensive in the south-west, and talking about how they should respond to this new round of aggression.

⌘

Just as the eastern sky had brightened Atibo and the residents were beginning their day, several fast moving and low flying jet aircraft shot overhead. Faces craned skyward in an attempt to catch sight of the noisy intruders. On one or two occasions in the past, ancient Mig-17s belonging to the government of Mozambique had flown over during training missions. Loud and fast aircraft were a rarity here, especially this early in the day. Even so, their presence provoked only mild interest.

Three 12.7 heavy machine guns with anti-aircraft globe sights were placed in rudimentary defensive positions on the outskirts of Atibo, but the gun emplacements were not manned. General Taderera thought that this was unnecessary given the relative safety of the location. As the planes passed overhead the stunned observers watched open mouthed as objects fell from their wings and bellies. These objects almost seemed to fall in slow motion at first, but because they were released at such a low altitude the delay was brief before they struck the ground. Then all hell broke loose.

A five-hundred-pound high-explosive bomb from the internal rotary bay of a Canberra bomber ploughed through the side wall of a main barracks building, exploding at its centre and killing or injuring more than forty people inside. The wooden structure caught fire and began to burn brightly in the dusky light. A Hawker Hunter dropped two containers from the roots of its wings. As the thin metal envelopes struck the ground at the edge of the camp, they broke open, releasing hundreds of green bomblets which were slightly larger than golf balls. The rubber-coated spheres employed the kinetic energy from the fall and bounced in all directions, exploding at random. Each exploding bomblet sprayed hundreds of white-hot metal fragments of steel wire, shredding anything nearby.

A ZANLA supply officer, Captain Maduki, heard the commotion and walked towards the door of his office just in time to see a little green ball bouncing across the ground, heading directly towards him. Instinctively he reached out to catch the curious object, but the ball exploded a foot from his outstretched hand. He died with his arm still extended.

General Taderera and his staff heard the sound of jets, quickly followed by explosions. They all scrambled up from their meeting and bolted from the building, running to the main square of the camp to assess what was happening. Having discharged their bomb loads, the Hawker Hunnter and Vampire fighter bombers then turned tight circles for a final strafing run on the camp before heading back to base. The 30mm explosive-tipped cannon shells burst into deadly fragments on impact. One of General Taderera's adjutants, a lieutenant colonel from the Gweru district, caught a cannon round in his midsection as he ran across the main square. His torso flew twenty feet to the rear while his pelvis and his legs were frozen in mid-stride.

Above the din, General Taderera began shouting orders for all of his soldiers to man the defensive positions. A training drill held the previous month for just this type of situation found the camp's performance inadequate, but at that time the general wasn't overly concerned. Atibo and Kitaya were located far beyond the reach of the Rhodesians, or so he thought. Taderera looked in dismay at the chaos around him. The air strike had reduced his best cadre to a collection of panicked civilians.

Taderera had a feeling that an air strike was inevitable given Rhodesia's penchant for aggression and desperate measures. He should have anticipated this! Then another thought raced through his mind. Maybe this was a good thing. It would allow him to restructure the defences and ask for more funds from the Central Committee. His mind was turning, Yes, good, it was good.

As his eyes swept the scene General Taderera caught the silhouette of a helicopter in the distance, several kilometres away but coming closer. The distinctive dragonfly shape of an Alouette II became apparent. As far as he knew neither the Mozambican nor Tanzanian governments had any of those. The Rhodesians did, but this was far beyond their range. Suddenly General Taderera felt the first symptoms of real fear, and acid rose in his throat. If Rhodesian helicopters were here so were the Rhodesian troops, probably the deadly Fireforce and the camp's defences were in total shambles. The general began to run as never before.

⌘

Kurt's K-Car approached Atibo just as the Hunters and Vampires finished their strafing run. The K-Car pilot was told to orbit the camp perimeter once so the overall situation could be assessed and active defensive positions identified. Kurt spotted a 12.7mm gun emplacement that was not firing, but two ZANLA soldiers were hastily preparing it for action. The chopper tech was told over the intercom to engage with the 20mm cannon. The helicopter manoeuvred into position and with several rounds of cannon fire, the gun was neutralized. Seconds later near the position, flashes were seen as crates of 12.7mm ammunition exploded nearby.

In the large main square located between the buildings and around the perimeters of the camp, soldiers and civilians were running around chaotically. There were non-combatants, including women and children, living in the camp with the soldiers. This outraged Kurt, who didn't like to see civilians hurt, whilst acknowledging that it was almost impossible to prevent innocent casualties in this type of situation. He watched as a woman wearing a long pale-blue chiffon dress flowing gracefully behind her, ran swiftly across the main square looking strangely like a beautiful butterfly, fleeing danger.

Green tracers from AK-47s flew sporadically through the pale morning sky. There was no evidence of organized defensive resistance against the surprise attack. Using air strikes to prep a target was a double-edged sword. It usually created a state of disorder among the occupants, but it also gave warning that something dramatic was happening and the element of surprise was lost. If the ground sweep wasn't fast enough following the aerial attack, the defenders might have enough time to consolidate and present resistance.

Kurt's radio crackled to life.

"Osprey this is Talon. We are two minutes out, be warned."

"Talon this is Osprey, reading you fours. Your release point is camp centre. Resistance is light, I repeat light ... over."

"I copy you, Osprey. Release point is camp centre ... out."

Kurt told the K-Car pilot to vector away from the centre of the camp to stay clear of the paratroop drops.

The two DC-3s flew in almost wing to wing at an altitude of just under 150 metres. Half a kilometre in front of the camp perimeter, the paratroopers began to simultaneously exit from both aircraft. At low altitude parachutes were only deployed shortly before the soldiers hit the ground and there was no time to use a reserve chute, should a main chute fail. The parachutes blossomed like fat green flowers in two rows leading into the centre of Atibo.

As they hit the ground, the paratroopers rolled out, detached their chutes and proceeded in pairs to neutralize resistance in the camp, prior to the ground sweep. There was firing followed by radio traffic indicating that pockets of armed resistance were being encountered.

⌘

Half an hour before, whilst still dark, the lone DC-3 containing the Kitaya assault force headed directly to the other side of the Kumva River, following a flight path designated so as not to over-fly Atibo. Kitaya was a ZANLA administrative centre and, according to Kurt's reconnaissance, very lightly defended. The plan was to pin down the Kitaya defenders with a minimum number of troops until the Atibo assault team had finished, who would then be airlifted across the river to clean up.

During the planning of the raid, even this division of forces was controversial, but Kurt was convinced that one reinforced stick of paratroopers was sufficient to hold Kitaya until the main assault force could arrive from across the river. Some of the staff recommended letting Kitaya go and only attacking Atibo, but Kurt had convinced them that a complete elimination of the ZANLA command would require destruction of both camps. There would be no second chance and Kurt's ideas had prevailed, amidst much scepticism.

The Kitaya assault team was led by John E. Earl and consisted of 3 Commando RLI soldiers, two mortar teams from RLI Support Commando and several members of the Scout assault force. The Kitaya attackers, by necessity, had to make their insertion before first light. They did not drop directly on the camp but landed approximately two kilometres outside the camp's perimeter. Because of the early hour and the location, the parachute drop did not alert people on the ground, and Earl's small team of paratroopers was able to approach Kitaya undetected. The mission called for setting up stop groups at the three principal camp exit points then, with directed small arms and mortar fire, resistance would be bottled up until reinforcements could be airlifted in to sweep the target.

During his initial reconnaissance of Kitaya, Kurt had spotted two heavy machine gun positions on the perimeter of the camp. These were quickly found by the paratroopers and silently neutralized by removing the bolts from the guns, with the intention that the weapons would be airlifted intact to Rhodesia after the battle. The soldiers moved into their assigned positions, and when they heard the first explosions from the air attack on Atibo located several kilometres away across the river, Support Commando mortar teams began lobbing 81mm HE shells inside the perimeter of Kitaya.

The results were predictable and initially went as planned. People began to run from the buildings into the streets of the camp just before sunrise. The mortar crew then fired parachute illumination flares, which lit up the sky and cast an intense light on the scene. Scout snipers positioned on the camp perimeter then fired on anyone who looked like a soldier moving on the streets, dropping someone with every shot. Within a few minutes nearly everyone in Kitaya had taken cover and were not about to move. All that the assault force had to do then was to keep their heads down, with intermittent fire, until reinforcements could arrive from Atibo.

⌘

Back in Atibo the paratroopers in the airborne force were engaging targets of opportunity, to keep the occupants scared and confused so there would be minimal resistance for the troops approaching by helicopter. There was random firing from some of the buildings and the bush at the camp perimeter, but these targets were quickly engaged by the paratroopers using FN rifles and light machine guns. So far, there were no reported friendly casualties, and Kurt wanted to keep it that way.

Kurt keyed his radio button: "Osprey to Mamba, Osprey to Mamba ... what is your ETA, over?"

The voice came back immediately, clearly, with no distortion.

"Osprey ... Mamba here reading you fives. We are on final approach ... insertion momentary."

"Roger, Mamba, tell combat team leaders to press attack immediately. I repeat, press attack immediately before resistance becomes organized."

There was a pause before the voice came back.

"Roger, Osprey, word has been passed. We are thirty seconds from insertion... out."

Kurt turned his head and saw the flight of Alouettes descending into their pre-selected landing sites outside the camp perimeter. Even before the helicopters could settle on the ground, Fireforce soldiers leapt from them and ran forward to form a sweep line.

Other helicopters containing Cobra stop groups were landing further away from Atibo. Their mission was to set up static ambush points on roads, paths and other likely exit points from the camp. The mission of the assault force was to kill every enemy soldier unless they were designated a prisoner. The Rhodesian troops were outnumbered by ZANLA forces by ten to one, so the attackers could not afford to be selective about targets. When so greatly outnumbered, aggression was essential for mission success.

From his airborne perch Kurt saw a jagged line of muzzle flashes and gun smoke on the south-west perimeter of Atibo. The RLI Fireforce and Scout assault elements had begun their ground sweep and they were moving steadily forward with minimal resistance.

Suddenly streaks of light were seen coming from the centre of the camp and heading toward the line of advancing troops. Immediately the distinctive drawl of Holliday's voice boomed over the radio.

"Osprey, Osprey, we have a big gun shootin' at us, probably a 12.7. I got one man down already and I can't see where the fire's coming from!"

"Roger, Mamba, I think I have the gun's location. Take cover until I can clear it."

Kurt followed the tracers back and saw where they originated. On top of a relatively intact building a concealed HMG position had been set up, covered by the thick bough of an overhanging hardwood tree. It was a tough shot from any angle. If the 20mm was used and the rounds struck the limb, the enemy operator might have time to elevate the barrel of the 12.7mm and put a round or two through the K-Car. A 12.7mm incendiary round would devastate the flimsy Alouette II. Kurt told the 20mm gunner to hold his fire and the pilot to orbit wide and low to come up behind the HMG position.

As the K-Car circled around and green tracers arced past them. Panicked ZANLA soldiers on the ground were firing at random, but they all knew that a random shot could be just as deadly as an intentional one. The chopper slowed to a hover and came in behind the roof-mounted 12.7mm heavy machine gun. The enemy operator's position was almost totally obscured by tree branches and leaves. Kurt thought that whoever set up this nest had done a good job.

They were almost at a hover, which made them extremely vulnerable to both ground fire and the 12.7 itself, if it was turned on them. Kurt leaned out of the side door of the K-Car and thumbed the selector switch of his FNC to semi-automatic. As the gun operator broke cover in an attempt to see what was happening to his rear, Kurt fired three rapid but aimed shots. The gunner rolled down the roof. The man was very large and had gold braid on his epaulettes. When the body fell off, a brief glimpse of his face left no doubt that the gunner was General Taderera himself, recognizable from the night when Kurt had stolen the red intelligence folder.

Kurt was surprised at who he had just shot, but quickly indicated for the chopper tech to fire the 20mm cannon into the camouflaged gun position. The short-barrelled 20mm barked several times. One of the cannon rounds struck some ordinance stored in the position and secondary explosions began to go off, setting the roof of the building alight.

Kurt keyed his radio.

"Mamba, this is Osprey. The gun had been neutralized. You can proceed with the sweep ... over."

"Much obliged, big bird," Holliday's drawl came over in his usual monotone. "Medics have been notified about the wounded man, looks like his wound isn't critical."

"Roger, Mamba, good luck ... out."

The K-Car increased altitude to seventy-five metres and again circled the outer boundary of the camp. RLI Support Commando had just arrived on the scene and from the camp perimeter were lobbing 81mm mortar shells in front of the troops conducting the sweep. The co-ordination had to be exact. The 81s were used like prepping artillery fire, by carefully walking exploding shells ahead of the advancing troops. Within minutes the sweep line was working their way through the camp centre with a solid wall of small-arms fire, encountering only light and sporadic resistance from enemy guns.

⌘

Back at Kitaya, the small airborne force assigned to bottle up the smaller camp unexpectedly began to take heavy fire from the direction of the village. This fire wasn't sporadic or intermittent as expected, but was intense and well directed. Unknown to the planners, a company-sized ZANLA reaction force had been placed outside Kitaya after Kurt's reconnaissance some weeks before. Now Earl's paratroopers were being pinned down by an unanticipated superior force.

Earl grabbed his radio mike and keyed it.

"Osprey, this is Adder. We are receiving intense fire from the direction of the village, both small arms and RPGs. I request air support if available ... over."

"I copy you, Adder. Negative to tactical air, they have all gone for refuelling. Give me specifics and I will try to help. Support force ETA is thirty to forty minutes ... over."

"Confirm transmission, Osprey. We're pinned down here and a large enemy force is closing on us. Mortar bombs are gone and ammo is short, situation is becoming critical ... over."

"Roger, Adder. I am heading your way. Keep transmission open." Kurt keyed his mike again,

"Mamba, come in Mamba."

"Mamba here, whaddya need, feathered friend?"

"Are you about done there, cowboy? The boys across the river could use some help. Heavy resistance has developed … over."

"Roger, Osprey, we're just cleaning up. Still some active pockets we have to deal with. Is the trouble serious … over?"

"It may be, Mamba. I'm heading across now. Get the troops together and follow me ASAP. Do you copy … over?"

"Will comply, Opsrey, but the choppers can't land until we clear out the remaining pockets. Don't bite off more than ya can chew, now. Wait on us if ya can."

"Roger, Mamba … I'll keep coms open … out."

Kurt ordered the K-Car pilot to head across the river to the Kitaya camp immediately.

"Sir, we are low on fuel. We have to go back to the fuel bladders at the support site."

"Negative," Kurt told the pilot over the internal mike. "Earl and the men are in imminent danger. We have to go now. If we run out of fuel we'll just have to put down somewhere"

"But, sir, I …

"Just fly this damned thing. There's no time for discussion."

The pilot banked the K-Car away from Atibo, and flew across the river into Tanzania. In a few minutes they were vectoring towards Kitaya. Plumes of smoke from the burning buildings made the target easy to see on the bright clear morning. Kurt knew the camp layout pretty well from his covert reconnaissance weeks ago. However, it took awhile to orientate himself and locate the pinned down troops, and the opposing force. Finally, distinctive flashes from AKs and RPD light machine guns gave away the position of the enemy. Kurt keyed his mike.

"Adder, I see your bogies. Looks like it's at least company sized. What is your status?"

Kurt had a difficult time hearing Earl's voice over the surrounding gunfire.

"We're holding off the bastards, Osprey, but the ammo will be finished shortly. Where the hell is Fireforce? Over."

"About twenty minutes, Adder. We can't get the choppers to them until they clear out the ground fire."

"We will be out of ammo and overrun by then, Osprey, it's not looking good."

"Hold tight, Adder, I have an idea."

"Well, it better be a good one, or we're in the shit."

"Make a low pass over the heads of our men and parallel to the enemy's line of advance." Kurt explained his plan to the pilot over the intercom.

"They'll shoot the hell out of us; sir we'll be a sitting duck."

"Maybe not. If we pass quick and low, it will take them by surprise. Get the cannon ready." Kurt pointed at the tech, "No point targets ... just chain fire it into their line. okay, here we go."

The Alouette banked sharply to port and decreased altitude until its skids were brushing the small branches on top of the trees. The helicopter then pulled hard to starboard, positioned to fly directly over the heads of Earl and his men. The moment the Alouette was poised, the Tech began firing the 20mm cannon as fast as its cyclic rate would allow. *Thud ... Thud ... Thud ... Thud*. The airframe shook as the cannon unleashed a stream of high explosive rounds into the bush occupied by the advancing enemy.

Kurt saw the high-explosive fragmenting projectiles explode into the tree line, sending small branches and leaves down in a shower. The fire was not directed and would not be effective in producing enemy casualties, but that was not the purpose of the exercise. Kurt was only trying to keep the enemy's heads down and slow their rate of advance so he could move in behind them.

Midway through the fly-by several ZANLA soldiers began to return fire. Green tracers arced up from the bush and zipped behind them. Then one RDP gunner swung ahead with an adequate lead and a bullet struck the front of the Alouette's Plexiglas windscreen and shattered it. Another bullet passed through the open door and hit the tech just above his left knee, causing him to fly backwards away from the cannon. Reacting to the impact the pilot instinctively swung the chopper away to avoid the incoming fire. Kurt placed his left hand on the pilot's shoulder, and with his right indicated for him to stay low, and continue steering to port in order to circle behind the enemy. The aircraft took several more hits from small-arms fire but none struck a vital area or the occupants. In seconds the helicopter was behind cover and out of sight of the ZANLA troops.

The K-Car was running with an empty fuel gauge so there was no option but to set the chopper down to the rear of the ZANLA reaction force. Kurt was surprised that such fierce opposition had been laying in wait, but this was no time for contemplation. Through the shattered Plexiglas windscreen a small clearing could be made out midway between the advancing reaction force and the village. Without room or time for a conventional landing approach, Kurt pointed to a hole in the trees, and the pilot pulled back to autorotate, or flop down, into the small clearing. The smell of jet fuel indicated one or more bullets had penetrated the tanks or fuel lines and they were fortunate the helicopter wasn't on fire. The chopper set down very hard, enough to jar their bones and bend the landing skids, but they were on the ground safely.

Kurt hustled the pilot and the technician out of the crumpled Alouette, fearing it might burst into flames at any moment, into a patch of low dense cover nearby.

When they reached the cover, Kurt quickly applied a compression bandage around the technician's leg to slow the bleeding; happily the bone seemed to be in one piece. He told the pilot and technician to stay in place until someone returned for them. Both crew members carried an issue Star Model B 9mm pistol for protection. This was hardly effective weaponry but in the circumstances, better than nothing at all. The pair looked frightened, but at least they had decent cover.

Bullets were raking over their heads, clipping off leaves and twigs which fell like green rain. Kurt charged the FNC with a fresh magazine and checked his combat vest to ensure all of the spare magazines and grenades were there and secure. Some of the ZANLA troops had turned around and were firing in their direction. Coming at them from behind had already upset their advance. Fortunately, the enemy had no way of knowing that the threat to their rear was only one man, with one rifle.

Kurt knew he faced the impossible but if he failed now many soldiers could be killed, and it was his plan. This thought put his mind into that red zone reserved for special occasions. Against all tactical logic he began to run, keeping low, charging directly into the confused and now disorganized ZANLA unit. Yet again there was the exhilaration of running on the jagged edge, where surprise and audacity were the only tickets to survival.

Holding the FNC .223 rifle low and in front, there was no need for sights. Each target was fired on whilst zigzagging through the bush, in no predictable pattern. By sprinting through the middle of the enemy position, Kurt caused a brief hesitation on the part of the enemy troops to fire in the direction of their fellow soldiers. This natural momentary reluctance to engage gave Kurt a slight but valuable advantage of seconds. Until now the ZANLA troops had been rapidly advancing on Earl's outnumbered stick, and had not taken cover. This made them easy targets for the most part.

On his first pass through the ranks, Kurt hit nine of the sixty ZANLA troops, cutting a swathe through the middle of their formation. Without stopping, he spun around and sliced through their rear security, downing another four. Every time the FNC fired the report was followed momentarily by a *whack* as a bullet hit flesh. Most of the ZANLA troops were green and this was their first fire fight. The psychological effect on them was devastating. They heard one of their own being hit with each round fired. This fear collapsed their momentum, turning a once-organized advance into a chaotic rout. Kurt took cover and, as the retreating troops passed, dropped more of the enemy with single shots or short bursts.

Earl and his troops sensed that the ZANLA opponents, who a short time ago threatened to overrun them, had stopped moving offensively and were now in retreat. Most of the ZANLA novices had dropped their weapons and taken to the bush when things started to turn bad. Even though his troops were critically short on ammunition, Earl took advantage of the situation. He quickly organized a counter assault, and using classic fire and movement tactics, manoeuvred against the retreating enemy. Sweeping the bush, the Rhodesians could hear the light short bursts from Kurt's .223, firing at retreating ZANLA troops unlucky enough to pass his position. Twenty minutes later, the threat had been neutralized.

Alouettes began arriving at the Kitaya site with troops airlifted from Atibo. The assault force, fresh from their morning victory across the river, made short work of the smaller camp's remaining defences. In another hour the operation was complete, and all gunfire stopped. Surviving enemy had either surrendered or fled into the bush. Flushed with this double victory, the Rhodesian troops began to celebrate, even though they were still deep into enemy territory. The victorious troops began to assemble at the west end of the Kitaya compound shouting congratulatory slogans to each other and whooping and jumping around like fans at a college ball game.

⌘

When the immediate threat was over, Kurt made his way back to the helicopter pilot and the wounded technician left in cover near the downed K-Car. The body of a ZANLA soldier was sprawled a few feet away. Evidently one of them shot the soldier when he came too close during the withdrawal. The pilot was still grasping a 9mm pistol in his right hand and intently staring towards the direction of the dead soldier. Kurt quietly approached to his rear and spoke.

"I think we're clear, guys. Who ... "

The pilot reeled around and fired his 9mm. In the fraction of a second before it happened, Kurt saw the gun swing towards him as well as the panicked look on the pilot's face. He began to move sideways, away from the direction of the pistol when there was a searing heat on his left arm, like a hot iron was suddenly pressed to it. The pilot immediately realized what he had just done, and tossed the pistol to the ground as though it had burned him.

"Oh God ... what have I done?" the pilot said in an anguished voice, putting his hands to his face.

At first Kurt looked at him as he would a pet dog that had suddenly bitten him, but then began to laugh and shake his head with disbelief.

"All of this," Kurt held out his right arm to indicate the battle zone, "all of this and I get shot by my own damn pilot ... Christ."

"I'm sorry, sir, I ... "

"Don't worry," Kurt told him. "I should have known better than to sneak up on downed airmen. I just stupidly broke a cardinal rule of special operations. It's my fault. Hey, I've an idea. We'll say that this guy over here," Kurt pointed to the dead ZANLA body, "was coming through the bush and I didn't see him. Then he fired one shot that wounded me but before he could finish me off, you shot him with your pistol."

"But, sir, I ... " the pilot began.

"Never mind the 'buts', Lieutenant, that's the way I saw the incident. Don't you agree, Sergeant?"

The technician nodded but did not speak.

"Good, if all our stories match then we'll get you a medal for heroism. After all, you did a great job of flying us in here."

The two men were still crouched down in the thick bush, looking miserable.

"Come on guys; let's join the others. It looks as though we may have won this one."

After wrapping his wounded arm with a piece of torn shirt, Kurt and the two airmen made their way back toward the collection of soldiers and equipment, to cheering and clapping. Word quickly circulated about the latest action. When it was mentioned, Kurt tried to relate how the pilot had saved his life, and that he was the real hero of the day, but no one seemed to listen. Hands were reaching out slapping them on the back, and men were putting their fists in the air, hooting and howling like wolves.

Despite exhaustion and throbbing pain in his arm, Kurt felt a glow and a rush travel through his body in a lingering wave. They had just pulled off an operation that many thought was impossible. Two enemy base camps were totally destroyed and the war could now take a new turn, offensive not defensive. If not historic, this battle was surely unique in history.

He remembered a scene from one of the few movies his grandfather had taken him to in that far-off Maine village. The movie was Lawrence of Arabia and the band of Arab irregulars, under the command of T.E. Lawrence, had just blown up an enemy supply train.

Kurt walked through the jubilant crowd to an Alouette that had landed in a clearing. Leaping onto the skid, he scrambled up to the rotor head on top of the helicopter. Extending his rifle with his right arm and, despite the wound, spread the other wide, then slowly turned around to face the assembled men. A wild shouting erupted. To his ears, it was more inspiring than the most beautiful music ever written.

⌘

Later that evening when all the operational forces had withdrawn across the Rhodesian border, Kurt was staring into a fire at JOC Mtoko. The party was already well underway and even though the hour was late, there would be no shortage of beer and food tonight. The estimated tally was seven friendly troops wounded and two killed by stray AK rounds, one Army and one Air Force. He would have to thank Bluie for a job well done when he saw him next. The enemy had suffered casualties of up to two-thousand killed with an unknown number wounded. The action would without doubt be recorded as one of the most dramatic one-sided victories in the annals of warfare.

He felt drained and stunned. The implications of it all had not yet sunk in, when someone approached from the rear. Kurt turned to see Colonel Donovan. The colonel's presence was unexpected but Kurt was glad to see his boss. He was smiling but in a reserved way, as was his manner.

"Excellent, Captain Christianson, you've done an incredible job. I'll debrief you formally at Inkomo tomorrow. The reason I came out here though has to do with another matter."

"What's that, sir?"

"A police inspector by the name of Greenfield insists on talking to you," Donovan replied. "I brought him out with me. He said it couldn't wait. I don't know what it's about; he said it's personal."

Colonel Donovan motioned with his right hand and another man stepped into the firelight. Neatly dressed in a police uniform he stuck out his hand to Kurt.

"I hear congratulations are in order, Captain Christianson," the policeman said with a smooth pleasant tone. "I know you must be exhausted but it's essential I talk with you tonight. I'm Inspector Greenfield of the BSAP, I won't keep you long."

"No problem," Kurt said with a little irritation in his voice. All he wanted to do now was to eat, drink and celebrate with his troops, not talk to this stiff.

"If you'll excuse us, Colonel," Greenfield said.

Greenfield indicated to Kurt to 'walk this way' and the two of them slowly moved over to a storage building at the edge of the compound. Light from the flickering fire vaguely, and intermittently, illuminated their forms but they were far enough away from the crowd to talk privately.

"Captain Christianson ... "

"Call me Kurt, Inspector, I prefer that."

"That's fine Kurt, I'm Robert. We can keep this informal; it's just between the two of us. I hate to interrupt your celebration here but this couldn't wait. I've been working the Ainsley case for several weeks now and ... "

Kurt tensed, and took a step back from Greenfield, who was carefully watching his body language.

"Let me preface my discussion by saying I've been an ardent admirer of you, Kurt. You've done great things for this country."

"Cut to the quick, Inspector; don't play games, I'm not in the mood."

"In due course, Kurt. I want to frame this in the best way. I just want to say that I believe I am as good at what I do as you are at what you do. We operate in different worlds but it has always been my basic inclination to understand things in detail. That is my passion and my job gives me that luxury. You have worked your way into a position in the military where you can plan and conduct war because that is your driving force. Information and understanding events are mine. I think we are equally driven."

"And," Kurt prompted impatiently.

"Like I said, I was assigned to the Colonel Ainsley murder case and I believe I have figured it out."

"Well good for you, Inspector," Kurt said. "It seems that it has been concluded, in the papers anyway, that Ainsley killed himself, and had motive to do it."

"Precisely, those were my official findings."

"Then what the hell are we talking about here?" Kurt replied, "You didn't come all the way out here tonight to tell me that."

"No, I didn't," Greenfield said. "I said those were my *official* findings. In fact, Kurt, I know that you killed Colonel Ainsley."

"Do you have proof of that, Inspector? Because if you don't you are treading on very dangerous ground here, you know that."

"Yes, I have proof," Greenfield said. "But rest assured that I will never implicate you for the murder. Ainsley was a very ... should we say ... untrustworthy man. However, he made the mistake of crossing *both* sides, and when he did that he was as good as dead. It was just a matter of time. Nobody was sad to see the last of him, including me."

"Then I'm still confused, Inspector, why are you telling me this?"

"I just wanted you to know Kurt that you didn't fool *me*. I worked it out pretty quickly. It was actually more difficult to make the evidence fit the cover story than it was to solve it in the first place."

"So, the question is still unanswered, Inspector, *why* are you telling me this?"

"Because it leads to my second point, and the real reason I'm here, Kurt."

"I'm listening."

"I'm not going to lie to you. You're too perceptive and I respect you too much, and I have the feeling you can take the truth, no matter how harsh." Greenfield paused and let the statement sink in before continuing.

"I told you my passion is trying to understand events and this is what I've discovered. Just after World War II there was a secret meeting between some very powerful people including financial interests, the heads of international corporations, heads of state and such. The purpose of the meeting was to prevent any more world catastrophes from occurring like world war. With atomic and biological weapons they feared that the next big war may be the last. It was not an unreasonable assumption."

"Still I fail to see the ... " Kurt said, now growing agitated.

"Hold on, I'll get to the point in a second," Greenfield replied. "After much study they concluded the common factor that caused these problems was what they termed 'the cult of personality.' Hitler, Stalin, Mao, Castro, the major headaches on the international stage were all set in motion by people who literally came out of nowhere and by the force of their personalities and ability to influence people brought the world to war, or the brink of war."

"Inspector, I don't see where this is going."

"Where it's going, Kurt, is that you've been identified by these people as having that potential."

Kurt was stunned by what he'd just heard.

"Me! That's insane. I'm not a Hitler or a Stalin. I'm just a simple goddamn soldier from a hardscrabble upbringing. How could I ...?"

"They are not saying you *will,* Kurt, just that you *could,* and their protocol says we can not take that chance. You don't play by the rules, people are mesmerized by you, you are gifted and you have extraordinary vision. These are all cardinal signs."

"Well, saying I believe you, which I don't, what will these people do? How will they stop me, or someone else, from achieving our destiny?"

"Whatever it takes, Kurt," Greenfield replied. "Death comes to mind, scandal, blackmail, disease, there are a multitude of ways to stop one person once that person has been identified."

"I suppose in my case, the Ainsley affair?"

Greenfield looked him directly in the eyes before answering.

"Possibly."

"Do you work for these people, Inspector," Kurt asked. "Or are you just their errand boy?"

"Neither, Kurt, and I'll overlook the insults, I know this is traumatic. Like I said, I just know things and I don't want to see anything happen to you. You are a national hero and I want you to exit as one. It's in the country's best interest."

"So what do you propose for me to do, Inspector? I suppose you've got that figured out too."

"If I were you I would go to that classy lady in Namibia, Kurt. Get a real life, have some kids, hunt, fish, have fun. You've had enough killing and war. Do the right thing."

Upon hearing the phrase Kurt's mind was back in the desert; he could smell the clean air, feel the dryness on his skin and a wave of perfect pleasure displaced all the other feelings in his tired and bruised body. He stood still for many seconds until the feeling slowly subsided.

"How did you know about her?" he almost whispered, "about Diana I mean?"

"I told you, Kurt, my job is to know things. I've even read your mail."

Kurt nodded to Inspector Greenfield and quietly walked off. He knew what his destiny would be. It had come to him in a flash and he knew there would be no regrets. It was *his* future ... and it was the right thing to do.

⌘

In the complexity of the modern world it became apparent that the most powerful men on earth were not the richest, nor the most influential, not even the most ruthless. They were people who could change the course of history with only spoken words. It was a rare ability, but the future of mankind would be altered in many ways by their secretive and subtle efforts.

Greenfield walked toward the parking area where his police Peugeot was parked. As he passed between the two buildings he saw a ghostly figure barely illuminated by the rising moon. He knew who it was. Next to the man sat a pig, a wild warthog, which was looking at its master with quiet reverence while he stroked between its ears. The pig had changed its ways lately and was finally becoming 'civilized' according to the Mad Medic.

As Greenfield passed no words were exchanged, but the Medic lifted up a white arm and gave the inspector a 'thumbs up' which, to the few that knew him, was his highest compliment.

Inspector Greenfield smiled to himself. It felt good to please the boss.

# EPILOGUE

In the tumultuous decades at the end of the twentieth century, great changes took place in all parts of the world, and no area was changed more dramatically than Africa. Military victories were inevitably nullified by political concessions, but this had become the way of the world. The colonial enclaves are now independent countries with local self-ruling governments. The promise of independence, however, was only the beginning of even more serious problems to surmount, such as unbridled population growth, sluggish economies and factional violence. These ongoing troubles are not easily resolved, and the future success of most of these countries remains uncertain.

⌘

Despite some beliefs, a single person cannot change the course of history. The more fortunate can ride a wave of existing tidal changes to glory if they are in the right place at the right time. An unfortunate person may just as easily be caught up and obliterated by the maelstrom of violence and war still so prevalent on our planet.

An overly cautious person avoids conflict at any cost. A reckless person is drawn to conflict for its own sake. A rare individual seeking the elusive secrets of truth and meaning may find both during a harrowing journey of personal discovery. However, it is easy to confuse the seeker with the reckless, because both bear the same scars.

As humans, we have come a long way from the shadows of our origins, but in many ways we are the same creatures that hunted animal flesh for survival and then for unknown reasons turned those deadly skills on our own kind. Knowledge of our past may allow eventual understanding of our present behaviour. Only by a deep and continual search of self may we one day become the rational beings we profess to be, but there is no guarantee.

⌘

Kurt started life anew in the deserts and rugged bush of Namibia. Andre, at the end of his military service, decided to pursue commercial aviation and had no time to continue with his game management job with the government. By way of some returned favours and pulled strings, Kurt was given Andre's old position and took to it like a fish to water. Kurt quickly became an integral part of the landscape he grew to love, and for the most part forgot about the war he was so drawn to early in life. For the first couple of years he would wake up in a cold sweat, dreaming of some battle, or images of the dead, but those events became more infrequent until they disappeared altogether.

Kurt and Diana were married the year after he left Rhodesia in the commissioner's office in Windhoek. The list of invitees was small, but Jack Malloy, Colonel Reed Donovan, and Dave Armstrong were present for the ceremony. Over the door of the ranch house in the isolated Namibian bush Kurt placed a carved wild olivewood plaque with the runic inscriptions as he remembered from the small house in Maine. Roughly translated they said:

*"Only by the force of man's will can the fire be kept burning in the cold forest."*

Kurt hired Xi and several other Bushman trackers to assist him in his job. As a result of their combined expertise, illegal poaching of game in the region was almost eradicated. The animal populations rebounded and the small family of Bushman felt secure about their ancient lifestyle, for the first time in their memory.

The Grand Cross of Valour Medal was placed on a nail in Kurt's study at the ranch. One day Xi made a rare visit to the house and saw it hanging there. His eyes were transfixed by the golden disc with the raised design of a lion. Kurt smiled when he saw Xi's interest, and lifted the medal and brightly coloured ribbon off of the nail and placed it around the Bushman's neck. Xi grinned, his filed teeth looking like spikes as he felt the weight of the piece and ran his fingers over the bold design.

"You may be the only one who appreciates this thing, Xi, I sure don't," Kurt said as he walked away.

⌘

In the late 1990s a group of wealthy American hunters were staying at a private safari camp that bordered a national game reserve in Namibia. Just before dusk after a successful day of hunting, the half-dozen hunters were drinking liquor and telling their hunting stories when three Bushmen silently moved into the camp. One of the men began to reach for his rifle but was rebuked by the guide.

"They are government game officers, damn it. Just stay put."

The leader of the three Bushman had a bright gold medal hanging on his chest held on by a finely braided leather rope. The cloth ribbon was frayed and bleached with sun exposure. One of the Americans pointed, but the guide put his hand up and shook his head.

"They are just checking out our kill," the guide told them softly.

The well-oiled hunters watched the Bushman as they carried out their business, and began to smirk and then laugh among themselves at these miniature people.

"Do you gentleman find something funny?" The deep resonating words came from behind.

The men stopped laughing, froze, then slowly turned towards the voice. The speaker was over six feet tall with skin as bronzed as burnished copper. The hair on his head was bleached white from the sun, and even in the fading light his piercing blue eyes looked not at, but through them. He wore only faded green shorts and a frayed vest of a similar material. Around his waist was a belt made out of exotic textured animal hide which supported revolver and knife scabbards of the same leather.

The man's body was unlike any the Americans had ever seen. The muscles in his legs and arms rippled like a large cat. The hunters stared at the imposing and frightening figure, but remained speechless.

"Oh hello, Eric," their guide said smiling as he walked toward the stranger, hand extended. "How's your family doing these days?"

"They are all fine thanks, Peter. Uncle Andre is still flying 747s on the London run. Mom and dad keep busy with the ranch of course, and they both teach part time. I've taken over most of dad's patrols; he doesn't move as well as he used to, I think some old injuries are catching up with him."

"Well, give them all my best, Eric, and tell them I'll try to stop by when things calm down a bit. Would you four like to stay for dinner? The cook always makes too much food, might as well not let it go to waste."

"Thanks for the invitation, Peter, but I promised Xi I would go to Bushman camp tonight; one of his sons has just had a child and there is a celebration. Every new life is precious to the Bushmen; there are so few of them left."

"Thanks for stopping by," Peter said. "I hope you've found everything in order?"

Eric turned to the Bushmen and fluently conversed with them in a soft clicking tongue, so exotic to the Western ear.

"They say everything is fine, Peter, as expected. I'll talk to you later."

"Bye, Eric, and be careful out there."

The men quietly slipped into the growing dusk.

The hunters' mouths were still agape. None of them said anything for a minute, until one broke the silence.

"Who the hell was that? Is he British, German or ...?"

Peter lit a bowl of pipe tobacco, always surprised at how naive these foreign hunters were. Oh well, it's a way to make a living out here, he thought.

"That was Eric Christianson," Peter said taking a long draw on his pipe. "He is an African."

⌘

"Sir, we need to go. They are waiting."

The finely suited and distinguished white-haired man stood in the dusty, stiflingly hot warehouse. It was an odd place for him to be. To his front stood a metal statue, but dust, grime and cobwebs had nearly obscured its surface. The statue was of a man, a soldier from a long-past and forgotten war.

"Sir, why are you looking at that old statue? It is just some junk they dug out recently, I hear its going to be melted down soon to make something useful."

"I'll be with you in a minute," the white-haired man said to his aide. "Just leave me for a moment. There are some things that you are too young to remember, which I need to deal with."

The man stood motionless for another minute. Although the stature was unwanted and discarded, it conjured up powerful images and feelings that could never be spoken of to anyone. This statue marked both the beginning and the end of his tumultuous second life.

"I have done as you said, Tokoloshe," the man spoke with a whisper. "It took a long time but it happened as you predicted, so now I must leave you."

Reaching up to his neck with his good arm, the man removed the braided necklace with three charms he had worn for the last forty years, and carefully hung it on the outstretched arm of the statue.

"I'm sorry, Prime Minister, but we must go now. Parliament is waiting for your arrival," the aide said, sounding frustrated.

The prime minister took one more look at the neglected statue and shook his head.

"How strange this world is ... goodbye, Tokoloshe."

The door of the warehouse closed and the statue was enveloped by darkness.

⌘

On a barren, lonely, windswept desert plain great luminous discs eternally point toward the heavens ... listening.

# Glossary of Terms

## Geography and politics

**Angola** – Was a Portuguese colony on the west coast of Africa. When the Portuguese suddenly pulled out in 1975, a guerrilla war ensued as several factions struggled for control. See MPLA, FNLA and UNITA.

**Luanda** – Largest city and capital of Angola.

**FNLA** – Frente Naçional de Libertaçao (Portuguese) or The National Front for the Liberation of Angola (English). The FNLA was a nationalist group founded in 1957 by Holden Roberto in 1957 as the Union of the Populations of Northern Angola.

**MPLA** – Movimento Popular de Libertaçao de Angola (Portuguese) or People's Movement for the Liberation of Angola (English). Founded in 1956 by the consolidation of several national liberation movements, the MPLA took over control of Angola when the Portuguese withdrew from the colony in 1975 and has ruled it ever since.

**UNITA** – Uniao Naçional para a Independencia Total de Angola (Portuguese) or National Union for the Total Independence of Angola (English). Founded by charismatic leader Jonas Savimbi, and backed by the US and South Africa. UNITA resisted the takeover by the MPLA in Angola's southern provinces well into the 1980s.

**Agency** – Is also known as the CIA (Central Intelligence Agency) or sometimes 'The Company'. Intelligence-gathering and covert action arm of the U.S. government that descended from the OSS (Office of Strategic Services) in WWII.

**Brazzaville** – The capital and largest city of the Republic of the Congo, it is located on the Congo River.

**Bushmen** – Also referred to as the San, are ancient hunter-gathers who are indigenous to southern and southwest Africa.

**Maine** – A state on the far northeast corner of the US, known for its picturesque seacoast and fishing.

**Mozambique** – For several hundred years was a Portuguese colony along the southeast coast of Africa. When Portugal pulled out unexpectedly in 1975, the liberation movement FRELIMO was handed power on a plate. Mozambique borders Rhodesia (Zimbabwe) to the east and harboured insurgents during the guerrilla war.

**New Mexico** – A state in the desert, south-west USA.

**Rhodesia** – A small landlocked country in south-central Africa named after Cecil Rhodes whose British South Africa Company acquired the land in the nineteenth century. Originally a colony of Britain it was a self-governing colony since the 1920s. Because of disagreement with Britain on majority rule in the 1960s, Rhodesia declared Unilateral Declaration of Independence (UDI) in 1965 and a bitter guerrilla war ensued. After popular elections were held in 1980 Rhodesia's name was changed to Zimbabwe.

**Salisbury** – Capital of Rhodesia, renamed Harare after Rhodesia became Zimbabwe in 1980.

**Senegal** – A country (formerly a French colony) on the far western tip of Africa.

**South West Africa** – Originally German Southwest Africa, this sparsely populated and arid land became a South African protectorate after WWI. In 1990 it became the independent Republic of Namibia.

**Windhoek** – Capital and largest city in Namibia.

**Tanzania** – A country in East Africa, the United Republic of Tanzania was formed when Tanganyika and the islands of Zanzibar consolidated in 1964.

**ZANLA** – Zimbabwe African National Liberation Army was the armed wing of the political movement ZANU (Zimbabwe African National Union). ZANU won the popular elections held in 1980, and has ruled the nation of Zimbabwe ever since.

## Military units

**BSAP** – British South Africa Police was the name of the Rhodesian national police force. They retained their historical name from the British South Africa Company, which governed the colony during its early history.

**RLI** – Rhodesian Light Infantry, an elite unit in the Rhodesian army organized into three commandos, a support group and a base group. Founded in 1961 and disbanded in 1980. One of the most effective fighting forces in history. Their loss to kill ratio was 500 to 1.

**SAS** – Special Air Service, an elite special operation unit founded in WWII Britain, organized into squadrons. C Squadron SAS operated in Rhodesia until it was disbanded in 1980.

**Selous Scouts** – Was a special forces regiment of the Rhodesian army which operated from 1973 until the introduction of majority rule and the country's independence as Zimbabwe in 1980. They were named after British explorer Frederick Courteney Selous (1851-1917). The charter of the Selous Scouts directed: 'The clandestine elimination of terrorists/terrorism both within and without the country.'

**Special Forces** – Also called SF or Green Berets, an elite unit in the US Army trained in counter-insurgency warfare and special operations missions. Like the CIA, Special Forces descended from the OSS of WWII.

**SOG** – Studies and Observation Group. A classified Special Forces cross-border reconnaissance unit that operated during the Vietnam War.

**CCN, CCC, CCS** – Command and Control elements of SOG in Vietnam. Designating: Command and Control North, Command and Control Central, and Command and Control South.

**Special Branch** – Is the arm of the BSAP that dealt with national security matters including terrorism, subversive and other extremist activity.

## Arms, munitions and equipment

**AK-47** – Automat Kalashnikova 1947 (Russian) standard 7.62mm military assault rifle designed by Mikhail Kalashnikov and manufactured in huge numbers in the Eastern Bloc during the Cold War.

**Browning High Power** – A 9mm semi-automatic high capacity pistol.

**Cloud XL** – An early model of the rectangular or 'square' parachute introduced in the 1970s.

**FN FAL  Fusil Automatique Léger** (Light Automatic Rifle) or **FAL** – Is a 7.62 × 51mm NATO self-loading, selective-fire rifle produced by the Belgian armaments manufacturer Fabrique Nationale de Herstal (FN) during the Cold War. The FN-FAL was used extensively in the Rhodesian bush war.

**FN MAG** (or **MAG-58**) – is a belt-fed 7.62 x 51mm machine gun manufactured by Fabrique Nationale (FN), Belgium. In production since 1958, and has become a widely adopted by more than 20 countries. MAG stands for *Mitrailleuse d'Appui General*, translated as 'general purpose machine gun' (GPMG).

**FNC** – a compact 5.56mm (.22 caliber) military carbine manufactured by FN.

**G3** – Stands for **Gewehr 3**, (*Rifle #3*) is a family of reliable select fire battle rifles manufactured by Heckler & Koch in Germany. It was adopted as the standard service rifle by the *Bundeswehr* in 1959, as well as several other countries. The G3 was chambered for the 7.62 × 51mm NATO cartridge.

**M16** – Is a lightweight 5.56mm air-cooled, gas-operated, magazine-fed rifle used extensively in the Vietnam era. Its improved fourth-generation variant, the M16A-4, is still the standard rifle of American military forces.

**M79** – Single shot, shoulder-fired 40mm grenade launcher used to US forces in Vietnam

**Minigun** – A 'Gatling style' rotary-barrelled cannon of 7.62 x 51mm that could fire at a sustained rate of 4,000 rounds a minute. Often aircraft mounted, it is called 'mini' because it is a downscaled version of the larger 20mm M-61 Vulcan rotary cannon.

**Mortar** – A muzzle-loading indirect weapon that fires shells at low velocities at short ranges and high trajectories. The 82mm mortar was used commonly by the Eastern Bloc and their allies.

**PC** – Para Commander, a round parachute made highly maneuverable by steering slots and control lines.

**Pencil (crush) detonator** – Is a time delay explosive detonator using a vial of corrosive liquid of varying concentrations that erodes through a steel wire and ignites a percussion cap. Mostly used in sabotage and clandestine operations.

**Puukko** – Is a small fix-bladed utility knife developed by the Laplanders in northern Scandinavia.

**Randall knife** – a hand-made custom knife made in the Randall shop in Orlando Florida.

**RB-15** – A tactical inflatable boat used by Special Operations forces for water infiltration, so named because it carries 15 men.

**RPD** – Is a belt-fed machine gun formerly manufactured in the Soviet Union and in China. The name stands for *Ruchnoy Pulemyot Degtyareva* (Russian for light machine gun). The RPD use as a squad automatic weapon (SAW), and entered service during the 1950s. The RPD is still widely used by many guerrilla organizations around the world.

**RPG-7** – *Ruchnoy Protivotankoviy Granatomet* (Russian) or Rocket Propelled Grenade (English) Type 69. Is a handheld anti-tank grenade launcher that is inexpensive to manufacture, easy to use, and very powerful. Manufactured in huge numbers in the USSR and the Eastern Bloc, it is still a very common weapon worldwide.

**Satchel charge** – A very powerful bundle of explosives consisting of 8 blocks of tetrol (pentaerythritol) linked by detonating cord. Developed in WWII it gave the infantry the capability to destroy bunkers and other hardened targets.

**SEAL** – Sea Air Land, US Navy special operations unit specializing in counter-insurgency warfare and covert direct action operations.

**Smith & Wesson** – Sometimes referred to as just 'Smith', has made high-quality handguns, most notably revolvers including the powerful .44 magnum, in the U.S. for over 150 years.

**Stoner System** – The Stoner 63 is a modular 5.56mm firearm system produced by Cadillac Gage and designed primarily by Eugene Stoner. Introduced in 1963 it is often known by its U.S. military designation Mk 23 Mod 0.

**Tokarev** – Or TT33 a 7.62 x 25mm semi-automatic pistol introduced in the 1930s and used extensively by the Soviets in WWII. The pistol was widely exported in the Cold War and widely carried by the Viet Cong and North Vietnamese.

**Weatherby** – a company based in California that builds high-quality hunting rifles.

**2.75-inch rockets** – The LAU-59 rocket pod holds seven 2.75-inch FFARs (folding-fin aircraft rockets) which were armed with various warheads depending on the mission. The rockets were unguided and usually fired in salvos against ground targets.

**12.7mm** – DShKM heavy machine gun is 12.7 x 114mm (51 caliber) was a common communist heavy support weapon used both in an anti-aircraft and infantry roles.

**14.5mm** – KPV heavy machine gun is a Soviet-designed 14.5 x 114mm weapon that first saw service in 1949. This weapon was used in both anti-aircraft and light anti-armour roles.

## Aircraft

**Alouette** – A light turbine-powered helicopter originally manufactured by Sud Aviation (later Aerospatiale) of France. Alouettes were extensively used in the Rhodesian War.

**Cobra** – Built by the Bell Helicopter Company (now Textron) the AH-1 Cobra was a light fast helicopter gunship based on the UH-1's engine, rotor and transmission unit. It first saw combat in Vietnam in the late 1960s, often referred to as 'Snakes' by the infantry.

**Canberra** – The English Electric Canberra was a first-generation jet bomber manufactured in large numbers through the 1950s. Able to carry a 3.6-tonne payload and having a service ceiling of 48,000 feet, it was used by many countries worldwide including Rhodesia and South Africa.

**DC-3** – A very successful two-engine piston-driven transport aircraft built by the Douglas Aircraft Company (later McDonnell Douglas) used extensively in WWII to drop paratroopers and also used civilian aviation until recent times. Called the Dakota by the British the name was commonly shortened to Dak by the Rhodesians.

**DC-8** – Large four-engine commercial jet aircraft used for both passenger and cargo-hauling, manufactured by McDonnell Douglas.

**Hawker Hunter** – A British-designed jet fighter built by Hawker Siddeley that was widely exported around the globe. A total of 1,972 were built. The Rhodesians used their Hawker FGA 9s extensively against insurgents from the late 1960s through the 1970s.

**Huey** – UH1H or Iroquois, a turbine-powered utility helicopter built by Bell Helicopter used extensively during the Vietnam War. UH1s were configured as both gunships and troop carriers informally called 'Slicks' because no guns protruded from them.

**MIG-17** – A Soviet jet fighter designed by the Mikoyan-Gurevich (MiG) design bureau which was used in many countries around the world aligned with the USSR, including Angola.

**Mirage III** – A supersonic fighter aircraft designed by Dassault aviation during the 1950s, and manufactured by France and under contract by other countries. Mirage IIIs were flown as interceptors in the South African Air Force (SAAF).

**Vampire** – The de Havilland DH 100 Vampire was an early British-designed jet fighter of the post-WWII era. Nearly 4,400 Vampires were built and it was the last modern military aircraft to use composite wood and metal construction. It has distinctive twin tail booms similar to the Lockheed P-38.